Sagas of
CONAN

The Conan Novels
in chronological order

Sagas of CONAN

Conan the Swordsman
Conan the Liberator
Conan and the Spider God

L. Sprague de Camp
Lin Carter
Björn Nyberg

TOR®

A Tom Doherty Associates Book
New York

This is a work of fiction. All the characters and events portrayed in the novels of this volume are either fictitious or are used fictitiously.

SAGAS OF CONAN

Map by Ellisa Mitchell

A Tor Book
Published by Tom Doherty Associates, LLC
175 Fifth Avenue
New York, NY 10010

www.tor.com

Tor® is a registered trademark of Tom Doherty Associates, LLC.

Library of Congress Cataloging-in-Publication Data

De Camp, L. Sprague (Lyon Sprague), 1907-
    Sagas of Conan / L. Sprague de Camp, Lin Carter, Björn Nyberg.—1st Tor pbk. ed.
      p. cm. — (Tor book)
    Contents: Conan the swordsman / by L. Sprague de Camp, Lin Carter & Björn
Nyberg—Conan the liberator / by L. Sprague de Camp & Lin Carter—Conan and the spider
god / by L. Sprague de Camp—"Hyborian names" / by L. Sprague de Camp.
    ISBN 0-765-31054-6
    1. Conan (Fictitious character)—Fiction.   2. Adventure stories, American.   3. Fantasy
fiction, American. I. Carter, Lin. II. Nyberg, Björn. III. Title. IV. Series.

PS3507.E2344A6 2004
813'.52—dc22

            2003057061

First Tor Paperback Edition: January 2004

Printed in the United States of America

0 9 8 7 6 5 4 3 2 1

Contents

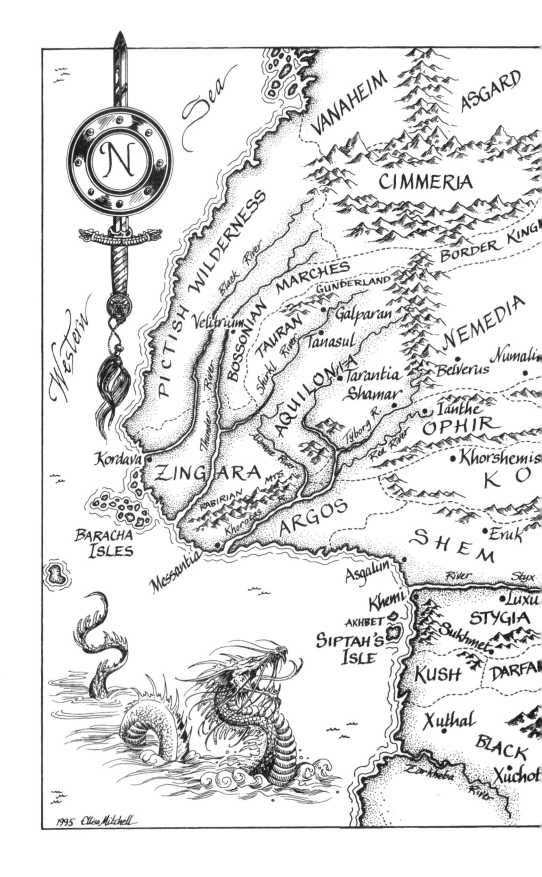

N

Western Sea

VANAHEIM

ASGARD

CIMMERIA

PICTISH WILDERNESS

BORDER KING

Black River

GUNDERLAND

MARCHES

BOSSONIAN

Velitrium

TAURAN

Galparan

Tanasul

Thunder River

Shirki River

AQUILONIA

NEMEDIA

Numali

Tarantia

Belverus

Shamar

Tybor R.

Ianthe

OPHIR

Kordava

ZINGARA

Red River

Khorshemis

KO

RABIRIAN

MTS

Khoraja

ARGOS

SHEM

Messantia

Asgalun

River

Styx

Luxu

BARACHA
ISLES

Khemi

AKHBET

SIPTAH'S
ISLE

Sukhmet

STYGIA

KUSH

DARFA

Xuthal

BLACK

Xuchot

1995 Ellisa Mitchell

Tundras
Haloga
Hyperborea
Deserts
Brythunia
Kezankian Mts.
Steppes
Hyrkania
Corinthia
Zamora
Karpash Mts.
Shadizar
Arenjun
Turan
Sultanapur
Vilayet Sea
Khitai
Isle of Iron Statues
Khauran
T H
Akit
Aghrapur
Khoraja
Deserts
Samara
Ibars Mts.
Shangara
Xapur
Zaporoska River
Zamboula
Khawarism
Pteion
Kuthchernes
Ilbars River
Kassali
Keshan
Punt
Vendhya
Kingdoms
Zembabwei
Iranistan

CONAN

The Swordsman

L. Sprague de Camp
Lin Carter
Björn Nyberg

Acknowledgments

The story "People of the Summit" is a rewritten version of a story by the same title, by Björn Nyberg, in *The Mighty Swordsmen* (New York: Lancer Books, 1970), copyright © 1970 by Hans Stefan Santesson.

Contents

The Conan Saga

How would you like to go to a world where men are mighty, women are beautiful, problems are simple, and life is adventurous? Where gleaming cities raise their shining spires against the stars; sorcerers cast sinister spells from subterranean lairs; baleful spirits stalk crumbling ruins of hoary antiquity; primeval monsters crash through jungle thickets; and the fate of kingdoms is balanced on the bloody blades of broadswords brandished by heroes of preternatural might and valor? And where nobody so much as mentions the income tax or the school-dropout problem or atmospheric pollution?

This is the world of heroic fantasy, or, as some prefer to call it, swordplay-and-sorcery fiction. We apply the name "heroic fantasy" to stories laid in an imaginary, preindustrial world — in the remote past, the remote future, another planet, or another dimension — where magic works, machinery has not been invented, and gods, demons, and other supernatural beings are real and portentous presences.

Fiction of this genre is pure entertainment. It is not intended to solve current social and economic problems; it has nothing to say about the faults of the foreign-aid program, or the woes of disadvantaged ethnics, or socialized medicine, or inflation. It is escape fiction of the purest kind, in which the reader escapes clear out of the real world. And why not? As J. R. R. Tolkien once said, a man in prison is not required to think of nothing but bars and cells and jailers.

The stories in this saga feature one of the most popular characters of heroic fantasy ever invented. This is Conan the Cimmerian, the gigantic, invincible, swashbuckling prehistoric adventurer. Conan was conceived in 1932 by Robert Ervin Howard (1906–36) of Cross Plains, Texas. Robert E. Howard was a leading author of adventure fiction for the pulp magazines, which flourished in the 1920s and 1930s, dwindled away during the paper shortage of the Second World War, and were replaced in popular reading after that war by the paperbacked book.

Howard wrote not only fantasies but also science fiction, Western, sport, detective, historical, and oriental stories. After an early struggle to establish himself, he attained a fair degree of success, earning what was in the Depression days of the early 1930s a respectable income. He had a few close friends in west-central Texas—none of whom cared for his stories—and a growing circle of admiring correspondents, including leading fantasists of the time like H. P. Lovecraft, Clark Ashton Smith, and August Derleth. Although a big, powerful man like his heroes, Howard had his private demons, including an excessive devotion to and dependence upon his mother. In 1936, when his aged mother lay dying, he ended a promising literary career by suicide.

Howard's stories, although not without fault, are distinguished by strong plots, a sound, taut, economical, colorful, vivid style, a marvelous sense of pace and action, and most of all by a singular emotional intensity, which sweeps the reader along. As his pen pal Lovecraft wrote in a letter to E. Hoffmann Price, "the real secret is that he himself is in every one of [his stories]." Rudyard Kipling, Jack London, Harold Lamb, Talbot Mundy, Arthur D. Howden Smith, and Sax Rohmer all influenced him, but Howard achieved his own unique synthesis.

Like most of Howard's stories, the tales of the Conan saga are somber in tone, with a keen sense of the inevitable tragedy of life and the harshness of existence in the medieval and ancient worlds. There is only a rare gleam of humor. Nevertheless, Howard was by no means humorless. He wrote many boxing and Western stories full of broad, slapstick, frontier humor, often hilarious. Even at his pulpiest, Howard is always fun to read. The term "natural storyteller" applies to Howard as strongly as it does to any writer, ancient or modern.

Howard wrote several fantasy series, most of which appeared in the magazine *Weird Tales,* which began publication in 1923. Of these series, the most popular by far have been those about Conan the Cimmerian. They have been printed and reprinted, in this and in at least seven foreign countries, long after the death of the original author and the demise of the magazine in which they were first published.

Howard was the leading American pioneer in heroic fantasy. Fiction of this kind was introduced in the 1880s by the British artist, writer, reformer, decorator, poet, manufacturer, and printer William Morris. In the early twentieth century, it was further developed by Lord Dunsany and Eric R. Eddison and, later, by J. R. R. Tolkien (*The Lord of the Rings*) and T. H. White (*The Once and Future King*). Besides Robert E. Howard, leading American practitioners of the genre include Clark Ashton Smith, Catherine L. Moore, and Fritz Leiber.

With the end of the magazines *Unknown Worlds* in 1943 and *Weird Tales* in 1954, it looked for a while as if fantasy had become a casualty of the machine age. In the 1950s, publication in hardcover of Tolkien's three-volume novel

The Lord of the Rings and the reprinting of the Conan stories began a modest revival. With the appearance both of the Tolkien and of the Howard stories in paperback came a tremendous upsurge of interest in fantasy. Millions of copies of both series have been sold, and other writers have composed fantastic tales obviously influenced by these two authors.

I became involved in this blooming of heroic fantasy in 1951, when I discovered a pile of unsold Howard manuscripts in the closet of a literary agent in New York. These included two unpublished Conan stories, one story originally written as a Conan story but actually published in a fan magazine with the hero's name changed, and several adventure stories with medieval and modern settings. By arrangement with the heirs of Robert E. Howard, I edited the rejected Conan stories and arranged for their publication. Later I rewrote four of the medieval and modern stories to turn them into Conan stories. I also collaborated with a Swedish fan, Björn Nyberg, on a novel, *The Return of Conan*.

A few years later, I was fortunate in being able to arrange for publication of the whole Conan saga in paperback, putting all the then-existing Conan stories in chronological order. More unpublished stories were discovered by Glenn Lord, agent for the Howard heirs. One was complete; the rest were fragments or synopses only. My colleagues Lin Carter, Björn Nyberg, and I have completed those unfinished Conan stories and, to fill the gaps in the saga, have written several Conan stories of our own, following the hints in Howard's letters and original stories. We have tried to copy Howard's style and type of plotting. How successful we have been in this endeavor, the reader must judge. Since the demand for Conan stories has become greater than Carter, Nyberg, and I could fill, other contemporary writers have also been enlisted to try their hands at Howard pastiches.

The first hint of the Conan stories came in a series of tales that Howard wrote in 1929, laid in the time of the supposed lost continent of Atlantis. His hero was a Stone Age Atlantean named Kull, who gets to the mainland, becomes a soldier in the civilized kingdom of Valusia, and rises to be king of that land. Howard wrote—or at least began—thirteen Kull stories but sold only three. One of these brought Kull by magical time travel to the historical era and involved him with another of Howard's heroes, the Pictish chieftain Bran Mak Morn of Roman times. Three Kull stories, left unfinished, were later completed by Lin Carter.

Since the Kull stories enjoyed only meager success, Howard put the idea aside. In 1931, however, Howard read a series of articles by a French writer on the Atlantis legend and was stimulated to try again his basic concept of a prehistoric adventure-fantasy world, this time in a more polished and carefully thought-out form. His hero would be named Conan, an old Celtic name borne by, among others, several dukes of medieval Brittany. Conan, Howard said, "simply grew up in my mind a few years ago when I was stopping in a little border town on the lower Rio Grande. . . . He simply stalked full grown out of oblivion and set me at work recording the saga of his adventures. . . . Some mechanism in my subconscious took the dominant characteristics of various prize-fighters, gunmen, bootleggers, oil field bullies, gamblers, and honest workmen I have come in contact with, and combining them all, produced the amalgamation I call Conan the Cimmerian."

As a stage for Conan to stride across, Howard devised a Hyborian Age, about twelve thousand years ago, between the sinking of Atlantis and the beginnings of recorded history. This period, Howard supposed, was one in which magic was rife and supernatural beings walked the earth. The records of this civilization were lost, save for myths and legends, as a result of barbarian invasions and natural catastrophes. Howard worked out a detailed fictional "history" of this Hyborian Age, covering several thousand years. In the midst of this time, Conan lived, loved, wandered, and battled his way to kingship.

Howard made it plain that this pseudo-history was invented for storytelling purposes and was not to be considered a serious theory of human prehistory. Howard had read widely in history and said he enjoyed writing historical fiction. It is sad that he did not survive to the 1950s, when such fiction was at the peak of its popularity.

Conan (Howard assumed) was a native of the bleak and barbarous northern land of Cimmeria. The Cimmerians he supposed to have been the ancestors of the historical Celts. Still farther north lay the subarctic lands of Vanaheim, Asgard, and Hyperborea. Adventuring with a band of Æsir from Asgard on a raid into Hyperborea, Conan was captured and imprisoned. Escaping, he made his way southward to the land of Zamora, east of the Hyborian nations. These nations—Aquilonia, Nemedia, Corinthia, Ophir, and Koth—had arisen after the Hyborians, another group of northern barbarians, had conquered the sorcerous kingdom of Acheron and built up their own kingdoms on its ruins, three thousand years before Conan's time.

In Zamora, Corinthia, and Nemedia, Conan led a precarious life as a thief, more notable for strength and daring than for skill and subtlety. Becoming weary of this starveling existence, he enlisted in the armies of Turan. This kingdom lay east of Zamora, along the western shores of the great inland Sea of Vilayet, whose shrunken remnants we today call the Caspian. The Turanians were one of the nomadic peoples of Hyrkania, which began east of the sea and stretched for thousands of miles to far Khitai. Hyrkania corresponded to the steppes and deserts of Central Asia today.

As a soldier of Turan, Conan learned horsemanship and archery and rose to commissioned rank. Trouble with a superior caused him to desert. After some unsuccessful treasure hunting, he wandered westward, serving as a *condottiere* in Nemedia, Ophir, and Argos. Again, trouble with the law compelled him to flee, this time to sea. When his ship was captured by a pirate vessel of the black corsairs, commanded by the seductive Shemitish she-pirate Bêlit, he joined Bêlit in piratical raiding of the Black Coast.

After Bêlit's death, Conan resumed his career ashore as a mercenary soldier, first in the black countries, then in Shem and the Hyborian nations. He paid occasional visits to his Cimmerian homeland and spent a period as leader of an outlaw band, the *kozaki* of the steppes between Turan and Zamora. When the Turanian army broke up the band, Conan fought his way to leadership of a crew of pirates plying the Vilayet Sea.

Next, Conan became a soldier in the army of the small southeasterly Hyborian kingdom of Khauran and, later, leader of the desert-dwelling Zuagir nomads. His wanderings took him as far east as Vendhya (corresponding to modern India) and south to the deserts between the sinister land of Stygia and the equatorial jungles. He joined the pirates of the Barachan Isles, then became captain of one of the privateering ships of the Zingaran buccaneers.

When Conan's ship was sunk by Zingaran rivals, he served as a mercenary for Stygia. He sought and almost found his hoped-for fortune in the semicivilized black countries of Keshan and Punt. At last he traveled northward, to resume life as a mercenary soldier in Aquilonia, the mightiest of the Hyborian kingdoms. He served on the Pictish frontier, was involved in bloody affrays with the fierce savages of Pictland, and for his success was promoted to general and called back to the capital, Tarantia.

In Tarantia, the depraved and jealous King Numedides imprisoned Conan in a dungeon. But Conan escaped and adventured in the Pictish Wilderness with the primitive natives and with two bands of pirates. Eventually he found himself (at about forty years of age) leading a revolt against Numedides, whom he killed and whose throne he usurped.

Other stories follow Conan's adventures into middle and old age, but of those you can read elsewhere. This synopsis will give you the framework needed to place the stories in this volume in time and place.

So let us whet our steel, pull on our boots, and be off on a galloping charger or the heeling deck of a carack, to follow Conan through some of his many sorcerous and sanguinary adventures.

CONAN
The Swordsman

Legions of the Dead

Conan, born in the bleak, cloud-oppressed northern hills of Cimmeria, was known as a fighter around the council fires before he had seen fifteen snows. In that year, the Cimmerian tribesmen forgot their feuds and joined forces to repel the Gundermen who, pushing across the Aquilonian frontier, had built the frontier post of Venarium and begun to colonize the southern marches of Cimmeria. Conan was one of the howling, blood-mad horde that swept out of the northern hills, stormed over the stockade with sword and torch, and drove the Aquilonians back to their former border.

At the sack of Venarium, still short of his full growth, Conan already stood six feet tall and weighed 180 pounds. He had the alertness and stealth of the born woodsman, the iron-hardness of the mountain man, the Herculean physique of his blacksmith father, and a practical familiarity with knife, axe, and sword.

After the plunder of the Aquilonian outpost, Conan returns for a time to his tribe. Restless under the conflicting urges of his adolescence, his traditions, and his times, he becomes involved in a local feud and is not sorry to leave his village. He joins a band of Æsir in raiding the Vanir and the Hyperboreans. Some of the Hyperborean citadels, however, are under control of a caste of widely feared magicians, called Witchmen, and it is against one of these strongholds that Conan finds himself taking part in a foray.

1 • Blood on the Snow

A deer paused at the brink of the shallow stream and raised its head, sniffing the frosty air. Water dripped from its muzzle like beads of crystal. The lingering sun gleamed on its tawny hide and glistened on the tines of its branching antlers.

Whatever faint sound or scent had disturbed the animal was not repeated. Presently it bent to drink again from the frigid water, which rushed and bubbled amid crusts of broken ice.

On either side of the stream, steep banks of earth lay mantled in the new-fallen snow of early winter. Thickets of leafless bush grew close together under the somber boughs of the neighboring pines; and from the forest beyond, nothing could be heard but the ceaseless drip, drip of melting snow. The featureless leaden sky of the dying day scarcely seemed to clear the tops of the trees.

From the shelter of the woods, a slender javelin darted with deadly precision; and at the end of its arc, the long shaft caught the stag off guard and sank behind its shoulder. The stricken creature bolted for the far side of the creek; then staggered, coughed blood, and fell. For a moment or two it lay on its side, kicking and struggling. Then its eyes glazed, its head hung limply, and its heaving flanks grew still. Blood, mixed with froth and foam, dribbled from its sagging jaws to stain the virgin snow a brilliant crimson.

Two men emerged from the trees and studied the snowy landscape with searching eyes. The larger and older, plainly in command, was a giant of a man with massive shoulders and long, heavily muscled arms. The swell of his mighty chest and shoulders was visible beneath the cloak of fur that enveloped his stalwart figure and the coarse, baggy woolens he wore beneath the cloak. A broad belt of rawhide with a golden buckle held his garments around him, and a hood of wolf fur, forming part of the cloak, obscured his face.

Now pushing back the hood to peer about, he revealed a head of curling golden hair, slightly streaked with gray. A short, roughly trimmed beard of the same hue clothed his broad cheeks and heavy jaw. The color of his hair, his fair skin and ruddy cheeks, and his bold blue eyes marked him as one of the Æsir.

The youth beside him differed from him in many ways. Scarcely more than a boy, he was tall and brawny for his age—almost as tall as the full-grown Northman beside him—but lean and wiry rather than massive. He was dark and sullen, with straight, coarse black hair hacked off at the nape, and the skin of his somber visage was either naturally swarthy or heavily tanned. Under heavy black brows, his eyes were as blue as those of the giant at his elbow; but whereas the golden warrior's eyes sparkled with the joy of the hunt and zest for the kill, those of the dark youth glowered like the eyes of some wild and hungry predator. Unlike his bearded companion, the young man's beard was shaven clean, although a dark stubble shadowed his square jaw.

The bearded man was Njal, a *jarl* or chieftain of the Æsir and leader of a band of raiders known and feared on the wintry borders between Asgard and Hyperborea. The youth was Conan, a renegade from the rugged, cloud-haunted hills of Cimmeria to the south.

Satisfied that they were unobserved, the two emerged from cover, descended the bank, and waded the icy current to the place where their kill lay lifeless on the blood-spotted snow. Weighing almost as much as the two men together, the stag was too heavy and, with its branching antlers, too cumbersome to bear back to their camp. So, while the youth watched broodingly, the chieftain bent and, with a long knife, swiftly butchered the beast, peeling back the hide and separating the shoulders, haunches, and ribs from the rest of the carcass.

"Dig a hole, boy, and make it deep," grunted the man.

The youth cut into the frozen slope of the bank, using the blade of the long-handled ax that had been strapped to his back. By the time that Njal had finished dressing the stag, Conan had hacked out a pit capacious enough to hide the offal. While the Northman cleaned the bloody quarters in the rushing stream, the youth buried all that was left of the carcass, and scraped the crimson snow into the pit along with the loosened soil. Then untying his fur cloak, the Cimmerian dragged it back and forth, obliterating the traces of his handiwork.

Njal wrapped the flesh of the deer in the freshly flayed hide of the beast and tied the mouth of the improvised sack with a thong brought along for the purpose. Conan cut a sapling with his ax and trimmed it down to a pole as long as a man, while the jarl cleansed his javelin by thrusting it into the sand in the bed of the stream. Njal tied the bag to the middle of the pole, which the two then hoisted to their shoulders. Dragging Conan's cloak behind them to erase their footprints, they climbed the farther slope and reentered the woods.

Here along the Hyperborean border, the pines grew tall, thick, and dark. Wherever a break in the forest afforded a vista, the ridges could be seen to roll endlessly away, covered with snowcapped pines of a green as dark as sable. Wolves skulked along the nighted forest trails, their burning eyes lambent green coals, while above floated great white owls on silent wings.

The two well-armed hunters had no fear of the local creatures; save that, when a bear ambled across the path ahead, they gave it a respectfully wide berth. Like ghosts they glided through the darkened woods to join their fellow raiders, who lay encamped beneath the shoulder of a hill. Since both were woodsmen born and bred, they made no noise and left little trace of their swift passage. Even the scrubby bushes did not rustle as they slipped through them.

So well concealed was the Æsir camp that their first knowledge of its presence was the murmur of voices around a hidden fire; yet the watchful sentinels had seen their coming. An elderly Northman, whose locks had turned to silver, rose from the fireside to greet them silently. One of his eyes was bright and keen; the other was an empty socket concealed by a leather patch. He was Gorm, a bard of the Æsir, over whose bent shoulders slept a harp in a sack of deerskin.

"What word from Egil?" demanded the raider chief, lowering the pole from his shoulder and motioning to the cook to take it away.

"No word, Jarl," said the one-eyed man somberly. "I like it not." He moved uneasily, as does a beast at the scent of danger.

Njal exchanged a glance with the silent Conan. Two days before, an advance party had left the camp under cover of a moonless night to spy out the great castle of Haloga, which lay not far beyond the hills that ringed the horizon to the southeast.

Thirty warriors, seasoned and canny veterans all, led by Egil the huntsman, had gone to scout the way and to study the fortifications of the forbidding Hyperborean stronghold. Conan, unasked, had brashly spoken out against the imprudence of so drastically dividing their strength thus near the enemy, and Njal had roughly bade the youth to hold his tongue. Later, regretting his harshness, the jarl had brought Conan with him in search of game as his rude way of making amends.

Egil's messengers should have returned many hours since. The fact that they had not stirred fear in the mind of Njal, and in the secret places of his heart, he wished that he had harkened to the young Cimmerian's warning.

Njal's shortness of temper and the urgency with which he had driven his men across the wilderness to the Hyperborean border were not without cause. Hyperborean slavers, a fortnight since—slavers with the red mark of Haloga on their black raiment—had carried off his only daughter, Rann.

Brooding over the fate of his beloved daughter and the whereabouts of his trusted scouts, the jarl repressed a shudder. The Witchmen of shadowy Hyperborea were feared far and wide for their uncanny mastery of the black arts; and Haloga's sadistic queen was feared like the Black Death.

Njal fought down the chill that clutched his heart and turned to Gorm the skald. "Tell the cook to broil the meat swiftly—and on charcoal, for we cannot risk the smoke of open fires. And bid the men eat fast. When night descends, we move."

2 • The Horror on the Parapet

All that night, like a band of wolves, the raiders from Asgard drifted in single file across the snowy hills into the clammy, swirling mists of Hyperborea. At first the night was star-decked only, but once they crossed the hills, cold mists blotted out even the wan and frosty glimmer of the stars. When at length the moon arose, the mists bedimmed it to a pearly blotch in the sky, like a moon reflected in wind-ruffled water.

Despite the gloom that drenched this barren, bog-infested, scantily inhabited land, the raiders took advantage of every slightest bit of cover, every leafless bush and stunted tree and inky patch of shadow. For Haloga was a mighty fortress, and doubtless guarded well. Desperate and vengeful as he was, Njal well knew in the depths of his heart that his only hope of success lay in surprise.

The moon and mists had fled together before they reached Haloga. The castle stood on a low rise in the center of a shallow, bowl-shaped valley. Huge were its frowning walls of dark stone, and massive the masonry around the lone and ponderous gate. Above the main walls rose a castellated parapet. A few windows were set high in the towers; nothing else but arrow slits broke the clifflike surface of the megalithic walls.

It would, Njal knew, be difficult to storm this place. And where were the men whom he had sent ahead to scout the way? No sign of them had been discerned, even by his keen-eyed trackers; for the newly fallen snow had obliterated their footprints.

"Shall we essay the walls, Jarl?" asked a warrior—an outlaw fled hither from Vanaheim, if his red beard was any token.

"Nay, the dawn approaches, curse the luck!" growled the chief. "We must wait for night again, or pray the gods will let the white-haired devils grow careless and raise the portcullis. Tell the men to sleep where they are and to sprinkle snow over their furs so none can see them. Tell Thror Ironhand his squad has the first watch."

Njal lay down, wrapped his furs around him, and closed his eyes. But sleep came not soon; and when it came, dreams of shadowy, chuckling menace made it hideous.

Conan slept not at all. Possessed by uneasy foreboding, the youth still resented Njal's gruff dismissal of his argument against the scouting party. He was a stranger among the Æsir freebooters, driven from his homeland by a blood feud, and had with difficulty won a precarious place among these blond warriors. They approved his ability to endure privation and hardship without complaint, and the bullies among them had learned to respect his heavy fists; for despite his youth, he fought with the ferocity of a cornered wildcat and needs must be dragged bodily from a foe once he had felled him. But still, as youths will, the Cimmerian burned to win the applause of his elders by some feat of daring or heroism.

Conan had observed the windows of the keep, which were much too high to reach by climbing, were it humanly possible to scale such walls without a ladder. He had mastered many sheer cliffs in his homeland; but those had at least afforded a toe- and finger-hold. The stones of Haloga were fitted and trimmed to a glassy smoothness that defied the climbing efforts of any creature larger than an insect.

The arrow slits, however, were set lower in the walls and thus seemed more accessible. Those of the lowest tier were little more than thrice a man's height above the ground, to give the archers a fair shot at besiegers who might cluster about the base of the wall. Plainly too narrow for a full-grown man of the bulk of most Æsir, were they too narrow for the smaller, slenderer Conan?

———

When dawn broke, one raider was missing from the camp—the young Cimmerian outlaw, Conan. Njal had other things to think about and so had little time to ponder the fate of a surly, black-visaged young runaway, who seemed to lack the stomach for this raid.

The jarl had just discovered his missing scouts. They hung from the parapet, clearly visible as dawn lit the empty sky and dispelled the clammy fogs that shrouded the air of this accursed land. The men were still alive, dancing in their death throes at the ends of thirty ropes.

Njal stared, then cursed until his voice was hoarse, and he dug his nails into his hard palms. Although he felt sick to the roots of his soul, he could not tear his eyes away.

The eternally young queen of Haloga, Vammatar the Cruel, stood on the parapet fair as the morning, with long bright hair and full breasts, which curved sweetly beneath her heavy white robes. A lazy, languorous smile parted her full red lips: The men who attended her were true Hyperboreans, unearthly in their gaunt, long-legged stature, with pale eyes and skeins of colorless silken hair.

As the hidden Æsir, sick with rage and fury and helpless horror, watched, the men of Egil's party were slowly done to death with merciless hooks and wickedly curved knives. They squealed and flopped and wriggled, those gory, mangled things that had been stalwart warriors two days before. It took them hours to die.

Njal, his lips bitten through, aged much during that endless, terrible morn. And there was nothing at all he could do. A leader cannot throw a small band of men against high walls with only hand weapons. If he has a large, well-found army capable of keeping the field for months, he can batter down the walls with rams and catapults, or undermine them with tunnels, or roll siege towers up to them and swarm across, or surround the stronghold and starve it out. Lacking such overmastering force, he needs at least scaling ladders as long as the wall is high, a force of archers or slingers to beat the defenders back from the ramparts, and above all surprise.

Surprise, the advantage on which Njal had counted, was now lost to him. However the Hyperboreans had captured Egil's scouting party, the mere fact of their capture had alerted the people of Haloga to the presence of Æsir in the vicinity. The Witchmen of this devil-haunted land must, by their weird arts, have known of the approach of the hostile force. The sinister legends about them were now proved true by the crimson evidence hanging against the red-stained stone of the parapet. Haloga had known that the Æsir were out there all the time, and not even the cold-hearted and vengeance-loving gods of the Northlands could help them now.

Then it was that the first plume of jet-black smoke drifted from the lofty windows of the keep, and the torturers broke, crying out in amazement, and scurried away with their black gowns flapping. The lazy, catlike smile vanished from the soft, curved lips of Haloga's queen. A feeble, flickering flame of hope leaped up within the breast of Njal of Asgard.

3 • Shadow of Vengeance

Scaling the wall had been neither easier nor harder than Conan had guessed. A rain spout, curved like the mouth of a vomiting dragon, caught and held the noose of his rope on the fifteenth or sixteenth try. The rope, knotted at intervals for better purchase, neither slipped nor broke beneath his weight.

When he had ascended to the level of the slit, Conan locked his legs about the rope and rocked back and forth, like a child on a swing. By throwing his weight from one side to the other, he increased the dimensions of the arc. It was slow going; but at last, at the end of a swing to the right, he came within reach of the slit.

The next time he swung, he shot out a hand and grasped the masonry. Still holding the rope in his free hand, he thrust a booted foot into the opening and followed it with the other. Slowly and carefully he shifted his weight until he was sitting on the sill of the arrow slit with his legs inside. He still grasped the rope with his left hand, for it occurred to him that, if he released it, his lifeline would fall away and hang out of reach when he would have need of it for a hasty departure.

The slit was too narrow for Conan to pass through in his present position. Already his lean hips were wedged into the opening, the sides of which were angled outward to give the defender a wider field of arrow shot. So, turning sideways, he wriggled his hips and midsection through the aperture. But when his arms and chest reached the narrow opening, his woolen tunic, bunched up beneath his armpits, arrested further progress. Would he not look an utter fool, he thought, if the Witchmen came upon him wedged in the arrow slit? He had visions of being caught forever in this stony vise. Even if undiscovered, he would perish of hunger and thirst and make good food for the ravens.

Gathering courage, he decided that by expelling all the breath from his lungs, he might just slip through. He took several deep breaths, as if preparing to swim under water, exhaled, and pushed ahead until his thrashing feet found a firm surface to stand on. Turning his head, he wormed it through the inner edges of the slit and collapsed on a rough wooden floor. In his excitement he had released the rope, which started to snake through the slit. He caught it just before it slipped away.

Conan found himself in a small circular chamber, an archer's roost that was unoccupied. As he peered around in the gloom, he sighted a rough stool, placed there for the comfort of the defender. He pulled the stool nearer and made the rope fast to it, so that the heavy wood might serve to anchor the rope during his escape. Then he stretched his cramped muscles. He must, he thought, have left a few square palms of skin on the stonework as he scraped through.

Across the room from the arrow slit, the masonry was interrupted by an arched doorway. Conan drew his long knife from its scabbard and stole through the aperture. Beyond the doorway a spiral stair led upward, and occasional torches set in wall brackets did little to dispel the almost palpable obscurity.

Moving a step at a time and flattening himself against the wall to listen, Conan slowly worked his way through many passages to the central keep, where prisoners of rank and worth might lodge. Day had dawned long since, although little light penetrated this massive pile of stone through the arrow slits and narrow windows. From the screams that filtered faintly through the thick walls, the Cimmerian youth had a grim notion of what occupied the Witchmen on the parapet.

In a corridor intermittently lit by torches set in brackets, Conan found his prey at last—two of them, in fact. They were guarding a cell and, from the look of them, he knew the old stories were true. He had seen Cimmerians and Gundermen and Aquilonians and Æsir and Vanir, but never before had he set eyes upon a Hyperborean at close quarters, and the sight chilled the blood in his veins.

Like devils from some lightless hell they seemed, long-jawed faces white as fungi, pale and soulless amber eyes, and hair of colorless flax. Their gaunt bodies were clad all in black, save that the red mark of Haloga was embroidered on their bony chests. It seemed to Conan's fancy that the marks were bloody tokens of hearts that had been torn from their breasts, leaving naught but a grisly stain behind. The superstitious youth almost believed the ancient legends that these men were mere cadavers, animated by demons from the depths of some black hell.

They did have hearts, however; and when cut, they bled. They could also be killed, as he found when he hurled himself upon them from the corridor. The first one squawked and went down, sprawling awkwardly under the thunderbolt impact of Conan's catlike leap, and died bubbling as the Cimmerian's knife pierced his breast.

The second guard, staring slack-jawed and blank-eyed, gaped for a heartbeat. Then he aimed a kick at the intruder and went for his sword. But Conan's knife, a serpent's tongue, flicked out and slashed the Hyperborean's throat, leaving a mirthless, red-rimmed smile below the guard's pale thin-lipped mouth.

When the two were dead, Conan stripped them of their weapons and, dragging the bodies to an empty cell, heaped upon them the straw that lay matted on the floor. Then he peered into the small compartment that they had guarded.

A tall, milk-skinned girl with clear blue eyes and long, smooth hair the color of sun-ripened wheat stood proudly in the center of the enclosure, awaiting a fate she knew not of. Although the maiden's high young breasts rose and fell in her agitation, there was no fear in her eyes.

"Who are you?" she asked.

"Conan, a Cimmerian, a member of your father's band," he said, speaking her tongue with an accent foreign to her. "If you are Njal's daughter, that is."

She lifted her chin. "I am indeed Rann Njalsdatter."

"Good," he grunted, thrusting into the lock a key snatched from the dead Witchmen. "I have come for you."

"Alone?" Her eyes widened, incredulously.

Conan nodded. Snatching her hand, he led the Æsir girl into the corridor and gave her one of the two swords of the slain Witchmen. With her behind him and his newfound weapon readied for action, he cautiously retraced his steps along the stone passageways through which he had come.

Down the long corridor he prowled, silent and wary as a jungle cat. Moving with every sense alert, his smoldering gaze swept the walls and the doors set in them. In the flickering torchlight, his eyes burned like those of some savage creature of the wild.

At any moment, Conan knew, the Witchmen might discover them, for surely not every denizen of the castle was on the parapet with the torturers. Deep in his primal heart, he breathed an unspoken prayer to Crom, the merciless god of his shadowy homeland, that he and the girl might, unobserved, attain the arrow slit whereby he had entered.

Like an insubstantial shadow, the young Cimmerian glided through the gloomy passageways, which now curved following the girdle of the curtain wall; and Rann, on little cat feet, followed after him. Torches smoldered and smoked in their brackets, but the dark intervals between the flickering lights were alive with evil.

They met no one; yet Conan was not satisfied. True, their luck had held thus far, but it might end at any moment. If two or three Witchmen fell upon them, they might still win through; for the women of the Æsir were not pampered playthings but skilled and daring swordswomen. Often in battle they stood shoulder to shoulder with their men; and when fight they must, they fought with the ferocity of tigresses.

But what if they were set upon by six or a dozen Witchmen? Young as he was, Conan knew no mortal man, however skillful with his sword, can face at once in all directions; and whilst they thrust and parried in these dark passages, the alarm would surely sound and rouse the castle.

A diversion was needed, and one of the torches they passed gave the youth an inspiration. The torches were soaked in tarry pitch to burn long and slowly, but they burned deep and were not easily extinguished. Conan glanced about. The walls of the castle were of stone, but the floor planks and the beams sup-

porting them were wooden. Across his grim face flitted a small smile of satisfaction.

Conan needed to find a storeroom, and as he prowled the corridors, he
peered into chambers whose doors were open. One was vacant. Another contained a pair of empty beds. A third appeared to be a storage place for broken
or damaged weapons and other metallic objects awaiting repair.

The door to the next room stood ajar, leaving a narrow crack of darkness in
the flickering torchlight. Conan pushed it, and the door swung open with a
faint squeal of hinges. Then he started back and hastily shut out the sight of
that dark chamber; for the room contained a bed, and on the bed lay a sleeping
Witchman. Beside him on a stool were several phials, which Conan supposed
held medications for a sick man. He left the fellow snoring.

The next chamber turned out to be the sought-for storeroom. As Conan
surveyed it from the hall, the rising sound of footsteps and voices caused him
to whirl about, lip lifted in a snarl. He gestured frantically to Rann.

"Inside!" he breathed.

The twain slipped into the storeroom, and Conan closed the door. Since the
room had no window, they waited in complete darkness, listening to the clatter
of the approaching Hyperboreans. Soon the party passed the door, speaking in
their guttural tongue, and their footsteps died away.

When all was silent again, Conan drew a long breath. Holding high his
Hyperborean sword, he opened the door a crack, then more widely as he
viewed naught but the empty corridor. With the door ajar, the dim light of
the torches pierced the gloom, and he could make out the contents of the
chamber. Here were a pile of fresh torches, a barrel of pitch, and in one corner,
a heap of straw to garnish the cell floors in lieu of carpets.

It was but the work of a moment for Conan to toss the pile of straw about
the chamber, overturn the barrel of pitch upon it, and spread the viscous stuff
around. Darting out into the passageway, he snatched a torch from the nearest
bracket and heaved it into the combustible mass that covered the floor of the
storeroom. Crackling lustily, the flames ate their way through the straw and
belched black smoke along the corridor.

Tarred from face to boots and coughing from the acrid fumes, Conan
caught Rann's hand, sprinted down the winding stairs, and regained the alcove
through which he had gained entry. How long before the Witchmen would
discover that their castle was ablaze, Conan knew not; but he trusted this diversion to occupy their full attention while the rescuer and rescued squirmed
through the narrow slit and clambered down the rope to the safety of the frozen ground.

4 • That Which Pursued

Jarl Njal bellowed with joy and seized the laughing, weeping girl in his arms, crushing her against his burly chest. But even in his joy, the chieftain paused to look deep into Conan's eyes and clap the youth on the shoulder with a friendly buffet that would have knocked most striplings off their feet.

As they hastened to the Asgard camp beneath the cover of the snow-tipped pines, the youth, in terse words, described the day's adventure. But words were scarcely needed. Behind them a raven cloud of soot besmudged the afternoon sky, and the crash of collapsing timbers and fire-blackened masonry resounded like distant thunder in the hills. The Witchmen would doubtless save part of their fortress; although many of the lank, flaxen-haired devils must have already perished in the conflagration.

Wasting no time, Njal ordered his men to begin the long trek back to Asgard. Not until he and his band were deep in their own land could the chief of the Æsir count himself safe from Hyperborean vengeance. There would, no doubt, be pursuit; but for the moment the dwellers in Haloga had other matters to busy them.

The Æsir made haste to depart, and in their hurry they sacrificed concealment to speed. Since the face of the wan sun was still pillowed on the treetops, they could with effort put leagues between themselves and the castle before the early fall of the northern night.

From the parapet of Haloga, the agelessly beautiful Queen Vammatar watched them go, her jasper eyes cold with hate as she smiled a slow and evil smile.

There was little greenery in this flat land of bog and hillock, and what there was lay blanketed in snow. As the sun neared the horizon, clammy coils of choking fog rose from the stagnant meres and laid a chill upon men's hearts. The travelers saw few signs of life, save for a couple of Hyperborean serfs who fled from the band and lost themselves in the mist.

From time to time, one or another of the Æsir set an ear to the ground, but no drumming of hooves could be heard. They hastened on, slipping and stumbling on the uncertain, frozen footing. But before day wrapped her icy cloak around her shoulders and departed, Conan glanced to the rear, and cried out: "Someone follows us!"

The Æsir halted and gazed in the direction that he indicated. At first they could see nothing but the endless, undulant plain, whose junction with the sky was hidden in the mists. Then a Northman with vision that transcended the sight of his fellows exclaimed:

"He is right. Men on foot pursue us, mayhap . . . mayhap a half a league behind."

"Come!" growled Njal. "We will not stop to camp this night. In these fogs, 'twere easy for a foe to creep upon us, no matter how many sentries we might post."

The band staggered on while the setting sun was swallowed by the voracious mists. After the Æsir had long trudged in darkness, a wan moon climbed above the mists that hemmed them in, and its light shone on a faint patch of rippling shade. It was the pursuing force, larger and nearer than ever.

Njal, a man of iron, strode forward with his exhausted daughter in his arms; nor would he entrust so precious a burden to another. Conan, full as he was with the vigor of youth, ached in every limb and sinew as he followed the giant jarl. The other raiders, uncomplaining, maintained the grueling pace. Yet their pursuers seemed to tire not at all. Indeed, the host from Haloga had not slowed, but was on the contrary gaining upon them. Njal cursed hoarsely and urged his men to greater speed. But however doggedly they struggled on, they were altogether played out. Soon they must turn and make a stand, albeit the jarl well knew that no seasoned warrior would choose to do battle on a strange terrain when overtaken by exhaustion. Still, their meager choice was plain: either fight or be cut down.

Each time they crested a low hill clad in winter's silvered garment, they could see the silent mass of moving men, twice their number, drawing nearer than before. There was something strange about these pursuers, but neither Njal nor Gorm nor any other of the company could quite tell what was wrong with them.

As the hunters drew closer, the hunted perceived that not all the members of the oncoming force were Witchmen, a race that tended to be taller and more slender than the Northmen. Many of the pursuing host had mighty shoulders and massive frames and wore the horned helmets of the Æsir and Vanir. Njal shivered, as from the icy touch of some uncanny premonition of despair.

The other strange thing about the pursuers was the way they walked. . . .

Ahead, Njal spied the loom of a hill, higher than most of the eminences of this flat land, and his weary eyes brightened. The crest of the hill would serve for a defensive position, although the chieftain wished it higher yet and steeper to force the enemy to charge uphill in the teeth of Æsir weapons. In any case, the foe was almost snapping at their heels, so stand they must, and soon.

Shouldering the girl, Njal turned to shout from a raw throat: "Men! Up yonder hill and speedily! There we shall make our stand."

The Æsir plodded up the misty slope, to assemble at the crest, well pleased to cease putting one road-weary foot before the other. And like true warriors everywhere, the prospect of a bloody battle brightened their flagging spirits.

Thror Ironhand and the other captains passed around leathern bottles of wine and water, albeit little enough was left of either. The raiders rested, caught their breath, and limbered their bows. Long shields of wicker and hide, which had been slung upon their backs, were cast loose and fitted together to form a veritable wall of shields, encircling the crest of the hill. One-eyed Gorm uncovered his harp and began in a strong, melodious voice to chant an ancient battle song:

> Our blades were forged in the flames that leap
>> From the burning heart of Hell,
> And were quenched in frozen rivers deep,
> Where the icy bones of dead men sleep,
>> Who fought our sires and fell.

The respite was short. Shouldering through the fog, a swarm of sinister figures emerged from the murk, and with steady, rhythmic steps stalked up the slope, like men walking in their sleep or puppets worked by strings. The flight of javelins that met the shambling attackers slowed them not at all, as they hurled themselves against the ring of shields. Naked steel flashed darkly in the wan moonlight. The attackers swung high sword and axe and war hammer and brought them whistling down upon the living wall, cleaving flesh and shattering bone.

In the van Njal, bellowing an ancient Æsir war cry, hewed mightily. Then he paused, blinking, and the heart in his bosom faltered. For the man he was fighting was none other than his own captain, Egil the huntsman, who had died that morn on the end of a rope, suspended from the walls of Haloga. The light of the pallid moon shone plainly on that familiar face and turned Jarl Njal's bones to water.

5 • "Men Cannot Die Twice!"

The face that stared stonily into his own was surely that of Njal's old comrade; for the white scar athwart the brow betokened a slash that Egil, five summers before, had suffered in a raid against the Vanir. But the blue eyes of Egil knew not his jarl. Those eyes were as cold and empty as the skies above the starless, misty night.

Glancing again, Njal saw the mangled flesh of Egil's naked breast, whence hours before the living heart had been untimely torn. Revolted by the thing he saw, Njal perceived that however much he wounded his adversary's flesh, these wounds would never bleed. Neither would his old friend's corpse feel the bitter kiss of steel.

Behind the dead but battling Æsir, a half-charred Witchman stumbled up the slope, his face a grinning mask of horror. Here, thought Njal, was a denizen of Haloga who had perished in the fire set by the wily Conan.

"Forgive, brother," whispered Njal through stiffened lips, as with a backhand stroke, he hamstrung Egil's walking corpse. Like a puppet with severed strings, the dismembered body flopped backward down the hill; but instantly the cadaver of the grinning Witchman took its place.

The Æsir chieftain fought mechanically but without hope. For when your foe can summon forth the very dead from hell to fight you, what victory can ensue?

All along the line, men shouted in hoarse surprise and consternation as they found themselves fighting the walking corpses of their own dead comrades who had perished under the cruel knives of the Hyperboreans. But the host that swarmed against them numbered others in their hideous ranks. Side by side with Witchmen crushed beneath collapsing walls or burned in the day's conflagration strode corpses long buried, from whose pale and tattered flesh grave worms wriggled or fell wetly to the ground. These hurled themselves, weaponless, upon the Æsir. The stench was sickening; and terror overwhelmed all but the hardiest.

Even old Gorm felt the icy clutch of fear at his heart. His war song faltered and died.

"May the gods help us all!" he muttered. "What hope have we when we pit our steel against the walking dead? Men cannot die twice!"

The Æsir line crumbled as wave after wave of walking corpses swept the warriors down, one by one, and crushed them into the viscid earth. These attackers bore no weapons but fought with naked hands, tearing living men asunder with their frigid grip.

The Cimmerian stood in the second rank. When the stout warrior before him fell, Conan, roaring with a voice as gusty as the north wind, leaped forward to fill the gap in the swaying line. With a sweep of the Hyperborean sword he bore, he severed the neck of a skeletal thing that was squeezing the life from the Northman at his feet. The skull-like head rolled grinning down the hill.

Then Conan's blood congealed with horror: for, headless or not, the long-dead cadaver rose and groped for him with its bony hands. With the nape of his neck tingling in primordial fear, Conan kicked out and stove in ribs that showed through the tattered flesh. The corpse staggered back, then came on again, talons clutching.

Gripping his sword hilt with both hands, Conan put all his young strength into a mighty slash. The sword bit through the lean and fleshless waist, severed the half-exposed spinal column, and sent the divided cadaver tumbling earthward. For the moment, he had no opponent. Breathing hard, he shook back his raven mane.

The Cimmerian glanced along the Æsir line. Njal had fallen, taking with him a dozen of the foe, hacked, like venison, into pieces. Howling like a wolf, old Gorm took his place in the wavering line, swinging a heavy axe with deadly skill. But now the line was breaking; the battle nearly done.

"Do not slay all!" a cold voice rang in the stillness, borne upon the icy wind. "Take such as you can for the slave pens."

Peering through the murk, Conan spied the speaker. On a tall black stallion sat Queen Vammatar in her flowing snow-white robes. Trembling in every limb, he knew the legions of the walking dead obeyed her least command.

Suddenly Rann appeared at Conan's side, her face wet with tears but blue eyes unafraid. She had seen Gorm and her father fall before the onslaught of the ghastly enemy and had pushed her way through the press to the young Cimmerian. She snatched up a discarded sword and prepared to die fighting. Then, like a gift from Crom, an idea shaped itself in Conan's despairing mind. The battle was already lost. He and the surviving Æsir were bound, as surely as day follows night, for the slave pens of Hyperborea. Something, however, might be saved from the wreck of all their hopes.

Whirling, Conan lifted the girl in his arms and tossed her over his shoulder. Then he kicked and hacked a path through the foe, down the corpse-littered slope to the foot of the hill, where the queen sat on her steed awaiting the end, an evil smile on her half-parted lips.

In the stable dark beneath the swirling coils of mist, the queen, eyes raised to watch the final struggle on the hilltop, failed to mark the noiseless approach of the Cimmerian. Nor did she see the girl he set upon the trampled snow. No premonition reached her senses until iron fingers closed about her forearm and thigh and hauled her, shrieking with dismay and fury, from her mount. With a mighty heave Conan hurled the queen from him, to fall with a splash into the chilly bosom of the bog. Then Conan lifted Rann and boosted her, protesting, into the vacant saddle.

Before he could vault up behind her on the prancing animal, several of the living corpses, obeying the furious commands of their mistress, seized Conan from behind and clung, leechlike, to his left arm.

With a superhuman effort, before he was dragged earthward by the putrid monsters, Conan struck the stallion's rump with the flat of his sword. "Ride, girl, ride!" he shouted. "To Asgard and safety!"

The black horse reared, neighing, and bolted across the foggy, snow-clad plain. Rann hugged the animal's neck, pressing her tear-stained cheek against its warm hide, and her long blond hair mingled with its flying mane.

As the steed swept around the base of the hill and off to the west, she cast one backward glance, just as the brave youth who twice had saved her life went down beneath a mound of fighting cadavers. Queen Vammatar, her white robes spattered with slime, stood in the frosty moonlight, smiling her evil smile. Then the loom of the hill and the rising fogs mercifully hid the scene of the carnage.

Across the plain, a score of Æsir survivors trudged eastward in the pallid moonlight, their wrists bound behind their backs with rawhide thongs. The walking dead—those who had not been cut to pieces in the fray—surrounded the captives. At the head of the weird procession marched two figures: Conan and Queen Vammatar.

With every step the queen, her handsome face twisted with fury, slashed at the Cimmerian youth with her riding whip. Red weals crisscrossed his face and body; but he walked with shoulders squared and head held high, although he knew that none returned from the slave pens of this accursed land. Easy it would have been to slay the queen when he threw her from her stallion, but in his natal land custom demanded chivalry toward women, and he could not forsake his childhood training.

As the eastern fogs paled with the approach of dawn, Rann Njalsdatter reached the borders of Asgard. Her heart was heavy, but she remembered the last stanza of the song that Gorm had chanted beneath the fog-dimmed moon:

> You can cut us down; we can bleed and die,
>   But men of the North are we:
> You can chain our flesh; you can blind our eye;
> You can break us under the iron sky,
>   But our hearts are proud and free!

The brave words of the song stiffened her back and lifted her spirits. With shoulders unbowed and bright head high, she rode home under the morning.

The People of the Summit

After a year or two of felonious life as a thief in Zamora, Corinthia, and Nemedia, Conan, who has just about turned twenty, undertakes to earn a more or less honest living as a mercenary soldier serving King Yildiz of Turan. Following the events of the story "The City of Skulls," the mighty Cimmerian, as a reward for his services to the king's daughter Zosara, is given a noncommissioned rank corresponding to that of sergeant. In this capacity he goes to the Khozgari Hills as part of the military escort of an emissary sent by the king to the restless tribesmen of that region, in hope of dissuading them by bribes and threats from raiding and plundering the Turanians of the lowlands. But the Khozgarians are warlike barbarians who respect only immediate and overwhelming force. They treacherously attack the detachment, killing the emissary and all but two of the soldiers. These two, Conan and Jamal, escape.

The lean Turanian, whose dusty crimson jerkin and stained white breeches testified to the rigors of his flight, reined in his mare at the signal. Turning questing black eyes upon his giant leader, he asked:

"Dare we tarry here?"

His companion, similarly garbed, save that the flowing left sleeve of his woolen shirt bore the golden scimitar of a sergeant in the Turanian frontier cavalry, scowled. Blue eyes blazing beneath the crimson turban that bound his spired helmet, he tossed aside the flap of cloth that protected his face from the swirling dust and spat before he answered.

"The beasts must rest."

The heaving flanks of the two animals and their foam-flecked mouths made plain the need for a halt.

"But, Conan," protested the Turanian, "what if those Khozgari devils still follow us?" Uneasily he studied the curved scimitar thrust into his sash, and his grip tightened on the lance resting in its leathern pouch beside his right stirrup. He was comforted by the weight of the double-curved bow and the full quiver of arrows slung upon his back.

"Damn that stupid emissary!" growled the Cimmerian. "Jamal, thrice I warned him of the treacherous Khozgari tribesmen; but his head was so full of trade treaties and caravan routes that he would not listen. Now that thick-skulled head of his hangs in the smokeroom of a chief's hut, along with seven of our company. Damn him to Hell, and damn the lieutenant for permitting the palaver in the rock village!"

"Aye, Conan, but what could our lieutenant do? The emissary had full power to command. Our task was to protect him and obey him, only. Had he countered the emissary's orders, the captain would have snapped his scimitar before the regiment and reduced him to the ranks. You know the captain's temper."

"Better broken to the ranks than dead," growled Conan, scowling. "We two were lucky to escape when the devils rushed us! Listen!" He held up his hand. "What was that?"

Conan rose in his stirrups, blue eyes sweeping the gorges and crevices for the source of the faint sound he had heard. As his companion silently unslung his great bow and nocked an arrow, Conan's hand closed on the hilt of his scimitar.

A moment later, he flung himself from the saddle and, like a charging bull, rushed toward the nearby rock wall; for in that fleeting space of time, a youth had raced across the narrow gorge and scaled the steep cliff with the agility of a monkey.

Conan swept to the granite wall, found purchase for reaching hands and feet, and clambered upward with the assurance born of long experience. He heaved himself over the rim of the rock and cast himself aside just as a club descended on the spot where, a moment earlier, his head had been. Rolling to his knees, he rose and gripped the arms of his assailant before another blow could fall. Then he stared.

It was a girl he held, dirty and disheveled but nevertheless a girl, and her body would have graced the statues of a king's sculptor. Her face was pretty even through the grime, although she was sobbing now in impotent rage as she twisted her slim arms savagely against the fierce grip of her captor.

Conan's voice was rough with suspicion. "You are a spy! What tribe?"

The girl's emerald eyes flamed as she hurled back her defiance:

"I am Shanya, daughter of Shaf Karaz, chief of the Khozgari and ruler of the mountains! He will spit you on his lance and roast you over his council fire for daring to lay hands on me!"

"A likely story!" taunted the Cimmerian. "A chief's daughter without an armed following, here, alone?"

"No one dares lay violent hands on Shanya. The Theggir and the Ghoufags cower in their huts as Shanya, daughter of Shaf Karaz, rides abroad to hunt the mountain goat. Dog of a Turanian! Let me loose!"

She twisted angrily, but Conan held her slim body in the vise of his arms.

"Not so fast, my pretty one! You'll make a fine hostage for our safe passage back to Samara. You will ride before me on the saddle all the way; and you'd best sit still, lest you make the journey bound and gagged." He grinned in cold indifference to her hot temper.

"Dog!" she cried. "I do as you say for the present. But have a care that you fall not into the hands of the Khozgari in the future!"

"We were surrounded by your tribesmen a scant two hours past," growled Conan. "But their bowmen could not hit the wall of a canyon. Jamal here could outshoot a dozen of them. Enough of this chatter! We move, and move fast. Keep your pretty mouth shut from now on; it is easy enough to gag."

The girl's lips curled with unspoken ire as the horses picked their careful way between the rocks and boulders.

"Which way do you plan to go, Conan?" Jamal's voice was anxious.

"We cannot go back. I don't trust this hostage business too much in the heat of ambush. We will ride straight south to the road of Garma and cross the Misty Mountains through the Bhambar Pass. That should put us within two days' journey of Samara."

The girl turned to stare at him, her face blanched with sudden fright.

"You fool! Are you so careless of life as to try to cross the Misty Mountains? They are the haunts of the People of the Summit. No traveler has ever entered their land and returned. The People emerged but once out of the mists during the reign of Angharzeb of Turan, and they defeated his whole army by magic and monsters, as the king strove to recover the burial grounds of the ancient Turanians. 'Tis a land of terror and death! Do not go there!"

Conan's reply was indifferent. "Everywhere there are old wives' tales of demons and monsters that no one living has ever seen. This is the safest and shortest way. If we make a detour, we shall have to spend a week in the guardhouse for dallying along the road." He urged his horse forward. The clatter of hooves on stone alone broke the silence as they wove their way among the towering cliffs.

This blasted fog is as thick as mare's milk!" exclaimed Jamal some time later.

The mist hung dank and impenetrable; the travelers could see a scant two yards ahead. The horses walked slowly, side by side, occasionally touching, feeling their way forward with careful steps. The thickness of the milky mist was inconstant; the whiteness wavered and billowed, and now and then the bleak walls of the mountain pass appeared for a fleeting moment.

Conan's senses were sharply tuned. One hand held the bared scimitar; the other clutched Shanya firmly. His eyes ranged the small field of vision, taking advantage of every opening to reconnoiter.

The girl's scream, ringing out with sudden shock, brought them to a halt. She pointed with a trembling finger, cowering in the saddle against Conan's massive chest.

"I saw something move! Just for a second! It was not human!"

Conan swept the scene with narrowed lids as a random billowing of the mist cleared the roadway in front for a moment. He stiffened in the saddle, then relaxed and urged the horses forward, saying:

"Naught for the daughter of a Khozgari chief to worry about!"

But the shape at the roadside was disturbing. A human skeleton danced from two poles, crossed slantwise. The bones were held together by some fluttering rags, bits of tendon, and shriveled skin. The skull lay on the ground, grinning, snapped from the neckbones and cracked open like a coconut.

A sound floated through the mists. It began as a demonic laugh that rose and fell, changing into angry chattering, and ending in an ululating wail. The girl responded with keening. Stiff with terror, her lips moved dryly.

"The—the demons of the Summit are calling for our flesh! Our bones will lie stripped in their stone dwelling before evening. Oh, save me! I do not want to die!"

Conan felt the hair rise on the nape of his neck; and chills ran down his spine on little lizard feet. But he shook off his fear of the unknown with a shrug of his great shoulders.

"We are here, and we have to get through. Let that howler come within reach of my blade, and he'll scream in another key."

As his horse stepped forward, a heavy crash and a groan caused Conan to glance back. At that moment, he felt a tug upon his weeping captive. Before he could grasp her more firmly, she rose screaming into the mists on the end of a snakelike rope. Conan's horse reared wildly, flinging him to the ground, and the clatter of its hooves died away as he staggered to his feet.

Nearby lay Jamal and his horse, both crushed beneath a giant boulder. The man's dead hand protruded from under the gray stone, still clutching the war bow and a quiver of arrows. These Conan scooped up in one swift motion. He wasted no time in mourning the death of his comrade; for here was deadly danger. Snarling like an angry panther, he slung the bow over his shoulder, stuck the arrows in his sash, and gripped his bared scimitar.

The thick mist swirled around him as he felt a noose drop over his head. Moving with the speed of lightning, he ducked, then seized the rope with his free hand, gave a tug, and voiced a gurgling cry like that of a strangling man. His eyes were slitted as he swung upward, hauled by an immense power whose source he knew not. The feel of the mist was wet in his nostrils.

Heavy hands gripped him as he reached the edge of the escarpment, but the figures he discerned in the thinning mist were shadows only. He shrugged free of the clutching fingers and drove in silent deadliness at the nearest shadow. Soft resistance and a shriek told him that his scimitar had entered living flesh. Then the shadows closed around him. Standing with his back to the edge of the abyss, he swung his great blade in devastating arcs.

Never had Conan battled in such eerie surroundings. His enemies disappeared into the misty whirls, only to return again and again, like insubstantial ghosts. Their blades flicked out like serpents' tongues, but he soon took the measure of their clumsy swordsmanship. With renewed self-confidence, he taunted his silent attackers.

"Time you learned something of the way of the sword, you jackals of the mist! Ambushing travelers does not make for skill with the scimitar. You need lessons. The undercut—like this! The overhand slash—there! The upward rip with the point into the throat—watch!"

His exclamations were accompanied by demonstrations that left many shadowy figures gurgling or shrieking on the rocks. The Cimmerian fought with cold and terrible control, and suddenly he carried the fight to his assailants in a swift and devastating charge. Two more figures fell to his vicious slashes, their crimson guts spilling out upon the moss. Suddenly the remaining foemen melted away in panicky flight.

Conan wiped the sweat off his forehead with the wide sleeve of his uniform. Then, bending down to stare at one of the corpses, he grunted in surprise. It was no human being that sprawled there with small, sightless eyes and flaring nostrils. The low forehead and receding jaw were those of an ape, but an ape unlike any he had seen in the forests on the shores of the Sea of Vilayet. This ape was hairless from head to toe, and its only accouterment was a heavy rope twisted around its bulging swagbelly.

Conan was puzzled. The great Vilayet apes never hunted in packs and lacked the intelligence to use arms and tools, save when trained for performances before the royal court in Aghrapur. Nor was the creature's sword of a crude design. Forged of the best Turanian steel, its curved blade was honed to a razor's edge. Conan noticed a penetrating, musky odor emanating from the dead ape. His nostrils widened as he inhaled the scent with care. He would smell out his escaped prey and, following its trail, win a path through the milky mist.

"I shall have to save that fool of a girl," he muttered in an undertone. "She may be the daughter of an enemy, but I will not leave a woman in the hands of hairless apes." Like a hunting leopard, he moved forward on the scent.

As the mists began to thin, he trod more carefully. The spoor of the scent twisted and turned, as if panic had wrought havoc with his quarry's sense of direction. Conan smiled grimly. Better to be the hunter than the hunted.

Here and there beside the path small pyramids of spherical stones the size of a man's head rose above the low-lying mists. These, Conan knew, were ancient places of the dead, graves of the chiefs of the early Turanian tribes. Neither time nor the apes had managed to demolish them. The Cimmerian stepped carefully around each grave, not only to avoid a possible ambush, but also to show reverence for those who rested there.

Only torn shreds of mist remained as he reached the upper heights. Here the path became a narrow walkway atop a mountain wall, which bisected a dizzying abyss. At the end of the walkway, at the very summit of the mountain, an imposing keep of mottled serpentine loomed like an index finger of evil against the backdrop of bleak and distant mountain ranges. Conan hid behind one of the graves along the path to spy out the situation. But he saw no sign of life.

Shanya woke in odd surroundings. She lay upon a divan draped in a rough black cloth. No fetters bound her, but she had been deprived of all her clothing. She stretched her supple body upon this strange bed to look around and recoiled from what she saw.

In a wooden armchair, curiously carved, sat a man, but he was like no man that she had ever seen. His ashen face seemed made of chalk and strangely stiff; his eyes were black with no white showing around the iris; his head was bald. He wore a kaftan of coarse black cloth and hid his hands within the ebon sleeves.

"It has been many long years since a beautiful woman last came to the abode of Shangara," he said in a sibilant whisper. "No new blood has infused the race of the People of the Summit for twice a hundred years. You are a fit mate for me and for my son."

Horror ignited a bright flame of anger in the breast of the proud barbarian girl.

"Think you that a daughter of a hundred chiefs would mate with one of your abominable race? Rather would I fling myself into the nearest gorge than dwell within your house! Release me, or these walls will tremble to the thunder of a thousand Khozgari spears!"

A mocking smile parted the pale lips of the ancient, pallid face.

"You are a headstrong hussy! No spears reach through the Bhambar mists. No mortal lives who dares to cross these mountains. Come to your senses, girl! Should you persist in stubbornness, no easy leap from a cliff's edge will be your fate. Your body will, instead, be used to nourish the most ancient inhabitant of this forgotten land—one who is bound in serfdom to the People of the Summit.

"He it was who helped smite down the Turanian king who once endeavored to conquer our domain. Then we, ourselves, were strong and could do battle.

Now we are few, our number dwindling through the centuries to a bare dozen who dwell here guarded by our cliff apes.

"Still we have no fear of enemies, for the ancient one lives, ready to come forth when peril threatens. You shall gaze upon his countenance. Then choose your fate!"

The aged man arose, shaking back the folds of kaftan, and clapped his claw-like hands. At the summons, two other white-faced, skull-eyed men entered the room, bowed, and grasped a pair of handles set into the stone wall. Two massive door halves rolled smoothly back, revealing a chamber filled with billowing mist. Like a scudding cloud, it swirled into the room, and as it thinned revealed the vague outline of a huge, unmoving shape.

As the mist roiled out, the girl perceived the *thing* inside. She screamed and fainted. Then the heavy doors were closed.

Conan, hidden behind a grave mound, fretted with impatience. During his long wait, no sign of life had appeared around the forbidding tower. Had he not scented the reek of musky ape, he would have deemed the tower to be deserted. Tensely he fondled the hilt of his scimitar and ran a hand along the curve of his bow.

At length a figure strode to the battlements and gazed out upon the crumpled brown terrain. Conan could not discern details at so great a distance, but the lean contours beneath the flowing robe revealed a human shape. Conan's mouth curved in a grim half-smile.

With a single motion, he drew and loosed an arrow; and the figure on the battlement flung up its arms and toppled, limp as a broken doll, over the crenellated wall into the depths below. He nocked another arrow and waited.

This time he had not long to wait. A pierced stone portal slowly opened, and a group of apes ran out, padding splayfooted along the narrow walkway. Conan loosed again and yet again, his marksmanship unerring. His merciless hail of arrows pitched them one after another into the shadowy gorge. But still the apes came on, with lolling tongues and slavering jaws.

Conan shot his last arrow and flung the bow aside. He rushed, sword raised, to meet the two that still defended the narrow, cliffside path. Ducking, he avoided the sword thrust of the first and lunged, shearing through flesh and bone. The remaining ape proved quicker. Conan had scarcely time to wrench his reddened blade from the hairless corpse and parry a vicious swipe aimed at his head. He staggered at the impact of the great ape's blow and fell to his knees. He saw with horror the dizzying depths of the precipice that beckoned him to doom. The ape's dull mind perceived the situation, and the creature rushed forward to sweep him into the bottomless abyss.

Still on his knees, Conan feinted swiftly and lashed out with a disembowling thrust, too fast for the eye to follow. His adversary, bellowing, pitched forward and, trailing a receding cry, plummeted into the shadowy depths.

Surefooted as a mountain goat, Conan dashed up the unprotected walkway and reached the open portal. Something hissed past his head as he threw himself sidewise, and in swift retaliation, he thrust his scimitar at a black-clad figure lurking in the gloom of the entrance. A muted gurgle was followed by the clatter of a fallen weapon.

Conan bent down to peer at the corpse. A tall, skeletal man with a curiously stiff face stared up at him through sightless eyes. He saw that the face was covered by a peculiar mask of some translucent substance. He snatched it off and studied it.

The Cimmerian had never seen anything remotely like it nor like the material of which it was fashioned. He tucked it into his sash and strode on into the silent hall.

Conan moved more warily along a curving corridor that he encountered farther on. The stones were damp when he laid a hand upon them, and the clammy air reminded him of the chill of morning fog. Then suddenly the circular passageway widened into a great chamber, where a strange assemblage confronted him.

Ten black-clad, corpselike people faced him, among whom he saw two women whose stringy, colorless hair framed chalky features. They stood like painted ghosts, save that each held a murderous knife with a sawtoothed edge.

Behind them on a black-draped catafalque, set in the middle of the chamber, reclined the naked body of a girl whom he recognized as Shanya. Motionless she lay, her heavy-lidded eyes closed beneath long fringed lashes, save that her full breasts rose and fell with her even breathing. And Conan knew that she was either drugged or in a faint.

He gripped his sword more firmly as he studied the spectral group, whose coal-black eyes burned with the fire of commingled fear and hatred.

A tall, bald man began to speak. Although his voice was but a whisper borne upon the wind, it carried with bell-like clarity.

"What is your purpose here? You are no Hyrkanian, nor are you a mountain man, although you wear the garb of a Turanian."

"I am Conan, a Cimmerian. That girl is my hostage, and I have come to take her back that I may continue on my journey."

"Cimmeria—a tongue-twisting name for a land we know not of. Do you jest with us?" whispered the strange man.

"Had you voyaged to the frozen North, you would know I do not jest. We are a fighting people. With half my tribe at my elbow, I should be ruler of Turan!" growled Conan.

"You lie," hissed the old man. "The land of the north wind is the edge of the world and stretches beneath a starless, eternal night. The girl is ours by right of conquest. She shall give our race new strength, breeding strong men from her youthful womb. You, who have dared to intrude upon the People of the Summit, shall feed the maw of our defender, the ancient one."

"If I die, you will precede me into Hell," growled the Cimmerian, raising his sword.

In answer, the ghostly man struck a silver gong a single blow that reverberated from the rafters. Two men silently left the group and, moving together to the farther wall, grasped the iron handles and began to open the heavy doors. Like a great calla lily unfolding at dawn, a thick white vapor billowed from the opening and swirled toward the center of the room.

Moving in unison, the beady-eyed ancients passed their left hands across their faces. Before the thickening vapor blotted out his view, Conan saw that each had donned a curious transparent mask like that worn by his earlier assailant.

Impelled by an instinct as old as time, the barbarian reached into his sash, snatched up the mask, and managed to put it on before the cloying mists swirled and eddied around him, hiding his sable-clad enemies. To his surprise, the substance of the mask hugged the skin of his forehead, cheeks, and lids and lay like gossamer across his very eyes. Looking around the room, he was astounded to discover that he could see clearly, as if a puff of campfire smoke had vanished into the ambient darkness.

His adversaries had crept forward behind their misty shield, and now two were almost upon him. Moving on a thread of time, Conan's curved steel blade whistled through the damp air of the misty hall.

It was a massacre. The remnants of a once powerful race stood little chance against the fury of the vengeful Cimmerian. Undulating knives glanced harmlessly off the whirling streak of his restless scimitar. Each time his blade licked out, a dark-robed figure sank dying to the floor. His rough code of chivalry tempted him to spare the white-haired crones; but when the women flung themselves upon him in unrelenting frenzy, he returned blow for blow.

At last Conan stood alone in the vaulted chamber, save for ten supine bodies and the still unconscious girl. Resting on his long, curved sword, he surveyed the scene with satisfaction. Then one of the bodies writhed and raised a gaunt, accusing hand. The head man, rekindling the last sparks of his departing life, glared and spoke through lips twisted with pain.

"Barbarian cur!" he hissed. "You have destroyed our race. But you shall not live to savor your victory. The ancient one will strip the meat from your foul bones and suck the marrow from their innards. Give me strength, O Ancient One . . ."

As Conan watched in fascination, the lean man with a hideous groan rose to his knees and exerted his last powers. He struggled, half crawling, to the scarcely opened doors, and with a clawlike hand tugged at one of the twin handles on the pair of heavy doors. With a roll of thunder, the door opened wide.

Conan's hair rose on his nape as he glimpsed the hulking form within the cavernous chamber. Huge and many-limbed was the body, and spiderlike, or like an egg with legs. Its stalked eyeballs and gaping jaw exuded an almost tangible power of evil, for it was a thing conceived in the dark eons before man ever walked the earth.

Mastering his horror, the Cimmerian flung himself forward and scooped up the body of Shanya, while a clawed and hairless limb fumbled at the other door to enlarge the opening. Bearing the limp body of the girl upon his shoulder, he sprinted down the long corridor leading to the outer portal. A wheezing snuffle followed him.

Conan had almost transversed the elongated walkway, balancing precariously in his great haste, when he ventured to look back. The monster, running agilely on its ten powerful legs, had reached the midpoint of the narrow path. Panting, Conan forced himself onward until he stood between two pyramidal grave mounds. Gently laying the unconscious girl at the foot of one mound, he turned to give battle.

Conan met the first onrush of the monster with a savage cut at one of the grasping limbs, but his blade splintered against the impenetrable horny hide of the creature. Although it fell back for a moment, it came on again with its weaving gait.

Desperate, Conan cast about for any weapon, and his eyes fastened upon the nearest mound of rounded stones. Flexing his great muscles, he lifted one of the spherical boulders above his head. And, straining his mighty thews, he hurled it at the terrible apparition that was almost upon him.

The forgotten spells chanted by unremembered Turanian sorcerers over the graves of long-dead chieftains had not lost their power against a monster that roamed the mountains before mankind was young. For, with a bloodcurdling shriek, the creature, half paralyzed, tugged at a limb crushed beneath insensate rock.

Conan snatched up a second boulder and flung it; pushed yet another, rolling it toward the thrashing monster; and hurled still another. Then the undermined pyramid of ponderous stones collapsed in a hurtling avalanche, which carried the many-limbed creature down into the abyss in a cloud of dust and shards.

Conan wiped his sweaty brow with a hand that trembled as much from revulsion as from exertion. He heard a stirring behind him and swung around. Shanya's eyes were open, and she gazed around her in bewilderment.

"Where am I? Where is the white-faced, evil man?" She shuddered. "He was going to feed me to . . ."

Conan's voice broke in roughly upon her. "I cleaned up that nest of mummified robbers. Their evil thing I returned to the abyss whence it came. Lucky for you that I arrived in time to save your pretty skin."

Shanya's emerald eyes flashed with haughty anger. "I should have managed to outwit them. My father would have saved me."

Conan grunted. "Had he found his way hither, that monster would have made mincemeat of his warriors. Only by luck I discovered a weapon that could kill the overgrown cockroach. Now we must move fast. I have to be in Samara before week's end. And I still need you as a hostage. Come!"

Shanya stared at the rugged barbarian as he stood outlined against the indigo sky, one strong arm outstretched to help her rise. Her green eyes softened. For a moment her lids drooped, and she blushed, suddenly aware of her nakedness. Then she tossed her proud head, shrugged her bare shoulders, and said:

"I will come, Conan, not as your hostage, but as your guide to the border region. You saved my life, and you shall have safe conduct through Khozgari country as your reward."

Conan caught a new, warm undertone in her now-gentled voice, as she added with a ghost of a smile: "It will be interesting to learn something of the ways of a northern barbarian."

Shanya stretched her splendid body, rose-tinted by the setting sun, and reached for his outstretched hand.

Conan looked at her with appreciation. "By the bones of Crom! Perhaps dallying a few days along the way will be worth a week in the guardhouse!"

Shadows in the Dark

After mercenary service in various countries and a spell of piracy with the black corsairs of the Kushite coast, Conan adventures in the black kingdoms. Returning north, he soldiers, first in Shem and then in the small Hyborian kingdom of Khoraja. Following the events of "Black Colossus," in which he defeats the armies of the terrible Natohk, a long-dead sorcerer revived by magic, Conan settles down as general of the armies of Khoraja. He is now in his late twenties. But complications arise. The princess-regent, Yasmela, whose lover he had thought to be, is too preoccupied with affairs of state to have time for him. Her brother, King Khossus, has been treacherously seized and imprisoned by the hostile king of Ophir, leaving Khoraja in perilous plight.

In the Street of Magicians in the Shemitish city of Eruk, practitioners of the arcane arts put away their paraphernalia and began to close their shops. The scryers wrapped up their crystal balls in lambs' wool; the pyromancers extinguished the flames in which they saw their visions; and the sorcerers mopped pentacles from the worn tiles of their floors.

Rhazes the astrologer was likewise busied with the closing of his stall when an Eruki in kaftan and turban approached him, saying:

"Do not close just yet, friend Rhazes! The king has bid me get a final word from you ere you set out for Khoraja."

Rhazes, a large, stout man, grunted his displeasure, then hid his feelings behind a suave smile. "Step in, step in, most eminent Dathan. What would His Majesty at this late hour?"

"He fain would know what the stars foretell about the fates of neighboring kings and kingdoms."

"You have brought my proper fee in silver?" asked the astrologer.

"Certainly, good sir. The king has found your prognostications worthy, and hence is loath to lose you."

"Were he so loath, why did he not do somewhat to abate the envy of my Eruki colleagues toward a foreigner and curb their harassments? But it is now too late for that; I'm off for Khoraja at dawn."

"Will naught persuade you otherwise?"

"Naught; for a greater prize awaits me there than this small city-state affords."

Dathan frowned. "Odd. Travelers say that Khoraja is much impoverished by the vanquishing of Natohk, may he fry in Hell."

Rhazes ignored this comment. "Now let's consult the stars. Pray, sit."

Dathan took a chair. Rhazes set before him a boxlike brazen object with slip rings and dials upon its vertical faces. Through apertures along its sides, a multitude of brass gear wheels were plain for all to see.

The astrologer made adjustments, then slowly turned a silver knob affixed to the outer end of a protruding shaft. He watched the dials intently until they reached a setting of his choosing. At length he spoke:

"I see portentous changes. The star of Mitra will soon conjoin with the star of Nergal, which is in the ascendance. Aye, changes there shall be in Khoraja.

"I see three persons, all royal, either now, or formerly, or yet in times to come. One is a beautiful woman, caught in a web like unto a spider's. Another is a young man of high estate surrounded by walls of massive stone.

"The third is a mighty man, older than the other but still youthful, and of vast and sanguinary prowess. The woman urges him to join her in the web, but he destroys it utterly. Meanwhile the young man beats his fists in vain against the wall.

"Now strange shapes move upon the astral plane. Witches ride the clouds by the light of a gibbous moon, and the ghosts of drowned men bubble up from stagnant swamps. And the Great Worm tunnels beneath the earth to seek the graves of kings."

Rhazes shook his head as if emerging from a trance. "So tell your master that changes portend in Khoraja and in the land of Koth. Now pray excuse me; I must finish my preparations for the coming journey. Farewell, and may your stars prove auspicious!"

Through the halls of the royal palace of Khoraja, on marble floors beneath vaults and domes of lapis lazuli, strode Conan the Cimmerian. With a thud of boot heels and a jingle of spurs, he came to the private apartments of Yasmela, princess-regent of the kingdom of Khoraja.

"Vateesa!" he roared. "Where is your lady?"

A dark-eyed lady-in-waiting parted the draperies. "General Conan," she said. "The princess prepares to receive the envoy from Shumir and cannot give you audience now."

"To the devil with the envoy from Shumir! I haven't seen Princess Yasmela alone since the last new moon, and that she knows full well. If she can afford time for some smooth-talking horse-thief from one of these piddling city-states, she can afford the time for me."

"Is aught amiss with the army?"

"Nay, little one. Most of the troublemakers who resented serving under a barbarian general fell at Shamla. Now I hear naught but the usual peacetime grumbles over scanty pay and slow promotion. But I want to see your lady, and by Crom, I'll—"

"Vatessa!" called a gentle voice. "Permit him entry. The envoy can await me for a while."

Conan marched into the chamber where Princess Yasmela sat before her dressing table in the full splendor of her royal habiliments. Two tiring-women assisted in her preparations, one delicately tinting her soft lips, while another settled a glittering tiara on her night-black hair.

When she had dismissed her handmaidens, she rose and faced the giant Cimmerian. Conan held out his brawny arms, but Yasmela stepped back with a minatory gesture.

"Not now, my love!" she breathed. "You'd crumple my courtly rainment."

"Good gods, woman!" growled the Cimmerian. "When can I have you to myself? I like you better, anyhow, without that frippery about you."

"Conan dear, I say again that which I said before. Much as I love you, I belong to the people of Khoraja. My enemies wait like birds of prey to take advantage of my least misjudgment. 'Twas folly, what we did in that ruined temple. If I gave myself to you again and the word took wings, the throne would rock beneath me—and worse did I conceive a child by you. Besides, so busied am I with affairs of state that at the close of day I am too weary even for love."

"Then come with me before your high priest of Ishtar and let him make us one."

Yasmela sighed and shook her head. "That cannot be, my love, so long as I am regent. Were my brother free, something might be arranged, even though marriage with a foreigner is much against our customs."

"You mean if I can loose King Khossus from Moranthes' prison cell, he would take over all this mummery that uses up your life and keeps you from me?"

Yasmela raised her hands, palms upward. "Surely the king would resume his daily tasks. Whether he would permit our union, I do not know. Methinks I could persuade him."

"And the kingdom cannot pay the ransom demanded by Moranthes?" asked Conan.

"Nay. Before the war with Natohk, we raised a sum that he would have then accepted. But Ophir's price has risen, whilst our treasury is depleted. And now I fear Moranthes will sell my brother to the king of Koth. Would that we had a wizard to conjure poor Khossus out of his prison cell! Now I must go, my dear. Promptness was ever the courtesy of kings, and I must uphold the traditions of my house."

Yasmela rang a little silver bell, and the two servants returned to give the final touches to the princess's attire. Conan bowed his way out; then at the door he paused and said: "Princess, your words have given me a thought."

"What thought, my General?"

"I'll tell you when you have the time to listen. Farewell for now."

Taurus the chancellor brushed back the white hair above a face lined with the cares of many years. He looked intently at Conan, sitting across from him in his cabinet of state. He said:

"You ask what would befall if Khossus were slain? Why then, the council would choose his successor. As he has no legitimate heir, his sister is the likely choice, since the Princess Yasmela is popular and conscientious."

"If she declined the honor?" said Conan.

"The succession would pass to her next of kin, her uncle Bardes. If, good Conan, you think to grasp the crown yourself, dismiss the thought. We Khorajis are a clannish folk; none would accept a foreigner like you. I mean no offense; I do but utter facts."

Conan waved away Taurus's apology. "I like an honest man. But what if a ninny came to sit upon the throne?"

"Better one ninny on whom all agree, than two able princes wasting the land in a struggle for power. But you came not to discuss the rule of kings but to advance some proposal, did you not?"

"I thought if I went secretly to Ophir and smuggled Khossus out, the kingdom would greatly profit, would it not?"

Experienced statesman though he was, Taurus's eyes widened. "Amazing that you voice this proposition! Only a few days since, a soothsayer broached a like suggestion. The stars foretold, he said, that Conan would embark on this adventure and carry it to success. Thinking naught of magic, I dismissed the matter. But perchance the undertaking might happily go forward."

"What mage was this?" asked Conan in surprise.

"Rhazes, a Corinthian, lately come from Eruk."

"I know him not," said Conan. "Something the princess said gave me the notion."

Taurus looked shrewdly at the barbarian general. He had heard rumors of the passion between Conan and Yasmela but thought it wiser not to mention the affair. The idea of a union between his adored princess and a rough barbarian mercenary made Taurus shudder. Still, despite his pride of class and ancestry, he tried to be fair-minded toward the savior of Khoraja. He said:

" 'Tis but a forlorn hope, this rescue of the king, yet we must act upon it soon or not at all. Since we cannot pay Moranthes the ransom he demands, I fear he will deliver our young king to Strabonus of Koth, who offers Ophir an advantageous treaty. Once the Kothian gets Khossus in his clutches, he'll doubt-less torture him until he signs an abdication in Strabonus's favor, making him ruler of our land. We'll fight, for certain; but a bitter end is foreordained."

"We beat Natohk's army," said Conan.

"Aye, thanks to you. But Strabonus commands in great numbers sound, well-disciplined troops, unlike Natohk's motley hordes."

"And if I free the king, what reward is mine?" asked Conan.

Taurus gave a wry smile. "You come straight to the point, do you not, General? Do you not hope to enjoy more of the princess's company, once her brother regains the throne?"

"What if I do?" growled Conan.

"No offense, no offense. But would not that reward suffice you?"

"It would not. If I am to win respect among your perfumed nobles, I shall need more than an officer's pay. I will accept half the sum you offered Mor-anthes for the king's return, ere he raised his price."

With another, Taurus would have bargained; but he judged Conan too shrewdly to think that he could gain by chaffering with him. The unpredictable Cimmerian might roar with laughter, or fly into a rage, storm out, and leave Khoraja just when the kingdom needed him.

"Very well," said Taurus. "At least, the money will stay within the kingdom. I'll send for this Rhazes, and we shall plan your expedition."

Conan strode in on Yasmela, Taurus, and another—a large, stout man of middle years, wearing a gauzy robe and a sleepy expression. At Conan's heels came a small and furtive man, skeletally thin, in ragged garments.

"Hail, Princess!" said Conan. "And hail, Chancellor. And good day to you, whoever you may be."

Taurus cleared his throat. "General Conan, I present Master Rhazes of Lim-nae, the eminent astrologer. And who is the gentleman who accompanies you?"

Conan gave a bark of laughter. "Know, friends, that this is no gentleman but Fronto, the most skillful thief in all your kingdom. I found him in a reeking dive last night when all you honest folk were sleeping."

Fronto bowed low, while Taurus seemed to be controlling his feelings of distaste.

"A thief?" said the chancellor. "What need have we for such an one in this enterprise?"

"Being one myself, once, I know something of thievish ways," said Conan quietly. "When I was in the trade, though, I never learned the art of picking locks. My fingers were too large and clumsy. But for our purposes now, we may need a lock-picker, and there is none more adroit at this than Fronto. I inquired among some other thieves I know."

"You have the most amazing acquaintances," said Taurus dryly. "But—but how can you rely upon persons of his character?"

Conan grinned. "Fronto has his reasons for helping us. Tell them, Fronto."

In a soft Ophirean accent, the thief spoke for the first time: "Know, good sirs and lady, that I have my own score to settle with King Moranthes of Ophir. I am, if not of noble blood, at least from a station in life higher than that wherein you see me. I am the only son of Hermion, in his time the foremost architect of Ophir.

"Some years ago, when Moranthes, then a stripling youth, came to the throne of Ophir, he chose to build a new and larger palace in Ianthe. For this task he hired my father. The king decreed that there should be a secret passage from the interior of the palace complex to a point outside the city walls, whereby he could escape a sudden uprising of the people or the destruction of his city by a foe.

"When the palace was complete, secret passage and all, the king ordered that the builders of the passageway be slain, so none should spread the secret. My father he did not slay. Deeming himself merciful, Moranthes merely had him blinded.

"The hideous injury broke my father's health. He died within the month. But ere he passed away, he revealed to me the secret of the passage, whereby I can lead the general into the palace. And since the passage opens into the dungeons and I can pick the lock of any door, we have a gambler's chance of rescuing the king."

"And what, good thief, are you asking for your services?" inquired Taurus.

"Besides revenge, I wish for a small pension—the kind Khoraja pays to her old soldiers."

"You shall have it," said the chancellor.

Conan shot a glance at the astrologer, asking: "What is your part in this, Master Rhazes?"

"I offer my services to your expedition, General. With my astronomical calculator," he said, pointing to the brass box fitted with dials and wheels that he set upon his palm, "I can seek out the most auspicious times for each step of your journey."

Rhazes held it forward and turned the silver knob. After frowning at the dials, he said: "A happy coincidence! The best time for departure for the next two months occurs upon the morrow. And while I am no sorcerer, I know a magical trick or two to aid you."

Conan growled: "I've managed not a few years without the aid of magical mummeries, and I see no reason to turn to them now."

"Furthermore," said Rhazes blandly, ignoring Conan's remark, "I know Koth well and speak the tongue without a trace of accent. Since we shall cross that vasty kingdom on our way to Ophir—"

"The devil with that!" said Conan. "Strabonus would love to get his hands on us. Nay, we shall skirt the borders of Koth, through Shem and Argos—"

"Rhazes has reason," Taurus broke in. "Time is of the essence, and the route you propose would add much to your journey."

Yasmela joined Taurus in the argument, until Conan with little grace agreed to take the shorter route and accepted the Corinthian as the third member of the party. Then the chancellor said:

"You will need personal guards and servants to do camp chores and care for your equipment—"

"No!" roared Conan, smiting the table in the audience room. "Every extra man is one more pair of eyes to see, ears to hear, and tongue to blab our secrets. I've camped out in many lands, in weather fair and foul, and Fronto also knows the rougher side of life. If Master Rhazes does not wish to share these trifling hardships, let him remain in Khoraja."

Taurus clucked. "It is unheard of for a man of your rank, General, to cross the country without even a varlet to clean his boots."

"I've done my own chores before, and it won't harm me to do them once again. On a journey of this kind, he travels the fastest who travels alone."

The fat astrologer sighed. "I will come alone, if I must. But ask me not to chop the firewood."

"Very well, then." Conan rose. "Chancellor, give Fronto a pass from the palace, lest some sentry assume the worst and clap him in irons." He flipped a coin to the thief, who caught it. "Fronto, buy yourself some clothes—decent but not gaudy—and meet me at the officers' quarters before the supper hour. Princess, permit me to escort you to your apartments."

When they neared Yasmela's rooms, Conan murmured: "May I come to you tonight?"

"I—I know not—the risk—"

"It may be our last time, you know."

"Oh, you wretched man to torment me so! Very well, I'll send my tiring-women away before the changing of the guard."

Three riders and their pack mule trotted up the gentle slope that led toward the northern branch of the Kothian Escarpment. Now and again the travelers passed traffic on the road: a peddler afoot with his pack on his back, a farmer in a cart drawn by plodding oxen, a train of camels guided by Shemites in striped robes and headcloths, a Khorajan aristocrat whipping his chariot team ahead of his cantering knot of retainers.

At last the rampart of the escarpment towered above them. From below it seemed a solid wall of rock, but as they came closer, the wall was seen to be fractured into bluffs, parted by narrow gorges.

The road led into one of these defiles, and as they walked their horses up the winding path cut in the canyon, the wall of rock blotted out the setting sun. When the travelers mounted the highest rampart, the sun had set.

To the west, the rounded Kothian hills stood out against the skyline like breasts of recumbent giantesses. In the distance Conan could discern the peak of Mount Khrosha, its plume of smoke colored an angry red by the glow of the seething fires within the crater.

Ahead the ground rolled gently, and here a group of armed men, wearing the golden helmet of Koth embroidered on their surcoats, halted them. The travelers had reached the border. Rhazes said:

"General Conan, let me manage this."

With a grunt, the stout magician lowered himself from the saddle and approached the commander of the border guard. He took the officer by the elbow, led him aside, and spoke rapidly in fluent Kothic, now and then gesturing toward his companions. The officer's stern face broke into a smile. Then, uttering a guffaw and slapping his thigh, he turned to Conan and Fronto and jerked a thumb.

"On your way!" he said.

When the border post had shriveled in the distance, Conan asked: "What did you tell those knaves, Rhazes?"

The astrologer smiled blandly. "I said that we are on our way to Asgalun and we heard tales of war among the western states of Shem."

"Aye, but what made the fellow laugh?"

"Oh, I said that Fronto was my son, and we were going to offer prayers at the temple of Derketo to enable him to beget a son. I said he suffered from— ah—certain bodily weakness."

"You bastard!" roared Conan, doubling up with raucous mirth, while Fronto kept his eyes upon the road and scowled.

The moon swelled to full, then shrank to a slender scimitar as they plodded over the endless leagues of Koth. They moved through a land of rolling prairie, where mounted neatherds tended longhorned cattle. They skirted the barrens of central Koth, where streams emptied into a lake so salt that the few plants marching along the marge were armed with spines and thorns. In time they reached more fertile country and stopped to rest.

Conan studied his companions. Fronto worried him. The little thief was a willing helper, active and adroit; but he muttered endlessly about his private woes and grudges.

"If the gods vouchsafe the chance," he said, "I'll slay that villain Moranthes, though afterwards they boil me in oil."

"I blame you not," said Conan. "Vengeance is sweet, and I, too, have enjoyed it. But one must survive to experience the pleasure of revenge.

"Remember that we come not to kill Moranthes, however much he may deserve it, but to get Khossus out of his confines. Later if you would fain go back to stalk the king, that's your affair."

But Fronto still muttered, chewing his lips and wringing his fingers in the intensity of his pent-up emotions.

Rhazes was different. The astrologer did no chores unless Conan bullied him, and he was so unhandy that he would have been but little help if willing. Always good-natured, he entertained the two with stories out of ancient myths and disquisitions on the arcane sciences.

Still, the astrologer had a way of evading answers to direct questions, slithering out from under them like a serpent wriggling away from a descending foot. Conan felt a vague distrust of the man; yet, however much he watched and listened, he could find nothing definite against him.

They were camped in a stretch of forest east of Khorshemish when Rhazes said: "I must cast our horoscope to ascertain if danger awaits us in the capital of Koth."

He took his calculating box from the large leathern sack, which contained his magical apparatus. He studied the stars overhead, peering through the branches of the surrounding trees, and turned the silver knob, watching the dials by the flickering firelight. At last he said:

"Indeed, peril awaits us in Khorshemish. We had best take the back roads around the city. I know the route." The astrologer frowned at his instrument, made small adjustments, and continued: "I am puzzled by an indication of another danger, close to hand."

"What sort?" said Conan.

"That I cannot tell, but we had best be on our guard." Rhazes carefully returned his machine to the sack, in which he fumbled and brought forth a length of rope. "I'll show you a trick of petty magic, which I learned from a sorcerer in Zamora. See you this? Catch it!"

He tossed the rope to Conan, who shot out a hand. Then Conan leaped up with a startled oath, hurling the object from him, for in midair it had turned into a writhing serpent. Falling to earth, the snake changed back to an inert piece of rope.

"Damn your hide, Rhazes!" snarled Conan, half drawing his sword. "Do you seek to murder me?"

The astrologer chuckled as he retrieved the rope. "Merely an illusion, my dear General. 'Twas never aught but a rope. Even if it had truly been a serpent, it was—as anyone could see—a snake of a harmless kind."

"To me, a snake is a snake," grunted Conan, resuming his seat. "Count yourself lucky your head still rides atop your shoulders."

Imperturbably, Rhazes returned the rope to his bag, saying: "I warn you not to pry into this pack. Some of the things therein are not so harmless. This casket, for example."

He drew out a small, ornately carved copper chest, larger than the calculating device, and soon returned it to the bag.

Fronto grinned an elfish grin. "So the mighty General Conan fears something after all!" he chortled.

"Indeed," growled Conan, "when we sight the towers of Ianthe, we shall see who fears—"

"Do not move!" said a harsh voice in Kothic. "You are covered by a dozen drawn bows."

Conan turned his eyes as a man stepped out of the shadows—a lean man in ragged finery, with a patch over one eye. A movement among the trees revealed the presence of his fellows.

"Who are you?" grated Conan.

"A distressed gentleman, collecting his fee for the use of his demesne, to wit: this greenwood," said the man, who called to his men, "Come closer, lads, and let them see the points of your shafts."

There were only seven archers in the robber band, but they were quite enough to keep three travelers covered.

Conan bent his knees beneath him, as if preparing to spring erect. Were he alone, he would have instantly attacked, trusting to the mail shirt beneath his tunic; but the fact that his comrades would surely perish if he did so made him hesitate.

"Ah!" said the leading robber, bending over Rhazes's leathern sack. "What have we here?" Thrusting in a hand, he brought out the copper casket. "Gold—not heavy enough. Jewels—mayhap. Let us see—"

"I warn you not to open it," said Rhazes.

The one-eyed man gave a small snort of laughter, fumbled with the catch, and raised the lid of the box. "Why," he exclaimed, " 'tis empty—or full of smoke—"

The robber chief broke off with a shrill scream and hurled the box away. From it had issued what looked in the firelight like a cloud of sooty smoke. The cloud, like a living thing, swelled to man-size and wrapped itself around the one-eyed robber, who staggered about, thrashing his arms and beating his clothes as if to put out enveloping flames. As he danced, he continued screaming. Rhazes sat motionless, muttering to himself.

The box lay open where it had fallen, and from it poured another animated cloud and yet another. Shapeless, amorphous presences, they billowed through the air, like some shapeless creatures swimming through the depths of the ocean. One fastened on a second robber, who also began to leap about and yell.

The remaining robbers loosed their arrows at the inky clouds, which continued to roll out of the copper casket, but the shafts met no resistance. The robber chief and the archer ceased writhing and lay still. In a trice, the remaining archers vanished from the firelight, their pounding feet and shouts of terror receding into the silence of the forest.

Rhazes pushed himself erect and recovered his box. Holding it open, he raised his voice in a weird chant, and one by one the smoky clouds drifted toward him and poured into the casket. They seemed to have no trouble crowding back into their pen.

At last Rhazes snapped shut the lid and turned the catch. "He cannot say I did not warn him," said the astrologer with a smile. "Or, I should say, his ghost cannot so accuse me."

"You're more of a sorcerer than you care to own," growled Conan. "What were those spooks?"

"Elemental spirits, trapped by a powerful spell on this material plane. In darkness they obey me, but they cannot endure the light of day. I won the casket from a magician of Luxur in Stygia." He shrugged. "The stars foretold that I should win the game."

"Seems like cheating to me," said Conan.

"Ah, but he tried to cheat me, too, by enchanting the dice."

"Well," said Conan, "I've gambled away more gold and silver than most men see in a lifetime; but Mitra save me from being lured by a wizard into a game of chance!" Conan poked the fire thoughtfully. "Your man-eating clouds saved our gear and perhaps our necks as well. But had I not been listening to your chatter, I should have heard the men approach and not been surprised like a newborn lamb. Now stop the talk and go to sleep. I'll take the first watch."

Rhazes guided the party over little-traveled roads around Khorshemish, until they were again on the main road to Ophir.

As the leagues fell behind them, Conan grew more and more uneasy. It was not the prospect of breaking into King Moranthes's stronghold that daunted him: he had survived many such episodes. Nor was it fear of torture; and death had been his companion for so long that he paid it less attention than he would a fly.

He finally found the source of his unease: their journey so far had been too free of trouble. Whenever they were stopped by road patrols, Rhazes talked their way past them as handily as with the border guards. There had been no magical menace, no desperate combat, no wild pursuit. Conan smiled at the irony of it. He had become so hardened to peril that its absence made him uncomfortable.

At last they came in sight of Ianthe, straddling the Red River. A short, sharp rainstorm had swept the air clean, and the setting sun sparkled on the metal ornaments that crowned the city's domes and towers. Over the wall stared the red-tiled roofs of the taller houses. Fronto said:

"To cross the river by the floating bridge, one must enter the city—a questionable plan. Or we can ride half a league upstream to the nearest ford."

"Is the tunnel entrance on the northern side?" asked Conan.

"Aye, General."

"Then we'll go upstream to cross."

Rhazes looked sharply at Fronto. "Can we reach the tunnel by midnight?"

"I'm sure of it."

The astrologer nodded.

The moon, a thick crescent waxing toward the half, flitted palely through the trees as the three men dismounted in a grove on the northeast side of the city. A bowshot away, the crenellated city walls rose black against the star-strewn sky. Conan took from his saddle bags a bundle of torches—long pine sticks with one end wrapped in rags that had been soaked in lard.

"Stay with the horses, Rhazes," muttered Conan. "Fronto and I will enter the tunnel."

"Oh, no, General!" said the astrologer firmly. "I'll go with you. The tethered beasts will be quite safe. And you may need my bag of magic tricks ere you get Khossus out alive."

"He's right, General," said Fronto the thief.

"He's too old and fat for acrobatics," said Conan.

"I am more active than you think," replied Rhazes. "Further, the stars foretell that you will require my aid to bring off your enterprise."

"Very well," growled Conan. In spite of himself, Conan had been impressed by some of Rhazes's prognostications about such things as weather and accommodations at inns. "But if you lag behind and Ophireans seize you, do not expect me return to rescue you!"

"I am prepared to take my chances," said Rhazes.

"Then let's go!" hissed Fronto, fidgeting. "I cannot wait to flesh my dagger in one of Moranthes's villains!"

"No stabbing for mere pleasure!" growled Conan. "This is no pleasure hunt in the greenwood. Come on."

Muttering, the thief led his companions through the grove and into a clump of shrubs a few yards beyond the palace wall. Above them, the moonlight twinkled on the helmet and spear of a sentry pacing his rounds upon the parapet. All three froze, like hunted animals; and they held their positions, scarcely breathing, until the sentry passed out of sight.

In the center of the thicket, shielded on all sides from view by the circle of bushes, they found a patch of earth where the grass grew thin. Fronto scrabbled in this meager ground cover until he found a bronzen ring. Seizing it, he tugged upward, but nothing moved.

"General," he breathed, "you are stronger than I; try raising it."

Conan took a deep breath, stooped, grasped the ring, and heaved. Slowly, with a grating sound, the buried trapdoor rose. Conan peered down into fetid darkness. The moonlight outlined a flight of stairs.

"My father planned the thing aright," whispered Fronto. "Even so tall a man as you, Conan, can walk upright without butting the ceiling."

"Stay here to lower the trapdoor, after I light a torch," said Conan, feeling his way down the steps.

At the bottom, he went to work with flint and steel. After striking sparks for some time without result he growled:

"Crom's devils! The rain has gotten into my tinder. Has anybody some that's dry?"

"I have that which will do in its stead," said Rhazes, leaning over Conan's shoulder. "Stand back, pray."

From his leather bag the astrologer produced a rod, which he pointed at the torch while muttering an incantation. The end of the rod glowed red, then yellow, then white. A beam of bright light speared the torch, which smoked, sputtered, and burst into flame. The rod's glow faded, and Rhazes returned the implement to his bag.

"Lower the trapdoor, Fronto!" said Conan. "Gently, you fool! Banging it down that way will alert the guards!"

"Sorry; my hand slipped," said Fronto, scuttling spiderlike down the stairs. "Give me the torch; I know the way."

In silence the three men plodded along the dark passage. It was lined with stone slabs on floor and sides and roofed with massive timbers. Moss and fungus splotched the crude stones and squelched noisomely underfoot. Rats squeaked and fled from their approach, red eyes glinting like accursed rubies in the blackness, claws scraping the damp stones as they fled.

Through the dripping darkness they proceeded, guided only by the flickering torch that Fronto held aloft. They said nothing. Was it out of inborn caution, or was it unwillingness to acknowledge the clammy breath of fear that followed them through the gloom and whispering darkness?

Conan looked about him, grimly. The flickering orange flames of the torch painted black shadows across the lichen-encrusted stones—shadows that swooped and billowed like enormous bats. The subterranean passage had for years been sealed away from the outside world; for now the air was vitiated and stifling, thick with the unwholesome odors of decay.

After a time Conan growled: "How much farther, Fronto? We must have walked clear across Ianthe and are beyond the city now."

"We are not halfway yet. The palace lies in the midst of the city, where once stood the citadel."

"What noise is that?" asked Rhazes when a rumble as of thunder reverberated overhead.

"Just an ox cart on Ishtar Street," said Fronto.

At last they reached the tunnel's end. Here a flight of steps led upward to a trapdoor like the other. Conan took the torch and examined the trap.

Conan asked softly: "Where in the dungeons does this passage lead?"

Fronto rubbed a reflective hand over a stubbled jaw. "To the far end of the south branch," he said.

"And King Khossus is held prisoner in the middle branch, parallel to this," murmured Rhazes from behind them. Conan, suddenly suspicious, shot him a glance.

"How do you come to know that?" he demanded sharply.

The plump seer spread both hands in a disarming gesture. "By my stars, General. How else?"

Conan muttered something that sounded like a curse.

The eager thief pushed up the trapdoor a finger's breadth at a time, pressing an attentive ear against the rough wood. At last he whispered: "There seem to be no guards in this part. Come."

Despite a faint squeal of hinges, he thrust the trap up all the way and beckoned to his companions.

Conan let his breath out with a sigh and set the torch down so that it leaned against the side of the tunnel and burned with a dim but welcome light. Then he followed Fronto to the dungeon. After him panted Rhazes.

They emerged into a corridor some twenty paces long and saw a row of untenanted cells on either side. The air was heavy with the prison stench of decay and mold and ordure. The only light came faintly from a torch mounted in a bracket on the wall of a transverse passage at the far end of their corridor, save that a roseate glow emanated from the torch Conan had set against the dank wall of the tunnel below them. To extinguish this telltale glow, Fronto began to lower the trap, but Conan hastily set a coin between the trap and the strut on which it rested, propping the door up ever so slightly; so that, by the slight irregularity of flooring, they could find it when they again had need of it.

Conan's sword whispered from its sheath as he turned and led his strange companions toward the distant torch. Under drawn brows, his blue eyes darted from side to side, scanning the cells. Most were empty, but in one a pile of bones gleamed whitely in the semidarkness. In another a living prisoner, ragged and filthy, his face all but invisible behind a tangled mass of grizzled hair, shuffled up to the bars and silently watched the invaders. So quietly did they move along the narrow hall that the very silence seemed to roar.

When they reached the corner of the corridor where the bracketed torch belched smoke, Fronto pointed to the right. Moving like a pride of hunting lionesses, they paced the cross-passage unseen, and turning left again, they reached another cell-lined passageway. As they proceeded noiselessly along it, Fronto jerked a thumb to draw Conan's attention.

This cell was twice the size of the others. In the dimness, Conan made out a chair, a small table, a washstand, and a bed. A man sitting on the bed rose as the three silent figures stopped outside the bars that held him. The man could not clearly be discerned, but from his stance and outline, Conan perceived that he was young and handsomely attired.

"Get to work, Fronto," whispered Conan.

The thief pulled from his boot a slender length of bent wire and inserted it into the keyhole, his feral eyes agleam in the flickering torchlight. After a momentary fumble, the lock clicked back and Conan shouldered in the door.

The prisoner recoiled as, sword in hand, Conan strode in. "Has Moranthes sent you here to murder me?" he whispered hoarsely.

"Nay, my lad; if you be Khossus of Khoraja, we've come to rescue you."

The young man stiffened. "You must not speak so to an annointed king! You should address me—"

"Lower your voice," snarled Conan. "Are you Khossus, or are you not?"

"I am he; but you should say 'Your Maj—'"

"We've no time for such courtesies. Will you come or stay?"

"I'll come," grumbled the youth. "But who are you?"

"I'm Conan, general of your army. Now come quickly and quietly."

"First lend me your sword, General."

"What for?" said Conan in astonishment.

"The captain of the guard here has used me with spite and contumely. He has insulted the honor of Khoraja, and I have sworn to fight him to the death. And I'll not leave until it's done!"

Khossus's voice rose as he spoke until it echoed in the narrow cell. Conan glanced at his companions, shook his touseled mane, and brought his huge fist up against Khossus's jaw. With a click, the king's teeth came together, and Khossus fell back against his cot.

An instant later, Conan, with the king's unconscious body draped across one shoulder, led his companions from the cell. As they turned into the transverse passageway, they heard the tramp of booted feet and the clank of metal accouterments.

"Run for the tunnel. I'll stand off the guard," hissed Conan.

"Nay, you bear the king. You go ahead; I'll harry the lout," whispered Rhazes, fumbling in his bag.

"What goes on there?" rumbled an angry voice, as its owner, sword unsheathed, appeared around the third prong of the cell block.

As Conan and Fronto sprinted toward the passage in which the trapdoor lay, the astrologer, billowing robes etched by the feeble light of the single torch, drew from his leathern sack that which appeared to be a hempen noose. The prison warden checked his pace and threw up a hand to catch the flying rope. Then shrieking at the writhing thing within his grasp, he flung the serpent from him, turned abruptly, and still yelling like a madman, vanished down the farthest corridor.

Then Rhazes trotted to the open trapdoor, where Conan, still bearing the unconscious king upon his shoulder, reached up a brawny arm to steady his descent. As the astrologer reset his bag strap across his back, Fronto scampered up the steps and lowered the trapdoor carefully.

Conan muttered: "Is there no bolt to secure the trap?"

"I see none," said Fronto. "The fact that the door is masked by several flagstones makes it nigh invisible from the upper passageway."

"Then we must run," said Conan, and shifting the weight of the slender king, he followed Fronto, who darted ahead with upheld torch. Rhazes, like some merchant ship sailing before the wind, panted after them.

During their flight, Khossus revived. When his head cleared, and he realized his undignified position, he complained:

"Why do you carry me like a sack of tubers on the way to market? Put me down instanter! This is no way to treat your king!"

Conan, never slackening his pace, grunted. "When you can run as fast as I, I'll set you down. Unless, perchance you prefer to be overtaken by the prison warden and returned to your cell—or to a worse one. Well?"

"Oh, all right," said the young king sulkily. "But you seem to have no feel for royal dignity."

At the exit from the tunnel, Conan set the king upon his feet and, pushing past Fronto, scrambled up the stairs. With a grunt and a mighty heave, he pushed open the trapdoor. Fronto was at his heels.

"Put out that torch!" he snapped. Fronto obeyed.

Then Conan stepped out into the starlight. The moon had set, and Conan realized that the rescue had taken longer than expected.

With his companions crowding behind him, Conan worked his way through the circle of shrubbery around the open trapdoor and halted. A few paces ahead, standing in the thicket, was a score or more of armed men with crossbows cocked and trained on the fugitives. Behind them, in the grove, he saw the flames of a brisk campfire.

"What's this?" demanded Conan, sweeping out his sword.

"Pray, General," wheezed Rhazes behind him, "I can explain."

"Come out, Rhazes," said one of the dark figures in Kothic, "we should not wish to shoot you by mistake."

The astrologer pushed past Conan and turned. "Dear simple General, you'd best surrender quietly. These are soldiers of my native Koth, whose king I have the honor loyally to serve. Arrangements for this ambuscade were made on our way hither by our border guards. We avoided Khorshemish lest some acquaintance hail me and disclose my small imposture. You have helped me pluck King Khossus out of Moranthes's clutches; and now we'll take the pair of you to Koth. Thus shall we remove the last obstacle to reuniting Khoraja with her mother country."

Conan tensed, rocking forward on the balls of his feet, preparing for action. He trusted to his mailshirt to deflect the crossbow bolts; and if that failed — well, no man can live forever.

"Drop your sword, General Conan!" ordered the soldier who had already spoken.

"You'll have to kill me first!" shouted Conan, rushing forward to meet the Kothian officer.

Then Fronto moved. With a scream of rage, the little thief leaped forward, eyes gleaming in reflected firelight, and drove his dagger into Rhazes's paunch — once, twice, thrice. Two crossbows snapped, but the bolts whistled harmlessly into the dark, as the arbalesters feared hitting their own men.

Silently Rhazes sank down, his fluttering garments billowing like pale fog in the starlight. His leather bag fell open on the ground beside him. Like a jumping spider, Fronto leaped sidewise, snatched up the bag, and ran for the grove of trees. Then another crossbow twanged. Fronto strangled on a blood-flecked cough and dropped headfirst into the fire. The bag he bore likewise landed in the embers.

Conan, defending Khossus, traded blows with several Kothians. His blade whirled and clanged against his foes', as the cold stars glimmered on the steel. One Kothian gave back with a hoarse scream, gripping the stump of his sword arm with his remaining hand. Another fell, his belly ripped open, spilling out his guts. Bounding ahead Khossus stooped and wrenched the sword from the severed hand in time to save the battling Cimmerian from a sword thrust in the back.

Then, despite the noise and confusion, Conan perceived the faint jingle of mail, the crackling of broken branches, the tramp of booted feet as more men pushed through the thicket. Drawing Khossus with him, Conan faded into the bushes as a party of Ophirean prison guards poured from the tunnel on the trail of their liberated prisoner. Bursting through the thicket, they found themselves face to face with the men of Koth. Conan and his king, hidden in the shadows, heard the snap of a crossbow and shrieks of pain as the new battle was joined.

All was confusion. Kothians fought Ophireans. Men shouted contradictory orders.

"Khossus!" barked the Cimmerian. "Run for the grove—on the left—the horses tethered there."

They broke from their shelter and ran. Then the Ophirean prison warden recognized the slender king and shouted to his men: "To me! Here's the prisoner—and his rescuer! Seize them!"

"Faster!" said Conan, wheeling around to stem the tide of pursuers. He parried a slash from one scarcely seen antagonist and wounded another. He was about to strike down another, a Kothian, when an Ophirean attacked the man, and the fight swirled off into the darkness. In the confusion, Conan and Khossus plunged out of the melee, reached the grove, jumped over the embers of the fire, and raced for their tethered horses.

"Stop them! Stop them!" shouted a chorus of voices as the fugitives disappeared among the trees. Behind them Kothians joined with Ophireans, each intent on recapturing their human prize and his barbarian protector. One Kothian leaped the fire, and Conan, wheeling, struck him down just as a tremendous report shook the earth and showered the fugitives with embers and debris. Rhazes' bag, simmering on the fire, had at last exploded.

As two Ophireans plunged into the grove in hot pursuit, black, smoky clouds boiled up from the ruptured fire. In wave after wave the shadows rose, like huge amoeboids swimming in the deep. One swooped down upon the first oncomer and engulfed him. The man gave a wild shriek of terror and lay still. The other pursuer, whirling in his haste to get away, stumbled over a root and sprawled beneath another undulating cloud.

"Rhazes's shadows," muttered Conan, as another howl of horror from a dying man floated upward. "Untie the horses, fast. Ride one and lead the other!" With trembling fingers, Khossus obeyed.

The next instant Conan and the king flung themselves into their saddles and spurred out of the grove, faces close to the horses' necks to avoid the lashing branches. But even in their mad flight, Conan looked back to see the billowing shadows hovering like wings of death, impartially, above both the men of Ophir and their Kothian adversaries, whose fleeing cries of pain and terror melded into one indistinguishable shriek.

Conan and the king came out upon a road, and the ringing of their horses' hooves drowned out the clangor of the rout.

———

As the flying hooves cleaved the still night, Khossus called out in a shaky voice: "Conan! This is not the way to Khoraja! We're on the road to Argos and Zingara!"

"Which way do you think they'll go to look for us?" snarled Conan. "Come on, kick some speed out of that nag!" He galloped westward with the king of Khoraja close behind him.

Although the flying pair made exceptional speed by frequent changes of mount, the following nightfall saw them still within the confines of Ophir. None challenged them, since their flight had outrun the news of their escape. They found a stretch of forest and made camp, eating dried fruits and biscuits from their saddle bags. Khossus, who had abandoned his efforts to make Conan address him in royal style, told how he came to be captured:

"Moranthes proposed an alliance against Strabonus of Koth, and that seemed logical to me. Like a fool, I went to parley with him with a small escort only, carefully bypassing Koth by traveling through the city-states of Shem. Taurus had warned me against Moranthes, but I was sure that no annointed king would sink to trickery. I know better now—for no sooner had I reached Ianthe than the scoundrel clapped me into prison.

"My lot was somewhat better than that of common prisoners. Now and then news of the outside world reached me. Thus I learned of your victory over Natohk at the Shamla Pass." The king peered narrowly at Conan. "I also heard that you had become my sister's lover. Be that true?"

Conan looked up from the fire with a slight suggestion of a smile. "If I had, it would be ungentle of me to admit it. Whilst no blushing virgin, I do not kiss and tell. But tell me, would you accept me as a brother-in-law?"

Khossus started. "Out of the question, my good General! You—a foreign barbarian and vulgar mercenary—nay, friend Conan, think not upon the matter. I appreciate your heroism and owe my life to you, but I could not admit you into the royal family. And now it is my royal wish to sleep, since I am weary to the bone."

"Very well, Your Majesty," grumbled Conan acidly. "Your royal will be done."

Long that night he sat beside the embers of the fire, his black brows drawn in night-dark thoughts.

The following day they crossed the Argossean border and put up at an inconspicuous inn. After supper, as they dawdled over jacks of ale, Khossus said:

"General, I have been thinking. You deserve well of me." He raised a hand as Conan opened his mouth for a reply. "Nay, deny it not, your rescue of your king from the Ophireans, the Kothians, and your treacherous friend Rhazes's elementals were feats worthy of an epic.

"A man like you should be well settled with a family, and I shall wish to keep you with us to direct our army. Since you cannot wed the princess Yasmela, I will find you an attractive maiden of the middle classes—some small landowner's daughter, perhaps—and unite the twain of you. And I shall likewise choose a royal marriage partner for my sister.

"However, while I wish you to direct our army, one of your lowly origins cannot continue to command Khoraja's knights and noblemen. You had trouble, did you not, with the unfortunate Count Thespides on that same score? So I shall choose a man of suitable rank to bear the name of general, yet he shall ever follow your advice. And I shall create some special, well-paid post, open to commoners, for your express benefit."

Conan looked at the king, his eyes inscrutable. "Your Majesty's generosity overwhelms me," he said.

Oblivious of the sarcasm, Khossus waved away a protest. " 'Tis but your due, good sir. How would the title sergeant-general suit you?"

"Let us leave that till we return," said Conan.

Lying awake in the dark room of the inn, Conan pondered his future. He had ever been one to live for the moment and let the future take care of itself. Yet, it was obvious now that his career in Khoraja was headed for trouble. This haughty but well-meaning young ass believed every word he spoke about his royal rights and duties.

True, he could quietly kill the king and return to Khoraja with some cock-and-bull story about the idiot's end. But to risk so much to rescue him, only to murder the fool, would be ridiculous. Yasmela would never forgive him. Besides, he had given his word to save the king, and—this he noted with some small surprise—his passion for Yasmela had begun to cool.

At Messantia, Khossus found a port official who knew him, and who, on the strength of his position, lent him two hundred Argossean gold dolphins, borrowed from a moneylender. The king handed the bag containing this small fortune to Conan for safekeeping, saying:

"It becomes not the dignity of a monarch to carry filthy money."

They found a ship about to sail for Asgalun, whence they could make their way through Shem to Khoraja. As the sailors manned the ropes preparing to cast off, Conan dug into the bag of gold and brought out a fistful of coins.

"Here," he said, handing the money over to Khossus. "You'll need these to get home."

"But—but—what are you doing? I thought—"

"I've changed my mind," said Conan. As the vessel left the pier, he leaped from the ship's rail to the quay. Then he turned and added, "It's time I visited my homeland, and there's a craft sailing for Kordava tomorrow."

"But my gold!" cried the king from the receding deck.

"Call it the price of your life," shouted Conan across the widening stretch of water. "And say farewell to Princess Yasmela for me!"

Whistling an air, he walked away without another backward look.

The Star of Khorala

*Conan survives adventures as a leader among the kozaki of the steppes east of Za-
mora and as a pirate captain on the Sea of Vilayet. He saves Queen Taramis of
Khauran from a plot by her evil twin sister, rules a desert band of Zuagir nomads,
and gains a fortune but quickly loses it in the stews and gambling houses of Zamboula.
He does, however, acquire, by a feat of sleight-of-hand, a ring of supposedly fabulous
magical powers—the Star of Khorala.*

*Conan is now about thirty-one years old. After the events of "Shadows in Zam-
boula," he rides westward with the Star into the meadowlands of Shem and across the
vast stretches of Koth on his way to Ophir, looking for a substantial reward from the
queen of Ophir for the return of her magical gem. He hopes, if not for the rumored
roomful of gold, at least for enough to keep him in comfort for a while, with an official
post of good pay and power thrown in. Instead, he finds neither the political situation
in Ophir nor the occult powers of the gem quite what he had expected.*

1 • The Road to Ianthe

The wanton river stretched lazily between the kingdoms of Koth and Ophir
and smiled at the cloudless sky, when a horse's hooves at the shallow ford
shattered the surface of the water into rainbows of spray. The flanks of the
mare, sweat-darkened, heaved as she lowered her head to drink; but her rider,
giving thought to her welfare, tightened the rein and guided her across to the
farther bank. Later, when she had cooled, it would be time enough for her to
drink the cold river water.

The rider's dusty face was streaked with runnels, and his attire, once black,
was powdered mouse-gray from the dusts of the road. Still, the hilt of the
serviceable broadsword, which hung from his belt, bore the luster of meticulous
care. For over a month Conan had been traveling the road from Zamboula,

pushing through the deserts and steppes of eastern Shem and picking his way along highways and byways of turbulent Koth. He had perforce to keep his weapon ready for instant use.

In his pouch lay a comfortable weight—the Star of Khorala, a great gem set in a ring of gold, which had been stolen some time past from the young queen of Ophir and snatched in turn by Conan from the satrap of Zamboula.

The mighty Cimmerian, ever adventurous, was stirred by the thought of returning the stone to the beautiful Queen Marala. Such service to the ruler of so great a kingdom should earn him—if not the fabled roomful of gold—at least some hundreds of gold coins, riches enough for many years' comfort. The reward, so ran his thinking, would buy him land, or a commission in a Hyborian army, or mayhap a title of nobility.

Conan despised the people of Ophir, whose kingdom had long been a cockpit of conflict among the feudal factions. The weakling ruler, Moranthes II, leaned for support on the strongest among his barons. It was said that, centuries before, a far-seeing count had sought to force the fractious nobles and their king to sign a charter. Many tales were told about this ancient effort to provide a stable government, but the present state of Ophir showed no lessening of its immemorial turmoil.

Conan chose the shortest route to Ianthe, the capital. His road wound through craggy borderland that huddled, lone and deserted, save for the ramshackle huts of peasants who eked out a bare living as goat-herds. Then, little by little, the country grew fertile; and after seven days of journeying within the kingdom, Conan rode among golden fields of ripening grain.

The countryfolk here, as before, remained surly and silent. Although they permitted the traveler to purchase food and lodging at wayside hostelries, they answered his questioning with grunts and monosyllables or not at all. While Conan himself was not a garrulous man, this reticence irritated him; and to discover the cause of it, he asked the landlord of an inn outside the capital of Ophir to share a cup of wine with him. He asked:

"What ails the people hereabouts? Never have I seen a folk so sour and silent, as if the worm of death were feeding on their guts! I hear of no war, and the land is bursting with fruit and ripening grain. What is wrong in the kingdom of Ophir?"

"The folk are frightened these days," replied the taverner. "We know not what will happen. Word travels on forked tongues that the king has imprisoned his queen because, quoth he, she excelled in lewdness whilst he was busy with his councillors. But she is a gentle lady, always just and kind to the common folk when she travels in the land, and never the hot breath of scandal has scorched her before.

"Lately the barons have kept to their castles, laying up supplies and preparing for war. We know not how the king's mind runs."

Conan grunted. "You mean, you wonder if the king has lost his sanity. What faction now rules this weakling?"

"The king's cousin, Rigello, is said to be in favor again. Five years since, he burned ten villages of his fief when the rains came not and folk could not deliver to their liege their quota of crops. He was therefore banished from the court; but now, they say, he has returned. If true, this bodes ill for the rest of us."

The door of the tavern opened; a gust of air and the jingle of bells interrupted the talk. Conan beheld a grizzled warrior in helmet and mail, with a star-shaped emblem on his chest, who shortly doffed his casque and threw it clanging on the floor.

"Wine, damn you," he said hoarsely. "Wine to slake my thirst and deaden my conscience!"

A tavern maid hurried to fetch a pitcher and goblet. Conan asked: "Who is that man?"

The host lowered his voice and, leaning forward, murmured: "Captain Garus, an officer of Queen Marala's guard. The regiment is now disbanded. I do but hope he has the wherewithal to pay for his victuals."

Conan took a silver coin from his pouch. "This will pay for his eating and drinking, and mine, too. The balance will cause you to forget our talk."

The taverner opened his mouth as if to speak, but after a glance at the grim eyes of the black-browed Cimmerian, he merely answered with a nod and scuttled back to his wine taps. Picking up his own pitcher and goblet, Conan carried them to the old soldier's table and seated himself boldly.

"I offer you health, Captain!" he said.

The ex-officer's faded eyes fixed themselves on Conan's face with unexpected sharpness.

"Do you try to make a fool of me, stranger? By Mitra, do you mock me? I know full well that I should have laid down my life defending my queen and that I failed to do so. You need not tell me this!"

Conan curbed the curt reply that trembled on his lips when the tavern door slammed open and four men in ebon mail stamped in, hands on sword hilts. Their leader, a gaunt fellow with a white scar stitched from ear to mouth, pointed a mail-gloved finger. "Seize the traitor!"

The old captain lumbered to his feet, tugging at his sword, as the grasping hands of two soldiers seized and tried to disarm him. Conan leaped to the table top, and with a sweeping kick, sent one of the intruders tumbling into a corner. The other aimed a cut at Conan's legs; but the Cimmerian leaped high with folded knees, and the blade whistled harmlessly beneath his feet. Then his booted heels slammed into the chest of the attacker, and both men hit the straw-covered floor in a whirl of thrashing limbs. The man collapsed with a scream of anguish as his ribs cracked under the blows of the mighty Cimmerian.

Conan rolled to his feet and swept his sword out of its scabbard just in time to parry a slash from the scar-faced officer's weapon. Out of the corner of his eye, he saw his drinking companion trading blows with the remaining invader; swords flashed in the firelight. The other patrons of the inn scrambled out of the way—bursting out the door, pressing against the oaken walls, or ducking under the stout tables.

Thrusting, slicing, and parrying with the scar-faced officer, Conan roared: "Why the devil do you interrupt my drinking?"

"You will find out in Count Rigello's dungeons!" panted the other. "Your drinking days are done."

Scarface, Conan realized, was a seasoned and skillful fighter. During a brief pause, the officer drew a poniard from his belt, and after deflecting one of Conan's furious attacks, he threw himself into a body-to-body bind, stabbing at Conan with his free left arm.

Catching the man's wrist, Conan dropped his blade. With a speed no civilized man could match, he clapped a hand to the other's thigh, hoisted him high above his head, and hurled him to the floor with an earth-shaking crash. The officer's weapons clattered away, and he lay, barely breathing, blood gushing from his mouth.

Conan retrieved his sword and turned to see how Garus fared. The old soldier's opponent had lost his weapon and now stood with back to wall, nursing a bloodstained arm and murmuring pleas for quarter.

"Have done with him!" shouted Conan. "Let us be off!"

Garus slapped the man's ear with a gusty blow to the side of his head, and the fellow, moaning, tumbled into the straw. The innkeeper and the bravest of the tavern's habitués clustered in the doorway, gaping at the carnage and the overturned tables; but Conan and Garus, ignoring their slack-jawed stares, sheathened their weapons and hastened out. Soon they were galloping toward Ianthe, hooves drumming on the clay roadbed, cloaks blown backward in the wind.

"Why did you, a stranger, save my hide?" grumbled Garus when they slackened their speed to a trot.

Conan's rude laugh floated back along the moonlit road. "I like not to be disturbed at my drinking. Besides, I have business with your queen, and I shall find your help of value to procure an audience."

He spurred his mount, and the horses plunged forward into the velvet night.

At dawn they thundered into the city, which straddled the Red River, a tributary of the Khorotas. The rising sun painted the windows of the tile-roofed buildings myriad shades of red, and the metallic ornaments on the domes and towers twinkled, jewel-like, in the clear morning light.

2 • "Fetch Me the Dragon's Feet"

Again a tavern, again a table, again a pitcher of wine. At the Wild Boar in Ianthe sat Conan and Garus, swathed in voluminous hooded robes, purchased with gold the Cimmerian had brought from Zamboula. The merchants of the city favored these garments because, Conan guessed, their sheer bulk aided many to cozen their customers. In this surmise, Conan was not altogether wrong; but the robes also lessened a man's chance of recognition by the minions of Lord Rigello, a useful aspect of the apparel.

The wine drinkers talked in low voices to a dark-skinned young woman in a servant's smock, of a quality that bespoke service in a wealthy household. The girl was red-eyed from weeping.

"I do so want to help my queen!" she said.

"Keep your voice down," growled Conan. "Where is she now?"

"In the West Tower of the royal palace. Ten of Count Rigello's men guard her door, and her chambermaid brings her food. The only person else allowed to visit her is her physician."

"What is his name?" said Conan, eyes glinting.

"The learned Doctor Khafrates, who dwells by the Corner Gate. He is an old and wise friend to the queen."

"Fear not, little one," said Conan. "We shall meet with the good doctor to see if he can cure the queen's affliction. But first let's have a look at this West Tower."

The young evening wore a wreath of rosy clouds in honor of the coming night, and the streets of Ianthe rang with the shouts and laughter of the populace. Conan and Garus strolled among them and unnoticed reached the West Tower of the royal palace. The tower formed a corner bastion of the curtain wall encircling the palace grounds. Its cylinder of masonry rose abruptly from the side of one of the city's major avenues. There were no openings on the four lower stories of the tower, but above that level, windows pierced the massive structure, some illuminated from within.

"Which is the queen's chamber?" whispered Conan.

"Let me see," said the girl. "It is that one, the second row up, third window from the right end." She pointed.

"Don't point, lass; you'll draw attention." Conan walked to the base of the wall and examined the masonry.

"Nobody could climb that wall," said Garus.

"No? You have not seen what a Cimmerian hillman can do." Conan fingered the grouting between the ashlars of stone. "You're right in one way, Garus. The recesses between the stones lack depth for toe- and finger-holds. Had I the world of time, I could scale this wall by digging mortar from between the stones to make my own holds as I climbed. Well, let us now find Doctor Khafrates."

The good doctor was a portly man with a vast gray beard that lay, like melting snow, upon his expansive chest. Thoughtfully he answered Conan's questions.

"In accordance with my oath, I treat all who come for healing, no matter on which side of the law they stand. So, in the course of timeless years, I have come to know the city's leading thieves. I would not reveal one name to any man, save for my queen. . . .

"I will accompany you to the lair of Torgrio the thief, who has but lately retired from his old profession. In his day he was a daring practitioner of his peculiar art. He was a burglar, apt at climbing lofty walls, who now lives on his ill-gotten gains, betimes selling stolen merchandise for younger colleagues. Come."

Torgrio's house, a small but well-kept structure, nestled between a magnate's mansion on one side and a pottery works on the other. It was a house to which a thrifty, hardworking tradesman might retire after a lifetime of scrimping; for it wore respectability like a garment. Torgrio was no man to make an ostentatious display of his felonious gains.

The man himself was of so spare a build as to remind Conan of a spider. When Khafrates introduced the newscomers and vouched for them, Torgrio smiled a snag-toothed grin.

"Like the good doctor, I have my principles," he said, "but this case admits of exceptions. What would you of me?"

"Means to climb the Western Tower," said Conan.

"Indeed?" said Torgrio, raising an eyebrow. "What means?"

"You know what I need," growled Conan. "There are such things in Ianthe. When I was in the business myself, I heard about them."

"I'll allow they do exist," said Torgrio.

"Then, will you show them to me?"

"Perhaps, for a consideration," said Torgrio with a shrug. He called across his shoulder, "Junia, fetch me the dragon's feet!"

Presently a middle-aged woman padded in, her arms full of steel devices. Torgrio took them and, fingering them, explained:

"This pair is clamped to your boots—if indeed they will cover feet as large as yours—while this pair is for your hands. First, you adjust the clamps to the size of the courses of stone. Then you place a dragon's foot against one course and pull the handle down, so, clamping these claws into the upper and lower edges of a stone. To release the device, you push the handle up, so. Always retain your grip with one hand and foot while moving upward to another course of stone."

Garus shuddered. "If Mitra himself commanded me to crawl up a wall like a fly, I could not."

Conan's laughter was like thunder in the hills. "I got my head for heights on the cliffs of my native land. Sometimes it was either climb or lose your life. Let's practice somewhat on your garden wall, Torgrio."

3 • The Wall No Fly Could Climb

The captain of the guardsmen halted the stout Khafrates outside the chamber assigned to the queen. Amid the guard's crude jests about his rotund figure, the physician endured their routine search. Then the heavy locks clanked open, and Khafrates entered the queen's apartment.

The dark-skinned slave girl, now in flowing robes, conducted him into the inner room. The apartment proved a luxurious prison. Tapestries from Iranistan and Vendhya adorned the walls; golden goblets and polished silver salvers gleamed on painted shelves above deep painted cupboards carved in high relief.

Queen Marala's shining hair poured a tousled, flaxen mass across her pillow as she lay weeping on her couch. The couch and cushions on which she lay were covered with Turanian cloth of gold, but the fine furnishings did nothing to assuage her sorrow. She exhaled in painful sighs, and her slender young body shivered beneath the whirlwind of her emotion.

The slave girl spoke softly but anxiously: "My Queen! The learned Doctor Khafrates is here. Will you receive him?"

Marala raised her head and wiped her eyes on a linen napkin. "Oh, yes! Come in, good Doctor! You are my only friend outside these walls; for you alone I trust. You may leave us, dear Rima."

Khafrates waddled in, briefly bent a knee, and grunted as he straightened it again. Marala motioned him to a settle near the pillows of her couch. As he sat down, she seized one of his hands in both of hers.

"It is so good to see you, Doctor Khafrates!" she said. "I grow desperate. I have now been here a month, friendless save for you and Rima.

"I have ever been loyal to Moranthes, but now his treatment of me has become too much to bear. Rima reports that Rigello's guards swagger about the palace and the city streets like conquerors, and my husband jumps when Rigello snaps his fingers.

"You must advise me, dear friend. You know my father persuaded me to wed King Moranthes to preserve the reigning blood line of this land. I cared not for the king, knowing him to be a weak and unstable vessel, but I did my patriotic duty. I think even Father had regrets before the nuptial feast, but he could not tell the king of them and hope to live.

"As it came to pass, Father's dreams of sturdy princelings for the throne of Ophir proved fruitless. Moranthes cares naught for women; his tastes run to. . . . in other directions. Then my troubles multiplied when, a year gone by, some worthless wight filched the Star of Khorala!"

Khafrates stroked his beard to collect his thoughts. Never had the queen addressed him with such candor. No courtier physician he, using his position for political gain, and for this reason he was still allowed to minister to the imprisoned queen. Yet now, he needs must risk that role and with it risk his very life.

He called to mind his recent conversation with the giant blue-eyed barbarian and the grizzled captain of the Queen's Guard who, in happier times, was wont to stride about his duties in the palace. His blood ran cold as he thought of the peril they had placed him in. Yet he loved the beautiful woman, hardly out of her girlhood, who now appealed to him for help. Suddenly he was glad that he had summoned up the courage to meet the would-be rescuers and abet their plot. He passed a soothing hand over the queen's forehead, saying:

"Despair not, Your Majesty! Your heart is pinched by long confinement, lack of human contact, and ignorance of the world outside. Help may be closer than you think."

Queen Marala sat up and swept her hair back from her face, as her inborn courage strove to conquer her depression.

"You are kind, Khafrates. Yet you must realize that when I possessed the Star, Moranthes feared its power. Now he fears it no more and cares not what becomes of me."

Khafrates lifted bushy eyebrows. "What then was the power of the gem, my Queen?"

"Was and is, though vulgar legend misinterprets it." She shrugged. "Moranthes imagined that the stone enabled me to enslave men as I wished. He so believed, and thus the people came, also, to believe it. But the legend is false."

She rose, drew herself up, and looked hard at the physician. "Think you that I need magic to persuade any man to my will—any normal, manly man, that is?"

Although Khafrates was old, he well knew the power to incite desire that lay within the queen's fine-chiseled lips and the sweet rondure of her lithe body—a body that her gown did little to conceal. He shook his head.

"I will tell you a story," said Marala, moving gracefully about the chamber, brows indrawn with thought. "Count Alarkar, my ancestor seven generations removed, first owned the Star of Khorala. A famous traveler of his time—and this was long before the present ruling house of Ophir ascended to the throne—he traveled in the East where no Ophirean had ere set foot. . . ."

Khafrates coughed an interruption. "Your Majesty, I have some urgent news. . . ."

Caught up in her recollections, the queen imperiously gestured him to silence. "When Alarkar traveled in the Vendhyan jungles, he came upon the ruined city of Khorala, inhabited only by a hermit. This hermit was nigh starved; for he had broken a leg and was unable to cultivate his garden patch.

"Alarkar nursed the injured man to health, while his retinue scoured the nearby forest aisles for food. In gratitude the lone old man disclosed a cache of treasure beneath the floor of a ruined temple thereabouts and told Alarkar to take whatever he wished. My ancestor chose a ring inset with a great gem-stone of azure, and in the sapphire heart of the jewel pulsed an everlasting fire confined within the sphere, like a silver star. This he chose and nothing more."

"Why did he not take many jewels?" asked Khafrates in amazement.

The queen smiled. "Count Alarkar was not a greedy man, nor was he with-out wide wealth at home. Besides, I suppose, he thought that if his retinue departed laden with the riches of the jungle city, they would run afoul of cut-throats and avaricious rulers. In any case, that single ring was all he asked.

"This proved a proper choice. The hermit was a wizard of ten-score years and more. Had robbers entered his abode, he would have instantly destroyed them by supernatural means. But the mage discerned my ancestor's virtue and, in return for his assistance, granted him a favor. He cast a mighty spell upon the gem."

"The Star of Khorala?"

"Aye. When the wizard completed his spell, he said, 'This ring, in the pos-session of a good man, will cause other good men to rally round him to fight in a good cause.' " She paused, remembering.

"But—this gem—what does it signify to us today?"

Marala collected herself. "About two hundred years ago, the gem enabled Alarkar to rally the support of king and nobles for a charter to establish the rights and duties of all subjects of the kingdom. Because of treachery, his move-ment failed, and . . ."

The window of the apartment burst inward with a crash and the tinkle of broken panes. A black-clad giant with blue eyes blazing leaped into the room, his sword upraised.

In his free hand the man carried a pair of curious contraptions, huge bird claws cunningly wrought of steel. These he placed gently on the carpet, along with his weapon; then, sitting on a footstool, he removed a pair of similar devices from his feet. Rising, he glided to the door of the apartment to listen briefly. Alarming as this apparition was, Marala could not but admire the catlike way he moved.

The intruder turned to Khafrates and the queen, flashing white teeth in a wide grin. Khafrates had lurched to his feet, uncertainly fluttering his hands. At last the physician pulled himself together.

"Conan!" he said. "I have not yet had time to tell Her Majesty our plan! You burst in here like a bull in one of the legendary porcelain shops of Khitai!"

Conan ignored him. With eyes devouring Marala's splendid form, he said:

"Your Majesty, you want your freedom from this prison, do you not?"

"Oh, yes—but how?"

"The same way that I entered—down the wall, with the use of these devices. You'll have to ride like a sack on my back."

"Whither would you take me, stranger?" The queen's eyes smoldered with excitement.

"First to a safe place where we can strike a bargain; and then wherever you choose."

"But what of me?" quavered Khafrates. "When the guards find Your Majesty gone, 'twill be the rack and boiling oil for me!"

Marala turned to Conan. "Can we not take him with us?"

The Cimmerian pondered. "Nay. These dragon's feet could not support the weight of more than two. But I shall give the good doctor an excuse for having failed to call the guard. We must hurry; Garus waits below with horses."

Marala's face betrayed her joy. "Is Garus still alive, then? I would entrust my life to him at any time!"

"Then let's be off, Lady! We have no time to lose."

Marala was unused to being addressed in a rough, peremptory manner, let alone by a foreigner with a barbarous accent. But she hastened to her dressing room and soon emerged in hunting dress to find Khafrates lying bound and gagged upon the carpet. The physician, who bore a purpling bruise about his jaw, knew neither where he was, nor what had befallen him.

Conan grinned as the queen approached him resolutely. "Your plan for Khafrates' safety was sound," she said. "I am ready."

The barbarian's ice-blue eyes warmed with admiration as much for her composure as for the lovely curves scarcely shrouded by a velvet riding jacket and silken pantaloons thrust into fine red-leather boots. Snatching up a broidered coverlet, he said:

"I shall tie you to my back, lass, like a babe in its mother's shawl. Put your arms around my neck and press your knees against my waist. If heights make you queasy, shut your eyes. Shift not your weight, and these dragon's feet will serve for both of us."

Conan sat down to clamp the devices to his boots; then enfolding the queen's slim body in the coverlet, he tied two ends around his chest and two around his hips. With Marala clinging to him, he backed carefully out the window, feeling for joints in the masonry to make fast his steel devices.

Conan moved slowly during the descent; for the strain was great both on the dragon's feet and on his gigantic frame. Moreover, his rude code of chivalry compelled him to cherish any woman who entrusted her safety to him.

Thus they descended foot by foot, while the city slept under a moonless sky and no dogs barked.

4 • A Fire on the Mountain

"Stranger, tell me, pray," said Marala, "who are you?"

After a long gallop away to the southwest, they were walking their horses to breathe them. There had been no surprises and no delays upon reaching the road where Garus awaited them with three horses and supplies for the journey. Nor had the thunder of their horses' hooves disturbed the sleep of prince or peasant as they rushed along the quiet streets of Ianthe and the ghost-haunted country lanes.

"I am Conan, a Cimmerian by birth—and a wanderer," said the hulking barbarian. "I have fought in more countries than most wise men know exist."

"And why did you rescue me?"

"I may have something you want, Lady, and I think you will offer a fair price for it."

"Methinks I shall never be able to offer anyone a fair price, even for a loaf of bread. I am a queen without a throne. But tell me, what is this desirable thing?"

"We'll talk of such matters later, when we stop to rest. We must not tarry now."

When night drew curtains of darkness around the long day of their flight, they built a small campfire in the cleft of a rock where the glow was well hidden from the road. Their horses, unsaddled and tethered nearby, slaked their thirst in a bubbling mountain spring and cropped the sparse grass. In the markets of Ianthe, Conan had purchased bread, fruit, and dried meat, together with a skin of Kothian wine; and now they supped amid the cheerful crackle of burning logs.

His hunger satiated, Conan leaned back against his saddle and contemplated the beautiful woman beside him. This weary but courageous girl, then, was the Queen of Ophir, she who was reputed to enslave men with the great gem now hidden in his pouch. He had often imagined how he would come to Ophir, obtain an audience with the queen, bowing like a courtier, and hand her the ring in exchange for a thousand pieces of gold and, perhaps, a military post of consequence. He found himself, instead, stretched out upon the greensward, like a common laborer in a strife-torn land, beside a queen who was a penniless refugee. He spoke bluntly:

"Khafrates, I see, did not explain things to you, nor, perhaps, to me. What of this gem they say you use to bend men to your will?"

The queen met his eyes with a level gaze. "Know, Conan, that Alarkar, my ancestor, received the jewel from a Vendhyan hermit long ago."

As she briefly repeated the story she had told to Khafrates, memories of ancient treachery made her voice heavy with unshed tears.

"Upon his return to Ophir, Count Alarkar, determined to strengthen the kingdom, called an assemblage of all the lords of the realm." She turned to Garus. "Captain, you have surely heard of the Battle of the Hundred and One Swords?"

Garus, half dozing, vanquished sleep, and his deep voice tolled:

"Aye, Your Majesty, I have heard of it, albeit as a legend, muddied by the passage of time. Count Alarkar called a meeting of these lords at his castle of Theringo, two hundred years agone. Each, with only his personal retinue, came to discuss the problems of the realm. They all met on the plain outside Theringo Castle but could agree on nothing. Then the count disappeared."

The queen broke in. "The remainder of the tale is known only to my family. I will tell it to you."

Conan sat still, intently listening. Marala went on:

"All the leading nobles gathered on the plain before the castle, but the conference proceeded at a snail's pace. Although my forbear feared the power of Koth and the growing might of Turan, he had no wish to command the magic ring save as a last resort."

Garus stirred the embers until they ignited a log fresh-laid upon the dying fire; and sparks, like fireflies, winged upward into the night. The queen took a swallow of wine before continuing:

"During the conference, the Count of Mecanta—from whom my kinsman Rigello descends—withdrew without a word. The Count of Frosol and the Barons of Terson and Lodier soon followed after him. All with their retainers saddled their mounts and sped away.

"A moment later, a rain of arbalest quarrels arced from the nearby woods, where Mecanta's crossbowmen lay hidden along the ridge. There were a hundred nobles and their knights unarmed upon the plain that day, and most of them were slain. Alarkar rallied the remainder, who mounted their horses and pursued the traitors."

Marala's eyes filled with tears, and Conan pulled her to him, cradling her against his shoulder.

"What then befell?" asked Conan eagerly.

"Alarkar and his men had gone but a bowshot from the camp below the castle, when they met the army of Mecanta and his partisans, charging at full gallop. Alarkar stood to the attack, defending the family banner, until he fell, pierced by a crossbow bolt." Her voice became silent at the memory of ancient wrongs.

Conan's deep bass recalled her to herself. "So," he said, "the same as always. Nobles quarrel and stab each other in the back. What's new about that?" His tone was deliberately abrasive to spur Marala to further talk about the Star of Khorala. She resumed:

"All were buried when they fell, and there they all remain. The castle was laid in ruins. The countess and a few retainers escaped through the postern when they saw the outcome of the battle. The son she carried was my forebear."

"And what of the Star of Khorala?" rumbled Conan softly.

"Alarkar did not use its magic. He trusted in the power of reason because his cause was clearly in the right. The Star was carried away in the bosom of his wife—his widow, rather—who later married in another land. Her son, when grown, returned to Ophir to claim his fief and found my family line. And so the legend has been remembered and the jewel handed down the generations. Now it is lost forever."

"What would you do if it were returned to you?" asked Conan casually.

"I would try to work the magic in it. I would gather the good men of the kingdom to free my feckless husband from the clutch of Rigello and his ruthless kind. Do you question that I would oust Rigello and unite the kingdom if I could?"

The fierce courage of the slender girl who, sitting beside the embers of a campfire in the wilderness with but a retinue of two, still spoke of ousting tyrants and intriguers from a kingdom, struck a receptive chord in Conan's barbaric spirit. He cleared his throat, embarrassed at his surge of deep emotion.

"My Lady," he said, "mayhap I can help you on your way." He groped in his pouch and drew out the Star of Khorala. "Here is your ancestral bauble. You have better use for it than I."

The queen's lips parted in astonishment. "You—you *give* me this?"

"Aye. I'm no saintly character like your ancestor, but I . . . I sometimes like to help a brave woman beset by troubles."

Marala took the ring and gazed upon the gem, from whose oval, sapphire eye, firelit, burst the beauty of the star within.

"You put me under vast obligation, Conan. How can I repay you?"

Conan's burning gaze roved up and down Marala's sweetly curving body. With queenly dignity, she moved away from his embracing arm to signal disapproval of his unspoken suggestion.

Looking away, he said: "You owe me naught just now, my Lady. If you regain your throne and I attend your court, you might offer me a generalship."

Marala looked a question at Garus, who nodded. "He is the man for it, my Queen. Mercenary captain, chief of a band of wild nomads, guard commander—a clever strategist and skilled with sword and dirk. He saved my life and gained you your liberty."

"So be it," said Marala.

5 • "Fetch My Horse; We Ride at Once"

Count Rigello was clad in ebon mail. His sword and dirk rattled at his side; his black casque rested on an inlaid table. King Moranthes regarded him with anxious eyes, for he knew the power of this arrogant descendant of the house of Mecanta.

The king, betimes, considered ordering the black count done away with. But he feared that Rigello's kinsmen and followers would avenge their leader on the person of their king. Besides, with Rigello gone, might he not fall into the power of nobles even more ruthless, or be toppled from his throne by some reckless usurper, such as his rascally cousin Amalrus?

Intensity etched Rigello's coarse and swollen features as he leaned forward, like a dog straining at its leash. "The queen was abducted from the tower last night, Your Majesty," he said. "I have a hundred men ready to ride upon your command."

Rigello knew that the call to action would be his, but a show of obsequious fealty to the delicate young king amused him. He continued:

"This abduction, I am sure, occurred with her consent. Her trusted physician was found senseless, bound and gagged in her apartment; and the window was shattered."

"How could anyone enter and leave the chamber by way of the window?" asked the king in his high-pitched voice. "There is a sheer drop of fifteen or twenty paces!"

"Exactly so, Sire," said Rigello. "The queen doubtless lowered a rope or its like to her abductors, first making one end fast to the furniture. 'Tis plain she plots against Your Majesty, as I have oftimes warned you. It is but a matter of time before she foments a rebellion."

Biting his thumbnail, the king searched his gilded throne chamber, seeking advice from the speechless walls. But, save for the count, there was none to give him counsel other than the statuesque guards standing motionless in the doorway. Rigello persisted:

"Your Majesty, now is the time to end the strife among the noble families, once and for all."

"Yes, yes." The king wallowed in indecision. "What think you I should do?"

"Order immediate pursuit. The queen and her retinue—whoever they may be—cannot be far from Ianthe. Even with good animals, they needs must rest from time to time. Each of my riders leads an extra horse, so we shall soon catch up with them."

"How know you which way they went?" asked the king querulously.

"The queen would surely head southwest toward her ancestral lands of Theringo. There, if anywhere in Ophir, could she hope to rally supporters."

"But if she has regained the Star of Khorala, no man can compel her to do aught against her will, and none can stand against her. How will you overcome the power of the gem?"

"Sire, no one has seen the Star since it was filched a twelve-month past. Had she possessed it, she would not have fled the tower; for she could have commanded the obedience of the guards and so regained her freedom."

The king's weak face brightened. "I thank you, Rigello; you anticipate my wishes. Ride like the wind! Bring the queen to my torture chambers and spare not the men who have aided her!"

Rigello smiled as he left the throne chamber, drew on a mailed gauntlet, and hitched his sword belt more tightly around his hips. When he captured Queen Marala, he thought, he would use her popularity with the citizenry to foment a revolt against Moranthes, and overthrow and slay him. Then he, himself, would wed Marala and reign as king of Ophir.

With what the queen might say to this plan Rigello was not much concerned. Surely, she would prefer a virile man like him to that effeminate noodlehead now huddled on the throne. If she resisted, there were less pleasant methods of persuasion. He smiled again.

Rigello stood for an instant in the hallway, admiring his stalwart figure in a full-length mirror. Then, drawing on his other gauntlet, he strode down the palace stairs to the courtyard.

"Barras! Fetch my horse. We ride at once!" he barked.

6 • "This Is Theringo Castle"

Conan left his horse with Garus below the crest of the hill and crept to the summit. He did not show his head above the bushes, but, instead, gently parted the foliage to study the land beyond.

Anxiously, Marala asked, "Why does he move so slowly? We are in haste to reach the Aquilonian border."

Garus replied: "He is the man who can bring you to safety if anyone can, my Lady. Although I take him to be little more than half my age, he has crowded into his youthful years a lifetime of battles and escapes. Trust him!"

Conan beckoned. When Marala and Garus reached the crest of the rise, they looked down upon a broad plain. In the middle distance, on a small hill, stood the ruins of a castle. Beyond, at the edge of the flat-land, a distant river snaked its silvered way among the feet of the forested hills that rose against the skyline.

"I know now whose seat this was," whispered Marala.

Studying the countryside, Conan said, "Once we cross that plain and, after that, the river, we shall be close upon the border of Aquilonia. I believe the line is drawn along the crest of yonder mountain range. Your king's men would have trouble capturing us there; for the Aquilonians have no love of armed invaders."

Swiftly, they returned to their horses and, mounting, labored up the rise and cantered down the other side. As they reached the plain, Conan caught the faint sound of rhythmic thudding. He turned in his saddle, then cried:

"Spur your horses! As fast as you can! Ophirean cavalry!"

The three beasts broke into a furious gallop toward the ruined castle and the safety of the river beyond. Yet the pursuing horsemen swiftly gained upon them. Instead of pounding down the road behind the fugitives, the pursuers spread out into a wide, crescent-shaped formation, with the horns of the crescent pointing forward.

"Damned Hyrkanian trick!" muttered Conan, driving his heels into his lathered beast.

The queen, a splendid horsewoman, rode hard between her escorts. Yet as they neared the ruined castle, the riders at the far ends of the pursuing crescent, traveling on light, fresh mounts, passed the structure and began to close a circle round about it.

Nearing the ruined castle, Conan roared: "Come, lass, here's a place we can defend! If this is to be our end, we'll take some of those bastards with us!"

They splashed through a small stream and pounded up the gentle slope. Dismounting, they led their winded animals through the rubble-clogged main gate. Within the crumbling curtain walls stood the keep, a massive cylinder of heavy masonry. The upper parts of the keep had fallen, leaving a talus of broken stone at its feet, but the walls of the lower stories still raised protecting masonry too high to scale without ladders. Although the guard towers that flanked the gate had fallen into ruin, spilling masonry into the space where the valves had been, man and beast could pick their way among the broken stones of the heaped remains.

"Mean you to make a stand here?" panted Marala, as they reached the inner courtyard.

"Nay; they'd climb the outer wall somehow and come at us from behind. The keep looks sound; that is our place to stand."

The wooden door had disappeared, but the arched doorway was narrow enough to ensure the entrance of no more than one invader at a time. Slapping the rumps of the horses to send them around to the rear, Conan roughly pushed Marala into the doorway of the keep. He turned in time to parry the attack of two horsemen, who had forced their mounts over the broken stone at the main gate and now rode at them, gleaming swords upraised.

Conan leaped up to slash one rider's sword arm and felt a satisfying crunch of cloven flesh and bone. He wheeled to meet the second, but Garus had already dived beneath the attacker's horse and ripped open its belly with an upward thrust of his knife. The screams of the rider echoed those of the plunging beast when Conan lopped off the fellow's leg as he toppled from the dying horse.

The next Ophirean rider who rushed at them was hurled headlong as his mount stumbled on the detritus in the gateway, and he spilled out his brains against a jagged stone. As the thrashing, fallen animal blocked the entrance,

Conan and Garus snatched up the weapons of the slain. Chief among them were a pair of crossbows with two quivers full of bolts.

"Inside!" cried Conan; and the two defenders scrambled through the doorway of the keep and turned to face the next attack. A few paces behind them, foot upon the winding stair, stood Marala, her lips curved in a happy smile, like one entranced. The Cimmerian turned and grasped her arm to waken her.

"What is it, lass?" His rough voice grew gentle.

"Know you where we are?" the queen replied.

"Close to Aquilonia. What of it? They'll attack at any time, and we can't flee."

She waved a hand to indicate the crumbling masonry. "Conan, this is Theringo Castle, where my ancestor Alarkar was betrayed."

Puzzled by her composure and the strange look in her amber eyes, Conan stepped back to the doorway to meet the next onslaught. Marala followed him, snatched up a crossbow, and said to Garus:

"Cock me both crossbows; I am not strong enough to do it."

When the weapons were readied, she carried them up the worn stone stair, which spiraled high inside the ruined tower. At the first turning, she discovered a small landing, dim-lit by a narrow window, scarce wider than an arrow slit.

Then the attack began.

7 • A Host on Horseback

Conan, Marala, and Garus leaned wearily upon the doorway of the keep. Twice they had beaten off attackers. In the second assault, they were almost overwhelmed by a mass of men pushing in with leveled spears. But so narrow was the opening that the crowded enemy could not wield their weapons, while Conan and Garus above them on the stairs grasped at spear points and hacked at heads and hands. Whereas Conan and Garus wore coats of stout chain mail, the soldiers of Ophir were armored in light leathern corselets to make possible a swift pursuit; and, unable to turn to flee the defenders' blows, many fell screaming in slippery pools of their own blood.

Marala, from the second-story window, picked off two attackers with her pair of crossbows. Although she was not a trained arbalester, the bolts she shot at the struggling mass of men near the doorway of the keep could not fail to find their mark. And after she discharged both weapons, she hurried down the stone stairs so that one or the other of her warriors could, in a moment of lull, recock them for her.

This steady attrition of their forces at last sent the surviving attackers streaming back through the main gate, leaving behind a tangled mass of maimed and dying men. Their broken bodies half blocked the doorway to the keep, and their shrieks and groans were horrible to hear. Conan pushed his way out, shoving dead and wounded aside, to retrieve their weapons.

Count Rigello, sitting his destrier on the slope below the ruin, received his officers impatiently. His black mail was dust-besmirched from the long ride, and his temper frayed by the ridiculous resistance of his quarry. A veteran captain, reining in his horse, saluted the count and said:

"Sir, the donjon is invincible. We have lost two-score men in the attempt to storm it. Others of our lads are like to bleed to death or to live crippled all their days. There is no way to bring our strength to bear."

"A hundred men against three, and one a woman?" sneered the count. "Pity your prospects when we return to Ianthe!"

"But, my Lord," said the captain earnestly, "this barbarian warrior is incredible. None can stand before his sword. And the woman in that window with her crossbows—if you would let our arbalesters pick off the woman . . ."

"Nay, she must be taken alive at any cost. But wait, how many arbalesters have we now?"

"Belike a score in condition to fight."

"Then hark. Order the lads to cock and load their weapons, then charge up the hill afoot. Let them enter the gate bent double to present a negligible target, and spread out before the keep, loosing their quarrels upon a single signal. If only one defender falls, our swordsmen can rush in and overpower the other. Fail not to kill the men, but take the woman captive."

Brows creased in doubt, the captain withdrew to order the attack. Rigello watched the preparations, stroking his mustache and imagining the silken cushions of the throne already at his back. Nothing, he thought, could stop him now.

The count's eyes suddenly grew wide. His men, dismounted, were advancing up the slope, when between them and the ruined castle walls appeared a host on horseback, clad in the armor of a fashion long gone by.

Rigello's men recoiled, amazed, as the newcomers started down the slope at a brisk trot, lances leveled and swords swinging. The arbalesters threw down their bows and, running for their horses, scrambled to their saddles and flogged their mounts into a mad retreat. The swordsmen held a moment longer, then joined the headlong flight.

"Mitra!" yelled Rigello, galloping against the ebbing tide of men. "What ails you? Stand and fight, you cowards! To me! To me!"

With courage born of desperation, Count Rigello spurred his palfrey up the slope, cutting a swath through the wrack of his army, and rode into the thick of the oncoming knights. Then a crossbow bolt split his skull.

8 • "Our Paths May Cross Some Day"

The three defenders stood, panting, at the ruined castle's gate, watching the rout of the Ophirean force.

"Good shot, girl!" cried Conan. Laughing, he added: "If you tire of playing queen, you can hire out as an arbalester in any army I command." Conan's mood changed and he frowned. "But I cannot understand this army that appeared from nowhere, chased away our foes, and vanished in a trice. Have you been working magic?"

Marala smiled serenely. "Aye, the magic of the Star of Khorala. The good men who fell here, two hundred years ago, were denied their chance to save their beloved kingdom. They waited till this day, when the Star and I—and you for giving it—released them to do their duty. Now Alarkar and his true men can rest at last."

"Those horsemen . . . were they solid flesh and blood or conjured phantoms, ghosts through which a man could pass like smoke?"

The queen raised her delicate hands, palms upward; and as she moved, the great jewel flashed its fire encased in azure ice.

"I know not, and I think none shall ever know. But you are hurt. Let me clean and bind your wounds—and Garus's, too, as best I may."

She led the two, unarmored now and limping wearily, down the slope to the brook that gurgled merrily along the bottom before it disappeared into the distant river. She helped them wash their battlesore bodies and bound their superficial wounds with strips of cloth torn from the garments of the dead.

Refreshed at last, Conan asked: "And what of you now, Lady? Rigello is dead, but others will scramble to control the king."

Marala tied the final bandage and stood back, biting her lower lip in thought.

"Mayhap the Star can rally the good men of the kingdom; but Ophir seems to lack good men—at least among the nobles of the realm. All the magnates whom I know are, like Rigello, greedy and unscrupulous. Of course, with the Star of Khorala . . ." She broke off, staring at her hand. "My ring! Where is it? It must have slipped off my finger whilst I dabbled in the chilly water!"

Until sundown the three sought the great jewel within the stream and along its banks; but the Star was not to be found. The rushing waters must have carried it downstream, or playfully buried it in the silver sand. When the search was ended, Marala burst into tears.

"Just when I had recovered it—to lose it again so soon!" Conan enfolded her in his strong arms to comfort her, saying: "There, there, lass. I never much liked magic anyway. You cannot trust the stuff."

"That settles it," said Marala, when at last her tears ran dry. "I had but feeble chance in Ophir when I possessed the Star; without it I should have no chance at all. Nor do I think that Mitra himself could make a man of Moranthes. I shall go to live in Aquilonia, where I have kin. Let the men of Ophir settle their feuds without me. And may Mitra help the people of my realm!"

"Have you money enough?" asked Conan with gruff concern.

"A moment, and I'll show you," said the queen with a flicker of a smile.

Turning away, she withdrew from her inner clothing a damask belt into which were sewn many pockets no larger than a fingernail. Tucked into these were sparkling jewels and coins of gold in dizzying profusion.

"You'll manage," growled Conan, "if some thief lightfingers not your wealth."

"For that, I shall rely on Garus." Turning to him prettily, she said: "You will go into exile with me, will you not?"

"My Lady," smiled the old soldier, "I would follow you into the very gates of Hell."

"I thank you, loyal friend," said Marala with a regal nod. "But what of you, Conan? I cannot offer you the promised generalship of Ophir's armies. Will you go to Aquilonia with me?"

Conan shook a somber head. "I, too, have changed my plans. I'll head north, to see my native land once more."

The queen studied Conan's solemn mien. "You do not sound as if you liked the prospect. Do you fear to return?"

Conan's harsh laugh rang out like the clash of steel on steel. "Save for some sorcery and certain supernatural beings I have met, there's naught I fear. I may come home to trouble with an ancient feud or two—but that does not disturb me. It is just . . . well, Cimmeria is a dull country after the southerly kingdoms."

Taking both her hands in his, he surveyed her golden hair above her heart-shaped face, her splendid bosom, and her proud and graceful carriage. His eyes burned with desire and his voice grew intimate.

"True it is that fair company shrinks the miles and warms the lonely heart."

Watching them, Garus tensed. Marala gently disengaged her hands and shook her lovely head.

"While Moranthes lives and I am yet his wife, I will be faithful to my vows. But neither state will last forever." She smiled a trifle sadly. "Why go you to that bleak northland, if you enjoy it not? The Hyborian kingdoms offer many opportunities for a brave and generous man like you."

"I go to pay a visit."

"To whom? Some sweetheart of former days?"

Conan turned a cool glance on Queen Marala, but his blue eyes betrayed his painful disappointment. He replied: "Say that I go to visit an old woman. Who is she, is my affair. But where in Aquilonia will you settle? Our paths may cross again some day."

Marala smiled fondly at the brawny Cimmerian. "My Aquilonian kin dwell in the county of Albiona, near Tarantia. They are old and childless and look upon me as a daughter. They intend to leave me title to their ancestral lands. I am no longer Queen of Ophir, but one day men may call me 'Countess Albiona'!"

The Gem in the Tower

After a visit to his northern homeland, Conan returns to the kozaki. When the energetic new king of Turan, Yezdigerd, scatters the outlaw bands, Conan serves as a mercenary in Iranistan and wanders east to the Himelian Mountains and the fabled land of Vendhya. On his return to the West, he explores a phantom city of living dead men and is briefly joint king of a black empire in the desert south of Stygia.

Following the events narrated in "Drums of Tombalku," Conan makes his way across the southern grasslands to the other black kingdoms. Here he is known of old, and Amra the Lion has no difficulty in reaching the coast, which he ravaged in his days with Bêlit. But Bêlit is now only a fading memory on the Black Coast. The ship that finally appears off the headland where Conan sits whetting his sword is manned by pirates of the Barachan Isles, off the coasts of Argos and Zingara. They, too, have heard of Conan and welcome his sword and experience. He is in his middle thirties when he joins the Barachan pirates, with whom he remains for some time. This story tells of one of his many adventures in this environment.

1 • Death on the Wind

The first longboat beached on the yellow strand near sundown, when all the West was a wild conflagration of crimson flame. As the boat attained the shallows, the crew, splashing through the breakers, dragged it up the beach so that the tide could not float it out to sea again.

The men were a ruffianly lot, Argosseans for the most part—stocky men with brown or tawny hair. Several among them were sallow-skinned Zingarans, with lean shanks and ebon locks; and not a few were hook-nosed Shemites, swart and muscular, with ringleted blue-black beards. All were clad in rough sea togs, but while some went barefoot, others wore high, well-greased sea boots; and cutlasses, scimitars, or dirks were thrust into the scarlet sashes wound about their waists.

With them came a lone Stygian, a lean, dark-skinned, thin-lipped man with a shaven pate and jet-black eyes, wearing a short half-tunic and sandals. This was Mena the conjuror, who despite his appearance and name was Stygian by courtesy only; for he was a half-breed, begotten by a wandering Shemite trader upon a woman of Khemi, the foremost city of the sinister land of Stygia.

At their leader's command, the crew hauled their boat into the shrubbery at the jungle's edge, where like a forbidding wall, trees crept down to edge the beach beyond the high-tide mark.

The man who gave the order was neither Zingarian nor Argossean, but a Cimmerian from the frigid, fog-bound hills to the north. He was a veritable giant in a tunic of supple leather and baggy silken breeches, with a cutlass on his hip and a poignard thrust into his scarlet sash. Tall was he and deep-chested, with powerful, sinewy arms and swelling thews. Unlike the other pirates, he was clean-shaven, and his coarse mane of straight raven hair was hacked off at the nape. Grim was his mien, and beneath his dark brows smoldered eyes with fires of volcanic blue. His name was Conan.

Now a second longboat, with silent, rhythmic oars, creased the azure waters of the little bay. Behind it, outlined against the crimson tapestry of the West, the lean-hulled carrack *Hawk* rode at anchor. The longboat, beached, was man-handled over the sand to the verdant bushes wherein the first lay hidden. The leader of the second crew joined Conan as he watched his men drape palm fronds over the sterns of both to conceal them utterly.

The newcomer was a true Zingaran, lean and elegant, with sallow features and an aquiline nose that seemed to reinforce his supercilious manner. Trim mustachios and a small beard framed his tight mouth and adorned his pointed chin. He was Gonzago, a freebooter of some repute among the Barachan pirates and captain of the *Hawk*. For the past month Conan had been his second mate.

"Get the men together and follow me," he said. The Cimmerian nodded and turned to wave the pirates on; but the conjuror touched his arm and halted him.

"What ails you?" demanded Conan gruffly. He did not like the Stygian's swarthy, vulpine features, shaven pate, and lackluster eyes. But then, he never had much use for wizards.

"Death," whispered the conjuror. "I smell death on the wind. . . ."

"Hush, you fool, before you panic the men!" growled Conan. He knew the Barachan corsairs for an unruly, quarrelsome, superstitious lot, and once again he wished that Captain Gonzago had heeded his advice not to enlist the Stygian magician for the expedition. But Gonzago was master here, not Conan.

"What holds you up?" snapped Gonzago, striding over to join them. "We have barely an hour of daylight left and must traverse this cursed jungle ere we can reach the tower. Every moment counts, so get the men moving."

Conan repeated the whispered warning, and the Zingaran looked at Mena the wizard.

"Can you not be more precise, man?" the captain grated. "What manner of death—and whose—and from what quarter?"

Mena shook his head, his eyes dull and haunted. "I cannot say," he replied. "But I regret that I have come to this dark isle with you. The Master Siptah is a high prince among magicians, and the spells of such an one are more powerful than any I command."

Gonzago spat a curse. Conan stood, arms folded on his mighty chest, and cast wary eyes about him. But innocent and normal seemed the yellow strand, the blue sea, and the red-streaked sky. Only the gloom-drenched forest, ominous with shadows, gave cause for hesitation. Its menace was merely of the unexplored, the wild, the savage—a matter of eyes gleaming with feral, hungry fires from the underbrush, or vipers gliding across the boles of fallen tree trunks, or quicksands and jungle fevers, or hostile natives and sudden storms.

Nothing in all these dangers was especially fearsome, for such were the ordinary hazards of the buccaneering trade. So far the weather had held fair; they had seen no sign of human habitation; and Conan's experience told him that, in general, small islands do not harbor dangerous animals.

Still, the wizard scented death upon the wind. And wizards sense things other men do not.

2 • Jewel of Wizardry

Before night drew her veil across the lingering light of day, the raiders gained the farther reaches of the island. A pair of pirates with bared blades plunged into the jungle ahead of their fellows, hacking away the lush vegetation and blazing the larger trees to mark a trail against their return. As one pair tired, another seized the task, and so the crew moved forward with little hesitation.

The trek proved neither difficult nor dangerous, and nothing occurred to fulfill Mena's dire prophecy. The men encountered no creature more fearsome than a sounder of small wild pigs, a few squawking parrots flaunting their vivid plumage, and a sluggish serpent, rope-coiled upon a root, which slithered away at the noisy approach of the pirates.

So easy was their progress that Conan felt a growing apprehension. He sensed a chilling air of unseen menace about the place, and like Mena began to wish that Gonzago had never undertaken the foray.

For longer than the memory of man, the tower that now loomed above the trees had stood upon the eastern coast of this small, nameless island off the shores of Stygia, south of Khemi. It was said to be inhabited by the Stygian sorcerer Siptah, and by him alone, save for diverse uncanny creatures from other planes and ancient worlds that he might summon by his spells. The pirates of the Barachan Archipelago whispered that the sorcerer concealed within his slender spire a fabulous treasure, gleaned through the years from troubled souls who sought the seer's advice and supernatural aid. But it was not to win this treasure trove that Gonzago had decided to attack the tower.

Legends told of a mysterious gem recovered long ago by the Stygian mage from deep within a desert tomb. A huge and glittering crystal it was said to be, graven with magic sigils in a language unknown to any living man. Immense and uncanny were the reputed powers of that gem, for it was common gossip among the merchants and seamen of the ports of Shem and Zingara that, by secret spells locked within the massy jewel, Siptah could command the spirits of air, earth, fire, and water, and the less savory demons of the underworld.

Those seafarers who had purchased the favor of Siptah sailed serenely forth into harbors, safe and hospitable. No storm or flood could touch them; neither were their ships becalmed, nor fell they prey to hostile monsters of the deep. The merchant princes of those sea-lapped cities would offer fortunes to possess the crystal, for with it in their hands they could enjoy the safety of the seas without the ruinous tribute demanded by the sorcerer. Deprived of that great gem, Siptah would be powerless to do them harm, since the very touch of the enchanted crystal was the key to all his demon-raising spells.

Now there were those who whispered that Siptah of Stygia was dead; for many months had passed since the merchants of the seacoast cities had received demands for tribute, and even longer since the sorcerer had replied to their petitions. Indeed, if he were living, Siptah the Stygian would be of an enormous age—but wizards can transcend the mortality of common men, warding off senility and death with their uncanny powers.

At length, anxious to render the rapacious Stygian powerless and to arrogate to themselves his mastery over wind and wave, a consortium of merchants had approached the more daring of the Barachan pirate captains to commission such a venture. If in truth Siptah was dead, they urgently desired possession of the gem, to which the spirits of Stygia were bound by terrible oaths. If another wizard gained the gem in the tower, he might prove even more extortionate in his demands than Siptah.

This scheme appealed to the daring of Gonzago, and to his greed. The merchants' plan had roused in his breast a lust to seize the fabulous gem, even if he must wrest it from the withered arms of the ancient sorcerer. For if the maritime merchants would pay him well to secure the gem, another sorcerer, lusting for Siptah's power, might reward him far more handsomely.

Yet Gonzago was no fool. Wizards are dangerous, and men seldom live to enjoy the treasures stolen from practitioners of the black arts. Gonzago would be careful.

3 • **Blood on the Sand**

In a waterfront tavern at Messantia, the pirate captain first encountered Mena. A cunning thought inflamed his greed: how better to fight magic than with magic? He had bought the conjuror's services on the spot and bade his officers to prepare the *Hawk* for a voyage to the lonely isle.

Now, as the pirates hacked a narrow path across the jungle and reached the eastern shore close to the tower, Gonzago knew his plans had been well laid. He had dropped anchor on the west side of the island lest the approaching carack and its ship's boats be seen from the sorcerer's stronghold. The raiders had transversed the jungle without loss of life and without discovery by the dreaded sorcerer—if in truth he still lived at all. Now that the blue-green of the sea shimmered through the trees, the men had but to rush the tower, batter their way in, and seize for themselves the gem and other treasures of the aged magician.

But Gonzago had not survived his hazardous trade thus long by acting rashly. So now he summoned the gaunt Stygian to his side.

"Can you cast a spell upon us, Master Mena, to ward off Siptah's magic?" he demanded.

Mena shrugged. "I can perchance becloud his vision so that he perceives not our approach until too late," he murmured.

Gonzago grinned, white teeth gleaming in his sallow, bearded face. "As you did in the tavern?" he suggested. For it had been this trick—a spell of seeming invisibility—that had inspired Gonzago to hire the conjuror to work his subtle arts against the Stygian mage. Mena nodded his shaven pate.

Without further words, the conjuror gathered dry twigs and built a little fire near the jungle's edge at a sheltered spot, where the trees ended and the sands ran out to meet the sea. As the curious pirates watched, Mena drew from his girdle small leathern bags and, with a tiny silver spoon, measured minute quantities of colored powders into a little copper pan. When the twigs had burned to a bed of glowing embers, he placed the pan upon the fire. A sharp and pungent vapor wafted seaward on the evening wind.

Conan sniffed and spat. He little liked such witcheries; his way would have simply been to charge the tower with naked steel, a band of fearless swordsmen at his back. But since Gonzago was master here, Conan held his tongue.

Mena sat cross-legged before the little mound of coals, whereon the nameless melded powders seethed in the copper pan and wafted perfumed smokes upon the evening breeze. Arms folded on his bony breast, the conjuror chanted a sonorous spell in a sibilant tongue.

The crimson embers cast a weird, rosy light on the sorcerer's fleshless face, lending it the aspect of a living skull. Deep-sunken in their sockets, the magician's eyes gleamed like the ghosts of long-dead stars. He bent to peer into his bubbling melt, and his singsong wail sank to the faintest whisper.

Then Mena ceased his incantation and crooked a finger at Gonzago. When the pirate captain bent his head to listen, Mena hissed:

"You and the men must leave me. The last step in the cantrip requires a stringent solitude."

Gonzago nodded and herded his men back upon the trail along which they had come. When all were out of sight of the magician, they sat on fallen logs or rested elbows on the ground, idly swatting flies as they waited the Stygian's call.

Time passed. The light drained from the sky. Suddenly a hoarse scream rent the evening quiet.

With muttered exclamations, Gonzago and Conan dashed back to the small clearing where the magician plied his trade. Mena lay facedown beside his little fire.

Cursing sulphurously, Gonzago clutched the conjuror's bony shoulder and turned the body over. What he saw by the glow of the dying coals made him cry out to his forgotten boyhood gods. For Mena's throat had been cleanly cut, and his blood trickled out and soaked into the humus of the forest floor.

This meant, thought Conan, either that Siptah still lived to guard his treasure, or that the spirits bound to the terrible gem yet served his will though he himself were dead. Either way, the knowledge enkindled grim forebodings.

Gonzago stared down upon the ghastly figure as fresh gore welled from the gaping wound. The crew behind them muttered, the whites of their eyes gleaming redly in the gloom.

Gonzago squatted, brooding with thoughtful eyes. Conan, shivering in the warm air, said nothing. Mena had spoken but the truth when he said he scented death upon the wind.

4 • Where None May Enter

Few of the men were willing to return to their ship empty-handed, though all felt the cold breath of mysterious menace at their backs. Gonzago was determined to attack the tower, confident that bright steel would triumph over even the darkest wizardry. Therefore he led his party through the tangled vines that edged the jungle and out upon the beach where the first stars of evening gleamed above an oily, darkling sea.

Their spirits cowed by Mena's strange and unexpected death, the pirates plodded along the strand, hugging the jungle's edge and speaking in hoarse, furtive whispers.

Presently Conan parted a clump of tall dune grass that rose from a small headland and studied a smooth stretch of beach that lay as pale and untrodden as a silver stream beneath the wan glimmer of the far, uncaring stars. There were few sounds to break the hush of night—only the plash of little waves against the sands, the mournful cry of a distant gull, and the buzz and chirp of nocturnal insects.

A bowshot's distance along the deserted beach, a black shape like a pointing finger pierced the starry sky, now paling in the east. As Conan watched, a silver slice of moon, just past its full, manifested itself above the seascape. The moon moved slowly up the sky, turning the tower into an ink-sketched silhouette backed by the silvery light. It was a simple, slender cylinder surrounded at its tapered height by a narrow parapet; and above this prominence sharply rose the spire.

There was no sign of light or life within the tower. The tower seemed untenanted and forlorn; but where magic is concerned, looks can ever be deceiving. Besides, thought Conan grimly, someone or something had slain the conjuror. Now the pirates had no recourse but to attack the tower directly, sure that the Stygian wizard had perceived their presence. Since the advantage of surprise was lost, little could be gained by further secrecy.

So Gonzago set his men to felling a slender palm tree, cutting notches down its trunk, and tying thereto small lengths of branches. Then, beneath the risen moon, they carried this crude ladder across the virgin sand to the base of the black tower. But at the spire's foot they halted, staring at each other in wild-eyed disbelief.

For Siptah's tower had neither doors nor windows. Sleek walls of black basalt rose windowless from the rugged rocks of its foundation to the small parapet that crowned its castled height. Although they strained their eyes, they could discern no opening, crack, or crevice in the satin-textured fitted stones.

"Crom and Mitra," rumbled Conan, his nape-hair lifting and scalp a tingle, "has this sorcerer wings?"

"Only Set knows," mused Gonzago.

"Mayhap we could scale the height by means of a grappling hook," said Conan.

"Too tall," replied the captain heavily.

They explored the rocks around the base of Siptah's spire and found nothing that was useful in their predicament. The tower thrust skyward from a shelf of naked rock that jutted into the sea's edge as the tide came in. There was no possibility of entrance there.

Yet some way of entry must exist, however well concealed; for every dwelling—if this was a dwelling—must have a mode of entrance and egress. Gonzago stood silent for a moment, the sea breeze ruffling his black cloak as he chewed his lower lip.

"Back up the beach, bullies," he said at last. "We can do naught at night, without tools and a plan. We'll camp two bowshots from this accursed tower, lest one loose arrows from the parapet. Behind a jungle screen, we'll wait for dawn."

The raiders plodded dispiritedly back along the beach, subdued but seemingly relieved. None, Conan noted with wry amusement, had been too eager to beard the wizard in his lair, such gentry being as notoriously unlucky to disturb as hibernating bears.

The pirates set up camp in a sheltered spot where the tree line met the sand. Conan ordered some to gather brush to build a fire, while Gonzago dispatched a pair to the far shore whereon the longboats lay hidden under palm fronds. Then, rowing to the *Hawk*, they must inform Gonzago's first mate, the Argossean Borus, of all that had befallen on the island and gather sacks of axes, hammers, chisels, drills, and other tools to aid in their attack upon the spire. Food, too, and flasks of wine were needed to replenish their supplies.

Under the fitful glimmer of the inconstant moon, the others sat about the fire, broiling what meat they had and grumbling at the scarcity of water. Their grumbling was muted, for their captain, not an easy man even in the best of times, was in the grip of icy fury. As the others fell asleep beside the dying fire, he sat apart, wrapped in his cloak, and brooded sulkily.

Conan set the watch and retired to the place that he had chosen for his rest. Thrusting his cutlass into the soil where it would be within reach of his hand, he leaned against a palm tree and prepared himself for slumber. But that night sleep did not come easily to the giant Cimmerian.

The playful waves ceased their chattering, and the jungle, like a crouching beast, silently watched and waited. Waited for *what*? Conan did not know, but he felt as tense as a coiled spring. With the finehoned senses of the barbarian, he detected menace lurking in the uncanny silence of the night.

Something was out there, that he knew. And it was stalking them.

5 • Dreams in the Night

Toward midnight Conan slept at last, but through his troubled sleep flitted dark, chaotic dreams. An ominous foreboding hovered about him, and in the darkness of his dreaming he saw a beach whereon he and others slept with readied swords. The men around him were rough and villainous seafarers—not unlike his comrades—but their faces were unfamiliar to him.

One face among them was familiar. This man was lean and elegant, with aristocratic bearing, and the long jaw and icy, cunning eyes of Captain Gonzago.

In his dream it seemed to Conan that Gonzago, wrapped in his long cloak, sat huddled on a log brooding over the coals of a dying fire. And as the dreaming Cimmerian watched, another form materialized out of the gloom at the edge of the silent jungle. Like the seated man of Conan's dream, the stranger, too, was swathed in the folds of a long black cloak, which concealed his shape entirely.

Tall and lean was this dark figure, and strangely misshapen, although Conan could discern no obvious deformity. Perhaps it was his high, hunched shoulders that lent his figure a suggestion of abnormality, or the crooked, bony jaw and slitted yellow eyes that glared from the mask of his face like the feral orbs of a savage beast. But the shadow of nameless, misshapen evil clung as tightly about his motionless form as the dark cloak that shrouded him.

Although the dreaming Conan clearly saw both the brooding man and the tall stranger hovering behind him, Gonzago seemed entirely unaware of the masked and evil presence. Then within the barbarian's brain flared up the bright blue flame of apprehension. He struggled in the toils of his unseemly vision, trying to cry out to warn the seated man of the imminence of danger. But he could neither speak, nor move, nor otherwise attract the attention of Gonzago, who sat bemused beside the dying fire.

Then, with startling suddenness, the cloaked figure sprang into motion. He hurled himself out of the jungle, amber eyes burning through the gloom. Straight for the back of the unknowing Gonzago the dark man launched himself, and coming, spread strange, slender arms with gaunt fingers hooked to rend and tear, like talons of some monstrous, predatory bird.

As the being spread his arms, Conan saw they were not arms at all and what he had perceived as the long folds of a dark cloak were the wings of an enormous bat.

And still Conan fought within the confines of his dream to rise, to shout to the oblivious figure of his captain, to warn him of the evil shape of darkness about to spring upon him with bared fangs and wicked claws extended.

Then a sudden scream ripped the unnatural stillness of the night, shattering the dream like tinkling shards of glass. For a timeless moment Conan lay propped against the palm tree, his heart thudding, not knowing whether he had waked or still lay trammeled within a nightmare's grasp.

That hoarse, despairing shriek aroused the other sleeping pirates with the same abruptness that wrenched Conan from his haunted slumbers. As the Cimmerian snatched up his cutlass and rolled to his feet, he sought the cause of the cry that had awakened him. His comrades likewise shambled from their earthen beds, fumbled with their weapons, and muttered confused questions.

The moon rode high in the sky, and in its opalescent light all eyes were drawn to the slumped figure of their captain. Silent and motionless, he sat upon his log before the gray-veiled embers, head bowed upon his knees. He alone had not been shocked awake by the scream that floated on the breeze. Deep indeed must be Gonzago's dreams if that terrible cry did not awaken him.

Conan's scalp prickled with a superstitious premonition as he strode to the captain and shook him by the shoulder. Gonzago sagged and tumbled forward as limp as a rag doll; and as he fell, his head flopped back upon one shoulder. Then Conan knew who had voiced that raw, despairing shriek, knew, too, that they were not alone on this small island. For Gonzago's throat, like Mena's, had been sliced across, as if by a hooked knife or by the talon of some monstrous bird of prey. Through the mask of blood that once had been a face, eyes stared forth sightlessly.

6 • Murder in the Moonlight

No raider slept for the remainder of that night. Not even the hardiest among them wanted again to risk the oblivion of slumber and an untimely end. So the men gathered more wood and built the fire again, piling the brush higher and higher still, until the flames licked the tops of the palms, and the rising smoke enveloped the unwinking and uncaring stars.

Conan had not spoken about his dreams, wherein he watched a hideous winged creature strike and slay from the dense shadows. Nor could the Cimmerian explain, even to himself, why he held his tongue in this matter. Perhaps it was simply that the men were frightened enough already by the weird demise of the conjuror and their captain; and it would be incautious of a commander to excite the primal superstitious fears of his unruly band. For were they to conceive the notion of a gaunt and murderous specter stalking the shadowy aisles of the jungle night, not even one such as the mighty Conan could hold them obedient to his orders.

With the death of Gonzago, command of the ill-starred expedition devolved upon Conan; for Borus, the first mate of the *Hawk*, was still aboard the pirate ship moored on the farther side of Siptah's isle. And even on his brawny shoulders the burden would rest uneasily.

Conan posted fresh sentries, twice as many as before, and sternly bade them to be vigilant. Gonzago's murder, he assured the men, had been the work of some strange jungle beast, which might still prowl abroad.

Conan was not entirely certain of the falsity of this explanation. A dream may be a dream and nothing more; yet the Cimmerian had never discredited the claims of those who read the future by means of a man's dreaming. And yet the slayer was more likely to be a little-known beast of prey brought by some unknown means from a distant coast of Stygia. Perhaps one of Gonzago's men, nursing a grudge against the captain, had stolen up behind him in the dark and cut his throat. Or, perhaps, again, the winged figure in his dream was some hybrid monstrosity, bred of an unholy experiment performed by the Stygian sorcerer. Who could say what creatures dwelt on such a nameless and unholy isle?

So meditated Conan, sitting among his sleepless men around the roaring fire. Then a strangled cry of horror ripped the velvet night.

Shuddering at the clammy touch of grisly premonition, Conan sprang, cursing, to his feet, his steel naked in the firelight. A running figure shouldered through the twisting jungle vines and, speechless, stopped before him.

It was no cloaked and amber-eyed thing with hunched and bony shoulders, but one of the posted sentries—a burly-chested, tawny-bearded Argossean named Fabio. The man's face was ghostly pale, and his hands shook as he pointed wordlessly into the jungle. Harshly bidding the others to remain, Conan followed the sentry back along the narrow path.

Up the jungle trail hacked out the previous day prowled the Cimmerian with a catlike gait behind the trembling sentry. As he strode forward, his blue eyes penetrated the darkness, and he sniffed the air for telltale odors. Then Fabio halted, pointing.

Dappled moonlight filtering through the foliage revealed two men sprawled upon the ground. Conan bent and rolled the corpses over, grimly certain of the cause of death. The sailors earlier dispatched for tools and provisions had been returning, laden, when met by pitiless death. For bulging canvas bags were strewn beside the bodies, which lay with faces mangled almost beyond recognition.

Conan frowned and knelt, dabbling his fingers in the trickling gore. The blood was fresh and warm, and just beginning to scum over as it dried. Thus he knew the hapless men had perished within the quarter hour, and like the captain, died by the same hand—or claw.

7 • Winged Horror

Conan and Fabio hastened to the clearing wherein the huddled crew awaited them. Now there was no concealing from the crew the nature of the thing that had thrice struck from the shadows; for the sentry had seen the killer crouched before its prey. And he babbled the tale excitedly to all who listened.

"Like a tall man, he was—a winged man—and bald, with the yellow eyes of a cat and a long, crooked jaw. At first I thought he wore a black cloak; but as I watched, he spread his arms wide—so—and I saw the cloak was a pair of wings, black wings, like those of a bat. An enormous bat."

"How tall was he?" growled Conan.

Fabio shrugged. "Taller than you even."

"What did he then?" asked the Cimmerian.

"He slashed with talons affixed within his wings, cutting their throats. And then he—he sprang into the air and disappeared," said Fabio, wetting dry lips.

Conan was silent, scowling. The men looked fearfully at one another. Never had they heard of a man-size bat that ripped out throats in the dark of the night. Unbelievable it was; yet there were three corpses to attest to the sentry's tale.

"Is it Siptah himself, think you, Conan?" a pirate asked.

Conan shook his raven mane. "From all that I have heard," he said, "Siptah is a Stygian sorcerer, naught more—a man like you or me, even though master of the blackest arts."

"What manner of beast, then?" asked another.

"I know not," growled the Cimmerian. "Maybe some demon Siptah has conjured out of the foulest pit of Hell to ward his tower against unwanted visitors. Or a survivor of some monstrous breed else vanished in the mists of long-forgotten ages. Whatever it is, it's made of solid flesh and blood, and so can die. Slay it we must, lest it destroy us one by one or force us to leave this misbegotten island empty-handed."

"How do we kill it, then?" demanded a hook-nosed Shemite named Abimael. "We know not where it lairs, and we must find it to attack it."

"Leave that to me," said Conan shortly. He studied the leaping flames of the roaring fire, and something in the seething fury of their crackling seemed to fascinate him. As he stared, an idea came to him.

"Surely, on all this isle the dwelling of the winged thing is in the tower of Siptah. For it occurs to me that a bird-man has no need of doors or windows."

"But the tower has a spire," said Abimael, "rising above yon parapet. How could it enter there?"

"In truth, I know not. But it seems the likeliest place. And the lair of every creature has an entrance, although we know not where," said Conan.

"If you be right, how can we reach the accursed thing?" asked Fabio. "*We* cannot fly, and the tower lacks doors or windows."

Conan nodded toward the fire and grinned. It was a mirthless thing, that smile: a wolfish baring of the teeth, white in a somber face suffused with fierce determination.

"We'll smoke the devil out."

8 • Death from Above

By dawn the men had finished their task, and weary but alert, they rested on the beach. Under the Cimmerian's direction, they had dragged piles of brush to join the driftwood on the beach. They felled trees and cut trunks apart to furnish logs and laid them in a ring around the tower's base. Frantically they labored, chopping and hauling, through the small hours of that terrible night.

When the east flamed with the approach of dawn, the makings of a tremendous bonfire circled the base of the black tower. Higher than a man the mass of logs and brush and leaves were heaped, and, Conan hoped, the coming conflagration would create such billowing smoke that no live thing within the tower could long endure the heat and choking fumes.

Surely the winged horror, if it nested in the tower, would emerge to fight or fly away; and then, in daylight, they could attack the demon-thing with manmade weaponry and hope to win. And to this end, Conan posted his finest archers so that they might command the tower's crest from every angle.

Dawn rose out of the sea in crimson and gold, as restless waves moaned against the strand and gulls circled the blue waters, uttering their harsh and lonesome cries. When the first rays of the rosy sun struck the tower's upper reaches, Conan shouted: "Fire!"

Men thrust torches into the high-piled brush, and flames leaped, like nimble dancers, from branch to branch. As the fire roared along the ebon stones, the tower shimmered before the gaze of the expectant watchers, who shielded their weary eyes against the glare of sun and flame. Clouds of pale gray smoke swirled beneath the parapet and vanished within the tower or wafted into the azure sky.

"Pile on more logs," ordered the Cimmerian.

"Surely," said Abimael the Shemite, "nothing can long endure within the tower now."

"We shall see," growled Conan. "It takes time to penetrate so vast a mass of stone. Pile on more fuel, buckos."

At last a bowman, shouting and waving to attract attention, pointed to the tower's upper reaches. Conan raised his eyes.

A dark, hunch-shouldered creature stood out against the morning sky, leaning like a gargoyle above the parapet to survey the beach with hate-filled yellow eyes. Conan heaved a gusty sigh of relief. Now it was all over but the killing!

"Ready with your bows," he roared.

A bowman yelled, as from the tower's crest the black-winged monster cast itself upon the ambient air. Colossal was the stretch of its batlike pinions; no earth-bred bird had ever soared the winds on wings so broad.

Tense bowstrings snapped, and swift arrows flicked about the soaring figure; but with the armor of enchantment around it, not one struck home. The creature wavered in a zigzag, batlike flight, so that no barbed shaft grazed its feathered flesh.

Conan stared skyward, eyes narrowed against the growing glare, and clearly saw the winged devil. The thing he saw was naked, with a pallid body, lean and fleshless. Its upper chest bulged forward to form a kind of keel; and on either side of its bird's breast bulged massive muscles. Its narrow, elongated skull was bald and shapen like that of some ancient, predatory reptile. Its translucent, leathern wings were supported by a structure that corresponded to a human wrist, whence were prolonged downward two free digits that ended in hooked and lethal claws.

Swooping like a striking hawk, the devil-thing approached the beach and slew a bowman as he nocked an arrow. The Cimmerian with a roar of rage rushed to meet it, his cutlass flashing in the morning sun. He aimed a blow that should have cloven the creature's skull in twain.

The blade snapped near the hilt, and only a small cut gaped in the creature's skin. Then Conan knew that he had struck no ordinary skull, but one of strange and sinister density.

Down came the taloned feet toward Conan's chest. With a mighty sweep of his left arm, he knocked aside the deadly claws and struck the devil's body with the brazen knuckle guard of his shattered sword. The grinning monster, ignoring Conan's hammerlike blows, closed in; and Conan fought for life against a relentless adversary. With superhuman strength, the wicked talons on feet and wings ripped the Cimmerian's leather jerkin, gashed his arms, and tore an opening in his scalp, streaking his face with crimson.

Beside him stood the Shemite Abimael, screaming curses as he slashed the winged form to no avail; and Conan realized with the clarity of the beleaguered that his life's span was measurable in minutes.

Half-blinded by his blood, Conan fought on, as other pirates, yelling and waving weapons, rushed toward him from all sides. And Conan knew, if he could but hold out a heartbeat more, the demon would be ringed with glittering steel, outnumbered, and cut down despite its unnatural vitality.

Suddenly, alerted to its peril, the otherworldly brute sprang away from Conan, turned, and spread its wings. But Conan, in a crimson fog of battle lust, refused to let it flap away, to attack again. With a howl of primal fury, he leaped upon its back and hooked an arm around its throat. He strove to break its neck or strangle it, but that lean neck was steel beneath its leathery skin.

The black wings spread, catching the shoreward breeze. Lean sinews writhed across the gaunt torso as the monster soared on laboring pinions with Conan on its back. A score of yards above the sea they rose, while Conan measured the languid, curling swells and wondered if he might survive a fall and swim ashore. And then he dug his iron fingers deeper into the gullet of his aerial steed. Behind them, pirates stared, eyes bulging in consternation, and none dared send an arrow after them, lest this seal Conan's doom.

The monster spiraled upward. Higher it rose with every turn, until at last it fanned the air adjacent to the parapet. The parapet, Conan saw, stood a mere foot above a flagstone walk. Over it, a cone-shaped roof, thrusting upward like a spire, was supported by four columns of black basalt. These strange supports were richly carved in high relief with creatures never before seen by mortal man. On one writhed squidlike beasts with reaching tentacles; another bore serpent bodies bedight with feathered pinions. A third showed horned beings with merciless eyes charging an unseen foe; and on the fourth were scribed narrow, manlike bodies with widespread batlike wings, which Conan recognized as like that which bore him now aloft.

Like some ungainly bird, the monster fluttered to the parapet and hopped upon the flagstoned walk. Conan slid free of its back. As the being whirled to face him, Conan snatched the poniard from his sash. It was a feeble weapon; but now that hope had fled, Conan prepared to sell his life as dearly as he might.

The thing came on, the claws of its bird-feet clicking on the flagstones, wings half-spread to reveal the knifelike digits on each wing joint. Conan crouched, his dirk held low, prepared for one last upward thrust.

Suddenly, with a cawing screech of pain, the monster lurched sidewise, one wing gone limp. The shaft of an arrow protruded from the fleshless shoulder, its point imbedded in a dorsal muscle. A cheer, wafting from the strand, did honor to this lucky shot by a Barachan archer. The winged devil was not so invulnerable as first appeared. If it could be hurt, it might be killed. Conan smiled grimly.

One wing outspread, the monster attacked again. It did not seem too discommoded by its wound. For a brief moment, Conan and the demon circled the stone pit that cut into the center of the flagstone pave. Then Conan, taking the offensive, ceased waiting for the creature to approach.

The Cimmerian, weary from the loss of blood and the past night's vigil, summoned his last reserves of strength. Pouncing like a tiger, he leaped forward toward his foe and drove the poniard deep into its chest, hoping to pierce the heart.

The blade sank to the hilt in a deep flying muscle, and beneath the forceful blow the devil crumpled. Squawking furiously, the creature twisted its disabled body, wrenching the hilt-buried knife from Conan's hand, and then lay prone upon the flagstones. Conan, gasping painfully, wiped the blood from his eyes and looked for signs of life. He saw none.

The Cimmerian looked closely at the pit centered beneath the columned pavillion and saw that it housed a circular stair of stone that led down to a room below. He had indeed smoked the devil out, for even now the dwindling plumes of smoke from the surrounding bonfires swirled like a whirlpool beneath the conical roof of the pavillion and were sucked into the stairwell.

Not knowing what he should encounter there, he set his feet upon the narrow steps and clambered down. Within the tower the air was hot and stifling, and the smoke obscured parts of the circular chamber in which he found himself.

Here was luxury indeed. The polished wooden floor, inlaid with lighter woods in curious designs, was embellished with small silken rugs in which were woven pentacles and circles and other mystic patterns. The chamber's curved stone walls were hung with tapestries and rich brocades; and worked into the fabric Conan saw threads of gold and silver gleaming brilliantly in the slanting rays of sunlight that, by some strange arrangement of mirrors, lit the room as if the sun itself shone in upon it. To one side stood a lectern of carved and polished wood upon which rested an open book of ancient parchment leaves. Farther along the wall an idol leered, its wolfish mien a frozen mask of menace.

Conan moved quickly around the room, searching for a weapon; but he found nothing. The circumferential chamber had several curtained alcoves, that he ascertained; and choosing one at random, he flung the curtains back. And stared.

The center of the alcove was occupied by a high-backed chair of creamy marble, intricately carved into a labyrinthine tangle of serpent bodies and devil's heads; and seated on this throne was Siptah the sorcerer, his expressionless eyes returning Conan's stare.

9 • Slave of the Crystal

Conan, who had tensed, prepared to fight again, let his breath out with a sigh of satisfaction. Siptah was dead. His eyes were dull and shriveled, and the flesh had fallen in upon his visage, so that his face was but a skull over which dried skin was tightly stretched. Conan sniffed but could not, above the odor of the wood smoke, detect any taint of carrion. Siptah had sat for months upon his throne while his muscles and organs dried and shriveled.

The shrunken figure wore a gown of emerald cloth; and in the bony up-turned hands resting in its lap was cradled a huge, unfaceted crystal, which glowed with topaz fire. This, Conan surmised, was the demon-dreaded gem whose quest had brought him and his comrades to this death-haunted isle.

Conan stepped forward to examine the crystal. To his untutored eyes it seemed but a glimmering sphere of glass lit by an inner glow. Yet so many men desired it that it must have value far beyond imagining. Demons were somehow bound to this pale sphere and could not be released from service save by this orb. But Conan knew not how. He did not understand such matters, and all that was clean and savage within him shrank from traffic with the powers of darkness.

The scrape of a clawed foot on flagstones roused the Cimmerian from his contemplation. He whirled. The creature did not descend the stairs in human fashion, but on half-opened wings dropped down the well to the floor below. Amazed, Conan saw the arrow still transfixing its shoulder and his poniard still sunk into the muscles of its breast; and yet it showed no lessening of its pre-ternatural vitality. A man, however strong, or a wild jungle beast would have been rendered helpless by such wounds; but not, it seemed, the guardian of Siptah's tower.

The creature raised a clawed forelimb and advanced upon him. Frantically, Conan leaped to the left and seized the lectern on which rested the ancient tome. The book crashed to the floor as the Cimmerian raised the heavy piece of furniture like an unwieldy club.

As the winged demon lurched toward him with taloned feet outstretched, Conan swung the clumsy weapon above his head and brought it down upon the monster's skull. The force of the blow sent the devil reeling back and smashed the lectern into a dozen shattered fragments.

Mewling and leaking blood from its crushed skull, the bat-man staggered slowly to its feet and once again advanced. Conan felt a momentary thrill of admiration for any being that sustained such crippling punishment and yet fought on. Still, his own plight was dire—a thing that would not die and Conan weaponless!

And then an idea, simple and audacious, exploded into consciousness; and Conan cursed himself for past stupidity. He turned and snatched the crystal from the mummy's lap, then hurled it at the oncoming monster.

Although Conan's aim was true, the wily creature ducked the missile; and it hurtled through the smoky air to land at last upon the lowest step of the stone staircase. And there, with a tinkling crash and a flash of amber light, the crystal shattered into a thousand pieces.

Then as Conan watched, slit-eyed and empty-handed, his adversary fell head-long to the floor. There was a puff of dust, an acrid odor. When the air cleared, he witnessed an amazing transformation: the monster's skin shriveled, curled up, and crumbled into powder. It was as if the process of decay were speeded up ten thousand times before his wondering eyes. He watched the membranes of the bat wings vanish and saw the bones disintegrate beneath the leathery hide. In a few minutes, nothing was left of the creature but an outline of its shape marked on the floor by little heaps and ridges of dust. And a spent arrow and Conan's dirk.

10 • Siptah's Treasure

The midday sun beat on the yellow sand when Conan's shaggy mane appeared above the parapet. A bloodstained bandage was wound around his head, and strips of sheeting staunched wounds on his arms and chest.

He waved to the cheering men below and, using a knotted strip of bedding for a rope, he lowered a small chest into their eager hands. Then grasping that self-same rope a trifle gingerly, he stiffly slid down into the ashes of the burned-out bonfire.

"Gods and devils, is there aught to drink in this accursed place?" he croaked.

"Here!" cried several corsairs, thrusting leathern wineskins toward him. Conan took a hearty swig, then greeted Borus, the first mate of the *Hawk*.

"While you were in the tower, the lads sent back for food and drink," explained the Argossean. "From what they told me, I thought it best to come ashore. What in the nine hells happened in the tower, Conan?"

"I'll tell you once I get these scratches cleaned and bandaged," growled the Cimmerian.

An hour later, Conan sat upon a stump, eating huge mouthfuls of brown bread and cheese and gulping red wine from the ship's stores.

"And so," he said, "the monster crumbled into dust in less time than it takes to tell of it. It must have been an ancient corpse kept living by Siptah's sorcery. The old he-witch laid some command upon it to drive all uninvited callers from the island; and under Siptah's spell, it followed the command long after its master's death."

"Is that the only treasure in the tower?" asked Abimael, pointing to the chest.

"Aye, all but the furnishings, and those we could not carry. I went through every alcove—where he cooked and worked his spells, where he stored supplies, even in his narrow bedchamber, but I found naught save this. 'Twill furnish all a good share-out—naught fabulous—and a good carouse in Port Tortage."

"Were there no secret doors?" said Fabio, when the men had ceased their shouts of laughter.

"None that I could find, and I hunted the place over. It stands to reason Siptah gained more gold than's in this little chest, but I saw no sign of it. Perhaps it's buried somewhere on this island, but without a map to guide us, we could dig a hundred years in vain." Conan took a gulp of wine and looked at Siptah's spire. "Methinks this tower was built centuries before the Stygian came with his black arts to conquer it."

"Whose was the tower, then?" asked Borus.

"My guess would be it was the winged man's, and others of his kind," said Conan somberly. "I think the devil was the last of a tribe that walked the earth—or flew the skies—before mankind appeared. Only winged men would build a tower with neither doors nor windows."

"And Siptah with his magic enslaved the bat-man?" asked Borus.

Conan shrugged. "That were my guess. The Stygian bound him to the magic crystal in some occult manner; and when the crystal broke, the spell was ended."

Abimael said: "Who knows? Mayhap the creature was not hostile after all, until the sorcerer compelled it to obey his cruel commands."

"To me a devil is a devil," said Conan, "but you may be right. That we shall never know. Let's get back to the *Hawk*, Borus, and trim sail for the Barachas. And once aboard, if any dog wakes me before I've slept my fill, I'll make him wish the bat-man had cut his throat instead!"

The Ivory Goddess

Among the Barachan pirates, Conan acquires more enemies than even he can handle. Fleeing the isles, he is picked up by a ship of the Zingaran buccaneers, whose captaincy he usurps. He makes himself welcome at the Zingaran court by rescuing the daughter of King Ferdrugo from captivity among the Black Amazons; but other Zingarans, jealous of his rise, sink his ship. Conan gets ashore, joins a band of condottieri soldiering for Stygia, and finds an ancient city whose people, divided into two factions, are waging a war of mutual extermination. Escaping the final massacre, Conan tries his luck in Keshan, a black kingdom rumored to harbor a set of priceless jewels in the ruined city of Alkmeenon. He wins the gems but loses them in a matter of minutes.

After the events of "Jewels of Gwahlur," Conan takes Muriela, the girl he picked up at Alkmeenon, eastward to Punt. He means to use the actress to swindle the Puntians out of some of their abundant gold. He is disconcerted to find that his Stygian enemy Thutmekri, like himself, has been compelled to flee from Keshan and has already reached Kassali, the capital of Punt. Thutmekri is deep in intrigues with King Lalibeha, which fact calls for a sudden change in Conan's plans.

Borne on winds from the west, the sound of drums beat against the temple tower, flamingo pink in the setting sun. On its sunlit wall the shadow of Zaramba, chief priest of Punt, stood transfixed, his attenuated form resembling a stork. The figure etched upon the wall was no darker than the black man whose shape it mimicked, although the outlined beak was but a pointed tuft of hair that decorated the front of his wooly pate.

Zaramba tossed back the cowl of his short purple robe and listened intently, straining to catch the message that pulsed out of the West. His drummer, clad only in a linen loin cloth, squatted beside two—now voiceless—hollow logs that served as temple drums, and marked each note as the distant roll of a great drum irregularly alternated with the clack of a lesser.

At length the drummer turned a somber face. "Bad news," he said.

"What says the message?" asked Zaramba.

"Keshan has been plagued by the intrigue of foreigners. The king has expelled all strangers. Priests of the shrine of Alkmeenon were massacred by demons, one priest alone escaping to tell the tale. The scoundrels who wrought this evil are on their way to Punt. Let the men of Punt beware!"

"I needs must tell the king," said Zaramba. "Send a message to our brother priests in Keshan to thank them for their warning."

The drummer raised his sticks and pounded the logs in a rattling code, as Zaramba hastened from the tower and bent his steps toward the royal palace of sun-dried mud, which raised its towers in the center of Kassali, the capital of Punt.

Days passed. The sun of late afternoon stood far down in the western sky, where long clouds lay athwart the deepening azure like red banners floating on the winds of war. From the grassy hill whereon the painted temple stood, the city stretched all around. The low sun gleamed on the gold and crystal ornaments that topped the dun-brown palace in the middle distance and lent sparkle to the temple on the hill.

Eastward, beyond the city, a stretch of forest encroached upon the uplands, and from the far side of these clustered trees now issued two figures mounted on wiry Stygian ponies.

In the lead rode a huge man, nearly naked, his massive arms, broad shoulders, and deeply arched chest burned to a bronzen hue. His only garments were a pair of ragged silken breeks, a leathern baldric, and sandals of rhinoceros hide. A belt of crocodile skin, which upheld the breeches, also supported a dirk in its sheath, and from the baldric hung a long, straight sword in a lacquered wooden scabbard.

The man's thick mane of coarse, blue-black hair was square-cut at the nape of his neck. Smoldering eyes of volcanic blue stared out beneath thick, drawn brows. The man scowled as a gust of wind disordered his sable mane. Not long before, he had worn a circlet of beaten silver around his brows, denoting him a general of the Keshani hosts. But the medal he had sold in Kassali to a Shemitish trader for food and other needfuls now carried in a sack, along with a meager roll of possessions, on the back of the pack horse he led.

Emerging from the forest cover, the man pulled up his pony and rose in his stirrups to stare about. Satisfied that they were unobserved, he gestured to his companion to follow.

This was a girl who slumped with exhaustion in her saddle. She was nearly as nude as the man, for generous areas of smooth, soft flesh gleamed through the rents in her scanty raiment of silken cloth. Her hair was a foam of jet-black curls, and her oval features framed eyes as lustrous as black opals.

As the weary girl caught up with him, the man thumped his heels against the ribs of his mount and trotted out upon the savanna. The westerly sun was setting in a sea of flame as they crossed the grassy flatland and reached the somber hills.

Conan of Cimmeria, soldier, adventurer, pirate, rogue, and thief, had come to the land of Punt with his love of the moment, the Corinthian dancing girl Muriela, former slave to Zargheba. They came to search for treasure, having escaped a hideous death at the hands of the priests of Keshan.

There Zargheba, his slave girl Muriela, and his Stygian partner Thutmekri had concocted a plan to steal from the temple of Alkmeenon a chest of precious gems just when Conan, then a hireling general in Keshan, had set afoot a similar scheme. When all their plots were foiled and Zargheba fell victim to the supernatural guardians of the shrine, Conan and Muriela fled together from Keshan ahead of the vengeful Thutmekri and the furious, scandalized priests.

When Muriela's impersonation of the goddess Yelaya became known throughout the land, Thutmekri and his retinue narrowly escaped being thrown to the royal crocodiles. The Stygian claimed innocence in the blasphemous plot and strove to lay the blame on his enemy Conan. But the incensed priests refused to listen to his plaints, and he and his men departed hastily under cover of darkness and came to the land of Punt.

In Punt, the Stygian made his way to Kassali, the capital, where the mud-brick palace of King Lalibeha reared its towers, spangled with ornaments of glass and gold, into the blue tropical sky. Arguing that the Keshanis planned an invasion of Punt, the wily Thutmekri offered his services to the black ruler.

The king's advisers scoffed. The armies of Punt and Keshan, they said, were too evenly matched for either to attack the other with reasonable hope of success. The Stygian then claimed that the King of Keshan had formed a secret alliance with the twin monarchs of the southeasterly kingdom of Zembabwei to grind Punt between them. He promised, if accorded gold and plunder, to train the black legions of Punt in the skills of civilized war and swore that he could lead the Puntish hosts to the destruction of Keshan.

Thutmekri was not alone in his search for wealth and power. The riches of Punt also drew Conan and Muriela; for there, it was said, people sieved golden nuggets the size of goose eggs in the sandy beds of sparkling mountain streams. There, too, the devout worshiped the goddess Nebethet, whose likeness was carved in ivory inlaid with diamonds, sapphires, and pearls from the farthest seas.

The flight from Alkmeenon had told upon the strength of Muriela, who had hoped to stop in Kassali long enough to recover; but when Conan learned that Thutmekri had preceded him thither, he abruptly changed his plans, bought a supply of food, and left the city. The Cimmerian now schemed to have the Corinthian girl, an accomplished actress, impersonate the goddess Nebethet, reasoning that the priests of Punt would not refuse to share their wealth when so instructed by their goddess. Conan would, in return, humbly obey the goddess's command to lead the Puntian army and defend the land against invasion.

Muriela doubted the wisdom of this plan. She pointed out that such a scheme had failed in the shrine of Alkmeenon and that their enemy, Thutmekri, had already arrived in Kassali and was closeted with King Lalibeha.

Conan growled: "Lucky that trader fellow, Nahor, warned us of Thutmekri's arrival before I sought an audience with the king. I could never match wits with that slippery devil. He would have denounced us to the king, and the fat would have been in the fire."

"Oh, Conan!" whimpered Muriela. "Give up this mad scheme! Nahor offered you a post in his caravan. . . ."

Conan snorted. "Take Nahor's piddling pay as a caravan guard, when there's a fortune for the finding here in Punt? Not I!"

Before the first stars ventured forth upon the plain of evening, Conan and Muriela reached the hill they sought. Here in an uninhabited place stood the shrine-temple of the Puntish divinity, Nebethet. There was something about the place—the emptiness, the silence, the somber gloom draping the hills in velvet cloaks—that sent a chill of premonition into Muriela's heart.

Nor was the sight of the shrine reassuring when, having wound up the steep slope, they caught their first glimpse of it. It was a round, domed building of white marble, rare in this land of dun mud-brick walls and roofs of thatch. The barred portal resembled a mouth with bared fangs and was flanked on the second story by two square windows like empty eye sockets. A great silver skull, the edifice grinned down on them in the light of the gibbous moon, a lonely sentinel guarding a grim and silent land that stretched away on either side in barren desolation.

Muriela shuddered. "The gate is barred. Let us go, Conan; we cannot enter here."

"We stay," muttered Conan. "We will go in if I have to carve a way into this skull-shaped pile. Hold the horses."

Conan swung off his mount, handed his reins to the trembling girl, and examined the entrance. The portal was blocked by a huge portcullis of bronze, green with age. Conan heaved upon the structure; but, although the massive muscles of his arms and chest writhed like pythons, the portcullis would not budge.

"If one way does not serve, we'll try another," he grunted, returning to Muriela and the horses. From the sack strapped to the spare horse, he took a coil of rope, to which was attached a small grapnell. Then he disappeared around a curve of the building, leaving the fearful girl alone in the eerie place. As time passed, her fear turned into stark terror; and when a low voice called her name, she cried aloud.

"Here, wench, here!"

Startled, she looked up. At one of the dark windows above the portal, Conan waved at her.

"Tie the nags," he said. "And forget not to loosen their girths."

When she had tethered the beasts to one of the bars of the toothy portal, he added, "Grasp this and sit in the loop I have made."

The rope snaked down, and when she was seated in the bight, he hauled her up, hand over hand. The grazing horses and the grinning entrance wobbled and spun beneath her in the light of the rising moon. She bit her lip and closed her eyes; and her knuckles were alabaster as she clung to the rope. Soon Conan's strong arms closed about her. She felt the cold slickness of the marble sill against her bare thighs as he drew her slim weight in through the casement. When at last the flooring held firm beneath her feet, she breathed a sigh of relief, and her eyes fluttered open.

There was nothing in her new surroundings to give rise to superstitious fear. She stood in a small empty room, the stone walls of which were bare of ornament. Across the room she saw the outlines of a trapdoor, propped open by a stick of wood.

"This way," said Conan, grasping her arm to steady her uncertain steps. "Careful, now. The planks of this floor are old and rotten."

Below the trapdoor, a ladder descended into the gloom. Fighting her queasiness, she let her companion precede her downward. They found themselves in a spacious rotunda, ghostly in the semidarkness. A circle of marble columns surrounded them, supporting the dome overhead.

"The modern Puntians could not have built this temple," muttered Conan. "This marble must have traveled a long way."

"Who built it, then, think you?" asked Muriela.

Conan shrugged. "I know not. A Nemedian I met—one of those learned men—told me entire civilizations rise and fall, leaving but a few scattered ruins and monuments to mark their passing. I have seen such in my travels, and this may be another. Let us strike a light before the moon goes down and it grows too dark to see."

Six small copper lamps hung from long chains beneath the circle of the dome, and reaching up, Conan unhooked one from its hanging.

"There's oil in it and a wick," he said. "That means someone tends these lamps. I wonder who?"

Conan struck sparks from flint and steel into a pinch of tinder, and flame sputtered into being. He caught the flame on the end of the wick and held up the lamp, whence issued a warm yellow glow. The outlines of the chamber sprang into view.

On the perimeter opposite the great portal, backed by a fretted marble screen, they saw a dais set upon three marble steps. A figure stood erect upon the dais.

"Nebethet herself!" announced Conan, grinning recklessly at the life-size idol.

Muriela shuddered. Revealed in the uncertain lamplight was a woman's beautiful naked body, well-rounded and seductive. But instead of a maiden's attractive features, the face of the statue was a fleshless skull. Muriela turned away in horror from the sight of that death's head, obscenely perched upon the voluptuous female form.

Conan, to whom death was an old acquaintance, was less affected. Nonetheless, the sight caused shivers to run along his spine. Raising the lamp, he saw with dismay that the statue was carved from a single piece of ivory. In his travels in Kush and Hyrkania, he had learned much of the elephant tribe; yet he could not imagine what sort of monster might have borne a tusk as thick as a small woman's body.

"Crom!" he grunted, staring at the grinning skull. "This means my scheme won't work. I planned to spirit away the statue and put you in its place to utter the auguries. But even a fool would never think you that skull-faced abortion come to life."

"Let us fly, then, whilst we still live!" implored Muriela, backing toward the ladder.

"Nonsense, girl! We'll find a way to persuade the black king to oust Thutmekri and shower rewards on us. Till then, we'll search out the rich offerings left here by the faithful. In rooms behind the idol, maybe, or in underground crypts. Let's explore. . . ."

"I cannot," said Muriela faintly. "I am fordone with weariness."

"Then stay here whilst I look around. But wander not away, and call to me if aught occurs!"

Lamp in hand, Conan slipped out of the room, leaving Muriela in the enveloping silence. When the dancer's eyes adjusted to the dark, she could see the outlines of the statue with its sweetly curved woman's body and its gaunt and ghoulish head. The idol was faintly illuminated by the rays of the moon, downthrusting through an opening in the dome; and as the tomblike silence seemed to take on a tangible shape, so the statue in the moonlight seemed to sway and waver. The beating of her heart became the tramp of ghostly feet.

Resolutely, Muriela turned her back upon the statue and sat, a small huddled shape, on the first step of the dais. The things she felt and saw, she told herself, were illusions wrought by fatigue, lack of food, and the weirdness of her surroundings. Still, her fear blossomed until she could have sworn before the gods of Corinthia that a dim, unholy phosphorescence lifted the gloom of the columned hall and that she heard the spectral shuffle of unseen presences.

Muriela felt a compelling need to turn and look behind her; for she had an uncanny sensation that something stood there, staring at her from the shadows. Time and again she resisted this temptation, urging herself not to succumb to foolish fears.

A dirty, skeletal hand, like the claw of some huge bird of prey, closed on the flesh of her naked shoulder. She shrieked as she turned to find herself looking at a sunken face, with bony, withered jaws, topped by a mat of tangled hair that was barely visible in the palpable-seeming darkness. As she jerked away and began to rise, a lumbering monstrosity materialized on her other side. It picked her up like a doll and pressed her against its hairy, muscular chest. With a scream of sheer terror, Muriela fainted.

In the dusty apartments behind the marble rotunda, Conan whirled like a startled jungle cat as the echo of that shriek invaded his senses. With a coarse oath, he sprang from the cubicle he had been investigating and raced back along the corridor, retracing his steps. If something had befallen Muriela, he thought, he was to blame for abandoning her in this ghastly place. He should have kept her with him while exploring the ancient shrine; but, aware that she was near the end of her strength, he had taken pity on her weakness.

When he reentered the central hall, sword in hand and lamp held high, there was nothing to be seen. The girl was no longer where he had left her, nor was she to be found behind one of the many moon-pale columns. Neither could his keen eyes discern any signs of a struggle. It was as if Muriela had evaporated into air.

A prickling of superstitious horror stirred the barbarian to the core. He paid little heed to the dogmas of priests or the oracular warnings of wizards. His Cimmerian gods did not much meddle in the affairs of mortals. But here in Punt, things might be different. Besides, he had survived enough encounters with presences from beyond earthly dimensions to have a healthy respect for their powers; and deep within him smoldered an atavistic fear of the supernatural.

Relighting his lamp, which had faltered and flickered out during his frantic survey of the great hall, he searched on, but with a sense of leaden futility. Wherever the girl might be, she had indeed gone from the rotunda.

———

Muriela slowly came to her senses and found herself slumped against a wall of smooth stone. She was surrounded by darkness so impenetrable that never since the world began, it seemed to her dazed mind, had light plumbed this abyss of gloom.

Rising, she felt her way along the wall until she came to an angle. She set off in a new direction, brushing her fingertips against the rough stone for guidance. She turned another angle, and still another, until it occurred to the frightened and bewildered girl that she had completed the circuit of a small chamber in which she had not detected any door or opening, a featureless cube of stone. How, then, had she come hither? Had she been lowered through a trapdoor? Was she, perchance, in some dark well set deep into the living rock of the hill itself? Was this place her grave?

Muriela shrank into a huddle, staring into the featureless darkness trying to recall what had happened before her swooning. Suddenly, the gates of memory burst open, flooding her mind with living horror. She remembered the touch of the withered claw of the shriveled creature that had crept upon her in the hall of the idol. She felt again the grasp of the hulking monstrosity that had caught her up against its hairy breast.

As memory returned, she cried out again, sobbing Conan's name.

Faint as was that beseeching cry, Conan heard it. His catlike senses, honed through centuries of savage heritage, recognized the echo of Muriela's voice. He whipped about and sought down the corridor in the direction whence the cry had come. The orange flame of his guttering lamp grew feeble, as the gloom of night through which he strode drank up the flickering light.

Although the stony corridors and gloomy chambers seemed untenanted, the Cimmerian was alert to the slightest sound. When he heard a faint rasp from the black mouth of a side passage, he stopped, wheeled, and thrust his lamp forward.

A wizened, shriveled thing, no taller than a child, leered, mummylike, from the lateral corridor. Ancient it seemed as the stones underfoot, and as dead, save for the fire in the bleary eyes set in cavernous sockets in the shrunken face. The thing cowered from the light of the lamp and threw up a skeletal hand as if to ward off a blow.

Then a second apparition took shape out of the darkness behind the first. The monstrous being pushed past the shriveled one and flung itself upon Conan, like a pouncing beast of prey. So swift was the assault that Conan had only a fleeting glimpse of a mountain of sable fur before the lamp was knocked from his hand, to go bouncing and clattering away. Conan found himself fighting for his life in absolute darkness.

Like a trapped leopard, his reaction was instinctive and violent. He tore himself loose from apelike arms, which tried to pinion him, and lashed out blindly with fists that thudded like triphammers. He was unable to discern the true nature of his assailant in the total darkness but assumed that it was some manner of two-legged beast. He felt the jolt of a solid hit travel up his arm and heard the satisfying crunch of a jawbone.

The unknown attacker came on again, swinging long arms. Conan sprang back, but not before the savage talons of the brute raked across his chest, laying his tanned hide open in long scarlet furrows. The cuts, stinging like fury, filled the Cimmerian with black barbaric rage. Needles of agony ripped away the veneer that civilization had placed upon his seething volcanic soul. Throwing back his tousled mane, he howled like a wolf and hurled himself upon his attacker, grappling breast to breast. Hot, fetid breath struck his face like the stinking fumes of a furnace. Sharp fangs slavered and snapped at his corded throat. Hands like clamps closed about his wrists, holding him at bay.

Conan brought his booted foot up in a mighty kick at the enemy's crotch. With a scream of pain, the creature staggered back, loosening his grip on Conan's arms. Conan wrenched loose from the clutching paws and, with a bestial growl, hurled himself forward, groping for the monster's throat. As he locked his hands on the unseen windpipe, the beast tore loose and closed its fanged jaws on Conan's forearm. Lowering his head like a pain-maddened bull, the Cimmerian butted the staggering form in the belly.

His opponent was taller than he by inches, and heavier by far, but its breath erupted with a gasp of anguish and it went down with a crash. Snatching out his dagger, Conan seized a handful of coarse hair and stabbed frantically again and again, driving the weapon into the creature's belly, chest, and throat until he had buffetted the last spark of life from its battered hulk.

Conan rose unsteadily to his feet, gasping and nauseated with the pain of many bites and scratches. When he stopped retching and regained his breath, he wiped his blade on the monster's hairy leg and sheathed it. Then he groped for his lamp. Although the lamp had gone out, a tiny blue flame danced above a puddle of spilled oil. By the feeble light of this elfin fire, Conan found his lamp and lit it.

The dead thing at his feet was a curious hybrid, neither man nor beast. Manlike in shape, it was covered with black hair, like a bear or a gorilla. Yet it was clearly not an ape. Its body and limbs were too manlike in proportions, while its head resembled nothing that Conan had ever looked upon. It had the sloping forehead and protruding snout of a baboon or dog, and its inky, rubbery lips were parted to reveal gleaming canine fangs. And yet, it must have had some link to humankind, for its private parts were covered by a filthy breechclout.

Trembling with terror, Muriela listened to the shouts, snarls, and scuffle of the battle in the passageway above her prison. When it was over, she renewed her plaintive cries. Following the sound of her whimperings, Conan located a niche in the corridor, floored by a flagstone to which was fastened a ring of bronze. He hoisted the slab, bent down, and caught the arms that Muriela reached up to him.

The girl gasped and shrank away from the bloody apparition that supported her, but the sound of Conan's familiar voice reassured her as he helped her step across the battered, hairy corpse that blocked the passage.

Haltingly she described the withered ancient who had laid hands upon her in the rotunda and told how the monster had seized and borne her off. Conan grunted.

"The old hag must be the priestess or oracle of this shrine," he said. "Her voice is the voice of the ivory goddess. There is a closet behind the idol with a door hidden in the fretted marble wall. Hiding there, she can see and speak to those who come to seek her counsel."

"And the monster; what of him?" quavered the girl.

Conan shrugged. "Crom knows! Mayhap her servitor, or some deformed brute the savages of Punt considered touched by the gods and marked for temple duty. Anyway, the thing is dead and the priestess has taken flight. Now we have naught to do but hide in the small room behind the statue when someone comes to hear the oracle."

"We might wait months. Perhaps no one will ever come."

"Nay, our friend Nahor told us the chiefs of Punt consult the ivory wench before each grave decision. Methinks you will play the skull-faced goddess after all."

"Oh, Conan, I am sore afraid. We cannot stay here, even if we would, for we shall starve," said Muriela.

"Nonsense, girl! Our pack horse carries food enough for many days, and this is as good a place to rest as any."

"But how about the priestess?" persisted the frightened girl.

"The old hag cannot harm us now that her monster is dead," said Conan cheerfully, adding, "If we use normal caution, that is. I would not accept a drink from her hand."

"So be it, then," said Muriela. A look of sadness crossed her beautiful face as she added, "In truth I am no oracle, but I foretell that this adventure will end badly for us both."

Conan put his arms around her to comfort her. And in the early morning light that stole through the opening of the dome, she saw the blood oozing from the razor cuts across his chest.

"My beloved, you are hurt and I knew it not! I must wash and bind your wounds."

"Just a few scratches," grumbled Conan. But he allowed her to lead him to the well in the little cloistered courtyard behind the skull-faced temple. There she washed the dried blood from his limbs and bandaged the beast's bites with strips of silk torn from her skirt. A half hour later, Conan and Muriela returned to the rotunda and rested behind a pillar out of sight of the ivory goddess. Keeping alternate watch, they slept all that day and the following night.

When Conan awoke, the golden rays of the rising sun were gilding the clouds of morning, and the East was ablaze with ruddy vapors. Muriela sat with her back to a pillar, cradling Conan's head in her arms.

He stretched. "I must go and get us some food," he said. "Here, take this dagger in case the old priestess returns."

Climbing the ladder to the small storeroom through whose window they had entered, he hooked the grapnell into the sill and prepared to descend the rope. Then he paused to peer westward, for he caught — or thought he caught — a glimpse of distant movement.

Beyond the hills that surrounded the temple-shrine lay a wide savanna, and at the far end of that grassy plain stood the city of Kassali, roof ornaments on temple and palace twinkling in the slanting sunlight. All seemed peaceful, the city asleep. Then Conan's keen eyes discerned a row of black dots moving across the plain. A faint plume of dust arose behind them.

"Our visitors are coming sooner than I thought," he growled. "I cannot leave the nags tethered here. The delegation would know at once that strangers occupied their temple."

He swung over the sill and let himself down swiftly. In a moment he had unhitched the horses. Tightening the girth on one, he vaulted into the saddle and departed at a gallop, leading the other two. A quarter hour later he returned, breathing hard from running up the long slope of the hill. He climbed the rope and drew it in, then made his way to the head of the ladder.

"Horsemen coming!" he gasped. "Tied the nags — in the woods — at the foot of the hill! Put on your goddess garb, and quickly." He tossed Muriela a bundle of female garments.

Returning to the window, he found that the line of dots had grown into a cavalcade, cantering toward the foot of the temple knoll. He raced to the ladder, clambered down, and said:

"Come; we have scarce time to hide ourselves in the oracle chamber. You remember your speech?"

"Y-yes; but I fear. It did not work when we tried it at Alkmeenon."

"There was a rascal then, and Bît-Yakin's accursed servants. This priestess lacks her monster, and I've seen no other temple denizens. This time, I'll stay beside you. Come!"

He took her hand and almost dragged her across the room. By the time the cavalcade reached the temple, Conan and Muriela were crowded into the small chamber behind the ivory goddess.

They heard the clop of hooves, the jingle of harness, and the mumble of distant voices as men dismounted. Presently Conan caught a slow mechanical rumble.

"That must be the portcullis," he whispered. "The priests must have some sort of key."

The voices grew louder, mingled with the tramp of many feet. Through the band of fretwork that ran across the door, Conan saw a procession file into the rotunda. First came a group of blacks in barbaric finery. In their midst paced a large, stout man with graying, wooly hair, on which rode an elaborate crown, made of sheets of gold hammered into the form of a hawk with outspread wings. This, Conan surmised, must be King Lalibeha. A very tall, lean man in a purple robe he took to be Zaramba, the high priest.

They were followed by a squad of Puntian spearmen with headdresses of ostrich plumes and rhinoceros-hide shields. Behind them strode Thutmekri the Stygian and a score of his personal retainers, among them Kushite spearmen and Shemitish archers armed with heavy double-curved bows.

Conan's neck hairs stiffened as he sighted his enemy.

Thutmekri the Stygian felt the morning breeze at his back. That same chill, or an echo of it, closed about his heart. Rogue and adventurer though he was, the tall Stygian cared little for this unexpected visit to the shrine of the ivory goddess. He remembered all too well the disaster that had befallen his partner in the temple of the goddess Yelaya at Alkmeenon.

Although Thutmekri had spoken plausibly about the possibility of war against Punt, King Lalibeha had remained doubtful and suspicious. Among the rulers of the northern tier of black countries, the old king was known as canny and cautious. To cap the king's doubts, his high priest Zaramba had received a drum message from his sacerdotal colleagues to westward, warning against certain pale-skinned troublemakers who were fleeing toward Punt. When the smooth-talking Stygian persisted, Zaramba proposed a visit to the oracular shrine of Nebethet, to seek the advice of the goddess.

Thus king and high priest with their attendants had set out at dawn and traveled into the sunrise. It behooved Thutmekri to go with them, much as he disliked the notion. The Stygian thought little of these southern gods, but he feared their fanatical priests, who might turn upon him, denouncing him as a foreign interloper. His debacle in Keshan had honed a fine edge on his fears. And as they rode toward the skull-shaped temple on that distant hill, he wondered whether the whole expedition was a pretext by Lalibeha and his high priest to trap and destroy him.

So they had come to the shrine of the goddess Nebethet. Zaramba released the hidden catch that enabled his servants to raise the portcullis, and in they went. The king placed Thutmekri and his men in the center of the solemn procession, in order, the Stygian suspected, to give the royal escort the advantage should a fracas begin.

Eyes gleamed with holy awe; the priest and the courtiers knelt and bowed low to the ground. On the dais before the ivory, skull-faced goddess, the king placed a small, lacquered casket; and as he opened it, jeweled fire spilled out into the pale morning light of the secluded place.

Long black arms rose in homage to the ivory woman. Zaramba intoned an invocation, while youthful acolytes with shaven heads swung golden censers, spreading clouds of fragrant smoke.

Thutmekri's nerves were on edge. He fancied that he felt the pressure of unseen eyes. As the priest spoke in an archaic dialect of Puntic, which he could not understand, his restlessness grew. His Stygian ancestry whispered that something was about to happen.

In a bell-like voice, the skull-faced woman spoke: "Beware, O King, of the wiles of Stygia! Beware, O Lalibeha, of the plots of blasphemers from distant, sinister lands! The man before you is no friend but a smooth-tongued traitor, come slinking out of Keshan to pave the road to your doom!"

Growling and lifting their feather-tufted spears, the Puntian warriors glared suspiciously at Thutmekri and his escort. The Stygian's men clustered together, the spearmen forming a circle of shields. Behind them, the Shemites reached back over their shoulders, ready to whip arrows from their quivers. In an instant, the hall might explode into a scene of scarlet carnage.

Thutmekri remained frozen. There was something familiar about that voice. He could have sworn that it was the voice of a much younger woman disguised to sound mature—a young woman whose voice, he was sure, he had heard before.

"Wait, O King!" he cried. "You are being cozened. . . ."

But the voice from the statue, continuing without pause, commanded the attention of all. "Choose, instead, as your general Conan the Cimmerian. He has fought from the snows of Vanaheim to the jungles of Kush; from the steppes of Hyrkania to the pirate isles of the Western Ocean. He is beloved of the gods, who have carried him victorious through all his battles. He alone can lead your legions to victory!"

As the voice ceased, Conan stepped out of the small chamber that opened on the rotunda. With a keen sense of the dramatic, he strode majestically forward, bowing formally to King Lalibeha and again to the high priest.

"The devil!" snarled Thutmekri. His face convulsed with rage, he told his archers: "Feather me yonder clown!"

As half a dozen Shemites pulled arrows from their quivers and nocked them, Conan's eye caught their action. He gathered his legs beneath him to spring behind the nearest pillar; for at that range, he would be an inevitable target for a volley of arrows. The king opened his mouth to shout a command.

At that moment the ivory statue of Nebethet creaked, groaned, and toppled forward, to crash down the steps of the dais. Where the statue had been now stood a woman on whom all eyes were fixed.

Staring with the rest, Conan saw that it was Muriela—yet it was not she. Nor was it merely the shimmering ankle-length gown or the few dabs of cosmetics. This woman seemed Muriela transfigured, taller, more majestic, even more beautiful. The air about her seemed to glow with a weird violet light, and the atmosphere of the rotunda was suddenly vibrant with life. The woman's voice was neither Muriela's light soprano nor her imitation of the ringing tones of the goddess she feigned to be. It was a deeper, more resonant voice—a voice which seemed to make the very floor vibrate like the plucked string of a lute.

"O King! Know that I am the true goddess Nebethet, albeit in the body of a mortal woman. Does any mortal contest this?"

Thutmekri, insensate with rage and frustration, growled to one of his Shemites, "Shoot her!"

As the man bent his bow, aiming over the head of the kneeling spearmen before him, the woman smiled slightly and pointed a finger. There was a flash and a sharp crack, and the Shemite fell dead among his comrades.

"Now do you believe?" she asked.

There was no reply. Every man in the chamber—king, priest, warriors, and the adventurers Conan and Thutmekri—sank to his knees and bowed his head. The goddess continued:

"Know, O King, that these two great rogues, Thutmekri and Conan, desire to gain whatever they can at your expense, as they sought and failed to cozen the priests in Keshan. The Stygian merits naught less than to be thrown to the crocodiles. The Cimmerian deserves no less a fate, but I would that he be leniently dealt with because he was kind to the woman whose body is my garment. Give him two days to leave the kingdom or become the reptiles' prey.

"I lay upon you one more command. My eidolon, cracked in its fall, was at best an ugly image. Set your artisans, O King, to carving me a new statue in the likeness of this woman whose form I now inhabit. I shall, in the interval, make my abode in her body. See that it be furnished with the best of food and drink. Forget not my commands. I grant you now permission to withdraw."

The purple light faded; the goddess stood motionless upon the dais. The men, bemused, rose silently to their feet and stood as men transfixed. Stealthily the Stygian and his retinue moved toward the open portal.

The king's command shattered the silence. "Take them!" he roared.

A long-bladed javelin soared from the hand of a king's man, to bury itself in the black breast of one of Thutmekri's Kushites. The victim screamed, lurched drunkenly, and sank sprawling on the marble floor, blood gushing from mouth and nose.

The next instant, the hall was alive with yelling, struggling men. Javelins arced, bowstrings twanged, spears jabbed. Jagged-bladed throwing knives whirled through the air, and hardwood clubs thudded on rhinoceros-hide shields and woolly-pated heads. Again and again the men of Punt hurled themselves upon the compact knot of Thutmekri's men. As each wave receded, wounded or dying men clutched at spurting arteries or writhed in their own spilled viscera.

Thutmekri whipped out his glittering scimitar. Thundering oaths and calling on Set and Yig and all the other devil-gods of the Stygian pantheon, he hewed like a madman among his attackers. Shortly, he cleared a space before and around him, the nearest Puntians giving back before his deadly strokes. Through the thinning press, Thutmekri sighted Conan, standing with sword in hand beside the dais.

Eyes glaring, mouth twisted with hate, Thutmekri broke out of the crowd and rushed upon the man he blamed for the collapse of all his schemes.

"This is for you, Cimmerian lout!" he screamed, aiming a decapitating slash at Conan's neck.

Conan parried, and the swords met with the clang of a bell. The blades sprang apart, circled, clashed, and ground. Sparks flew from the steel. Breathing heavily, the antagonists circled, thrusting and slashing in a frenzy of action.

After a quick feint, Conan struck home against Thutmekri's flank. With a groan, the Stygian doubled over, dropping his sword and clutching at his cloven side. Blood gushed across his fingers. A second blow sent his head leaping from his shoulders and rolling along the floor, while his body slumped into a swiftly widening pool of its own blood.

When their leader fell, Thutmekri's men—such as were still standing—broke for the exit. In a mass, they crowded through the encircling Puntians, pushing some aside and trampling others. In a trice they were through the portal.

"After them!" shouted King Lalibeha. "Slay all!"

King, priests, and warriors streamed out after the fugitives. When Conan reached the portcullis, the grassy slope and the plain beyond were alive with men, some galloping on horseback and some running afoot like madmen. Some of the fugitives vanished into the forest that lapped the hill to southward.

Back in the shrine, Conan stepped over the silent dead and the groaning wounded to approach the dais. Muriela still stood motionless where once had stood the ivory statue. Conan said:

"Come, Muriela, we must be gone. How did you manage that purple glow?"

"Muriela?" said the woman, looking full upon his face. The violet radiance returned as she spoke. There was about her a chill remoteness of tone and manner far beyond the capacity of Muriela's not unskillful acting. "Do not presume, mortal, unless you wish the fate accorded that unfortunate Shemite."

Conan's skin crawled. Awe shone in the blue eyes he turned upon the goddess.

"You are truly Nebethet?"

"Aye, so some men call me."

"But—but what is to become of Muriela? I cannot just abandon her."

"Your concern does credit to you, Conan. But fear not for her. She shall be my garment as long as I wish. When I wish otherwise, I will see that she is well provided for. Now you had best be on your way, unless you prefer to end up in the bellies of Lalibeha's crocodiles."

Seldom in his turbulent life had Conan deferred to any human being, no matter how exalted. Now, for once, he became respectful, almost humble.

"On my way whither?" he said. "Your Divinity knows that I am out of money. I cannot return to Kassali to take up Nahor's offer, for my welcome either in Punt or in Keshan would be something less than hearty."

"Then bend your steps toward Zembabwei. Nahor of Asgalun has a nephew in the city of New Zembabwei, who may have a post for you as caravan guard. Now go, ere I bethink me of the blasphemies you plotted in my name!"

Conan bowed, backed away from the dais, turned, and strode out. As he walked beneath the raised portcullis, a shuffling sound behind made him whirl, hand on hilt.

From the darkness within, a withered, bent, and shrunken figure tottered into the light. It had once been a woman.

The aged priestess of the temple of Nebethet shook a bony fist at Conan. From her toothless jaws came a harsh, grating speech:

"My son! Ye have slain my son! The curse of the goddess upon thee! The curse of the child's father, the demon Jamankh, upon thee! I call upon Jamankh, the hyena-demon, to blast and rend this murderer, this blasphemer! May your eyeballs rot in your head! May your bowels be drawn from your belly, inch by inch! May ye be staked out over an anthill! Come, Jamankh! Avenge—"

A fit of coughing racked the aged frame. The crone pressed both bony hands to her chest, and her faded eyes widened in their cavernous sockets. Then she fell headlong upon the marble.

Conan stepped forward and touched the ancient body. Dead, he mused; she was so old that any shock would slay her. *Perchance her demon lover, who begat the monstrosity on her, will come after me and perchance not. In any case, I must be on my way.*

He closed the staring eyes of the corpse, strode out of the temple, and swung down the grassy slope to the place in the forest where he had left the horses.

Moon of Blood

Failing to obtain his long-sought fortune in Punt, Conan travels north to Aquilonia and takes service as a scout on the western frontier, on the edge of the Pictish Wilderness. After the events of "Beyond the Black River," he rises rapidly in the Aquilonian service. As captain of regular troops, he is in the thick of the fighting that rages all over the province of Conajohara, from Velitrium to the Black River. These fights are skirmishes between the retreating Aquilonians and the oncoming Picts, reoccupying the territory they had enjoyed before the Aquilonians drove them out of it. Rumor says that the feuding Pictish clans have united and plan to attack Velitrium itself. So Conan and another captain are sent out with detachments to probe deep into the lost province and to find out what the Picts are up to.

1 • The Owl that Cried by Day

The forest was strangely silent. Wind whispered through the jade-green leaves of spring, but no sound came from the beasts and birds who dwelt within these verdant solitudes. It was as if the forest, with its thousand eyes and ears, sensed the presence of an intruder.

Then through the aisles of giant oaks came the rustling of armed men on the move—the tramp of feet, the muted jingle of metal armament, the murmur of voices.

Suddenly the leaves parted and a burnished giant of a man entered a clearing. He was armed as if for war; a plain steel helm covered his mane of coarse black hair; and his deep chest and knotted arms were protected by a hauberk of chain mail. The dented helm framed a dark, scarred face bronzed by strange suns, wherein blazed eyes of smouldering volcanic blue.

He did not tramp along, but glided from bush to bush, now and again stopping to peer, to listen, and to sniff the air. He had about him the tense and wary look of one who expects an ambush. Soon a second man appeared behind the first—a well-built, blond young man of medium height, wearing the war harness of a lieutenant in the Golden Lions, a regiment in the Frontier Guard of Numedides, King of Aquilonia.

The difference between the two was striking. The black-maned giant, obviously a Cimmerian from the savage wildernesses to the north, was vigilant but at ease; the younger officer, starting at every sound and swatting the myriad flies, appeared clumsy and nervous. He addressed the older man with deference:

"Captain Conan, Captain Arno asks if all is well forward of our position. He waits your signal to advance the troops."

Conan grunted, saying nothing. The lieutenant glanced uneasily about the glade. "It seems quiet enough to me," he added.

Conan shrugged. "Too quiet for my taste. These woods at midday should be alive with birdsong and the chattering of squirrels. But it's as silent hereabouts as any graveyard."

"Mayhap the presence of our troops has affrighted the forest creatures," suggested the Aquilonian.

"Or," said Conan, "mayhap the presence of a Pictish force, though as yet I have seen no certain sign. They may be here, or they may not. Tell me, Flavius, have any of our scouts returned?"

"Not yet, sir," said the young lieutenant. "But the scouts sent out by General Lucian report no Picts are in the forest."

Conan bared his fangs in a mirthless wolf's grin. "Aye, the General's scouts swear there's not a living Pict in all of Conajohara, that I know. They conclude the painted devils anticipate our strike in force and have withdrawn. But . . ."

"You distrust the scouts, Captain?"

Conan glanced briefly at the lieutenant. "I know them not. Nor whence Lucian brought them, nor how trustworthy their opinions may be. I'd trust the word of my own scouts—the men I had before Fort Tuscelan fell."

Flavius blinked, incredulous. "Do you suspect Viscount Lucian of wishing us ill?"

Conan's face became a mask as, slit-eyed, he studied his companion. "I've said naught to that effect. But I've seen enough of this world to trust few men. Go, tell Captain Arno. . . . Wait, here comes one of Lucian's vagabonds."

A lean man, with a brown skin seamed by a hundred small wrinkles, stepped from behind the trunk of a huge oak—an oak that was already old when the Picts ruled all the Westermarck. The man was clad in buckskin and bore a bow and hunting falchion.

"Well?" said Conan in lieu of other greeting.

"Not a sign of a Pict the whole length of South Creek," said the scout.

"Who is on our flanks?"

The scout repeated several names. "No Picts anywhere. There's the creek ahead of you," he said, pointing.

"That I know," said Conan, dryly.

As Flavius, peering through the massive tree trunks, discovered a glimmer of silver in the middle distance, the scout faded back into the forest.

The sounds of moving men grew louder as the head of the column appeared on the trail behind them. Of the hundred-odd Aquilonian soldiers, who traveled in ones and twos along the narrow trail, half were pikemen and half archers. The pikemen, mostly stocky, tawny-haired Gundermen, wore helmets and mail shirts. The archers, mainly Bossonians, walked unarmored save for hauberks of leather studded with bronzen rings or buttons, and here and there, a light steel cap. Arno, it seemed, had wearied of waiting.

A stocky, brown-haired officer hurried up to Conan, sweat running down his round, red face. The new arrival pushed back his helmet and said:

"Captain Conan, my pig-stickers begin to tire. They need a short rest."

"They find this a hard march? Ha! They need hardening, Arno, the way I've been hardening my archers. Let them rest for a moment. And go stop their loose tongues. If there's a Pict within a league, he'd know where and how many we are."

Captain Arno slapped at a fly on his neck. "Few men have legs as long as yours, Conan, or tongues as short." He returned to his soldiers, shaking his head.

" 'Reconnaisance in force,' forsooth!" growled Conan to Flavius. "Under these conditions, it invites disaster."

"The general's orders were positive," said Flavius.

"Aye, but that makes them no less foolish. To war with Picts, you need news before the fight and numbers during it. So you scatter your scouts to seek the size and position of the foe, then concentrate your troops to hit them hard."

"That, sir, takes careful timing, does it not?"

"Aye, that it does. If you miscalculate, you're dead. Timing, lad, is half the art of war—what Numedides's gilded generals call strategy. But sending two half-companies thus along the creek, with no force to back us up in case of trouble, when the Picts can bring together thousands. . . ."

Conan's deepset blue eyes pierced the long aisles between the ancient trees, as if by staring hard he could penetrate the massive boles and see into the shadowy, hidden distances. He liked nothing about this expedition, which seemed to him foolhardy to the point of insanity. Soldiers long in the service of King Numedides never questioned their orders or the wisdom of their superiors. But Conan the Cimmerian was no common Aquilonian soldier, although for more than a year he had served as a mercenary here, fighting the country's wars for hire. He was beginning to regret his acceptance of a command in the Frontier Guard, although at the time it had seemed the wisest course. The sharing of command with Captain Arno partly accounted for his change of heart; but this blind expedition into an unknown and hostile wilderness irked him more. Every savage instinct in his primitive soul cried out in warning against so foolish a plan.

"Well, time to move on," he growled. "Flavius, return to Arno and have him get his pikemen on their feet."

Through the long morning, the troops with muted tread made their way over rocks and roots of trees along the trail to South Creek, the boundary of water that divided the province of Schohira from the lost Conajohara, now overrun by painted Picts.

Returning up the line of marching men, Flavius rejoined Conan at the front and delivered his message: "Captain Arno will hold the pace you set until you signal otherwise."

Conan nodded curtly, lips parted in a sour smile. "Praise be to Crom," he said.

"For what?" asked Flavius.

"For Arno's good sense to know that he knows not the frontier. So he takes my advice. In other circumstance, two commanders of one force would be an invitation to the gods of disaster."

"General Lucian insisted there be two of you."

"Still I like it not. Something stinks about this whole foray."

As the trail approached the creek, Conan turned to the soldiers in the van. "Fill your water jugs and skins, all of you. Pass the word along, but whisper it."

When the sun looked down from the center of the sky, the troop had covered another league along South Creek as it tumbled over its rocky bed in its haste to reach its junction with the Black River. Aside from the rippling of the water, the forest was as silent as a tomb.

Suddenly a sound broke the quiet. It was the hoot of an owl. Conan whirled and dashed back toward the disorderly column of marching men.

"Form square for attack!" he roared. "Archers, hold your shots till you see your targets plain."

Running after him, Flavius panted: "It was but an owl, Captain. There is no . . ."

"Whoever heard an owl at midday?" snarled Conan, as a chorus of yells from trees ahead half drowned his words.

2 • Death from the Trees

Arno, too, shouted orders, and the snakelike column dissolved into a shapeless mass of men. Then in accordance with the maneuvers that Conan had drilled into them, the mass shook itself out into a hollow square. The perimeter bristled with the low-held points of fifty-odd pikemen, and behind each stood an archer, bow in hand and arrow nocked. The pikemen knelt on the soft, leaf-covered forest floor, their pikes butt to the ground, shafts slanting forward, points waist-high.

The wall of men had scarce been formed when a horde of painted savages erupted from the woods. Naked but for breech clouts and moccasins, and feathers in their tangled manes of knotted hair, the Picts charged the Aquilonians, shooting arrows as they came. Formidable they were, these swarthy, muscular men armed with copper-bladed hatchets and copper-headed spears. Some bore weapons of fine Aquilonian steel, stolen from the dead after the fall of Fort Tuscelan.

"Mitra! There must be thousands of them," breathed Flavius.

"Go to yonder corner of the square," said Conan as he positioned himself at the corner to the right. Arno and Arno's lieutenant occupied the remaining corners, facing outward toward the fast-surrounding hordes.

Several Picts fell before the withering rain of Bossonian arrows. Then the Picts were upon them. Some, in their warlike fury, impaled themselves on the points of the pikes. Others danced beyond the spears, yelling war cries and brandishing weapons. A few dropped to the ground and tried to roll beneath the jagged line of spears; but these were soon dispatched.

Defending his corner of the square, Conan whirled his heavy broadsword, lopping off a head here, an arm there. The archers, with the relentless rhythm of automatons, nocked arrows and loosed them into the surging mass. Pict after Pict fell screaming, trying to draw a shaft from his chest or writhing in his death throes. Blood flowed unchecked across last winter's leaves and soaked into the thick humus of the forest floor. The motionless air drank in the stench of blood and sweat and fear.

The screech of a bone whistle cut through the roar of battle. Pictish chiefs ran among the battle-crazed savages, pulling them back and shouting unintelligible commands. The frenzied tribesmen were not readily commanded; but at last they turned their backs on the foe. Trotting down the forest aisle, limping or hobbling away, or staggering beneath the weight of wounded comrades, they faded into the budding branches and were gone.

Around the armored square lay more than two-score dead and wounded Picts, some moaning, others feebly trying to crawl to safety. Conan wiped the blood and sweat from his face and turned to confront his soldiers, who stood expectantly beside the fallen members of the company.

"You! And you!" barked Conan, indicating two of the pikemen. "Fall out and dispatch me those dogs who still move. If it's a Pict, spear it; they are good at shamming dead. The rest of you, keep your places. Throw our dead out of the square. Tend our wounded."

Conan designated three archers to leave the square to gather up the spent arrows lying on the ground or sunk in Pictish flesh. Arno asked:

"Why have the savages quit when they outnumbered us ten to one?"

"Crom only knows. They've probably withdrawn to plan some other devil-ment. Don't break formation yet."

A gentle breeze carried the sound of a drum and a rattle shaken by a swarthy hand. The Aquilonians sighed in relief, wiped sweat from their faces, and drank deeply from their water jugs and skins. When some doffed helmets and mail-shirts, Conan roared:

"Put back your harness, dolts! How think you we slew so many more than we, ourselves, have lost?"

In the airless afternoon, flies swarmed around the bodies of the fallen, form-ing black clusters on the bloody wounds; and the drumming and rattling of the savages droned on. The four officers gathered apart from the square of restless, weary men to confer in lowered voices. Conan said:

"I heard they have a new wizard, Sagayetha, nephew of old Zogar Zag. Methinks that racket means he's there among them directing the next attack."

"Beware, Conan!" hissed Arno. "If the men suspect there's sorcery afoot . . ."

"Anyone who wars with Picts fights sorcery," said Conan. " 'Tis the natural condition of the frontier. They cannot stand against good Aquilonian steel, the steel that plucked the Westermarck out of Pictish hands. So they turn to their black devil-magic to even up the odds."

"What mean you, 'plucked'?" said Arno with indignation. "The land was bought from them, piece by piece, by legal treaties bearing royal seals."

Conan snorted: "I know those treaties, signed by some Pictish drunken ne'er-do-well who knew not what he placed his mark upon. I love not Picts, but I can understand the fury that drives them now. We'd best march back in columns of fours, pikes without and archers within. Should they again attack, we can reform our hedgehog."

The officers returned to their posts, but before the column had proceeded a hundred paces, the rattling and drumming ceased abruptly. The marchers paused, disquieted by the sudden silence.

A piercing scream ripped through the garment of uncanny silence. A man staggered out of ranks and fell writhing among the twisted roots. Another likewise fell; and suddenly the line vibrated with fearful cries of horror.

Snakes—Pictish vipers, some as long as a man, with wedge-shaped heads and diamond patterns down their thick, scaly bodies—dropped from the trees among the Aquilonians. On the forest floor they coiled, heads swaying, and lunged at the nearest soldier. Then slithering to their next victim, they coiled and struck again.

"Swords!" shouted Conan. "Kill them! Keep your ranks, but kill them!"

Conan's blade divided a six-foot serpent into writhing halves; but there seemed no end to the rain of snakes. An archer, shrieking in mindless terror, dropped his bow and broke into a run.

"Back in the ranks, you!" roared Conan.

The flat of his sword felled the fleeing Aquilonian. But it was too late; panic had taken hold. Arno, snake-bitten, lay writhing on the ground.

The Frontier Guards dissolved into a stream of fugitives, casting aside armor and weapons in their headlong flight. The Picts swarmed out of the forest cover and rushed after them, hacking, stabbing, and cudgeling those they overtook.

Conan's whirling broadsword struck down two Picts. "Flavius!" he cried. "This way!"

The young lieutenant fought through the press to join Conan, as the Cimmerian strode away from the fleeing Aquilonians.

"Are you mad?" panted Flavius; catching a Pictish hatchet blow on his buckler and missing a swipe at the wielder.

"See for yourself," growled Conan, running another Pict through the body. "If you'd leave this place alive, follow me."

The two hastened northwestward. Suddenly, there were no more Picts ahead, the nearest having given a wide berth to the two mailed warriors with bloody blades. Conan and Flavius ran down the trail and were soon out of sight of the battlefield.

The savages sprinted after the bulk of the Aquilonians, fleeing back toward Velitrium. But the Picts avoided the area where the Aquilonians had formed their square, for there lay bodies heaped and serpents still slithered and coiled and struck.

3 • Blood Money

In time the creek spread itself voluptuously beneath the blue sky, which it caught in reflected splendor. As Conan and Flavius pushed through the lush greenery cradling its shores, a sharp clap shattered the stillness. A splash roiled the placid surface of the pond, and drops of water leaped up the slanting rays of the afternoon sun, glittering like topaz.

"Fish?" whispered Flavius.

"Beaver. They splash with tails like broadswords to warn the others when danger approaches. See you their dam downstream of the pond? That's their abode."

"Mean you they live beneath the water?"

"Nay, in dry nests of twigs above the surface within the confines of the dam. Can you see that opening beyond the dam?"

On the right bank of South Creek, below the beaver dam, Flavius saw a clearing. Once neglected and overgrown, it had been lately cleared again.

Through the trees that crowned this promontory, Flavius glimpsed the steel-blue water of the Black River.

In the midst of the clearing rose a granite statue twice the height of a man. Little more than a large upright boulder, it was roughly trimmed to suggest a human shape. In front of this rude eidolon, a smaller flat-topped boulder appeared above the long grass.

"The Council Rocks," muttered Conan. "The Picts were wont to meet here before the Aquilonians drove them out of Conajohara. Now they've cleared the place again and use it for their gatherings. We'll hide behind the beaver house to watch and listen. They'll hold a council, now that our forces are in disarray."

"But they'll spy us, Conan, and take us prisoner or worse!"

"I think not." Conan pulled ferns and water plants from the margin of the pond and fastened them about his helmet. "Tie plants about your helm, like mine."

"This hides our heads full well," said Flavius. "But what about mail-clad bodies?"

"All is invisible in blackish water, son."

"Mean you we must lurk within this pond, in all our harness, like some scaly creatures of the deep?"

"That's it. Better wet than dead."

Flavius sighed. "I suppose you are right."

"The day I'm wrong, they'll hang my head in one of their altar huts. Come on!"

Conan stepped into water no deeper than his waist and led his young companion across the pond to the beaver house, a wide mound of sticks two feet above the water. As they approached, a turtle, sunning itself on the wattled dam, slipped off into the water and vanished.

As they crouched until the water reached their chins, only their heads, all but undetectable under the leafy disguises, showed above the surface.

"I'd rather pray to Mitra in a temple than kneel on this dank leaf mold," said Flavius with a wry little smile.

"Be still; our lives depend upon it. Can you hold this pose for hours if need be?"

"I'll try," said the lieutenant gamely.

Conan grunted approvingly, and like a crouching leopard, ceased to move.

Insects hummed around them, and the frogs, which had fallen silent when the men appeared, resumed their croaking chorus. A red sun hung low above the fan of greenery that dabbled its feet in the roseate water. Slowly the woods darkened.

Flavius whispered desperately, "Something is biting me."

"Bloodsucker," said Conan. "Fear not; it will not steal enough of your blood to weaken you."

With a shudder, Flavius pinched the writhing leech and cast it from him.

"Hist! They come," murmured Conan.

Flavius quieted, hardly daring to breathe, as Picts in ones and twos flitted among the darkening trees, whooping with laughter. Flavius was surprised. From what he had seen of Picts, he deemed them a dour and silent folk. Evidently these savages could rejoice as well as other men.

The clearing filled as Picts, in clan regalia, squatted in rows and passed around skins of weak native beer, amid chatter and boasting.

"I see Wolves, Hawks, Turtles, Wildcats, and Ravens," whispered Flavius, "all in seeming amity."

"They are learning to put aside their clannish feuds," muttered Conan. "If ever the tribes unite at once, let Aquilonia beware. Ha! Look at those twain!"

Two figures, distinct from the throng of nearly naked savages, stepped into the clearing. One was a Pictish shaman, wearing a harness of leather in which was set a score of tinted ostrich feathers. These plumes, Flavius knew, must have been borne for nearly a thousand leagues over trade routes that wound like ribbons through the deserts and savannas of the south.

The other man was a lean, weatherbeaten Aquilonian in buckskins. Conan whispered:

"Sagayetha, and—by Crom—that's Edric, the scout whom Lucian foisted on us!"

Cutting a path through the squatting warriors, who swayed like fields of grain to let them pass, the shaman and the scout came through the throng and climbed the smaller boulder. The Aquilonian spoke in his native language to the Picts, pausing betimes for Sagayetha to translate.

"You have seen, my children," began Edric, "that your great and loyal friend, General Viscount Lucian, is not one whose words are straw. He said he would betray a company of Aquilonians into your hands, and did he not? Even so, when he promises you all of Schohira, he will not fail you.

"Now the time has come for the reckoning. In return for aiding you to recover the land that was stolen from you but a few decades ago, he now asks payment of the promised treasure."

Sagayetha translated the last phrase and ripped out a short speech of his own.

"What says he?" whispered Flavius.

"He told them to fetch the money. Now hush."

Four Picts appeared, staggering under a stout chest slung from a pole, which the Picts carried on their shoulders. As they lowered the chest to the ground, Sagayetha and Edric jumped down from the boulder and raised the lid. From their watery lurking place, Conan and Flavius could not see the contents; but Edric dipped a hand in, brought up a fistful of the gleaming coins, and let them trickle back into the container. Flavius could hear the metallic clatter.

"Where would the Picts get so much gold and silver?" he whispered. "They use not coins, save now and then for trading with the Aquilonians."

"Valannus's pay chest," muttered Conan. "A full one had arrived at Fort Tuscelan just before it fell, and the Picts got their hands on it before it could be paid out to the soldiers."

"Why in the name of all the gods would Lucian betray his own folk and sell their land to savages?"

"I know not, albeit I have some ideas."

"I will slay those villains or die trying. One quick rush might reach them ere they struck me down—"

"Try it and I'll throttle you," growled Conan. "This news we hear is more important than aught that you could do. If we live not, it will never reach Velitrium. Now keep your head low and stay your tongue."

The two men in the beaver pond watched in silence as the four Picts hoisted the pole, from which hung the chest, and set off with Edric into the forest. Sagayetha mounted the boulder again and launched into an oration, telling the Picts of their past heroism and future glories. His gaudy plumage swayed and flapped with his fiery gestures.

Before Sagayetha finished, the sun had set, leaving overhead a scattering of scarlet clouds in a sapphire sky. In the gathering dark, the Picts began a victory dance, hopping, shuffling, and stamping in long lines, while others applied themselves to the beerskins.

By the time a few stars appeared through the canopy of leaves, the dance had become a savage thing of leaping, shadowy figures. Maddened by the liquor of their victory, the Picts cast off restraint, reverting to the beast that sleeps within all men. As the roistering became obscene, Conan grunted in disgust.

The moon was high when the forest grew still, save for the croaking of frogs and the hum of mosquitoes. Fireflies flashed their elfin lights as they soared above the recumbent Picts. Conan said:

"They're all asleep. We go."

Across the beaver pond they waded, bent low to shield their passage from the sight of any waking Pict. As they emerged dripping and sought the shelter of the trees, Flavius shivered in the chilly evening air. He suppressed a groan as he stretched his stiffened muscles and fought down an urge to sneeze.

Conan struck out along the trail that had led them to the beaver pond. The Cimmerian seemed to possess the ability to see in darkness as well as by day, and moved through the trees with catlike ease. So little moonlight penetrated the dense cover that Flavius had much ado to keep from straying off the path or blundering into clumps of brush or trunks of trees. The best way to travel, Flavius found, was to follow Conan closely and trust blindly in his barbarian instincts.

The forest was alive with the chirp and buzz and twitter of nocturnal insects, as they passed the site of the past day's battle, where rotting corpses had already begun to exude a fetid stench. Flavius started at the sound of some unseen beast crashing through the darkness.

When Flavius began to gasp at the stiff pace set by Conan's long legs, the Cimmerian halted to rest his young companion. When his breath returned, Flavius said:

"Why did Lucian turn traitor to his country? You said you knew."

" 'Tis plain enough," said Conan, drawing his sword to cleanse it of the water of the pond. "After the fall of Tuscelan, Lucian became the temporary governor of Conajohara and commander of what troops remain in this rump province."

"True," said Flavius. "It's nothing but a strip along Thunder River, joining Conawaga and Schohira with Oriskonie . . . and the city of Velitrium."

"Aye. And this rump province will not keep its independence long, for Thasperas of Schohira and Brocas of Conawaga have gone to Tarantia to press before the king their claims to this poor remnant.

"Lucian well knows that his governorship will end when King Numedides bestows the land on one or the other or, perchance, gives parts to each of them. It's said that Thasperas and Lucian hate each other, so he gains both fortune and revenge by betraying Schohira to the Picts. That pay chest held a half-year's pay for nigh a thousand men—a tidy sum indeed. Lucian is said to be a gambler and, belike, is to his jowls in debt."

"But, Conan, what fate will overtake the common folk of Schohira?"

"Lucian cares not a fig for them. He works for General Viscount Lucian first and last, as do most feudal lordlings."

"Baron Thasperas would do no thing so foul, I know," said Flavius.

"At least Thasperas did not recall the companies he sent us as reinforcements after Tuscelan, and that cannot be said of Brocas. Still, I trust none of them. Besides, Lucian's plot is no less fair than that whereby you Aquilonians took the Westermarck—at least, so think the savages."

Anger tore at Flavius's devotion to his captain. "If you so despise us Aquilonians, why do you risk your neck, fighting for us against the Picts?"

Conan shrugged, there in the moonless forest. "I do not despise you, Flavius, or any of the other good men I have met among your people. But good men are hard to find in any land. The quarrels of lords and kings mean nothing to me, for I am a mercenary. I sell my sword to the highest bidder. So long as he pays me, I give him fair value in strength and strokes. Now, get up, young sir. We cannot stay here babbling all night."

4 • Moonlight on Gold

In the officers' quarters in the barracks at Velitrium, the fortress-headquarters of the Golden Lion regiment, four men sat in the yellow light of a brazen oil lamp, which swung from the sooty ceiling. Two were Conan and Flavius, both red-speckled from the myriad bites of mosquitoes. Conan, little affected by the grueling day and night that he had survived in the wilderness, spoke forcefully. Flavius fought the tides of sleep that threatened to engulf him. Each time he jerked himself awake, he forced his attention back to the two men, who stared at him with searching eyes. Then his eyelids would droop, his body slump, and his head nod until he jerked himself awake again.

The other two men wore parts of the uniform of Aquilonian officers. Neither was fully dressed, since both had been aroused from bed. One was a heavy-set man with a grizzled beard and a battle-scarred face. The other was younger, tall and handsome in a patrician way, with wavy blond hair that hung to his shoulders. The blond man spoke:

" 'Tis incredible, Captain Conan, what you tell us! That one of gentle blood, like General Lucian, should so foully betray his trust and his own soldiers! I cannot believe it. Were you to make such accusation publicly, I should feel obliged to denounce *you* as a traitor."

Conan snorted. "Believe what you like, Laodamas; but Flavius and I saw what we saw."

Laodamas appealed to the older officer. "Good Glyco, tell me, am I hearing treason, or have they both gone mad?"

Glyco took his time about replying. "It is a serious charge, surely. On the other hand, Flavius is one of our better junior officers, and our Cimmerian friend here showed his loyalty in the fighting last autumn. This Lucian I know not, save in the way of duty since he came here to command us. I say naught against him without evidence, but naught for him, either."

"But Lucian is a *nobleman!*" persisted Laodamas.

"So?" growled Conan. "Laodamas, if you believe a title renders a man above ordinary temptation, you have much to learn about your fellow beings."

"Well, if this fantastic tale be true, . . . wait!" said Laodamas as Conan's blue eyes flashed menace and a deep growl arose in his throat. "I gave not the lie to your story, Captain. I only said *if*. Now if it be true, what would you propose? We cannot go to our commander and say: 'Traitor, dismiss yourself from command and reside in the guardhouse pending trial.' "

Conan uttered a short bark of laughter. "I won't hazard anyone's neck without evidence. That pay chest should come across yon Thunder River soon, to be delivered unseen to the general. Flavius and I walked half the night to arrive ahead of it, reckoning the weight would delay those who bore it. If you two will finish dressing, we can intercept it ere it reaches the shore."

———

Muffled in cloaks against the chill and talking in low tones, the four officers stood about the narrow pier that jutted out from the Velitrium waterfront. Several small boats, tied to the pier, bobbed gently on the sinuous tide of the river. The moon, nearly full, hung a misshapen disk of luminous silver in the west. Overhead, white stars wheeled slowly, while from the surface of the river, a ghostly mist was rising. Above the mist could be seen the shaggy silhouettes of trees on the farther bank.

There was little sound save the lapping of water against the piles of the pier and the faint scrape of the small boats as they nudged each other in the current. The cry of a loon came from afar. The other three looked a question at Conan, who shook his head.

"That's a real call," he said, "not a Pictish signal."

"Flavius!" said Laodamas sharply. The lieutenant had slumped down with his back against a post.

"Let the lad have his nap," said Conan. "He has earned it thrice over."

Soon Flavius was snoring gently. Laodamas looked toward the east and asked: "The sky has paled a little. Is it dawn so soon?"

Conan shook his head. "That's the false dawn, as they call it. The real won't come for yet another hour."

Silence fell again, and the waiting officers paced noiselessly back and forth. As he paused to make a turn in his pacing, Conan came up short.

"Listen!"

After a moment, he said: "Oars! Take your posts."

He nudged Flavius awake with the toe of his boot, and the four retreated to the base of the pier, crouching behind such cover as they could find.

"Quiet, now!" said Conan.

Again there was silence. The moon had set, and without its competition, the stars blazed brightly. Then they dimmed again as the eastern sky paled with the approach of day.

A faint rhythmic splashing and creaking became audible, and a black shape took form out of the mist and resolved itself into a rowboat. As it came closer, the heads of five men could be discerned, rising from the indeterminate mass.

As the boat pulled up to the end of the pier, a man leaped out and made the painter fast to a cleat. With few words and much grunting, the oarsmen manhandled a heavy, bulky object out of the craft.

Four men, manning a carrying pole, hoisted the load to their shoulders. The fifth led them shoreward along the neck of the pier. In the waxing light, a keen eye could discern that the five wore the buckskin garb of Aquilonian scouts. At some time in the portage, thought Flavius, the Picts must have transferred their burden to these men.

As the five neared the base of the pier, Conan leaped out in front of them, drawing his sword.

"Stand or you're dead men!" he grated sharply.

The three other officers closed in with bared blades. For a heartbeat, there was silence.

The bearers dropped the chest with a crash. As a single being, they raced back to the end of the pier and leaped into their boat, rocking it perilously. One cut the painter with a knife; others snatched up oars and shoved off.

The leader also leaped back before the apparition of the giant Cimmerian, but he collided with the chest and toppled backward over it. In a flash, Conan was upon him, catching his scrawny neck in an iron grip and pointing the blade of his sword against the fellow's throat.

"One word and you'll never speak another," said Conan, eyes blazing through the shredded mists of dawn.

The other officers pushed past Conan and his hostage and reached the end of the pier. But the waterborne scouts were already rowing away, soon to be lost in the fog.

"Let the dogs go," growled Conan. "This one is Edric, the traitor who steered us into yesterday's trap. He'll tell us what we want to know, eh, Edric?"

When the scout remained silent, Conan said, "Never mind. I'll have him talking soon enough."

"What now, Conan?" asked Glyco.

"Back to barracks. We'll use your room."

Flavius said: "Conan, how can we get both man and chest back to barracks? It takes four to carry the chest, leaving no guard for our prisoner."

"Flavius, take this dog's knife away and bind his hands behind his back. His belt will serve. Now you take charge of him."

Releasing his grip on the traitorous scout, Conan straightened his great back and heaved on the chest. "Glyco and Laodamas, hoist this thing up so I can get my shoulder under it."

The two officers put their shoulders under the ends of the pole and, grunting, straightened up. Conan crouched, set his shoulder beneath the chest and, with taut muscles cracking, rose.

"By the gods!" said Laodamas, "I never thought mortal man could bear such weight."

"Help Flavius bring the prisoner to the barracks. I cannot hold this thing till the sun comes up."

In the pallid light, they set out along the muddy streets. First came the scout, with Glyco and Laodamas on either side while Flavius walked behind, sword point goading the man's unwilling steps. Conan followed, weaving and staggering, but holding the chest fast upon his shoulder with arms like knotted ropes.

They reached the barracks as the first bird songs greeted the dawn. The sentry stared but, recognizing officers, saluted without comment.

5 • The General Is Shaved

Minutes later, the five men sat in Glyco's quarters. The chest, lid raised to show its glittering contents, stood in the center of the small room. Edric sat on the rough boards with his wrists and ankles lashed together.

"There's your evidence," said Conan, still breathing deeply. He turned to Edric. "Now, fellow, will you talk, or must I try some Pictish persuasion?"

The sullen prisoner remained silent.

"Very well," said Conan. "Flavius, give me yon fellow's knife."

Flavius drew the scout's knife from his boot top and handed it to the Cimmerian, who thumbed it purposefully.

"I mislike to use my own blade," he mused, "because heating it to red takes the temper out of steel. Now, set the brazier here."

"I'll talk," whined the prisoner. "A devil like you could wring a confession from a dead man." Edric drew a deep breath. "We of Oriskonie," he said, "live far from the rest of the Westermarck and care little about the other provinces. Besides, the general promised to make us rich after we had delivered Schohira to the Picts. What have we had from our baron, or from the rest of you lordlings for that matter, but robbery and abuse?"

"It is your place to obey your natural lords . . ." began Laodamas, but Conan cut him off with a sharp gesture.

"Go on, Edric," said Conan. "Never mind the rights and wrongs of it."

Edric explained how General Lucian had put him and other scouts to work guiding the Aquilonians at Velitrium into Pictish traps.

"We set the trap at South Creek so that the general could show good faith to his Pictish allies and get the pay chest from them."

"How can a man like you betray your own countrymen for gold?" demanded Laodamas hotly.

Conan, brows knit, turned to the officer. "Quiet, Laodamas. Edric, what was this trap the general set?"

"The wizard, Sagayetha, can master serpents from afar. His people say he puts his soul into the body of a serpent, but I . . . I do not understand such matters of vile witchery."

"Nor I, nor any man," said Conan. "Think you Lucian would in truth deliver Schohira to the Picts?"

Edric shrugged. "I know not. I had not thought so far ahead."

"Is it not likely that he would have betrayed you, too? Have you and your comrades slain, lest any bear tales of his treachery to the throne of Aquilonia?"

"Mitra! I never thought of that!" gasped Edric, turning his head to hide his frightened eyes.

"Perhaps this wretch lies, and Lucian is a loyal Aquilonian after all," said Laodamas. "Then we need not . . ."

"Fool!" exploded Conan. "A loyal Aquilonian, to sacrifice a company of good men merely to bait a trap? Glyco, how many survived the rout?"

"Two score straggled back ere nightfall," said Glyco. "We hope a few more may . . ."

"But—" began Laodamas.

Conan smote his palm with a clenched fist.

"They were my men!" he snarled. "I had trained them, and I knew each one. Arno was a good man and my friend. Heads will pay for this treachery, whatever scheme the general may have had in mind. Glyco and Laodamas, go to your companies and choose a dozen men you can trust. Tell them it's a perilous action against treachery in high places, and if they want revenge for South Creek, they must follow orders. Meet me on the drill ground in half an hour. Flavius, take our prisoner to the lockup and then join me."

"Conan," said Laodamas, "whilst I concede your plan is sound, it is I should command the venture. I am of noble blood and stand above you on the promotion list. This is irregular . . ."

"And I stand above you, young man," snapped Glyco. "If you make an issue of rank, *I'll* take command. Lead on, Conan; you seem to know what you're about."

"If he does not," said Laodamas, sulkily, "we shall all hang for mutiny. Suppose the general cries to the men: 'Seize me those traitors!' Whom will they obey?"

"That," said Conan, "is a question time will answer. Come!"

On the drill ground, the three officers and their lieutenants lined up their two-score soldiers. Briefly, Conan explained the Pictish trap and who had planned the massacre. He told four men to carry the chest and said:

"Follow me."

The sun had mounted the tops of the rolling Bossonian hills when Conan's group arrived at the generous dwelling wherein lived the commander of the Frontier Guard of Conajohara. Built on a slope, the house fronted on a high terrace, reached by a dozen steps from street level. At the officers' approach, two sentries on the terrace snapped to attention.

Conan stamped up the steps. "Fetch the general!" he barked.

"But, sir, the general has not yet arisen," said a sentry.

"Fetch him anyway. This matter brooks no delay."

After a searching look at the grim faces of the officers, the sentry turned and entered the house. A groom appeared in the muddy street, leading one of the general's chargers.

"Why the beast?" asked Conan of the remaining sentry.

"His Lordship oft goes cantering before his morning meal," replied the sentry.

"A magnificent animal," said Conan.

The first sentry reappeared and said, "The general is being shaved, sir. He begs you wait . . ."

"To hell with him! If he comes not forth to treat with us, then we shall go to him. Go, tell his Lordship that!"

With a small sigh, the sentry reentered the house. Presently, General Viscount Lucian appeared with a towel around his neck. Although he wore breeches and boots, his upper torso was bare. He was a short, stocky man of middle age, whose well-developed muscles were growing flabby; and his black mustache, usually a pair of waxed points, looked—without the morning's pomade—frayed and drooping.

"Well, gentlemen," said Lucian haughtily, "to what emergency do I owe this untimely visit?" To a sentry he said, "Fetch a stool. Hermius can finish my shave whilst I listen to my early visitors. Captain Conan, if I remember aright. You seem the leader here. What is it you would say to me?"

"Few words, indeed, my lord Viscount," growled Conan. "But we have something to show you."

He gestured savagely, and the soldiers waiting in the street below moved briskly up the steps and deposited the chest on the mosaic floor of the terrace. Then they stepped back.

Glyco and Laodamas studied the general's face like scribes deciphering an ancient parchment. At the first glimpse of the chest, Lucian started, his face went pale, and he bit his underlip. But he stared at the bulky object, saying naught. There was no doubt in the hearts of those who watched him that the general recognized the chest, for the wine-red leather whereof it was fashioned and the gilt-tipped design of dragons incised upon it were unmistakable.

Then Conan lashed out with his booted foot, kicking the lid back upon its creaking hinges. The sentries blinked and Lucian flinched as the golden coins glittered in the sunlight.

"The time for lies is past, Viscount," said Conan grimly, his steel-blue eyes boring into those of his superior. "The evidence of your crime is here before you. I doubt me not that King Numedides will call it treason; I have other words for it: foul treachery. Foulest treachery to betray into a death trap your own soldiers who fought for you valiantly and blindly, trusting in you!"

Lucian made no move, save that he wet his lips with the tip of his tongue, as delicately as a cat. His eyes were bright and unwinking.

Conan's eyes narrowed to slits through which burned naked hate.

"We saw the Picts give yonder pay chest to your man Edric, and we have a full confession from him. You are under arrest. . . ."

Holding the bowl of scalding water under the general's chin, the barber lifted his razor to make a stroke. Like a striking serpent, Lucian moved. He snatched the bowl from the astonished barber and hurled it into Conan's face.

With amazing speed, Lucian rose and, placing both hands upon the chest, gave it a mighty shove. It toppled off the terrace, lid flapping; and turning over in its descent, it spewed forth a golden shower of coins, a veritable rain of flashing precious disks.

A collective gasp of sheer delight came from the soldiers who had followed Conan and his fellow mutineers. As the chest crashed to earth, sending more coins bouncing and rolling along the street, the soldiers broke ranks to scramble for the money.

Lucian brushed past Conan, who stood half blinded by the scalding, soapy water, took the steps two at a time, rushed through the scattered soldiers, and flung himself into the saddle of his stallion. By the time that Conan could see again, the horse was disappearing down the street at a mad gallop, clods of mud flying from its hooves.

Laodamas shouted to his dismounted cavalrymen to run to the barracks, mount, and pursue the fugitive.

"You'll never catch him," said Conan. "That's the best horse in all the Westermarck. Not that it matters greatly; when our sworn statements reach Tarantia, we shall at least be free of Lucian here. Whether the king chops off his head or inflicts him on some other province—that is his affair.

"Right now we have to stop the Picts from ravishing all of Schohira and drenching it in blood." To the waiting men below the terrace, he said:

"Gather up this money as best you may, ere it is lost in the mire. Then back to barracks to await my orders. Who comes with me to save the land for Mitra and Numedides?"

6 • Massacre Meadow

"Snakes do not terrify me, but I'll not vouch for my pikemen if those vile things begin to fall on them. All the troops now know about this Pictish magic from yesterday's survivors," said Glyco.

Laodamas shuddered. "In battle I am no worse a coward than most, but serpents . . . 'Tis no knightly way of war. Let's lure the Picts into open land where there are no trees for serpents to fall from and where my horsemen could cut the savages to bits."

"I see not how," grunted Conan. "Their next thrust is like to be across South Creek into Schohira, since that's the province Lucian sold to them; and for many leagues southwest that land is naught but forests. The Aquilonians have yet to clear and settle it."

"Then," persisted Laodamas, "why not muster our forces at Schondara, where the open land invites the use of cavalry?"

"We cannot force the Picts to seek us out on ground of our own choosing," said Conan. "The settlements of Schohira are scattered, and the Picts could swallow up the rest of the province while we sat like statues awaiting their attack. They flow through woods as water flows through gravel, while our men must be mustered and marched in battle array."

"What is your plan, then?" asked Glyco.

"I have picked from my archers scouts with forest experience. When they report back, I'll seek the place where the enemy plans to cross the creek and strike them there."

"But the serpents . . ." began Laodamas.

"Devils swallow the serpents! Whoever told you that soldiering was a safe trade? The snakes will cease to plague us when Sagayetha is dead. If I can slay him, that I will do. Meanwhile, we must do what we can with what we have. Crom and Mitra grant that we have enough."

Along the trail above the Council Rocks, South Creek ran through a patch of level ground, swampy on both sides of its serpentine bed. Since the creek was broad and shallow and easy to cross at this point, several trails converged there. The boggy flatland supported grasses and brush, but trees were rare. Still, Massacre Meadow, as it was known, was more open than most of the great Pictish wilderness.

Back from the open space, where dense forest began, Conan posted his army. Pikemen and archers were arrayed in a crescent beneath the trees, while Laodamas's horses were positioned on Conan's right flank. The riders sat on the ground, throwing dice, and the tethered animals stamped and switched their tails to discourage the tormenting flies.

Conan walked up and down his line, inspecting equipment, encouraging the fearful with rude jokes, and issuing orders.

"Glyco," he called. "Have you told off the men who are to make torches of their pikes?"

"They are preparing them now," said Glyco, pointing toward the dozen Aquilonians who were binding brushwood to the heads of their spears.

"Good. Light not the fire until the Picts are in sight, lest we reveal ourselves without need."

Conan strolled on. "Laodamas! If I'm not here to give the command, order your charge when the Picts are halfway across the creek."

"That would be taking unfair advantage," said Laodamas. " 'Twere not chivalrous."

"Crom and Mitra, man, this is no tournament! You have your orders."

Back among the infantry, he sighted Flavius and said: "Captain Flavius, are your men ready?"

Flavius beamed at hearing the title of his temporary rank. "Aye, sir; the extra quivers are laid out."

"Good. Whether an army is in more peril from having in command an honest idiot like Laodamas or a clever jackal like Lucian, I know not. You I can count upon." Flavius smiled broadly.

The afternoon wore on amid buzzing flies and grumbling men. Water jugs passed from hand to hand. Conan, sitting on a fallen log, made marks upon a sheet of bark as scouts came to him, reporting the position of the Pictish force. At length he had a rude sketch map from which to plan the coming fray.

As the sun was setting, the first Picts appeared across Massacre Meadow, yelling defiance and brandishing their weapons. More and more poured out of the forest until the low ground beyond South Creek was thronged with naked, painted men.

Flavius murmured to Conan: "We are outnumbered here as much as at the battle of the serpents."

Conan shrugged and rose. Commands rang up and down the Aquilonian line. The pikemen designated as snake destroyers kindled a fire from which to light their improvised torches, while archers drew arrows from their quivers and thrust them into the ground before them.

A drum began to beat like a throbbing heart. Yelping war cries, the Picts splashed across the creek, trotted across the boggy land on the southwest side of the meadow, and closed with the Aquilonians. Amid the savage whoops and the shouts of command, arrows whistled across the meadow, like specters of the damned.

Knots of painted Picts dashed themselves against the lines of pikemen. When one savage was transfixed by a pike and his weight dragged the weapon down, others pushed in through the gap thus created, thrusting with spears and slashing with hatchets. Pikemen of the second line, sweating and cursing, thrust them back. About the meadow, the wounded crawled, twitched, shrieked, or lay still.

Conan himself held the center of the line, towering like a giant above the stockier Gundermen and Aquilonians. Armed with a steel-shafted axe, he reaped a gory harvest of the foe. They came at him like yelping hounds seeking to drag down a boar. But the dreadful axe, which he wielded as tirelessly as if it were a willow wand, split skulls, crushed ribs, and lopped off heads and arms with merciless precision. Roaring a tuneless song, he fought, and the mounds of dead grew around him like grain after the scything.

Before long the Picts began to avoid the center where he stood unconquerable above the heaped corpses. Ferocious, blood-mad fighters though they were, it seeped into their wild consciousness that the giant figure sheathed in iron and splattered from head to foot with gore was not to be overcome by such as they.

The fighting ebbed for a moment, in one of those lulls that sometimes comes in the midst of battle. As Conan leaned upon his axe to catch his breath, his new-made captain hurried over to him.

"Conan," called Flavius, "we are sore beset! When will the horses charge?"

"Not yet, Flavius. Look yonder, on the distant meadow. Not a quarter of the painted ones have yet crossed the stream. This is but a skirmish to probe for our weakness. They'll draw off presently."

Soon whistles sounded. The Picts trotted back across the meadow and swam the creek, pursued by Aquilonian arrows.

"Archers!" shouted Conan. "Two men from each squad harvest arrows."

The archers hastened to push through the pikemen and pull spent shafts from the ground or from the blood-soaked bodies of the fallen, while the remainder cleansed their equipment or drank deeply from the waterskins.

"Whew!" said Flavius, doffing his helmet to wipe his blood-spattered face. "If that be but a skirmish, I hate to contemplate the onslaught. How knew you when the fiends would fall back?"

"When savages find a plan that works, they often repeat it blindly," replied the Cimmerian. "Sagayetha's earlier attack destroyed us, so belike he follows the same scheme now. Some civilized officers do likewise."

"Then will the next assault be one of serpents?"

"No doubt. Hark!"

From the deep woods came the distant sound of a drum and a rattle pounded in the same rhythm as that which preceded the magical assault of the previous battle.

" 'Twill soon be full dark," said Flavius, fearfully. "We shall not see the Picts to shoot nor the snakes to burn."

"You can do your best," growled Conan. "I'm going after that devil Sagayetha. Pass the word to the other officers."

Conan strode swiftly down the line to the glade wherein Glyco stood. To this seasoned veteran, Conan repeated his intention.

"But, Conan . . ."

"Seek not to dissuade me, man! I, alone, may hope to discover the lair of this hyena. The rest of you have orders; to you I give command till I return."

"If you return," muttered Glyco, but he found himself addressing empty air. Conan had vanished.

7 • Serpent Magic

The night air throbbed with the songs of insects. Skirting the lines of Aquilonians, Conan picked up the trail to Velitrium and jogged along it until he was well away from combatants. When the trail wandered close to South Creek, he left it and forded the stream, cursing beneath his breath as he stepped into a hole and went in up to his neck. Wading and swimming, he gained the other side and pushed through heavy undergrowth along the waterway until he reached the open aisles of the virgin forest beyond.

The moon, grown to a great silver disk since the defeat on South Creek, rode high in the sky. Guiding his steps by her light, Conan followed a circular course, calculated to bring him around to the rear of the Pictish army. He walked softly, pausing from time to time to listen and taste the air. Although afire with impatience to confront the wizard, he was enough of a seasoned warrior to know that haste would gain him only a swift demise.

Presently he picked up the sound of the drum and rattle, and stood, holding his breath and cocking his head to locate the direction whence it came. Then he set forth once more.

The rumble of the Pictish army reached his ears, as the bulk of the savages continued to gather on the northeast side of Massacre Meadow, across the creek from the Aquilonian force. Conan moved with more care than before, lest Pictish sentries discover him.

He met no Picts until the drumming and rattling became loud enough to locate the precise source of the clatter. Conan felt sure that in daylight he could have seen the wizard's tent from afar. But he was almost upon it before he found it, standing in the deepest gloom between two giant oaks in a glade feebly lit by a few dots of moonlight. Conan's nerves tingled in the presence of magic, like those of a jungle beast at the throat of unknown danger.

Then his keen eyes spied a Pict, leaning against a tree and staring in the direction of the massing savages. With exquisite care, Conan approached the fellow from the rear. The savage heard a twig snap behind him and whirled just in time to receive Conan's axe full in his war-painted face. The savage fell, twitching, his head split open like a melon.

Conan froze, fearing the sound of the blow and the fall might have alerted Sagayetha. There was, however, no immediate letup in the rhythmic pounding. Conan approached the tent, but as he raised his hand to lift the flap, the ear-splitting sounds died away. At the former battle of the serpents, this silence presaged the serpentine attack from the trees.

Conan lifted the tent flap and stepped in, his nostrils quivering from the reptilian stench. The dim red glow from the coals of a small fire in the center of the tent provided the only illumination, and beyond the fire, vaguely visible in the roseate dimness, sat a hunched figure.

As Conan stepped around the fire, preparing a swift blow that should end this menace once and for all, the silent figure remained motionless. He saw that it was indeed Sagayetha, in breech clout and moccasins, sitting upright with his eyes closed. He must, thought Conan, be in a trance, sending his spirit out to control the snakes. So much the better! Conan took another step.

Something moved on the floor of the tent. As Conan bent to see more closely, he felt a sharp sting on his left arm below the short sleeve of his mail-shirt.

Conan jerked back. A huge viper, he saw, had its fangs imbedded in his forearm. This must be king of all Pictish vipers; the creature was longer by a foot than the giant Cimmerian was tall. As he jerked back, he dragged the serpent half clear of the earthen floor.

With a gasp of revulsion. Conan struck with his axe. Although ragged and notched from the day's fighting, the blade sheared through the reptile's neck a foot below its head. With a violent shake of his injured arm, he sent the head and neck flying, while the serpent's severed body squirmed and coiled upon the earthen flooring. In its writhings, it threw itself into the fire, scattering coals; and the smell of roasting flesh filled the confined space.

Conan stared at his forearm, cold sweat beading his brow. Two red spots appeared where the fangs had pierced his naked flesh, and a drop of blood oozed from each puncture. The skin around the punctures was darkening fast, and a fierce pain spread to his shoulder.

He dropped the axe so that the spike on its head buried itself in the dirt. Then he drew his knife to incise the skin at the site of the wounds. Before he could do so, the seated figure stirred. Sagayetha's eyes opened, cold and deadly as the eyes of serpents.

"Cimmerian!" said the shaman. The word sounded like the hiss of a monstrous snake. "You have slain that into which I sent my soul, but I shall . . ."

Conan hurled his knife. The wizard swayed to one side, so that the implement struck the skin of the tent and stuck there. Sagayetha rose and pointed a skinny arm.

Before the wizard could utter a curse, Conan snatched up his axe and reached him with a single bound. A whistling blow ended in a meaty thud. Sagayetha's head flew off, rolled toward the embers, and came to rest on the hard-packed dirt. Blood poured from the collapsing body, soaking into the earth and hissing as it flooded over the hot coals in the center of the tent. Sinister vapors rose in the dim rosy light.

Conan recovered his knife and slashed at his bitten arm. He sucked blood from the wound and spat it out, sucked and spat, again and again. The dark discoloration had spread over most of his forearm, and the pain was agonizing.

He took but an instant to strip the corpse of the belt that supported its loin cloth and made of it a crude tourniquet, which he placed on his upper arm.

As he continued to suck the venom from the wound, the rising roar of battle came to him from afar. Evidently the Picts, impatient at the delay of their serpentine allies, had launched their own attack. Conan fretted to be gone, to join in the slaughter. But he knew that for a man freshly bitten by a venomous snake to set out at a run would mean immediate death. With a mighty effort of will, he forced himself to continue sucking and spitting.

At last the purplish stain seemed to spread no farther. When it receded a little, he bandaged the arm with cloth found among the wizard's effects. Carrying his axe in his good hand and swinging Sagayetha's head by its hair in the other, he left the tent.

8 • Blood on the Moon

Under the high-riding, heartless moon, an endless stream of Picts crossed South Creek to assail the embattled Aquilonians. Bodies of Aquilonians joined those of Picts in heaps on Massacre Meadow.

"Laodamas!" said a deep, harsh voice in the shadows. Sitting his horse, the cavalry commander turned in his saddle.

"Mitra save us!" he cried. "Conan!"

"Whom did you expect?" growled Conan.

As the full moon, now near its zenith, fell on Conan's upturned face, Laodamas saw that Conan staggered as he approached. In that face, he saw signs of exhaustion, as if Conan had pushed himself beyond the limits of endurance. Perhaps it was a trick of the silvery light, he thought, but Conan's mien was deathly pale.

"Why in Hell haven't you charged?" continued Conan. "More than half the Picts have crossed the creek."

"I will not!" said Laodamas. "To take such advantage of the foe while he is thus divided, were unknightly conduct. 'Tis clean against the rules of chivalry."

"Ass!" shouted Conan. "Then we must do it another way!"

Setting down his grisly burden and his weapons, he grasped Laodamas's ankle, jerked it out of the stirrup, and heaved it up.

"What . . ." cried Laodamas. Then he was tossed out of the saddle, to fall with a crash of armor into the soft soil on the far side of his horse.

An instant later, Conan swung into the empty saddle. He raised his axe on the spike of which he had impaled Sagayetha's head.

"Here's your Pictish wizard!" he roared. "Come on, my friends, by squads, advance!"

The trumpeter winded his horn. Aquilonian horsemen, chafing at Laodamas's long delay, spurred their mounts with a clatter of armor and a creaking of harness. Conan bellowed:

"Cry 'Sagayetha is dead!' Sound the charge, trumpeter!"

Conan held his gruesome banner high as the troop poured out of the forest, yelling at the footmen to get out of the way. They scrambled off, and the cavalry thundered through the gap.

The squads of mailed horsemen plowed through the loose knots of Picts, like an armored thunderbolt. At their fore rode Conan, his gory axe held in the crook of his left arm, so that the wizard's severed head thrust up above his shoulder, a ghastly standard. With his good right hand, he held the reins and guided the charger he had commandeered.

At his swift heels hurtled the iron-sheathed cavalry, thrusting and smiting to right and left. As they smote the reeling ranks of the foe, they chanted hoarsely the battle-song, "Sagayetha is dead! Sagayetha is dead!" Although the Picts knew not their words, the moonlight silvered the grisly visage of the dead shaman affixed to the shaft of Conan's axe, and they understood the meaning.

Now the infantry took up the chant in a deep, resonant cry. Stout Gunderman and sturdy Aquilonian yeomen armed with pikes splashed across the ford behind the horsemen. Yammering at one another, the savages pointed to the hideous head atop the shaft of Conan's axe; and, wailing in dismay, they broke away on every side, ignoring the shouting of their chiefs. The battle turned into a rout. The lines of painted, howling savages disintegrated into fleeing forms, glimpsed through the shafts of moonlight among the distant trees.

In a single broad front, the troop pounded through the marsh and meadow, riding down the masses of fleeing Picts. The Aquilonian pikemen and archers advanced behind the horse, spearing and stabbing, like avenging angels; and the Pictish army dissolved into a panicky mob. The face of the moon, reflected in the surface of the creek, was red with the blood of the dead and dying.

At length, Conan drew his horsemen up and shouted orders to the trumpeter. On signal, the riders wheeled into columns of squads and cantered toward the sheltered field whence they had come. Conan knew that at night in dense forest, horsemen would be useless.

"Press on, Glyco!" he shouted. "Give them no chance to rally!"

Glyco waved acknowledgement as he and his men charged into the woods after the fleeing Picts. Conan spurred his borrowed mount to overtake the head of the column. Then the world dissolved in whirling blackness. He had pressed himself too far—beyond the limits of his fading vigor.

Glyco and Flavius sat in Conan's bedroom in the barracks at Velitrium. Propped up in bed, Conan with ill grace accepted the ministrations of the army's physician. Old Sura fussed about his patient, changing dressings on

Conan's left arm, which bore from wrist to shoulder a rainbow pattern of red, blue, and purple discolorations.

"The wonder is to me," said Glyco, "how you managed to support that axe with the wizard's head upon it, with such an arm as this."

Conan spat. "I did what I had need to do." Then, turning to the doctor, he asked: "How long will you keep me here, swaddled like an infant, good Sura? I have things to do."

"A few days of care will see you restored to duty, General," said the gray-haired doctor. "If you overdo before then, you risk a relapse."

Conan growled a barbaric oath. "What was the final tale of the battle?"

Glyco replied: "After you swooned and fell from your horse—Laodamas's horse, I should say—we harried the painted devils till the last of them vanished, like smoke, into the forest depths. While we lost not a few good men, we slaughtered many more."

"I must be getting old," said Conan, "to faint from a mere snakebite and a bit of action. Who was it called me 'general'?"

Flavius spoke: "Whilst you lay here unconscious, we sent a messenger to the king bearing a report of our successes in the province of Schohira, and a memorial praying him to confirm you as our new commanding officer. Our choice was unanimous—albeit we put no small pressure on Laodamas to make him sign it. He was much angered with you for usurping his horse and his authority and talked of challenging you to a duel."

Conan laughed enormously—a laugh that spread and resonated like the sound of trumpets blown at dawn. "I'd have been sorry to carve up the young ninnyhammer. The lad means well, but he lacks sense."

A knock preceded the opening of the door, and a lean man in the tight leather garments of a royal messenger entered.

"General Conan?" he asked.

"Aye. What is it?"

"I have the honor to deliver this missive from His Majesty." The messenger handed over a scroll with a deferential bow.

Conan broke the seal, unrolled the scroll, and peered at the writing thereon.

"Bring that candle nearer, Sura," he said. "This light is poor for reading." His friends watched with eager interest as he sat in silence, moving his lips.

"Well," he drawled at last, "the king confirms my appointment. What's more, he bids me to Tarantia for an official investiture and a royal feast."

Conan grinned and stretched his great body beneath the bedclothes.

"After a year of dodging Picts through trackless forests and unmasking traitorous commanders, the fleshpots of Tarantia sound tempting. Whatever Numedides' shortcomings, 'tis said his cooks are superb. And I could use some fine wine and a bouncing, highbred damsel in place of the bellywash we get here and your slatternly camp followers!"

"My patient must rest now, sirs," said the doctor.

Glyco and Flavius rose. The old soldier said: "Till later, then, Conan. But have a care. At court, they say, there's a scorpion under every silken cushion."

"I'll take care, fear not. But if neither Zogar Sag nor Sagayetha, for all their uncanny powers, could slay me, I think the hero of Velitrium will be in little peril at the court of Aquilonia's king!"

CONAN

The Liberator

L. Sprague de Camp
& Lin Carter

Contents

Introduction

Conan the Cimmerian, hero of heroes, was first conceived by Robert Ervin Howard (1906–36) of Cross Plains, Texas. Howard was an active pulp writer, and his career coincided with the greatest expansion of the pulp-magazine field. There were scores of such periodicals, all in the same format (about 6.5 × 10 inches) and printed on grayish uncoated paper. Now these magazines have disappeared, save for a few that still carry the old titles under a different format.

During the brief decade of his writing career, Howard wrote fantasy, science fiction, Westerns, sports stories, detective stories, historical fiction, stories of oriental adventure, and verse. But of all his heroes, the one with the widest appeal is Conan the Cimmerian. In the genre of fantasy, the Conan stories have made Howard's work second only to that of J. R. R. Tolkien in popularity.

Born in Peaster, Texas, Howard lived all his short life in that state except for brief visits to adjacent states and to Mexico. His father was a frontier physician from Arkansas; a man of brusque, domineering manner, he was well regarded as an able country doctor. Robert Howard's mother, born in Dallas, Texas, thought herself socially above her husband and, for that matter, above all the folk of Cross Plains, where the family settled in 1919.

Both parents, but more especially the mother, were extremely possessive toward their only child. When Robert was a boy, his mother kept a vigilant watch over him and decided what friendships to permit him. When he grew to manhood, she actively discouraged any interest on his part in girls, although he did manage to date one young woman, a teacher, frequently during his last two years. Robert grew up slavishly devoted to his intermittently sickly mother; when he bought an automobile, he took her with him on long trips around Texas.

Puny and bullied as a small boy, Robert matured into a large, powerful man. He weighed nearly two hundred pounds, most of it muscle. He kept himself in shape by bag punching and weight lifting. His favorite sport, both active and passive, was boxing; he also became a football fan. Despite his rugged exterior, Robert Howard was a voracious bookworm. A fast and omnivorous reader, he would race through an entire shelf in a public library in a few hours.

While still an adolescent, he determined to pursue a writing career. When in 1928 he finished one year of noncredit courses at Howard Payne Academy in Brownwood, Texas, his father agreed to let him try freelance writing for a year before putting pressure on him to get a more conventional job. At the end of that time his sales, while modest, had been encouraging enough for his family to let him follow his bent.

Robert also grew up extremely moody, alternating between moments of wit, charm, and spellbinding garrulity and spells of black depression, despair, and misanthropy. He was hardly out of adolescence when he became fascinated with suicide. This obsession grew and deepened all his life. By hints and casual remarks, he let his parents and several friends know that he did not intend to survive his mother; but nobody took these veiled threats seriously.

In 1936, Robert Howard was a leading pulp writer with the best earnings of any man in Cross Plains. He enjoyed good health and had a congenial occupation, an adequate income, a growing circle of friends and admirers, and a promising literary future. But his mother lay dying of tuberculosis. When he learned that she was in a terminal coma, he went out, got into his car, and shot himself through the head.

From 1926 to 1930, Robert Howard wrote a series of fantasies about a hero called Kull, a barbarian from lost Atlantis who becomes king of a mainland realm. Howard had only meager success with these stories; of the nine Kull stories he completed, he sold only three. These appeared in *Weird Tales*, a magazine of fantasy and science fiction published from 1923 to 1954. Although its word rates were low and its payments often late, *Weird Tales* nevertheless proved Howard's most reliable market.

In 1932, after the unsold Kull stories had languished in the trunk that Howard used as a filing cabinet, he rewrote one of these stories, changing the protagonist to Conan and adding a supernatural element; 'The Phoenix on the Sword' was published in *Weird Tales* for December 1932. The story attained instant popularity, and for several years Conan stories occupied a large part of Howard's working time. Eighteen of these stories appeared during Howard's lifetime; others were either rejected or unfinished. In some late letters, Howard considered dropping Conan to devote all his time to Westerns.

Conan was both a development of King Kull and an idealization of Robert Howard himself—a picture of Howard as he would like to have been. Howard idealized barbarians and the barbarian life as did Rudyard Kipling, Jack London and Edgar Rice Burroughs, all of whom influenced Robert E. Howard. Conan is the rough, tough, rootless, violent, far-traveled, irresponsible adventurer, of gigantic strength and stature, that Howard—whose own life was quiet, reclusive, aloof and introverted—liked to imagine himself. Conan combines the qualities of the Texan frontier hero Bigfoot Wallace, Burroughs's Tarzan, and A. D. Howden Smith's Viking hero Swain, with a dash of Howard's own sombre moodiness.

Howard himself spoke, in a letter to H. P. Lovecraft, of Conan's having "stalked full grown out of oblivion and set me to work recording the saga of his adventures . . . He is simply a combination of a number of men I have known . . . prize-fighters, gunmen, bootleggers, oil-field bullies, gamblers and honest workmen I have come in contact with, and combining them all, produced the amalgamation I call Conan the Cimmerian."

After Howard's death, some of his stories were published posthumously in the pulp magazines. Then the paper shortage of the Second World War slaughtered the pulps, and the Conan stories were forgotten save by a small circle of enthusiasts. In the 1950s, a New York publisher issued the Conan stories in small printings as a series of clothbound volumes.

The present writer became involved in this enterprise as a result of finding some unpublished Howard material in the hands of a New York literary agent and adapting it for publication as part of this series. A decade later I arranged for paperback publication of the whole series, including several new adventures of Conan written in collaboration with my colleagues Lin Carter and Björn Nyberg. For years we have toiled to accommodate our own styles to Howard's, with what success the reader must judge. The present novel, to which my wife Catherine Crook de Camp has contributed extensive editorial assistance, is the latest of these efforts.

Meanwhile Glenn Lord, literary agent for the Howard heirs, by clever and persistent detective work, tracked down the trunk containing Howard's papers, which had disappeared after his death. This cache included more Conan stories or fragments of stories. These were also incorporated in the series, the incomplete tales being finished by Carter or me. Lord also arranged publication of scores of Howard's non-Conan stories, some reprinted from the pulps and some previously unpublished. While Howard's posthumous success has been gratifying, those who have taken part in it cannot help a feeling of sadness that Howard himself did not live to enjoy it.

There are several explanations for the extraordinary surge in Robert Howard's posthumous popularity. Some attribute it to the *Zeitgeist*. Many readers have grown tired of the anti-heroes, the heavily subjective, psychological stories, and the focus on contemporary socioeconomic problems that colored so much fiction in the 1950s and '60s. For a time it looked as if fantasy had become a casualty of the Machine Age; but the success of Tolkien's *The Lord of the Rings* three-decker showed that a revival of fantasy was due. The Conan stories were among the first in the genre to benefit from this revival, and since their publication they have begotten a host of imitations.

Equal credit for their success must go to Howard's own ability as a writer. He was a natural storyteller, and this is the *sine qua non* of fiction writing. With this talent, many of any writer's faults may be overlooked; without it, no other virtues make up the lack.

Although self-taught, Howard achieved a notable and distinctive style—taut, colourful, rhythmic, and eloquent. While using adjectives but sparingly, he achieved effects of color and movement by lavish use of active verbs and personification; as can be seen at the start of his one full-length Conan novel: "Know, O Prince, that between the years when the oceans drank Atlantis and the gleaming cities . . . there was an Age undreamed of, when shining kingdoms lay spread across the world like blue mantles beneath the stars . . ." With Howard's perfervid imagination, ingenious plots, hypnotic style, headlong narrative drive, and the intensity with which he put himself into his characters, even his pulpit tales—his boxing and Western stories—are fun to read.

The fifty-odd Conan stories so far published relate the life of Conan from adolescence to old age. As a stage for his hero to stride across, sword in hand, Howard invented a Hyborian Age, set twelve thousand years ago between the sinking of Atlantis and the rise of recorded history. He postulated that barbarian invasions and natural catastrophes destroyed all records of this era, save for fragments appearing in later ages as myths and legends. He assured his readers that this was a purely fictional construct, not to be taken as a serious theory of prehistory.

In the Hyborian Age, magic worked and supernatural beings stalked the earth. The western part of the main continent, whose outlines differed signally from those on the modern map, was divided among a number of kingdoms, modeled on various realms of real ancient and medieval history. Thus Aquilonia corresponds more or less to medieval France, with Poitain as its Provence; Zingara resembles Spain; Asgard and Vanaheim answer to Viking Scandinavia; Shem with its warring city-states echoes the ancient Near East; while Stygia is a fictional version of ancient Egypt.

Conan is a native of Cimmeria, a bleak, hilly, cloudy northern land whose people are proto-Celts. Conan (whose name is Celtic) arrives as a youth at the easterly kingdom of Zamora and for several years makes his living as a thief. Then he serves as a mercenary soldier, first in the Oriental realm of Turan and then in several Hyborian kingdoms. Forced to flee from Argos, he becomes a pirate along the coast of Kush, with a Shemitish she-pirate and a crew of black corsairs.

Later Conan serves as a mercenary in various lands. He adventures among the nomadic *kozaks* of the eastern steppes and the pirates of the Vilayet Sea, the larger predecessor of the Caspian. He becomes a chieftain among the hill tribes of the Himellian Mountains, coruler of a desert city south of Stygia, a pirate of the Barachan Isles, and captain of a ship of Zingaran buccaneers.

Eventually he resumes the trade of soldier in the service of Aquilonia; the mightiest Hyborian kingdom of them all. He defeats the savage Picts on the western frontier, rises to general, but is forced to flee the murderous intentions of the depraved and jealous King Numedides.

After further adventures, Conan (now about forty years old) is rescued from the coast of Pictland by a ship bearing the leaders of a revolt against the tyrannical and eccentric rule of Numedides. They have chosen Conan as commander-in-chief of the rebellion, and here the present story opens.

L. Sprague de Camp

Villanova, Pennsylvania
July 1978

CONAN
The Liberator

chapter  i

When Madness Wears the Crown

Night hovered on black and filmy wings above the spires of royal Tarantia. Along fog-silenced streets cressets burned with the feral eyes of beasts of prey in primal wilderness. Few there were who walked abroad on nights like this, although the veiled darkness was redolent with the scent of early spring. Those few whom dire necessity drove out of doors stole forth like thieves on furtive feet and tensed at every shadow.

On the acropolis, round which sprawled the Old City, the palace of many kings lifted its crenelated crest against the wan and pallid stars. This castled capitol crouched upon its hill like some fantastic monster out of ages past, glaring at the Outer City walls, whose great stones held it captive.

On glittering suite and marble hall within the sullen palace, silence lay as thick as dust in mouldering Stygian tombs. Servants and pages cowered behind locked doors, and none bestrode the long corridors and curving stairs except the royal guard. Even these scarred and battle-seasoned veterans were loath to stare too deeply into shadows and winced at every unexpected sound.

Two guards stood motionless before a portal draped in rich hangings of brocaded purple. They stiffened and blanched as an eerie, muffled cry escaped from the apartment. It sang a thin, pitiful song of agony, which pierced like an icy needle the stout hearts of the guardsmen.

"Mitra save us all," whispered the guard on the left, through pinched lips pale with tension.

His comrade said naught, but his thudding heart echoed the fervent prayer and added: "Mitra save us all, and the land as well. . . ."

For they had a saying in Aquilonia, the proudest kingdom of the Hyborian world: "The bravest cower when madness wears the crown." And the king of Aquilonia was mad.

Numedides was his name, nephew and successor to Vilerus III and the scion of an ancient royal line. For six years the kingdom had groaned beneath his heavy hand. Superstitious, ignorant, self-indulgent and cruel was Numedides; but heretofore his sins were merely those of any royal voluptuary with a taste for soft flesh, the crack of the lash, and the cries of cringing supplicants. For some time Numedides had been content to let his ministers rule the people in his name while he wallowed in the sensual pleasures of his harem and his torture chamber.

All this had changed with the coming of Thulandra Thuu. Who he was, this lean, dark man of many mysteries, none could say. Neither knew they whence or why he had come into Aquilonia out of the shadowy East.

Some whispered that he was a Witchman from the mist-veiled land of Hyperboria; others, that he had crept from haunted shadows beneath the crumbling palaces of Stygia or Shem. A few even believed him a Vendhyan, as his name—if it truly were his name—suggested. Many were the theories; but no one knew the truth.

For more than a year, Thulandra Thuu had dwelt in the palace, living on the bounty of the king and enjoying the powers and perquisites of a royal favorite. Some said he was a philosopher, an alchemist seeking to transmute iron into gold or to concoct a universal panacea. Others called him a sorcerer, steeped in the black arts of goëtia. A few of the more progressive nobles thought him naught but a clever charlatan, avid for power.

None, though, denied that he had cast a spell over King Numedides. Whether his vaunted mastery of alchemical science with its lure of infinite wealth had aroused the king's cupidity, or whether he had in sooth enmeshed the monarch in a web of sorcerous spells, none could be sure. But all could see that Thulandra Thuu, not Numedides, ruled from the Ruby Throne. His slightest whim had now become the law. Even the king's chancellor, Vibius Latro, had been instructed to take orders from Thulandra as if they had been issued from the king himself.

Meanwhile Numedides's conduct had grown increasingly strange. He ordered the golden coinage in his treasury cast into statues of himself adorned with royal jewels, and oft held converse with the blossoming trees and nodding flowers that graced his garden walks. Woe unto any kingdom when the crown is worn by a madman—a madman who, moreover, is the puppet of a crafty and unscrupulous favorite, whether a genuine magician or clever mountebank!

Behind the brocaded hangings of the guarded portal lay a suite whose walls were hung with mystic purple. Here a bizarre tableau unfolded.

In a translucent sarcophagus of alabaster, the king lay as if in deepest slumber. His gross body was unclothed. Even in the slackness of repose, his form testified to a life besmirched with vicious self-indulgence. His skin was blotched; his moist lips sagged; and his eyes were deeply pouched. Above the edge of the coffin bulged his bloated paunch, obscene and toadlike.

Suspended by her ankles, a naked twelve-year-old girl hung head down above the open casket. Her tender flesh bore the marks of instruments of torture. These instruments now lay among the glowing embers in a copper brazier that stood before a thronelike chair of sable iron, inlaid with cryptic sigils wrought in softly glowing silver.

The girl's throat had been neatly cut, and now bright blood ran down her inverted face and bedrabbed her ash-blonde hair. The casket beneath the corpse was awash with steaming blood, and in this scarlet bath the corpulent body of King Numedides lay partially immersed.

Set in a precise ellipse around the sarcophagus, to illuminate its contents, stood nineteen massive candles, each as tall as a half-grown boy. These candles had been fashioned, so rumor ran among the palace servants, of tallow stripped from human cadavers. But none knew whence they came.

Upon the black iron throne brooded Thulandra Thuu, a slender man of ascetic build and, seemingly, of middle years. His hair, bound by a fillet of ruddy gold, wrought in the likeness of a wreath of intertwining serpents, was silver gray; and serpentine were his cold, thick-lidded eyes. His mien declared him a philosopher, but his unwinking stare bespoke the zealot.

The bones of his narrow face seemed molded by a sculptor. His skin was dark as teakwood; and from time to time he moistened his thin lips with a darting, pointed tongue. His spare torso was confined by an ample length of mulberry brocade, wrapped round and round and draped across one shoulder, leaving the other bare and exposing to view both of his scrawny arms.

At intervals he raised his eyes from the ancient, python-bound tome that lay upon his lap to stare thoughtfully into the alabaster casket, wherein the bloated body of King Numedides rested in its bath of virgin's blood. Then, frowning, he would again return to the pages of his book. The parchment of this monstrous volume was inscribed in a spidery hand in a language unknown to scholars of the West. Row upon row of hooked and cursive characters marched down the page in columns. And many of the glyphs were writ in inks of emerald, amethyst, and vermillion, unfaded by the passage of the years.

A water clock of gold and crystal, set on a nearby taboret, chimed with a silvery tinkle. Thulandra Thuu once more looked deep into the casket. The tight-lipped expression on his dark visage bore wordless testimony to the failure of his undertaking. The rich, red bath of blood was darkening; the surface became dull with scum as vitality faded from the cooling fluid.

Abruptly the sorcerer rose and, with an angry gesture of frustration, hurled the book aside. It struck the hangings on the wall and fell open, facedown upon the marble floor. Had anyone been present to study the inscription on the spine and understand its cryptic signary, he would have discovered that this arcane volume was entitled: *The Secrets of Immortality, According to Guchupta of Shamballah.*

Awakened from his hypnotic trance, King Numedides clambered out of the sarcophagus and stepped into a tub of flower-scented water. He wiped his coarse features with a thirsty towel while Thulandra Thuu sponged the blood from his heavy body. The sorcerer would allow no one, not even the king's tiring men, into his oratory during his magical operations; therefore he must himself attend to the cleansing and tiring of the monarch. The king stared into the brooding, hooded eyes of the magician.

"Well?" demanded Numedides hoarsely. "What were the results? Did the *signum vitalis* enter my body when drained from that little brat?"

"Some, great king," replied Thulandra Thuu in a toneless, staccato voice. "Some—but not enough."

Numedides grunted, scratching a hairy paunch with an unpared fingernail. The thick, curly hair of his belly, like that of his short beard, was rusty red, fading into gray. "Well, shall we continue, then? Aquilonia has many girls whose kin would never dare report their loss, and my agents are adept."

"Allow me to consider, O King. I must consult the scroll of Amendarath to make certain that my partial failure lies not in an adverse conjunction or opposition of the planets. And I fain would cast your horoscope again. The stars foretoken ominous times."

The king, who had struggled into a scarlet robe, picked up a beaker of empurpled wine, upon which floated the crimson buds of poppies, and downed the exotic drink.

"I know, I know," he growled. "Troubles flaring at the border, plots afoot in half the noble houses . . . But fear not, my trepidatious thaumaturge! This royal house has lasted long and will survive long after you are dust."

The king's eyes glazed and a small smile played at the corner of his mouth as he muttered: "Dust—dust—all is dust. All save Numedides." Then seeming to recover himself, he demanded irritably: "Can you not give answer to my question? Would you have another girl-child for your experiments?"

"Aye, O King," replied Thulandra Thuu after a moment of reflection. "I have bethought me of a refinement in the procedure that, I am convinced, will bring us to our goal."

The king grinned broadly and thumped a hairy hand against the sorcerer's lean back. The unexpected blow staggered the slender mage. A flicker of anger danced across the alchemist's dark features and was instantly extinguished, as by an unseen hand.

"Good, sir magician!" roared Numedides. "Make me immortal to rule forever this fair land, and I will give you a treasury of gold. Already I feel the stirrings of divinity—albeit I will not yet proclaim my theophany to my steadfast and devoted subjects."

"But Majesty!" said the startled sorcerer, recovering his composure. "The country's plight is of more moment than you appear to know. The people grow restless. There are signs of insurrection from the south and from the sea. I understand not—"

The king waved him aside. "I've put down treasonous rascals oft ere this, and I shall counter them again."

What the king dismissed as trifling inconveniences were, in truth, matters worthy of a monarch's grave concern. More than one revolt simmered along the western borders of Aquilonia, where the land was rent asunder by wars and rivalries among the petty barons. The populace groaned beneath their ruler's obduracy and cried out for relief from oppressive taxation and monstrous maltreatment by agents of the king. But the worries of the common folk concerned their monarch little; he turned a deaf ear to their cries.

Yet Numedides was not so wedded to his peculiar pleasures that he failed to mark the findings of his spies, collected for him by his able minister, Vibius Latro. The chancellor reported rumours of no less a leader of the commons than the rich and powerful Count Trocero of Poitain. Trocero was no man idly to be dismissed—not with his peerless force of armored cavalry and a warlike, fiercely loyal people ready to rise at his beckoning.

"Trocero," mused the king, "must be destroyed, it's true; but he's too strong for open confrontation. We must needs seek out a skilfull poisoner. . . . Meanwhile, my faithful, hardfisted Amulius Procas is stationed in the southern border region. He has crushed more than one arrogant landowner who dared turn revolutionary."

Inscrutable were the cold black eyes of Thulandra Thuu. "Omens of danger overwhelming to your general I read upon the face of heaven. We must concern ourselves—"

Numedides ceased to listen. His trancelike slumber, together with the stimulus of the poppied wine, had flogged his sensual appetite. His harem newly housed a delectable, full-breasted Kushite girl, and a torture—yet unnamed—was forming in his twisted brain.

"I'm off," he said abruptly. "Detain me not, lest I blast you with my shafts of lightning."

The king pointed a taut forefinger at Thulandra Thuu and made a guttural sound. Then, roaring with boorish mirth, he pushed aside a panel behind the purple arras and slipped through. Thence a secret passage led to that part of the harem whispered of, with loathing, as the House of Pain and Pleasure. The sorcerer watched him go with the shadow of a smile and thoughtfully snuffed out the nineteen massive candles.

"O King of Toads," he muttered in his unknown tongue. "You speak the very truth, save that you have the characters reversed. Numedides shall crumble into dust, and Thulandra Thuu shall rule the West from an eternal throne, when Father Set and Mother Kali teach their loving son to wrest from the dark pages of the vast Unknown the secret of eternal life. . . ."

The thin voice pulsed through the darkened chamber like the dry rustle of a serpent's scales, slithering over the pallid bones of murdered men.

chapter  ii

The Lions Gather

Far south of Aquilonia, a slender war galley cleft the stormy waters of the Western Ocean. The ship, of Argossean lines, was headed shoreward, where the lights of Messantia glimmered through the twilight. A band of luminescent green along the western horizon marked the passing of the day; and overhead, the first stars of evening bejewelled the sapphire sky, then paled before the rising of the moon.

On the forecastle, leaning upon the rail above the bow, stood seven persons cloaked against chill bursts of spray that fountained as the bronzen ram rose and dipped, cleaving the waves asunder. One of the seven was Dexitheus; a calm-eyed, grave-faced man of mature years, dressed in the flowing robes of a priest of Mitra.

Beside him stood a broad-shouldered, slim-hipped nobleman with dark hair tinged with gray, who wore a silvered cuirass, on the breast of which the three leopards of Poitain were curiously worked in gold. This was Trocero, Count of Poitain, and his motif of three crimson leopards was repeated on the banner that fluttered from the foremast high above his head.

At Count Trocero's elbow, a younger man of aristocratic bearing, elegantly clad in velvet beneath a silvered shirt of mail, fingered his small beard. He moved quickly, and his ready smile masked with gaiety the metal of a seasoned and skilfull soldier. This was Prospero, a former general of the Aquilonian army. A stout and balding man, wearing neither sword nor armor and unmindful of the failing light, worked sums with a stylus on a set of waxed tablets, braced against the rail. Publius had been the royal treasurer of Aquilonia before his resignation in despairing protest against his monarch's policies of unlimited taxation and unrestrained expenditure.

Nearby, two girls clutched the inconstant rail. One was Belesa of Korzetta, a noblewoman of Zingara, slender and exquisite and but recently come to womanhood. Her long black hair streamed in the sea-wind like a silken banner.

Nestled against her in the curve of one arm, a pale, flaxen-haired child stared wide-eyed at the lights that rimmed the waterfront. An Ophirean slave, Tina had been rescued from a brutal master by the Lady Belesa, niece of the late Count Valenso. Mistress and slave, inseparable, had shared the moody count's self-exile in the Pictish wilderness.

Above them towered a grim-faced man of gigantic stature. His smoldering eyes of volcanic blue and the black mane of coarse, straight hair that brushed his massive shoulders suggested the controlled ferocity of a lion in repose. He was a Cimmerian, and Conan was his name.

Conan's sea boots, tight breeches and torn silken shirt disclosed his magnificent physique. These garments he had looted from the chests of the dead pirate admiral, Bloody Tranicos, where in a cave on a hill in Pictland, the corpses of Tranicos and his captains still sat around a table heaped with the treasure of a Stygian prince. The clothes, small for so large a man, were faded, ripped, and stained with dirt and blood; but no one looking at the towering Cimmerian and the heavy broadsword at his side would mistake him for a beggar.

"If we offer the treasure of Tranicos in the open marketplace," mused Count Trocero, "King Milo may regard us with disfavor. Hitherto he has entreated us fairly; but when rumors of our hoard of rubies, emeralds, amethysts, and such-like trinkets set in gold do buzz about his ears, he may decree that the treasure shall escheat to the crown of Argos."

Prospero nodded. "Aye, Milo of Argos loves a well-filled treasury as well as any monarch. And if we approach the goldsmiths and moneylenders of Messantia, the secret will be shouted about the town within an hour's time."

"To whom, then, shall we sell the jewels?" asked Trocero.

"Ask our commander-in-chief," Prospero laughed slyly. "Correct me if I'm wrong, General Conan, but did you not once have acquaintance with—ah—"

Conan shrugged. "You mean, was I not once a bloody pirate with a fence in every port? Aye, so I was; and that I might have once again become, had you not arrived in time to plant my feet on the road to respectability." He spoke Aquilonian fluently but with a barbarous accent.

After a moment's pause, Conan continued: "My plan is this. Publius shall go to the treasurer of Argos and recover the deposit advanced upon the usage of this galley, minus the proper fee. Meanwhile, I'll take our treasure to a discreet dealer whom I knew in former days. Old Varro always gave me a fair price for plunder."

"Men say," quoth Prospero, "that the gems of Tranicos have greater worth than all the other jewels in all the world. Men such as he of whom you speak would give us but a fraction of their value."

"Prepare for disappointment," said Publius. "The value of such baubles ever gains in the telling but shrinks in the selling."

Conan grinned wolfishly. "I'll get what I can, fear not. Remember I have often dealt beneath the counter. Besides, even a fraction of the treasure is enough to set swinging all the swords in Aquilonia." Conan looked back at the quarterdeck, where stood the captain and the steersman.

"Ho there," Captain Zeno!" he roared in Argossean. "Tell your rowers that if they put us ashore ere the taverns shutter for the night, it's a silver penny apiece for them, above their promised wage! I see the lights of the pilot boat ahead."

Conan turned back to his companions and lowered his voice. "Now, friends, we must guard our tongues as concerns our riches. A stray word, overheard, might cost us the wherewithal to buy the men we need. Forget it not!"

The harbor boat, a gig rowed by six burly Argosseans, approached the galley. In the bow a cloak-wrapped figure wagged a lantern to and fro, and the captain waved an answer to the signal. As Conan moved to go below and gather his possessions, Belesa laid a slender hand upon his arm. Her gentle eyes sought his face, and there was anguish in her voice.

"Do you still intend to send us to Zingara?" she asked.

"It is best to part thus, Lady. Wars and rebellions are no places for gentle-women. From the gems I gave you, you should realize enough to live on, with enough to spare for your dowry. If you wish, I'll see to converting them to coin. Now I have matters to attend to in my cabin."

Wordlessly, Belesa handed Conan a small bag of soft leather, containing the rubies that Conan had taken from a chest in the cave of Tranicos. As he strode aft along the catwalk to his cabin in the poop, Belesa watched him go. All that was woman within her responded to the virility that emanated from him, like heat from a roaring blaze. Could she have had her unspoken wish, there would have been no need for a dowry. But, ever since Conan had rescued her and the girl Tina from the Picts, he had been to them no more than a friend and protector.

Conan, she realized with a twinge of regret, was wiser than she in such matters. He knew that a delicate, highborn lady, imbued with Zingaran ideals of womanly modesty and purity, could never adapt herself to the wild, rough life of an adventurer. Moreover, if he were slain or if he tired of her, she would become an outcast, for the princely houses of Zingara would never admit a barbarian mercenary's drab into their marble halls.

With a small sigh, she touched the girl who nestled beside her. "Time to go below, Tina, and gather our belongings."

———

Amid shouts and hails, the slender galley inched up to the quay. Publius paid the harbor tax and rewarded the pilot. He settled his debt to Captain Zeno and his crew and, reminding him of the secrecy of the mission, bade the Argossean skipper a ceremonious farewell.

As the captain barked his orders, the sail was lowered to the deck and stowed beneath the catwalk; the oars were shipped amid oaths and clatter and placed under the benches. The crew—officers, sailors, and rowers—streamed merrily ashore, where bright lights blazed in inns and taverns; and painted slatterns, beckoning from second-story windows, exchanged raillery and cheerful obscenities with the expectant mariners.

Men loitered about the waterfront street. Some lurched drunkenly along the roadway, while others snored in doorways or relieved themselves in the dark mouths of alleys.

One among the loiterers was neither so drunk nor so bleary-eyed as he appeared. A lean, hatchet-faced Zingaran he was, who called himself Quesado. Limp blue-black ringlets framed his narrow face, and his heavy-lidded eyes gave him a deceptive look of sleepy indolence. In shabby garments of sober black, he lounged in a doorway as if time itself stood still; and when accosted by a pair of drunken mariners, he retorted with a well-worn jest that sent them chuckling on their way.

Quesado closely observed the galley as it tied up to the quay. He noted that, after the crew had roistered off, a small group of armed men accompanied by two women disembarked and paused as they reached the pier, until several loungers hurried up to proffer their services. Soon the curious party disappeared, followed by a line of porters with chests and sea bags slung across their shoulders or balanced on their heads.

When darkness had swallowed up the final porter, Quesado sauntered over to a wineshop, where several crewmen from the ship had gathered. He found a cosy place beside the fire, ordered wine, and eyed the seamen. Eventually he chose a muscular, sunburned Argossean rower, already in his cups, and struck up a conversation. He bought the youth a jack of ale and told a bawdy jest.

The rower laughed uproariously, and when he had ceased chuckling, the Zingaran said indifferently: "Aren't you from that big galley moored at the third pier?"

The Argossean nodded, gulping down his ale.

"Merchant galley, isn't she?"

The rower jerked back his tousled head and stared contemptuously. "Trust a damned foreigner not to know one ship from another!" he snorted. "She's a ship-o'-war, you spindle-shanked fool! That's the *Arianus*, pride of King Milo's navy."

Quesado clapped a hand to his forehead. "Oh, gods, how stupid of me!

She's been abroad so long I scarce recognized her. But when she put in, was she not flying some device with lions on it?"

"Those be the crimson leopards of Poitain, my friend," the oarsman said importantly. "And the Count of Poitain, no less, hired the ship and himself commanded her."

"I can scarcely credit it!" exclaimed Quesado, acting much amazed. "Some weighty diplomatic mission, that I'll warrant . . ."

The drunken rower, puffed by the wind of his hearer's rapt attention, rushed on: "We've been on the damndest voyage—a thousand leagues or more—and it's a wonder we didn't get our throats cut by the savage Picts—"

He broke off as a hard-faced officer from the *Arianus* clapped a heavy hand upon his shoulder.

"Hold your tongue, you babbling idiot!" snapped the mate, glancing suspiciously at the Zingaran. "The captain warned us to keep close-mouthed, especially with strangers. Now shut your gob!"

"Aye, aye," mumbled the rower. Avoiding Quesado's eye, he buried his face in his jack of ale.

"It's naught to me, mates," yawned Quesado with a careless shrug. "Little has happened in Messantia of late, so I but thought to nibble on some gossip." He rose lazily to his feet, paid up, and sauntered out the door.

Outside, Quesado lost his air of sleepy idleness. He strode briskly along the pierside street until he reached a seedy roominghouse wherein he rented a chamber that overlooked the harbor. Moving like a thief in the night, he climbed the narrow stairs to his second-story room.

Swiftly he bolted the door behind him, drew tattered curtains across the dormer windows, and lit a candle stub from the glowing coals in a small iron brazier. Then he hunched over a rickety table, forming tiny letters with a fine-pointed quill on a slender strip of papyrus.

His message written, the Zingaran rolled up the bit of flattened reed and cleverly inserted it into a brazen cylinder no larger than a fingernail. Then he scrambled to his feet, thrust open a cage that leaned against the seaward wall, and brought out a fat, sleepy pigeon. To one of its feet he secured the tiny cylinder; and gliding to the window, he drew aside the drape, opened the pane, and tossed the bird out into the night. As it circled the harbor and vanished, Quesado smiled, knowing that his carrier pigeon would find a safe roost and set out on its long journey northward with the coming of the dawn.

In Tarantia, nine days later, Vibius Latro, chancellor to King Numedides and chief of his intelligence service, received the brass tube from the royal pigeon-keeper. He unrolled the fragile papyrus with careful fingers and held it in the narrow band of sunlight that slanted through his office window. He read:

The Count of Poitain, with a small entourage, has arrived from a distant port on a secret mission. Q.

There is a destiny that hovers over kings, and signs and omens presage the fall of ancient dynasties and the doom of mighty realms. It did not require the sorceries of such as Thulandra Thuu to sense that the house of Numedides stood in grave peril. The signs of its impending fall were everywhere.

Messages came out of Messantia, traveling northward by dusty roads and by the unseen pathways of the air. To Poitain and the other feudal demesnes along the troubled and strife-torn borders of Aquilonia, these missives found their way; some even penetrated the palisaded camps and fortresses of the loyal Aquilonian army. For stationed there were swordsmen and pikemen, horsemen and archers who had served with Conan when he was an officer of King Numedides—men who had fought at Conan's side in the great battle of Velitrium, and even before that, at Massacre Meadow, when Conan first broke the hosts of savage Picts—men of his old regiment, the Lions, who well remembered him. And like the beasts whose name they bore, they remained loyal to the leader of the pride. Others who harkened to the call were wearied of service to a royal maniac who shrugged aside the business of his kingdom to indulge his unnatural lusts and to pursue mad dreams of eternal life.

In the months after Conan's arrival in Messantia, many Aquilonian veterans of the Pictish wars resigned or deserted from their units and drifted south to Argos. With them down the long and lonesome roads tramped Poitanians and Bossonians, Gundermen from the North, yeomen of the Tauran, petty nobles from Tarantia, impoverished knights from distant provinces, and many a penniless adventurer.

"Whence come they all?" marveled Publius as he stood with Conan near the large tent of the commander-in-chief, watching a band of ragtail knights ride into the rebel camp. Their horses were lean, their trappings ragged, their armor rusty, and they were caked with dust and dried mud. Some bore bandaged wounds.

"Your mad king has made many enemies," grumbled Conan. "I get reports of knights whose lands he has seized, nobles whose wives or daughters he has outraged, sons of merchants whom he has stripped of their pelf—even common workmen and peasants, stout-hearted enough to take up arms against the royal madman. Those knights yonder are outlaws driven into exile for speaking out against the tyrant."

"Tyranny oft breeds its own downfall," said Publius. "How many have we now?"

"Over ten thousand, by yesterday's reckoning."

Publius whistled. "So many? We had better limit our recruits ere they devour all the coin in our treasury. Vast as is the sum that you obtained for the jewels of Tranicos, 'twill melt like snow in the springtime if we enlist more men than we can afford to pay."

Conan clapped the stout civilian on the back. "It's your task as treasurer, good Publius, to make our purse outlast this feast of vultures. Only today I importuned King Milo for more camp space. Instead, he drenched me with a cataract of complaints. Our men crowd Messantia; they overtax the facilities of the city; they drive up prices; some commit crimes against the citizens. He wants us hence, either to a new camp or on our way to Aquilonia."

Publius frowned. "Whilst our troops train, we must remain close to the city and the sea, for access to supplies. Ten thousand men grow exceedingly hungry when drilled as you drill them. And ten thousand bellies require much food, or their owners grow surly and desert."

Conan shrugged. "No help for it. Trocero and I ride forth on the morrow to scout for a new site. The next full moon should see us on the road to Aquilonia."

"Who is that?" murmured Publius, indicating a soldier who, released from the morning's drill, was sauntering by, close to the general's tent. The man, clad in shabby black, had swilled a tankardful that afternoon; for his lean legs wobbled beneath him, and once he tripped over a stone that lay athwart his path. Sighting Conan and Publius, he swept off his battered cap, bowed so low that he quite unbalanced himself, recovered, and proceeded on his way.

Conan said: "A Zingaran who turned up at the recruiting tent a few days past. He seemed a mousy little fellow—no warrior—but he has proved a fair swordsman, an excellent horseman, and an artist with a throwing knife; so Prospero signed him on with all the rest. He called himself—I think it was Quesado."

"Your reputation, like a lodestone, draws men from near and far," said Publius.

"So I had better win this war," replied Conan. "In the old days, if I lost a battle, I could slip away to lands that knew me not and start over again with nobody the wiser. That were not so easy now; too many men have heard of me."

" 'Tis good news for the rest of us," grinned Publius, "that fame robs leaders of the chance to flee."

Conan said nothing. Parading through his memory marched the arduous years since he had plunged out of the wintry North, a ragged, starveling youth. He had warred and wandered the length and breadth of the Thurian continent. Thief, pirate, bandit, primitive chieftain—all these he had been; and common soldier, too, rising to general and falling again with the ebb of Fortune. From the savage wilderness of Pictland to the steppes of Hyrkania, from the snows of Nordheim to the steaming jungles of Kush, his name and fame were legend.

Hence warriors flocked from distant lands to serve beneath his banner.

Conan's banner now proudly rode the breeze atop the central pole of the general's tent. Its device, a golden lion rampant on a field of sable silk, was Conan's own design. Son of a Cimmerian blacksmith, Conan was not at all of armigerous blood; but he had gained his greatest recognition as commander of the Lion Regiment in the battle at Velitrium. Its ensign he had adopted as his own, knowing that soldiers need a flag to fight for. It was following this victory that King Numedides, holding the Cimmerian's fame a threat to his own supremacy, had sought to trap and destroy his popular general, in whom he sensed a potential rival. Conan's growing reputation for invincibility he envied; his magnetic leadership he feared.

After eluding the snare Numedides had set for him, thus forfeiting his command, the Cimmerian looked back upon his days with the Lions with fond nostalgia. And now the banner under which he had won his mightiest victories flew above his head again, a symbol of his past glories and a rallying point for his cause.

He would need even mightier victories in the months ahead, and the golden lion on a field of black was to him an auspicious omen. For Conan was not without his superstitions. Although he had brawled and swaggered over half the earth, exploring distant lands and the exotic lore of foreign peoples, and had gained wisdom in the ways of kings and priests, wizards and warriors, magnates and beggars, the primitive beliefs of his Cimmerian heritage still smoldered in the depths of his soul.

Meanwhile, the spy Quesado, having passed beyond the purlieu of the commander's tent, miraculously regained his full sobriety. No longer staggering, he walked briskly along the rutted road toward the North Gate of Messantia.

The spy had prudently retained his waterfront room when he took up soldier's quarters in the tent city outside the walls. And in that room, pushed under the rough-hewn door, he found a letter. It was unsigned, but Quesado knew the hand of Vibius Latro.

Having fed his pigeons, Quesado sat down to decipher the simple code that masked the meaning of the message. It seemed a jumble of domestic trivia; but, by marking every fourth word, Quesado learned that his master had sent him an accomplice. She was, the letter said, a woman of seductive beauty.

Quesado allowed himself a thin, discreet smile. Then he penned his usual report on a slender strip of papyrus and sent it winging north to far Tarantia.

While the army drilled, sweated, and increased in size, Conan bade farewell to the Lady Belesa and her youthful protégée. He saw their carriage go rattling off along the coastal road to Zingara, with a squad of sturdy guards riding before and behind. Hidden in the baggage, an iron-bound box enclosed sufficient gold to keep Belesa and Tina in comfort for many years, and Conan hoped that he would see no more of them.

Although the burly Cimmerian was sensible of Belesa's charms, he intended at this point to become entangled with no woman, least of all with a delicate gentlewoman, for whom there was no place in the wardrooms of war. Later, should the rebellion triumph, he might require a royal marriage to secure his throne. For thrones, however high their cost in common blood, must ofttimes be defended by the mystic power engendered by the blood of kings.

Still, Conan felt the pangs of lust no less than any active, virile man. Long had he been without a woman, and he showed his deprivation by curt words, sullen moods, and stormy explosions of temper. At last Prospero, divining the cause of these black moods, ventured to suggest that Conan might do well to set his eyes upon the tavern trulls of Messantia.

"With luck and discernment, General," he said, "you could find a bedmate to your fancy."

Prospero was unaware that his words buzzed like horseflies in the ears of a lank Zingaran mercenary, who huddled nearby with his back against a tent-stake, head bowed forward on his knees, apparently asleep.

Conan, equally unmindful, shrugged off his friend's suggestion. But as the days passed, desire battled with his self-control. And with every passing night, his need waxed more compelling.

Day by day, the army grew. Archers from the Bossonian Marches, pikemen from Gunderland, light horse from Poitain, and men of high and low degree from all of Aquilonia streamed in. The drill field resounded to the shouts of commands, the tramp of infantry, the thunder of cavalry, the snap of bowstrings and the whistle of arrows. Conan, Prospero, and Trocero labored ceaselessly to forge their raw recruits into a well-trained army. But whether this force, cobbled together from far-flung lands and never battle-tested, could withstand the crack troops of the hard-riding, hard-fighting, and victorious Amulius Procas, no man knew.

Meanwhile, Publius organized a rebel spy service. His agents penetrated far into Aquilonia. Some merely sought for news. Some spread reports of the depravity of King Numedides—reports which the rumormongers found needed no exaggeration. Some begged for monetary aid from nobles who, while sympathetic to the rebel cause, had not yet dared declare themselves in favor of rebellion.

Each day, at noon, Conan reviewed his troops. Then, in rotation, he took his midday meal in the mess tent of each company; for a good leader knows many of his men by name and strengthens their loyalty by personal contact. A few days after Prospero's talk about the public women of Messantia, Conan dined with a company of light cavalry. He sat among the common soldiers and traded bawdy jests as he shared their meat, bread, and bitter ale.

At the sound of a sibilant voice, suddenly upraised, Conan turned his head. Nearby, a narrow-faced Zingaran, whom Conan remembered having seen before, was orating with grandiloquent gestures. Conan left a joke caught in an endless pause and listened closely; for the fellow was talking about women, and Conan felt a stirring in his blood.

"There's a certain dancing girl," cried the Zingaran, "with hair as black as a raven's wing and eyes of emerald, green. And there is a witchery in her soft red lips and in her limber body, and her breasts are like ripe pomegranates!" Here he cupped the ambient air with mobile hands.

"Every night she dances for thrown coppers at the Inn of the Nine Swords and bares her swaying body to the eyes of men. But she is a rare one, this Alcina—a haughty, fastidious minx who denies to all men her embrace. She has not met the man who could arouse her passion—or so she claims."

"Of course," added Quesado, winking lewdly, "there are doubtless lusty warriors in this very tent who could woo and win that haughty lass. Why, our gallant general himself—"

At that instant Quesado caught Conan's eye upon him. He broke off, bent his head, and said: "A thousand pardons, noble general! Your excellent beer so loosened my poor tongue that I forgot myself. Pray, ignore my indiscretion, I beg you, my good lord—"

"I'll forget it," growled Conan and turned back frowning to his food.

But that very evening, he asked his servants for the way to an inn called the Nine Swords. As he swung into the saddle and, with a single mounted groom for escort, pounded off toward the North Gate, Quesado, skulking in the shadows, smiled a small, complacent smile.

chapter  iii

Emerald Eyes

When dawn came laughing to the azure sky, a silver-throated trumpet heralded the arrival of an envoy from King Milo. Brave in embroidered tabard, the herald trotted into the rebel camp on a bay mare, brandishing aloft a sealed and beribboned scroll. The messenger sniffed disdainfully at the bustling drill ground, where a motley host was lining up for roll call. When he thundered his demand for escort to General Conan's tent, one of Trocero's men led the beast toward the center of the camp.

"This means trouble," murmured Trocero to the priest Dexitheus as they gazed after the Argossean herald.

The lean, bald Mitran priest fingered his beads. "We should be used to trouble by now, my lord Count," he replied. "And much more trouble lies ahead, as well you know."

"You mean Numedides?" asked the count with a wry smile. "My good friend, for that kind of trouble we are ready. I speak of difficulties with the King of Argos. For all that he gave me leave to muster here, I feel that Milo grows uneasy with so many men, pledged to a foreign cause, encamped outside his capital. Meseems His Majesty begins to repent him of his offer of a comfortable venue for our camp."

"Aye," added Publius, as the stout paymaster strolled up to join the other two. "I doubt not that the stews and alleys of Messantia already crawl with spies from Tarantia. Numedides will put a subtle pressure on the King of Argos to persuade him to turn against us now."

"The king were a fool to do so," mused Trocero, "with our army close by and lusting for a fight."

Publius shrugged. The monarch of Messantia has hitherto been our friend," he said. "But kings are given to perfidy, and expediency rules the hearts of even the noblest of them. We must needs wait and see . . . I wonder what ill news that haughty herald bore?"

Publius and Trocero strolled off to attend their duties, leaving Dexitheus absently fingering his prayer beads. When he had spoken of future troubles, he thought not only of the coming clash but also of another portent.

The night before, his slumbers had been roiled by a disturbing dream. Lord Mitra often granted his loyal suppliants foreknowledge of events through dreams, and Dexitheus wondered if his dream had been a prophecy.

In this dream, General Conan confronted the enemy on a battlefield, harking on his soldiers with brandished sword; but behind the giant Cimmerian lurked a shadowy form, slender and furtive. Naught could the sleeper discern of this stealthy presence save that in its hood-shadowed visage burned catlike eyes of emerald green, and that it ever stood at Conan's unprotected back.

Although the risen sun had warmed the mild spring morning, Dexitheus shivered. He did not like such dreams; they cast pebbles into the deep well of his serenity. Besides, no recruit in the rebel camp had eyes of such a brilliant green, or he would have noticed the oddity.

Along the dusty road back to Messantia cantered the herald, as messengers went forth to summon the leaders of the rebel host to council.

In his tent, the giant Cimmerian barely checked his anger as his squires strapped him into his harness for his morning exercise with arms. When Prospero, Trocero, Dexitheus, Publius, and the others were assembled, he spoke sharply, biting off his words.

"Briefly, friends," he rumbled, "it is His Majesty's pleasure that we withdraw north to the grassy plains, at least nine leagues from Messantia. King Milo feels our nearness to his capital endangers both his city and our cause. Some of our troops, quoth he, have been enjoying themselves a bit too rowdily of late, shattering the king's peace and giving trouble to the civic guard."

"I feared as much," sighed Dexitheus. "Our warriors are much given to the pleasures of the goblet and the couch. Still and all, it asks too much of human nature to expect soldiers—especially a mixed crowd like ours—to behave with the meekness of hooded monks."

"True," said Trocero. "And luckily we are not unprepared to go. When shall we move, General?"

Conan buckled his sword belt with a savage gesture. His blue eyes glared lionlike beneath his square-cut black mane.

"He gives us ten days to be gone," he grunted, "but I am fain to move at once. Messantia has too many eyes and ears to please me, and too many of our soldiery have limber tongues, which a stoup of wine sets wagging. I'll move, not nine leagues but ninety, from this nest of spies.

"So let's be off, my lords. Cancel all leaves and drag our men out of the wineshops, by force if need be. This night I shall proceed with a picked troop to study the route and choose a new campsite. Trocero, you shall command until I rejoin the army."

They saluted and left. All the rest of that day, soldiers were rounded up, provisions readied, and gear piled into wagons. Before the next morning's sun had touched the gilded pinnacles of Messantia with its lances of light, tents were struck and companies formed for the line of march. While the ghosts of fog still floated on the lowlands, the army got under way—knight and yeoman, archer and pikeman, all well guarded by scouts and flankers before, behind, and on the sides.

Conan and his troop of Poitanian light horse had trotted off to northward, while darkness veiled the land. The barbarian general did not entirely trust King Milo's friendship. Many considerations mold the acts of kings; and Numedides's agents might have already persuaded the Argossean monarch to ally himself with the ruler of Aquilonia, rather than espouse the unpredictable fortunes of the rebels. Surely Argos knew that, if the insurrection failed, Aquilonia's vengeance would be swift and devastating. And, if a king is bent upon destruction, an army is best attacked while on the march, with the men strung out and encumbered by their gear. . . .

So, the Lions moved north. Company by company, the unseasoned army tramped the dusty road, splashed across the fords of shallow rivers, and snaked through the low Didymian Hills. No one ambushed, attacked, or harassed the marching men. Perhaps Conan's suspicions of King Milo were unjustified; perhaps the army was too strong for the Argosseans to try conclusions with them. Or perhaps the king awaited a more felicitous moment to hurl his strength against the rebels. Whether he were friend or secret foe, Conan rejoiced in his precautions.

When his forces had covered the first day's march without interference, Conan, cantering back from his chosen campsite, relaxed a little. They were now beyond the reach of the spies that infested the winding alleys of Messantia. His scouts and outriders traveled far and wide; if unfriendly eyes watched the army in the countryside, Conan looked to his scouts to sniff their owners out. None was discovered.

The giant Cimmerian trusted few men and those never lightly. His long years of war and outlawry had reinforced his feline wariness. Still, he knew these men who followed him, and his cause was theirs. Thus it never occurred to him that spies might be already in his camp and ill-wishers at his very back.

Two days later, the rebels forded the River Astar in Hypsonia and entered the Plain of Pallos. To the north loomed the Rabirian Mountains, a serrated line of purple peaks marching like giants into the sunset. The army made its camp at the edge of the plain, on a low, rounded hillock that would offer some protection when fortified around the top by ditch and palisade. Here, so long as supplies came regularly from Messantia or from nearby farms, the warriors could perfect their skills before crossing the Alimane into Poitain, the south-ernmost province of Aquilonia.

During the long day after their arrival, the grumbling soldiers laboured with pick, shovel and mattock to surround the camp with a protective rampart. Meanwhile a troop of light horse cantered back along the road by which they had come, to escort the plodding supply wagons.

But during the second watch of that night, a slender figure glided from the darkness of Conan's tent into a pool of moonlight. It was robed and muffled in a long, full caftan of amber wool, which blended into the raw earth beneath its feet. This figure came upon another, shrouded in the shadow of a nearby tent.

The two exchanged a muttered word of recognition. Then slim, beringed fingers pressed a scrap of parchment into the other's labor-grimed hands.

"On this map I have marked the passes that the rebels will take into Aqui-lonia," said the girl in the silken, sibilant whisper of a purring cat. "Also the disposition of the regiments."

"I'll send the word," murmured the other. "Our master will see that it gets to Procas. You have done well, Lady Alcina."

"There is much more to do, Quesado," said the girl. "We must not be seen together."

The Zingaran nodded and vanished into the darkest shadows. The dancer threw back her hood and looked up at the argent moon. Although she had just come from the lusty arms of Conan the Cimmerian, her moonlit features were icily unmoved. Like a mask carved from yellow ivory was that pallid oval face; and in the cool depths of her emerald eyes lurked traces of amusement, malice, and disdain.

That night, as the rebel army slept upon the Plain of Pallos in the embrace of the Rabirian Mountains, one recruit deserted. His absence was not discovered until roll call the next morning; and when it was, Trocero deemed it a matter of small moment. The man, a Zingaran named Quesado, was reputedly a lazy malingerer whose loss would be of little consequence.

Despite his feckless manner, Quesado was in truth anything but lazy. The most diligent of spies, he masked with seeming indolence his busy watching, listening, and compiling of terse but accurate reports. And that night, while the encampment slumbered, he stole a horse from the paddock, eluded the sentinels, and galloped northward hour after weary hour.

Ten days later, splashed with mud, covered with dust, and staggering with exhaustion, Quesado reached the great gates of Tarantia. The sight of the sigil he wore above his heart gained him swift access to Vibius Latro, Numedides's chancellor.

The master of spies frowned over the map that Alcina had slipped into Quesado's hand and that the Zingaran now handed to him. Sternly he asked:

"Why did you bring it yourself? You know you are needed with the rebel army."

The Zingaran shrugged. "It was impossible to send it by carrier pigeon, my lord. When I joined that gaggle of rebels, I had to leave my birds in Messantia, under care of my replacement, Fadius the Kothian."

Vibius Latro stared coldly. "Then, why did you not take the map to Fadius, who could have flown it hither in the accustomed manner? You could have remained in that nest of traitors to follow the winds of change. I counted on your knife at Conan's back."

Quesado gestured helplessly. "When the lady Alcina obtained this copy of the map, Master, the army was already three days' ride beyond Messantia. I could scarce request a six-day leave to go thither and return without arousing suspicion, whilst to go as a deserter would have meant searches and questions by the Argosseans. Nor could I rejoin the army once I had departed without leave. And pigeons do betimes get lost, or are slain by falcons or wildcats or hunters. For a document of such moment, I deemed it better to carry it myself."

The chancellor grunted, pursing his lips. "Why, then, did you not bear it straightway to General Procas?"

Quesado was now perspiring freely. His sallow brow and bestubbled cheeks glistened with moisture. Vibius Latro was no man lightly to displease.

"General P-Procas knows me not." The spy's voice grew querulous. "My sigil would mean naught to him. Only you, my lord, command all channels for transmission of such intelligence to the military chiefs."

A small, thin-lipped smile flickered across the other's enigmatic features. "Quite so," he said. "You have done adequately. I should have liked it better had Alcina obtained the map ere the rebels marched north from Messantia."

"Methinks the rebel leaders had not fully chosen their route before the night of my departure," said Quesado. He did not know this for a fact, but it had a reasonable ring.

Vibius Latro dismissed the spy and summoned his secretary. Studying the map, he dictated a brief message to General Amulius Procas, with a copy for the king. While the secretary copied Alcina's crude sketch, Latro summoned a page and gave him both copies of each document.

"Take these to the king's secretary," the chancellor said, "and ask that His

Majesty impress his seal upon one set. Then, if there be no objection, ride with that set to Amulius Procas in Poitain. Here is a pass to the royal stables. Choose the swiftest horse, and change mounts at each post inn."

The message came not to the king's secretary. It was, instead, delivered into the thin, dark hands of Thulandra Thuu by his Khitan servant, Hsiao. As the king's sorcerer read the message and examined the map in the light of a corpse-fat candle, he smiled coldly, nodding approval to the Khitan.

"It fell out as you predicted, Master," said Hsiao. "I told the page that His Majesty and his scribe were closeted with you, so he handed the scrolls to me."

"You have done well, good Hsiao," said Thulandra Thuu. "Fetch me the wax; I will seal the scrolls myself. There is no need to distract His Majesty from his pleasures for a trifle."

From a locked coffer the sorcerer took a duplicate of the king's seal ring and, folding together one copy each of map and message, he lit a taper from one of the massive candles. Touching the sealing wax to the flame, he dripped the molten wax along the open edge of the packet. Thulandra then stamped the cooling wax with the duplicate seal ring and handed the package to the Khitan.

"Give this to Latro's courier," he said, "and tell him that His Majesty desires it to go post-haste to General Procas. Then draft me a letter to Count Ascalante of Thune, at present commanding the Fourth Tauranian Regiment at Palaea. I require his presence here."

Hsiao hesitated. "Dread lord!" he said.

Thulandra Thuu looked at his servant sharply. "Well?"

"It is not unknown to this unworthy person that you and General Procas are not always in accord. Permit me to ask: Is it your wish that he shall triumph over the barbarian rebel?"

Thulandra Thuu smiled thinly. Hsiao knew that the wizard and the general were fierce rivals for the King's regard, and Hsiao was the only person in the world in whom the sorcerer was willing to confide. Thulandra murmured:

"For the time being. As long as Procas remains in the southern provinces, far from Tarantia, he cannot threaten my position here. And I must risk that he add another victory to his swollen list, since neither he nor I would welcome Conan at the gates of Tarantia.

"Procas stands betwixt the rebels and their march upon the capital. I intend that he shall crush the insurrection, aye; but in such wise that the credit shall fall to me. Then, perchance, an accident may take our heroic general from us in his moment of victory, ere he can return in triumph to Tarantia. Now be on your way."

Hsiao bowed low and silently withdrew. Thulandra Thuu unlocked a chest of ebon and placed therein his copies of the documents.

Trocero stared in puzzlement at his commander, who paced the tent like a caged tiger, angry impatience smoldering in his fierce blue eyes.

"What ails you, General Conan?" he demanded. "I thought it was lack of a woman, but since you carried off the dancing girl, that explanation is a punctured wineskin. What troubles you?"

Conan ceased his restless pacing and came over to the field table. Glowering, he poured himself a cup of wine.

"Naught that I can set a name to," he growled. "But of late I grow fretful, starting at shadows."

He broke off, eyes suddenly alert, as he stared into one corner of the tent. Then he forced a gruff laugh and threw himself back in his leather campaign chair.

"Crom, I'm as restless as a bitch in heat!" he said. "Forsooth, I know not what is gnawing at my vitals. Sometimes, when we confer, I half believe that the very shadows listen to our words."

"Shadows do betimes have ears," said Trocero. "And eyes as well."

Conan shrugged. "I know there be none here save you and me, with the lass at rest, and my two squires burnishing my armor, and the sentries tramping outside the tent," he muttered. "Still and all, I sense a listening presence."

Trocero did not scoff, and foreboding grew upon him. He had learned to trust the Cimmerian's primitive instincts, knowing them keener by far than those of civilized men like himself.

But Trocero was not without instincts of his own; and one of these bade him distrust the supple dancing girl whom Conan had borne off as his willing mistress. Something about her bothered Trocero, although he could not put his finger on the reason. Certainly she was beautiful—if anything, too beautiful to dance for thrown coppers in a Messantian pier-side tavern. Also, she was too silent and secretive for his taste. Trocero could usually charm a woman into a babbling stream of confidences; but, when he had tried to draw Alcina out, he had no success at all. She answered his questions politely but concommittally, leaving him no wiser than before.

He shrugged, poured himself another cup, and consigned all such perturbations to the nine hells of Mitra. "The inaction chafes you, Conan," he said. "Once we are on the march, with the Lion banner floating overhead, you'll feel yourself again. No more listening shadows then!"

"Aye," grunted Conan.

What Trocero had said was true enough. Give Conan an enemy of flesh and blood, put cold steel in his hand, and he would dare the deadliest odds with a

high heart. But, when he strove against impalpable foes and insubstantial shadows, the primitive superstitions of his tribal ancestors crowded into his mind.

In the rear of the tent, behind a curtain, Alcina smiled a slow, catlike smile,
while her slim fingers played with a curious talisman, which hung by a delicate
chain about her neck. There was only one match to it in all the world.

Far to the north, beyond the plains and the mountains and the River Alimane,
Thulandra Thuu sat upon his wrought-iron throne. On his lap, partly unrolled,
he held a scroll inscribed with astrological diagrams and symbols. Before him
on a taboret stood an oval mirror of black volcanic glass. From one edge of
this mystic mirror, a semicircular chip was missing, and it was this half-disc of
obsidian, bound to the main glass by subtle linkages of psychic force, that hung
between the rounded breasts of Alcina the dancing girl.

As the sorcerer studied the chart on his knee, he raised his head betimes to
glance at the small water dock of gilt and crystal, which stood beside the mirror.
From this rare instrument came a steady drip, drip, inaudible to all but the
keenest ears.

When the silver bell within the clock chimed the hour, Thulandra Thuu
released the scroll. He moved a clawlike hand before the mirror, muttering an
exotic charm in an unknown tongue. Gazing into the mirror's depths, he became one in mind and soul with his servant, the lady Alcina; for when a mystic
trance linked the twain, at a moment determined by certain aspects of the
heavenly bodies, the sights Alcina saw and the words she uttered were trans-
mitted magically to the sorcerer in Tarantia.

Truly, the mage had little need of the men of Vibius Latro's corps of spies.
And truly Conan's keen senses served him well: even the shadows in his tent
had eyes and ears.

chapter  iv

The Bloody Arrow

Each dawn the brazen trumpets routed the men from slumber to drill for hours upon the Plain of Pallos and, with the setting sun, dismissed them to their night's repose; and still the army grew. And with the newcomers came news and gossip from Messantia. The moon had shrunk from a silver coin to a sickle of steel when the captains of the rebellion gathered in Conan's tent for supper. After washing down their coarse campaign fare with draughts of weak green beer, the leaders of the host consulted.

"Daily," mused Trocero, "it seems King Milo grows more restive."

Publius nodded. "Aye, it pleases him not to have within his borders so great an armed force, under another's leadership. Be like he fears that we shall turn upon him, as easier prey than the Aquilonian tyrant."

Dexitheus, priest of Mitra, smiled. "Kings are a suspicious lot at best, ever fearful for their crowns. King Milo is no different from the rest."

"Think you he'll seek to attack us in the rear?" growled Conan.

The black-robed priest turned up a narrow hand. "Who can say? Even I, trained by my holy office to read the hearts of men, dare hazard no guess as to the shrouded thoughts that lurk in King Milo's mind. But I advise that we cross the Alimane, and soon."

"The army is prepared," said Prospero. "The men are trained and as ready to fight as ever they will be. It were well they were blooded soon, ere inaction dulls the edge of their fighting spirit."

Conan nodded sombrely. Experience had taught him that an army, over-trained and under-used, is often splintered into quarreling factions by those same forces of pride and militancy that its trainers have so painstakingly instilled. Or it rots, like overripe fruit.

"I agree, Prospero," said the Cimmerian. "But an equal peril lies in too early a move. Surely Procas in Aquilonia has spies to tell him that we lodge in the mountains of northern Argos. And a general less shrewd than he would guess that we mean to cross the Alimane into Poitain, the most disaffected of all the provinces of Aquilonia. He needs but to mount a heavy guard at every ford and keep his Border Legion mobile, ready to march to any threatened crossing."

Trocero swept back his graying hair with confident fingers. "All Poitain will rise to march with us; but my partisans keep silent, lest word reach the vigilant Procas in time to act."

The others exchanged significant glances, wherein hope and skepticism mingled. Days before, messengers had left the rebel camp to enter Poitain in the guise of merchants, tinkers, and peddlars. Their mission was to urge Count Trocero's liegemen and supporters to prepare for forays and diversions, to confuse the royalists or to draw them off in futile pursuit of raiding bands. Once these agents had carried out their mission, a signal to move would reach the rebel army—a Poitanian arrow dipped in blood. Meanwhile, waiting for the message stretched nerves taut.

Prospero said: "I am less concerned about the rising of Poitain, which is as certain as aught can be in this chancy world, than I am about the promised deputation from the northern barons. If we be not at Culario by the ninth day of the vernal month, they may withdraw, since planting time will be upon them."

Conan grunted and drained his goblet. The northern lordlings, in smoldering revolt against Numedides, had vowed to support the rebels but would not openly commit themselves to a rebellion stigmatized by failure. If the Lion banner were broken at the Alimane, or if the Poitanian revolt failed to take fire, no bond would tie these self-serving nobles to the rebel cause.

The barons' caution was understandable; but uncertainty drove sharp spurs into the rebel leaders' souls. If they must linger on the Plain of Pallos until the Poitanians sent their secret signal, would there be time to reach Culario on the appointed day? Despite the headstrong urgings of his barbaric nature, Conan counseled patience until the Poitanian signal came. But his officers remained uncertain or offered diverse plans.

So the rebel leaders argued far into the night. Prospero wished to split the army into three contingents and hurl them all at once upon the three best fords: those of Mevano, Nogara, and Tunais.

Conan shook his head. "Procas will expect just that," he said.

"What, then?" Prospero frowned.

Conan spread the map and with a scarred forefinger pointed to the middle ford, Nogara. "We'll feint here, with two or three companies only. You know tricks to convince the foe that our numbers are vaster than they truly are. We'll set up empty tents, light extra campfires, and parade companies within view of the foe and then swing them out of sight behind a copse and around the circuit again. We'll unlimber a couple of ballistas on the river bank to harass the crossing guards. Those screeching darts should entice Procas and his army thither in a hurry.

"You, Prospero, shall command the diversion," Conan added. Learning that he would miss the main battle, the young commander began to object, but Conan silenced him: "Trocero, you and I shall take the remaining troops, half to Mevano and the balance to Tunais, and force the two crossings. With luck, we may catch Procas in a nutcracker."

"Perchance you're right," murmured Trocero. "With our Poitanians in revolt in Procas's rear . . ."

"May the gods smile upon your plan, General," said Publius, mopping his brow. "If not, all is lost!"

"Ah, gloomy one!" said Trocero. "War is a chancy trade, and we have no less to lose than you. Win or lose, we all must stand together."

"Aye, even at the foot of the gallows," muttered Publius.

Behind the partition in Conan's tent, his mistress lay couched on a bed of furs, her slender body gleaming in the feeble light of a single candle, whose wavering flame reflected strangely in her emerald eyes and in the clouded depths of the small obsidian talisman that reposed in the scented valley of her breasts. She smiled a catlike smile.

Before dawn, Trocero was roused from his couch by the urgent hand of a sentry. The count yawned, stretched, blinked, and irritably struck the guard's hand aside.

"Enough!" he barked. "I am awake, lout, though it scarcely seems light enough for roll call. . . ."

His face went blank and his voice died as he saw what the guard held out to him. It was a Poitanian arrow, coated from barb to feathers with dried blood.

"How came this here?" he asked. "And when?"

"A short time past, my Lord Count, borne by a rider from the north," replied the guard.

"So! Summon my squires! Sound the alarm and bear the arrow forthwith to General Conan!" cried Trocero, heaving himself to his feet.

The guard saluted and left. Soon two squires, knuckling sleep from their eyes, hastened in to attire the count and buckle on his armor.

"Action at last, by Mitra, Ishtar, and Crom of the Cimmerians!" cried Trocero. "You there, Mnester! Summon my captains to council! And you, boy, has Black Lady been fed and watered? See to her saddling, and quickly. Draw the girth tight! I've no wish for a cold bath in the waters of the Alimane!"

Before a ruby sun inflamed the forested crests of the Rabirian Mountains, the tents were struck, the sentries recalled, and the wains laden. By the time bright day had chased away the laggard morning mists, the army was on the march in three long columns, heading for Saxula Pass through the mountains and beyond it for Aquilonia and war. The land grew rugged and the road tortuous. On either side rose barren rondures toothed with stony outcrops. These were the foothills of the Rabirians, which scurried westward following the stately tread of the adjacent mountains.

Hour after hour, warriors and camp servants trudged up the long slopes and down the farther sides. The hot sun beat upon them as they manhandled heavy vehicles over steep rises, clustering about the wains like bees around a hive to push, heave, and pull. On the downward slopes, each teamster belayed one wheel with a length of chain, so that, unable to rotate, it served to brake the vehicle. Dust devils eddied skyward, besmudging the crystalline mountain air.

As they crested each rise, the main range receded miragelike before them. But, when the purple shadows of late afternoon fingered the eastern slope of every hill, the mountains opened out, like curtains drawn aside. They parted to disclose Saxula Pass, a deep cleft in the central ridge, as if made by a blow from an axe in the hand of an angry god.

As the army struggled upward toward the pass, Conan commanded a contingent of his scouts to clamber up the steep sides of the opening to make sure no ambush awaited his coming. The scouts signaled that all was clear, and the army tramped on through. The footfalls of men, the rattle of equipment, the drum of hooves, and the creak of axles reverberated from the rocky cliffs on either hand.

As the men emerged from the confines of the pass, the road wound downward, losing itself in the thick stands of cedar and pine that masked the northern slopes. In the distance, beyond the intermediate ranges, the men glimpsed the Alimane, coiling through the flatlands like a silvery serpent warmed by the last rays of the setting sun.

Down the winding slope they went, with wheels lashed to hold the wagons back. As the stars throbbed in the darkening sky, they reached a fork in the road beyond the pass. Here the army halted and set up camp. Conan flung his sentinels out wide, to guard against a night attack from the foe across the river. But nothing disturbed the weary troopers' rest except the snarl of a prowling leopard, which fled at a sentry's shout.

The following morning, Trocero and his contingent departed along the right branch of the fork, headed for the ford of Tunais. Conan and Prospero, with their forces, continued down the left branch until, shortly before noon, they reached another fork. Here Prospero with his small detachment bore to the right, for the central ford of Nogara. Conan, with the remaining horse and foot, continued westward to seek out the ford of Mevano.

Section by section, squad by squad, Conan's rebels filed down the narrow roads. They camped one more night in the hills and went on. As they descended the final range of foothills, between clumps of conifers they again caught glimpses of the broad Alimane, which sundered Argos from Poitain. True, Argos claimed a tract of land on the northern side of the river—a tract extending to the junction of the Alimane with the Khorotas. But under Vilerus III the Aquilonians had overrun the area and, being the stronger, still retained possession.

As Conan's division reached the flatlands, the Cimmerian ordered his men to speak but little and only in low voices. As far as possible, they were to quiet the jingle of their gear. The wagons halted under heavy stands of trees, and the men pitched camp out of sight of the ford of Mevano. Scouts sent ahead reported no sign of any foe, but they brought back the unwelcome news that the river was in flood, rampant with the springtime melting of the highland snows.

Well before the dawn of a cloud-darkened day, Conan's officers routed the men from their tents. Grumbling, the soldiers bolted an uncooked breakfast and fell into formation. Conan stalked about, snarling curses and threatening those who raised their voices or dropped their weapons. To his apprehensive ears, it seemed as if the clatter could be heard for leagues above the purl of the river. A better-trained force, he thought sourly, would move on cats' paws.

To diminish the noise, commands were passed from captains to men by hand signals instead of by shouts and trumpet calls; and this caused some confusion. One company, signaled to march, cut through the ranks of another. Fisticuffs erupted and noses bled before the officers ended the fracas.

A heavy overcast blanketed road and river as Conan's troops neared the banks of the Alimane. Mounted on his black stallion Fury, Conan drew rein and peered through the curtaining drizzle toward the farther bank. Beyond his horse's hooves, the high water, brown with sediment, gurgled past.

Conan signaled to his aide Alaricus, a promising young Aquilonian captain. Alaricus maneuvred his horse close to that of his general.

"How deep, think you?" muttered Conan.

"More than knee-deep, General," replied Alaricus. "Perhaps chest-high. Let me put my mount into it to see."

"Try not to fall into a mudhole," cautioned Conan.

The young captain urged his bay gelding into the swirling flood. The animal balked, then waded obediently toward the northern shore. By midstream, the murky water was curling over the toes of Alaricus's boots; and when he looked back, Conan beckoned him.

"We shall have to chance it," growled the Cimmerian when the aide had rejoined him. "Pass the word for Dio's light horse to make the first crossing and scout the farther woods. Then the foot shall go single file, each man grasping the belt of the man before him. Some of these clodhoppers would drown if they lost their footing whilst weighted with their gear."

As sunless day paled into the somber sky, the company of light horse splashed into the stream. Reaching the farther bank, Captain Dio waved to indicate that the woods harbored no foe.

Conan had watched intently as the troopers' horses sank into the swirling flume, noting the depth of the water. When it was plain that the river bed shoaled beyond midstream and that the other bank was clear, he signaled the first company of foot to cross. Soon two companies of pikemen and one of archers breasted the flood. Each soldier gripped the man in front, while the archers held aloft their bows to keep them dry.

Conan brought his stallion close to Alaricus, saying: "Tell the heavy horse to ford the stream, and then start the baggage train across, with Cerco's company of foot to haul them out of mudholes. I'm going out to midstream."

Fury stumbled into the river, gaskin-deep in the rushing brown water. When the charger flinched and whinnied, as if sensing unseen danger, Conan tightened his grip on the reins and forced the beast through the deepest part of the central channel.

His keen eyes searched the jade-green foliage along the northern shore, where a riot of flowering shrubs, their colors muted by the overcast, surrounded the boles of ancient trees. The road became a dark tunnel amid the new-leaved oaks, which seemed to bear the weight of the leaden sky. Here was ample room for concealment, thought Conan somberly. The light cavalry still waited, bunched into the small clearing where the road dipped into the river, although they should have searched far into the surrounding woods before the first foot soldiers reached the northern bank. Conan gestured angrily.

"Dio!" he roared from the midstream shallows. If any foe was present, he would long since have observed the crossing, so Conan saw no point in keeping silence. "Spread out and beat the bushes! Move, damn your soul!"

The three companies of infantry scrambled out on the northern bank, muddy and dripping, while Dio's horsemen broke into squads and pushed into the thickets on either side of the road. An army is at its most vulnerable when fording a stream, this Conan knew; and foreboding swelled in his barbaric heart.

He wheeled his beast about to survey the southern shore. The heavy cavalry was already knee-deep in the stream, and the leading wains of the baggage train were struggling through the flood. A couple had bogged down in the mud of the river bottom; soldiers, heaving on the wheels, manhandled them along.

A sudden cry ripped the heavy air. As Conan swung around, he caught a flicker of movement in the bushes at the junction of road and river. With a short bark of warning, Conan reined his steed, and an arrow meant for him flashed past his breast and, swift as a striking viper, buried itself in the neck of the young officer behind him. As the dying man slumped into the roiling water, Conan spurred his horse forward, bellowing orders. He must, he thought, command the troops in contact with the foe, whether they faced a paltry crossing guard or the full might of Procas's army.

Suddenly Fury reared and staggered beneath the impact of another arrow. With a shriek, the animal fell to its knees, hurling Conan from the saddle. The Cimmerian gulped a swirl of muddy water and struggled to his feet, coughing curses. Another arrow struck his cuirass, glanced off, and tumbled into the torrent. All about him, the stagnant calm of the leaden day hung in tatters. Men howled war cries, screamed in fear and pain, and cursed the very gods above.

Blinking water from his stinging eyes, Conan perceived a triple line of archers and crossbowmen in the blue surcoats of the Border Legion. As one man, they had leaped from the lush foliage to rake the floundering riverbound rebels with a hail of arrows.

The screeching whistle of arrows mingled with the deeper thrum of crossbow bolts. Although the arbalesters could not shoot their cumbersome weapons so fast as the longbowmen, their crossbows had the greater range, and their iron bolts could pierce the stoutest armor. Man after man fell, screaming or silent, as the muddy waters closed over their heads and rolled their bodies along the scoured shoals.

Wading shoreward, Conan searched out a trumpeter to call his milling men into battle formations. In the shallows he found one, a tow-headed Gunderman, staring dumbly at the carnage. Growling curses, Conan splashed toward the awestruck lout; but as he sought to seize the fellow's jerkin, the Gunderman doubled up and pitched headfirst into the water, a bolt buried in his vitals. The trumpet fell from his flaccid grip and was tumbled out of reach by the current.

As Conan paused to catch his breath, glaring about like a cornered lion, an augmented clatter from the clearing riveted his attention. Aquilonian cavalry— armored lancers and swordsmen on sturdy mounts—thundered out of the woods and swept down upon the milling mass of rebel light horse and infantry. The smaller horses of the rebel scouts were brushed aside; the men on foot were ridden down and trampled. In a trice the north bank was cleared of rebels. Then, with clocklike precision, Procas's armored squadrons opened out into a troop-wide rank of horsemen, which plunged into the water to assail those rebels who struggled in the deeps.

"To me!" roared Conan, brandishing his sword. "Form squares!"

But now the survivors of the débâcle, who had been swept back into the river by the Aquilonian cavalry, thrashed through the water in panicked flight, pushing aside or knocking over comrades who floundered northward. Through the turbulent current pounded Procas' horse amid fountains of spray. Behind the second line, a third line opened out, and then another and another. And from the flanks, Procas' archers continued their barrage of missiles, to which the rebel archers, with unstrung bows, could not reply.

"General!" cried Alaricus. Conan looked around to see the young captain breasting the water toward him. "Save yourself! They're broken here, but you can rally the men for a stand on the southern bank. Take my horse!"

Conan spat a curse at the fast-approaching line of armored horsemen. For an instant he hesitated, the thought of rushing among them single-handed, hewing right and left, flickering in his mind. But the idea was banished as soon as it appeared. In an earlier day, Conan might have essayed such a mad attack. Now he was a general, responsible for the lives of other men, and experience had tempered his youthful recklessness with caution. As Alaricus started to dismount, Conan seized the aide's stirrup with his left hand, growling:

"Stay up there lad! Go on, head for the south bank, Crom blast it!"

Alaricus spurred his horse, which struggled toward the Argossean shore. Conan, gripping the stirrup, accompanied him with long, half-leaping strides, amid the retreating mass of rebels, horsed and afoot, all plunging southward in confused and abject flight.

Behind them rode the Aquilonians, spearing and swording the laggards as they fought the flood. Already the muddy waters of the Alimane ran red below the ford of Mevano. Only the fact that the pursuers, too, were hampered by the swirling stream saved Conan's advance units from utter annihilation.

At length the fugitives reached a company of heavy cavalry that had broached the river behind the rebel infantry. The fleeing men pushed between the on-coming horses, yammering their terror. Thus beset, the frightened beasts reared and plunged until their riders, also, joined the retreat. Behind them, mired in the river bottom, teamsters strove to turn their cumbersome supply wagons around or, in despair, abandoned them to leap into the water and splash back toward the southern shore. Coming upon the abandoned vehicles, the Aquilonians butchered the bellowing oxen and pressed on. Sodden corpses, rolled along by the current, wedged together into grisly human log jams. Wagons were overturned; their loads of tent canvas and poles, bundles of spears, and sheaves of arrows floated downstream on the relentless flood.

Conan, shouting himself hoarse, struggled out on the south bank, where the remaining companies had awaited their turn to cross. He tried to rally them into defensive formations, but everywhere the rebel host was crumbling into formless clots of fleeing men. Throwing away pikes, shields, and helmets, they sought safety, running in all directions out of the shallows and across the flats that bordered the river. All discipline, so painfully inculcated during the preceding months, was lost in the terror of the moment.

A few knots of men stood firm as the Aquilonian cavalry reached them and fought with stubborn ferocity, but they were ridden down and slain or scattered.

Conan found Publius in the crush and seized him by the shoulder, shouting in his ear. Unable to hear his commander above the uproar, the treasurer shrugged helplessly, pointing. At his feet lay the body of Conan's aide, which Publius was shielding from the rough boots of the fleeing soldiery. Alaricus's horse had disappeared.

With an angry bellow, Conan dispersed the crowd around him by striking about with the flat of his blade. Then he hoisted Alaricus to his shoulder and headed southward at a jog trot. The stout Publius ran puffing beside him. Not far behind, the Aquilonian cavalry clambered out of the river to pursue the retreating rebels. They enveloped the line of wains drawn up along the shore, awaiting their turn to breast the flood.

Farther inland, some of the teamsters managed to turn their clumsy carts and lashed their oxen into a shambling run back toward the safety of the hills. The road south was black with fleeing men, while hundreds of others darted off across the meadows to lose themselves in the sheltering woods.

Since the day was young and the Aquilonian forces fresh, Conan's division faced annihilation at the hands of their well-mounted pursuers. But here occurred a check—not a great one, but enough to give the fugitives some small advantage. The Aquilonians who had surrounded the supply wagons, instead of pushing on, pulled up to loot the vehicles, despite the shouted commands of their officers. Hearing them, Conan panted:

"Publius? Where's the pay chest?"

"I—know—not," gasped the treasurer. " 'Twas in one of the last wains, so perchance it escaped the wreck. I—can—run—no further. Go on, Conan."

"Don't be a fool!" snarled Conan. "I need a man who can reckon sums, and my young mealsack here regains his wits."

As Conan set down his burden, Alaricus opened his eyes and groaned. Conan, hastily examining him for wounds, found none. The captain, it transpired, had been stunned by a crossbow bolt, which merely grazed his head and dented his helmet. Conan hauled him to his feet.

"I've carried you, my lad," said the Cimmerian. "Now 'tis your turn to help me carry our fat friend."

Soon the three set out again for the safety of the hills, Publius staggering between the other two with an arm about the neck of each. Rain began to fall, gently at first and then in torrents.

The winds of misfortune blew cold on Conan's head that night as he sat in a hollow of the Rabirian Mountains. The day was plainly lost, his men dispersed—those who had survived the battle and the bloody vengeance meted out by the royalist general and his searching parties. In a few hours, it seemed, their very cause had foundered, sunk in the muddy, bloodstained waters of the River Alimane.

Here in a rocky hollow, hidden amid oak and pine, Conan, Publius, and five-score other rebels waited out the dark and hopeless night. The refugees were a mixed lot: renegade Aquilonian knights, staunch yeomen, armed outlaws, and soldiers of fortune. Some were hurt, though few mortally, and many hearts pounded drumbeats of despair.

The legions of Amulius Procas, Conan knew, were sniffing through the hills, bent on slaughtering every survivor. The victorious Aquilonian evidently meant to smash the rebellion for all time by dealing speedy death to every rebel he could catch. Conan grudgingly gave the veteran commander credit for his plan. Had Conan been in Amulius Procas's place, he would have followed much the same course.

Sunk in silent gloom, Conan fretted over the fate of Prospero and Trocero. Prospero was to have feinted at the ford of Nogara, drawing thither the bulk of Procas's troops, so that Conan and Trocero should have only minor contingents of crossing guards to contend with. Instead, Procas's massed warriors had erupted out of concealment when Conan's van, waist-deep in the Alimane, was at a hopeless disadvantage. Conan wondered how Procas had so cleverly divined the rebels' plans.

Gathered around their fugitive leader, in the lonely dark, huddled men who had been soaked by rain and river. They dared not light a fire lest it become a beacon guiding forces for their destruction. The coughs and sneezes of the fugitives tolled the knell of their hopes. When someone cursed the weather, Conan growled:

"Thank your gods for that rain! Had the day been fair, Procas would have butchered the lot of us. No fire!" he barked at a soldier who tried to strike a light with flint and steel. "Would you draw Procas's hounds upon us? How many are we? Sound off, but softly. Count them, Publius."

Men responded "Here!" "Here!" while Publius kept track with his fingers. When the last "Here!" had been heard, he said:

"One hundred thirteen, General, not counting ourselves."

Conan grunted. Brightly though the lust for revenge burned in his barbarian heart, it seemed impossible that such a paltry number could form the nucleus of another army. While he put up a bold front before his rebel remnant, the vulture of despondency clawed at his weary flesh.

He set out sentries, and during the night exhausted men, guided by these sentinels, stumbled into the hollow in ones and twos and threes. Toward midnight came Dexitheus, the priest of Mitra, limping along on an improvised crutch, leaning heavily on the arm of the sentry who guided him, and wincing with the pain of a wrenched ankle.

Now there were nearly twice a hundred fugitives, some gravely wounded, gathered in the hollow. The Mitraist priest, despite the pain of his own injury, set to work to tend the wounded, drawing arrows from limbs and bandaging wounds for hours, until Conan brusquely commanded him to rest.

The camp was rude, its comforts primitive; and, Conan knew, the rebels had little chance of seeing another nightfall. But at least they were alive, most still bore arms, and many could put up a savage fight if Procas should discover their hiding place. And so, at last, Conan slept.

Dawn mounted a sky where clouds were breaking up and dwindling, leaving a clear blue vault. Conan was awakened by the subdued chatter of many armed men. The newcomers were Prospero and his diversionary detachment, five hundred strong.

"Prospero!" cried Conan, struggling to his feet to clasp his friend in a mighty embrace. Then he led the officer aside and spoke in a low voice, lest ill tidings should further depress the spirits of the men. "Thank Mitra! How went your day? How did you find us? What of Trocero?"

"One at a time, General," said Prospero, catching his breath. "We found naught but a few crossing guards at Nogara, and they fled before us. For a whole day, we marched in circles, blew trumpets, and beat drums, but no royalists could we draw to the ford. Thinking this strange, I sent a galloper downstream to Tunais. He reported a hard fight there, with Trocero's division in retreat. Then a fugitive from your command fell in with us and spoke of your disaster. So, not wishing my small force to be caught between the millstones of two enemy divisions, I fell back into the uplands. There, other runagates told us of the direction they had seen you take. Now, what of you?"

Conan clenched his teeth to stifle his self reproach. "I played the fool this time, Prospero, and led us into Procas's jaws. I should have waited until Dio had probed the forest ere starting my lads across. It's well that Dio fell at the first onslaught—had he not, I'd have made him wish he had. He and his men milled around like sheep for a snailish time ere pushing out to beat the undergrowth. But still, I was at fault to let impatience sway me. Procas had watchers in the trees, to signal the attack. Now all is lost."

"Not so, Conan," said Prospero. "As you are wont to say, naught is hopeless until the last man chews the dust or knuckles under; and in every war the gods throw boons and banes to either side. Let us fall back to the Plain of Pallos and our base camp. We may join Trocero along the way. We are now several hundred strong, and we shall count to thousands when we sweep up the other stragglers. A hundred gullies in these hills must shelter groups like ours."

"Procas far outnumbers us," said Conan somberly, "and his well-found forces carry high spirits from their victories. What can a few thousand, downcast by defeat, achieve against them? Besides, he will have seized the passes through the Rabirians, or at least the main pass at Saxula."

"Doubtless," said Prospero, "but Procas's troops are scattered wide, searching for fugitives. Our hungry pride of lions could one by one devour his packs of bloodhounds. In sooth, we came upon one such on our way hither—a squad of light horse—and slew the lot. Come, General! You of all men are the indomitable one—the man who never quits. You've built a band of brigands into an army and shaken thrones ere now; you can do the same again. So be of good cheer!"

Conan took a deep breath and squared his massive shoulders. "You're right, by Crom! I'll mewl no longer like a starving beldame. We've lost one engagement, but our cause remains whilst there be two of us to stand back to back and fight for it. And we have this, at least."

He reached into the shadows and drew from a crevice in the rocks the Lion banner, the symbol of the rebellion. His standard bearer, though mortally wounded, had borne it to the hollow in the hills. After the man had succumbed, Conan had rolled up the banner and thrust it out of sight. Now he unfurled it in the pale light of dawn.

"It's little enough to salvage from the rout of an army," he rumbled, "but thrones have been won with less." And Conan smiled a grim, determined smile.

chapter  v

The Purple Locus

The smiling day revealed that Fate had not entirely forsaken the army of the rebellion. For the night had been heavily overcast, and in the gloom the weary warriors of Amulius Procas had failed to root out many scattered pockets of survivors, like that which Conan had gathered around him. Thus, as the morning sun rolled back its blanket of clouds, bands of heartsore rebels, who had either eluded the search parties or routed those they encountered, began to filter back across the Rabirian range.

Night was nigh when Conan and his remnant approached the pass of Saxula. Conan dispatched men ahead to scout, since he was convinced he would have to fight his way through. He snorted with surprise when the scouts reported back that there was no evidence of the Border Legion anywhere near the pass. There were signs—the ashes of campfires and other debris—that a force of Procas's men had camped in the pass, but they were nowhere to be seen.

"Crom! What means this?" Conan mused, staring up at the great notch in the ridge. "Unless Procas has sent his men on, deeper into Argos."

"I think not," said Publius. "That would mean open war with Milo. More likely, he ordered his men back across the Alimane before the court at Messantia could hear of his incursion. Then, if King Milo protests, Procas can aver that not one Aquilonian soldier remains on Argossean soil."

"Let's hope you are right," said Conan. "Forward, men!"

By the next midday, Conan's band had gathered up several full companies that had fled unscathed from the ambush at Mevano. But the rebels' greatest prize was Count Trocero himself, camped on a hilltop with two hundred horse and foot. Having built a rude palisade, the Count of Poitain was prepared to hold his little fort against Procas and all his iron legions. Trocero emotionally embraced Conan and Prospero.

"Thank Mitra you live!" he cried. "I heard that you had fallen to an arrow and that your division fled southward like wintering wildfowl."

"You hear many things about a battle, perhaps one tenth of them true," said Conan. He told the tale of the ambush at Mevano and asked: "How fared you at Tunais?"

"Procas smashed us as badly as he shattered you. I believe that he himself commanded. He laid his ambush on the south bank of the river and assailed us from both sides as we prepared to cross. I had not thought that he would dare so grossly to violate Argossean territory."

"Amulius Procas is nobody's fool," said Conan, "nor does he scruple to snatch at a long chance when he must. But how came you hither? Through Saxula Pass?"

"Nay. When we approached it, a strong force of Procas's men were there encamped. Luckily, one of my horsemen, a smuggler by trade, knew a narrow, little-used opening through which he led us. It was a dizzy climb, but we got through with the loss of but two beasts. Now, say you that Saxula Pass is open?"

"It was last night, at least," said Conan. He looked around. "Let's go on, posthaste, back to our base camp on the Plain of Pallos. My men together with yours make above a thousand fighters."

"A thousand scarce an army makes," grumbled Publius. " 'Tis but a remnant of the ten thousand who marched northward with us."

"It's a beginning," said Conan, whose gloom of the night before had vanished with the light of day. "I can recall when our whole enterprise numbered only five stout hearts."

A s the remnant of the rebels marched, more bands that had escaped the slaughter joined the host, and individual survivors and small groups came straggling in. Conan kept glancing back with apprehension, expecting at any moment to see Procas's whole Border Legion pour down the Rabirian Hills in hot pursuit. But Publius thought differently.

"Look you, General," he said. "King Milo has not yet betrayed us or turned against us, or surely he would have come pounding at our rear whilst Procas engaged us in the van. Methinks not even the mad King of Aquilonia dare risk a full and open war with the sovereign state of Argos; the Argosseans are a hardy lot. Amulius Procas knows his politics; he would not have so long survived in Numedides's service had he rashly affronted neighboring kingdoms. Once we regain our base camp and shore up our barricades, we should be safe for the moment. The reserve supplies and the camp followers await us."

Conan scowled. "Until Numedides bribes or bullies Milo into turning his hand against us."

In a sense, Conan was right. For even at that hour, the agents of Aquilonia were closeted with King Milo and his councilmen. Chief among these agents was Quesado the Zingaran, who had reached Messantia with his party by a long, hard ride from Tarantia, swinging wide of the embattled armies.

Quesado, now resplendent in black velvet with boots of fine red Kordavan leather, had changed; and the change was not to his employer's advantage. Hearing of the spy's exploits in the service of Vibius Latro, a delighted King Numedides had insisted on promoting Quesado to the diplomatic corps. This proved a mistake.

The Zingaran had been an excellent spy, long trained to affect an unassuming, inconspicuous air. Now suddenly raised in pay and prestige, he let his façade of humility crumble, and the pompous pride and hauteur of a would-be Zingaran gentleman began to show through the gaps. Looking down his beak of a nose, he endeavored by thinly veiled threats to persuade King Milo and his councilors that it were wiser to court the favor of the King of Aquilonia than to support his raggle-taggle foes.

"My lord King and gentlemen," said Quesado in a sharp, schoolmasterish voice, "surely you know that, if you choose to be no friend of my master, you must be counted amongst his enemies. And the longer you permit your realm to shelter our rebellious foes, the more you will be tainted with the poison of treason against my sovereign lord, the mighty King of Aquilonia."

King Milo's broad face flushed with anger, and he sat up sharply. A heavy-set man of middle years, whose luxuriant gray beard overspread his chest, Milo gave the impression of stolid taciturnity, more like some honest peasant than the ruler of a rich and sophisticated realm. Slow to make up his mind, he could be exceedingly stubborn once he had reached his decision. Glaring at Quesado, he snapped:

"Argos is a free and sovereign state, sirrah! We have never been and, Mitra willing, never shall be subject to the King of Aquilonia. Treason means a misdeed of a subject against his overlord. Do you claim that fat Numedides is overlord of Argos?"

Quesado began to perspire; his bony forehead gleamed damply in the soft light that streamed in ribbons of azure, vert, and scarlet through the stained-glass windows of the council chamber.

"Such was not my intention, Your Majesty," he hastily apologized. More humbly, he pleaded: "But with all respect, sire, I must point out that my master can hardly overlook assistance given by a neighboring brother monarch to rebels against his divinely established Ruby Throne."

"We have given them no help," said Milo, glowering. "Your spies will have apprized you that their remnants are encamped upon the Plain of Pallos and, lacking supplies from Messantia, are desperately scouring the countryside for food. Their famed Bossonian archers employ their skill in pursuing ducks and deer. You say your General Procas's victory was decisive? What, then, has mighty Aquilonia to fear from a gaggle of fugitives, reduced by starvation to mere banditry? We are told they have but a tithe of their original strength and that desertions further reduce their numbers day by day."

"True, my lord King," said Quesado, who had recovered his poise. "But, by the same token, what has cultured Argos to gain by sheltering such a band? Unable to assail their rightful ruler, they must needs maintain themselves by depredations against your own loyal subjects."

Scowling, Milo lapsed into silence, for he had no convincing answer to Quesado's argument. He could hardly say, that he had given his word to an old friend, Count Trocero, to let the rebels use his land as a base for operations against a neighboring king. Moreover, he resented the Aquilonian envoy's efforts to rush him into a decision. He liked to make up his own mind in his own time, without hectoring.

Lumbering to his feet, the king curtly adjourned the session: "We will consider the requests of our brother monarch, Ambassador Quesado. Our gentlemen shall inform you of our decision at our pleasure. You have our leave to withdraw."

Lips curled in a false smile, Quesado bowed his way out, but venom ate at his heart. Fortune had favored the rebellious Cimmerian this time, he thought, but the next throw of the dice might have a different outcome. For though he knew it not, Conan nursed a viper in his bosom.

The Army of the Lion was in no wise so enfeebled or reduced to famine as Milo and Quesado believed. Now numbering over fifteen hundred, it daily rebuilt its strength and gathered supplies. The lean horses grazed on the long grass of the plain; the women camp followers, who had been left at the base camp when the army marched northward, nursed the wounded. Much of the baggage train had been salvaged, and ragged survivors continued to limp and straggle in, to swell the thin but resolute ranks of the rebellion. The forests whispered to the footfalls of hunters and rang to the axes of woodcutters, while in the camp, fletchers whittled spear and arrow shafts, and the anvils of blacksmiths clanged with the beat of hammers on point and blade.

Most encouraging was the tale that the rear guard, a thousand strong under the Aquilonian Baron Groder, had escaped the débâcle at Tunais and was wandering in the mountains to the east. To investigate, Conan sent Prospero with a troop of light horse to search for their lost comrades and guide them to the base. Dexitheus prayed to Mitra that this rumor might prove true, for the addition of Groder's force would nearly double their strength. Kingdoms had fallen ere this to fewer than three thousand determined warriors.

A full moon glared down upon the Plain of Pallos like the yellow eye of an angry god. A chill, uneasy wind rustled through the tall meadow grasses and plucked with ghostly fingers at the cloaks of sentries, who stood watch about the rebel camp.

In his candle-lit tent, Conan sat late over a flagon of ale, listening to his officers. Some, still downcast by their recent defeat, were reluctant to contemplate further conflicts at this time. Others, avid for revenge, urged an early assault, even with their present diminished might.

"Look you, General," said Count Trocero. "Amulius Procas will never expect an attack so soon upon the heels of our disaster, so we shall take him by surprise. Once across the Alimane, we shall be joined by our Poitanian friends, who only await our coming to raise the province."

Conan's savage soul incited him to heed his friend's advice. To strike across the border now, at the very ebb of their fortunes, would wrest victory from defeat with a vengeance. He urgently needed a vigorous sally to mend the men's morale. Already some were drifting away, deserting what they viewed as a hopeless cause. Unless he could shore up the dykes of loyalty with hopes of triumph, the leakage of the disaffected would soon become a flood, leaching his army away to nothing.

Yet the mighty Cimmerian had, during his years of campaigning, grown wise in the ways of war. Experience cautioned him to rein in his eagerness, rather than commit his remaining strength — at least until Prospero returned with word of Baron Groder and his force. Once Conan knew he could count upon this powerful reinforcement, he could then determine whether the moment for assault was at hand.

Dismissing his commanders, Conan sought the warm arms and soft breasts of Alcina. The golden dancing girl had entranced him with her wily ways of assuaging his passions; but this night she laughingly eluded his embrace, to proffer a goblet of wine.

" 'Tis time, my lord, that you enjoyed a gentleman's drink, instead of swilling bitter beer like any peasant," she said. "I brought a flask of fine wine from Messantia for your especial pleasure."

"Crom and Mitra, girl, I've drunk enough this night! I thirst now for the wine of your lips, not for the pressings of the grape."

"It is but a gentle stimulant, lord, to augment your desires — and my enjoyment of them," she wheedled. Standing in the candlelight in a length of sheer saffron silk, which did little to hide the lush lines of her body, she smiled seductively and thrust the goblet toward him, saying: "It contains spices from my homeland to rouse your senses. Will you not drink it, my lord, to please me?"

Looking eagerly upon the moon-pale oval of her face, Conan said: "I need no rousing when I smell the perfume of your hair. But give it to me; I'll drink to this night's delights."

He drank the wine in three great gulps, ignoring the faintly acrid taste of the spices, and slammed the goblet down. Then he reached for the delectable girl, whose wide-set eyes were fixed upon him.

But, when he sought to seize her in his arms, the tent reeled crazily about him, and a searing pain bloomed in his vitals. He snatched at the tent pole, missed, and fell heavily.

Alcina leaned over his supine body. In his blurring vision, her features melted into a mist, through which her green eyes burned like incandescent emeralds.

"Crom's blood, wench!" Conan gasped. "You've poisoned me!"

He struggled to rise, but it seemed to the Cimmerian that his body had turned to lead. Although the veins in his temples throbbed, his face purpled with effort, and his thews stood out along his limbs like ship's cables, he could not regain his feet. He fell back, gulping air. Then his vision dimmed until he seemed to drift from the lamplit interior of the tent into a trancelike waking dream. He could neither speak nor stir.

"Conan!" the girl murmured, bending over him; but he made no reply. In a silken whisper, she said: "So much for you, barbarian pig! And soon your wretched remnant of an army will follow you back to the hells whence you and they once crawled!"

Calmly seating herself, she drew forth the amulet she bore between her breasts. A glance at the time candle on a taboret showed that half an hour must yet elapse before she could commune with her master. In sphinxlike silence she sat, unmoving, until the time approached. Then she focused her mind upon the obsidian fragment.

In far-off Tarantia, Thulandra Thuu, gazing into his magical mirror, gave a dry chuckle as he observed the quiescent form of the giant Cimmerian. Rising, he replaced the mirror in its cabinet, roused his servant, and sent him with a message to the king.

Hsiao found Numedides, unclothed, enjoying a massage by four handsome naked girls. Keeping his modest eyes fixed upon the marble floor, Hsiao bowed low and said:

"My master respectfully informs Your Majesty that the bandit rebel Conan is slain in Argos by my master's otherworldly powers."

With a grunt, Numedides sat up, pushing the girls away. "Eh? Dead, you say?"

"Aye, my lord King."

"Excellent news, excellent news." With a loud guffaw, Numedides slapped his bare thigh. "When I become a—but enough of that. What else?"

"My master asks your permission to send a message to General Amulius Procas, informing him of this event and authorizing him to cross into Argos, to scatter the rebel remnants ere they can choose another leader."

Numedides waved the Khitan away. "Begone, yellow dog, and tell your master to do as he thinks best. Now let us continue, girls."

Thus, later that night, a courier set out along the far-flung road to General Procas' headquarters on the Argossean frontier. The message, which bore the seal of King Numedides, would in less than a fortnight loose the fury of the Border Legion upon the leaderless men who followed the Lion banner.

In Conan's tent, Alcina opened her traveling chest and dug out a page's costume, into which she changed. Under the garments in the chest lay a small copper casket, which she opened by twisting the silver dragon that bestrode the lid. The casket contained a choice assortment of rings, bracelets, necklaces, earrings and other gem-encrusted finery. Alcina burrowed into the jewelery until she found a small oblong of copper, inscribed in Argossean. This token—a forgery provided by Quesado—entitled the bearer to change horses at the royal post stations. She made a quick selection of the jewelery, tucking the better pieces into her girdle, and filled the small purse depending from her belt with coins of gold and silver.

Then she extinguished the candle and boldly left the darkened tent. Demurely she addressed the sentry: "The general sleeps; but he has asked me to bear an urgent message to the court of Argos. Will you kindly order the grooms to saddle a horse, forthwith, and fetch it hither?"

The sentry called the corporal of the guard, who sent a man to comply with Alcina's request, while the girl waited silently at the entrance to the tent. The soldiers, who were used to the comings and goings of the general's mistress and admired her splendid figure and easy ways, hastened to do her bidding.

When the horse was brought, she mounted swiftly and followed the sentry assigned to her beyond the limits of the camp. Then, at a spanking trot, she vanished into the moonlit distance.

Four days later, Alcina arrived in Messantia. She hastened to Quesado's hideaway, where she found the spy's replacement, Fadius the Kothian, feeding Quesado's carrier pigeons. She asked:

"Pray, where is Quesado?"

"Have you not heard?" replied Fadius. "He's an ambassador now, too proud to spare time for the likes of us. He's been here but once since he arrived on his embassy."

"Well, grandee or no grandee, I must see him at once. I bear news of the greatest import."

Grumbling, Fadius led Alcina to the hostelry in Messantia where the Aquilonians lodged. Quesado's servant was pulling off his master's boots and preparing him for bed when Alcina and Fadius burst in unannounced.

"Damme!" cried Quesado. "What sort of ill-bred rabble are you, to intrude on a gentleman retiring for the night?"

"You know well enough who we are," said Alcina. "I came to tell you Conan is dead."

Quesado paused with his mouth open, then closed it slowly. "Well!" he said at last. "That casts a different light on many matters. Pull on my boots again, Narses. I must go to the palace forthwith. What has befallen, Mistress Alcina?"

A little time later, Quesado presented himself at the palace with a peremptory demand to see the king. The Zingaran intended to urge an instant attack on Conan's army by the forces of Argos. He felt sure that the rebels, demoralized by the fall of their leader, would crumble before any vigorous assault.

Fate, however, ordained that events should march to a different tune. Roused from slumber, King Milo flew into a rage at Quesado's insolence in demanding a midnight audience.

"His Majesty," reported the head page to Quesado, "commands that you depart instanter and return at a more seemly time. He suggests an hour before noon tomorrow."

Quesado flushed with the anger of frustration. Looking down his nose, he said: "My good man, you do not seem to realize who and what I am."

The page laughed, matching Quesado's impudence with his own. "Aye, sir, we all know who you are—and what you were." Derisive grins spread to the faces of the guards flanking the page, who continued: "Now pray depart hence, and speedily, on pain of my sovereign lord's displeasure!"

"You shall rue those words, varlet!" snarled Quesado, turning away. He tramped the cobbled streets to his former headquarters on the waterfront, where he found Fadius and Alcina awaiting him. There he prepared a furious dispatch to the King of Aquilonia, telling of Milo's rebuff, and sent it on its way wired to the leg of a pigeon.

In a few days, the former spy's report reached Vibius Latro, who brought it to his king's attention. Numedides, seldom able to restrain his passions under the easiest of circumstances, read of the recalcitrance of the King of Argos toward his mighty neighbor and sent another courier posthaste to General Amulius Procas. This dispatch did more than authorize an incursion into Argos, as had the previous message. In exigent terms, it commanded the general at once to attack across the borders of Argos, with whatever force he needed, to stamp out the last embers of the rebellion.

Procas, a tough and canny old campaigner, winced at the royal command. On the night that followed his victorious battles on the Alimane, he had quickly withdrawn from Argossean territory the detachments he had sent across the river to harry the fleeing rebels. Those incursions could be excused on grounds of hot pursuit. But now, if he mounted a new invasion, the open violation of the border would almost certainly turn King Milo's sympathies from cautious neutrality into open hostility to the royal Aquilonian cause.

But the royal command admitted of no argument or refusal. If he wished his head to continue to ride his shoulders, Procas must attack, although every instinct in his soldierly bosom cried out against this hasty, ill-timed instruction.

Procas delayed his advance for several days, hoping that the king, on second thoughts, would countermand his order. But no communication came, and Procas dared wait no longer. And so, on a bright spring morning, Amulius Procas crossed the Alimane in force. The river, which had subsided somewhat from its flood, offered no obstacle to his squadrons of glittering, panoplied knights, stolid mailed spearmen and leather-coated archers. They splashed across and marched implacably up the winding road that led to Saxula Pass through the Rabirian range, and thence to the rebel camp on the Plain of Pallos.

Not until the morning after Alcina's departure did Conan's officers learn of the fall of their leader. They gathered round him, laid him on his bed, and searched him for wounds. Dexitheus, still limping on a walking stick, sniffed at the dregs in the goblet from which Conan had drunk Alcina's potion.

"That drink," he said, "was laced with the juice of the purple lotus of Stygia. By rights, our general should be as dead as King Tuthamon; yet he lives, albeit no more than a living corpse with open eyes."

Publius flicked his fingers as he did mental sums and mused: "Perchance the poisoner used only so much of the drug as would suffice to slay an ordinary man, unmindful of Conan's great size and strength."

" 'Twas that green-eyed witch!" cried Trocero. "I've never trusted her, and her disappearance last night proclaims her guilt. Were she in my power, I'd burn her at the stake!"

Dexitheus turned on the count. "Green eyes, quotha? A woman with green eyes?"

"Aye, as green as emeralds. But what of it? Surely you know Conan's con-cubine, the fair Alcina."

Dexitheus shook his head with a frown of foreboding. "I heard that our general had taken a dancing girl from the wineshops of Argos," he murmured, "but I try to ignore such whoredoms among my sons, and Conan tactfully kept her out of my sight. Woe unto our cause! For the lord Mitra warned me in a dream to beware a green-eyed shadow hovering near our leader, although I knew not that the evil one already walked amongst us. Woe unto me, who failed to confide the warning to my comrades!"

"Enough of this," said Publius. "Conan lives, and we can thank our gods that our fair poisoner is no arithmetician. Let none but his squires attend him or even enter the tent. We must tell the men that he is ill of a minor tisick, whilst we continue to rebuild our force. If he recovers, he recovers; but meanwhile you must take command, Trocero."

The Poitanian count nodded somberly. "I'll do what I can, since I am second in command. You, Publius, must mend the nets of your spy system, so that we shall have warning of Procas' moves. It's time for morning roll call, so I must be off. I'll drill the lads as hard as Conan ever drilled them, aye and more!"

By the time Procas began his invasion, the Lions again had their watching eyes and listening ears abroad. Reports of the strength of the invaders reached the leaders of the rebel army, who had gathered in Conan's tent. Trocero, wearing the silvery badge of age and the lines of weariness but self-assured withal, asked Publius:

"What know we of the numbers of the foe?"

Publius bent his head to work sums on his waxen tablets. When he raised his eyes, his expression showed alarm. "Thrice our strength and more," he said heavily. "This is a black day, my friends. We can do little save make a final stand."

"Be of good cheer!" said the count, slapping the stout treasurer on the back. "You'd never make a general, Publius; you'd assure the soldiers they were beaten before the fray began." He turned to Dexitheus. "How does our patient?"

"He regains some slight awareness, but as yet he cannot move. I now think he will live, praise Mitra."

"Well, if he cannot sit a horse when the battle trumpet blows, I must sit it for him. Have we any word of Prospero?"

Publius and Dexitheus shook their heads. Trocero shrugged, saying: "Then we must make do with what we have. The foe will close within striking distance on the morrow, and we must needs decide whether to fight or flee."

Down from the mountains streamed the armored cavalry and infantry of the Border Legion. A swirl of galloping scouts preceded them, and in their midst rode General Amulius Procas in his chariot. Drawn up to confront them, the rebels formed their battle lines in the midst of the plain.

The still air offered no respite from the myriad fears and silent prayers of the waiting men. The broad front of the superior Aquilonian force allowed Count Trocero no opportunity for clever flanking or enveloping moves. Yet, to retreat now would mean the instant dissolution of the rebel force. The count knew there could be no shrewdly timed withdrawal, with rear-guard actions to delay pursuit. Such a fighting retreat was only for well-trained, self-confident troops. These men, discouraged by their fortune on the Alimane, would simply flee, every man for himself, while the Aquilonian light horse rode down the fugitives, slaying and slaying until nightfall sheltered the survivors beneath its dragon wings.

Trocero, scanning the oncoming host from his command post on a hillock, presently signaled his groom to fetch his charger. He adjusted a strap on his armor and heaved himself into the saddle. To the few hundred horsemen who gathered around him, he said:

"You know our plan, my friends. 'Tis a slim chance, but our only one."

For Trocero had decided that their only hope lay in a suicidal charge into the Aquilonian array, in a mad effort to reach Amulius Procas himself. He knew that the enemy commander, a stout man of middle years slowed by ancient wounds, found riding hard on his aging joints and preferred to travel by chariot. He knew, too, that the general's charioteer would have difficulty in maneuvring the clumsy vehicle in the press of battle. Thus, if the rebel horse could by some miracle reach and slay the Aquilonian general, his troops might falter and break.

The outlook, as Trocero had said, was black, but the plan was the best he could devise. Meanwhile he strove to give his subordinates no sign of his discomfiture. He laughed and joked as if he faced certain victory instead of a forlorn attempt to vanquish thrice their number of the world's best soldiery.

Once again, Destiny intervened on the side of the rebels, in the royal person of Milo, King of Argos. Even before the Aquilonian invasion began, an Argossean spy, killing three horses in his haste to reach Messantia, brought word to the court of Numedides's command to violate the territory of Argos. Thus King Milo learned of the planned attack as soon as did the rebel commanders. Already affronted by the arrogance of Ambassador Quesado, the usually even-tempered Milo flew into a rage. At once he commanded the nearest division of his army to speed north on forced marches to intercept the invasion.

In a calmer moment, Milo might have temporized. Since he did not think that Numedides meant to seize a portion of his land, as the late King Vilerus had done, he had sound reasons for delaying any irrevocable action. But, by the time his temper had cooled, his troops were already on the march northward, and with his usual stubbornness the king refused to change his decision.

Amulius Procas had halted his army and was meticulously ordering his troops for an assault when a breathless scout galloped up to his chariot.

"General!" he cried, gasping for breath. "A great cloud of dust is rising from the southern road; it is as if another army approached!"

Procas made the scout repeat his message. Then, blueing the air with curses, he tugged off his helmet and hurled it with a clang to the floor of his chariot. It was as he had feared; King Milo had got wind of the invasion and was sending troops to block it. To his aides he barked:

"Tell the men to stand at ease, and see that they have water. Order the scouts to swing around the rebel army and probe to southward, to learn the numbers and composition of the approaching force. Pitch a tent, and call my high officers to a conference."

When, an hour later, the scouts reported that a thousand cavalry were on the march, Amulius Procas found himself caught on the horns of a dilemma. Without explicit orders from his king, he dared not provoke Argos into open warfare. Neither did he dare disobey a direct command from Numedides without some overriding reason.

True, Procas's army could doubtless crush the rebels and chase Milo's cavalry back to Messantia. But such an action would presage a major war, for which Aquilonia was ill-prepared. While his country was the larger and more populous kingdom, her king was, at least, eccentric; and his rule had gravely weakened mighty Aquilonia. The Argosseans, moreover, fighting with righteous indignation an invader on their native soil, might with the aid of a small rebel force, like that assembled beneath the Lion banner, tip the scales against Procas's homeland.

Neither could Procas retreat. Since his troops outnumbered the combined rebel and Argossean forces, King Numedides might readily read his withdrawal as an act of cowardice or treachery and shorten him by a head for his disobedience.

As the sun rode down the western sky, Procas, deep in discussion with his officers, still delayed his decision. At last he said:

"'Tis too late to start an action this day. We shall withdraw to northward, where we have left the baggage train, and set up a fortified camp. Send a man to order the engineers to begin digging." Trocero, narrowly watching the royalists from his rise, had long since dismounted. Beside him stood Publius, munching on a fowl's leg. At last the treasurer said:

"What in Mitra's name is Procas doing? He had us where he wanted us, and now he pulls back and pitches camp. Is he mad? For aught he knows, we might slip away in the coming night, or steal past him to enter Aquilonia."

Trocero shrugged. "Belike the report we had, of Argosseans approaching, has something to do with his actions. It remains to be seen whether these Argossean horsemen mean to help or harm us. We could be caught between the two forces and ground to powder, unless Procas counts on the Argosseans to do his dirty work for him."

Even as the count spoke, hoofbeats summoned his glance southward across the plain. Soon a small party of mounted men cantered up the rise—a group of Argosseans, guided in by a rebel cavalryman. Two of these new arrivals dismounted with a clank of armor and strode forward. One was tall, lean, and leathery of visage, with the look of a professional soldier. His companion was younger and short of stature, with a wide-cheeked, snub-nosed face and bright, interested eyes. He wore a gilded cuirass and a purple cloak edged with scarlet, and purple-and-scarlet were the plumes that danced on the crest of his helm.

The lean veteran spoke first: "Hail, Count Trocero! I am Arcadio, senior captain of the Royal Guard, at your service, sir. May I present Prince Cassio of Argos, heir apparent to the throne? We desire a council with your general, Conan the Cimmerian."

Nodding to the officer and making a slight bow to the Prince of Argos, Trocero said: "I remember you well, Prince Cassio, as a mischievous child and a harum-scarum youth. As for General Conan, I regret to say he is indisposed. But you may state the purpose of your visit to me as second-in-command."

"Our purpose, Count Trocero," said the prince, "is to thwart this Aquilonian violation of our territorial integrity. To that endeavor, my royal father has sent me hither with such force as could readily be mustered. I assume my officers and I may consider you and your followers as allies?"

Trocero smiled. "Thrice welcome, Prince Cassio! From your aspect, you have had a long and dusty ride. Will you and Captain Arcadio come to our command tent for refreshment, while your escort take their ease? Our wine has long since gone, but we still have ale."

On the way back to the tent, Trocero spoke privately to Publius: "This explains Procas's withdrawal when he all but had us in his jaws. He dare not attack for fear of starting an unauthorized war with Argos, and he dare not retreat lest he be branded a poltroon. So he camps where he is, awaiting—"

"Trocero!" A deep roar came from within the tent. "Who is it you are talking to, besides Publius? Fetch him in!"

"That's General Conan," said Trocero, dissembling his startlement. "Will you step inside, gentlemen?"

They found Conan, in shirt and short breeks, propped up on his bunk. Under the ministrations of Dexitheus, he had recovered full consciousness, his mighty frame having thrown off the worst effects of a draught that would have doomed an ordinary man. While he could think and speak, he could do little else; for the residue of the poison still chained his brawny limbs. Unable to rise without help, he chafed at his confinement.

"Gods and devils!" he fumed. "Could I but stand and lift a sword, I'd show Procas how to cut and thrust! And who are these Argosseans?"

Trocero introduced Prince Cassio and Captain Arcadio and recounted Procas's latest move. Conan snarled:

"This I will see for myself. Squires! Raise me to my feet. Procas may be shamming a withdrawal, the better to surprise us by a night attack."

With an arm around the neck of each squire, Conan tottered to the entrance. The sun, impaled upon the peaks of the Rabirian Hills to westward, spilled dark shadows down the mountainsides. In the middle distance, the departing rays struck scarlet sparks from the armor of the Aquilonians as they labored to set up a camp. The tap of mallets on tent pegs came softly through the evening air.

"Will Procas seek a parley, think you?" asked Conan. The others shrugged.

"He has sent no message yet; he may never do so," said Trocero. "We must wait and see."

"We've waited all day," growled Conan, "keeping our lads standing in harness in the sun. I, for one, would that something happened—anything, to end this dawdling."

"Methinks our general is about to have his wish," murmured Dexitheus, shading his eyes with his hand as he peered at the distant royalist camp. The other stared at him.

"What now, sir priest?" said Conan.

"Behold!" said Dexitheus, pointing.

"Ishtar!" breathed Captain Arcadio. "Fry my guts if they're not running away!"

And so they were; if not running, they were at least beginning an orderly retreat. Trumpets sounded, thin and far away. Instead of continuing to strengthen the fortification of their camp, the men of the Border Legion, antlike in the distance, were striking the tents they had just set up, loading the supply wagons, and streaming out, company by company, toward the pass in the Rabirian Hills. Conan and his comrades looked at one another in perplexity.

The cause of this withdrawal soon transpired. Marching briskly from the east, a fourth host came around the slope of a hill. More than fifteen hundred strong, as Trocero estimated them, the newcomers deployed and advanced on a broad front, ready for battle.

A rebel scout, lashing his horse up the slope, threw himself off his mount, saluted Conan, and gasped: "My lord General, they fly the leopards of Poitain and the arms of Baron Groder of Aquilonia!"

"Crom and Mitra!" whispered Conan. Then his face cleared and his laughter echoed among the hills. For it was indeed Prospero with the rebel force that he had searched for in the east.

"No wonder Procas runs!" said Trocero. "Now that we outnumber him, he can do so without arousing his sovereign's ire. He'll tell Numedides that three armies would have surrounded him at once and overwhelmed him."

"General Conan," said Dexitheus, "you must return to your bed to rest. We cannot afford to have you suffer a relapse."

As the squires lowered Conan to his pallet, the Cimmerian whispered: "Prospero, Prospero! For this I will make you a knight of the throne, if ever Aquilonia be mine!"

In Fadius's dingy room in Messantia, Alcina sat alone, holding her obsidian amulet before her and watching the alternate black-and-white bands of the time candle. Fadius was out prowling the nighted streets of the city; Alcina had brusquely ordered him forth so that she could privately commune with her master.

The flickering flame sank lower as the candle burned down through one of the black stripes in the wax. As the last of the sable band dissolved into molten wax and the flame wavered above a white band, the witch-dancer raised her talisman and focused her thoughts. Faintly, like words spoken in a dream, there came into her receptive mind the dry tones of Thulandra Thuu; while before her, barely visible in the dim-lit chamber, appeared a vision of the sorcerer himself, seated in his iron chair.

Thulandra Thuu's speech rustled so softly through Alcina's mind that it demanded rapt attention, together with a constant surveillance of the lips and the gestures of the vision, to grasp the magician's message: "You have done well, my daughter. Has aught befallen in Messantia?"

She shook her head, and the ghostly whisper continued: "Then I have another task for you. With the morn's first light, you shall don your page's garb, take horse, and follow the road north—"

Alcina gave a small cry of dismay. "Must I wear those ugly rags and plunge again into the wilderness, with ants and beetles for bedmates? I beg you, Master, let me stay here and be a woman yet a while!"

The sorcerer raised a sardonic eyebrow. "You prefer the fleshpots of Messantia?" he responded.

She nodded vigorously.

That cannot be, alas. Your duties there are finished, and I need you to watch the Border Legion and its general. If you find the going rough, bear in mind the future glories I have promised you.

"The troops dispatched by the Argossean King should now have reached the Plain of Pallos. Ere the sun rises twice again, Amulius Procas will in all likelihood have concluded a retreat back across the Alimane into Poitain. He will, I predict, cross at the ford of Nogara; so set you forth, swinging wide of the armies, to approach this place from the north, traveling southward on the road from Cularion. Then report to me again at the next favorable conjunction."

The murmuring voice fell silent and the filmy vision faded, leaving Alcina alone and brooding.

Then came a thunderous knock, and in lurched Fadius. The Kothian had spent more of his time and Vibius Latro's money in a Messantian wineshop than was prudent. Arms out, he staggered toward Alcina, babbling:

"Come, my little passion flower! I weary of sleeping on the bare floor, and 'tis time you accorded your comrade the same kindness you extend to barbarian bullies—"

Alcina leaped to her feet and backed away. "Have a care, Master Fadius!" she warned. "I take not kindly to presumption from such a one as you!"

"Come on, my pretty," mumbled Fadius. "I'll not hurt you—"

Alcina's hand flicked to the bodice of her gown. As by magic, a slender dagger appeared in her jeweled hand. "Stand back!" she cried. "One prick of this, and you're a dying spy!"

The threat penetrated Fadius's sodden wits, and he recoiled from the blade. He knew the lightning speed with which the dancer-witch could move and stab. "But—but—my dear little—"

"Get out!" said Alcina. "And come not back until you're sober!"

Cursing under his breath, Fadius went. In the chamber, among the cages of roosting pigeons, Alcina rummaged in her chest for the garments in which she would set out upon the morrow.

chapter  vi

The Chamber of Sphinxes

Between sunset and midnight, the men of Argos, rank upon rank, marched into camp amid ruffles of drums and rebel cheers. Salted Messantian meat, coarse barley bread and skins of ale from the rebels' dwindling stores were handed round to Baron Groder's starveling regiment and Prospero's weary troop. Horses were watered, hobbled, and turned out to pasture on the lush grass, as the rebels and their new allies lit campfires and settled down to their evening repast. Soon the fitful glow of fires scattered about the Plain of Pallos rivaled the twinkling stars upon the plain of heaven; and the shouts and laughter of four thousand men, wafted northward on the evening breeze, crashed like the dissonant chords of a dirge on the ears of Procas' retreating regulars.

In the command tent, Prince Cassio, Captain Arcadio, and the rebel leaders gathered near Conan's bed to share a frugal meal and draft the morrow's plans.

"We'll all after them at dawn!" cried Trocero.

"Nay," the young prince replied. The instructions from my royal father are explicit. Only if General Procas leads his forces further into our territory are we to join battle with him. The king hopes our presence will deter Procas from such rashness; and so it seems, since the Aquilonians are now in flight."

Conan said nothing, but the volcanic blaze in his blue eyes betrayed his angry disappointment. The prince glanced at him, half in awe and half in sympathy.

"I comprehend your feelings, General Conan," he said gently. "But you must understand our position, too. We do not wish to war with Aquilonia, which outnumbers us two to one. Indeed, we have risked enough already, giving haven to your force within our borders."

With a hand that trembled from effort, Conan grasped his cup of ale and brought it slowly to his lips. Sweat beaded his forehead, as if the flagon weighed half a hundredweight. He spilled some of the contents, drank the rest, and let the empty vessel fall to the floor.

"Then let us pursue Procas on our own," urged Trocero. "We can harry him back across the Alimane; and every man we fell will be one fewer to oppose us when we raise Poitain. If the survivors stand to make a battle of it — well, victory lies ever on the laps of the fickle gods."

Conan was tempted. Every belligerent instinct in his barbaric soul enticed him to send his men in headlong pursuit of the royalists, to worry them like a pack of hounds, to pick them off by ones and twos all the way back beyond the Alimane. The Rabirian range seemed designed by Destiny for just the sort of action he could wage against the outnumbering invaders. Cloven into a thousand gullies and ravines, those wrinkled hills and soaring peaks begged him to ambush every fleeing soldier.

But should Procas's troops turn to make a stand, Fate might not grant her guerdon to Conan's rebels. They were poor in provisions and weak in weaponry even now; and the regiment that Prospero had rescued was worn and weary, on gaunt, shambling mounts, after days of hiding out and foraging in the field. Moreover, a general who cannot ride a horse or wield a sword cannot greatly inspire his followers to deeds of dash and daring. Enfeebled as he still was by Alcina's poison, Conan knew full well that he had no choice except to remain in camp or to travel in a litter as a spectator at the fray.

As night slipped into misty dawn and trumpets sounded the reveille, Conan, supported by two squires, looked out across the waking camp and pondered his position. He must not let Procas get back to Aquilonia unscathed. At the same time, to overcome the mighty Border Legion, he must devise some unexpected manner of warfare — some innovation to give advantage to his lesser numbers. He required a force that was mobile and swiftly maneuvrable, yet able to strike the foe from a distance.

As Conan stared at the mustering men, his brooding gaze alighted upon a single Bossonian, who flung himself upon a horse and galloped toward the palisaded gate. He must bear a message to the sentries at the circumference of the camp, Conan mused, and that message must be urgent; for the fellow had not bothered to remove the unstrung bow that hung slantwise across his shoulders nor to discard the heavy quiver of arrows that slapped against his thigh.

Years of service with the King of Turan flooded Conan's memory. In that army, mounted archers formed the largest single contingent: men who could shoot their double-curved bows of horn and sinew from the back of a galloping steed as accurately as most men could shoot with feet firmly fixed upon the ground. Such a skill his Bossonian archers could not master without a decade of practice; and besides, the Bossonian longbow was much too cumbersome to be handled from horseback.

Suddenly, in his mind's eye, Conan saw a host of mounted archers pursuing the fleeing foe until, coming within range, they dismounted to loose shaft after deadly shaft, before spurring away when at last the goaded enemy turned to engage their tormentors. Conan's explosive roar of laughter startled his camp servants, who gaped like yokels at a circus while Captain Alaricus ran to waken the physician-priest.

When Dexitheus, clad in scanty clothing, rushed to Conan's tent, Conan grinned at his bewilderment.

"No," he chuckled, "the purple lotus has not addled my wits, my friend. But the lord Mitra, or Crom, or some such blessed god has given me an inspiration. Send someone posthaste to bid the Argossean leaders hither."

When Prince Cassio and Captain Arcadio, already armed and armored, plodded up the slope to the headquarters tent, Conan roared a greeting, adding: "You say King Milo forbids you to attack the retreating Aquilonians. Does the royal fiat encompass your horses, too?"

"Our *horses*, General?" repeated Arcadio blankly.

Conan nodded impatiently. "Aye, your beasts. Quickly, Captain, an answer, if you will. Our steeds—the few we have—are underfed, as you can see by counting their poor ribs. But yours are fresh and of an excellent breed. Lend us five hundred mounts, and we'll forswear the service of a single Argossean soldier to send Amulius Procas home with his tail between his legs."

As Conan outlined his plan, Prince Cassio grinned. More and ever more he liked this grim-visaged barbarian from the North, who made war in ways as ingenious as implausible.

"Lend him five hundred horses, Arcadio," he said. "The king, my father, said naught of that."

The Argossean officer clanked off to issue orders. And presently, below them on the flat where the Bossonian archers lined up for morning roll call, ten-score Argossean wranglers led saddled horses into the field behind them. Trocero and Prospero converged upon the startled and disordered foot soldiers and by their authority restored them to disciplined ranks.

"Fetch me my stallion and strap me to the saddle," growled Conan. "I must explain my plan to those who'll carry it out."

"General!" cried Dexitheus. "You should not, in your present state—"

"Spare me your cautions, Reverence. For a month the men have seen me not and doubtless wonder if I'm still alive."

As Conan's squires, with many helping hands, strained to boost Conan's massive body into the saddle, the Cimmerian chafed at the sluggishness that chained his mighty limbs. His blue eyes blazed with the fire of unconquerable will, and his broad brows drew together with the fury of his effort to drive vitality back into his flaccid thews. Strive as he would, the blood flowed but feebly through his numbed flesh; for Alcina had concocted the deadly draught with consummate care.

At length his squires strapped Conan to his saddle, he raving oaths the while and calling upon his somber Northern gods to avenge this foul indignity. And though the palsy shook his burly body, his eyes, seething with elemental fury, commanded every upturned face to show him neither courtesy nor pity, but only the respect that was his due.

All this Prince Cassio watched, held spellbound by amazement. Back in Messantia, the courtiers had sneered at Conan as a savage, an untutored barbarian whom the Aquilonian rebel nobles had unaccountably chosen to manage their revolt. Now the prince sensed the primal power of the man, his deep reservoirs of elemental vigor. He perceived the Cimmerian's driving purpose, his originality of thought, his dynamic presence—qualities that transformed nobles and common soldiers alike into willing captives of his personality. This man, thought Cassio, was created to command—was born to be a king.

Supported by a mounted squire on either side, Conan paced his charger slowly down the ranks toward the battalion of Bossonian archers. Although his face contorted with the effort, he managed to raise a hand in greeting as he passed row upon row of loyal followers. The men burst into frantic cheers.

Half a league to the north, a pair of royalist scouts, left behind to watch the rebel army, were breaking fast along the road that led to Saxula Pass. The cheers came faintly to their ears, and they exchanged glances of alarm.

"What betides yonder?" asked the younger man.

The other shaded his eyes. " 'Tis too far to see, but something must have happened to hearten the rebel host. One of us had best report to General Procas. I'll go; you stay."

The second speaker gulped his last bite, rose, untied his horse from a nearby tree, and mounted. The morning air echoed the fading drumbeat of hooves as he vanished up the road.

Quieting his men with a small motion of his upraised hand, Conan addressed the lines of archers. They were selected, he told them, from the entire army to inflict destruction on the retreating invaders. They were to move on silent hooves against pockets of the enemy and then dismount and nock their shafts. Shooting from cover in twos and threes, they could pick off scores of fleeing men; and when at last the enemy turned at bay, they, unencumbered by heavy armor, could quickly remount and soon outdistance the heavy-laden Aquilonian knights sent in pursuit.

Each squad would be commanded by an experienced cavalryman, who would make certain that the beasts were well handled and would hold the horses while the archers were dismounted. As for those who had seldom ridden—here Conan smiled a trifle grimly—they had but to grip the saddle or the horse's mane; for such temporarily mounted infantry, fine horsemanship was unimportant.

Under the command of an Aquilonian soldier-of-fortune named Pallantides, who had once trained with Turanian horse-archers and who had lately deserted from the royalists, the newly mounted Bossonians swept out of the camp at a steady canter and headed north along the climbing road that led toward Aquilonia.

They caught up with the rear guard of the royalist army in the foothills of the Rabirians, short of Saxula Pass; for Procas' retreat was slowed by his baggage train and his companies of plodding infantry. Spying the enemy, the Bossonians spread out, eased their horses through the brush to shooting range, and then went to work. A score of royalist spearmen fell, screaming or silent, or cursed less lethal wounds, before the clatter of armored horsemen told the rebel archers that Procas's cavalry was coming to disperse the attack and to cover his withdrawal. Thereupon the Bossonians unstrung their bows and, dashing back to their tethered beasts, silently mounted and scattered through the forest. Their only casualty was an injury to one archer who, unused to horseback, fell off and broke his collarbone.

For the next three days, the Bossonians harried the retreating Aquilonians, like hounds snapping at the heels of fleeing criminals. They struck from the shadows; and when the royalists turned to challenge them, they were gone — hidden in a thousand hollows etched by wind and weather upon the wrinkled face of the terrain.

Amulius Procas and his officers cursed themselves hoarse, but little could they do. An arrow would whistle from behind a boulder. Sometimes it missed, merely causing the marching men to flinch and duck. Sometimes it buried itself in a horse's flank, inciting the stricken animal to rear and plunge, unseating its rider. Sometimes a soldier screamed in pain as a shaft transfixed his body; or a horseman, with a clang of armor, toppled from his saddle to lie where he fell. From the heights above, unseen in the gloaming, a sudden rain of arrows would slay or cripple thrice a dozen men.

Amulius Procas had few choices. He could not camp near Saxula Pass, because there little open ground and inadequate supplies of water could be found. Neither could he attack in close order, where his weight of numbers and armor would give him the advantage, because the enemy refused to close with him. If he threw his whole army against them, he could doubtless sweep away these pestilent rebels like chaff upon the wind; but such an action would carry him back to the Plain of Pallos and thus embroil him with the Argosseans.

So there was nothing for Amulius Procas to do but plod grimly on, sending out his light horse to drive away the enemy whenever they revealed their presence by a flight of arrows. Numerically his losses were trivial, only a fraction of the death toll of a joined battle. But the constant attrition depressed his men's morale; and the wind of chill foreboding, sweeping across his heart, whispered that King Numedides would not forget and still less forgive the failure of the expedition launched at the king's express command.

In the throat of Saxula Pass, an avalanche of boulders crashed down upon the hapless royalists. Procas glumly ordered the wreckage cleared, the smashed wagons abandoned, and the mortally wounded men and beasts mercifully put to the sword. On the far side of the pass, his troops moved faster, but the harassment continued unabated.

Procas realized that his Cimmerian opponent was a master of this irregular warfare; and he shook with shame that his enforced withdrawal had spurred the barbarian's fecund inventiveness. This stain upon his honor, he swore, he would wash out in rebel blood.

On the third day of the retreat, as the gray skies turned to lead, the disheartened, exhausted royalists gathered on the southern bank of the Alimane at the ford of Nogara. There for a time Procas lingered, tormented by indecision. Even though the floods of spring had subsided, the river's reach invited an attack when his fording men were least disposed to counter it. It would be a cruel jest of the capricious gods to ensnare the Aquilonian general in the very trap in which, not two months earlier, he had all but crushed the rebels. Moreover, to essay a crossing in the gloom of coming night would involve an almost certain loss of men and equipment.

Yet to pitch a camp on the Argossean side would doom sentries and sleeping men to death by flights of phantom arrows from the forest. Procas gnawed his lip. Since his troops could not effectively defend themselves against such tactics, the sooner he led them across the Alimane the safer they would sleep. Although the river was broad and swift, making the fords formidable, it would at least place his army beyond bowshots from the southern shore.

While these thoughts shambled through the mind of Amulius Procas, one of his officers approached the chariot in which he stood, atop a small rise along the river bank. The officer, a heavy-shouldered giant of a man—a Bossonian from his accent—with a surly expression on his coarse-featured face, saluted.

"Sir, we await your orders to begin the fording," he said. "The longer we stay, the more of our men will those damnable hidden archers wing."

"I am aware of that, Gromel," said the general stiffly. Then he heaved a sigh and made a curt gesture. "Very well, get on with it! Naught's to be gained by loitering here. But it goes against my grain to let these starveling rascals harry us home without repaying them in their own coin. Were it not for political considerations . . ."

Gromel raked the hills behind them with a contemptuous glance. "Curse these politics, which tie the soldier's hands!" he growled. "The cowards will not stand and fight, knowing we should wipe them out. So there is nothing for it save to gather on the soil of Poitain, there to stand ready to crush them if they essay the fords again."

"We shall be ready," said Procas sternly. "Sound the trumpets."

The retreat across the Alimane proceeded in good order, although night dimmed the twilight before the last company splashed into the river bed. As the men moved away from the southern bank, ten-score archers, lurking in the undergrowth, stepped into view with bows strung and arrows nocked.

Procas had left his chariot to heave himself, grunting with pain from ancient wounds, into the saddle of his charger. Commanding a small rear guard of light horse, the dour old veteran was among the last to wade his steed into the darkling flood, while arrows from shore whistled past like angry insects.

In midstream the general suddenly exclaimed, clapping a hand to his leg. At his cry, the Bossonian officer who had addressed him earlier rode nigh and reined in. He opened thick lips to ask what was amiss, then spied the rebel arrow that had pierced the old man's thigh above the knee. A gleam of satisfaction flickered in Gromel's porcine eyes and quickly vanished; for he was a man implacably bent on pursuit of promotion, however he might attain it.

Stoically, Procas sat his steed across the river; but once amid the bushes that fringed the northern shore, he suffered his aides to lift him from the beast while Gromel trotted ahead to summon the surgeon.

After plucking forth the barb and binding the wound, the physician said: "It will be many days, General, ere you will be well enough to travel again."

"Very well," said Procas stolidly. "Pitch my tent on yonder hillock. Here we shall camp and let the rebels come to us, if they've got the stomach for it."

Ghostly among the shadows of the trees nearby, a slender figure clad in the garments of a page, much worn and travel-stained, watched and listened. Had any viewer with catlike eyes perceived the swelling rondure of that youthful figure, he would have recognized a lithe and lovely woman. Now, with a mirthless smile, she unhitched her horse and quietly led the animal to a prudent distance from the camp that the Border Legion was hastily erecting.

That his rival, Amulius Procas, had been wounded during a cowardly retreat before a rabble would be pleasing news for Thulandra Thuu, thought the Lady Alcina. Now that the mighty Cimmerian was dead, Procas had served his purpose and could safely be sacrificed to her master's vaulting ambition. She must get word to the wizard as soon as the aspects of the stars and planets again permitted the use of her obsidian talisman. She melted into the darkness and vanished from the scene.

Bending toward his magical mirror of burnished obsidian, Thulandra Thuu learned with delight of the injury to General Procas. As the image of Alcina faded from the gleaming glass, the sorcerer thoughtfully stroked the bridge of his hawklike nose. Reaching out a slender hand, he raised a metal mallet and smote the skull-shaped gong that hung beside his iron throne, and its sonorous note echoed dully through the purple-shrouded chamber.

Presently the draperies drew aside, revealing Hsiao the Khitan. Arms tucked into the voluminous sleeves of his green silk robe, he bowed, silently awaiting his master's commands.

"Does the Count of Thune still wait upon me in the ante-chamber?" the sorcerer enquired.

"Master, Count Ascalante attends your pleasure," murmured the yellow servant.

Thulandra Thuu nodded. "Excellent! I will speak to him forthwith. Inform him that I shall receive him in the Chamber of the Sphinxes, and go yourself to notify the king that I shall presently request an audience upon urgent business of state. You have my leave to go."

Hsiao bowed and withdrew, and the draperies fell back into place, concealing the door through which the Khitan had passed.

The Chamber of the Sphinxes, which Thulandra Thuu had converted to his own use from a disused room in the palace, was aptly named. Tomblike in its barrenness, it was walled and floored in roseate marble and contained no visible furnishings beyond a limestone seat, placed against the farther wall. This seat, shaped like a throne, was upheld by a pair of stone supports carved in the likeness of feline monsters with human heads. This motif was repeated in the matching tapestries that hung in rich array against the wall behind the throne. Here, cunningly crafted in glittering threads, two catlike beasts with manlike faces, bearded and imperious, stared out with cold and supercilious eyes. The only light in this chill chamber was provided by a pair of copper torcheres, the flames of which danced in the silver mirrors set into the wall behind them.

Not unlike the sphinxes was Ascalante, officer-adventurer and self-styled Count of Thune. A tall and supple man, elegantly clad in plum-colored velvet, he prowled around the chamber with a feline grace. For all his military bearing and debonair deportment, his eyes, like those of the embroidered monsters, were cold and supercilious; but they were wary, too, and a trifle apprehensive.

For some time now, Ascalante had awaited an audience with the all-powerful sorcerer of unknown origin. Although Thulandra Thuu had recalled Ascalante from the eastern frontier and demanded his daily presence at court, the magician had let him cool his heels outside the audience chamber for several days. Now it might be that his fortunes were about to change.

Suddenly Ascalante froze, his hand instinctively darting to the hilt of his dagger. One of the tapestries lifted to reveal a narrow doorway, within which stood a slender, dark-skinned man, silently regarding him. The cool, amused intelligence behind those hooded eyes seemed capable of reading a man's thoughts as if they were painted on his forehead. Recovering his composure, Ascalante made a courtly obeisance as Thulandra Thuu entered the room. The sorcerer bore an ornately carven staff, which writhed with intertwined inscriptions in characters unknown to Ascalante.

Thulandra strode unhurriedly across the chamber and seated himself on the sphinx-supported throne. He acknowledged the other's bow with a nod and the shadow of a smile, saying: "I trust you are well, Count, and that your enforced inactivity has not wearied you?"

Ascalante murmured a polite reply.

"Count Ascalante," said the magician, "your experience and accomplishments have not eluded those who serve as my eyes and ears in distant places. Neither, I may add, has your lust for high office, nor a certain lack of scruple as regards the means whereby you hope to attain it. I hasten to assure you that the king and I approve of your ambition and of your—ah—practicality."

"I thank you, my lord," replied the count with a show of composure that aped the suavity of the sorcerer.

"I shall come directly to the point," said Thulandra Thuu, "for events move ever forward through the passing hours, and mortal men must scurry to keep abreast of them. Briefly, this is the situation: it has pleased His Majesty to withdraw his favor from the honorable Amulius Procas, commander of the Border Legion."

Amazement burned in the inscrutable eyes of Ascalante, for the news astounded him. All knew that Procas was the ablest commander Aquilonia could put in the field, now that Conan had left the king's service. If anyone could subdue the restive barons in the North and crush the rebellion in the South, it was Amulius Procas. To remove him from command at such a time, before either menace had been obliterated, was madness.

"I can divine the feelings that your loyalty reins in," purred Thulandra with a narrow smile. "The fact is that our General Procas has led a rash and ill-planned raid across the Alimane, thus risking open war with Milo, King of Argos."

"Forgive me, lord, but I find this almost impossible of credence," said Ascalante. "To invade a friendly neighboring state without our monarch's express command is tantamount to treason!"

"It is precisely that," smiled the sorcerer. "And that the king imprudently did order a punitive expedition into Argos is a datum that, I fear, history will fail to record, since every copy of the document has strangely disappeared. You take my meaning, sir?"

Amusement gleamed in Ascalante's eyes. "I believe I do, my lord. But pray continue." The Count of Thune appreciated a subtle act of villainy much as a connoisseur of wines might savor a rare vintage.

"The general might have avoided censure," Thulandra Thuu added with mock regret, "if he had stamped out the last sparks of the rebellion; for the rumors you have heard about the self-styled Army of Liberation, now gathered north of the Rabirians, are true. An adventurer who called himself Conan the Cimmerian—"

"That giant of a man who last year led the Lion Regiment of Aquilonia to victory over the marauding Picts?" cried Ascalante.

"The same," replied Thulandra. "But time presses and affords us little leisure for profitless gossip, however diverting. Had General Procas shattered the rebel remnant and then retreated across the Alimane before King Milo learned of the incursion, all had been well. But Procas bungled the mission, stirred up the wrath of Argos, and fled from the field of battle without spilling a single drop of rebel blood. He so botched the fording of the Alimane that rebel archers targeted scores of our finest soldiers. And his errors were compounded in Messantia by the blunders of a stupid spy of Vibius Latro—a Zingaran named Quesado—whom His Majesty had impulsively urged upon the diplomatic corps.

"The upshot was that, during the retreat, the general himself was wounded—so severely that, I fear, he is no longer able to command. Fortunately for us, the rebel leader Conan also perished. So to return to you, my dear Count—"

"To me?" murmured Ascalante, affecting an air of infinite modesty.

"To yourself," said the sorcerer with a sliver of a smile. "Your service on the Ophirean and Nemedian frontiers, I find, qualifies you to take command of the Border Legion, which has fallen from the failing hands of General Procas—or shortly will, once he receives this document."

The sorcerer paused and withdrew from the deep sleeve of his garment a scroll, richly embellished with azure and topaz ribbons, upon which the royal seal blazed like a clot of freshly shed blood.

"I begin to understand," said Ascalante. And eagerness welled up within his heart, like a bubbling spring beneath a stone.

"You have long awaited the call of opportunity to ascend to high office in the realm and earn the preferment of your king. That opportunity approaches. But—" and here Thulandra raised a warning finger and continued in a voice sibilant with emphasis—"you must fully understand me, Count Ascalante."

"My lord?"

"I am aware that the Herald's Court has not as yet approved your assumption of the Countship of Thune, and that certain—ah—irregularities surround the demise of your elder brother, the late lamented count, who perished in a 'hunting accident.'"

Flushing, Ascalante opened his lips to make an impassioned protest; but the sorcerer silenced him with lifted hand and a bland, uncaring smile.

"These are but minor disagreements, which shall be swept away in the acclaim that greets the laureled victor. I will see you well rewarded for your service to the crown," Thulandra Thuu continued craftily. "But you must obey my orders to the letter, or the County of Thune will never fall to you.

"I am aware that you have little actual experience in border warfare, or in commanding more men than constitute a regiment. The actual command of the Border Legion, then, I shall place in the hands of a certain senior officer, Gromel the Bossonian by name, who has been well blooded in our recent warfare against the Picts. I have long had Gromel under observation, and I plan to bind him to me with hopes of recompense. Therefore, while he shall deploy and order the actual battle lines, you will retain the nominal command. Is this quite understood?"

"It is, my lord," hissed Ascalante between clenched teeth.

"Good. Now that Conan lies dead, you and Gromel between you can easily immobilize the remaining rebels south of the Alimane until the fractious horde disintegrates from hunger and lack of accomplishment."

Thulandra Thuu proffered the scroll, saying: "Here are your orders. An escort awaits you at the South Gate. Ride for the ford of Nogara on the Alimane with all dispatch."

"And what, lord, if Amulius Procas refuses to accept my bona fides?" enquired Ascalante, who liked to make certain that he held all the winning pieces in any game of fortune.

"A tragic accident may befall our gallant general before your arrival to assume command," smiled Thulandra Thuu. "An accident which—when you officially report it—will be termed a suicide due to despondency over cowardice in the face of insubstantial foemen and repentance for provoking hostilities against a neighboring realm. When this occurs, be sure to send the body home to Tarantia. Alive, Procas would not have been altogether welcome here; dead, he will play the leading role in a magnificent funeral.

"Now be on your way, good sir, and forget not to obey orders to be given to you from time to time by one Alcina, a trusted green-eyed woman in my service."

Grasping the embossed scroll, Ascalante bowed deeply and departed from the Chamber of Sphinxes.

Watching his departure, Thulandra Thuu smiled a slow and mirthless smile. The instruments that served his will were all weak and flawed, he knew; but a flawed instrument is all the more dispensable should it need to be discarded after use.

chapter  vii

Death in the Dark

For many days, the presence of the army of Amulius Procas on the far side of the Alimane deterred the rebels from attempts to ford river. Although Procas himself, injured and unable to walk or ride, remained secluded in his tent, his seasoned officers kept a vigilant eye alert for any movement of the rebel forces. Conan's men marched daily up and down the river's southern shore, feinting at crossing one or another ford; but Procas' scouts remarked every move, and naught occurred to give pleasure to the Cimmerian or his cohorts.

"Stalemate!" groaned the restive Prospero. "I feared that it might come to this!"

"What we require for our success," suggested Dexitheus, "is a diversion of some kind, but on a colossal scale—some sudden intervention of the gods, perchance."

"In a lifetime devoted to the arts of war," responded the Count of Poitain, "I have learned to rely less upon the deities than on my own poor wits. Excuse me, Your Reverence, but methinks if any diversion were to deter Amulius Procas, it would be one of our own making. And I believe I know what that diversion well may be; for our spies report that the pot of my native county is coming to the boil."

That night, with the approval of the general, a man clad all in black swam the deeper reaches of the Alimane, crept dripping into the underbrush, and vanished. The night was heavily overcast, dark, and moonless; and a clammy drizzle herded the royalist sentries beneath the cover of the trees and shut out the small night sounds that might otherwise have alarmed them.

The swimmer in dark raiment was a Poitanian, a yeoman of Count Trocero's desmesne. He bore against his breast an envelope of oiled silk, carefully folded, in which lay a letter penned in the count's own hand and addressed to the leaders of the simmering Poitanian revolt.

Amulius Procas did not sleep that night. The rain, sluiced against the fabric of his tent, depressed his fallen spirits and inflamed his aching wound. Growling barbarous oaths recalled from years spent as a junior officer along the frontiers of Aquilonia, the old general sipped hot spiced wine to ward off the chills and fever and distracted his melancholy with a board game played against one of his aides, a sergeant. His wounded leg, swathed in bandages, rested uneasily on a rude footstool.

The grumble of thunder caused the army veteran to lift his grizzled head.

" 'Tis only thunder, sir," said the sergeant. "The night's a stormy one."

"A perfect night for Conan's rebels to attempt a crossing of the fords," said Procas. "I trust the sentries have received instruction to walk their rounds, instead of lurking under trees?"

"They have been so instructed, sir," the sergeant assured him. "Your play, sir; observe that my queen has you in check."

"So she has; so she has," muttered Procas, frowning at the board. Uneasily he wondered why a cold chill pierced his heart at hearing those harmless words, "my queen has you in check." Then he scoffed at these womanish night fears and downed a swallow of wine. It was not for old soldiers like Amulius Procas to flinch from frivolous omens! But still, would that he had been in fettle personally to inspect the sentries, who inevitably grew slack in the absence of a vigilant commander . . .

The tent flap twitched aside, revealing a tall soldier.

"What is it, man?" asked Procas. "Do the rebels stir?"

"Nay, General; but you have a visitor."

"A visitor, you say?" repeated Procas in perplexity. "Well, send him in; send him in!"

"It's 'her,' sir, not 'him,'" said the soldier. As Procas gestured for the entry of the unknown visitor, his partner at the board game rose, saluted, and left the tent.

Presently the soldier ushered in a girl attired in the vestments of a page. She had boldly approached the sentries, claiming to be an agent of King Numedides' ministers. None asked how she had traveled thither, being impressed by her icy air of calm authority and by the strange light that burned in her wide-set emerald eyes.

Procas studied her dubiously. The sigil that she showed meant little to him; such baubles can be forged or stolen. Neither gave he much credence to the documents she bore. But when she claimed to carry a message from Thulandra Thuu, his curiosity was aroused. He knew and feared the lean, dark sorcerer, whose hold over Numedides he had long envied, distrusted, and tried to counteract.

"Well," growled Amulius Procas at length, "say on."

Alcina glanced at the two sentries standing at her elbows, with hands on sword hilts. "It is for your ears only, my general," she said gently.

Procas thought a moment, then nodded to the sentries. "Very well, men; wait outside!"

"But, sir!" said the elder of the two, "we ought not to leave you alone with this woman. Who knows what tricks that son of evil, Conan, may be up to—"

"Conan!" cried Alcina. "But he's dead!" No sooner had she uttered those impetuous words than she would have gladly bitten off her tongue could she have thus recalled them.

The older sentry smiled. "Nay, lass; the barbarian has more lives than a cat. They say he suffered a wasting illness in the rebel camp for a while; but when we crossed the river, there he was behind us on his horse, shouting to his archers to make hedgehogs of us."

Amulius Procas rumbled: "The young woman evidently thinks that Conan perished; and I am fain to learn the reason for her view. Leave us, men; I am not yet such a drooling dotard that I need fear a wisp of a girl."

When the sentries had saluted and withdrawn, Amulius Procas said to Alcina with a chuckle: "My lads seize every opportunity to stay in out of the rain. And now repeat to me the message from Thulandra Thuu. Then we shall investigate the other matters."

Rain pounded on the tent, and thunder rolled as Alcina fumbled at the fastenings of the silken shirt she wore beneath her rain-soaked page's tunic. Presently she said:

"The message from my master, sir, is . . ."

A bolt of lightning and a crash of thunder drowned her following words. At the same time, she dropped her voice to just above a whisper. Procas leaned forward, thrusting his graying head to within a hand's breadth of her face in an effort to hear. She continued in that same sweet murmur:

"—that the time—has come—"

With the speed of a striking serpent, she drove her slender dagger into Amulius Procas's chest, aiming for the heart.

"—for you to die!" she finished, leaping back to escape the flailing sweep of the wounded general's arms.

True though her thrust had been, it encountered a check. Beneath his tunic, Procas wore a shirt of fine mesh-mail. Although the point of the dagger pierced one of the links and drove between the general's ribs, as the blade widened it became wedged within the link and so penetrated less than a finger's breadth. And, in her frantic struggle to wrench it free, Alcina snapped off the blade's tip, which remained lodged in the general's breast.

With a hoarse cry, the old soldier rose to his feet despite his injury and lunged, spreading his arms to seize the girl. Alcina backed away and, upsetting the taboret on which the candle stood, snuffed out the flame and plunged the tent into darkness deeper than the tomb.

Amulius Procas limped about in the ebon dark, until his strong hands chanced to grasp a handful of silken raiment. For a fleeting instant Alcina thought that she was doomed to die choking beneath the general's thick, gnarled fingers; but as the fabric ripped, the old soldier gasped and staggered. His injured leg gave way, and death rattled in his throat as he fell full-length across the carpet. The venom on Alcina's blade had done its work.

Alcina hastened to the entrance and looked out through a crack in the tent flap. A flash of lightning limned the two sentries, huddled in their sodden cloaks, standing like statues to the left and right. She perceived with satisfaction that the rumble of the storm had masked the sounds of struggle within the general's tent.

Fumbling in the darkness, Alcina discovered flint, steel, and tinder, and, with great difficulty, relighted the candle. Quickly she examined the general's body, then curled his fingers around the jeweled hilt of her broken dagger. Darting back to the tent flap, she peered at the soldiers standing stiffly still and began to croon a tender song, slowly raising her voice until the flowing rhythm carried to the sentinels.

The song she sang was a kind of lullaby, whose pattern of sound had been carefully assembled to hypnotize the hearer. Little by little, unaware of the fragile, otherworldly music, the sentries slipped into a catatonic lethargy, in which they no longer heard the rain that spattered on their helmets.

An hour later, having eluded the guards at the boundaries of the camp, Alcina regained her own small tent on a wooded hilltop near the river. With a gasp of fatigue, she threw herself into the shelter and began to doff her rain-soaked garments. The shirt was torn—a ruin . . .

Then she clapped a hand to her breast, where had reposed the obsidian talisman; but there it lay no longer. Appalled, she realized that Procas, in seizing her in the darkness, had grasped the slender chain on which it hung and snapped it off. The glassy half-circle must now be lying on the rug that floored the general's tent; but how could she recover it? When they discovered their leader's body, the royalists would swarm out like angry hornets. And at the camp hard-eyed sentries would be everywhere, with orders instantly to destroy a black-haired, green-eyed woman in the clothing of a page.

Shivering with terror and uncertainty, Alcina endured the angry rolls of thunder and the drumming fingers of the rain. But her thoughts raced on. Did Thulandra Thuu know that Conan had survived her poison? Her master had revealed no hint of such unwelcome knowledge that last time they conferred by means of the lost talisman. If the news of the Cimmerian's recovery had not yet reached the sorcerer, she must get word to him forthwith. But without her magical fragment of obsidian, she could report only by repairing to Tarantia.

Further black thoughts intruded on her mind. If Thulandra Thuu had known that Conan lived, would he have ordered her to slay Amulius Procas? Might he not be angry with her for killing the general, even though he had himself ordained the act, now that Procas's leadership was needed to save the royalist cause? Worse, might the sorcerer not punish her for failing to give the rebel chieftain a sufficient dose of poison? Worse of all, what vengeance might he not exact from her who lost his magical amulet? Stranded weaponless, without communication with her mentor, resourceless save for her puny knowledge of the elementary forms of witchcraft, Alcina lost heart and for a moment wavered between returning to Tarantia and fleeing to a foreign land.

But then, she reflected, Thulandra Thuu had always used her kindly and paid her well. She recalled his hinted promises of instruction in the higher arts of witchcraft, his talk of conferring on her immortality like his own, and—when he became sole ruler over Aquilonia, to reign forever—his assurance that she would be his surrogate.

Alcina decided to return to the capital and chance her master's wrath. Besides, being both beautiful and shrewd, she had a way with men, no matter what their station. Smiling, she slept, prepared to set forth with the coming of the light.

Toward dawn, an Aquilonian captain approached the general's tent to have him sign the orders of the day. The two sentries of the night before, wearily anticipating the conclusion of their tour of duty, saluted their superior before one stepped forward to open the tent flap and usher the captain in.

But General Procas would sign no further orders, save perchance in hell. He sprawled facedown in a pool of his congealing blood, clasping in his hand the stump of the slim-bladed poniard that had stilled the voice of Aquilonia's mightiest warrior.

The two soldiers turned over the corpse and stared at it. Procas's iron-gray hair, now dappled with dried blood, lay in disorder, partly masking his dormant features.

"I shall never believe our general took his own life," whispered the captain, deeply moved. "It was not his way."

"Nor I, sir," said the sentry. "What man determined to kill himself would plunge a dagger into a shirt of mail? It must have been that woman."

"Woman? What woman?" barked the captain.

"The green-eyed one I led here late last night. She said she brought a message from the king. See, there is one of her footprints." The soldier pointed to an outline of a small, booted foot etched in dried mud upon the carpet. "We urged the general to let us stay during the interview, but he ordered us out regardless."

"What became of the woman?"

The sentry turned up helpless hands. "Gone, I know not how. I assure you, sir, that she did not pass us on her way out. Sergius and I were wide awake and at our posts from the time we left the general till you came just now for orders. You can ask the watch."

"Hm," said the captain. "Only a devil can vanish from the midst of an armed and guarded camp of war."

"Then perhaps the devil is a woman, sir," muttered the sentry, biting his lip. "Look there on the rug: a half-moon of rock-glass, black as the depths of hell."

The captain toed the bit of obsidian, then kicked it aside impatiently. "Some fribbling amulet, such as the superstitious wear. Devil or no, we must not stand here babbling. You guard the general's body, whilst I call up a squad to search the camp and the surrounding hills. Sergius, fetch me a trumpeter! If I ever catch that she-devil . . ."

Alone in the tent, the sentry furtively searched among the shadows on the rug and found the amulet. He examined his find, tied the broken ends of chain together, and slipped it over his head. If the ornament was not much to look at, it might at least bring him good luck. Somebody must have thought so, and a soldier needs all the good fortune that the gods bestow.

Conan leaned above the rim of a great rock and studied the disposition of the royalist troops, still encamped along the northern bank of the Alimane. Only the day before, something unsettling had occurred among them; for there had been much shouting and noisy confusion. But from his aerie not even the keen-eyed Cimmerian could discern the nature of the disturbance.

Keeping his eyes fixed on the scene across the river, Conan accepted a joint of cold meat from his squire and gnawed on it with a lusty appetite. He felt full of renewed vigor, now that he had shaken off the lingering effects of the poisoned wine; and the days of harrying the Border Legion home had much appeased his rage over the lost battle amid the waters of the Alimane, where so many of his faithful followers had perished in the swirling flood.

Years had passed since the Cimmerian adventurer had last fought a guerrilla war—striking from the shadows, ambushing stragglers, hounding a stronger force from the security of darkness. Then he had commanded a brigand band in the Zuagir desert. Pleased he was that the skills were still with him, trammelled in his memory, razor-sharp in spite of long disuse.

Still, now that the enemy had crossed the Alimane and were encamped upon the farther bank, the problems of the war he fought had changed again—and, thought the impatient Cimmerian, changed for the worse.

The hosts beneath the Lion banner could not ford the Alimane so long as the royalists stood ready to repel each assault. For such an attack to succeed in the face of vigorous resistance would require, as in scaling the walls of a fortress, overwhelming numbers; and these the rebels did not have. Nor could they rely upon guerilla tactics and the novel employment of mounted archers. Moreover, their supplies were running low.

Conan scowled as he moodily munched the cold meat. At least, he reflected, the troops of Amulius Procas displayed no inclination to recross the river to do battle. And for the twentieth time he pondered the nature of the event that, the day before, had so disturbed the orderly calm of the enemy camp.

The Border Legion had enlarged the open space on the farther side of the river, where the Culario road met the water; they had felled trees, extending the clearing up and down the stream to make room for their camp. Beyond the camp, the forest was a wall of monotonous green, now that the springtime flowers on tree and shrub had faded. As Conan watched, a party of mounted men entered the encampment, and the song of trumpets foretold a visitation of some moment.

Conan shaded his eyes, frowned at the distant camp, and turned to his squire. "Go fetch Melias the scout, and quickly."

The squire trotted off, soon to return with a lean and leathery oldster. Conan glanced up, his face warm with greeting. Melias had served with Conan years before on the Pictish frontier. His eye was keener than any hawk's, and his moccasined feet slipped through dry underbrush as silently as a serpent.

"Who is it enters yonder camp, old man?" Conan enquired, nodding toward the royalist encampment.

The scout stared fixedly at the party moving down the company street. At length he said: "A general officer—field rank, at any rate, from the size of his escort. And of the nobility, too, from his blazonry."

Conan dispatched his page to fetch Dexitheus, who made a hobby of unraveling heraldic symbols. As the scout described the insignia embroidered on the newcomer's surcoat, the priest-physician rubbed his nose with a slow finger, as if to stimulate his memory.

"Methinks," he said at last, "that is the coat of arms of the Count of Thune."

Conan shrugged irritably. "The name is not unfamiliar to me, but I am sure I have never met the man. What know you of him?"

Dexitheus pondered. "Thune is an eastern county of Aquilonia. But I have not encountered the present holder of the title. I recall some rumor—perhaps a year ago—of a scandal in connection with his accession; but further details I fail to recollect."

Back at the rebel camp, Conan sought out the other leaders, to query them about the new arrival. But they could tell him little more than he already knew about the Count of Thune, save that the man had served as an officer on the peaceful eastern frontiers, with, so far as they knew, neither fabulous heroism nor crushing disgrace to his name.

By midafternoon, Melias reported that the troops of the Border Legion were ranked in parade formation and that, presently, the Count of Thune appeared and began to read aloud from documents bearing impressive seals and ribbons. Prospero and an aide slipped out of camp and, screened by foliage along the river bank, listened to the proceedings. Since a royalist sergeant repeated every phrase of the proclamation in a stentorian voice, which carried across the water, the astounded rebels learned that their adversary had died by his own hand and that Ascalante, Count of Thune, had been appointed in his place to command the Border Legion. This startling news they relayed with all dispatch to the other rebel chiefs.

"Procas a suicide?" growled Conan, bristling. "Never, by Crom! The old man, for all he was my enemy, was a soldier through and through, and the best officer in all of Aquilonia. Such as Procas sell their lives dearly; they do not slough them off! I smell the stench of treachery in this; how say the rest of you?"

"As for myself," muttered Dexitheus, fingering his prayer beads, "in this I see the sly hand of Thulandra Thuu, who long nursed hatred for the general."

"Does none of you know more of this Count Ascalante?" demanded Conan. "Can he lead troops in battle? Has combat seasoned him, or is he just another perfumed hanger-on of mad Numedides?" When the others shook their heads, Conan added: "Well, send your sergeants to enquire among the troops, whether any man of them has served beneath the count, and what manner of officer he was."

"Think you," asked Prospero, "that this new commander of the Border Legion may unwittingly serve our cause?"

Conan shrugged. "Perhaps; and perhaps not. We shall see. If Trocero's promised diversion comes to pass . . ."

Count Trocero smiled a secret smile.

The following morning, the rebel leaders, gathered on the lookout prominence, stared across the river in somber fascination. While the Border Legion stood in parade formation, a small party of mounted men moved slowly through the camp and vanished up the Culario road. In their midst a pair of black horses, driven by General Procas' charioteer, trundled the general's chariot along at a slow and solemn pace. Across the rear of the vehicle was lashed a large wooden box or coffin.

Conan grunted: "That's the last we shall ever see of old Amulius. If *he* had been king of Aquilonia, things would be quite different here today."

A few nights later, when fog lay heavy on the surface of the Alimane, the black-clad swimmer, whom Count Trocero had sent across the river several days before, returned. Again he bore a letter sewn into an envelope of well-oiled silk.

That very night the Lion Banner rose against the silver splendor of the watchful moon.

chapter  viii

Swords Across the Alimane

For several months, the friends of Count Trocero had done their work, and well. In marketplace and roadside inn, in village and hamlet, in town and city, the whisper winged across the province of Poitain: "The Liberator comes!"

Such was the title given to Conan by Count Trocero's partisans, men who remembered trembling tales of the giant Cimmerian from years gone by. They had heard how he thrust and cut amidst the silvery flood of Thunder River to break the will of the savage Picts, lest they swarm in their thousands across the border to loot and slay and ravish the Bossonian Marches. Poitanians who knew these stories now looked to the indomitable figure of Conan to wrest them from the clutches of their bloody tyrant.

For weeks, archers and yeomen and men-at-arms had filtered southward, ever southward, toward the Alimane. In the villages, men muttered over mugs of ale, their shaggy heads bent close together, of the invasion to come.

Now, at last, the Liberator neared. The moment loomed to free Poitain and, in good time, all of Aquilonia, prostrate now beneath the heavy heel of mad Numedides. The word so eagerly awaited had arrived in an oiled-silk envelope, stamped with the seal of their beloved count. And they were ready.

Chilled by the raw and foggy night, the sentinel, a youth from Gunderland, sneezed as he stamped his booted feet and slapped his shoulders. Sentry-go was a tedious tour of duty in the best of times, but on a damp night during a cold snap, it could be cursed uncomfortable.

If only he had not foolishly let himself be caught blowing kisses in the ear of the captain's mistress, thought the Gunderman gloomily, he might even now be carousing in the cheerful warmth of the sergeants' mess with his luckier comrades. What need, after all, to guard the main gate to the barracks of Cu-lario on such a night as this? Did the commandant think an army was stealing upon the base from Koth, or Nemedia, or even far Vanaheim?

Wistfully he told himself, had he enjoyed the fortune of a landed sire and birth into the gentry, he would now be an officer, swanking in satin and gilded steel at the officers' ball. So deep was he in dreams that he failed to remark a slight scuff of feet behind him on the cobblestones. He was aware of nothing untoward until a leathern thong settled about his plump throat, drew quickly tight, and strangled him.

The officers' ball throbbed with merriment. Chandeliers blazed with the light of a thousand candles, which sparkled and shimmered in the silvered pier glasses. Splendid in parade uniforms, junior officers vied for the favors of the local belles, who fluttered prettily, giggling at the honeyed whispers of their partners, while their mothers watched benignly from rows of gilded chairs along the pilastered walls.

The party was past its peak. The royal governor, Sir Conradin, had made his requisite appearance to open the festivities and long since had departed in his carriage. Senior Captain Armandius, commandant of the Culario garrison, yawned and nodded over a goblet of Poitain's choicest vintage. From his red velvet seat, he stared down sourly upon the dancers, thinking that all this prancing, bowing, and circling was a pastime fit for children only. In another hour, he decided, it would not seem remiss to take his leave. His thoughts turned to his dark-eyed Zingaran mistress, who doubtless waited impatiently for him. He smiled sleepily, picturing her soft lips and other charms. And then he dozed.

A servant first smelled smoke and thrust open the front door, to see a pile of burning brush stacked high against the walls of the officers' barracks. He bawled an alarm.

In the space of a few breaths, the king's officers swarmed out of the burning building, like bees smoked out of their hive by honey-seeking boys. The men and their ladies, furious or bewildered, found the courtyard already full—crowded by silent, somber men with grim eyes in their work-worn faces and naked steel in their sun-browned hands.

Alas for the officers; they wore only their daggers, more ornamental than useful, and so stood little chance against the well-armed rebels. Within the hour, Culario was free; and the banner of the Count of Poitain, with its crimson leopards, flew beside a strange new flag that bore the blazon of a golden lion on a sable field.

In a private room in Culario's best-regarded inn, the royal governor sat gaming with his crony, the Aquilonian tax assessor for the southern region. Both were deep in their cups, and consistent losses had rendered the governor surly and

short tempered. Still, having escaped from the officers' ball, Sir Conradin preferred to shun his home for yet a while, knowing that his wife would accord
him an unpleasant welcome. The presence of the sentry stationed in the doorway so fanned his irritation that he brusquely commanded the soldier to stand
out of sight beyond the entrance to the inn.

"Give a man some privacy," he grumbled.

"Especially when he's losing, eh?" teased the assessor. He guessed that the
sentry would not have to brave the clammy mists for long, for Sir Conradin's
purse was nearly empty.

Continuing their game, engrossed in the dance of ivory cubes and the whim-
sical twists of fortune, neither player noticed a dull thud and the sound of a
falling body beyond the heavy wooden portal.

An instant later, booted feet kicked open the door of the inn; and a fierce-
eyed mob of rustics, armed with clubs and rakes and scythes as well as more
conventional weapons, burst in to drag the gamesters from their table to the
crude gallows newly set in the center of the market square.

The men of the Border Legion received their first warning that the province
seethed with insurrection when an officer of the guard, yawning as he strolled
about the perimeter of the camp to assure himself that every sentry stood alert
and at his post, discovered one such sentinel slumbering in the shadow of a
baggage wain.

With an oath, the captain sent his booted toe thudding against the shirker's
ribs. When this failed to arouse the sleeper, the officer squatted to examine the
man. A feeling of dampness on his fingers caused him to snatch away his hand;
and he stared incredulously at the stain that darkened it and at the welling gash
that bridged the fellow's throat. Then he straightened his back and filled his
lungs to bellow an alarm, just in time to take an arrow through the heart.

Fog drifted across the rippling waters of the Alimane, to twist and coil
around the boles of trees and the tents of sleeping men. Fog also swirled about
the edges of the camp, where dark and somber forests stood knee-deep in purple
gloom. The ghostly tendrils wreathed the trunks of immemorial oaks, and
through the coils there drifted a wraithlike host of crouching figures in drab
clothing, with knives in their hands and strung bows draped across their shoulders. These shadowy figures breasted the curtaining fog, going from tent to
tent, entering softly, and emerging moments later with blood upon the blades
of their silent knives.

As these intruders stole among the sleeping men, other dark figures struggled
through the clutching waters of the Alimane. These, too, were armed.

———————

Ascalante, Count of Thune, was roused from heavy slumber by a shapeless cry as of a man in agony. The cry was followed by a score of shouts, and then the horns of chaos blared across the camp. For a moment, the Aquilonian adventurer thought himself immersed in bloody dreams. Then there sounded through the dripping night the screams of men in mortal combat, the shrieks of the injured, the gurgle of the dying, the tramp of many feet, the hiss of arrows, and the clangor of steel.

Cursing, the count sprang half-naked from his cot, flung wide the tent flap, and stared out upon a scene of roaring carnage. Burning tents cast a lurid light across a phantasmagoria of indescribable confusion. Corpses lay tossed about and trampled in the slimy mud, like toys discarded by the careless hands of children. Half-clothed Aquilonian soldiers fought with the frenzy of despair against mail-suited men armed with spear, sword, and axe, and others who plied longbows at such close range that every arrow thudded home. Royalist captains and sergeants strove heroically to force their pikemen into formation and to arm those who had issued unprepared from their shelters.

Then a terrible figure loomed up before the tent wherein the Count of Thune stood frozen with astonishment and horror. It was Gromel, the burly Bossonian, from whose thick lips poured a steady stream of curses. Ascalante blinked at him in amazement. The officer was clad in nothing but a loin cloth and a knee-length coat of mail. That mail was rent and hacked in at least a dozen places, baring Gromel's mightily muscled torso, which seemed to the fastidious count to be incarnadined with gore.

"Are we betrayed?" gasped Ascalante, clutching at Gromel's blood-encrusted sword arm.

Gromel shook off the grasping hand and spat blood. "Betrayed or surprised, or both—by the slimy guts of Nergal!" growled the Bossonian. "The province has risen. Our sentries are slain; our horses chased into the woods. The road north is blocked. The rebels have snaked across the river, unseen in these accursed fogs. Most of the sentries have had their throats cut by the countryfolk. We're caught between the two forces and helpless to fight back."

"What's to be done, then?" whispered Ascalante.

"Flee for your life, man," spat Gromel. "Or surrender, as I intend to do. Here, help me to bind up these wounds, ere I bleed to death."

First, hidden by the fog, Conan had led his pikemen across the ford of Nogara. Once the fight had started, Trocero, Prospero, and Pallantides followed with the archers and mounted troops. Before a wan moon broke through the deep-piled clouds, the Count of Poitain found himself engaged in a pitched battle; for enough of the Legionnaires had gathered to make a wall of shields, behind which their long spears bristled like a giant thorn bush. Trocero led his ar-

mored knights against this barrier of interlocking shields and, after several unsuccessful tries, broke through. Then the slaughter began.

The Numedidean camp was a makeshift affair, strung out along the northern
bank of the Alimane and backed against the forest. Its elongated shape made
it difficult to defend. As a rule, Aquilonian soldiers built square encampments,
walled with earthworks or palisades of logs. Neither of these defenses was prac-
ticable in the present case, and thus the camp of the Border Legion was vulnerable. The conformation of the land, together with the complete surprise
effected by the Army of Liberation (as it came to be called) tipped the balance
in favor of the rebels, even though the Legionnaires still outnumbered the
combined forces of Conan and the revolting Poitanians.

Besides, the morale of the Legion had declined, so that Aquilonia's finest
soldiers for once failed to deserve their reputation. Ascalante had reported to
his officers that their former chief, Amulius Procas, died by his own hand,
despondent over his sorry showing in the Argossean incursion. The soldiers of
the Legion could scarcely credit this canard. They knew and loved their old
general, for all his strict discipline and crusty ways.

To the officers and men, Ascalante seemed a fop and a poseur. True, the
Count of Thune had some experience with the military, but in garrison duty
only and on quiet frontiers. And also true, any general stepping up to greatness
over battle-hardened senior officers needs time to cool the hot breath of rancor
in those whom he commands. But the languid ways and courtly airs of the new
arrival did little to conciliate his staff; and their discontent was wordlessly trans-
mitted to the soldiers of the line.

The attack was well planned. When the Poitanian peasants had spilled the
blood of the sentries, fired the tents, and driven off the horses from their makeshift corral, the sleeping troops, roused at last to their peril, formed ranks to
challenge their attackers along the northern boundary of the camp. But when
they were simultaneously battered from the south by Conan's unexpected
forces, their lines of defense crumbled and the song of swords became a deathly
clamor.

General Ascalante was nowhere to be found. Descrying a horse, the courtier
had flung himself astride the unsaddled beast and, lacking spurs, had lashed the
animal into motion with a length of branch torn from a nearby tree. He eluded
the Poitanian foresters by a hair's breadth and galloped off into the night.

A cunning opportunist like Gromel might curry favor with the victors by
surrendering himself and his contingent; but for Ascalante it was quite another
matter. He had a noble's pride. Besides, the count divined what Thulandra
Thuu would do when he learned of the débâcle. The sorcerer had expected his
appointee to hold the rebels south of the Alimane—a task not too difficult
under ordinary circumstances for a commander with a modicum of military
training. But the magician's arts had somehow failed to warn him of the up-

rising of the Poitanians—an event that would have daunted an officer more seasoned than the Count of Thune. And now his camp was charred and cindered, and defeat was imminent. Ascalante, thus, could only quit the lieu and put as much distance as he could between himself and both the crafty rebel leader and the dark, lean necromancer in Tarantia.

Throughout the moonless night, the Count of Thune thundered through a tunnel of tall trees, and dawn found him nine leagues east of the site of the disaster. Spurred by the thought of Thulandra's incalculable wrath, he pushed ahead as fast as he dared go on his exhausted mount. There were places in the eastern deserts where, he hoped, even the vengeful sorcerer would never find him.

But as the hours passed, Ascalante conceived a fierce and abiding hatred of Conan the Cimmerian, on whom he laid the blame for his defeat and flight. In his heart the Count of Thune vowed some day in like manner to repay the Liberator.

Toward dawn Conan bestrode the Border Legion's ruined camp, receiving information from his captains. Hundreds of Legionnaires lay dead or dying, and hundreds more had sought the safety of the forest, whence Trocero's partisans were now dislodging them. But a full regiment of royalist soldiery, seven hundred strong, had come over to Conan's cause, having been persuaded by circumstances and a Bossonian officer named Gromel. The surrender of these troops—Poitanians and Bossonians, with a sprinkling of Gundermen and a few score other Aquilonians among them—pleased the Cimmerian mightily; for seasoned, well-trained professionals would bolster his fighting strength and stiffen the resolve of his motley followers.

A shrewd judge of men, Conan suspected Gromel, whom he had briefly known along the Pictish frontier, of being both a formidable fighter and a wily opportunist; but opportunism is forgivable when it serves one's turn. And so he congratulated the burly captain on his change of heart and appointed him an officer in the Army of Liberation.

Squads of weary men labored to strip the dead of usable equipment and stack the corpses in a funeral pyre, when Prospero strode up. His armor, splashed with dried blood, was ruddy in the roseate light of dawn, and he seemed in rare good humor.

"What word?" asked Conan gruffly.

"Nothing but good, General," grinned the other. "We have captured their entire baggage train, with supplies and weapons enough for twice our strength."

"Good work!" grunted Conan. "What of the enemy's horses?"

"The foresters have rounded up the beasts they let run free, so we have mounts again. And we have taken several thousand prisoners, who threw down their arms when they saw their cause was hopeless. Pallantides fain would know what he's to do with them."

"Offer them enlistment in our forces. If they refuse, let them go where they will. Unarmed men can harm us not," said Conan indifferently. "If we do win this war, we shall need all the good will we can muster. Tell Pallantides to let each choose his course."

"Very well, General; what other orders?" asked Prospero.

"We ride this morn for Culario. Trocero's partisans report there's not a royalist still under arms between here and the town, which waits to welcome us."

"Then we shall have an easy march to Tarantia," grinned Prospero.

"Perhaps, and perhaps not," Conan replied, narrowing his lids. "It will be days before news of the royalist rout arrives in Bossonia and Gunderland and the garrisons there head south to intercept us. But they will come in time."

"Aye. Under Count Ulric of Raman, I'll wager," said Prospero. Then, as Trocero joined his fellow officers, he added: "What is your guess, my lord Count?"

"Ulric, I have no doubt," said Trocero. "A pity we missed our meeting with the northern barons. They would have held him back for quite a while."

Conan shrugged his massive shoulders. "Prepare the men to move by noon. I'll take a look at Pallantides's prisoners."

A short while later, Conan stalked down the line of disarmed royalist soldiery, stopping now and then to ask a sharp question: "You wish to serve in the Army of Liberation? Why?"

In the course of this inspection, his eye caught the reflected sparkle of the morning sun on the hairy chest of a ragged prisoner. Looking more closely, he perceived that the light bounced off a small half-circle of obsidian, hung on a slender chain around the man's burly neck. For an instant Conan stared, struggling to remember where it was that he had seen the trinket. Taking the object between thumb and forefinger, he asked the soldier with a hidden snarl:

"Where did you get this bauble?"

"May it please you, General, I picked it up in General Procas's tent the morning after the general was—after he died. I thought it might be an amulet to bring me luck."

Conan studied the man through narrowed lids. "It surely brought no luck to General Procas. Give it to me."

The soldier hastily stripped off the ornament and, trembling, handed it to Conan. At that moment Trocero approached, and Conan, holding up the object to his gaze, muttered. "I know where I have seen this thing before. The dancer Alcina wore it around her neck."

Trocero's eyebrows rose. "Aha! then that explains—"

"Later," said Conan. And nodding to the prisoner, he continued his inspection.

As the level shafts of the morning sun inflamed the clouds that lingered in the eastern sky, Conan's baggage train and rear guard lumbered across the Alimane; and soon thereafter the Army of Liberation began its march across Poitain to Culario and thence toward great Tarantia and the palace of its kings. To tread the soil of Aquilonia after so many months of scaling crags in a lost and hostile land heartened the rebel warriors. Bone-weary as they were after a night of slaughter, they bellowed a marching song as they threaded their way north among the towering Poitanian oaks.

Ahead, swifter than the wind, flew the glad tidings: The Liberator comes! From farm and hamlet to town and city, it winged its way—a mere whisper at first, but swelling as it went into a mighty shout—a cry that monarchs dread, presaging as it does the toppling of a throne or the downfall of a dynasty.

Conan and his officers, pacing the van on fine horseflesh, were jubilant. The progress through Count Trocero's demesne would be, as it were, on eagles' wings. The nearest royalist forces, unapprised of their arrival, lay several hundred leagues away. And since Amulius Procas was in his grave, they had no enemy to fear until they reached the very gates of fair Tarantia. There they would find the city portals locked and barred against them, this they knew; and the Black Dragons, the monarch's household guard, in harness to defend their king and capital. But because the people stood behind them and a throne lay before, they would hack down all defenses and trample every foe.

In this the rebels were mistaken. One foe remained of whom they knew but little. This was the sorcerer Thulandra Thuu.

In his purple-pendant oratory, lighted by corpse-tallow candles, Thulandra Thuu brooded on his sable throne. He stared into his obsidian mirror, seeking by sheer intensity of purpose to wrest from the opaque pane bright visions of persons and events in distant places. At length with a small sigh, he settled back and rested his tired eyes. Then, frowning, he once again studied the sheet of parchment on which, in his spidery hand, were inscribed the astrological aspects he deemed conducive to communication by this occult means. He peered at the gilded crystal water clock and found no error of day or hour to explain his unsuccess. Whatever the cause, Alcina had failed to commune with him at the appointed time, now and for many days gone by.

A knock disturbed his melancholy meditation. "Enter!" said Thulandra Thuu through lips livid with frustration.

The drapery parted, and Hsiao stood on the marble threshold. Bowing, the

Khitan intoned in his quavering voice: "Master, the Lady Alcina would confer with you."

"Alcina!" The sharpness of the sorcerer's tone betrayed his agitation. "Show her in at once!"

The hangings fell together silently, then parted once again. Alcina staggered in. Her page's garb, tattered and torn, was gray with dust and caked with sun-dried mud. Her black hair formed a tangled web around a face stiff with soil and apprehension. She dragged weary feet, scarce able to support her drooping frame. The beautiful girl, who had gallantly set off for Messantia, now seemed a worn woman in the winter of her years.

"Alcina!" cried the wizard. "Whence come you? What brings you here?"

In a scarcely audible whisper, she replied: "Master, may I sit? I am fordone."

"Be seated, then." As Alcina sank down upon a marble bench and closed her eyes, Thulandra Thuu projected his sibilant voice across the echoing chamber: "Hsiao! Wine for Mistress Alcina. Now, good wench, relate all that has befallen you."

The girl drew a sobbing breath. "I have been eight days on the road, scarce halting to snatch a cat nap and a bite to eat."

"Ah, so! And wherefore?"

"I came to say—to tell you—that Amulius Procas is dead—"

"Good!" said Thulandra Thuu, pinwheels of light dancing in his hooded eyes.

"—but Conan lives!"

At this astounding information, the sorcerer for the second time that day lost his composure. "Set and Kali!" he cried. "How did that happen? Out with it, girl; out with it!"

Before answering, Alcina paused to sip from the cup of saffron wine that Hsiao handed her. Then, haltingly, she recounted her adventures in the camp of the Border Legion—how she stabbed Procas; how she learned that Conan lived; and how she escaped the guard.

"And so," she concluded, "fearing that you knew not of the barbarian's miraculous survival, I deemed it my duty to report to you forthwith."

Brows drawn in a ferocious frown, the sorcerer contemplated Alcina with his hypnotic gaze. Then he purred with the controlled rage of an angry feline: "Instead of undertaking this weary journey, why did you not withdraw a prudent distance from the Legion's camp, and commune with me at the appropriate hour by means of your fragment of yonder mirror?"

"I could not, Master." Alcina wrung her hands distractedly.

"Wherefore not?" Thulandra Thuu's voice suddenly jabbed like a thrown knife. "Have you mislaid the table of positions of the planets, with which I did supply you?"

"Nay, my lord; it's worse than that. I lost my fragment of the mirror—I lost my talisman!"

Lips drawn back in a snarl, Thulandra uttered an ophidian hiss. "By Nergal's demons!" he grated. "You little fool! What devil of carelessness possessed you? Are you mad? Or did you set your silly heart on some lusty lout, like unto a she-cat in heat? For this I will punish you in ways unknown to mortal men! I will not only flog your body but flay your very soul! You shall live the pains of all your previous lives, from the first bit of protoplasmal slime up through the worm, the fish, and the ape! You shall beg me for death, but—"

"Pray, Master, do but listen!" cried Alcina, falling to her knees. "You know men's lusts mean naught to me, save as I rouse them in your service." Weeping, she told of the death struggle in the dark with Amulius Procas and of her later discovery of the loss of the talisman.

Thulandra Thuu bit his lip to master his rising wrath. "I see," he said at length. "But when striking for great prizes, one cannot afford mistakes. Had your dagger traveled true, Procas would not have lingered long enough to seize your amulet."

"I knew not that he wore a shirt of mail beneath his tunic. Can you not cut another fragment from the master mirror?"

"I could, but the enchantment of the fragment for transmitting distant messages is such a tedious process that the war were over ere it was completed." Thulandra Thuu stroked his sharp chin. "Did you make certain of Procas's death?"

"Yes. I felt his pulse and listened for his heartbeat."

"Aye. But you did not so with the Cimmerian! That was the greater error."

Alcina made a gesture of despair. "I served him with sufficient poison to have slain two ordinary men; but betwixt his great size and the unnatural vitality that propelled him . . ." She drooped abjectly at her master's feet and let her voice trail off.

Thulandra Thuu rose; and towering above the trembling girl, pointed a skinny forefinger toward heaven. "Father Set, can none of my servants carry out my simplest demand?" Then, turning his sudden anger on the huddled girl, he added: "Little idiot, would you feed a boarhound on a lap-dog's rations?"

"Master, you warned me not, and who am I to calculate the grains of lotus venom needed for a giant?" Alcina's voice rose and fury rode upon it. "You sit in comfort in your palace, whilst this poor servant courses the countryside in good and evil weather, risking her skin to do your desperate deeds. And not a kindly word have you to offer her!"

Thulandra Thuu spread his arms wide, palms upturned in a gesture of forgiveness. "Now, now, my dear Alcina, let us speak no ill of one another. When allies part, the enemy wins the battle by default. If I ask you to poison another of my foes, I'll send along a clerk skilled in reckoning to calculate the dose."

He seated himself with a thin and rueful smile. "Truly, the gods must laugh like fiends at the irony of it. Having sent Amulius Procas to whatever nether world the Fates decreed, I earnestly wish that the old ruffian were alive again; for on none but him can I rely to defeat the barbarian and his rebel following.

"I thought that Ascalante and Gromel could together thwart the insurgents' efforts to cross the Alimane; and so they could have, were not Conan in command. Now I must find an abler general for the Border Legion. This needs some thinking on. Count Ulric of Raman has the Army of the North in Gunderland, watching the Cimmerians. An able commander, he; but the moon must wax and wane ere he receives an order and rides the length of Aquilonia. Prince Numitor lies closer on the Pictish frontier, but—"

Hsiao's tactful knock echoed like a tiny brazen bell. Entering, he said: "A pigeon-borne dispatch from Messantia, Master, newly received by Vibius Latro." Bowing, he handed the small scroll to the wizard.

Thulandra Thuu rose and held the scroll close to one of the huge candles, and reading, pressed his lips together until his mouth became a thin slit in his dusky face. At last he said:

"Well, Mistress Alcina, it seems the gods of my far distant island are careless of the welfare of their favored child."

"What has befallen now?" asked Alcina, rising to her feet.

"Prince Cassio, quoth Fadius, has sent a messenger from the Rabirian Mountains back to his sire in Messantia. Conan, it seems, fully recovered from an illness that struck him down, has crossed the Alimane and, with the aid of Poitanian lords and peasants, has utterly destroyed the Border Legion. Senior Captain Gromel and his men have deserted to the rebels; Ascalante may have fled, for neither he nor his exanimate body can be found."

The wizard crumpled the missive and glared at Alcina; and the eyes he fixed upon her burned red with a rage such as she had never seen in any living eyes. He snarled: "Betimes you tempt me, wench, to snuff out your miserable life, as a man extinguishes a lighted candle. I have a silent spell that turns mine enemy into a petty pile of ashes, with never a flame nor a plume of smoke—"

Alcina shrank away and crossed her arms upon her breast, but there was no escape from the sorcerer's hypnotic stare. Her body burned as from the licking tongues of flame that lapped the open door of a furnace. The magical emanations pierced her inmost being, and she closed her eyes as if to shut out the cruel radiations. When she opened them once more, she threw up her hands to ward off a blow and shrieked hysterically.

Where the sorcerer had stood, now reared a monstrous serpent. From its upraised head, swaying on a level with her own, slit-pupiled eyes poured maleficent rays into her soul, while a reptilian stench inflamed her nostrils. The scaly jaws gaped wide, revealing a pair of dagger-pointed fangs as the great head lunged toward her. Flinching, she blinked again; and when she ventured to open her eyes, it was Thulandra Thuu who stood before her.

With a crooked smile on his narrow face, the wizard said: "Fear not, girl; I do not wantonly blunt my tools whilst they still possess a cutting edge."

Still shuddering, Alcina recovered herself enough to ask: "Did—did you in truth take the form of a serpent, Master, or did you but cast an image of reality upon me?"

Thulandra Thuu evaded her question. "I did but remind you which of us is master here and which apprentice."

Alcina was content to change the subject. Pointing to the crumpled parchment, she asked: "How came Fadius by Prince Cassio's information?"

"Milo of Argos declared a public celebration, and the reason was no secret. It is plain which side the old fool favors. And one item more: Milo ordered that clodpate Quesado banished from his kingdom, and our would-be diplomat was last seen traveling with an escort of Milo's household guard along the road to Aquilonia. I shall urge Vibius Latro to set the fellow working as a collector of offal; he is good for nothing else.

"And now, perhaps, our meddlesome mad king will leave affairs of state to me and confine himself to his besotted pleasures. I must ponder my next move in this board game with Fate, wherein a kingdom is the prize. And so, Alcina, you have my leave to go. Hsiao will provide you with food, drink, a much-needed bath, and woman's raiment."

The league-long glittering river that was the Army of Liberation wound around tree-crowned hills, past fields and steads, and up to the gates of Culario. Conan, in the lead, reined in his black stallion at the sight of the gaping opening. From the gate towers flapped flags bearing the crimson leopards of Poitain; but the black heraldic eagle of Aquilonia was nowhere to be seen. Inside the city walls people lined both sides of the narrow street. In Conan's agile mind stirred the barbarian's suspicion of the trickery of civilized men.

Turning to Trocero, who rode a white gelding at his side, Conan muttered: "You're certain it's not a royalist trap they've set for us?"

"My head on it!" replied the count fervently. "I know my people well."

Conan studied the scene before him and rasped: "Me thinks I'd best not look too much the conqueror. Wait a little."

He unbuckled the chin strap of his helmet, pulled off the headpiece, and hung it on the pommel of his saddle. Then he dismounted with a clank of armor and strode toward the gate on foot, leading his horse.

Thus Conan the Liberator entered unpretentiously into Culario, nodding gravely to the citizens ranked on either side. Petals of fragrant flowers showered upon him; cheers resounded down the winding corridor. Following him on horseback, Prospero pulled to Trocero and whispered in his comrade's ear:

"Were we not fools the other night to wonder who should succeed Numedides?"

Count Trocero replied with a wry smile and a shrug of his iron-clad shoulders as he raised a hand in salutation to his fond and loyal subjects.

In his sanctum, Thulandra Thuu bent over a map, unrolled upon a taboret with weights of precious metals holding its edges down. He addressed himself to Alcina, now well rested from her journey and resplendent in a flowing robe of yellow satin, which clung to her fine-molded body and glorified her raven hair.

"One of Latro's spies reports that Conan and his army are in Culario, resting from their battle and forced march. In time they will strike north, following the Khorotas to Tarantia." He pointed with a long, well-pared fingernail. "The place to stop them is at the Imirian Escarpment in Poitain, which lies athwart their path. The only force that has both weight and time enough to accomplish such a task is Prince Numitor's Royal Frontiersmen, based at Fort Thandara in the Westermarck of Bossonia."

Alcina peered at the map and said: "Then should you not order Prince Numitor to march south-east with all dispatch, taking all but a small garrison?"

The wizard chuckled drily. "We shall make a general of you yet, good wench. The rider bearing that message in his pouch set off ere dawn." Thulandra Thuu then measured off distances with his fingers, rotating his hand as if it were a draughtsman's compass. "But, as you see, if Conan marches within the next two days, Numitor can in no way reach the escarpment in advance of him. We must cause him to delay."

"Yes, Master, but how?"

"I am not unacquainted with weather magic and can control the spirits of the air. I shall contrive a scheme to hold the Cimmerian in Culario. Fetch hither yonder powders and potions, girl, and we shall test the power of my wizardry."

Conan stood on the city wall beside the newly elected mayor of Culario. The day had been fair when they began their promenade; but now they gazed at an indigo sky across which clouds of leaden gray rolled in endless procession.

"I like it not, sir," said the mayor. "The summer has been wet, and this looks like the start of another spell. Too much rain can be as bad for the crops as none at all. And here it comes!" he finished, wiping a large drop from his forehead.

As the two men descended the spiral stair that wound around the tower, an agitated Prospero confronted them. "General!" he cried. "You slipped away from your bodyguard again!"

"By Crom, I like to get off by myself sometimes!" growled Conan. "I need no nursemaid looking after me."

"It is the price of power, General," said Prospero. "More than our leader, you've become our symbol and our inspiration. We must guard you as we would our banner or another sacred relic; for if the enemy could strike you down, his fight were three-fourths won. I assure you, spies of Vibius Latro lurk in Culario, watching for a chance to slip a poison into your wine, or a poniard between your ribs."

"Those vermin!" snorted Conan.

"Aye, but you can die from such a creature's sting as readily as any common man. Thus, General, we have no choice but to cosset you as carefully as a newborn prince. These trifling inconveniences you must learn to endure."

Conan heaved a gusty sigh. "There's much to be said for the life of a foot-loose wanderer, such as once I was. Let's back to the governor's palace ere this cloudburst wash us all away."

Conan and Prospero strode swiftly over the cobblestones, the stout mayor panting to keep pace. Overhead, a meandering crack of violet light cleft the sky, and thunder crashed like the roll of a thousand drums. The rain came down in sheets.

chapter  ix

The Iron Stallion

While Poitain writhed beneath the lash of the most violent storm in the memory of living men, a benign sun smiled on fair Tarantia. Standing in its salubrious rays on a palace balcony, Thulandra Thuu, attended by Alcina and Hsiao, looked out across the gently rolling fields of central Aquilonia, where summer wheat was ripening into spears of gold. To the dancer, now young and beautiful once more, with jewels atwinkle in her night-black hair and a gown of clinging satin sheathing her shapely form, the wizard said:

"The wheel of heaven reveals to me that the spirits of the air have served me well. My storm progresses apace; and after it subsides, the southern roads and every ford will be impassable. Numitor hastens from the Westermarck, and I must forth to join him."

Alcina stared. "You mean to travel to the field of battle, Master? Ishtar! That's not your wont. May I ask why?"

"Numitor will be outnumbered by the rebel forces; and despite forced marches, Ulric of Raman cannot reach Poitain until at least a fortnight after the prince arrives. Moreover, Prince Numitor is but an honest blockhead— doubtless the reason why our knavish king has let his cousin live when he has slain or exiled all his other kin. Nay, I cannot trust the prince to hold the Imirian Escarpment until Count Ulric arrives. He will require the assistance of my arcane arts."

The sorcerer turned to his servant, the inscrutable slit-eyed one who had followed him from lands beyond the seas. "Hsiao, prepare my chariot and gather the necessaries for our journey. We shall depart upon the morrow."

Bowing, the man withdrew. Turning to Alcina, Thulandra Thuu continued: "Since the spirits of the air have well obeyed me, I shall discover what the spirits of the earth will do to aid my cause. And you, good wench, I leave here as my deputy."

"Me? No, Master; I lack the skills to take your place."

"I will instruct you. First, you will learn to use the Mirror of Ptahmesu to commune with me."

"But we are without the necessary talisman!"

"I can project images by the propellant power of my mind, though you could not. Come, we have no time to waste."

From the royal paddocks Hsiao led out the single horse that drew his master's carriage. To a casual observer, the animal appeared to be a large black stallion; but a closer inspection of its hide revealed a strange, metallic sheen. The beast, moreover, neither pawed the ground nor lashed its tail at flies. In fact, no flies alighted on it, although the stable yard buzzed with their myriad wings. The stallion stood quiescent until Hsiao uttered a command unintelligible to any who might hear it; then the creature obeyed him instantly.

Hsiao now led the ebon stallion to the carriage house and backed it into the stall where stood Thulandra's chariot. When a careless hoof struck against one of the lowered carriage shafts, a metallic ring reverberated through the silent air.

The vehicle, a boxlike two-wheeled cart, lacquered in vermillion and emblazed with a frieze of writhing serpents worked in gold, was furnished with a seat across the back. A pair of carven posts, upthrust on either side, supported an arched wooden frame, covered with canvas. No ordinary cover this; it was embroidered with strange symbols beyond the ken of all who gazed upon it, save that the astute among them might discern the likeness of the moon and the major constellations of the southern hemisphere.

Into the chest beneath the seat of this singular vehicle, Hsiao placed all manner of supplies, and on the broad expanse above, he piled silken cushions in profusion. And as he worked, he hummed a plaintive song of Khitai, full of curious quarter-tones.

Conan and Trocero watched the sheeting rain from the governor's mansion. At length Conan growled: "I knew not that your country lay at the bottom of an inland sea, my lord."

The count shook his head. "Never in half a century of living have I seen a storm of such intensity. Naught but sorcery could account for it. Think you Thulandra Thuu—"

Conan clapped his companion on the shoulder. "You Aquilonians see magic lurking in every passing shadow! If you stub your toe, it's Thulandra's doing. In my dealings with these wizards, I've seldom found them so formidable as they would wish us to believe. . . . Aye, Prospero?" he added, as the officer bustled in.

"The scouts have returned, General, and report all roads are utterly impassable. Even the smallest creeks are bursting into raging torrents. It were useless to send the column forward; they'd not advance a league beyond the city."

Conan cursed. "Your suspicion of that he-witch in Tarantia begins to carry weight, Trocero."

"And we have visitors," continued Prospero. "The northern barons, who set out for home before we reached C[u]lario, have been overtaken by the storm and forced to return hither."

A smile illumined Conan's dark, scarred face. "Thank Crom, good news at last! Show them in."

Prospero ushered in five men in damp woolen traveling garments of good quality, mud-splattered from top to booted toe. Trocero presented the Baron Roaldo of Imirus, whose demesne lay in northern Poitain. A former officer in the royal army, this hardy, gray-haired noble had guided the other barons and their escorts to Culario and now introduced them to the Cimmerian.

Conan judged the lordlings to be men of diverse characters: one stout, red-faced and full of boisterous good humor; another slim and elegant; still another fat and obviously privy to the pleasures of the table and the jug; and two of somber mien and given to few words. Differing though they did among themselves, all heartily supported the rebellion; for their tempers were rubbed raw by Numedides's grasping tax collectors, and their ancient pride affronted by the royal troops stationed on their demesnes to wrest a yearly tribute from landowner and peasant. They avidly desired the downfall of the tyrant, and their questing gaze sought to discover Numedides's successor, so they might court their future monarch's favor.

After the barons had rested and donned fresh raiment, Conan and his friends heard their tally of complaints and drew out their hidden hopes. Conan promised little, but his sympathetic demeanor left each with the impression that, in a new regime, he would occupy a position of importance.

"Be warned, my lords," said Conan, "Ulric, Count of Raman, will move his troops across your lands as he travels south to confront our rebel army."

"What troops does that graybeard count command?" snorted Baron Roaldo. "A ragtail lot, I'll warrant. The Cimmerian frontier has long been peaceful and needs but a weak force to keep it safe."

"Not so," replied the Count of Poitain. "I am informed that the Army of the North is nearly up to strength and boasts veterans of many a border clash. Indeed, Raman himself is a master strategist who escaped from the sack of Venarium, many years ago."

Conan smiled grimly. As a stripling, he had joined the wild Cimmerian horde that plundered Fort Venarium, but of this he made no mention. Instead, he told the northern barons:

"Numedides will, I doubt not, send troops from the Westermarck; and being nearer, they will arrive the sooner. You must harry these northern contingents in a delaying action, at least until we rout the Bossonian royalists."

Count Trocero eyed the barons keenly. "Canst raise a fighting force without alerting the king's men stationed amongst you?"

Said Baron Ammian of Ronda: "Those human grasshoppers swarm only at harvest time to consume the fruit of our labors. They'll not arrive, the gods willing, for another month or two."

"But," argued the fat Baron Justin of Armavir, "such a conflict, waged on our lands, will ruin both our purses and our people. Perchance we can delay Sir Ulric, but only till he burns our fields, scatters our folk, and wrecks vengeance on our persons."

"If General Conan fails to take Tarantia, we are beggared in any case," countered the hard-featured Roaldo. "Word will soon reach the tyrant's spies that we have joined the rebel cause. Better to game for a golden eagle than for a copper penny."

"He speaks sooth," said Ammian of Ronda. "Unless we topple the tyrant, we shall all have our necks either lengthened or shortened, no matter what we do. So let us dare the hazard, and from encompassing dangers boldly pluck our safety!"

At last the five agreed, some with enthusiasm, others doubtfully. And so it was decided that, as soon as the weather cleared, the barons would hasten northward to their baronies, like chaff blown before an oncoming storm, to harass Count Ulric's Army of the North when it sought passage through their property.

After the barons had retired for the night, Prospero asked Conan: "Think you they will arrive in time?"

"For that matter," added Trocero, "will they hold true to their new alliance, if Numedides strews our path with steel or if Tarantia stands firm against us?"

Conan shrugged. "I am no prophet. The gods alone can read the hearts of men."

The sorcerer's chariot rumbled through the streets of Tarantia, with Hsiao, legs braced against the floorboards, gripping the reins and Thulandra Thuu in hooded cloak seated on the pillow-padded bench. Citizens who remarked the vehicle's approach turned away their faces. To meet the dark sorcerer's eyes might focus his attention, and all deemed it expedient to escape the magician's notice. For none there was who failed to hear rumors of his black experiments and tales of missing maidens.

The great bronze portals of the South Gate swung open at the vehicle's approach and closed behind it. Along the open country road, the strange steed paced at twice the speed of ordinary horseflesh, while the chariot bounced and swayed, trailing a thin plume of dust. More than forty leagues of white road unrolled with every passing day; and neither heat, nor rain, nor gloom of night stayed the iron stallion from its appointed task. When Hsiao wearied, his master grasped the reins. During these periods of rest, the yellow man devoured cold meats and snatched a spell of fitful sleep. Whether his master ever closed his eyes, Hsiao knew not.

After following the east bank of the River Khorotas for several days, Thulandra Thuu's chariot neared the great bridge that King Vilerus I had flung across the river. Here the Road of Kings, after swinging around two serpentine bends in the river, rejoined the stream and promptly crossed it to the western bank. The bridge, upraised on six stone piers that towered up from the river bed, was furnished with a wooden deck and a steeply sloping ramp on either end.

At the sight of the emblazoned chariot, the toll taker bowed low and waved the carriage through; and as the vehicle ascended to the deck, Thulandra scanned the countryside. When he perceived a cloud of dust, swirling aloft from the road ahead, a meager smile of satisfaction creased his saturnine visage. If the pounding hooves of Prince Numitor's cavalry roiled the loose soil and bore it skyward, his careful calculations of time and distance had been correct. They would meet where the Bossonian Road conjoined with the highway to Poitain.

The chariot thundered down the western ramp and continued southward, and within the hour Thulandra overtook a column of horsemen. As the painted chariot neared, a trooper at the column's tail recognized the vehicle. When word ran up the ranks, the cavalrymen hastily pulled their mounts aside, leaving an unobstructed path for the royal sorcerer. The horses shied and danced as the black metallic steed sped past, and the milling remounts and frightened pack animals reared and plunged and much discomfited their handlers.

At the head of the column, the magician found Prince Numitor astride a massive gelding. Like his royal cousin the king, the prince was a man of heavy build, with a reddish tinge to hair and beard. Otherwise he presented quite a different aspect; guileless blue eyes graced a broad-browed, sun-browned face that bore the stamp of easygoing geniality.

"Why, Mage Thulandra!" exclaimed Numitor in amazement, when Hsiao reined in his singular steed. "What brings you hither? Do you bear some urgent message from the king?"

"Prince Numitor, you will require my sorcerous arts to check the rebels' northward march."

The prince's eyes clouded with perplexity. "I like not magic in my warfare; it's not a manly way to fight. But if my royal cousin sent you, I must make the best of it."

A glint of malice flared up in the sorcerer's hooded eyes. "I speak for the true ruler of Aquilonia," he said. "And my commands must be obeyed. If we proceed with haste, we can reach the Imirian Escarpment before the rebels. Are these two regiments of horse all that you bring with you?"

"Nay, four regiments of foot follow. They have not yet reached the junction of the Bossonian Road with this."

"None too many, although we face naught but a rabble of undisciplined rogues. If we can hold them below the cliff wall until Count Ulric arrives, we shall pluck their fangs. When we attain the crest of the escarpment, I wish you to detail five of your men—experienced hunters all—for a certain task."

"What task is that, sir?"

"Of this I shall inform you later. Suffice it to say that skilled woodsmen are necessary to the spell I have in mind."

At last the rain ceased in Culario. The northern barons and their entourage slogged along the muddy road, where vapor steamed from puddles drying in the summer sun. Shortly thereafter, the Army of Liberation set out upon the same highway, leading northward to the central provinces and thence to proud Tarantia on the far bank of the Khorotas.

At every town and hamlet that they passed, the legions of the Liberator were infused with new recruits: old knights, eager to take part in one last glorious affray; battle-battered ex-soldiers who had served with Conan on the Pictish frontier; lean foresters and huntsmen who saw in Conan a nature-lover like themselves; outlaws and exiles, drawn by the promise of amnesty for those who fought beneath the Golden Lion; yeomen, tradesmen, and mechanics; wood-cutters, charcoal burners, smiths, masons, pavers, weavers, fullers, minstrels, clerks—all hard-eyed men eager to adventure in the army of the Liberator. They so drained the armory of weapons that Conan at last insisted each recruit come already armed, if only with a woodsman's axe.

Conan and his officers plunged into the arduous task of welding these eager volunteers into some semblance of a military force. They told the men off into squads and companies and appointed sergeants and captains from those experienced in war. During halts, these new officers exercised their road-weary men in simple drills; for, as Conan warned them:

"Without constant practice, a horde of raw recruits like these dissolve into a mass of shrieking fugitives when the first blood is shed."

Between the farm lands of southern Poitain and the Imirian Escarpment stretched the great Brocellian Forest, through which the highway glided like a serpent amid a bed of ferns. As the rebels neared the forest, the songs of the Poitanian volunteers diminished. More and more, Conan noted, the recruits tramped along in glum silence, apprehensively eyeing the overarching foliage.

"What ails them?" Conan asked Trocero as they sat of an evening in the command tent. "Anyone would think these woods writhed with venomous serpents."

The gray-haired count smiled indulgently. "We have only the common viper in Poitain, and few of those. But the folk hereabouts are full of peasant superstitions, holding the forest to harbor supernatural beings who may work magic on them. Such beliefs are not without advantage; they preserve a splendid hunting ground for my barons and my friends."

Conan grunted. "Once we scale the escarpment and gain the Imirian Plateau, they'll doubtless find some new hobgoblin to obsess them. I have not seen this part of Aquilonia before, but by my reckoning the cliff wall rises less than a day's march ahead. How runs the pass to the plateau?"

"There's a deep cleft in the cliff, where the turbulent Bitaxa River, a tributary of the Alimane, cascades across the wall of rock. The road, winding upward to the plateau, is borne upon a rock ledge thrust out from one side of the cleft. The gorge below—which we call the Giant's Notch—is slippery, steep, and narrow. An evil place to meet a cliff-top foe! Pray to your Crom that Numitor's Frontiersmen do not reach the Notch ahead of us."

"Crom cares but little for the prayers of men," said Conan, "or so they told me when I was a boy. He breathes into each mortal man the strength to face his enemies; and that's all a man can reasonably ask of gods, who have their own concerns. But we must not risk attack in this murderous trap. Tomorrow at dawn, take a strong party of mounted scouts to reconnoiter the escarpment."

Publius waddled in, arms full of ledgers, and Trocero left Conan studying the inventory of supplies. The count sought out the tents of his Poitanian horsemen and chose from amongst them forty skilled swordsmen for the morrow's reconnaissance.

The Giant's Notch loomed high above Trocero's company, its beetling cliffs hiding black wells of darkness from the midday sun. The count and his scouts sat their saddles, staring upward at the crest, searching in vain for the telltale sparkle of sunlight on armor. Neither could they observe upon the elevation the smoke of any campfires. At length Trocero said:

"We shall circle round the woods and meet again upon the road, a quarter-league back, where a high rock ledge overhangs the forest path. Vopisco, take your half of the detachment east and meet me thither within the hour. I shall go westward."

The detachment divided, and the horsemen forced their mounts through the dense foliage that spilled out into the road. Once past this obstacle, they encountered little underbrush beneath the thick trunks of the virgin oaks.

For a short while Trocero's party rode in silence, their horses' hooves soundless on the thick carpet of moldering leaves. Suddenly the forester in the lead flung up a hand, turned in his saddle, and murmured: "Men ahead, my lord. Mounted, I think."

The troop drew together, the men tense and apprehensive, their horses motionless. Through the shadowed ranks of trees Trocero's eyes detected a disquieting movement; his ears, a mutter of strange voices.

"Swords!" whispered the count. "Prepare to charge, but strike not till I command. We know not whether they be friend or foe."

Twenty swords hissed from their scabbards, as the riders eased their beasts to right or left, until they formed a line among the trees. The voices waxed louder, and a group of horsemen sprang into view beyond the rugged boles of immemorial oaks. His upraised sword a pointing finger, Trocero signaled the attack.

Weaving around the trees, the score of Poitanians rode at the strangers. In a few heartbeats they came within plain sight of them.

"Yield!" shouted Trocero, then reined his horse in blank amazement. The animal reared, eyes rolling, forelegs pawing the insubstantial air.

Five mounted men, unarmored but wearing white surcoats adorned with the black eagle of Aquilonia, paused to stare. All but one led captive creatures by cruel ropes noosed tightly about their necks. The captives—three males and a female—were no larger than half-grown children, their nakedness partly veiled by a thin coat of fawnlike, light-brown fur. Above each snub-nosed, humanoid face rose a pair of pointed ears. When their captors dropped the leashing ropes to draw their swords, and the freed creatures turned to run, Trocero saw each bore a short, furry tail, like that of a deer, white on the underside.

The leader of the Aquilonians, recovering his composure, shouted an order to his men. Instantly, they spurred their mounts and charged.

"Kill them!" cried Trocero.

As the five royalists, bending low over their horses' necks, pounded toward the Poitanians, death rode in their grim eyes. The rebel swordsmen could not present a solid line, spread out as they were among the trees, so the Aquilonians aimed for the gaps. The leader rode at Trocero, his blade thrust outward like a lance. To right and left, the count's men, avenging furies, rushed headlong at the foe.

There was an instant of wild confusion, raked by shouts and illumined by the white light of terror in the eyes of men flogged by the fury of their desperation. Two troopers converged upon a galloping Aquilonian, whose upraised sword whirled murderously above his tousled head. One drove his steel into the soldier's sword arm; the other struck downward with all his might, tearing a long gash in the speeding horse's side. But the screaming animal pressed forward, and the man ran free.

A rebel's sword darted past a blade that sought to slash him and sheathed six inches of its point into an eagle-emblemed midriff. The lean, muscle-knotted

Aquilonian leader lunged at Trocero, who parried with a clang, and the hum of steel on steel was a song of death. Then the five horses were through and away, like autumn leaves in a gale, with four of their riders. The fifth lay supine on the leaf mold of the forest floor, with a bloodstain spreading slowly across his white surcoat.

"Gremio!" shouted the count. "Take your squad and pursue! Try to capture one alive!"

Trocero turned back to the trampled turf, which bore mute testimony to the furious encounter. Spying the fallen man, he said: "Sergeant, see if that fellow lives."

As the sergeant dismounted, another trooper said: "Please, my lord, he spitted himself on my steel as he rode past. I know he's dead."

"He is," nodded the sergeant, after a quick examination.

Trocero cursed. "We needed him for questioning!"

"Here's one of their captives," said the sergeant, kneeling beside the nude creature, flung like a discarded garment against a fallen log. "Me thinks it was knocked down by a flying hoof and stunned in the mêlée."

Trocero bit his underlip in thought. "It is. I do believe, a fabled satyr, whereof the countryfolk tell fearsome old-wives' tales."

A look of superstitious terror crossed the sergeant's face, and he snatched back his questing hands. "What shall I do with it, sir," he said, rising and stepping backward.

The satyr, whose wrists were bound together by a narrow thong, opened its eyes, perceived the ring of hostile mounted men, and scrambled to its feet. Trembling, it sought to run; but the sergeant, grabbing the rope that trailed from its neck, tugged and brought it down.

When it had been subdued, Trocero addressed it: "Creature, can you talk?"

"Aye," the captive said in broken Aquilonian. "Talk good. Talk my tongue; talk little yours. What you do to me?"

"That's for our general to decide," replied Trocero.

"You no cut throat, like other men?"

"I have no wish to cut your throat. Why think you that those others so would do?"

"Others catch us for magic sacrifice."

The count grunted. "I see. You need fear naught of that from us. But we must bring you back to camp. Have you a name?"

"Me Gola," said the satyr in his gentle voice.

"Then, Gola, you shall ride pillion behind one of my men. Do you understand?"

The satyr looked downcast. "Me fear horse."

"You must overcome your fear," said Trocero, giving his sergeant a signal.

"Up you go," said the soldier, swinging the small form aloft; and, lifting the noose from Gola's neck, he bound the rope firmly about the satyr's waist and that of the trooper on whose horse the creature sat.

"You'll be quite safe," he laughed. Swinging into his saddle, he turned the column around.

The squad sent in pursuit of the royalists arrived at the base of the Giant's Notch in time to see the fugitives disappear up the steep tunnel of the gorge. Fearing ambush, the Poitanians pressed the pursuit no farther.

Later, in the command tent, Trocero reported on his mission to the assembled leaders of the rebellion. Conan surveyed the captive and said: "That binding on your wrists seems tight, friend Gola. We need it not."

He drew his dagger and approached the satyr, who cringed and screamed in mortal terror: "No cut throat! Man promise, no cut throat!"

"Forget your precious throat!" growled Conan, seizing the captive's wrists in one gigantic hand. "I would not harm you." He slashed the thong and sheathed his poinard, while Gola flexed his fingers and winced at the pain of returning circulation.

"That's better, eh?" said Conan, seating himself at the trestle table and beckoning the satyr to join him. "Do you like wine, Gola?"

The satyr smiled and nodded; and Conan signaled to his squire.

"General!" exclaimed Publius, holding up a finger to stay the execution of the order. "Our wine is nearly gone. A few flagons more and we're all back on beer."

"No matter," said Conan. "Wine we shall have. The Nemedians have a saying, 'In wine is truth,' and this I am about to test."

Publius, Trocero, and Prospero exchanged glances. Since he first clapped eyes upon the satyr, Conan displayed a curious affinity for this subhuman being. It was as if, a scarce-tamed creature of the wild himself, he felt instinctive sympathy for another child of nature, dragged from its native haunts by civilized men whose ways and motives must be utterly incomprehensible.

Half a wineskin later, Conan discovered that two regiments of royalist cavalry held the plateau above the Imirian Escarpment. They were encamped, not at the cliff-top where they could attack if the rebels ascended the flume of the Giant's Notch, but several bowshots—perhaps a quarter-league—back from the edge. And for several days royalist hunting parties had clambered down the Notch to sweep the neighboring woods for satyrs. Those they caught, they dragged alive back to their camp and penned them, still bound, in a stockade built for the purpose.

"My folk move from Notch," said Gola, sadly. "Had no pipes ready."

Ignoring that strange remark, Conan asked: "How know you that they plan to use your people's blood for magical sacrifices?"

The satyr gave Conan a sly, sidelong glance. "We know. We, too, have magic. Big magician on cliffs above."

Conan pondered, studying the small creature intently. "Gola, if we push the bad men from the upper plain, you need no longer fear mistreatment. If you help us, we will restore your woods to you."

"How know I what big men do? Big men kill our people."

"Nay, we are your friends. See, you are free to go." Conan pointed to the tent flap, arms spread wide.

A glow of childlike joy suffused the satyr's face. Conan waited for the glow to fade, then said: "Now that we've saved some of your folk from the wizard's cauldron, we may ask help from you. How can I reach you?"

Gola showed Conan a small tube made of bone that was suspended from a vine entwined about his neck. "Go in woods and blow." The satyr put the whistle to his lips and puffed his cheeks.

"I hear no sound," said Conan.

"Nay, but satyr hear. You take."

Conan stared at the tiny whistle as it lay in his huge palm, while the others frowned, thinking the bit of bone a useless toy intended to cozen their general. Presently, Conan slipped the whistle into his pouch, saying gravely: "I thank you, little friend." Then calling his squires and the nearest sentry, he said: "Escort Gola into the woods beyond the camp. Let none molest him—some of our superstitious soldiers might deem him an embodied evil spirit and take a cut at him. Farewell."

When the satyr had departed, Conan addressed his comrades: "Numitor lies beyond the Notch, waiting for us to climb the slope ere he signals attack! What make you of it?"

Prospero shrugged. "Meseems he relies much on that 'big magician'—the king's sorcerer, I have no doubt."

Trocero shook his head. "More likely, he's fain to give us a clear path to the top, so that we can face him on equal terms. He is a well-meaning gentleman who thinks to fight a war by rules of chivalry."

"He must know we outnumber him," said Publius, perplexed.

"Aye," retorted Trocero, "but his troops are Aquilonia's best, whereas half our motley horde are babes playing at warfare. So he relies on dash and discipline . . ."

The argument was long and inconclusive. As twilight deepened into night, Conan banged his goblet on the table. "We cannot sit below the cliffs for ay, attempting to read Numitor's mind. Tomorrow we shall scale the Giant's Notch, prepared for instant action."

chapter  x

Sacyrs' Blood

Prince Numitor paced restlessly about the royalist camp. The cooking fires were dying down, and the regiments of Royal Frontiersmen had turned in for the night. The new moon set, and in the gathering darkness the stars wheeled slowly westward like diamonds stitched upon the night-blue cloak of a dancing girl. To the west, where twilight lingered, the dodging shape of a foraging bat besmudged the horizon, while overhead the clap of a nightjar's wings shattered the silence.

The prince passed the line of sentries and strolled toward the edge of the escarpment, where Thulandra Thuu had placed things needful for his magic. Behind him the camp vanished into forest-shadowed darkness. Ahead the precipice fell sharply away. And leftward yawned the black canyon that was called the Giant's Notch.

Although the prince's placid ears picked up no sound of movement in the gorge, something about the camp's location disturbed him; but for a time he could not put a finger on the source of his unease.

After walking several bowshots' distance, Prince Numitor sighted the dancing flames of a small fire. He hastened toward it. Thulandra Thuu, hooded and cloaked in black, like some bird of ill omen, was bending over the fire, while Hsiao, on his knees, fed the blaze with twigs. A metal tripod, from the apex of which a small brazen pot was suspended by a chain, straddled the fickle fire. To one side a large copper cauldron squatted in the grass.

As Numitor approached, the sorcerer moved away from the firelight and, fumbling in a leathern wallet, extracted a crystal phial. This he unstoppered, muttering an incantation in an unknown tongue, and poured the contents into the heated vessel. A sudden hissing and a plume of smoke, shot through with rainbow hues, issued from the pot.

Thulandra Thuu glanced at the prince, said a brief "Good even, my lord!" and reached again into his wallet.

"Master Thulandra!" said Numitor.

"Sir?" The sorcerer paused in his searching.

"You insisted that the camp be set far from the precipice; I wonder at your reasoning. Should the rebels steal into the Giant's Notch, they would be upon us ere they were discovered. Why not move the camp here on the morrow, where our men can readily assail the foe with missiles from above?"

The eyes beneath the sorcerer's cowl were veiled in purple darkness, but the prince fancied that they glowed deep in that cavernous hollow, like the night eyes of beasts of prey. Thulandra purred: "My lord Prince, if the demons I unleash perform their proper function, my spell would put your men in danger should they stand where we stand now. The final stage I shall commence at midnight, a scant three hours hence. Hsiao will inform you in good time."

The magician shook more powder into the steaming pot and stirred the molten mixture with a slender silver rod. "Now I crave your pardon, my good lord, but I must ask you to stand back whilst I construct my pentacle."

Hsiao handed Thulandra Thuu the wooden staff, ornately carved, which served him as a walking stick when he stalked about the camp. While his servant piled fresh fuel upon the dying fire, the sorcerer paced off certain distances about the conflagration and marked the bare earth with the ferule of his staff. Muttering, he drew a circle, a dozen paces in diameter, then etched deep lines back and forth across the space enclosed. Following an arcane ritual, he inscribed a symbol in each angle of the pentacle. The prince understood neither the diagram nor the lettering thereon, but felt no desire to plumb the wizard's unholy mysteries.

Now Thulandra rose up and stood beside his fire, his back to the precipice. He intoned an utterance—a prayer or incantation—in a singsong foreign tongue. Then, facing east, he repeated his invocation, and in this wise completed one rotation. Numitor saw the stars grow dim and shapeless shadows flutter through the clear night air. He heard the sinister thunder of unseen beating wings. Thinking it better not to view more of the uncanny preparations of his cousin's favorite, he stumbled back to camp. To his captains he gave orders to rouse the men an hour before midnight to comply with the sorcerer's directions. Then he turned in.

Three hours later Hsiao spoke to a sentry, who sent another to awaken the sleeping prince. As Numitor made his way to the cliff whereon the wizard prepared his magical spell, he came upon the column of soldiers ordered by Thulandra Thuu. Each man-at-arms gripped a bound and captive satyr. A dozen of the furry forest folk whimpered and wailed as their captors brutally hustled them into line.

Hsiao had built up the fire, and the brazen pot bubbled merrily, sending a cloud of varicolored smoke into the starlit sky. Upon Thulandra's curt command, the first soldier in the line dragged his squirming captive to the copper cauldron standing upon the grass and forced the bleating creature's head down over the vessel's rim. As the darkness throbbed to the beat of an inaudible drum—or was it the beat of the awestruck soldiers' hearts?—the sorcerer deftly slashed the satyr's throat. At a signal, the man-at-arms lifted the sacrificial victim by its ankles and drained its blood into the large container. Then, in obedience to a low command, he tossed the small cadaver over the precipice.

A pause ensued while Thulandra added more powders to his sinister brew and pronounced another incantation. At length he beckoned to the next man in line, who dragged his satyr forward to be slain. The other soldiers shifted uneasy feet. One muttered:

"This takes longer than a coronation! Would he'd get on with it and let us back to bed."

The eastern sky was paling when the last satyr died. The fire beneath the brazen pot had burned to a bed of embers. Hsiao, at his master's command, unhooked the steaming pot and poured its boiling contents into the blood-filled cauldron. The nearest soldiers saw—or thought they saw—ghostly forms rise from the latter vessel; but others perceived only great clouds of vapor. In the deceptive predawn half-light, none could be sure of what he saw.

Faintly in the distance those on the cliff-top heard the sound of men in motion. Among the marching men no word was spoken, but the jingle of harness and the tramp of many feet cried defiance to the silent morning air.

Thulandra Thuu raised a voice shrill with tension: "My lord! Prince Numitor! Order your men away!"

Startled out of his sleepy lethargy, the prince barked the command: "Stand to arms! Back to camp!"

The sounds of an approaching army grew. The sorcerer raised his arms and droned an invocation. Hsiao handed him a dipper, with which he scooped up liquid from the cauldron and poured the fluid into a deep crack in the rocks. He stepped back, raised imploring arms against the lightening sky, and cried out again in unknown tongues. Then he ladled out another dipperful, and another.

Along the road from Culario, before that sandy ribbon disappeared beneath a canopy of leaves, the mage could see a pair of mounted men. They trotted toward the Giant's Notch, and as they went they studied the rock wall and the woods below it. Then a whole troop of cavalry came into view; and following them, files of infantry, swinging along with weapons balanced on their shoulders.

Thulandra Thuu hastily ladled out more liquid from the cauldron and once more raised his skinny arms to heaven.

———

Leading the first rank of rebel horse, Conan rose in his stirrups to peer about. His scouts had seen no royalists in the greenery along the forest road, or at the Giant's Notch, or atop the towering cliffs. The Cimmerian's eagle glance raked the summit, now tipped a rosy pink by the slanting rays of the morning sun. Conan's apprehension of hidden traps stirred in his savage soul. Prince Numitor was no genius, this he knew; but even such a one as he would make ready to defend the Notch.

Yet he saw no sign of a royalist mustering. Would Numitor, indeed, allow the rebels to reach the Imirian Plateau to lessen the odds against them? Conan knew the nobles of this land professed obedience to the rules of chivalry; but in all his years of war, no general had ever risked a certain chance of victory for such an abstract principle. Nay, the enemy had the upper hand; a trap was obvious! Experience with the hypocrisies of civilized men made the Cimmerian cynical about the ideals they so eloquently proclaimed. The barbarians among whom he had grown to manhood were quite as treacherous; but they did not seek to gild their bloody actions with noble sentiments.

One scout reported a strange discovery. At the base of the escarpment, left-ward of the Giant's Notch, he had come upon a heap of satyr corpses, each with its throat ripped open. The bodies, smashed and scattered, had fallen from the heights above.

"Sorcery afoot!" muttered Trocero. "The king's he-witch has joined with Numitor, I'll wager."

As the two lead horsemen neared the Notch, they spurred their steeds and vanished up the road that paralleled the turgid River Bitaxa. Soon they reappeared upon a rocky ledge and signaled all was quiet. Conan scanned the summit once again. He thought he caught a hint of movement—a mere black speck that might have been a trick of light or of tired eyes. Turning, he motioned the leader of the troop, Captain Morenus, to enter the tunnel of the Notch.

Conan sat his mount beside the road, watching intently. As the horsemen trotted past, his heart swelled at the soldierly appearance they made, thanks to the driving force of his incessant drilling. His own horse, a bay gelding, seemed restless, stamping its hooves and dancing sideways. Conan stroked the creature's neck to gentle it, but the bay continued to fidget. He first thought the animal was impatient to move forward with the others of the troop; but as the horse became more agitated, a premonition took shape in Conan's mind.

After another glance at the escarpment Conan, a scowl on his scarred face, swung off his beast and dropped with a clash of armor to the ground. Gripping his reins, he shut his eyes. His barbarian senses, keener than those of city-bred men, had not deceived him. Through the soles of his boots he felt a faint quivering in the earth. Not the vibration that a group of galloping horsemen sends through the ground, this was something slower, more deliberate, with more actual motion, as if the earth had waked to yawn and stretch.

Conan hesitated no longer. Cupping his hands around his mouth and filling his great lungs, he bellowed: "Morenus, come back! Get out of the Notch! Spur your horses, all! Come back!"

There was a moment of confusion in the Notch, as the command was passed along and the soldiers sought to turn their steeds on the narrow way. Above them on the cliff, the sorcerer shrieked a final invocation and struck the rocks outside his pentacle with his curiously carven staff.

A rumble—a deep-toned roll that scarcely could be heard—issued from the earth. Above the retreating cavalrymen, the cliffs swayed. Pieces of black basalt detached themselves and toppled, with deceptive slowness, then faster and faster, striking ledges, shattering, and bounding off to crash into the gorge. From the River Bitaxa, towering jets of spray fountained aloft to dwarf the downward fall of the cascade.

Conan found his stirrup with some difficulty, as his terror-stricken beast danced around him in a circle. His foot secured, he swung cursing into the saddle and wheeled to face the column of infantry, still marching briskly toward the Notch.

"Get back! Get back!" he roared, but his words were lost in the grumbling, grinding thunder of the earthquake. He moved his horse into the column's path, making frantic gestures. The lead men understood and checked their gait; but those behind continued to press forward, so that the column bunched up into a milling mass.

Within the Notch the cliffs swayed, reeled, and crumbled. With the roar of an angry god, millions of tons of rock cascaded into the gap. The earth beneath the soldiers' feet so swayed and bounced that men clutched one another to stay erect; a few fell, their weapons clattering to the rocky ground.

Down from the deadly flume raced Conan's troop of cavalry, lashed by their panic. The leaders crashed into the infantry column, downing some horses, spilling riders from their saddles, and injuring many foot soldiers caught in the pincer's jaws. Men's shouts and horses' screams soared above the thunder of the 'quake.

The Bitaxa River foamed out of its bed, as waves sent downstream by the fall of rock spread out on the flatlands below and lapped across the road. Soldiers splashed ankle-deep in water and prayed to their assorted gods.

Controling his frantic mount by a savage grip on the reins, Conan sought to restore order. "Morenus!" he shouted. "Did all your men get out?"

"All but a dozen or so in the van, General."

Glowering at the Giant's Notch, Conan cursed the loss. A vast cloud of dust obscured the pass, until a wind sprang up and swept it out. As the dust thinned, Conan saw that the Notch was now much wider than before and that its slopes were less than vertical. The flume was filled with a huge talus of broken rock—

stones of all sizes, from pebbles to fragments as large as a tent. From time to time small slides continued to issue from the sloping walls and clatter down upon the talus. Any man caught beneath that fall of rock would be entombed forever.

One section in the left side of the cliff had curiously remained in place; it now rose from the slope like a narrow buttress. At the pinnacle of this strange formation, Conan saw a pair of small figures, black-robed and cowled. One tossed its arms on high, as if in supplication.

"That's the king's sorcerer, Thulandra Thuu, or I'm a Stygian!" rasped a voice nearby.

Conan turned to see Gromel at his elbow. "Think you he sent the earthquake?"

"Aye. And if he'd waited till we were all within the Notch, we'd all be dead. He's too far for a bowshot; but if I had a bow, I'd chance it."

An archer heard and handed up his bow, saying: "Try mine, sir!"

Gromel dismounted, drew an arrow to the head, shifted aim by a hair's breadth, and let fly. The arrow arced high and struck the cliff a score of paces below the top. The small figures vanished.

"A good try," grunted Conan. "We should have set up a ballista. Gromel, there are broken bones in need of splints; see that the physicians do their work."

Under lowering brows Conan stared at the talus. His barbarian instincts told him to rally his men, dismount the cavalry, and lead them all in a headlong charge up the steep incline, leaping from rock to rock with naked steel in hand. But experience warned him that this would be a futile gesture, throwing away men's lives to no good purpose. Progress would be slow and laborious; the struggling climbers would be raked by arrows from above; those who survived the climb would be too winded to do battle.

He looked around. "Ho there, Trocero! Prospero! Morenus, send a trooper to tell Publius and Pallantides that I want them here. Now, friends, what next?"

Count Trocero reined his horse closer to Conan's and studied the mass of broken rock. "The army can in no way ascend the slope. Men afoot might slowly pick their way up—if Numitor did not assail them and the sorcerer cast no other deadly spell. But horses never, nor yet the wains."

"Could we build our own road, replacing the rock-ledge path that lies beneath the rocks?" suggested Prospero.

Trocero considered the idea. "With a thousand workmen, several months, and gold to spare, I'd build you as fine a road as you could wish."

"We do not have such time, nor money either," rumbled Conan. "If we cannot go through the Notch, we must go over, under, or around it. Order the men to march a quarter-league back along the road and pitch camp under the forest trees."

In the royalist camp Thulandra Thuu confronted a furious prince. The exhausted sorcerer, looking much older than was his wont, leaned on Hsiao's sturdy shoulder. The area on which his pentacle was marked had not fallen with the balance of the cliff, and he had walked the narrow bridge to safety.

"You fool necromancer!" grumbled Numitor. "Since you would resort to magic, you should have waited till the Notch was filled with rebels. Thus we had slain them all. Now they have fled with little scathe."

"You do not understand these matters, Prince," replied Thulandra coolly. "I withheld the final step of the enchantment until I saw that something—or someone—had warned the rebel leader of the trap and the rebels had begun to flee. Had I withheld my hand the longer, they would have all escaped scot-free. In any case the flume is blocked. The rebels must needs march east to the Khorotas or west to the Alimane, for they cannot now breach the escarpment.

"And now Your Highness must excuse me. The spell has drained my psychic forces, and I must rest."

"I never did think much of miracle-mongers," growled Numitor as he turned away.

In the sheltered forest camp that evening, Conan and his officers reviewed a map. "To bypass the escarpment," said Conan, "we must return to the village of Pedassa, whence the roads depart for the two rivers. But that's a lengthy march."

"If there were some little-known break in the long cliff wall," said Prospero wistfully, "we could, by moving quietly through the woods, steal a march on Numitor and fall upon him unawares."

Conan frowned. "This map shows no such pass; but long ago I learned not to trust mapmakers. You're lucky if they show the rivers flowing in the true direction. Trocero, know you any alternate route?"

Trocero shook his head. "Nay."

"There must be streams other than the Bitaxa that cut a channel in the cliff."

Trocero shrugged helplessly. Pallantides entered, saying: "Your pardon, General, but two men of Serdicus's company have deserted."

Conan snorted. "Every time we win, men desert from the royalists to join us; every time we lose, they desert us for the king. It is like a game of chance, following Fate's decree. Send scouts to look for them and hang them if you catch them; but do not make a public matter of it. Order woodsman at dawn to study the cliff face in both directions for the distance of a league to see if they can find a pathway to the top. And now, friends, leave me to ponder further on the matter."

———

Beside his camp bed Conan brooded over a flagon of ale. He restudied the map and cudgeled his brain for a way his army might surmount the escarpment.

Absently he fingered the half-circle of obsidian, which once had hung between the opulent breasts of the dancing girl Alcina, and which was now clasped around his massive neck. He stared down at the object, thinking how right had been his friend Trocero's suspicion that she had caused the death of old Amulius Procas.

Little by little, the pieces of the puzzle fitted together. Alcina had been sent—either by the king's spymaster or by the royal sorcerer—to try to murder him. Later she succeeded in slaying General Procas. Why Procas? Because with Conan in his grave, Procas was no longer needed to defend Aquilonia's mad king. Hence, neither she nor her master knew, at the time of Procas's death, that Conan had recovered from her deadly elixir.

Well, thought Conan, not without bitterness, he must hereafter be more cautious in choosing his bedmates. But why should Procas die? Because Alcina's master, whoever he might be, wanted the old man out of his way. This thought led Conan to Thulandra Thuu, for the rivalry between the sorcerer and the general for the king's favor was notorious.

Conan gripped the ebon talisman as this enlightenment burst upon him. And as he did so, he became aware of a curious sensation. It seemed that voices carried on a dialogue within his skull.

A shadowy form took shape before his eyes. As Conan tensed to snatch his sword, the vision solidified, and he saw a female figure sitting on a black wrought-iron throne. The vision was to some extent transparent—Conan could dimly see the tent wall behind the image—and too nebulous to recognize the woman's features. But in the shadowy face burned eyes of emerald green.

With every nerve atingle, Conan watched the figure and harkened to the voices. One was a woman's dusky voice, and her words followed the movements of the shadow's lips. The voice was Alcina's but she seemed unaware of Conan's scrutiny.

The other voice was dry, metallic, passionless, and spoke Aquilonian with a sibilant slur. Conan had never exchanged a word with Thulandra Thuu, although he had seen the mage across the throne room during courtly functions in Tarantia when he was general to the king. But from descriptions of the wizard, he imagined the king's favorite would speak thus. The voice proceeded;

". . . I know not who betrayed my plan; but some treacher must have forewarned the rebel chieftain."

Alcina replied: "Perhaps not, Master. The barbarian pig has senses keener than those of ordinary men; he might have detected the coming cataclysm by some stirring of the air above the earth. What do you now?"

"I must needs remain here to guard that ninny Numitor against some asinine misjudgment, until Count Ulric arrives. The stars inform me of his coming in three days' time. Yet I am weary. Calling up the spirits of the earth has prostrated me. I can work no further spells until I recoup my psychic forces."

"Then, pray, come back forthwith!" urged the vision of Alcina. "Ulric will surely arrive before the rebels can surmount the cliffs, and I have need of your protection."

"Protection? Why so?"

"His maggotty Majesty, the King, importunes me constantly to join him in his bestial amusements. I am afraid."

"What has this walking heap of excrement been urging you to do?"

"His desires beggar all description, Master. At your command, some men I have lain with, and some I have slain. But this I will not do."

"Set and Kali!" exclaimed the dry male voice. "When I have finished with Numedides, he'll wish he were in hell! I shall set forth for Tarantia on the morrow."

"Have a care that you fall not into rebel hands along the way! Insurgent bands have been reported along the Road of Kings, and the barbarian pig might lead a swift raid into loyal territory. He is a worthy adversary."

The male voice chuckled faintly. "Fear not for me, my dear Alcina. Even in my present depleted state, I can with my peculiar powers slay any mortal at close quarters. And now, farewell."

The voices fell silent, and the vision faded. Conan shook himself like one awakening from a vivid dream. With Thulandra gone from the scene of battle and Ulric not yet arrived, he had a chance to fall on Numitor's army and rout it—if only he could reach the plains above before the Count of Raman came with reinforcements.

He needed air to clear his rampant thoughts and rose to leave his narrow sleeping quarters. In the adjacent section of the tent, the bodyguards whom Prospero had assigned him were so engrossed in a game of chance that none looked up as Conan, soundless as a shadow, glided past them.

Outside, the sentries, used to his night prowls, supposed that he was making an inspection. They saluted as he wandered to the edge of the encampment and continued into the nighted woods. Prospero, he thought with a grim smile, would be perturbed to know that Conan once again had given his bodyguards the slip.

He fumbled in his wallet for the bone whistle Gola had given him, retrieved it, and fingered it. The satyr had said that if he ever wanted help from the people of these woods, he had but to blow upon it. Half in jest, he put the tiny whistle to his lips and blew. Nothing happened. More urgently, he blew another silent blast.

Perhaps the remnant of the satyrs had departed from the scene of their destruction. Even if they heard the call, they might need time to come to him. Conan stood motionless with the wary patience of a crouching panther waiting for its prey, listening to the buzz and chirp of insects and the rustle of a passing breeze. Now and then he put the soundless whistle to his lips and blew again.

At length he felt a movement in the shrubbery. "Who you, blow whistle call satyr?" asked a small high-pitched voice in broken Aquilonian.

"Gola?"

"Nay, me Zudik, chief. Who you?" The shrubbery parted.

"Conan the Cimmerian. Do you know Gola?" Conan, whose eyes had adjusted to the darkness, could see this was a bent and ancient satyr, whose pelt was tinged with silver.

"Aye," replied the satyr chieftain. "He tell about you. Save him and four others. What you want?"

"Your help to kill the men atop the cliff."

"How Zudik help big man like you?"

"We need a pathway to the top," said Conan, "now that the Giant's Notch is filled with rocks. Know you another way?"

The night sang with the sound of insects in the silence. Then Zudik answered slowly: "Is small path that way." The satyr pointed eastward.

"How far?"

The satyr replied in his own language, and his words were like the caws of crows.

Puzzled, the Cimmerian asked: "Can we get there within a day's march?"

"Walk hard. Can do."

"Will you show us the way?"

"Aye. Be ready before sun-up."

Later Conan sought out Publius and said: "We move at dawn for a path the satyrs say leads to the bluff; but it's too narrow for the wagons. You will take the baggage train back to Pedassa and follow the road thence to the Khorotas. If we join you on the road to Tarantia, we shall have vanquished Numitor; if not—" Conan drew a finger across his throat—"you'll go alone."

The second gap in the escarpment was much narrower than the Giant's Notch. From below it was invisible, hidden by lush greenery and overhanging rocks. The horsemen had to lead their mounts across the brook that gurgled at the bottom of the cleft and up the rocky way. More than one horse, frightened by the narrowing canyon walls, held up the others while it whinnied, rolled frightened eyes, and reared.

The men afoot, walking in single file, could just squeeze through. When dusk made the path darker and more sinister, Conan urged each man to grasp the garments of the man ahead and stumble forward. Morning saw the last man through.

While the Army of Liberation rested from their forced march and arduous climb, Conan sent scouts to probe Numitor's position. On their return the leader reported:

"Numitor has struck his camp and fallen back for several leagues along the road. His men have pitched camp in the forest, straddling the highway."

Conan looked a question at his officers. Pallantides said: "What's this? Even if Numitor is stupid, I've never heard he was a coward!"

"More likely," Trocero put in, "he learned that we have found a way up the escarpment and feared we would drive him to the precipice."

"The sorcerer might have warned him," ventured Prospero.

"That is not all, General," said the chief scout. "Four more regiments have arrived to reinforce the enemy. We recognized their banners."

Conan grunted. "Numitor has stripped the Westermarck of regulars, leaving the defense against the Picts to the local militia. So we are again outnumbered; and the Royal Frontiersmen are skilfull fighting men. I've fought beside them and I know." He paused a moment, then added: "Friends, that satyr Gola said something about using pipes against a foe. What think you that he meant?"

None knew. At last Conan said: "I see I must consult our little folk again."

As dusk drew a gray veil of mist along the tumbling stream, Conan worked his way down the narrow path up which his men had so laboriously clambered. He stood alone in the enshrouding dark of the Brocellian Forest, listening in vain for any footfall. He blew on the bone whistle and, as before, he waited in the shadow of an ancient tree. When at last his call was answered, he was relieved to find it was Zudik, the satyr who had directed his army to the pass. In answer to a question, Zudik said:

"Aye, we use pipes. Make your men stop up ears."

"Plug up our ears?" asked Conan wonderingly.

"Aye. Use beeswax, cloth, clay—so can no longer hear. Then we help you."

Numitor's Frontiersmen lay in a crescent across the highway to Tarantia. The prince seemed prepared to stand on the defensive until the arrival of Count Ulric. His men were digging earthworks with implanted pointed stakes to impede an attacker. Because of the dense stands of trees, the rebels could not outflank the royalists's long line.

Silently, the Army of Liberation spread out before the crescent, their presence hidden by the shrubbery. But when a royal sentry perceived a movement in the bushes, he sounded an alarm. Men dropped their shovels, snatched weapons, and took positions on the line.

Conan signaled to his aides, whose ears were plugged, to tell the archers to ply the foe with arrows; and presently, the thrum of bowstrings and the whistle of arrows rent the air. But Conan's men heard nothing.

To the royalist defenders on the ends of the line came a chilling sound—a shrill, ululating, unearthly piping. It came from nowhere into everywhere. It made men's teeth ache and imbued them with a strange, unreasoning panic. Soldiers dropped their weapons to clutch at pain-racked heads. Some burst into hysterical laughter; others dissolved in tears.

As the sound drew nearer, the feeling of dire doom expanded until it overflowed their souls. The impulse to be gone, which at first they mastered, overcame their years of battle training. Here and there a man turned from his position on the line to run, screaming madly, to the rear. More joined the flight, until the outer limits of the line dissolved into a mass of terrified fugitives, running from they knew not what. As the prince's flanks were swept away, the unseen pipers moved toward the center, until that, too, disintegrated. Trocero's cavalry rode down the fleeing men, slaying and taking prisoners.

"Anyway," said Conan as he looked at the abandoned royalist camp, "they left us weapons enough for twice our number. So now we can recruit whatever volunteers we find."

"That was an easy victory," exulted Prospero.

"Too easy," replied Conan grimly. "An easy victory is oft as false as a courtier's smile. I'll say the road to Tarantia is open when I see the city walls, and not before."

chapter  xi

The Key to the City

The Army of Liberation tramped unopposed through the smiling land, where Poitain's herds of fine horses and cattle grazed on luxuriant grass, and castles reared their crenelated towers of crimson and purple and gold. The rebel army serpentined its way through pillow-rounded mountains, lush with vegetation, and at last approached the border between Poitain and the central provinces of Aquilonis.

But as Conan sat his charger on an embankment to watch his soldiers pass before him, his gaze was somber. For, although Numitor's Frontiersmen had scattered like leaves in an autumn gale, a new foe, against which he had no defense, now assailed his army. This was sickness. A malady, which caused men to break out in scarlet spots and prostrated them with chills and fever, raced through his ranks, an invisible demon, felling more soldiers than a hard-fought battle. Many men were left abed in villages along the way; many, fearing the dread disease, deserted; many died.

"What do we number now?" Conan asked Publius of an evening, as the army neared the border village of Elymia.

The former chancellor studied his reports. "About eight thousand, counting the walking sick, who number nigh a thousand."

"Crom! We were ten thousand when we left the Alimane, and hundreds more have joined since then. What has become of them?"

Trocero said: "Some come to us in a roseate glow, like a bridegroom to his bride, but think better of their bargain when they have sweated and slogged a few leagues from their native heath. They fret about their families and getting home to harvest."

"And this spotted sickness has claimed thousands," added Dexitheus. "I, and the physicians under me, have tried every herb and purge to no avail. It seems magic is at work. Else an evil destiny doth shape our ends."

Conan bit back scornful words of incredulity. After the earthquake he dared not underestimate the potent magic of his enemy or the wanton cruelty of the gods.

"Could we have persuaded the satyrs to march with us, bringing their pipes," said Prospero, "our paltry numbers would be of little moment."

"But they would not leave their homes in the Brocellian Forest," said Conan.

Prospero replied: "You could have seized their old Zudik as a hostage, to compel them."

"That's not my way," growled Conan. "Zudik proved a friend in need. I would not use him ill."

Trocero smiled gently. "And are you not the man who scorned Prince Numitor for his high-flown ideals of chivalry?"

Conan grunted. "With savages, the chief has little power; I have dwelt amongst them, and I know. Besides, I doubt if even great love for their chieftain's weal would overcome the little people's fear of open country. But let us face the future and not raise ghosts from the dead past. Have the scouts reported signs of Ulric's army?"

"No reports," said Trocero, "save that today they glimpsed a few riders from afar, who quickly galloped out of sight. We know not who they are; but I would wager that the northern barons delay Count Ulric still."

"Tomorrow," said Conan, "I shall take Gyrto's troop to scout the border of Poitain, whilst the rest march for Elymia."

"General," objected Prospero. "You should not use yourself so recklessly. A commander should stay behind the lines, where he can control his units, and not risk his life like a landless adventurer."

Conan frowned. "If I am commander here, I must command as I think best!" Seeing Prospero's stricken face, he added with a smile: "Fear not; I'll do naught foolish. But even a general must betimes share the dangers of his men. Besides, am I not myself a landless adventurer?"

"Methinks," grumbled Prospero, "you merely indulge your barbarian lust for combat hand-to-hand." Conan's grin widened wolfishly, but he ignored the comment.

The road was a golden ribbon before them, as Conan's troop trotted through the misty morning. At the column's head rode Conan, clad in chain mail like the others, and Captain Gyrto rode at his side. With lance fixed into a stirrup boot, each cavalryman rode proudly through the rolling countryside. A few detached outriders cantered in wide circles across the fallow fields but skirted the simple farmsteads and the stands of ripening grain.

Rustics at work on furrow or vine paused in their labors to lean on rake or hoe and stare, as the armed men rode past. One or two raised a cautious cheer, but most remained stolidly noncommittal and silent. Now and then Conan caught a flash of red or yellow petticoat, as a woman rushed to hide herself from the passing soldiery.

"They wait to see who wins," said Gyrto.

"And well they might," said Conan, "for, if we lose, all who aided us will suffer for it."

Beyond the next rise, Elymia squatted in a shallow vale. A small stream meandered sluggishly past the mud-brick houses, wending its way eastward toward the Khorotas, while willows contemplated their reflections in the dark, slow-moving water.

The village, which sheltered less than two hundred souls, lacked protection; for decades of peace had so beguiled the villagers that they allowed the old wall of sun-dried brick to crumble utterly. Inhabitants—if any there were who labored in the hamlet—were nowhere to be seen.

"It's too quiet for me," muttered Conan. "People should be up and about on a fair day like this."

"Perchance they are sleeping off their midday meal," suggested Gyrto. "Or all but the babes and ancient crones are working in the fields."

"Too late for that," growled Conan. "I like it not."

"Or perchance they are in hiding, fearing robbery or murder."

Conan said: "Send two scouts through the village; we'll wait here."

Two troopers hastened down the gentle slope and disappeared into the maw of the narrow, winding street. Soon the street disgorged them; and galloping toward their fellows, they signaled that all was quiet.

"Let's take a look ourselves," growled Conan. And Gyrto waved his hundred lancers forward at a brisk trot.

The sun was a gigantic orange disc as it slipped to the western horizon; and the houses of Elymia stood black and sinister against its fiery glow. The rebels glanced about them with a touch of apprehension; for still there was no sign of human habitation in the squalid street or behind the shuttered doorways.

"Perhaps," suggested Gyrto, "the people heard of two approaching armies and fled, fearing to be caught betwixt hammer and anvil."

Conan shrugged, loosening his sword in its scabbard. On each side of the roadway rose low cottages, their roofs thick-thatched. The front of one house was open, with a counter set before it. A painted mug above the humble door proclaimed it the village ale shop, the town being too small to boast an inn. Down the short street a barnlike building thrust itself back from the road. Scattered iron bars, a pincers, and a brazier proved it a smithy; but no clang of metal issued from it. Something—he knew not what—raised the hairs on Conan's nape.

Conan twisted in the saddle to look back, as the last of his double column trotted into the deserted street. The pairs of horses pressed close against the walls of crowding houses, so meager was the way.

"A mean place for an attack," said Conan. "Signal the men to hurry through."

Gyrto waved an order to his trumpeter, when another trumpet blared, close at hand. Instantly the doors of all the cottages burst open, and royalist soldiers boiled out, rending the dusk hideous with battle cries. They struck at Conan's troop from either side, their swords and pikes thirsty for blood.

Ahead three ranks of pikemen sprang into position, blocking the road with a wall of pointed steel. Slowly they moved forward, with battle lust in their eyes and spearheads glowing a dull crimson in the rays of the setting sun.

"Crom and Ishtar!" yelled Conan, sweeping out his sword, "we're in Death's pocket! Gyrto, turn the men around!"

The din of battle rose—the shouts of angry men, the neighs of plunging steeds, the grind of steel on steel, the clash of swords on riven shields, and the dull thud of fallen bodies. Attacked from three sides by superior numbers, Conan's troopers were at a disadvantage. The confined space prevented them from bunching into a compact formation or working up speed for a charge. A lance in the hand of a charging horseman is more formidable than in the hand of that same horseman forced to halt.

The rebel troopers, spurred by fear and fury, set their lances and jabbed at their assailants. Some dropped their lances and, drawing swords, slashed downward at their attackers, raining well-aimed blows. Men swore loud oaths to their assorted gods. Injured horses reared and screamed like fiends in hell. One, disemboweled, fell kicking, pinning its rider; and the royalists swarmed upon the man, slashing and battering, until he lay incarnadined with gore.

Another rider, caught by an upflung spearhead, was lofted out of his saddle and tossed beneath the steel-shod hooves of a plunging steed. Still another was unhorsed, but he set his back to the wall of a house and stood off his attackers with the darting tongue of his sweeping blade.

Some of Count Ulric's soldiers went down beneath the rebels' lancepoints and swinging swords. Blood laid the dust on the earthern road, as wounded men shrieked in agony, the death rattle in their throats.

Roaring like a lion, Conan beat his way back along the column, squeezing between his milling men and the enclosing walls. His great sword swung upward and descended; with nearly every blow, a royalist crumpled or fell dead. Thrice his down-directed cuts sheared arms from shoulders, and thrice blood spurted bubbling from the ghastly wounds. As Conan hewed, he shouted lustily.

"Out! Out! To the rear, march! Out of the village! Rally on the road!"

Powerful as was his voice, his words were drowned in a torrent of cacophony. But little by little his men wrenched their horses' heads around and pushed southward. Behind Conan, Captain Gyrto and two veteran lancers fought a desperate rear-guard action against the massed pikemen who pressed forward behind their bristling steel. Lances at the ready, they spurred their terror-stricken beasts against the wall of steel; but as one spearman fell, another leaped in to take his place. And so, despite their grim intent to win or die, they could not overwhelm the relentless surge of steel-clad men. And there one lancer died.

Conan's steed stumbled over a supine body. He jerked up on the bridle to prevent the animal's inadvertent fall. He swung a back-hand blow at a royalist swordsman, who caught the vicious stroke on his shield; but the sheer force of the blow hurled the soldier to his knees in a battered doorway, and kneeling, he cradled a broken arm, tears streaming down his face.

Finally, Conan glimpsed the last remnant of his troopers fighting free of their attackers and galloping up the slope beyond the scene of the débâcle. Between him and the retreating men, the narrow street was filled with royalists afoot, slipping on the bloodstained entrails of men and horses, swaying with fatigue, but like human bloodhounds, smelling out their prey, coming closer, ever closer to the three horsemen caught in the cruel jaws of the clever trap. Glancing to the right, Conan perceived between two cottages a narrow alley, a mere footpath among the weeds.

"Gyrto!" bellowed Conan. "This way! Follow me!"

Abruptly turning his horse into that meager alley, Conan paused only long enough to make sure the others followed closely. The lengthening shadows of a cottage enshrouded the fleeing men in darkness, and for a moment there was no yapping at their heels.

In the momentary respite, Conan reined in his exhausted mount and allowed the beast to pick its way among the crumpled vegetation. Suddenly, despite the gloaming, he descried a pigsty, its entrance barred by a battered panel, rope-bound to the adjacent fencing. With his bloodstained blade he severed the heavy rope, and the crude door swung open.

Gyrto and his companion stood aghast, wondering whether the heat of battle or a heavy blow had unseated their leader's reason. Then with an upraised finger pointing forward, Conan spurred his horse and, followed closely by his loyal troopers, sped down the narrow passageway.

A wave of racing royalist foot soldiers, interspersed with mounted men-at-arms, swirled round the corner of the cottage and crested in the slender channel of the alley.

Gyrto yelled to Conan: "Ride man, ride! They're hot upon our trail."

Conan bent low above his horse's neck, face buried in the creature's flowing mane. And then, at the alley's end, a tall fence, scarce visible in the gathering gloom, barred the way to safety.

Conan's horse, gathering its mighty haunches, rose magnificently and cleared the obstruction, with Gyrto's partner Sardus close upon its flying tail. But Gyrto was less lucky. His animal, too weary to take the jump, slammed into the barrier, and screamed with the agony of a broken neck.

Gyrto, thrown clear, leaped to his feet and drew his sword, prepared to sell his life dearly. Suddenly, the pursuing riders drew rein and swore at their rearing, dancing mounts, which in their panic pressed swordsmen against the cottage walls or struck them wicked blows from flailing hooves.

Gyrto marveled at the hiatus in his almost sure destruction. "Magic again?" he muttered between clenched teeth.

Then he spied the cause of his salvation. A sow and twenty piglets had ambled from their pen and, coated with evil-smelling muck, ran squealing through the weeds, rooting for edibles.

He heard Conan call: "Climb the fence, man, quickly!" And, hesitating no longer, he flung himself at the rough barricade, dragged himself up, and scrambled over, just as the royalists reached the other side.

"Catch my stirrup!" roared Conan. "Don't try to mount!"

Gyrto seized Conan's stirrup strap and bounded along with giant strides as the spurred beast gathered speed. At an easy canter they crossed the darkling fields, leaving the royalists behind.

When the village grew small in the distance, Conan pulled up. Peering about the fading landscape, he said, "We shall catch up with the column presently. First I want a look at the enemy base. That hillock yonder may give a view of it."

From the hilltop Conan stared across the intervening swells and hollows of the earth; and north of the village, he discovered a field encampment. It had been hidden from the village by a low rise; but seen from this height, its large expanse was evident. Scores of cooking fires twinkled in the twilight, and thin blue plumes of smoke wavered in the gentle breeze.

"There's Count Ulric's army," said Conan. "How many would you judge there be, Gyrto?"

The captain thought the matter over. "From the number of fires and the size of the camp, General, I should say a dozen regiments. What say you, Sardus?"

"At least twenty thousand men, sir," said the veteran cavalryman. "What standard's that, flapping atop a flagstaff over to the right?"

Conan squinted, forcing his catlike eyes to see despite the gathering dark. Then he exclaimed: "Damn me for a Stygian, if that is not the standard of the Black Dragons!"

"Not the king's household guard, General?" exclaimed Gyrto. "That cannot be, unless Numedides himself is marching with Count Ulric."

"I do not see the royal standard, so I doubt it," rumbled Conan. "Time we rejoined our comrades. It's a long road back to camp."

Sardus mounted behind his footsore captain, and the trio began a cautious sweep around the village, wherein lay so many of their dead. Reaching the road at length, they hastened toward a stand of trees beneath which the survivors of the battle waited. At least a third of the sixty men were missing. Many wearing bandages helped to bind up their comrades' wounds.

As Conan, Gyrto, and Sardus trotted up, the dispirited troopers raised a faint hurrah. Conan growled:

"I thank you all, but save your cheers for victory. I should have searched the houses ere leading you into a tyro's trap. Still, lads, you gave them better than you got. Now let's be on our way and hope to find our army camp by dawn."

Next morning Conan told the tale of his adventures. Prospero whistled. "Twenty thousand men! In a pitched battle they'd eat us alive."

After swallowing a huge mouthful from a joint of beef, Conan said: "Breathe not such thoughts, lest the prophecy invite its own fulfillment. Rout the men out—all save the scouts who fought at Elymia—and set them to fortifying the camp. With such numbers, Count Ulric might risk a night attack. Without ditch or stockade to detain him, he could crush us like insects beneath a wagon wheel."

"But the Black Dragons!" cried Trocero. "It is a thing incredible that Numedides should send his household troops to strengthen Ulric, leaving his person unprotected!"

Conan shrugged. "I am sure of what I saw. No other unit carries for its symbol a winged monster on a field of black."

Pallantides said: "Sending the Black Dragons hither may leave Numedides vulnerable to attack, but it does naught to lessen our present problem."

"If anything, their coming aggravates it," added Trocero.

"Then be on your way, friends, and start the fortifications," said Conan. "We have no time to lose."

A gentle morning breeze fanned a hastily erected palisade and cooled the bloodshot eyes and aching bodies of its builders. When the camp followers—sutlers, water boys, women, and children—sought to carry water from a nearby stream, a company of royalist cavalry appeared over a rise, galloped down upon them, and sent them flying for their lives. One old man and one young child, slow to move, were slain.

A rebel scouting party was overtaken and forced to flee. When they regained the camp, their pursuers galloped past it, shouting taunts and hurling javelins into the stockade. Conan's archers, summoned hastily, brought down two of the enemy's horses, but comrades snatched their riders up and carried them away. Thus, although no real attack was launched against the rebels, Conan's weary men were worn down by tensions and alarums.

At the evening conference Publius said: "While I am not a military man, General, I think we ought to slip away during the night, ere Ulric brings us down or starves us out. He has the force to do his will, since sickness, like a gray ghost, stalks amongst us."

"I say," said Trocero, banging the table with his fist, "hold our position while my Poitanians raise the countryside. If Ulric surrounds us then, the countryfolk can throw a bigger ring around him."

"With harvest time approaching," Publius retorted, "you'll find it difficult to raise a thousand. And farmers armed with naught but axe and pitchfork cannot withstand a charge of Ulric's armored regulars. Would we were back in the Brocellian Forest, where our satyr friends could help us once again!"

Prospero put in: "Aye, till the royalists learn to plug their ears — not longer. I say to launch a surprise attack this night on Ulric's camp."

Pallantides shook his head. "Naught more easily falls into confusion, with friend striking down friend, than a night attack with half-trained men like ours."

The argument went round and round with no conclusion, while Conan sat somberly, frowning but saying little. Then a sentry announced:

"A royalist officer and some fifty men have come in under a flag of truce, General. The officer asks to speak to you."

"Disarm him and send him in," said Conan, straightening in his chair.

The tent flap gaped, and in stalked a man in armor. The black heraldic eagle of Aquilonia was spread upon the breast of his white surcoat, while from his helmet rose the brazen wyvern of the Black Dragons. The officer saluted stiffly.

"General Conan? I am Captain Silvanus of the Black Dragons. I have come to join you with most of my troop, if you will have us."

Conan looked the captain up and down through narrowed lids. He saw a tall, well-built, blond man, rather young for his captain's rating.

"Welcome, Captain Silvanus," he said at last. "I thank you for the offer. But before I accept it, I must know more of you."

"Certainly, General. Do but ask."

"First, what brings you to change sides at this juncture? You must know that our position is precarious, that Ulric outnumbers us, and that he is a competent commander. So wherefore turn your coat today?"

"It is simple, General Conan. My men and I have chosen a risk of death in the rebel cause over a safe life under that madman — if any life under the king's standard can be called safe."

"But why at this particular time?"

"This is our first opportunity. The Dragons reached Elymia yestereve, before the skirmish twixt Ulric's men and yours. Had we set out from Tarantia to join you, forces loyal to the king would have barred our way and destroyed us."

Conan asked: "Has Numedides sent the whole of the Black Dragon regiment hither?"

"Aye, save for a few young lads in training."

"Why does that dog denude himself of his personal guardians?"

"Numedides has proclaimed himself a god. He thinks himself immortal; and being invulnerable, has no need of bodyguards. Besides, he is determined to crush your rebellion and throws all contingents into Count Ulric's army. More march hither from the Eastern frontiers."

"What of Thulandra Thuu, the king's magician?"

Silvanus's face grew pale. "Demons are sometimes summoned by mention of their names, General Conan. During the madness of Numedides, the sorcerer rules the kingdom; and if less foolish than the king, he is as heartless and rapacious. His sacrifice of virgins for his unsavory experiments is known to all." Fumbling in his wallet, he brought out a miniature painted on alabaster and hung on a golden chain. The painting showed a girl of perhaps ten years of age.

"My daughter. She's dead," said Silvanus. "He took her. If the gods vouchsafe me a single chance, I will tear his throat out with my very teeth." The captain's voice shook, and his hands trembled with the intensity of his emotion.

A savage gleam of blue balefire shone in Conan's eyes. His officers stirred uneasily, knowing that mistreatment of women roused the ruthless Cimmerian's furious indignation. He showed the miniature around and returned it to Silvanus, saying:

"We want more information on Count Ulric's army. How many are they?"

"Nearly twenty-five thousand, I believe."

"Whence did Ulric get so many? The Army of the North had no such strength when I left the mad king's service."

"Many of Prince Numitor's Frontiersmen, when they recovered from their panic, rallied and joined Count Ulric. And the regiment of the Black Dragons was ordered from Tarantia."

"What befell Numitor after the rout?"

"He slew himself in despair over his failure."

"Are you certain?" asked Conan. "Amulius Procas was said to have killed himself, but I know that he was murdered."

"There is no doubt of it, sir. Prince Numitor stabbed himself before witnesses."

"A pity," said Trocero. "He was the most decent of the lot, if too simplehearted for a bloody civil war."

Conan rumbled: "This calls for discussion. Pallantides, find sleeping quarters for Captain Silvanus and his men; then rejoin us here. Good night, Captain."

Publius, who had said little, now spoke up: "A moment, if you please, Captain Silvanus. Who was your father?"

The officer, at the tent flap, turned. "Silvius Macro, sir. Why do you ask?"

"I knew him when I served the king as treasurer. Good night."

———

When the captain had departed, Conan said: "Well, what think you? At least, it's good to have men deserting to us—not from us—for a change."

"I think," said Prospero, "that Thulandra Thuu seeks to plant a new assassin in our midst. He'll but await the chance to slide a knife between your ribs, then ride like a fiend from hell."

Trocero said: "I disagree. He looked to me like a straightforward young officer, not like one of Numedides's fellow-debauchees or Thulandra's ensorcelled minions."

"You cannot trust appearances," rejoined Prospero. "An apple may look never so rosy and still be filled with worms."

"If you will permit me," interrupted Publius, "I knew the young man's father. He was a fine, upstanding citizen—and still is, if he lives."

"Like father not always is like son," grumbled Prospero.

"Prospero," said Conan, "your concern for my safety does me honor. But a man must take his chances, especially in war. However much you guard me against a secret dagger, Ulric is like to kill us one and all, unless by some sudden stroke we can reverse our fortunes."

For an instant there was silence as Conan sat brooding, his deep-set blue eyes focused on the ground before him. At last he said:

"I have a plan—a perilous plan, yet fraught with no more danger than our present situation. Tarantia is defenseless, stripped of her soldiery, whilst mad Numedides plays immortal god upon his throne. A band of desperate men, disguised as Dragons of the Household Guard, might reach the palace and—"

"Conan!" shouted Trocero. "An inspiration from the gods! I'll lead the foray."

"You are too important to Poitain, my lord," said Prospero. "It is I who—"

"Neither of you goes," said Conan firmly. "Poitanians are not greatly loved in the central provinces, whose people have not forgotten your invasion of their land during the war with King Vilerus."

"Who then?" asked Trocero. "Pallantides?"

Conan shook his full black mane, and his face glowed with the lust of battle. "I shall perform this task as best I may, or die in the trying. I'll choose a squad of seasoned veterans, and we'll borrow surcoats, and helmets from Captain Silvanus' men. Silvanus—I'll bring him, also, to identify us at the gates. Aye, he is the key to the city."

Publius held up a cautionary hand. "A moment, gentlemen. Conan's plan might well succeed in ordinary warfare. But in Tarantia you deal not merely with a demented king but also with a malevolent sorcerer, whose mystic passes and words of magic can move mountains and call demons from the earth or sea or sky."

"Wizards don't terrify me," said Conan. "Years ago, in Khoraja, I faced one of the deadliest and slew him despite his flutterings and mutterings."

"How did you that?" asked Trocero.

"I threw my sword at him."

"Do not count on such a feat again," said Publius. "Your strength is great and your senses keener than those of common men; but fortune is not always kind, even to heroes."

"When my time comes, it comes," growled Conan.

"But your time may well be our time, too," said Prospero. "Let me send for Dexitheus. A Mitrian priest knows more of the world beyond than we ordinary mortals do."

Conan gave in, albeit with ill grace.

Dexitheus listened with folded hands to Conan's plan. At length he spoke gravely: "Publius is right, Conan. Do not underestimate the power of Thulandra Thuu. We of the priesthood have some notion of the dark, nameless forces beyond man's fathoming."

"Whence comes this pestilent thaumaturge?" asked Trocero. "Men say he is a Vendhyan; others, a Stygian."

"Neither," replied Dexitheus. "In my priestly brotherhood we call him a Lemurian, coming—I know not how—from islands far beyond the known world, eastward, in the ocean beyond Khitai. These shrouded isles are all that remains of a once spacious land that sank beneath the waves. To outwit a sorcerer with powers such as his, our general needs more than material arms and armor."

Trocero asked: "Are there no wizards in this camp who would accept this service?"

"Nay!" snorted Conan. "I have no use for tricksters such as those. I would not harbor one or seek his aid."

Dexitheus's expression became doleful. "General, though you know it not, I am much discomfited."

"How so, Reverence?" said Conan. "I owe you much and would not distress you without cause. Speak not in riddles, good friend."

"You have no use for wizards, General, calling them charlatans and quacks; yet there is one you count among your friends. You have need of a magician; yet you refuse the help of such a one." Dexitheus paused and Conan beckoned him to continue.

"Know, then, that in my youth I studied the black arts, albeit I advanced little beyond the lowest grades of sorcery. Later I saw the light of Mitra and forswore all dealings with demons and the forces of the occult. Had the priesthood learned of my wizardly past, I should not have been admitted to their order. Therefore, when I accompany you on this perilous mission—"

"What, you?" cried Conan, frowning. "Wizard or no, you are too old to gallop a hundred leagues! You would not survive it."

"On the contrary, I am of tougher fiber than you think. The ascetic life lends me a vigor far beyond my years, and you will need me to cast a counter-spell or two. But when I accompany you, my secret will come out. I shall be forced to resign my holy office—a sad ending to my life's career."

"Meseems the use of magic for a worthy end is a forgivable sin," said Conan.

"To you, sir; not to my order, which is most intolerant in the matter. But I have no alternative; I shall use what powers I have for Aquilonia." His sigh was heavy with tears too deep for thought.

"After it's over," said Conan, "perchance I can persuade your priesthood to make exception to the rigor of their rules. Prepare, good friend, to leave within the hour."

"This very night?"

"When better? If we wait upon the morrow, we may find the camp hemmed in by royalists. Prospero, pick me a troop of your most skillful mounted fighters. See that each man has not one horse, but two, to allow for frequent changes. But do it quietly. We must outrun the news of our departure. As for the rest of you, keep the men busy improving our defenses whilst I am gone. To all of you, farewell!"

The half-moon barely cleared the treetops when a column of horsemen, each leading a spare mount, issued stealthily from the rebel camp. In the lead rode was Conan, wearing the helmet and white surcoat of the Black Dragons. With him rode Captain Silvanus, and behind them trotted Dexitheus, priest of Mitra, likewise attired. Fifty of Conan's most trusted troopers followed, disguised in the same manner as their leaders.

Under Silvanus's guidance, the column swung wide of the royalist encampment. When they were once again on the Tarantia road, they broke into a steady trot. The moon set, and black night swallowed up the line of desperate men.

chapter  xii

Darkness in the Moonlight

The sun had set, and overhead a brilliant half-moon hung suspended in a cloudless sky. At the royal palace of Tarantia, the king's solitary supper, served on gold platters in his private dining-room, had been cleared away. Save for a taster standing behind the royal armchair, two bodyguards stationed at the silver-studded doorway, and the footmen who served the royal meats, none had attended him to join in the repast.

Thousands of lamps and candles blazed in the royal chambers—so bountiful the light that a stranger, entering, would wonder whether a coronation or a neighboring monarch's visit occasioned this opulent display.

Yet the palace seemed curiously deserted. Instead of the chatter of lovely ladies, chivalrous youths, and high-ranking nobles of the kingdom, echoes from the past reverberated down the marble halls, empty save for a few guards, on whose silvered breastplates the multitude of candles were reflected. The guards were either adolescent boys or graybeard oldsters; for when the household guard marched south to confront the rebels, the king's officials had hastily replaced the corps of the Black Dragons with lads in training and retired veterans.

The lamps and candles burned all night, as the king—fancying himself a sun god—deemed naught but the light of day at night worthy of his exalted station. Thus, scurrying servants hastened from lamp to lamp to assure sufficient oil in each and carried armfuls of candles from chandelier to chandelier to replace those that flickered out.

As the king's madness waxed, the courtiers and civil servants, normally in attendance, stole away. Foremost among these was Vibius Latro, who had offices and living quarters in the palace. The chancellor had sent a message to Numedides, begging a short leave of absence. His health, the note continued, was breaking down from long hours of work, and without a brief respite at his country seat, he feared he could no longer further the interests of His Majesty.

Having just flogged one of his concubines to death, Numedides, in rare good humor, granted his request. Latro forthwith loaded his family into a traveling carriage and set out for his estates, north of Tarantia. At the first crossroads, he veered eastward and, lashing his horses, raced for the Nemedian border two hundred leagues away. Other members of the king's official family likewise found compelling reasons for a leave of absence and speedily departed.

Numedides's throne in the Chamber of Private Audience stood upon a patterned Iranistani carpet, woven of fine wools artfully dyed to the color of rubies, jades, amethysts, and sapphires and shot through with threads of gold. The chair itself, an ornate structure, though less imposing than the Ruby Throne in the Public Throne Room, was tastelessly embellished with dragons, lions, swords, and stars. The heraldic eagle of the Numedidean dynasty soared up from the tall back, its wings and eyes studded with precious stones that sparkled in the generous candlelight.

The king's silver scepter—the ceremonial symbol of kingship—lay across the purple-pillowed seat, while the Sword of State, a great two-handed weapon, bejewelled of hilt and scabbard, reposed on one of the chair's broad arms.

Two persons stood in the chamber: King Numedides, wearing the slender golden circlet that was the crown of Aquilonia and a crimson robe bespotted with stains of food, wine, and vomit; and Alcina, clad in a clinging gown of sea-green silk.

From opposite sides of the gilt throne they glared at each other. Alcina hissed:

"You mangy old dog! I will die before I submit to your perversions! You cannot catch me, you old, fat, filthy heap of offal! Go find a bitch or a sow to vent your lusts upon! Like to like!"

"I said I would not hurt you, little spitfire!" wheezed Numedides. "But catch you I will! None can escape the desires of a king, let alone a god! Come here!"

Numedides suddenly moved sidewise, in a feint at which he showed himself surprisingly nimble. Caught unawares, Alcina leaped back, losing the protection of the ornate chair. Then, with outspread arms and clutching hands, the king herded her into a corner far removed from either pair of double doors, whose pilastered frames adorned the walls to left and right of the ostentatious throne.

Alcina's fingers flew to her bodice and whipped out a slender dagger, tipped with the same poison that had slain Amulius Procas. "Keep back, I warn you!" she cried. "One prick of this, and you will die!"

Numedides gave back a step. "You little fool, know you not that I am impervious to your envenomed bodkin?"

"We shall soon see whether you are or not, if you approach me closer."

The king retreated to his throne and caught up his scepter. Then once more he stalked the trembling girl. When Alcina raised her dagger, he struck a blow with his silver club, hitting her hand. The dagger spun away and bounced across the carpet, while Alcina, with a cry of anguish, caught her bruised hand to her breast.

"Now, you little witch," said Numedides, "we shall—"

The pair of doors on the right side of the audience chamber sprang open. Thulandra Thuu, leaning on his carven staff, stood on the threshold.

"How came you here?" thundered Numedides. "The doors were locked!"

The dark-skinned sorcerer's sibilant voice was the crack of a whip. "Your Majesty! I warned you not to molest my servants!"

The king scowled. "We were just playing a harmless game. And who are you to warn a god of aught? Who is the ruler here?"

Thulandra Thuu smiled a thin and bitter smile. "You reign here, but you do not rule. I do."

Numedides's jowls empurpled with his waxing wrath. "You blasphemous ghoul! Out of my sight, ere I blast you with my lightnings!"

"Calm yourself, Majesty. I have news—"

The king's voice rose to a scream: "I said *get out*! I'll show you—"

Numedides's groping hand brushed the hilt of the Sword of State. He drew the ponderous blade from its jeweled scabbard and advanced upon Thulandra Thuu, swinging the weapon with both hands. The sorcerer calmly awaited his approach.

With an incoherent shriek, the king whirled the sword in a decapitating blow. At the last instant Thulandra, whose expression had not changed, brought up his staff to parry. Steel and carven wood met with a ringing crash, as if Thulandra, too, wielded a massive sword. With a dexterous twirl of his staff, the sorcerer whipped the weapon from the king's hands and sent it flying upward, turning over and over in the air. As it descended, the blade struck Numedides in the face, laying open a finger-long gash in the king's cheek. Blood trickled into his rusty beard.

Numedides clapped a hand to his cheek and stared stupidly at the blood dripping from his fingers. "I bleed, just like a mortal!" he mumbled. "How can that be?"

"You have a distance yet to go ere you wear the mantle of divinity," said Thulandra Thuu with a narrow smile.

The king bellowed in a sudden rage of fear: "Slaves! Pages! Phaedo! Manius! Where in the nine hells are you? Your divine master is being murdered!"

"It will do him no good," said Alcina, evenly. "He told me that he had ordered all his servants elsewhere in the palace, so I might scream my head off to no avail." And she tossed back her night-tipped hair with her uninjured hand.

"Where are my loyal subjects?" whimpered Numedides. "Valerius! Procas!

Thespius! Gromel! Volmana! Where are my courtiers? Where is Vibius Latro? Has everyone deserted me? Does no one love me anymore, despite all I have done for Aquilonia?" The abandoned monarch began to weep.

"As you know in your more lucid moments," the sorcerer said sternly, "Procas is dead; Vibius Latro has fled; and Gromel has deserted to the enemy. Volmana is fighting under Count Ulric, as are the others. Now, pray sit down and listen; I have things of moment to relate."

Waddling to the throne, Numedides sank down, his spotted robe billowing about him. He pulled a dirty kerchief from his sleeve and pressed it to his wounded cheek, where it grew red with blood.

"Unless you can better control yourself," said Thulandra Thuu, "I shall have to do away with you and rule directly, instead of through you as before."

"You never will be king!" mumbled Numedides. "Not a man in Aquilonia would obey you. You are not of royal blood. You are not an Aquilonian. You are not even a Hyborian. I begin to doubt if you are even a human being." He paused, glowering. "So even if we hate each other, you need me as much as I need you.

"Well, what is this news at which you hint? Good news, I hope. Speak up, sir sorcerer; do not keep me in suspense!"

"If you will but listen . . . I cast our horoscopes this afternoon and discovered the imminence of deadly peril."

"Peril? From what source?"

"That I cannot say; the indications were unclear. It surely cannot be the rebel army. My visions on the astral plane, confirmed by yesterday's message from Count Ulric, inform me that the rebels are penned beyond Elymia. They will soon retreat in the face of hopeless odds, disperse in despair, or suffer annihilation. We have naught to fear from them."

"Could that devil Conan have slipped past Count Ulric?"

"Alas, my astral visions are not clear enough to distinguish individuals from afar. But the barbarian is a resourceful rascal; when you drove him into flight, I warned you might not have seen the last of him."

"I have had reports of bands of traitors within sight of the city walls," said the king, lips quivering in petulant uncertainty.

"That is gossip and not truth, unless some new leader has arisen among the disaffected of the Central Provinces."

"Suppose such scum does wash ashore and lap the city walls? What can we do with the Black Dragons far away? It was your idea to have them join Count Ulric." The king's voice grew shrill, as fear and rage snapped the thin thread of his composure. He ranted on:

"I left the management of this campaign to you, because you claim a store of arcane wisdom. Now I see that in military matters you are the merest tyro. You have bungled everything! When you sent Procas into Argos, you said that this incursion would snuff out the rebel menace, once and for all; but it did not. You assured me that the rabble would never cross the Alimane, and lo! the Border Legion was broken and dispersed. Quoth you, they had no chance of passing the Imirian Escarpment, and yet the rebels did. Finally, the plague you sent among them, you said, would surely wipe the upstarts out, and yet—"

"Your Majesty!" A young voice severed the king's recriminations. "Pray, let me in! It is a dire emergency!"

"That is one of my pages; I know his voice," said Numedides, rising and going to the still-locked door on the left side of the throne. When he had turned the key, a youth in page's garb burst in, gasping: "My lord! The rebel Conan has seized the palace!"

"Conan!" cried the king. "What has befallen? Speak!"

"A troop of the Black Dragons—or men appareled in their garb—galloped up to the palace gates, crying that they had urgent messages from the front. The guards thought nothing of it and passed them through, but I recognized the huge Cimmerian when I saw his scarred face in the lighted anteroom. I knew him in the Westermarck, ere I came to Tarantia to serve Your Majesty. And so I ran to warn you."

"Mean you he is about to burst upon us, with no guards in the palace save a scrawny pack of striplings and their grandsires?" Eyes ablaze with fury, he turned to Thulandra Thuu. "Well, you sorcerous scoundrel, work a deterrent spell!"

The magician was already making passes with his staff and speaking in a sibilant, unknown tongue. As the sonorous sentences rolled out, a strange phenomenon occurred. The candles dimmed, as if the room were filled with swirling smoke or roiling fogs from evening marshes, dank with decay. Darker and darker grew the atmosphere, until the Chamber of Private Audience became as black as a dungeon rock-sealed for centuries.

The king cried out in terror: "Have you blinded me?"

"Quiet, Majesty! I have cast a spell of darkness over the palace, a magical defense. If we do lock the doors and speak in whispers, the invaders will not discover us."

The page felt his way across the wide expanse of carpet and turned the great key in the left pair of doors, while Alcina, lithe as a jaguar, likewise barred the right-hand portal. The king retreated to his throne and sat in silence, too terrified to speak. Alcina sought the slender body of the sorcerer and huddled at his feet in mute supplication. The page, uncertain of his whereabouts, shrank back from the door whose key he turned and wished himself home in the humble alleys of Tarantia. The silence was complete, save for the beating of four frightened hearts.

Suddenly the page's door sprang open, and a chant could be heard in the ancient Hyborian tongue. The blackness thinned and rolled away, and the light of many candles once more flooded the utmost corners of the audience chamber.

In the open doorway stood Conan the Cimmerian, bloody sword in hand; and at his side Dexitheus, the priest of Mitra, still crooned the final phrases of his potent incantation.

"Slay them, Thulandra," shrieked Numedides, eyes starting at the sight of his former general. He held the bloody kerchief to his injured cheek and moaned. Alcina shrank closer to her mentor and stared with baleful eyes upon the man who had survived her deadly potion.

Thulandra Thuu raised his carven staff, thrust it at Conan, and, in the language of his undiscoverable bourn, spat out a curse or else a ringing invocation to an unknown god. A rippling flash of light, like a blue streak of living fire, sped from the staff tip toward the Cimmerian's armored breast. With the dread rattling of a thunderclap, the bolt shattered against an unseen barrier, spattering sparks.

Frowning, Thulandra Thuu repeated his cantrip, louder and in a voice of deep authority, shifting his aim to Dexitheus. Again the blue flame zigzagged across the intervening space and spread out, like water tossed against a pane of glass.

As Conan started for the sorcerer, his blue eyes blazing with the lust to kill, Captain Silvanus jostled past him, shouting:

"You who slew my daughter! I seek revenge!"

Silvanus, with madness glinting in his bloodshot eyes, rushed at the sorcerer, sword raised above his head. But before he had gone three paces, the magician pointed his staff and once again cried out. Again the blue lightning illumined the room with its awful radiance; and Silvanus, uttering a scream of horror, pitched forward on his face.

A hole the thickness of a man's thumb opened on the back plate of his cuirass, and the blackened steel curled into the petals of a rose of death. A red stain slowly spread over the Iranistani carpet and mingled with the jeweled tones of its weaving.

Conan wasted no time lamenting his companion but strode briskly toward the sorcerer, his sword upraised to strike. The page, ashen-pale, scuttled behind the throne; Alcina and the king flattened themselves against opposing walls.

But Thulandra Thuu had not exhausted his resources. He gripped the two ends of his staff in his bony hands and held it at arm's length in front of him, chanting the while in a tongue that was old when the seas swallowed Lemuria. As Conan took another step, he encountered a strange resistance that brought him to a halt.

Elastic and yielding was this invisible surface; yet it confounded Conan's most strenuous attack. The cords in his massive neck stood out; his face darkened with his almost superhuman effort; his muscles writhed like pythons. Yet the formless barrier held. As he thrust his sword into that invisible substance, he saw Thulandra's staff bend in the middle, as if impelled by an opposing force, but it did not break. Dexitheus's mightiest magic had no power against the staff and the protection it afforded to Thulandra Thuu.

At last the sorcerer spoke, and his voice was weary with the weight of many years. "I see yon renegade priest of Mitra has armored you against my bolts; but for all his puny magic, he cannot destroy me. Aquilonia is unworthy of my efforts. I shall remove to a land beyond the sunrise, where people will value my experiments and the gift of life eternal. Farewell!"

"Master! Master! Take me with you!" cried Alcina, raising her arms in humble supplication.

"Nay, girl, stay back! I have no further use for you."

Thulandra Thuu edged to the door by which he had entered the audience chamber. As he moved, the elastic barrier he maintained retreated also. Lips bared in a mirthless grin, blue eyes ablaze, Conan followed the lean sorcerer step by step. His magnificent body quivered with the controlled fury of a lion deprived of its prey.

As they reached the doorway whence the sorcerer had entered, Thulandra Thuu began to sway, then to revolve. He spun faster and faster, until his dark figure became a blur. Suddenly he vanished.

As the wizard disappeared, the unseen barrier faded. Conan sprang forward, his sword upraised for a murderous slash. With a blistering curse, he rushed into the corridor. But the hall was empty. He listened, but he could detect no footfall.

Shaking his tousled mane as if to put a dream to flight, Conan turned back to the Chamber of Private Audience. He found Dexitheus guarding the other door, Alcina pressed against the farther wall, and King Numedides seated on his throne, dabbing his injured face with his bloody kerchief. Conan strode quickly to the throne to confront the king.

"Stand, mortal!" bawled Numedides, pointing a pudgy forefinger. "Know that I am a god! I am King of Aquilonia!"

Conan shot out an arm in which the hard muscles writhed like serpents. Seizing the king's robe, he hauled the madman to his feet. "You mean," he snarled, "you were king. Have you aught to say before you die?"

Numedides wilted, a pool of molten tallow in a burned-out candle. Tears coursed down his flabby face to mingle with the blood that still oozed from his wound. He sank to his knees, babbling:

"Pray, do not slay me, gallant Conan! Though I have committed errors, I intended only well for Aquilonia! Send me into exile, and I shall not return. You cannot kill an aging, unarmed man!"

With a contemptuous snort, Conan hurled Numedides to the floor. He wiped his sword on the hem of the fallen monarch's garment and sheathed it. Turning on his heel, he said:

"I do not hunt mice. Tie up this scum until we find a madhouse to confine him."

A sudden flicker of movement seen beyond the corner of his eye and sharp intake of breath by Dexitheus warned Conan of impending danger. Numedides had found the poisoned dagger dropped by Alcina and now, weapon in hand, he rose to make one last, desperate lunge to stab the Liberator in the back.

Conan wheeled, shot out his left hand and caught the descending wrist. His right hand seized Numedides's flaccid throat and, straining the mighty muscles in his arm, Conan forced his attacker down upon the throne. With his free hand the king wrenched in vain at Conan's obdurate wrist. His legs thrashed spasmodically.

As Conan's iron fingers dug deeper into the pudgy neck, Numedides's eyes bulged. His mouth gaped, but no sound issued forth. Deeper and deeper sank Conan's python grip, until the others in the room, standing with suspended breath, heard the cartilage crack. Blood trickled from the corner of the king's mouth, to mingle with the sanguine rheum that had besmeared his face and beard and hair.

Numedides's face turned blue, and little by little his flailing arms went limp. The poisoned dagger thudded to the floor and spun into a corner. Conan maintained his crushing grip until all life had fled.

At last Conan released the corpse, which tumbled off the throne in a disheveled heap. The Cimmerian drew a long breath, then spun around and whipped his blade from its scabbard, as running feet and rattling armor clattered down the hall. A score of his men, who had been wandering around the palace in search of him, crowded into the doorway to the chamber. All voices stilled, all eyes were turned upon him, as he stood, legs spread and sword in hand, beside the throne of Aquilonia, a look of triumph in his blazing eyes.

What thoughts raced through Conan's mind at that moment, none ever knew. But finally he sheathed his sword, bent down, and tore the bloody crown from the bedraggled head of dead Numedides. Holding the slender circlet in one hand, he unbuckled the chin strap of his helmet with the other and tugged the headpiece off. Then he raised the crown in both his hands and placed it on his head.

"Well," he said, "how does it look?"

Dexitheus spoke up: "Hail, King Conan of Aquilonia!"

The others took up the cry; and at last even the page, who stared owl-eyed from his hiding place behind the throne, joined in.

Alcina, moving forward with the seductive dancer's grace that had so excited Conan in Messantia, glided in front of him and fell prettily to her knees.

"Oh, Conan!" she cried, "it was ever you I loved. But alas, I was ensorcelled and forced to do the bidding of that wicked thaumaturge. Forgive me and I will be your faithful servant forevermore!"

Frowning, Conan looked down upon her, and his voice was thunder rumbling in the hills. "When someone has sought to murder me, I'd be a fool to give that one a second chance. Were you a man, I'd slay you here and now. But I do not war on women, so begone.

"If after this night you are found within those parts that have declared for me, you'll lose your pretty head. Elatus, accompany her to the stables, saddle her a horse, and see her to the outskirts of Tarantia."

Alcina went, the black cloud of her silken hair hiding her countenance. At the door she turned back to look once more at Conan, tears glistening on her cheeks. Then she was gone.

Conan kicked the corpse of Numedides. "Stick this carrion's head on a spear and display it in the city, then carry it to Count Ulric in Elymia, to convince him and his army that a new king rules in Aquilonia."

One of Conan's troopers shouldered his way into the crowded room. "General Conan!"

"Well?"

The man paused to catch his breath. His eyes were big as buttons. "You ordered Cadmus and me to guard the palace gates. Well, just now we heard a horse and chariot coming from the stables, but neither beast nor carriage did we see. Then Cadmus pointed to the ground, and there was a shadow on the moonlit road, like to a horse and cart. It ran along the ground, but naught there was to cast the shadow!"

"What did you?"

"Did, sir? What could we do? The shadow passed through the open gates and vanished down the street. So I came arunning to tell you."

"The late king's sorcerer and his man, I doubt not," said Conan to his assembled company. "Let them go; the he-witch said he would betake himself to some distant eastern bourn. He'll trouble us no more." Then turning to Dexitheus, he said: "We must set up a government on the morrow, and you shall be my chancellor."

The priest cried out in great distress. "Oh, no, Gen—Your Majesty! I must take up a hermit's life, to atone for my resort to magic despite the regulations of my order."

"When Publius joins us, you may do so with my blessing. In the interim we need a government, and you are wise in matters politic. Round up the officials and their clerks by noon."

Dexitheus sighed. "Very well, my lord King." He looked down on Silvanus's body and sadly shook his head. "I much regret the death of this young man, but I could not maintain defensive fields around you both."

"He died a soldier's death; we'll bury him with honors," Conan said. "Where can one take a bath in this marble barn?"

Newly shaven and shorn, his mighty frame arrayed in ebon velvet, Conan rested on the purple-pillowed throne in the Chamber of Private Audience. All traces of violence had been erased—the bodies removed, the poisoned dagger buried, the carpet scrubbed free of bloodstains. An expectant smile lit Conan's craggy countenance.

Then Chancellor Publius bustled in with several scrolls under his velvet-coated arm. "My lord," he began, "I have here—"

"Crom's devils!" Conan burst out. "Cannot that business wait? Prospero is bringing in a score of beauties who have volunteered to be the king's companions. I am to choose among them."

"Sire!" said Publius sternly. "Some of these matters require immediate attention. 'Twill not hurt the young women to wait a while.

"Here, for example, is a petition from the barony of Castria, begging to be forgiven their arrears in taxes. Here are the treasury accounts. And here the advocates' briefs in the lawsuit of Phinteas versus Arius Priscus, which is being appealed before the throne. The suit has continued undecided for sixteen years.

"Here is a letter from one Quesado of Kordava, a former spy of Vibius Latro. Meseems that we had dealings with him before."

"What does that dog want?" snorted Conan.

"He begs employment in his former capacity, as intelligence agent to His Majesty."

"Aye, he was good at skulking around and acting like a winesop or an idiot. Give him a post—on trial, but never send him as an envoy to a fellow monarch."

"Yes, sire. Here is the petition for pardon for Galenus Selo. And here is another petition, this one from the coppersmiths' guild. They want—"

"Gods and devils!" shouted Conan, slamming a hairy fist into his other hand. "Why did no one tell me that kingship entails this dreary drudgery? I'd almost rather be a pirate on the main!"

Publius smiled. "Even the lightest crown sits heavily betimes. A ruler has to rule, or another will govern in his stead. The late Numedides shirked his proper tasks, and he was—"

Conan sighed. "Yes, yes. I suppose you're right, Crom curse it. Page! Fetch a table and spread out these documents. Now, Publius, the treasury statements first . . ."

CONAN

and the
Spider God

L. Sprague de Camp

Contents

Introduction

Conan, the magnificent barbarian adventurer, grew up in the mind of Robert Ervin Howard, the Texan pulp writer, in 1932. As Howard put it, the character "grew up in my mind . . . when I was stopping in a little border town on the lower Rio Grande. . . . He simply stalked full-grown out of oblivion and set me to work recording the saga of his adventures. . . . Some mechanism in my subconsciousness took the dominant characteristics of various prize-fighters, gunmen, bootleggers, oil-field bullies, gamblers, and honest workmen I have come in contact with, and combining them all, produced the amalgamation I call Conan the Cimmerian."

This is undoubtedly true. Yet, at the same time, Conan is an obvious idealization of Howard himself — Howard as he wished he were: a hell-raising, irresponsible adventurer, devoted to wine, women, and strife. For all his burly build — he was five feet eleven inches tall and weighed nearly two hundred pounds, most of it muscle — Robert Howard and the great Cimmerian were as different as day and night.

While both Howard and his hero had hot tempers and a chivalrous attitude towards women, Conan is portrayed as a pure extrovert, a roughneck with few inhibitions and a rudimentary conscience. His creator, on the other hand, was a morally upright man, meticulously law-abiding; courteous and tenderhearted; shy, bookish, introverted, and — although he denied it — a genuine intellectual. A moody man, he alternated between periods of cheerful, spellbinding garrulity and spells of depression and despair. At the age of thirty, with a promising literary career opening out before him, he took his own life on the occasion of his aged mother's death.

Born in Peaster, Texas, in 1906, Robert E. Howard spent his adult years in the small town of Cross Plains, Texas, in the center of the state. A shy and lonely child, he became a voracious bookworm and a bodybuilder who enhanced his naturally powerful physique by boxing, weight-lifting, and riding. Among his favorite authors were Edgar Rice Burroughs, Rudyard Kipling, Harold Lamb, Jack London, and Talbot Mundy. With these interests, it is not surprising that he wrote boxing stories, Western stories, tales of oriental adventure, and a goodly volume of memorable verse.

Transcending all these, both in volume and in popularity, were his fantasy stories. It was Howard's misfortune that during the brief decade of his productive literary life, fantasy was held in low esteem. He did not live to see any of his works appear in book form. Most of his imaginative tales were published in *Weird Tales*, a magazine that led a precarious existence from 1923 to 1954. Although its rates were low and payments often late, Howard found it his most reliable market.

In the late 1920s, Howard wrote a series of fantasies about King Kull, a native of lost Atlantis who becomes the ruler of a mainland kingdom. The series had only limited success; of the ten Kull stories he completed, Howard sold three.

Later he rewrote an unsold Kull story, "By This Axe I Rule!" The new tale, "The Phoenix on the Sword," was set in a later imaginary period, Howard's Hyborian Age, a time between the sinking of Atlantis and the beginnings of recorded history. Howard gave his new hero the old Celtic name of Conan; for, being of partly Irish ancestry himself, Howard harbored an intense interest in and admiration for the Celts.

"The Phoenix on the Sword" became a smash hit with the readers of *Weird Tales*. Hence, from 1932 to 1936, most of Howard's writing time was devoted to Conan stories, although shortly before his death, he spoke of giving up fantasy to concentrate on Westerns.

Of Howard's several heroes, Conan proved the most popular. Howard saw the publication of eighteen stories about the gigantic barbarian, who wades through rivers of gore to overthrow foes both natural and supernatural, and who at last becomes the ruler of the mightiest Hyborian kingdom.

Since Howard's death, several unpublished Conan stories, from complete manuscripts to mere fragments and synopses, have come to light through the efforts of Glenn Lord and myself. My colleague, Lin Carter, and I have completed the unfinished tales, and Carter and Björn Nyberg have collaborated with me on new Conan stories to fill the gaps in the saga.

In addition, several other colleagues—Karl Edward Wagner, Andrew Offutt, and Poul Anderson—have also tried their hands at Conan pastiches, a venerable form of literature in which a living author tries to recapture both the spirit and the style of a predecessor, as Virgil in his *Aeneid* did with Homer's epics. *Conan and the Spider God* is such a novel. To what extent any of us can re-create the vividness of Howard's narratives and the excellence of his style, the reader must judge for himself.

The Conan stories belong to a subgenre of fantasy called heroic fantasy, or swordplay-and-sorcery fiction. This art form was originated in the 1880s by William Morris, the British artist, poet, decorator, manufacturer, and reformer, as a modern imitation of the medieval romance, which had been moribund since Cervantes burlesqued it with his *Don Quixote*. Morris was followed in the United Kingdom in the early twentieth century by Lord Dunsany and Eric Rücker Eddison, and in the United States by Robert Howard, Clark Ashton Smith, and many others.

Heroic fantasies are laid in an imaginary world—either long ago, or far into the future, or on another planet—where magic works, supernatural beings abound, and machinery does not exist. An adult fairy tale of this kind provides pure escape fiction. In such a world, gleaming cities raise their silver spires against the stars; sorcerers cast sinister spells from subterranean lairs; baleful spirits stalk crumbling ruins of immemorial antiquity; primeval monsters crash through jungle thickets; and the fate of kingdoms is balanced on the blades of broadswords brandished by heroes of preternatural strength and valor. Men are mighty, women are beautiful, problems are simple, life is adventurous, and nobody has ever heard of inflation, the petroleum shortage, or atmospheric pollution.

In other words, heroic fantasy sings of a world not as it is, but as it ought to be. Its aim is to entertain, not to display the author's cleverness, nor to uplift the reader, nor to expose the shortcomings of the world we live in. On the subject of pure escapism, J. R. R. Tolkien once remarked, "Why should a man be scorned if, finding himself in prison . . . he thinks and talks about other topics than jailers and prison-walls?"

During the Second World War, it appeared that fantasy had become a casualty of the machine age. Then, with the publication in the 1950s of Tolkien's three-volume novel *The Lord of the Rings*, and its later reprinting in paperback as a runaway bestseller, the future of modern fantasy was assured.

In the 1960s, I managed to interest a paperback publisher in the whole series of the Conan stories, so that for the first time Howard's remarkable tales reached a mass audience. The resulting twelve volumes proved second only to *The Lord of the Rings* in popularity among works of fantasy, for here is a hero who bestrides the world, untrammeled by petty laws and hindrances; here is a tale told in vigorous, colorful style; here is man triumphant over soul-searing trials and tribulations. Here is the stuff that dreams are made of.

In the saga, Conan, the son of a blacksmith, is born in the bleak, barbarous northern land of Cimmeria. Forced by a feud to flee his tribe, he travels north

to the subarctic land of Asgard, where he joins the Æsir in battles with the
Vanir of Vanaheim to the west and the Hyperboreans to the east. In one of
these forays he is captured and enslaved by the Hyperboreans. He escapes and
makes his way south to the ancient land of Zamora. Lawless and green to the
ways of civilization, Conan occupies himself for a couple of years as a thief,
more daring than adroit, not only in Zamora but also in the neighboring realms
of Corinthia and Nemedia.

Disgusted with this starveling, outcast existence, Conan treks eastward and
enlists in the army of the mighty oriental kingdom of Turan, then ruled by the
good-natured but ineffectual King Yildiz. Here he serves as a soldier for about
two years, learning archery and horsemanship and traveling widely, once as far
east as fabled Khitai.

As the present story opens, Conan, still in his early twenties, has risen to
the rank of captain and has obtained a long-coveted transfer to the Royal Guard
in the capital city of Aghrapur. As usual, trouble is his bedfellow; and circumstances soon compel him to seek his fortune elsewhere.

L. Sprague de Camp

Villanova, Pennsylvania

CONAN
and the
Spider God

chapter  i

Lust and Death

A tall, immensely powerful man—almost a giant—stood motionless in the shadows of the courtyard. Although he could see the candle that the Turanian woman had placed in the window as a sign that the coast was clear, and to a hillman the climb was child's play, he waited. He had no desire to be caught halfway up the wall, clinging like a beetle to the ivy that mantled the ancient edifice. While the civic guard would hesitate to arrest one of King Yildiz's officers, word of his escapade would surely reach the ears of Narkia's protector. And this protector was Senior Captain Orkhan, the large man's commanding officer.

With alert blue eyes, Conan of Cimmeria, a captain in the Royal Guard, scanned the sky above, where the full moon dusted the domes and towers of Aghrapur with powdered silver. A cloud was bearing down upon the luminary; but this wind-borne galleon of the sky was inadequate for the Cimmerian's purpose. It would dim the moonlight for only half the time required to clamber up the ivy. A much larger cloud, he observed with satisfaction, sailed in the wake of the first.

When the moon had veiled her face behind the more voluminous cloud, Conan hitched his baldric around so that the sword hung down between his shoulders. He slipped off his sandals and tucked them into his belt; then, grasping the heavy, knotted vines with fingers and toes, he mounted with catlike agility.

Across the shadowed spires and roofs lay a ghostly silence, broken but rarely by the sound of hurrying feet; while overhead the cloud, outlined in vermeil, billowed slowly past. The climber felt a thin wind stir his square-cut black mane, and a tiny shiver shook him. He remembered the words of the astrologer whom he had consulted three days before.

"Beware of launching an enterprise at the next full of the moon," the gray-beard had said. "The stellar aspects imply that you would thus set in motion wheels within wheels of cause and effect—a vast concatenation of dire changes."

"Will the result be good or bad?" demanded Conan.

The astrologer shrugged the bony shoulders under his patched robe. "That cannot be foreseen; save that it would be something drastic. There would ensure great overturns."

"Can't you even tell whether I shall end up on the top of the heap or at the bottom?"

"Nay, Captain. Since I see in the stars no great benison for you, meseems the bottom were more likely."

Grumbling at this uninspiring prediction, Conan paid up and departed. He did not disbelieve in any form of magic, sorcery, or spiritism; but he had an equal faith in the fallibility of individual occultists. Their ranks, he thought, were at least as full of fakers and blunderers as any other occupation. So, when Narkia had sent him a note inviting him to call while her protector was away, he had not let the astrologer's warning stop him.

The candle vanished, and the window creaked open. The giant eeled through and slid to his feet. He stared hungrily at the Turanian woman who stood before him. Her black hair cascaded down her supple shoulders, while the glow of the candle, now resting on the taboret beside her, revealed her splendid body through her diaphanous gown of amethyst silk.

"Well, here I am," rumbled Conan.

Narkia's feline eyes sparkled with amusement as they rested on the man who towered over her in a cheap woolen tunic and patched, baggy pantaloons.

"I have awaited your coming, Conan," she replied, moving forward with welcoming arms outstretched. "Though, in sooth, I did not expect to find you looking like a stable hand. Where are your splendid cream-and-scarlet uniform and silver-spurred boots?"

"I didn't think it sensible to wear them tonight," he said abruptly, lifting his baldric over his head and laying his sword carelessly on the carpet. Beneath his square-cut black mane, deep-set blue eyes under heavy black brows burned in a scarred and swarthy face. Although he was only in his early twenties, the vicissitudes of a wild, hard life had stamped him with the harsh appearance of maturity.

With the lithe motion of a tiger, Conan glided forward, gathered the wench into his brawny arms, and wheeled her toward the bed. But Narkia resisted, pushing her palms against his massive chest.

"Stay!" she breathed. "You barbarians are too impulsive. First, we needs must cultivate our acquaintance. Sit on yonder stool and have a sip of wine!"

"If I must," grumbled Conan, speaking Hyrkanian with a barbarous accent. Unwillingly he sat and, in three gulps, drained the proffered goblet of golden fluid.

"My thanks, girl," he muttered, setting the empty vessel down on the little table.

Narkia clucked. "Really, Captain Conan, you are a boor! A fine vintage from Iranistan should be sipped and savored slowly, but you pour it down like bitter beer. Will you never become civilized?"

"I doubt it," grunted Conan. "What I have seen of your so-called civilization in the last few years has not filled me with any great love of it."

"Then why stay here in Turan? You could return to your barbarous home-land—wherever that be."

With a wry grin, Conan clasped his massive hands behind his shaggy head and leaned back against the tapestried wall. "Why do I stay?" he shrugged. "I suppose because there is more gold to be gathered here, one way or another; also more things to see and do. Life in a Cimmerian village grows dull after a while—the same old round, day after day, save for petty quarrels with the other villagers and now and then a feud with a neighboring clan. Now, here—what's that?"

Booted feet tramped upon the stair, and in an instant the door burst open. In the black opening stood Senior Captain Orkhan, jaw sagging with astonish-ment beneath his spired, turban-wound helmet. Orkhan was a tall, hawk-featured man, less massive than Conan but strong and lithe, although the first gray hairs had begun to sprout in his close-cut dark beard.

As he studied the tableau, and recognition replaced astonishment, Orkhan's face reddened with rising wrath. "So!" he grated. "When the cat's away . . ." His hand went to the hilt of his scimitar.

The instant the door swung open, Narkia had thrown herself back on the bed. As Orkhan spoke, she cried: "Rape! This savage burst in, threatening to kill—"

In confusion, Conan glanced from one to the other before his brain, caught up in the whirl of events, grew clear. As Orkhan's sword sang from its sheath, the Cimmerian sprang to his feet, snatched up the stool on which he had been sitting, and hurled it at his assailant. The missile struck the Turanian in the belly, sending him staggering back. Meanwhile, Conan dove for his own sword, lying in its scabbard on the floor. By the time Orkhan had recovered, Conan was up and armed.

"Thank Erlik you've come, my lord!" gasped Narkia, huddling back on the bed. "He would have—"

As she spoke, Conan met a whirlwind attack by Orkhan, who bored in, striking forehand, backhand, and overhand in rapid succession. Conan grimly parried each vicious cut. The blades clashed, clanged, and ground together, striking sparks. The swordplay was all cut-and-parry, since the curved Turanian saber was ill-adapted to thrusting.

"Stop it, you fool!" roared Conan. "The woman lies! I came at her invitation, and we have done naught—"

Narkia screamed something that Conan failed to comprehend; for, as Orkhan pressed his attack, red battle rage surged up in Conan's veins. He struck harder and faster, until Orkhan, skilled swordsman though he was, fell back breathing heavily.

Then Conan's sword, flashing past Orkhan's guard, sheared through the links of the Turanian's mesh-mail vest and sliced into his side. Orkhan staggered, dropping his weapon and pressing a hand against his wound, while blood seeped out between his fingers. Conan followed the first telling blow with a slash that bit deeply into Orkhan's neck. The Turanian fell heavily, shuddered, and lay still, while dark stains spread across the carpet on which he sprawled.

"You've slain him!" shrieked Narkia. "Tughril will have your head for that. Why could you not have stunned him with the flat?"

"When you're fighting for your life," grunted Conan, wiping and sheathing his blade, "you cannot measure out your strokes with the nicety of an apothecary compounding a potion. It's as much your fault as mine. Why did you accuse me of rape, girl?"

Narkia shrugged. With a trace of a mischievous smile, she said: "Because I knew not which of you would win; and had I not accused you, and he slew you, he'd have killed me for good measure."

"That's civilization for you!" sneered Conan. Before lifting his baldric to slide it over his head, he whirled and slapped Narkia on the haunch with the scabbarded blade, bowling her over in an untidy heap. She shrank back, eyes big with fear.

"If you were not a woman," he growled, "it would go hard with you. I warn you to give me an hour ere you cry the alarm. If you do not . . ." Scowling, he drew a finger across his throat and backed to the window. An instant later he was swarming down the ivy, while Narkia's curses floated after him on the moonlit air.

Lyco of Khorshemish, lieutenant in the King's Light Horse, was playing a plaintive air on his flute when Conan burst into the room they shared on Maypur Alley. Muttering a hasty greeting, Conan hurriedly changed from civilian garb into his officer's uniform. Then he spread his blanket on the floor and began placing his meager possessions upon it. He opened a locked chest and drew out a small bag of coin.

"Whither away?" asked Lyco, a stocky, dark man of about Conan's age. "One would think you were leaving for good. Is some fiend after you?"

"I am and it is," grunted Conan.

"What have you been up to? Raiding the King's harem? Why in the name of the gods, when you have at last attained the easy duty you've been angling for?"

Conan hesitated, then said: "You might as well know, since I shall be hence ere you could betray me."

Lyco started a hot protest, but Conan waved him to silence. "I did but jest, Lyco. I've just killed Orkhan." Tersely, he gave an account of the evening's events.

Lyco whistled. "That spills the stew-pot into the fire! The High Priest of Erlik is his sire. Old Tughril will have your heart's blood, even if you could win the King's forgiveness."

"I know it," gritted Conan, tying up his blanket roll. "That's why I'm in a hurry."

"Had you also slain the woman, you could have made it seem an ordinary robbery, with nobody the wiser."

"Trust a Kothian to think of that!" snarled Conan. "I'm not yet civilized enough to kill women out of hand. If I stay long enough in these southlands, I may yet learn."

"Well, trust a thick-headed Cimmerian to blunder into traps, one after another! I told you the omens were unfavorable tonight, and that my dream of last night boded ill."

"Aye; you dreamed some foolishness that had naught to do with me—about a wizard seizing a priceless gem. You should have been a seer rather than a soldier, my lad."

Lyco rose. "Do you need more coin?"

Conan shook his head. "That is good of you; but I have enough to get me to some other kingdom. Thank Erlik, I've saved a little from my pay. If you pull the right strings, Lyco, you might get promoted to my post."

"I might; but I'd rather have my old comrade-in-arms about to trade insults with. What shall I tell people?"

Conan paused, frowning. "Crom, what a complicated business! Tell them I came in with some cock-and-bull story of a royal message to be carried to— to—what's that little border kingdom southeast of Koth?"

"Khauran?"

"Aye, a message to the King of Khauran."

"They have a queen there."

"The queen, then. Farewell, and in a fight never forget to guard your crotch!"

They made their adieus in bluff, soldierly fashion, wringing hands, slapping backs, and punching each other's shoulders. Then Conan was gone, in a swirl of saffron cloak.

———

The rotund moon, declining in the western sky, gazed placidly down upon the West Gate of Aghrapur as Conan trotted up on his big black destrier, Egil. His belongings in the blanket roll were lashed securely to his saddle, behind the cantle.

"Open up!" he called. "I'm Captain Conan of the King's Royal Guard, on a royal commission!"

"What is your mission, Captain?" demanded the officer of the gate guard.

Conan held up a roll of parchment. "A message from His Majesty to the Queen of Khauran. I must deliver it forthwith."

While grunting soldiers pulled on the bronze-studded oaken portal, Conan tucked the parchment into the wallet that hung from his belt. The scroll was in reality a short treatise on swordsmanship, on which Conan had been practicing his limited knowledge of written Hyrkanian, and he had counted upon the guards' not bothering to inspect it. Even if they had, he felt sure that few, if any, of them could read the document, especially by lantern light.

At last the gate creaked open. With a wave, Conan trotted through and broke into a canter. He followed the broad highway, which some in these parts called the Road of Kings—one of several thoroughfares so named—leading westward to Zamora and the Hyborian kingdoms. He rode steadily through the dying night, past fields of young spring wheat, past luxuriant pastures where shepherds watched their flocks and neatherds tended their cattle.

Before the road reached Shadizar, the capital of Zamora, a path led up into the hills bordering Khauran. Conan, however, had no intention of going to Khauran. As soon as he was out of sight of Aghrapur, he pulled off the road at a place where scrubby trees bordered a watercourse. Out of sight of passersby he dismounted, tethered his horse, stripped off his handsome uniform, and donned the shabby civilian tunic and trews in which he had made his ill-fated visit to Narkia.

As Conan changed clothes, he cursed himself for an addlepated fool. Lyco was right; he was a fool. The woman had slipped him a note, inviting him to her apartment while her protector was away in Shahpur; and, tired of tavern wenches, Conan aspired to a courtesan of higher rank and quality. For this, and for the boyish thrill of stealing his commander's girl out from under that officer's nose, he had cut short a promising career. He had never imagined that Orkhan might return from Shahpur earlier than expected. The worst of it was that he had never disliked the fellow; a strict officer but a fair one. . . .

Sunk in melancholy gloom, Conan unwound the turban from his spired helmet and draped the cloth over his head in imitation of a Zuagir kaffiyya, tucking the ends inside his tunic. Then he repacked his belongings, mounted, and set out briskly—but not back to the Road of Kings. Instead, he headed north across country, over fields and through woods where none could track his horse's hoofprints.

He smiled grimly when, far behind, he heard the drumming of hooves as a body of horsemen raced westward along the main road. Traveling in that direction, they would never catch him.

Half an hour later, in the violet dawn, Conan was walking his horse northward along a minor road that was little more than a track through a region of scrubby second growth. So full was his head of alternative plans and routes that for an instant he failed to mark the sound of hooves, the creak of harness, and the jingle of accouterments of approaching horsemen. Before he had time to turn his horse into the concealing scrub, the riders galloped around a bend in the track and rode straight for him. They were a squad of King Yildiz's horse archers on foam-flecked mounts.

Cursing his inattention, Conan pulled off to the roadside, uncertain whether to fight or flee. But the soldiers clattered past with scarcely a glance in his direction. The last man in the column, an officer, pulled up long enough to shout:

"You there, fellow! Have you seen a party of travelers with a woman?"

"Why—" Conan started an angry retort before he remembered that he was no longer Captain Conan of the King's Royal Guard. "Nay, sir, I have not," he growled, with an unconvincing show of humility.

Cursing by his gods, the officer spurred his horse after the rest of the squad. For Conan, as he resumed his northward trot, astonishment trod on the heels of relief. Something must have happened in Aghrapur—something of more moment than his affair with Orkhan. The squad that had rushed past had not even been interested in ascertaining his identity. Could it be that the force pounding westward along the Road of Kings also pursued some quarry other than the renegade Captain Conan?

Perhaps he would unravel the tangle in Sultanapur.

chapter  ii

The Swamp Cat

Traveling through the Marshes of Mehar proved no less onerous than guiding a camel across a featureless desert or conning a boat on the boundless sea. On all sides reeds, taller than Conan's horse, stretched away to infinity. The yellowed canes of last year's crop rattled monotonously whenever a breeze rippled across them; while below, the tender green shoots of the new growth crowded the earth and provided Egil with fodder.

A rider through the marshes was forced to set his course by sun and stars. A man afoot would find this task all but impossible, for the towering reeds would obscure all view save that of the sky directly overhead.

From the back of his stallion, Conan could look out across the tops of the reeds, which undulated gently like the waves of a placid sea. When he reached one of the rare rises of ground, he sometimes glimpsed the Vilayet Sea afar to his right. On his left he often sighted the tops of the low hills that sundered the Marshes of Mehar from the Turanian steppe.

Conan had swum his horse across the Ilbars River below Akif and headed north, keeping the sea in view. He reasoned that, to escape his pursuers' notice, he must either lose himself in an urban crowd or seek the solitude of some uninhabited place, whence he could be forewarned of his pursuers if they picked up his trail.

Conan had never before seen the Marshes of Mehar. Rumor reported them as solitary a lieu as any place on earth. The waterlogged soil was useless for farming. Timber was limited to a few dwarfish, twisted trees, crowning occasional knobby knolls. Biting insects were alleged to swarm in such numbers that even hunters, who might otherwise have invaded the marshes in pursuit of wild swine and other game, forswore to seek their prey there.

The marshes, moreover, were said to be the abode of a dangerous predator, vaguely referred to as the "swamp cat." Although Conan had never met anyone who claimed to have seen such a creature, all agreed that it was as deadly as a tiger.

Still, the dismal solitude of the marshes exceeded Conan's expectations. Here no sound broke the silence save the plashing of Egil's muddy hooves, the rustling of the reeds, and the buzz and hum of clouds of insects, which swirled up from the agitated canes. With his turban cloth securely wrapped around his head and face and his uniform gauntlets on his hands, Conan was well protected; but his miserable mount kept lashing his tail and shaking his mane to dislodge the myriad pests.

For days on end, Conan plodded through the changeless reeds. Once he started a sounder of swine of a large, rust-red species. Avid for some fresh pork to vary his dwindling supply of salted meat and hard biscuits, he reached for his bow; but by the time he had pulled the short, double-curved Hyrkanian weapon from its case, the pigs had vanished. Conan decided against the unwelcome delay of an extended hunt.

For three days Conan forged ahead, while the reeds before him still stretched to the horizon. Toward the close of the third day, when a hillock afforded a vista, he found that both the sea on his right and the hills on the western horizon had moved closer than before. Guessing that he was nearing the northern end of the marshes and, beyond that, the city of Sultanapur, he clucked Egil to a trot.

Then, thin in the distance, he heard a human cry; he thought he detected several voices shouting. Turning his head, he located the source of the commotion on a hillock to his left, whence a plume of blue smoke ascended lazily into the sky. Prudence told Conan to ride on, regardless of the cause of the disturbance. The fewer who saw him while he was still in Turan, the better were his chances of escaping that kingdom unscathed.

But prudence had never occupied the first rank among Conan's counselors; and a camp implied a fresh-cooked meal, and, beyond that, the possibility of loot or legitimate employment. Besides, his curiosity was aroused. While Conan was capable of ruthless action in pursuit of his own interests, he could also, on a quixotic impulse, throw himself into some affair that was none of his business when his barbaric notions of honor required it.

On this occasion, curiosity and thoughts of food vanquished caution. Conan turned Egil's head toward the hillock and heeled the horse into a fast trot. As he approached, he described some agitated figures rushing about on the crest of the knoll, among clumps of spring wildflowers whose scarlet, golden, and violet blooms lent a rare touch of color to the drab landscape.

As he came closer, he perceived that there were five men, moving around a small tent adjacent to their campfire. Their beasts of burden—four asses, two

horses, and a camel—had been securely tethered to a gnarled, dwarfish tree;
now terrified, they were bucking and straining at their tethers despite the efforts
of one of the men to calm them.

"What's the matter?" Conan roared across the rustle of the reeds.

"Beware! Swamp cat!" shouted one of the men, a lean fellow in a white
turban.

"Where?" yelled Conan.

The men around the tent babbled all at once, pointing in various directions.
Then a spitting snarl ripped the air on Conan's right, and out of the reeds
bounded a tawny creature whose like Conan had never beheld. The head and
forequarters were those of a large member of the cat tribe, but the hindlegs
were twice as long as those of a normal feline. The beast progressed by gigantic
leaps, its heavy tail held stiffly out behind for balance, presenting to view a
bizarre combination of a panther and a gigantic hare.

Sighting the approaching menace, the stallion whinnied in fear and leaped
convulsively to one side. During his two years of service with the Turanian
army, Conan had become an accomplished rider; but he still lacked the consummate skill of a Hyrkanian nomad, reared in the saddle. Caught by surprise,
Conan pitched headlong off his mount, landing heavily on his shoulder in a
mass of reeds. With a thunder of hooves, Egil vanished.

In a flash, Conan rolled to his feet and whipped out his scimitar. The swamp
cat had alighted within a spear's length of the Cimmerian, with its fur erect
and its eyes ablaze. Bracing himself for the attack, Conan raised his weapon
and uttered the fearsome battle cry of the Cimmerian tribes.

At that dreadful, inhuman scream, the cat paused, snarling. Then it leaped—
but not at Conan. The beast sprang away at an angle and began to circle the
knoll. On the crest of the low eminence, the five travelers rushed to intercept
it, armed with spears, daggers, and a solitary sword. But the swamp cat was
more interested in the travelers' tethered animals than in human prey.

Conan dashed up the slope to the top of the rise, where the campfire crackled
cheerfully. Seizing a blazing faggot, he sped on, heading straight for the swamp
cat, which crouched in preparation for another of its gargantuan leaps. Conan's
quick movement caused the log to blaze up, and he thrust the blazing end into
the cat's face.

With a shriek, the creature sprang back, turned, and bounded mewling away
into the reeds, leaving a faint trail of smoke from its singed hair and whiskers.

As Conan walked back up the slope, the traveler with the sword and turban
stepped forward to greet him. This man, a slender fellow of early middle age,
with a pointed black beard, seemed better accoutered than the others and somewhat taller, although all five were small, dark, and slender—mere pygmies compared to the giant Cimmerian.

"We are grateful, sir," the turbaned man began. "The beast would have borne off one or more of our mounts, leaving us stranded in this devil-haunted wilderness."

Conan nodded curtly. "It's naught. Who will help me to catch my nag, if the swamp cat hasn't eaten him?"

"Take my horse, sir," said the leader. "Dinak, saddle the baggage horse and accompany our visitor."

As the tethered animal was still skittish from its confrontation with the swamp cat, Conan had much ado to calm it. Eventually he swung into the saddle and set out after Egil, with Dinak trotting behind him. The trail through the trampled reeds was not hard to follow, and Conan turned in the saddle to say:

"You're Zamorians, are you not?"

"Aye, sir."

"I thought I knew that accent. Who is your leader, the man with the turban?"

"He is called Harpagus. We are merchants. And you, sir?"

"Merely an out-of-work mercenary."

It was on the tip of Conan's tongue to ask Dinak why the Zamorians were taking an unmarked route through this inhospitable wilderness instead of following the highway that paralleled their course beyond the westward hills. But when it occurred to him that the Zamorian might well ask the same question of him, Conan held his peace and bent his attention to the trail.

As the red ball of the sun hung above the dark line of the western hills, they caught up with Conan's horse nibbling on reed sprouts. Before night had swallowed the twilight, Conan had led the truant Egil back to the encampment. One of the Zamorians was roasting a leg of lamb for dinner, and Conan's nostrils quivered at the scent. He and Dinak unsaddled their mounts and tethered them within easy reach of the clumps of flower-bearing herbs that dotted the hillock.

"Join us, I pray you," invited Harpagus.

"Gladly," said Conan. "I haven't tasted a cooked repast since entering this forsaken marsh. Who lies within?" He jerked a thumb toward the tent, whence a slender hand was reaching out to take a plate of provender.

Harpagus paused before answering. "A lady," he said at last, "who does not wish to be seen by strangers."

Conan shrugged and addressed himself to his food. He could have eaten twice the portions that the Zamorians had served him, but he stretched his meager meal with a couple of stale biscuits from his saddle bags.

One Zamorian produced a skin of wine, which the men passed around, taking gulps from the muzzle. Combing his beard with his fingers, one of which bore a huge, ornate ring, Harpagus said:

"If I may be so bold, young sir, who are you and how came you upon us so opportunely?"

Conan shrugged. "Mere happenstance. As I told Dinak here, I am only a wandering soldier."

"Then you should be traveling toward Aghrapur instead of away from it. That is where you will find the recruiting officers for King Yildiz's army."

"I have other plans," said Conan shortly, wishing he were quick-witted enough to think up plausible lies. Then, suddenly, Harpagus turned, alerted by the soft crunch of a foot on the dried stems of last year's vegetation. Following the Zamorian's glance, Conan saw that a slender female figure had emerged from the obscurity of the tent.

Illumined by the flickering firelight, the woman appeared to be a decade older than Conan, comely of person, and richly clad in garments more suitable for a lordly Hyrkanian's harem than for travel in the wilderness. The firelight was reflected in the links of a golden chain about her columnar neck; and from the chain hung an enormous gem, of purplish hue, in an ornate setting. While the light was too weak for Conan to pick out details, such an ornament, he knew, bespoke the wealth of princes. As the woman slowly approached the fire, Conan perceived her curiously blank stare, like that of a sleepwalker.

"Ja—my lady!" Harpagus's voice rose sharply. "You were bidden to remain within the tent."

"It's cold," murmured the woman. "Cold in the tent." She stretched pale hands toward the flames, glancing unseeingly at Conan and away again into the night.

Harpagus rose, grasped the woman's shoulders, and turned her around. "Look!" he said. Before the woman's face he waved a hand that bore a ring with a great fiery gemstone, muttering: "You shall reenter the tent. You shall speak to no one. You shall forget all that you have seen. You shall reenter the tent. . . ."

After several repetitions, the woman bowed her head and silently retraced her steps, dropping the tent flap behind her. Conan glanced from Harpagus to the tent and back. He urgently wished for an explanation of the scene he had witnessed. Was the woman drugged, or was she under a spell? Were the Zamorians carrying her off? If so, whither? From the few words she had spoken, Conan thought the woman must be a high-born Turanian, for her Hyrkanian speech was accent-free.

Conan was, however, sufficiently seasoned in plots and intrigues not to utter his suspicions. First, his assumptions might be wrong; the woman's presence might be perfectly legitimate. Secondly, even if a plot were afoot, Harpagus would concoct a dozen plausible lies to explain his actions. Thirdly, while Conan had no fear of the small Zamorians, he did have scruples against picking a quarrel with men with whom he had just eaten and whose hospitality he had enjoyed.

Conan decided to wait until the others had bedded down for the night and then have a look in the tent. Although the Zamorians had been friendly, his barbarian instincts told him that something was amiss. For one thing, there was no sign of the usual stock-in-trade that such a party of merchants would normally carry with them. Also, these people were too silent and secretive for ordinary merchants, who, in Conan's experience, would chatter about prices and boast to one another of their sharp bargainings.

Conan's years in Zamora had given him an abiding mistrust of the folk of that nation. They were an ancient, long-settled civilized folk and, from what he had seen of them, notably given to evil. The King, Mithridates VIII, was said to be a drunkard manipulated by the various priesthoods, who struggled and competed with one another for control of the King.

As the evening progressed, one Zamorian produced a stringed instrument and twanged a few chords. Three others joined him in a wailing song, while Harpagus sat in silent dignity. Then a Zamorian asked:

"Can you give us a song, stranger?"

Conan shook his head with a shamefaced grin. "I am no musician. I can shoe a horse, scale a cliff, or split a skull; but I've no skill at singing."

The others persisted in urging him until at last Conan took the instrument and plucked the strings. "Forsooth," he said, "this thing is not unlike the harps of my native land." In a deep bass, he launched into a song:

"We're born with sword and axe in hand,
    For men of the North are we. . . ."

When Conan finished, Harpagus asked: "In what language did you sing? I know it not."

"The tongue of the Æsir," said Conan.

"Who are they?"

"A nation of northern barbarians, far from here."

"Are you one of that tribe?"

"Nay, but I have dwelt amongst them." Conan handed the instrument back and yawned elaborately to cut off further questions. "It's time I were abed."

As if inspired by Conan's example, the Zamorians, yawning in their turn, composed themselves for sleep—all but the one told off for sentry duty. Conan wrapped himself in his blanket, lay down with his head pillowed on his saddle, and closed his eyes.

When the gibbous moon had risen well above the eastern horizon and the four Zamorians were snoring lustily, Conan cautiously raised his head. The sentry paced slowly around the encampment with spear on shoulder. Conan noted that, on the northern side of the rise, for a considerable time during every round of the camp, the sentry passed out of sight.

The next time the sentry disappeared, Conan slid to his feet and, stalking in a crouch, approached the tent, moving as silently as a shadow. The fire had burned down to a bed of coals.

"You find it difficult to sleep?" purred a Zamorian voice behind him. Conan whirled, to find Harpagus standing in the light of the rising moon. Even Conan's keen barbarian senses had not heard the man's approach.

"Yes—I—it is a mere call of nature," growled Conan.

Harpagus clucked sympathetically. "Sleeplessness can be a grave affliction. I will see to it that you sleep soundly the rest of the night."

"No potions!" exclaimed Conan sharply. He had a vision of being drugged or poisoned.

"Fear not, good sir; I had no such thing in mind," said Harpagus gently. "Do but look closely at me."

Conan's eyes met those of the Zamorian. Something in the man's gaze riveted the Cimmerian's attention and held it captive. Harpagus's eyes seemed to grow strangely large and luminous. Conan felt as if he were suspended in a black, starless space, with nothing visible save those huge, glowing eyes.

Harpagus slowly passed the prismatic gem in his ring back and forth in front of Conan's face. In a hypnotic monotone the Zamorian murmured: "You shall go back to sleep. You shall sleep soundly for many hours. When you awaken, you shall have forgotten all about the Zamorian merchants you encamped with. You shall go back to sleep. . . ."

Conan awoke with a start to find the sun high in the heavens. He rolled to his feet, glaring wildly, and shook the air with his curses. Not only were the Zamorians and their animals gone, but his horse had vanished also. His saddle and saddle bags still lay on the ground where he had made his rude bed, but the little leather bag of gold pieces was missing from his wallet.

The worst of it was that he could not remember whom he had companied with the previous night. He recalled the journey from Aghrapur and the fight with the swamp cat. The remains of the campfire and the traces of riding animals proved that he had shared the high ground with several other persons, but he had no memory of who they were or what they had looked like. He had a fleeting recollection of singing a song, accompanied by a borrowed stringed instrument; but the people whom he had serenaded were less than insubstantial shadows in his memory. There had been such folk, of that he was certain; but he recalled no detail of their clothing or countenances.

He remembered that he was on his way to Sultanapur. So, after venting his rage on the indifferent wilderness, he shouldered his burdens and grimly set out northward, tramping through the crowding reeds with saddle bags slung over one massive shoulder and his saddle balanced on the other. If he could no longer navigate by sun and stars, being afoot, he could at least follow the trail of his erstwhile companions by the track they had left through the trampled reeds.

chapter  iii

The Blind Seer

Four days after Conan's encounter with the Zamorians, a heavy knock sounded on the door of the house of Kushad the Seer, in the port city of Sultanapur. When Kushad's daughter swung open the portal, she started back in alarm.

Before the door stood a haggard giant of a man, unshaven and mud-caked, carrying a saddle, a pair of saddle bags, a bow in its case, and a blanket roll. Although he presented a horrific aspect, the man grinned broadly through sweat and dirt.

"Hail, Tahmina!" he croaked. "You've grown since I saw you last; in a few years you'll be a woman, ripe for the plucking. Don't you know me?"

"Can it be—you must be Captain Conan, the Cimmerian!" she stammered. "Come in! My father will rejoice to see you."

"He may be less joyful when he hears my story," grunted Conan, setting down his burdens. "How fares the old fellow?"

"He is well, though his sight is nearly gone. He has no client at the moment, so come with me."

Conan followed the girl back to a chamber in which a small, white-bearded man sat cross-legged on a cushion. As Conan entered, the man stared from eyes clouded by cataract.

"Are you not Conan?" said the old man. "I discern your form but not your features. No other man has so shaken my house with the weight of his tread."

"I am indeed Conan, friend Kushad," said the Cimmerian. "You told me once that if I were ever on the dodge, I could seek asylum here."

Kushad chuckled. "So I did; so I did. But it was only a fair return for saving me from that gang of young ruffians. I recall how you scoffed at the notion that you, now a full captain in His Majesty's forces and a pillar of the kingdom, should ever again be forced to flee and hide. But you seem to draw trouble as offal attracts flies. Sit down and tell me what mischief you have been up to now. You do not require me to employ my astral vision for the finding of a lost coin, I trust?"

"Nay; but to find a whole sackful of them and a fine horse as well," growled Conan. While Tahmina went to fetch a jug of wine, Conan related his misadventure with Narkia, his flight from Aghrapur, and his encounter with the Zamorians.

"The strange thing was," he continued, "that for two whole days I could not remember with whom I had spent the night on that knoll. The memory was wiped clean from my mind, as by some devilish enchantment. Then yesterday, the scenes began to return, a little at a time, until I could picture the whole encounter. What, think you, befell me?"

"Hypnotism," said Kushad. "Your Zamorian must be skilled in the art—a priest or sorcerer, mayhap. Zamora crawls with them as does an inn with bedbugs."

"I know," grunted Conan.

"You displayed great resistance to the sorcerer's wiles, or you would not remember the Zamorians even now. You Westerners lack the fatalism that ofttimes palsies the will of us of the East. Yet I can teach you to guard yourself against such manipulation. Tell me more of these so-called Zamorian merchants."

Conan described the group, adding: "Besides, there was a woman in the tent, who came forth to warm her hands at the fire but was ordered back by the leader, Harpagus. She acted like one demented or under an enchantment."

Kushad's eyebrows arched. "A woman! What manner of female was she?"

"The light was poor; but I could see that she was tall and dark. Somewhat above thirty years of age and well-favored; wearing fluffy silken things, unsuited to—"

"By Erlik!" cried Kushad. "Know you not who the lady was?"

"Nay; who?"

"I do forget! You have been out of touch with mankind for a fortnight. Had you not heard that Jamilah, the favorite wife of King Yildiz, has been abducted?"

"No, by Crom, I hadn't! Now that I think on it, the night I fled, a company of Yildiz's horsemen galloped past without pausing to question me. I thought at first that such gentry would be searching for me on account of Orkhan's death; then I idly wondered if they were not on the trail of bigger game."

"It is your misfortune that you knew not of this kidnapping. Had you rescued the lady, your recent indiscretion would have been forgiven. His Majesty's men have turned the kingdom upside down in search of her."

"When I served at the palace," mused Conan, "I heard rumors of this favorite, but I never clapped eyes upon her. It was said that Yildiz was a simple, easygoing fellow who relied on this particular wife to make all his hard decisions. She was more king than he. I daresay the camel was her mount. But even had I rescued the lady from the Zamorians, I have no wish to continue in Yildiz's service."

"Why so?"

Conan grinned. "When I was galloping about the Hyrkanian steppe, being roasted and frozen and chased by wolves and dodging the arrows of nomads, my heart's desire was duty with the palace guard. I thought I should have naught to do but swagger about in well-polished armor and ogle the ladies.

"But when I became Captain of the Guard, I found it a terrible bore. Save for a little drill each morning, there was naught to do but stand like a statue, saluting the King and his officials, and looking for spots on the uniforms of my men. As much as anything, 'twas to escape the tedium of my post that I commenced my intrigue with that bitch Narkia.

"Besides, the unfortunate Orkhan, it appears, was a son of Tughril, High Priest of Erlik. If I know priests, he'd sooner or later find means of revenge, with or without the King's approval—poisoned needles in my bedding, or a dagger between the shoulder blades some moonless night. Anyway, two years with one master is long enough for me; especially since, as a foreigner, I could never rise to general in Turan."

"The rosiest apple oft harbors the biggest worm," said Kushad. "What would you now?"

Conan shrugged and took a gulp of Kushad's wine. "I had meant to flee to Zamora, where I know people from my old days as a thief. But the cursed Zamorians stole my horse—"

"You mean King Yildiz's horse, do you not?"

Conan shrugged. "Oh, he had horses to spare. The thieving devils got not only the beast but also the little gold I had hoarded. You it was who persuaded me to save a part of each month's pay; but see what good that's done me! I might as well have spent it on women and wine; I should then at least have pleasant memories."

"Count yourself lucky they did not cut your throat whilst you slept." Turning, Kushad called: "Tahmina!" When the girl appeared, he said: "Pull up the board and give me what lies beneath it."

Tahmina thrust a finger into a knothole in one of the floor boards and raised it. Crouching, she put an arm into the orifice and brought out a small but heavy sack. This she gave to Kushad, who handed it to Conan.

"Take what you think you'll need for a new horse, with enough besides to get you to Zamora," said the seer.

Conan untied the sack, inserted a hand, and brought out a fistful of coins. "Why do you this for me?" he asked gruffly.

"Because you were a friend when I needed a friend; and I, too, have my code of honor. Go on, take what you need instead of gaping at me like a stranded fish."

"How knew you I was gaping?"

"I see with the eyes of the mind, now that those of the body have failed me."

"I have met cursed few men in my wanderings who would do such a thing, or whom I could truly call 'friend,'" said Conan. "All the rest seize whatever they have power to take and keep whatever they can. I will pay you back when I am able."

"If you can repay me, good; if not, do not fret. I have enough to see me through this life. Daughter, draw the curtains and fetch my tripod. I must try to perceive with the eye of the spirit whither these Zamorians have gone. Conan, my preparations will take some time. You must be hungry."

"Hungry!" roared Conan. "I could eat a horse, hair, hide, bones, and all. I haven't eaten for two days, because the loss of my beast so delayed me that I ran out of provender."

"Tahmina shall prepare you a meal, and then you may wish to patronize the bathhouse down the street. Take my old cloak and keep your face within the hood. The King's agents may be on the watch for you."

An hour and a half later, Conan returned to Kushad's house. Tahmina whispered: "Hush, Captain Conan; my father is in his trance. He said you may join him if you will do so quietly."

"Then give these boots a pull, like a good girl, will you?" said Conan, thrusting out a leg.

Carrying his boots, Conan stole into the sanctum. Kushad sat cross-legged as before, but now in front of him stood a small brass tripod supporting a tiny bowl, in which some nameless substance smoldered. A thin plume of greenish smoke spiraled up from the vessel, wavering and swaying like a ghostly serpent seeking an exit from the darkened chamber.

Conan seated himself on the floor to watch. Kushad stared blankly before him. At length the seer murmured:

"Conan, you are near. Answer not; I feel your presence. I see a small caravan crossing a sandy steppe. There are—I must position myself closer—there are four asses, three horses, and a camel. One horse, a big black stallion, serves as a pack animal. That must be your mount. The camel has a tented saddle, so I cannot see who rides within; but I suspect that it be the lady Jamilah."

"Where are they?" whispered Conan.

"On a flat, boundless plain, stretching to the horizon."

"The vegetation?"

"It is all short grass, with a few thorny shrubs. They move toward the setting sun. That is all I can tell you." Slowly the aged seer shook off his trance.

Conan mused: "They must be crossing the steppe country between the western bourn of Turan and the Kezankian Mountains, which border Zamora. The kings of Turan talk much of extending their sway over this masterless land, to crush the nomads and outlaws who dwell there. But they have done naught. The kidnappers have moved fast; they're more than halfway to Zamora. I doubt I could catch them with the fleetest horse ere they were well within that realm. But catch them I will, to get my horse and money back—or, failing that, to wreak revenge."

"If chance enable you to rescue the lady Jamilah, by all means do so. The kingdom has need of her."

"If I can return her without losing my head in the process. But why should Zamorians abduct one of Yildiz's women? For ransom? For royal spite? If aught would stir this do-nothing King to action, that's it. And Turan's might is far greater than Zamora's."

Kushad shook his turbaned head. "I am sure the King of Zamora is not behind this. Mithridates knows the strength of his kingdom as well as we, and in any event he is but a tool of the priesthoods. The deep sleep that Harpagus cast upon you suggests the involvement of priests. Are you resolved upon going to Zamora?"

"Aye, that I am."

"Then stay hidden in my house, whilst I teach you some of the tricks of my trade."

Conan scowled. "I've always found a stout, sharp blade a better defense than magical mummeries."

"Your strong right arm failed you in the Marshes of Mehar, did it not? Now use your wits, young man! When you were stationed at Sultanapur, you told me how you had scorned the bow as an unmanly weapon until you learned its value in Turan. You will make the same discovery with the mental training that I intend to give you."

"I'll steer clear of priests and wizards," growled Conan.

"Ah, but will they steer clear of you? How can you avoid them if you do pursue them to recover your property?"

Conan grunted. "I understand your meaning."

"Where you are going, you will need every shaft your quiver can hold. You may wonder how Harpagus and his confederates could so easily escape from Turan. Had a squad of the King's men caught up with them, Harpagus and his ilk could readily have cast an illusion to send their pursuers haring off in the opposite direction. And they could do the same to you."

"Uh," said Conan suspiciously. "What is it that you propose to teach me?"

Kushad smiled. "Merely to defend yourself against the occult wiles of others. I cannot cast an illusion quite so well as when I had the full sight of my orbs,

yet I lack not all resource. Let us step out into the garden for a moment."
When Conan had followed the seer out into the flower and vegetable garden
in back of the house, Kushad turned and said: "Look at me!"

Conan stared and found that Kushad's nearly blind eyes caught and held his
vision as firmly as had the sharp eyes of Harpagus. Kushad waved a hand to
and fro, muttering softly.

Of a sudden, Conan found himself standing in a dense jungle, among the
massive boles of orchid-hung trees, whose buttressed roots spread writhing
across the jungle floor. A sound as of sawing wood caused him to whirl, hand
on his sword hilt. Ten paces off, the head of a huge tiger protruded from a
patch of long grass. With a low rumble, the tiger drew back its lips in a snarl,
showing fangs like curved Zuagir daggers. Then it charged.

Conan whipped out his scimitar. To his horror, he felt sentient life within
his grasp. Staring, he saw that he held not a curved Turanian saber, but the
neck of a writhing serpent. The snake's head strained this way and that as it
sought to flesh its needle-like fangs in Conan's hand and wrist.

With a yell of revulsion, Conan hurled the serpent from him and threw
himself sideways, out of the path of the tiger's hurtling body. His hand sought
his dagger. Knowing how puny was the strength of even the strongest man
compared to that of a giant cat, he was sure that death, which he had narrowly
foiled so often, had at last caught up with him. . . .

He found himself lying among the shrubs of Kushad's garden. Grumbling,
he staggered to his feet.

"See you what I mean?" said the blind seer, smiling thinly. "I must be more
circumspect with my illusions; you nearly took my head off when you threw
your sword. Happen I had you at a disadvantage, for you are fatigued from
your recent journey. Go; you will find a bed prepared. Tomorrow we shall
begin our lessons."

A re you ready?" said Kushad, as sunbeams played among the trellises of the
garden. "Remember your numbers, and clutch the mental picture of this courtyard firmly in your mind. Now look!"

Kushad waved a hand and muttered. The small court faded away. Conan
stood on the edge of a boundless swamp, lit by the eery crimson light of a
setting sun. Yellowed patches of swamp grass and dried reeds alternated with
pools and meres of still waters, lying jet-black beneath the bloody reflection of
the scarlet eye of heaven. Strange flying creatures, like gigantic bats with lizard
heads, soared overhead.

Directly in front of Conan, a huge reptilian head, as large as that of the bull
aurochs whose neck Conan had broken as a stripling in Cimmeria, parted the
surface of the slimy, stagnant water. As the gigantic head reared up against the

red disk of the sun, there seemed to be no end of the serpentine neck supporting it. Up—up—up it went. . . .

At first sight of the creature, Conan's hand instinctively flew to his sword. But then he recalled that his weapon was within the house; Kushad had insisted that he face his trial unarmed.

Still the head rose on its colossal neck, until it towered upward thrice the height of a man. Frantically searching the shards of his memory to piece together the seer's teachings, Conan concentrated on the picture of Kushad's garden, with the small, white-bearded seer sitting placidly on a cushion laid beside the path. Little by little, the image solidified and merged with that of the actual courtyard. Conan muttered to himself, "Four threes are twelve; four fours are sixteen; four fives . . ."

Slowly the swamp and its reptilian denizens faded from view, and Conan found himself back in Kushad's garden. He drew his sleeve across his sweat-beaded forehead, saying: "I feel as if I had been fighting a battle for an hour."

"Labor of the mind can be as strenuous as that of the body," said Kushad gently. "You are learning, my son, but you were slow to bring your mental forces to bear. We must try again."

"Not just yet, pray," said Conan. "I am fordone, as if I had run ten leagues."

"You may rest for the nonce. What will you call yourself henceforth?"

"Call myself?" snorted Conan. "What's the matter with Conan of Cimmeria?"

"Be not wroth. If there be not a price on your head now, there soon will be. A client full of bazaar gossip reports that you are accounted Jamilah's abductor, since you and she both vanished on the selfsame night."

"Going under a false name is cowardly; and besides, I'm sure to forget to answer to it."

"One gets used to an assumed name sooner than one thinks. Anyway, you needs must take another identity, at least until you reach a land where your repute has not preceded you. What name would you choose—something not incongruous with your aspect?"

Conan, scowling, pondered. At last he said: "My father was Nial the smith. He was a good man."

"Excellent! You shall be Nial, at least for the nonce. Tahmina! I sense that our guest hungers again. Fetch him wherewith to stay his pangs."

"You must think I eat enough for three," said Conan, sinking large white teeth into the loaf the girl proffered. "I am still making up for my dinnerless detour through the Marshes of Mehar. Thank you, Tahmina." He took a gulp of ale.

"Captain Conan," said the girl, "I—I had a dream last night, which perchance concerns you."

"What's this, my young seeress?" asked Kushad. "Why did you not inform us sooner?"

" 'Tis the first chance I have had, with you two locked in talk and saying you would fain not be disturbed."

"What of your dream, girl?" said Conan. "I scoff not at such portents; too many prophetic dreams have visited my kin."

"I dreamt I saw you running down a tunnel, deep inside the earth. Some creature did pursue you. It was too dark to see aright, but the thing was big—as large as an ox. As you ran, it gained upon you."

"Tell me more, my little one," persisted Conan. "Describe it in detail."

"I—I cannot, save that it had glowing eyes. There were eight such eyes, gleaming like great fiery jewels."

"Perhaps a pack of famished wolves?" suggested Conan.

"Nay, it was a single creature. But it did not move the way a large animal normally moves. It—I know not how to say it—it seemed to scurry along like a walking nightmare. And it came closer and closer, and I knew that in an instant it would catch you. . . ."

"Well?" barked Conan. "What then?"

"Then I awoke. That is all."

Kushad questioned his daughter, but elicited no further information. He said: "So, young Nial, meseems the dream is a symbol of something; but of what? Dreams can be interpreted in many ways, and any way may be right. Mayhap you had better avoid subterranean tunnels, in case this were a premonition of some real, material menace. Now, if you have eaten, we shall begin another trial of your powers of psychical resistance."

Several days later, Conan, wearing Kushad's hooded cloak, led his new horse to the seer's portal. The beast was a shaggy, stocky, Hyrkanian pony, shorter in the leg than the stolen Egil. Conan knew that, while the animal could easily be outdistanced by the slender-legged western breeds, it offset this shortcoming by endurance and an ability to thrive on coarse and scanty fare.

He bade Kushad and his daughter a brisk but affectionate farewell. Tahmina smiled bravely and wiped away a trembling tear. In a way, Conan was glad to leave. The young girl, whose form had just begun to fill out, had been casting sheep's eyes at him; and from a remark by Kushad, the Cimmerian gathered that the old man would welcome him as a son-in-law, if Conan ever gave up his wild, headstrong ways, got on the right side of the law, and settled down in Sultanapur to wait for the child to reach a marriageable age.

But Conan had no intention of settling down, or of tying himself to any woman. Neither did his sense of honor permit him to take advantage of Tahmina's girlish infatuation. So it was with a small sigh of relief that he strapped his gear to Ymir, his new horse, embraced his mentor and his youthful hostess, tightened the girth, and trotted smartly off.

chapter iv

The Golden Dragon

Westward Conan wended his way at the steady pace of the seasoned rider: walk, trot, canter, trot, walk, over and over. Every third day he paused long enough to give his steed several solid hours of grazing. Failure to do this, he knew, would wear the animal out and perhaps even kill it before he arrived at his destination.

He had reached the short-grass country of western Turan, where the plain glowed with clumps of wildflowers of scarlet and gold and blue, while the air above the greensward quivered with the flutter of countless iridescent butterflies. Here the land stretched for leagues with only slight rolls and undulations. The traveler in these parts came upon few signs of human life, save an occasional neatherd with his cattle or a shepherd with his flock. Once or twice a day, Conan encountered a caravan of camels sounding the silvery tinkle of bells, and the creaking leather and jingling mail of hired horse guards. More rarely, a lone trader jogged along on his ass, leading another piled with his gear and stock of goods.

Soon, Conan knew, he would reach the border. There King Yildiz's blockhouses and patrols warded the kingdom against the nomads and outlaws who roamed the unclaimed prairie to the west. The protection they afforded the kingdom was far from perfect. One of Conan's first assignments after promotion to a regular army unit had been to chase marauders back into this sparsely-settled west country. Sometimes the troop caught the raiders and rode proudly back to their fort with severed heads on their lances. More often the pillagers gave them the slip; and they returned on lathered steeds, with glum looks on their faces and grim jokes on their lips.

The border guards, Conan was well aware, had other duties, too. They questioned all travelers who sought to enter or leave the kingdom and apprehended felons and persons wanted by the authorities. The road that Conan followed had dwindled to a sandy track; and for a mounted man there was scant choice between this track and the boundless virgin prairie. After some deliberation Conan decided not to try to bluff his way past the border guard, but to detour around the blockhouse. So he angled northwest and soon lost sight of the beaten way.

The following afternoon, a black speck atop a nearby rise attracted his attention. Approaching, he discovered a pile of rocks, which betimes the kings of Turan ordered erected to define the bounds of the kingdom. But so vague was the site of the border that the cairn might be a dozen leagues beyond, or half a dozen short, of the line that appeared on the maps in Aghrapur.

Conan continued westward, and that evening staked out his horse to graze and stretched himself upon his blanket, assured that he was now beyond the bourn of Turan.

A stealthy footstep awakened him; but, before he could spring to his feet, something clinging fell upon him. When he struggled up, it tripped and hampered him. It was a game net, such as the Hyrkanians used in their periodic mass hunts. Before he could fight his way out of the entanglement, a club smashed down upon his head, bringing a shower of shooting stars followed by blackness.

When Conan regained consciousness, he found that his wrists were firmly lashed behind him. Looking up, he saw a circle of men in the King's uniforms, some mounted and some afoot, surrounding him in the starlight. One, bearing the insignia of a Turanian officer, commanded, "On your feet, vagabond!"

Grunting, Conan rolled over and tried to rise. He discovered that, when a man is lying down with his hands tied behind him, it is difficult or even impossible for him to arise without assistance. After several tries, he sank back on the grass.

"Someone will have to boost me up," he growled.

"Help him, Arslan," said the officer. "Aidin, stand ready with your club in case he tries to bite or run."

On his feet at last, Conan roared: "What is the meaning of this? It's an outrage on a harmless traveler!"

"We shall see about that," said the officer. "Honest travelers stop for questioning at the border post, which you obviously avoided. Luckily, we had word from a shepherd who saw you straying from the road, and the night was clear enough to track you down. Now come along, and we shall learn just how harmless you are."

A trooper slipped a Hyrkanian lasso—a pole with a running noose on the end—over Conan's head and tightened it around the Cimmerian's neck. The troopers mounted and set out across the steppe, one leading Ymir while Conan stumbled along on foot.

At the blockhouse, the soldiers pushed Conan into a small, crowded room. Six men with ready weapons watched him, while their commanding officer settled himself at a rough trestle table.

"Here's the blackguard, Captain," said the lieutenant who had brought Conan in.

"Did he put up a fight?" asked the captain.

"Nay; we caught him sleeping. But I do not think—"

"Never mind what you do or do not think," snapped the captain. "You, fellow!"

"Yes?" snarled Conan, staring at the officer through narrowed lids.

"Who are you?"

"Nial, a soldier of Turan."

"You are no Hyrkanian; that is plain from your aspect and barbarous accent. Whence came you?"

"I am a native of the Border Kingdom," said Conan, who had rehearsed his lies on the trek back to the blockhouse.

"What land is that?"

"A country far to the northwest, near Hyperborea."

"In what unit of the army do you serve?"

"Captain Shendin's cuirassiers, stationed at Khawarizm." This was a real unit and one with which Conan was familiar. Conan was thankful now that he had, however unwillingly, followed Kushad's advice and left most of his handsome uniform at the seer's house in Sultanapur. Had it been packed with the rest of his belongings and had the troopers found it, his imposture would have been shattered in an instant.

"Why are you departing from Turan? A deserter, eh?"

"Nay, I applied for leave because I learned that my aged mother is sick at home. I am returning thither and shall be back at my duties within three months. Send to ask Captain Shendin if you believe me not."

"Then why did you avoid the border post?"

"So as not to waste time answering foolish questions," grated Conan.

The captain reddened with quick anger. As he paused before replying, the lieutenant spoke again: "I do not think this man can be the renegade Conan, Captain, even though he somewhat answers the description. First, he does not have the King's lady with him. Second, he does not try to flatter or conciliate us, as would a guilty fugitive. And finally, this Conan is said to have such keen senses and mighty strength that we could not so easily have taken him alive."

The captain pondered for a moment, then said: "Very well; you seem to have the right of it. But I am still minded to have him flogged for insolence and for putting us to needless trouble."

"Pray, sir, the men are weary. Besides, if he be truly a soldier on leave—which he may well be—such a course might cause us trouble with the commander of his unit."

The captain sighed. "Release his bonds. Next time, Master Nial, do not try such tricks upon us, and count yourself lucky to get off without at least a beating. You may go."

Growling a surly word of thanks, Conan recovered his sword from the soldier who held it and started for the door. He was crowding past the troopers when another lieutenant appeared in the hallway before him. This man's eyes widened.

"Why, Conan!" cried the newcomer. "What do you here? Don't you remember Khusro, your old—"

Conan reacted instantly. Lowering his head in a bull-like rush, he lunged at the lieutenant, giving him so violent a push in the chest with his open hand that the man, hurled back, crashed against the wall and fell supine. Leaping over the sprawling body, Conan dashed out into the night.

Ymir was tied to a hitching post in front of the blockhouse. Without taking time to draw sword or dagger, Conan snapped the stout leather reins with a terrific jerk, vaulted into the saddle, and savagely pounded his heels against the horse's ribs.

By the time the shouting troopers had boiled out of the blockhouse, run to the paddock, saddled their mounts, and set out in pursuit, Conan was a distant speck in the starlight. As soon as a roll in the landscape hid him from view, he galloped off at right angles to the narrow road. Before the sun had thrust its ruddy limb above the level eastern horizon, he had shaken off his pursuers.

In the Zamorian language, the word *maul* denoted the most shabby, disreputable part of a city. Each of the two principal cities of Zamora, Shadizar and Arenjun, had its maul; and even some of the smaller towns boasted such unwholesome districts. The maul was an area of bitter poverty; a slum of tumbledown old houses ripe for razing; a section of starving folk defeated by life and sinking into oblivion; a quarter for new arrivals, fresh from the village and desperately struggling for a foothold in the life of the community; a haunt of thieves and outlaws who preyed alike on the rich outside the maul and on the poor within; and the repository of ill-gotten wealth.

The stench of the winding alleys of the maul of Shadizar brought Conan vivid memories of his days as a thief in Zamora. Although he had adapted himself to a soldier's life during the past two years, the smell of the maul in his nostrils roused the lawless devil in his blood. He felt a nostalgic yearning for the days when he owed no master and yielded to no discipline, save as his vestigial conscience and barbaric sense of honor dictated. Impatient of all restraint, he had often thought, during his employment as a mercenary, that the perfect freedom he dreamed of was worth the periods of starvation he had suffered as a thief.

Following directions received at Eriakes's Inn, Conan strode through the forbidding alleys, lit feebly by cressets and lamps set into the walls at distant, irregular intervals. His boots squidged in mud and refuse as he brushed aside beggars and pimps. A couple of knots of bravos eyed him with hostile or predatory stares. When he scowled at them, they turned away; his towering size and the stout scimitar at his side dissuaded them from their felonious intentions.

He reached a doorway over which, illumined by a pair of smoking cressets, hung a dark board on which a yellow dragon was crudely depicted. The sign identified the Golden Dragon, a wineshop and alehouse. Shouldering his way in, Conan swept the common room with his wary glance.

Suspended from the low, soot-blackened ceiling, a pair of brass lamps, burning liquid bitumen, cast a cheerful glow. At the tables and benches sat the usual raffish crowd: a pair of drunken soldiers, loudly boasting of herculean feats of venery; a trio of desert Zuagirs in kaffiyyas, who revealed by nervous sidelong glances that they were strange to cities; a poor mad creature talking to himself in an endless mumbling monotone; a well-dressed man who, Conan guessed, was the head of a local syndicate of thieves; a dedicated astrologer working celestial calculations on a sheet of papyrus. . . .

Conan headed for the counter, behind which stood a brawny middle-aged woman. "Is Tigranes in?" he asked.

"He just stepped out. He'll be back soon. What will you have?"

"Wine. The ordinary."

The woman uncovered a tub, dipped up a scoop, and filled a leather drinking jack, which she pushed toward Conan. The Cimmerian put down a coin, took his change, and surveyed the room. Only one seat was vacant, at a small table for two. The other occupant was a young Zamorian, slight and dark, who stared unseeingly over his mug of ale. Conan walked to the table and sat down. When the young man frowned at him, he growled: "Mind?"

The youth shook an unwilling head. "Nay; you are welcome."

Conan drank, wiped his mouth, and asked: "What's news in Shadizar these days?"

"I know not. I have just come from the North."

"Oh? Tell me, then, what news from the North?"

The young man grunted. "I was in the temple guard at Yezud, but the god-rotted priests have dismissed all the native guardsmen. They say Feridun will hire only foreigners, curse him." With a glance at Conan, the Zamorian added, "Excuse me, I see you are a foreigner. Naught personal."

"It matters not. Who is Feridun?"

"The High Priest of Zath."

Conan searched his memory. "Is not Zath the spider-god of Yezud?"

"Aye."

"But why should the priesthood prefer to be guarded by foreigners?"

The Zamorian shrugged. "They say they want men of larger stature, but I suspect some power maneuver in the ceaseless war of the priesthoods."

"So they're knifing one another in the back as usual?"

"Aye, verily! For the moment, the priests of Urud have the ear of the King, and the priests of Zath are fain to oust them and usurp their place."

"In a confrontation between the Zathites and the King," mused Conan, "perchance the Zathites think they would find foreign mercenaries more trustworthy than native Zamorians. What do you now?"

"Look for employment. I am Azanes the son of Vologas, and I have been thought a good man of my hands, even though I lack your bulk. Do you know of any openings?"

Conan shook his head. "I, too, have just arrived in Shadizar the Wicked; so I am in as fine a fix as you. They say the Turanians are recruiting mercenaries in Aghrapur—hold; there's the man I came to see."

Conan gulped his wine, rose, and returned to the counter, where a bald, potbellied fellow had taken the place of the brawny matron. Conan said: "Hail, Tigranes!"

The bald man, beaming, started to cry: "Co—" but Conan stopped him with an upraised hand. "My name is Nial," he said, "and forget it not. How do you? You still had hair on your pate when last I saw you."

"Alas, it's gone the way of all things mortal, friend. How long have you been in Shadizar? Where dwell you? How did you find me?"

"One at a time," grinned Conan. "First, let's find a place where we can talk less publicly."

"Right you are. Atossa!" When the woman took Tigranes's place behind the counter, Tigranes grasped Conan by the elbow and steered him into a curtained cubicle behind the counter.

"This one is on the house," he said, pouring two goblets of wine. "Now tell me about yourself. What have you been doing the last few years?"

"I've been a soldier in Turan, but I had to leave in haste."

The taverner chuckled. "Same old Conan—I mean Nial. Where are you staying?"

"At Eriakes's Inn, on the edge of the maul. I asked after you, and they directed me hither."

"What are you doing now?"

"Looking for gainful employment, honest or otherwise."

"If you seek a fence to dispose of your loot, do not look at me! I gave all that up after the Chief Inquisitor had me arrested. I escaped the scaffold only by bribing him with all I'd saved, to the last farthing. Well, *almost* to the last farthing." Tigranes cast a significant glance toward the curtained doorway.

Conan shook his head. "I've had enough of that starveling life, save as a last resort. But I have soldiered all the way from Shahpur to Khitai, and that should count for something."

"Speaking of Turan," said Tigranes, "a party of Turanians was here yesterday, asking questions. They said they were looking for a man of your description, accompanied by a woman. Has that aught to do with you?"

"It might or it might not. How looked these Turanians?"

"The leader was a short, square fellow with a little gray beard, who called himself Parvez. He had several fellow countrymen in tow, and an escort of a brace of King Mithridates's guards. His snooping evidently has our King's approval."

"I know who Parvez is," said Conan. "One of Yildiz's diplomats. A gang of Zamorians abducted Yildiz's favorite wife, and the King is frantic for her return. I had naught to do with that jape, but the Turanians seem to think I did. Methinks I had better shake the dust of Shadizar from my boots."

"That were not the only reason," said Tigranes. "The law remembers you all too well, despite the years you have been away. And your size makes you conspicuous, no matter by what name you call yourself." Tigranes's eyes narrowed speculatively, and the demon of greed peered out from his small, piglike orbs.

"I had thought of going to—" began Conan, but paused as suspicion crackled in his mind. His experience with the Zamorian underworld had taught him that the "honor amongst thieves," to which the denizens of the maul paid lip service, was in fact as rare as fur on serpents or feathers on fish.

"No matter," he said negligently. "I'll remain in hiding here for a few days ere I decide upon my next move. I shall visit you again."

Concealing his apprehension with a rough jest, Conan left the Golden Dragon and returned to Eriakes's Inn. Instead of going to bed, he roused Eriakes, paid his scot, got his horse from the stable, and by dawn was well away on the road to Yezud.

Next morning Tigranes, who had mulled things over during the night, went to the nearest police post. He told the sergeant that the notorious Conan, wanted for sundry breaches of Zamorian law in years gone by as well as for questioning by the Turanian envoy, was to be found at Eriakes's Inn.

But when the sergeant with a squad of regulars invaded Eriakes's establishment, they found that Conan had departed hours before, leaving no word of his destination. Thus Tigranes, instead of an informer's fee, received a beating for tardiness in reporting his news. Nursing his bruises, he returned to his inn, vowing vengeance on the Cimmerian, whom he illogically blamed for his mis-hap.

Meanwhile, Conan sped north on Ymir as fast as he dared to push his sturdy steed.

At Zamindi, the villagers were preparing for a spectacle. All the folk, in their patched brown and gray and rusty black woolens, had turned out; some boosted their children to their shoulders, the better to view the event. The much-anticipated spectacle was the burning of Nyssa the witch.

The old woman had been tied to a dead tree a bowshot from the outskirts of the town. In a ragged shift, her white hair blowing, she watched in sullen silence as a dozen men piled sticks and faggots around her. The ropes bound her tightly, but they did not sink into her flesh only because her withered form retained no fat beneath her mottled skin.

So intent upon the sight were the villagers that none remarked the clop of hooves along the path that led from the road to Shadizar. As the headman thrust his torch into the pile of firewood, the horse, a stocky Hyrkanian sorrel, nosed his way among the rearmost members of the crowd.

The smaller sticks caught fire and blazed up with a cheerful crackle. Nyssa looked down silently, her rheumy old eyes glazed with resignation.

Feeling a nudge and hearing a snuffling sound, one villager, munching an apple, turned and recoiled. The nudge was from the velvety nose of Ymir, who was begging for a bite of the apple. The man's startled gaze traveled along the horse's back to encompass a giant figure astride the beast. Conan rasped:

"What goes on here?"

"We burn a witch," replied the man shortly, with a scowl of suspicion.

"What has she done?"

"Put a curse upon us, that's what, so three children and a cow died, all in the same night. Who are you, stranger, to question me?"

"Had there been a feud between you?"

"Nay, if it be any of your affair," replied the man testily. "She used to be our healer; but some devil possessed her and caused these deaths."

The larger faggots were now catching fire, and the rising smoke made Nyssa cough.

"Men and beasts die all the time," ruminated Conan. "What makes you think these deaths unnatural?"

The man turned to confront Conan. "Look you, stranger, you mind your business whilst we mind ours. Now get along, if you would not be hurt!"

Conan had no love of witches. Neither had he any idea of civilized laws and rules of evidence. But still it seemed to him that the villagers were venting their grief on the aged crone more because she was old, ugly, and helpless than because they had reason to think her guilty. The Cimmerian seldom interfered in others' affairs where neither honor drove nor profit beckoned. If the villager had spoken him fair, he might have shrugged and gone his way.

But Conan was impulsive and easily roused to anger. And the protection of women, regardless of age, form, or station, was one of the few imperatives of his barbarian code. The villager's threat tipped the balance in the old woman's favor.

Conan backed his horse a few steps, wheeled the animal, and rode away from the crowd. Then he swung Ymir around, swept out his scimitar, and heeled the horse. As Ymir broke into a canter, headed straight for the tree to which the witch was tied, Conan uttered a fearful scream—the ancient Cimmerian war cry.

Startled faces turned; the villagers scrambled out of the way. Several were knocked down by the plunging beast.

Reaching the fire-ringed victim, the frightened animal rolled its eyes and reared. Conan soothed Ymir as he leaned into the smoke to smite the bindings that encircled the tree. The strands parted easily, for the villagers had thriftily chosen old and rotten rope for the burning.

As a collective growl arose from the thwarted peasants, Conan extended his free arm, roaring: "Catch hold, grandmother!"

Nyssa seized the brawny forearm and clung to it as, with a mighty heave, Conan swung her up on the horse's withers, before the saddle.

"Hold on!" shouted Conan, pressing the oldster against his chest and urging Ymir into a run again.

Once more the crowd, which had started to converge and advance, parted and scattered. Even as Conan plowed through them, he saw some of the more active men run to their crofts. As Ymir carried his double burden away from the village, Conan glanced back. Raging, the men were reemerging with scythes, pitchforks, and a couple of spears.

"Where do you want to go?" Conan asked the witch.

"I have no home to call my own," she replied in a quavery voice. "They have already burned my hut."

"Then whither?"

"Pray, whither you go, sir."

"I'm bound for Yezud; but I cannot take you with me all the way."

"If you will return to the main road and turn left, you will soon come upon another track, which leads uphill to my hiding place. Though I know not if your horse can bear the both of us up so steep a slope."

"Can he walk if I lead him?"

"Aye, sir; of that I am sure. But hurry! I do hear the dogs barking behind us."

A distant baying wafted to Conan's ears. Keen though his senses were, those of the old woman had earlier identified the sound.

"Your hearing is good for one of your years," he remarked.

"I have ways of reinforcing my mortal senses."

"If they have set dogs after us, what's to stop them from following us to your hideaway?"

"Let me but once reach the place, and I have means to lead them astray."

As they came out upon the main road, the sounds of pursuit grew louder, for Ymir was slowed by the weight of his double burden. Another quarter-hour, and Nyssa indicated the track to her refuge.

For a while, Ymir trotted up the steep path, which rose and dipped and wound through broken country. The baying increased apace, and Conan more and more disliked the situation. On the flat, with room to maneuver, he did not fear a villageful of yokels armed with improvised weapons. But on this uncertain footing, if the pursuers were brave enough to close in even after he had slain the foremost, they could swarm around him, hamstring his mount, and cut him to pieces.

"Those fellows must have horses," he muttered between clenched teeth.

"Aye, sir; the village breeds them and has a score of the beasts. And the lads are spry afoot; they beat the other villages in foot races at every fair. I used to be proud of my village."

Conan knew that, if he abandoned Nyssa, he could escape his pursuers even if they tried to run him to earth after they had recaptured the aged witch. But having committed himself to the crone's rescue, he gave no thought to any other course. In such matters he could be obstinate indeed.

The track thrust upward, ever steeper and more rugged. Conan pulled up and swung off the weary horse, saying: "I'll walk; you ride. How much farther goes this path?"

"A quarter of a league. Near the end, I needs must also walk."

On they plodded, Conan leading Ymir by the reins, while behind them the baying waxed louder as men and dogs gained on their quarry. Conan expected to sight their pursuers at any time.

"Here I must dismount," quavered Nyssa. "Kindly help me down, good sir."

When the witch had regained her uncertain footing, she pointed up a trackless slope and started up it vigorously, although each breath she drew was inhaled as a painful gasp.

Glancing back across the waste of tumbled rock and scanty vegetation, Conan caught the ominous blink of sun on steel. He gritted: "We must move faster. Let me carry you, grandmother!"

When she protested, he swept her frail form into his strong arms and hurried up the slope. Sweat rolled down his face, and his own breath came harder.

"Through yonder notch," murmured the witch, pointing.

Still carrying the old woman and leading Ymir, Conan found himself in a narrow canyon or gully, the sides of which supported a few scrubby pines. The bottom of the gulch was a jumble of stream-rounded stones of all sizes, among which gurgled and murmured a shrunken creek. Conan had to leap from boulder to boulder, while Ymir staggered and stumbled along behind him.

"H-here!" whispered Nyssa.

Around a slight bend in the gorge, Conan sighted the mouth of a cave, all but hidden by shrubs and overhanging vines. As the woman sank down, gasping, Conan said:

"Cast your spell quickly, grandmother; for the villagers are close upon our heels."

"Help me to start a fire," she wheezed.

Conan gathered some dry leaves and small sticks and started a little blaze with flint and steel. Then he turned to speak to Nyssa, but she had disappeared into the cave.

Soon she tottered out to the fire again, carrying a leathern bag in one bony fist. This she opened and, from one of its many internal compartments, extracted a pinch of powder, which she sprinkled on the blaze. As the fire flared and sputtered, a curious purple smoke arose, twisting and writhing like a serpent in its death throes. In a low voice, she muttered an incantation in a dialect so archaic that Conan could catch no more than a word or two.

"Hasten, grandmother," he growled, cocking an ear toward the ever-rising tumult of the pursuit. "They'll be upon us any time, now."

"Interrupt me not, boy!" she snapped. It had been years since anyone had dared thus to address Conan, but he meekly submitted to the affront.

From where he sat on a boulder, Conan could sight the end of the gorge, where it opened out into the broader valley up which they had ascended. As his eyes caught a flash of motion, he sprang to his feet and swept out his scimitar. In so narrow a cleft, his foes could come at him only one or two at a time—provided they did not scale the cliff to attack him above, or to get behind him, and provided they had no bows and arrows. Conan was wearing no armor, and he knew that not even his pantherlike agility would enable him to dodge arrows loosed at close range.

Nyssa was still muttering over the fire, when Conan snarled: "Here they come!"

"Speak not, and put away that sword," quavered the witch. "Now look again!" she said with a note of triumph in her shrill old voice.

Conan stared. The peasants and their dogs were streaming past the mouth of the gully.

"Hold your tongue, boy, and they'll not hear us!" she hissed.

Soon the rush of dogs, men, and horses had swept past the mouth of the gorge, and the clatter of their passing died away.

"How did you do that, grandmother?" asked Conan in wonderment.

"I cast a glamour, so to those folk the mouth of this ravine appeared as solid rock. If you had shouted, or if the flash of the sun on your blade had reached them, or if one of them had thrust a tool against that seeming wall of rock, the illusion would have been destroyed like a fog beneath the morning sun." She leaned back wearily against the wall of the gorge. "Help me back into the cave, I pray. I am fordone."

Conan assisted the old woman into the cavern, in which provisions, bundles of herbs, and other possessions were piled haphazardly. As she sank down, she said: "Young man, I must ask you for one more boon. Can you cook? I am too feeble even to get your supper."

"Aye, I can cook in my own fashion," said Conan. "It will be no banquet royal, I assure you; but I've camped alone in the wilds often enough to know the rudiments." He rummaged among the witch's supplies, then built up the smoldering fire. As he worked, he asked: "Tell me, grandmother, what befell between you and the village?"

She coughed, caught her breath, and spoke: "I am Nyssa of Komath. For many years I have earned a scanty living as the white witch of Zamindi, curing ills of man and beast, foretelling the prospects of young lovers seeking to wed, and predicting the changing seasons. But, as I have told the folk many a time and oft, naught is certain in occult matters, and the final decisions rest ever with the gods.

"Then a disease struck Zamindi. Many were sick, and one night three bairns died. I did what I could, but neither my simples nor my spells availed them. Then voices rose against me, saying that I had cast a malignant spell.

" 'Twas naught but a rumor set in motion by the headman, Babur, who long had coveted the little patch of land on which my poor hut stood. I enraged him by refusing to sell it to him, even at a reasonable price; so this is his revenge." A spasm of coughing shook her. "I cast my horoscope yestereve and saw that it portended peril. This morn I was gathering my last supplies to bring to this shelter, which I had prepared for emergencies long ago. But the villeins were too quick for me; they came and dragged me to the village." She cackled. "But you and I have cheated the omens, at least for the nonce. Now what of you, young man?"

Conan told Nyssa as much of his recent history as he thought expedient, adding: "What of my future?"

Her faded old eyes took on a faraway look. "Some things about you I already sense. You are a man of blood. Strife follows you and seeks you out, even when you would fain avoid it. There is great force about you. Nor am I the last old woman whom you will come upon in dire need and rescue." After a pause, she added: "Beware to whom or what you give your heart. Many times you will believe that you have attained your heart's desire, only to have it slip through your fingers and vanish like a puff of morning mist.

"But more of that anon. My poor old heart has been sorely strained this day, and I must needs have rest. I am not one of those who have added to their mortal span by the practice of arcane arts.

"Tomorrow I shall work a powerful conjuration for you, to try to part the veil that enshrouds the future. But meanwhile I will give you a token of my gratitude."

"You need not, grandmother—" began Conan, but she silenced him with a gesture.

"None shall say that Nyssa fails to pay her debts," she said. " 'Tis but a small thing I give you, yet it is all I have to give this night, what with the hazards and confusion of this turbulent day."

She fumbled among her disorderly piles of belongings and turned again to Conan, holding a small pouch, which she pressed upon him. "This," she explained, "is a spoonful of the powder of Forgetfulness. If an enemy close in upon you, thinking he has you at his mercy, throw a pinch into his face. When he breathes this dust, 'twill be as if he had never beheld you or had knowledge of you."

"What should I do with the fellow then?" asked Conan. "If he'd wronged me, my natural wont would be to slay him; but it would seem cowardly to strike him down, and him not knowing the reason for the quarrel."

"I would say to let him go and think no more about the matter. To slay him under such conditions were like killing a babe because you quarreled with his father. A heartless sort of revenge, indeed."

Conan grunted a puzzled assent, although in fact he had never before thought about the rights and wrongs of the matter. Among his fellow Cimmerians, it was customary to seek revenge upon a member of another clan by slaying the offender's kin.

Conan was tempted to refuse the proffered pouch, claiming that he had only contempt for magic and wanted nothing to do with it. But the old woman seemed so eager for him to have her gift that he accepted it with a growl of thanks rather than hurt her feelings.

When Conan awoke the next morning, he found Nyssa's body stiff and cold. She had not cheated the omens after all.

chapter  v

The City on the Crag

The sun had slipped behind the humped backs of the Karpash Mountains when Conan guided Ymir into the narrow valley that led to Yezud, city of the spider-god. The deepening shadows cast a black pall over the defile. Here little vegetation clothed the rocky soil; for the central, snowcapped ridge of the Karpashes, stretching from north to south for a hundred leagues without a single pass, had wrung the moisture from the western winds before they swept on east to Zamora. Ymir's shod hooves rang a metallic tattoo on the stones, save when the horse picked his way through slippery seepages of liquid bitumen. Below the path, a shrunken remnant of a stream gurgled as it played hide-and-seek among the boulders.

For the most part, the ever-rising path was wide enough to accommodate only a single horseman. Whenever it spread itself more generously, Conan passed knots of people waiting to resume their downward passage. One trader, delayed at such a turnout, led four asses, each laden with two bulky casks of bitumen. In the lowlands of southern Zamora, this dark mineral oil was put to sundry uses; it served as a purgative for people, a lubricant for wagon wheels, a base for paint, a fuel for lamps, and a cure for mange.

Conan caught up with a plodding procession of cattle, shambling upward on the path to Yezud. When the curvature of the slope revealed the serpentine path ahead, Conan marveled at the size of the herd. There must, he thought, be eighty to a hundred animals, pulled or prodded along by a dozen neatherds. The sloth of the cumbersome beasts irritated the Cimmerian, since nowhere could he pass them while the narrow track continued its winding way.

Although the departure of the sun had cast black gloom within the gorge, the sky above was still a bright cerulean blue when the ravine at last opened out into a narrow plain. Here a hamlet huddled at the roadside. Beyond it, where the canyon split in twain, a walled city or acropolis perched upon the shoulder of a crag formed by the divergent gorges; and like a monarch's crown, the marble temple of Zath reared up to tower above the roseate roofs of the fortified city. This lofty citadel bore the name of Yezud, whereas the lower village or suburb was known as Khesron.

As soon as the widened path permitted, Conan cantered past the herd of cattle and trotted briskly through the huddled village, where dirty children scampered from the road and barking dogs ran out to worry Ymir's hooves. The lone public building in Khesron, rising a story above the score of other dingy structures of the community, proclaimed itself an inn by means of a branch nailed to a board above the lintel of the front door.

The Cimmerian continued onward toward the rocky shoulder on which stood the walled city of Yezud, along a steeply sloping roadway cut into the stone of the hillside. Conan perceived that the only means of entry into the citadel was this same roadway and that Yezud, if resolutely defended, would be virtually impregnable. The steep sides of the eminence, which bore the citadel aloft and which merged into Mount Ghaf behind, were so nearly vertical that only a party of Cimmerian hillmen, unencumbered by armor, could hope to scale this formidable bastion.

Ymir balked on the hillside path. Although Conan spurred him forward, the animal refused to move. At last the Cimmerian dismounted and plodded up the incline, pulling Ymir along by his bridle. All the climbing way, the horse rolled his eyes, pricked up his ears, and behaved as if he sensed some evil beyond the comprehension of his human companion.

Man and unwilling horse at last reached the small stone platform before the city portal, a dizzy height above the plain. A pair of armed men, of greater stature than most Zamorians, stood guard before the open valves of the imposing bronze-studded gates.

"Your name and business?" snapped one of the guards, eyeing Conan hardily.

"Nial, a mercenary soldier," replied Conan. "I heard that such as I are being hired."

"They *were*," replied the soldier, his lip curling slightly with the shadow of a sneer. "But no more. You have tardy come."

"You mean the places are all filled?"

"And you have had your journey all for naught." The man spoke Zamorian with an unfamiliar accent.

"Are you two amongst those lately hired, then?" asked Conan.

"Aye; we are men of Captain Catigern's Free Company."

Although nettled by the soldier's surly manner, Conan kept his outward calm. "Well then, friend, whence hail you?"

"We are Brythunians."

"Indeed? I've traveled many lands, but never yet Brythunia. I crave a word with the man who hired you, whoever he may be."

"Too late for that today. Try again in the morning."

Conan grunted. "Well, is there an inn in Yezúd where I can take lodging and stable my horse?"

The soldier laughed scornfully. "Any fool knows that only the priests and those who work for them may rest their heads overnight within the walls of Yezúd!"

The quick flame of Conan's anger flared up. He had been in no pleasant mood as a result of the delay occasioned by the herd of cattle and the balkiness of his mount, and now the man's insolence raised his hot temper to the boiling point. With an effort he choked off a sharp retort, but he memorized the man's face should the future provide him with a chance for retaliation. As calmly as he could, the barbarian asked:

"Where, then, do travelers lie of nights?"

"Try Bartakes's Inn in Khesron. If that be full of pilgrims, the stars must be your roof."

"They've served me thus ere now," growled Conan. He turned to find the downward path blocked by the same scrambling herd of cattle that he had passed on his upward climb to Yezúd. Mooing and groaning, the animals were being prodded up the slope in single file by cursing herdsmen.

"Stand aside, lout, and let the cattle in!" barked the soldier.

Conan lips tightened and his hand itched for his sword hilt, but he remembered the flatness of his purse and held his peace. Unable to descend the path while the cattle occupied it, he waited, fuming, on the flat as the beasts were driven through the gate, one after another. Before the last animal had stumbled into the citadel and the gate slammed shut, stars had begun to twinkle in a darkling sky. Leading Ymir, Conan picked his way down the path, peering into the gloaming lest a misstep send him or his mount over the edge and down the cliffside.

Bartakes's Inn had plenty of room, because the flux of pilgrims swelled only at certain seasons of year, during the great festivals in the temple of Zath. The spring festival had come and gone, while the Festival of All Gods still lay ahead. So there were empty beds in the sleeping rooms and empty stalls in the stable.

Conan shouldered in the front door and glanced about the common room, where a few patrons sat at tables, eating, drinking, or gaming. Several were men of goodly size, with brown or tawny hair; from their garb, Conan guessed them to be members of the company of Brythunian mercenaries. Others were nondescript locals, save for one slender, swarthy fellow with a shaven head, wrapped in a monkish robe that fell below his ankles. Conan had seen such men before, in Corinthia and Nemedia, where he had been informed that they were Stygian priests, or acolytes, or simply students. This one was absorbed in

his sheaf of writing material—a mixture of sheets of parchment, rolls of papyrus, and thin slabs of wood—spread out on the table before him.

Behind the counter stood a plump, wavy-haired young woman, pouring ale
from a dipper into the leathern drinking jack of a patron. As Conan approached,
she turned her head and called: "Father!"

A fat taverner, wiping his hands on his apron, strolled out from the kitchen.
"Yes, sir?" he said invitingly.

Conan arranged for dinner and bed for himself and a bucket of grain and a
stall for Ymir. He bought a stoup of ale with his meal and retired early.

The rising sun saw him again before the gates of Yezud. When the portals
swung apart, Conan found himself confronting two unfamiliar guards and a
man who, from his bearing and handsome equipment, appeared to be an officer. This man was massive, almost as tall as Conan, and his bristling red
mustache curled upward at the ends. Seeing the Cimmerian, he said:

"Ho! You must be the fellow who came here at closing time last night,
asking about a post in Yezud. There is naught here for a fighting man; my boys
have taken over the protection of the citadel."

"You must be Captain Catigern," said Conan dourly.

"Aye. So?"

"Captain, I still desire to speak with the man who does the hiring. I can do
a few things other than splitting skulls."

The captain studied Conan carefully, with a frown born of suspicion. "It is
not likely he'll have aught for you. Are you friendly to the worship of Zath?"

"I'm friendly to all who buy my services and pay that which they promise,"
grunted Conan.

Lips pursed, Catigern contemplated the huge Cimmerian. Then he turned
to one of the guards, saying: "Morcant! Take this man to the Vicar. Let him
decide whether the fellow is to be trusted within. And you, stranger, leave your
sword with us until these matters are resolved."

Conan silently handed over his scimitar and followed Morcant into the
city. The buildings were of severely plain design—row upon row of neat,
whitewashed, red-roofed shops and dwellings, hardly to be distinguished one
from another. The streets were swept cleaner than any Conan had come
upon in other cities; the main thoroughfare appeared impeccable despite the
drove of cattle that had plodded along it but a few hours before. Conan
asked Morcant:

"Yestereve I saw above eighty head of cattle entering the city. Would the
folk have need of so much beef? Judging from the size of the town, it would
require a month for the citizens to eat it all."

"No questions, stranger," snapped the Brythunian.

Conan darted discreet glances to right and left from beneath his heavy brows, looking for signs of a stockyard in which the cattle might be confined. But although they passed stables and workshops of all descriptions, he saw no sign of a pen or corral.

At last they reached the precinct of the temple of Zath. Conan craned his neck and stared like a yokel at the largest building he had ever beheld—an edifice even more imposing than the temples and palaces of Shadizar and Aghrapur. The structure was built of great blocks of opalescent marble, gleaming golden in the sun-washed light of morning. From the huge central nucleus projected eight wings, each bedight with mosaic-inlaid columns and pilasters. Except where broad steps led up to the main entrance, lengths of polished granite wall joined the outer end of each wing to that of its neighbors. A vast central dome towered over all, and the early morning sun reflected with blinding intensity the gold leaf that covered the dome.

Before the main portal—an enormous pair of doors embellished with bronzen reliefs—two Brythunian guards stood rigidly at attention, their crimson uniforms spotless, their mailshirts agleam, and their halberds grounded at their sides. Morcant announced:

"A man to see the Vicar."

One guard pushed open a small door let into one of the huge bronze valves of the main portal. Conan ducked under the lintel and found himself in a spacious carpeted vestibule, whence passages led off to either side. Facing the wide entranceway, another pair of giant doors, these ornamented with exquisite gilded reliefs, towered above the visitors. Before the inner doors were stationed another pair of halberd-bearing guards.

Morcant nodded to these sentinels and led Conan down one of the side passages. As they proceeded, Conan became conscious of a faint odor of carrion. This, he knew, was not uncommon in temples where animals were either sacrificed to the god or eviscerated for purposes of divination. So he paid scant attention to the disagreeable smell.

After conducting the Cimmerian through a bewildering maze of corridors, Morcant stopped at an oaken door, before which stood another Brythunian mercenary, and knocked. When a voice called: "Enter!" he opened the door and waved Conan in.

A seated figure in a white turban bent over an ornate, flat-topped desk, writing by the light of a bitumen lamp. As Conan came to attention before him, the man raised his head. "Yes, my son?"

Conan started and reached for the sword that no longer hung at his side. For the man was Harpagus, he who had cast Conan into a hypnotic sleep in the Marshes of Mehar.

Harpagus gave no sign of recognition. Gathering his wits, Conan realized that, when he had encountered the Zamorians in the marshes, his face had been obscured by the turban cloth wound about his head. Even when he had shared a dinner with Harpagus and his men, he had not, because of the swarms of biting insects, removed the cloth altogether; he had merely raised the part that covered his mouth and chin and tucked it into the upper folds.

Struggling to hide the hatred that welled in his barbarian breast for the man who had tricked and robbed him, Conan forced himself to speak calmly: "I am Nial, a mercenary from the Border Kingdom. Hearing that the temple was hiring soldiers, I have come in hope of finding a post."

The turbaned man gently shook his head. "You are too late by a fortnight, my son. Captain Catigern likewise learned of the opportunity and, there being no wars at present in Brythunia, brought his Free Company hither."

"So I've been told. Nonetheless, sir, I need employment; for my money is nearly gone, and I must find more ere leaving to seek a post in other lieus."

Harpagus stroked his narrow chin. "The temple needs a clerk skilled in the casting of accounts, to keep our books. Are you a man trained to that task?"

It was Conan's turn to shake his shaggy head. "Not I! I cannot add a column of numbers twice and arrive at the same sum."

"Well, then—ah! We do have need of a blacksmith, at least for a time; since ours lies dying of a wasting distemperature. Perchance you know that skill?"

Conan's teeth flashed whitely in a sudden grin. "My father was a smith, and I was apprenticed to him for years when I was young."

"Good; excellent! You have the thews for the task, at least. You may start work today. The Brythunian will show you to your smithy, now in the care of Pariskas's bellows boy. He shall serve you in like capacity."

After settling such matters as Conan's wage, living quarters for himself, and stabling for his horse, Harpagus said: "We are then agreed, my son. But you must understand that, for those who dwell in holy Yezud, there shall be no drinking of fermented liquors, no gambling, and no fornication. And all do promise to attend the services of holy Zath at least once every ten-day." The Vicar paused, his brow furrowed. "Have I not met you on some previous occasion?"

Conan felt his nape-hairs rise, but he spoke with a negligent air. "I think not, sir—unless it were a chance encounter in Nemedia or Brythunia, where I have served as a mercenary."

Harpagus shook his head. "Nay, I have never traveled to those lands. Still, your voice reminds me of someone I knew briefly. . . . No matter. Go with the guard to your new quarters. You will find enough accumulated tasks to keep you busy."

"One thing more, sir. I want my sword, now in the custody of the gate guards."

Harpagus smiled thinly. "You shall have it. Forbidding a blacksmith his weapon were like confiscating a poet's verses; he'll only make another."

As the Brythunian led Conan through the narrow streets, the Cimmerian growled: "Is the Vicar's name Harpagus?"

"Aye."

"So I thought. Did I understand him aright, that in Yezud there is no wine, nor beer, nor gambling, nor light love?"

Morcant grinned. His manner had thawed to friendliness since learning that Conan would be a fellow employee of the temple. "High Priest Feridun is a very righteous man—a dolorously righteous man, and he hopes to impose his principles on all in Zamora. We of the Free Company go down to Bartakes's Inn for our sinful amusements. Feridun would like to close down that place, too. But he does not dare, knowing that the Free Company would go on the road if such constraints were imposed upon us."

Conan gave a rumble of mirth, knowing full well that brigandage was the usual occupation of mercenary companies out of military employment; but rarely was it so plainly named.

"I see no cause for merriment," said Morcant crisply with a reproving stare.

"No offense meant," said Conan, wiping the smile from his lips. "But I've been a hired sword myself and know somewhat of the ways of mercenaries."

The smithy was a simple, one-story affair, of which the larger section, open to the street, housed a forge, while a small apartment to the left did duty as the smith's domestic quarters. As Conan entered the smithy, a Zamorian boy of perhaps twelve years, who had been perched on the anvil, whittling a stick, jumped to his feet. Conan explained his presence.

"I am Lar, son of Yazdates," said the boy. "Pray, Nial sir, I hope you will teach me some smithery whilst I do work for you. The old smith would never let me handle his tools. Belike he feared I should grow up to take his post from him."

"We shall see," replied Conan. "It depends on how able a man of your hands you prove to be."

"Oh, I am very able, sir, for my age. I have practiced on the sly when old Pariskas was not looking. Sometimes he caught me at it and beat me." The boy looked apprehensively at the giant who was to be his new master.

"If I ever beat you, it won't be for trying to improve yourself," growled Conan. "Let's see to the tools."

Conan had not worked as a smith since, years before, a feud had driven him forth from his Cimmerian tribe. But, as he swung the heavy hammers and handled the stout iron tongs, he felt a thrill of familiarity. It would not be long, he felt sure, before he regained his half-remembered skill.

"Lar," he said, "I am going down to Khesron to fetch my horse and my belongings. While I'm gone, you shall start up the furnace, and we'll tackle this work today. By the way, where went all those cattle, which I saw driven into Yezud yestereve?"

"They went through a doorway on the western side of the temple," said Lar.

"A small town like this scarce needs so many beasts for food," mused Conan.

"Oh, sir, they are not meat for the townsfolk; not even the priests! They are for Zath."

"Forsooth?" said Conan. "That I can hardly believe. I have seen much of temples and more of priests. In those where the worshipers bring animals to sacrifice, the holy men slay the creatures, offer the skin and bones and offal to the god, and feast on the good flesh themselves. Why do you think your priests do not the same?"

"But, sir, everybody in Yezud knows the cattle are devoured by Zath! Have you been in the naos of the temple?"

"Not yet. What's there?"

"You will see all when you attend your first service. There stands the statue of Zath, in the likeness of a huge spider carven of black stone. Its body is enormous, and its legs—its legs . . ." The boy broke off with a shudder.

"A statue cannot eat cattle," remarked Conan, surprised at the boy's display of fear.

"Each night the statue comes to life," the lad continued. "It descends through a trapdoor in the holy place and enters the tunnels below, where it seizes upon the animals that have been driven in to assuage its appetite. So say the priests."

Conan ruminated. "I've seen many strange things in my travels, but never a statue that came to life. Even if this tale be true, what would such a spider want with a hundred head of cattle at a time? I have never kept a spider as a pet; but I do know something of the habits of other beasts of prey. I should think one ox would suffice a creature like Zath for a fortnight at the least."

"Oh, sir, these are holy mysteries! You must not pry into that which the gods do not intend us mortals to know." As he spoke, the boy reverently bowed his head and touched his fingertips to his forehead.

Conan grunted. "That's as may be. Now start up the forge, lad, while I go to get my gear from the inn."

Some time later, leading Ymir, Conan approached the common stable where he had been allotted a stall. As Conan was instructing the stable boy in the care of Ymir, a commotion arose in one of the more distant stalls. A horse was rearing, pawing the air, and squealing frantically.

"What's that?" asked Conan.

The groom looked around. "It's that accursed black stallion the Vicar bought in Turan," he said. "We have not been able to exercise him properly, because no man durst try to ride him."

"Hm," said Conan. "I'll take a look." He strolled down to the stall of the fractious stallion and recognized Egil. The horse whinnied with delight and nuzzled him.

Not daring to address the horse directly, Conan turned to the groom. "He seems to like me, the gods know why."

The groom leaned on his shovel while his sluggish thoughts took form. At last he mumbled: "Perhaps, sir, you could ride him. Are you fain to undertake his exercising? If the priests agreed, that is."

It was on the tip of Conan's tongue to say yes; but then it struck him that, if word got back to Harpagus, the Vicar might suspect that his new blacksmith and the former owner of Egil were one and the same. Instead he replied:

"We shall see. Just now I can barely spare time to keep my own nag in condition."

chapter  vi

The Temple of the Spider

Since Yezud was provided with no inn or eating-house and Conan did not wish to plod down to Khesron for each repast, he made arrangements for Lar's mother to cook his meals. At sundown, Conan washed the soot from his face and arms and followed Lar to the small house where the boy and his widowed mother dwelt. The house, freshly whitewashed, was neat within and furnished in the rear with a small, well-tended vegetable garden.

Amytis, a middle-aged woman with a weary face and graying hair, cooked an adequate meal, albeit Conan grumbled at the lack of ale with which to wash it down. He listened in dour silence as Amytis prattled on about her ancestry, her skin, and her well-remembered husband.

" 'Twas bitter hard after he died, poor man," she sighed. "But with the money you pay my Lar, and the stipend my daughter earns at the temple, and the coppers I make by taking in washing, we manage."

"You have a daughter?" asked Conan, eyeing the woman with the first faint stir of interest.

"Aye, Rudabeh is chief of the temple's dancing girls and has other responsibilities besides. A very capable maid; the man will be lucky who gets her to wife."

"The dancers are allowed to wed?"

"After their discharge, aye. In fact the priests approve of it; they give each girl a dowry when her service ends—if she has behaved herself, that is."

"How do they choose temple dancers?" Conan inquired idly, spooning out a portion of pudding.

"The priests hold a contest every year," explained Amytis, "to pick the two likeliest dancers. Families come from as far away as Shadizar, bringing their prettiest maidens, for the competition; but most come from the towns nearby. It is accounted an honor to have a daughter in the service of Zath."

"How long is their term of service?"

"The winners serve the temple for five years."

Conan glanced at young Lar. "Why didn't you tell me that you had a sister?"

The boy grimaced. "I did not think a great man like you would be interested in a *girl*."

Conan turned back to Amytis to hide his grin from his youthful hero-worshiper and asked: "Does your daughter ever visit you?"

"Oh, aye; four times in a month she is granted leave and comes here to sup. She spent an evening with us but three nights agone."

With an ostentatious show of unconcern, Conan yawned, stretched, and rose. "Lar," he said carelessly, "you must take me to the temple one day and explain the rituals. The Vicar commanded me to attend not less than thrice a month, and I must needs obey him."

Excusing himself, Conan returned to his smithy. He thought briefly of repairing to Bartakes's Inn to enliven the evening, but an afternoon of wielding the heavy tools of his new trade had left him more than willing to retire early.

The next day was spent at forge and anvil. While Lar manned the bellows, Conan shod several horses, welded a broken scythe blade, hammered a dent out of a helmet belonging to one of the Brythunians, and in odd moments made several score of nails. He was pleased to find the skills he had learned in boyhood so readily returning to him.

The following morning, Conan accompanied Lar to the temple of Zath, into which many dwellers of the citadel were streaming. Now the huge inner doors, as well as the outer portals, stood open to the worshipers. The halberd-bearing guards stood stiffly at attention, but their lusty glances followed many a well-favored woman who tempered her piety with smiles.

Towering above the crowd, Conan entered the naos. The odor of carrion was stronger here; one less hardened to the smell of death than the Cimmerian might have found it nauseating. The circular chamber of the naos, in the hub of the huge temple complex, was capable of accommodating thousands of the faithful. But, since this was not a time of festival, only a few hundred had foregathered in the capacious rotunda.

Conan observed that the entire floor was inlaid with delicate mosaics, skillfully patterned into the form of a series of connecting spiderwebs. Each web occupied a space scarcely larger than the width of a man's shoulders; and at the center of one web Lar took his stand, gesturing to Conan to do likewise.

Conan's appraising eye sought out the gilded piers that rose at intervals to support the lofty domed ceiling. Everywhere the spiderweb pattern was repeated. It festooned the plastered walls, wreathed around the pillars, and on a larger scale spread out across the inner surface of the gilded dome. Here the design was realized in black on white; there in white on black; elsewhere in red

THE TEMPLE OF THE SPIDER

on blue, or gold on green, or purple on silver, or some other chromatic combination.

The glitter of gold leaf, reflecting the light of a hundred gilded lamps suspended on bronzen chains from the shadowy recesses of the ceiling, and the endless repetition of the spoked cobweb pattern induced hypnotic immobility. Conan closed his eyes to shut out the reeling lights and painted swirls and forced himself to concentrate upon the peaceful garden of the seer Kushad.

When Conan trusted himself to reopen his eyes, his gaze became fixed upon the scene before him. Partly recessed into the wall surrounding the rotunda and partly projecting into the circle of the naos stood a sacred enclosure, square in plan. This holy place, raised above the level of the floor of the naos for better viewing by the congregated faithful, was fronted by three broad marble steps, which stretched across the full width of the sacred area. A pierced railing of polished brass, the height of a woman's waist, curved forward from the bottom step to separate the sacred precinct from the section allotted the worshipers.

Above the steps and on the right side of the stage stood a massive, timeworn ebon chest fitted with bronzen clasps, green with age. This ancient container was decorated with the ubiquitous spiderwebs, formed by slender silver wires cunningly inlaid into the polished wood.

Balancing this venerable repository, on the left side of the platform, a block of golden marble rose altarlike; and all around this plinth were carven cryptic sigils in the old Zamorian script. Upon this splendid base rested a bowl of chalcedony; and in the translucent basin danced an eternal flame, connected, Conan knew not how, with the worship of the spider-god.

In the center of the raised enclosure, the far end of which was cloaked in a blood-red arras, towered the statue of Zath; behind it, in the far left corner, the wall of the sacred area was recessed. The idol, graven of black onyx, was wrought with such fidelity to nature that Conan was half tempted to believe that the statue could indeed possess the power of life at night. The heavy ovoid body, supported by some sort of frame or table draped in crimson velvet to match the incarnadined wall behind it, seemed in the flickering light to stand without support, while each of the spider's eight jointed limbs, stouter than a galley's oar, rested on the marble pave. The statue reminded Conan unpleasantly of the giant spider he had fought in the Elephant Tower several years before, save that the arachnid here depicted was more than twice the size of that remembered monster.

Across the front of the creature's head—or what would have been its head if members of the spider tribe had possessed heads distinct from the forward segment of their bodies—a row of four great eyes gleamed with a bluish radiance in the lamplight. From where he stood, Conan could perceive that, in addition, Zath had four additional eyes, one pair on the sides of its body and the other pair on top. The sight stirred Conan's predatory instincts, and he whispered to Lar:

"What are those eyes composed of, boy?"

"Sh!" admonished Lar. "Here come the priests."

The walls of the sacred enclosure were pierced by two doors, one on each side beyond the chest and the altar. A staid procession emerged from the left-hand door: a dozen men in silken turbans and brocaded robes, each carrying a staff with a jewel-encrusted knob of gold or silver. In the lead strode one taller than the rest, a man clad in a flowing white garment and a night-black turban, whose bristling black brows, eagle's beak of a nose, and voluminous white beard endowed him with a formidable air.

Rainbow-hued were the vestments of the other priests. One wore a scarlet gown and azure headgear; another a purple robe topped by a saffron turban; and yet another a gown of sapphire blue surmounted by a headdress of pale celadon. Conan recognized the Vicar, Harpagus, by his sable robe and snowy turban.

The twelve priests formed a line before the spider-god. At a gesture from Harpagus, the congregation raised their arms aloft and cried in unison: "Hail Zath, god of all! Hail Feridun, apostle of Zath!"

Next, led by a young priest whose long, tapering fingers beat rhythmically upon the fetid air, the congregation sang a hymn. Conan comprehended but a few snatches of the paean, but he gathered that the refrain proclaimed Zath's purity, which stretched across Zamora like a vast spiderweb.

Four priests then moved majestically forward to surround the eternal flame. Each produced an object from the flowing sleeves of his garment. Conan glimpsed a silver chalice, a dagger with a jeweled hilt, a bronzen mirror, and a golden key. The priests performed some complex rite, causing the flame to emit a curling column of smoke; they passed the symbolic objects through the billowing curls of the smoke, chanting incantations in words that Conan could not understand.

Then the priests, with measured tread, formed two lines along the side walls of the sanctum, as through the right-hand door eight dancing girls approached the spider-god. All were naked save for enormous strings of jet-black beads, intricately threaded to resemble the webs of spiders. Jewels flashed in their ebon hair and on their graceful fingers like dewdrops in the morning sun.

He who wore the sapphire robe produced a flute and played a haunting melody, to which the girls performed a stately dance around the mammoth idol, their strings of beads jingling and clashing as their slender bodies swayed and undulated. Conan whispered:

"I thought Zath was a god of purity. Those lassies look not to me like a preachment for chastity."

"Sh, sir! You do not understand," breathed the boy, his eyes alight with religious fervor. "This is a sacred dance, ancient and honorable. The virtue of our dancing girls is guarded with the utmost vigilance."

Conan's devil whispered to him that, if such were the case, to carry off one of the maidens as his leman were a boastworthy feat. He persisted: "Which one is your sister?"

"That one—to the left of the center—now she's gone behind the statue. She is taller than the others."

"A handsome filly," muttered Conan to himself, "if she be the one I think she is." The girl was indeed taller and more voluptuously formed than the majority of the small, spare Zamorian women, and Conan felt his blood stir as he watched.

The dance ended with the eight girls prostrating themselves around the idol, one at the tip of each of the spidery legs. Then, rising and holding hands to form a chain, they filed out of the sanctum, while High Priest Feridun strode forward to rest the knuckles of his left hand upon the lid of the ancient chest. Commanding silence with a raised right hand, he launched into a sermon:

"Dearly beloved: We have expounded before on the sad state into which the once-great nation of Zamora hath fallen. We of the priesthood have expatiated—so far in vain, alas—upon the sins and depravity of the people. Corruption spreadeth amongst you, its source being the throne of your kings, and daily transformeth our once-proud nation into a cauldron of crime, intrigue, and other wickedness. All about us theft, murder, bribery, drunkenness, and fornication prevail. The cults of the other gods, which claim to combat this degeneracy, have either failed in their duty or—woe unto Zamora!—have joined in the scramble for illicit wealth and condoned men's wallowing in sensual pleasure."

The old priest's hortatory tones irritated Conan, arousing in him a perverse desire to cry out that, while the folk of Zamora were surely wicked enough, they were not so much worse than those of other nations. But aware that one man cannot fight hundreds inflamed with religious fanaticism, he held his tongue. High Priest Feridun continued:

"Only the True Faith of Zath hath retained its integrity of motive and of practice. Only the True Faith of Zath can purify the realm and restore Zamora to its ancient greatness. We do assure you, dearly beloved, that the day of cleansing draweth nigh. All of you standing devoutly here shall live to witness it. There shall be a great overturn, a destruction of the wicked, the like of which the world hath never witnessed; but ye shall see it. The flame of the great purification shall sweep across the land, consuming the sinful like insects dropped into a roaring fire! It cometh apace! Hold yourselves ready, dear ones, to serve as soldiers in the holy army of Zath. . . ."

As Feridun continued in this vein, Conan fidgeted with impatience, until at last the High Priest terminated his oratory with a chanted prayer. Then the eight girls, now clad in voluminous, if gauzy, robes of rainbow hues, filed solemnly out and sang a hymn to the wail of the flute in the hands of him who wore the sapphire robe and celadon turban. Meanwhile, acolytes in emerald tunics circulated among the congregation, shaking their offering bowls. The tinkle of coins furnished a cheerful if irregular accompaniment to the high-pitched chorus of maidens.

One acolyte thrust a bowl at Conan. Peering into its depths, the Cimmerian perceived a heap of coins of various denominations. Grumbling, he dug a small copper out of his well-worn purse and dropped it on the heap.

The acolyte sniffed disdainfully. "You are not overgenerous to the god, stranger," he murmured.

"Let the priests increase the sum they pay me as smith," growled Conan, "and I'll give you more." The acolyte opened his mouth, as for a sharp reply; but Conan's glower persuaded him to bite back his words and pass on to gather the next gratuity.

When the last offerings had been collected, the temple maidens ended their song and disappeared. High Priest Feridun stepped to the chest, ceremoniously unlocked it, and raised the lid. The acolytes paraded past, each emptying his bowl of coins, and the ringing clash of their falling echoed from the temple's gilded dome.

Feridun intoned another prayer, blessing the offerings, and relocked the re-plenished coffer. Again the congregation lifted their voices in song; Zath was once more hailed with upraised arms, and the service came to its end.

As Conan and the boy left the temple enclosure, Lar, bubbling with youthful enthusiasm, ventured: "Isn't High Priest Feridun a wonderful man? Does he not fill your heart with spiritual inspiration?"

Conan paused before answering. "I have not found priests much different from other men. All work for their own wealth, power, and glory, like the rest of us, however much they mask ambition by pious chatter."

"Oh, sir!" ejaculated the boy. "Let not such impious sentiments come to the ears of the priests of Zath! True, they might excuse you as naught but an ignorant foreigner; but you should never speak lightly of the god and his min-isters in holy Yezud—not, that is, unless you would fain serve as fodder for the spider-god."

"Is that the fate of malefactors here?" queried Conan.

"Aye, sir. It is our regular form of execution."

"How is it done?"

"The acolytes throw the criminal into the tunnels beneath the temple. Then, when immortal Zath takes on his mortal form at night, he descends thither to devour the miscreant."

"Who has seen Zath thus scuttling about?"

"Only the priests, sir."

"Has any plain citizen of Yezud witnessed this miracle?"

"N-no, sir. None dares enter the haunts of the spider-god, save the highest ranks of the priesthood. I did hear a tale last year, that one impious wight secretly entered the tunnels, hoping to find valuables to steal. You know what they say about Zamorian thieves?"

"That they are the most skillful in the world and the most faithful to their trust. What befell this venturesome fellow? Did Zath devour him?"

"Nay; he escaped." The boy shuddered. "But he came out raving mad and died a few days thereafter."

"Hm. No place to tarry for one's health, meseems. Tell me, Lar, of what substance are the eyes of Zath composed?"

"Why, of the same stuff as yours and mine, I suppose; save that when Zath returns to his pedestal and settles into his stony form, his eyes must become some sort of bluish mineral. More I cannot tell."

Conan walked in silence to Lar's home for the midday meal, his nimble mind already scheming. The eyes of Zath were certainly gems of some kind. If he could manage to steal some of them, he would command enough wealth for a lifetime. Usually Conan trod lightly in the presence of strange gods; but he found it difficult to attribute divinity to any spider, however formidable. Whether or not the statue possessed the power to transform itself into a sentient being, Conan could not bring himself to accord it godhood. He felt sure that the priests of Zath were swindling the credulous Zamorians, and that it would be simple justice for him to deprive them of part of their ill-gotten gains.

After the evening repast, Conan, weary of the sobriety of Yezud, strapped on his sword and strode down the rocky ramp to Bartakes's Inn in Khesron. He was pleased to find few other patrons in the common room, for he wished to be alone to think.

Conan carried his jack of wine from the innkeeper's counter and settled down in a corner. He regretted having spoken so cynically to young Lar about gods and priests because, he realized, his incautious words had given the pious and impressionable boy a hold upon him. If they should ever quarrel, or if Lar did something stupid and Conan cuffed him for it, Lar might run to the priests with an exaggerated tale of the blacksmith's heresies. Of the many hard lessons he was being forced to learn in order to make his way in civilized lands, Conan found guarding his tongue and weighing his words the hardest.

The Cimmerian's dour musings were interrupted by the crackle of sharp words across the dim-lit room, where a man and a woman sat with an empty bottle of wine between them. The woman, clad in a tight dress of red and white checked cotton, cut to display a generous expanse of bosom, Conan recognized as Bartakes's daughter Mandana. The man—Conan tensed, for he should have recognized the bristling red mustache immediately upon entering the common room—was Captain Catigern. Preoccupied with his own thoughts, Conan had overlooked the mercenary officer.

Catigern had obviously drunk more than he could handle, and the woman was berating him for his sodden condition. In the midst of her scolding, he made a rude noise, laid his head on his forearms, and went to sleep.

The woman pushed back her stool and, glancing boldly around the room, strolled over to Conan's table, saying: "May I join you, Master Nial?"

"Certes," said Conan. "What's your trouble, lass?"

"You can see for yourself." She jerked a thumb toward the somnolent Catigern. "He promised me a glorious evening, and what does he do but drink himself into a brutish stupor! I am sure that you, at least, would not fall asleep when came the time to pleasure your woman." She smiled provocatively and settled the bodice of her dress until her bulging breasts almost burst from their scanty covering.

Conan raised his heavy eyebrows. "Oho!" he murmured in a voice thickening with desire. "If that be the pleasure you require, I'm your man! Just name the time and place."

"Shortly, in my chambers upstairs. But let us drink a little first; and then you must pay my father's tariff for my affections." With a nod of her head she indicated the counter, behind which Bartakes stood.

Conan's eyes grew wary. "How much does he demand?"

"Ten coppers. By the bye, you returned not to the inn after your first night here; did you then gain employment with the priests of Yezud?"

"Aye; I'm now the temple's blacksmith," answered Conan, digging into his purse and counting out coins. "As peaceful trades go, it is not bad—"

Conan left his sentence hanging. Captain Catigern had awakened, lurched to his feet, and now towered above the table at which Conan and Mandana sat. He roared:

"What are you doing with my girl, you oaf?"

Conan studied the speaker with narrowed eyes, gauging the degree of the captain's insobriety. "You can go to hell, Captain," he said evenly. "The wench sought me out of her own free will, whilst you lay snoring in a stupor." He picked up his mug and took a lingering sip.

"Insolent puppy!" shouted Catigern, aiming a backhanded blow at Conan's face. The knuckles of the Brythunian's open hand struck Conan's upraised forearm, splashing his wine. With deliberation, Conan set down the mug, rose as lithely as a jungle cat, and shot his left fist into Catigern's face. The captain's head snapped back; he staggered and fell heavily. The blow would have deprived an ordinary man of consciousness, if it did not do him more substantial damage; but Catigern was an unusually large and powerful man. Hence he was up again in an instant, lugging out his sword.

"I'll carve out your liver and feed it to my dogs!" he snarled, rushing at Conan.

Ignoring a shouted plea from the taverner, Conan met Catigern halfway with his drawn Turanian scimitar, and their clanging blades flashed in the yellow lamplight. Several patrons ducked beneath their tables as the two large men circled, slashing and parrying. The ring of steel upon steel, mingled with the shouts of excited spectators, echoed like a demoniac uproar upon the evening air.

After the first whirlwind exchange of cuts and parries, when Captain Catigern had begun to pant for breath, he changed his tactics. His sword, like most of those used in the West, was straight, whereas Conan's scimitar, heavier than most Turanian blades, was curved like a crescent moon, and therefore useless for thrusting. Now the Brythunian, instead of trading cuts, began to aim swift, deadly thrusts between his hasty parries.

While Conan had ofttimes handled Western swords before coming to Turan, for the past two years all his training and practice had been with the curving saber. Thrice, only his pantherlike agility, combined with desperate parries, saved him from being spitted on Catigern's fine-honed blade. One thrust, like the strike of a serpent, ripped Conan's tunic and scored a bloody scratch across his shoulder.

The Brythunian, he realized, was an experienced fighter, not easily worsted even when rendered unsteady by drink. Although Conan was taller, stronger, faster, and younger, he deemed it fortunate that the skillful mercenary was not quite sober.

Bartakes danced about the combatants in an agony of apprehension, wringing his pudgy hands and crying: "Outside, I pray, gentlemen! Do not fight within my premises! You will bring ruin upon me!"

The duellists ignored him. Then, from a dark corner of the common room, a small, shadowy figure glided toward Catigern's back; and Conan caught the gleam of a dagger in the lamplight.

While Conan would willingly kill his adversary in a fair fight, a stab in the back of a man who faced another foe affronted his code of honor. Yet if Conan cried a warning of the danger, the Brythunian would think it merely a cunning distraction so that his antagonist could sword him with impunity.

All this flashed through Conan's mind in less time than it took him to swing his curved sword. With the lightning speed of a leaping leopard, he bounded backward, at the same time grounding the point of his scimitar.

"Behind you!" he bellowed. "Treachery!"

Finding himself momentarily beyond Conan's reach, Catigern whirled to glance behind him. As he whipped around, the unknown assassin threw up his dagger arm to drive a long poniard into the Brythunian's body. With a furious curse, Catigern sent a terrific backhand slash into the assassin's side. The blade sank in between the man's ribs and pelvis, almost severing his spine. The impact hurled the slender man against a trestle table, to strike the floor in a welter of blood and entrails. He moaned briefly and lay still.

"A mighty stroke," commented Conan, his point still fixed upon the floor. "Do you want to fight some more?"

"If you two great idiots—" began Bartakes, but his words were lost on the steely-eyed twain.

"Nay, nay," replied Catigern. He wiped his blade on a corner of the dead man's tunic and started to sheathe it, pausing only to assure himself that Conan was doing likewise. "I cannot kill a man who has just saved my life, even if he tried to slay me but a moment earlier. As to the girl—why, where the devil is the chit?"

Bartakes said: "Whilst you two were fighting, she slipped away to her chamber with another patron—one of your company, I believe, Captain." The innkeeper turned to shout for his sons to remove the body and scrub the floorboards clean. Then, shaking his head, he muttered: "Zath save me from another such pair of young fools!"

Catigern gave a wry smile. "You are right, my friend; we *were* fools, sure enough, to risk our lives over a public woman." He yawned. "As for me—"

"Wait," growled Conan. "Let's see who wanted to stick a knife into you. Fetch one of those lamps, innkeeper."

Turning over the mangled body, Conan saw that the man was a typical Zamorian, small, slight, and dark. Conan asked: "Know you this man, Bartakes?"

"Surely!" replied the taverner. "He rode in on a mule only today and took a bed, giving his name as Varathran of Shadizar."

"Had you ever clapped eyes upon him ere today?"

"Never. But folk from every corner of Zamora come here to do honor to the spider-god."

Conan ran practiced hands over the corpse. Suspended from Varathran's belt he found a wallet, containing a handful of silver and copper coinage and a small roll of parchment. Conan unrolled the parchment and frowned over it. At last he said:

"Catigern, do you read Zamorian?"

"Not I! I can scarcely read the writing of my native land. What of you?"

"I once learned a few Zamorian characters, but I've forgotten what little I once knew."

"Let me see that," said the innkeeper. Holding the parchment close to the lamp and silently moving his lips, he pored over the spidery script. At last, with a shrug of despair, he returned the roll to Conan.

"It's penned in Old Zamorian," he said, "a script gone clean out of use since Mithridates the First revised our system of writing. Perchance a priest in Yezud could decipher it; I cannot."

"May I see it?" purred a soft, high-pitched voice with a peculiar accent. The Stygian, whom Conan had earlier beheld seated among his scrolls and tablets, now stood expectantly at his shoulder. "I may be of some assistance to you, sir."

Conan frowned. "And who might you be?"

The shaven-headed one smiled. "I am called Psamitek of Luxur, a poor student of arcane arts."

With a grunt, Conan handed over the scroll, and the Stygian studied it in the flickering lamplight. "Let me see: 'I—Tughril—High Priest—of Erlik—do hereby swear—by my god—to pay—ten thousand—pieces of gold—for the head—what is this name? C-co—nan—the Cimmerian.' What make you of it, sirs? Who is this Conan? Is any here so named?"

Catigern cast a fleet glance about the room; then he and Conan shook their heads. Bartakes spoke: "I mind me that two years agone, when I visited Shadizar, I heard of a notorious thief, hight Conan. I had forgotten the story until yon parchment named him. 'Twas said the fellow's depredations were so outrageous that every guard and watchman in Zamora was sworn to seek him out. At last he fled the country and disappeared."

The Stygian murmured: "So? I doubt not there is some connection, however mysterious it seem. This Conan's head must have some singular quality, that a Turanian priest should offer a royal ransom for it. With such a sum, one could accumulate the greatest library of occult works in all of Stygia." With a sigh, he rolled up the parchment and slipped it into his pouch. "Since the message does not concern those present, none will object to my keeping this sheet, I am sure. Good parchment is costly, and this I can pumice off and use again. A good night to you all."

The Stygian bowed obsequiously and withdrew. Conan opened his mouth to demand the return of the scroll; but realizing that he could not make an issue of the matter without exposing his true identity, he ground his teeth in silent vexation. To cover his discomfiture, he turned to Catigern. "Captain, let's have a drink together while our host cleans up. Methinks we've earned it, and what better way to spend this little treasure trove?"

"Good!" said Catigern. "Tomorrow I shall have to report this slaying to the Vicar. You may be called in to testify on my account."

"Is not civilization hell?" grunted Conan. "You cannot even kill a man in honest self-defense without accounting for it to some damned nosy official!"

Later that night, the men of the Free Company on guard duty at the gates of Yezud were startled to see, by starlight, their captain and the town blacksmith, with arms around each other's necks, staggering up the cliff-side path. They were singing in powerful bass voices—singing not one song but two.

chapter  vii

Wine of Kyros

Three days later, when Conan accompanied Lar to Amytis's house for supper, he found Rudabeh there. Lar said:

"Hail, sister! This is our new blacksmith, the mighty Master Nial. He lets me hold the workpiece on the anvil, to get the feel of the tools, whilst he smites the iron. And today he explained the color changes in the metal as it heats and cools. I shall be a smith yet."

"That is good of you, Master Nial," said Rudabeh with a radiant smile.

Conan's eyes burned a volcanic blue as he looked at the girl. She was tall for a Zamorian and handsome—not the sort of fabulous beauty that kings chose for their seraglios, but clean, healthy, and regular-featured. Nor did the plain tunic and baggy pantaloons of the Zamorian woman's street attire entirely mask her supple, well-rounded dancer's body. She continued:

"Mother has repeated to me some of the tales of high adventure wherewith you have regaled my family. Are they indeed all true?"

"Close enough," grinned Conan, "albeit a good storyteller must stretch a few details for the sake of his art. Did I not see you dance before Zath at the last service in the temple?"

"If you were amongst the worshipers, you did."

"You look more warmly clad now than you were then, girl."

She smiled, seemingly unperturbed. "That is so. But let not my temple costume stir lascivious thoughts within your bosom. I will not become a feast for Zath to furnish any man with momentary pleasure."

Conan growled: "Anyone who tried to feed you to that overgrown bug would answer to me!"

"Your words are fine and brave, Master Nial, but you could not forestall my fate if the priests decided upon it." She gave a little sigh. "Sometimes methinks the holy fathers carry virtue to the point of vice; but, having chosen my route, I must travel it to the end."

"When does your term of service run out?"

"Eight months hence."

"What will you do then?" asked Conan as Amytis set the fleshpot on the table and the diners began spooning out portions of stew.

"Marry some local lad, I ween. Several have made sheep's eyes at me, but I have given the matter little thought. My temple duties fully occupy my waking hours."

"How do you pass your days?"

"As leader of the troupe, I lead the other girls in the sacred songs and dances and train the novices. When we are neither dancing nor singing, we act as handmaidens to the priests and clean the rooms within the temple.

"But these are not my only duties. The old Master of the Properties has lately died, and they have designated me Mistress of the Properties in his stead. The priests could not agree upon one of their own number for the post, so they pushed the task off on me."

"What does the Mistress of the Properties do?"

"I am responsible for all the surfaces of the temple and all the movables therein. I count and polish ornaments and furniture and sacred vessels and the like, and keep lists. So busy am I that I scarce can visit Mother once a fort-night."

"Do you spend the night at home on such occasions?"

"Nay; I must return to the temple ere midnight."

For a while, Conan ate in silence. When Amytis carried off the plates and sent Lar to the well for a bucket of water to wash them with, Conan said:

"Have you ever been to Bartakes's Inn in Khesron, Rudabeh?"

"Once, years ago, when Father lived, he took us all there. I do not remember much about it."

"They have a new harper, said to be good. May I escort you thither for the evening? I'll see you get back to the temple in ample time."

She sighed again. "How I should love it! But during my term of temple service, I am forbidden to set foot outside Yezud, unless accompanied by a priest. They would whip me if they caught me out of bounds."

"Oh, come on! Wear a veil or a cloak with a hood, and do not show your face. A girl like you should have some life outside her duties."

"You tempt me, sir; I have seen so little of the outer world. But still . . ."

In low voices, they argued back and forth. Eventually Rudabeh gave in. "Wait here but a moment," she said.

When she reappeared, she was bundled up to the eyes. "Crom!" exclaimed Conan. "You look like one of the mummies of Stygia they tell about. Well, come along; the night grows no younger."

———

The common room of Bartakes's Inn throbbed with the sound of many voices. Conan's fierce blue eyes roved among the tables, seeking the face of anyone who might cause trouble for the girl or for himself, before he led the heavily veiled Rudabeh to a dark corner and seated her.

The Stygian scholar sat by himself, studying scrolls and tables as before. A party of new arrivals occupied an adjacent table—four men in Hyrkanian traveling dress, their trews tucked into heavy boots, their sheepskin caps, with upturned brims, perched at jaunty angles on their shaven skulls. They were noisily throwing dice as they quaffed great jacks of ale.

Probably Turanians, thought Conan; certainly the fifth newcomer, seated at a small table by himself, was from Turan. Of all the branches of the Hyrkanian race, the Turanians, deeming themselves the most civilized, scorned their nomadic kinsmen, who roamed the boundless steppes east of the Vilayet Sea. Yet these same Turanians retained the physical features and many of the customs and attitudes of their barbaric forebears and present kinsmen.

The solitary Turanian, hunched over several sheets of parchment, was short and squarely built, with a neatly trimmed gray beard. Much finer than the clothing of the other four was his attire; and an embroidered black velvet skullcap, richly strewn with luminescent pearls, rested on his close-cut graying hair. He had pushed aside the platter with the cold remains of his dinner to make room for the documents on which he focused his attention.

Conan had a lingering impression that he had seen the man before, but he could not recall the circumstances. At least, he was sure it was not in Yezud, so he dismissed the matter from his mind. He snapped his fingers to summon Bartakes's daughter Mandana, who at the moment manned the wine counter. Keeping his voice low, he murmured:

"Wine for the lady and me—a fine wine, none of your ordinary slop. What have you?"

Mandana shot a hostile glance at the veiled figure and answered: "We have Numalian red, and Ianthic red, and white of Akkharia."

"Are those the choicest in the house?"

Mandana gave a disdainful little sniff. " 'Tis true we have a cask of the white of Kyros, but that is for high-born ladies and gentlemen. *You* could never afford—"

"The contents of my purse are no concern of yours!" growled Conan, slapping down a handful of silver. "Bring out the best."

Mandana flounced off. For the moment, Conan enjoyed an unaccustomed prosperity, for he had made a discovery about his present situation. During the illness of Pariskas, smithery work had so piled up that Conan's patrons, eager to obtain their work out of its proper turn, thrust upon him sizable sums, over and above the stipend paid him by the temple.

Soon two goblets of golden Kyrian appeared on his table. Instead of draining his goblet in three gulps, as was his usual wont, Conan endeavored to pursue the civilized custom of sniffing the aroma and delicately savoring each sip. Considering the cost of the beverage, even Conan, careless though he was with money, wanted to make each drink last awhile.

"This wine is wonderful!" whispered Rudabeh, who had partly raised her veil. "I have never tasted aught like it in my life."

"I thought you might enjoy it," said Conan expansively. "How go the intrigues at te—at your place of employment?"

"Something is brewing," she replied thoughtfully, barely above a whisper. "When my master talks of cleansing the kingdom, he is not merely casting words upon the wind. He has some terrible plan in mind and hints that he will shortly act—perhaps within a month."

Conan leaned forward to murmur: "What sort of wight is the High Priest?"

Rudabeh shuddered delicately. "We all fear him," she breathed. "He is a stern, unbending taskmaster—just according to his reckoning, but without mercy when he deems himself in the right, and he always thinks himself in the right."

Conan looked at Rudabeh through narrowed eyes, his heavy brows drawn in concentration. "What action does he plan?"

"I know not. And then there is this visit by—" She nodded toward the tables whereat lounged the four in sheepskin caps and the lone gray-bearded scholar in the pearl-spangled cap.

"What do you know of those fellows?" asked Conan.

"They come from Aghrapur, sent by King Yildiz on some mission to the temple. I do not know the names of those four ruffians; but the older man is Lord Parvez, a Turanian diplomat."

Conan clapped a large, muscular hand against his forehead. "Of course! I—" He checked himself in time to avoid blurting out that he had seen Parvez at Yildiz's court, a place where—according to his present story, he had never set foot. To cover his confusion, he signaled Mandana to refill their goblets. Rudabeh, noting Conan's discomfiture, whispered:

"Why, know you this Parvez?"

"Nay, I did but hear of him in Shadizar," muttered Conan lamely. "What can he want with Feridun? Kings send ambassadors to other kings, not to the priests of foreign lands."

"Again, I know not; but it might have some connection with the veiled woman."

"Veiled woman? What veiled woman?" asked Conan sharply. An idea was forming in his agile mind, just beyond the bounds of consciousness.

"Ere you came to Yezud, the Vicar returned from a lengthy journey, bringing with him a woman swathed in many-colored veils. He hustled her into the temple, where she remains in a locked chamber, seen by none save the priests of the highest rank and a single slave. This servant, a swarthy wench, comes from some far country and speaks no tongue I know."

Like a meteor, the idea burst upon Conan's consciousness: the woman must be the princess Jamilah, favorite wife of King Yildiz. He pressed his lips together lest he divulge his knowledge of Jamilah's abduction. Trying to seem casual, he said: "This woman, now—might your priests have kidnapped her for ransom?"

Rudabeh shook her head. "Nay; Zath and those who serve him are enormously rich. The coins in the offering chest are but a token of the temple's wealth. The real treasures of Zath—the vessels of gold and silver, set with diamonds and emeralds and rubies; the stacks of bars of precious metal; the heaps of uncut gems—are held in triple-locked and guarded crypts. Besides the tithes of the faithful and the gifts of the king, the temple controls the traffic in bitumen, which bubbles from the ground hereabouts and lies in pools until the folk, under the watchful eyes of the priests, scoop it up to sell. Such are the riches of Zath that not even a king's ransom would tempt them to such an outrage. Perchance the woman is some well-born fugitive, who has fled a brutal husband."

"Or poisoned him and now seeks sanctuary," added Conan.

Although Rudabeh's words gave Conan material for furious thought and set his eyes agleam with avarice, he dared not pursue the subject of the temple's wealth and the sequestered queen lest he arouse suspicion in the mind of his companion or of the company around them. To mask his thoughts, he affected a careless smile, drained his goblet of wine, and signaled Mandana to refill the tumblers. When the sullen girl had fulfilled her task, she stared insolently at Rudabeh before withdrawing. The dancer drew down her half-raised veil and shrank back into the corner. Conan said:

"Pay the wench no heed. Her nose is out of joint with envy of your handsome cloak, no more. Now tell me how you spend the hours of your day."

Rudabeh, he found, was a lively talker: intelligent, clear-sighted, and not without wit. The women he had known since leaving Cimmeria had all chattered foolishly, regarding talk only as a preliminary to lovemaking, or to refusal, as the case might be. He enjoyed Rudabeh's talk for its own sake, and the contact with her keen mind proved a new and stimulating experience. She told him softly:

"One of my tasks is to keep watch on the reservoir whence feeds the sacred flame."

"How is that done?"

"The flame burns bitumen from a wick of braided fabric, set in oil in a hollow in the block of marble, beneath the chalcedony bowl. In the recess by the door whence the priests enter the naos for services, a pipe juts out, to which a bronzen valve is affixed. I turn the valve to the left, and oil flows; to the right, and the flow ceases."

"An ingenious device," mused Conan. "I have seen royal palaces that had been better off for such amenities. How is the reservoir filled?"

"Every day," she continued, "I must needs inspect the reservoir to see how low the oil has sunk. When it is low—say, after three days—I inform the priest whose duty it is. He fills a pitcher at the pipe and pours the bitumen into the reservoir.

"Last year, saying they had more work than they could accomplish, the priests appointed me to perform that task. But the first time I tried it, being new to the job, I spilled some bitumen, and the High Priest was furious. You'd have thought I had stolen one of the Eyes of Zath. Later he blamed me when the priest Mirzes set fire to his robe, claiming I had not cleaned up the oil sufficiently so that Mirzes slipped on the marble."

"How could that start a fire?" asked Conan.

"Mirzes got careless during the Presentation of the Telesms—when they bring out the sacred key and mirror and so on—and waved his arm across the eternal flame. His fluttery sleeve caught fire, and there was much dashing about and shouting ere they beat the fire out."

"What was the upshot?"

"Mirzes had his arm in bandages for a fortnight. As soon as he was well, the High Priest gave him the task of filling the reservoir, saying that he, if anyone, would appreciate the need for care. I did not mind escaping that chore, albeit I resented Feridun's barbed comments on the stupidity of women."

"Whence comes this oil?"

"I know not for certain, but one told me the pipe lies beneath the ground outside the temple and leads up to a gorge, wherein the bitumen seeps from the soil and forms a pool."

Conan nodded his understanding. "And speaking of the Eyes of Zath, they must be gems of some sort—at least when Zath is in his stony form. Do you know what sort?"

" 'Tis said they are eight matchless specimens of the Kambujan girasol, or as some say, fire opal. Their value must be as great as all the rest of the treasure of Zath." Glancing around, Rudabeh suddenly stiffened and caught Conan's hand in a convulsive grip. "Nial! We must flee!"

"Why? What's up, lass?"

"See you that man who just entered?" She moved her head slightly to indicate direction. "Nay, do not stare; but that man is Darius, one of the priests! If he sees me, I am undone!"

The individual indicated was one of the younger priests, a slim, ascetic-looking man not much older than Conan, clad in an amber robe and an emerald turban. Paying no attention to the other patrons, Darius walked quietly across the floor to where sat the Stygian scholar. The two greeted each other with bows and stately gestures before the priest pulled up a stool and sat facing Psamitek. The priest and the Stygian spoke in low voices, while Psamitek made notes on a waxed wooden tablet.

"I've heard of this Stygian," murmured Rudabeh. "He travels about, studying the cults of many gods; and now he wishes instruction in the theology of Zathism. I suppose Darius is imparting it to him. Now shall we go?"

Conan shook his head slightly. "We must not leap up and depart in haste, for that would draw attention. Besides, he seems completely absorbed in what he's telling the Stygian."

"At least," breathed Rudabeh, "Darius is one of whom I have little fear. He is unworldly and idealistic, and gossip says he is at outs with the High Priest and the Vicar. Behold, here comes the harper. Dare we wait to hear him?"

"Surely!" said Conan. "I'll order one more cup for each of us ere he begins." He waved to Mandana.

Rudabeh yawned, then smiled through her veil. "I ought not to drink so much, but this wine is so refreshing. What is it called?"

"Wine of Kyros, from the coast of Shem. I hear the combination of climate and soil makes it the world's best; and if there be a better, I have yet to taste it."

The harper sat on his stool and tuned his instrument. Sweeping skilled hands across the strings, he sang a tragic lament in a voice quivering with despair. At the end he got a brief round of applause. He acknowledged it with a bow, then passed around the room, holding out his cap for donations.

His next song was a rollicking ballad about a fabled robber who stole from the rich but gave to the poor. But now a dispute broke out among the four Turanians, whose angry voices nearly drowned out the delicate chords of the harp and the fluting voice of the singer. Several patrons tried to quiet them, but they paid no heed. Since they were speaking Hyrkanian, Conan could follow the thrust of the dispute.

The Turanians were arguing over who should enjoy the favors of Mandana for the night. Conan had been discomfited to learn that Bartakes rented out his daughter for this purpose. Although he had shed most of the stern moral code of his barbaric homeland, Conan considered it dishonorable for any man to prostitute his kinswoman. But then, he told himself, what could one expect of decadent Zamorians? Besides, he admitted, before he met Rudabeh he had intended to avail himself of the tavern wench's services.

The dispute was at length referred to the dice box, and for a while the twang of the harp competed with the rattle of dice. Then a shout announced the winner, and the other three congratulated him with loud, lewd jests.

Rudabeh, taking a sip of her wine, said: "It is—it is a shame we cannot hear the music. Nial, can naught be done to quiet those louts?"

Conan had resolved not to let himself be drawn into any brawls that night. He feared that either his identity or that of his companion might be exposed, or that—if nothing worse—Bartakes would forbid him the premises. On the other hand, it went against his nature to sit supinely by while a woman in distress appealed to him for aid.

Before he could decide which impulse to follow, one of the Turanians rose unsteadily to his feet and lurched across the common room to Conan's table. He slapped Conan on the shoulders and barked in broken Zamorian:

"You, fellow! How much you take for loan of your woman for this night?"

Keeping a tight rein on his volcanic temper, Conan replied: "My woman, as you call her, is not for sale or rent. Besides, I thought you had already gained the innkeeper's daughter?"

Swaying, the Turanian spat on the floor. "That was Tutush won her, not me. Here I am, randy as goat and no woman. What you take? I pay good money."

"I have told you," grated Conan, "the lady is not for sale."

The Turanian gave Conan a cuff on the shoulder that was somewhere between a friendly pat and a hostile blow. "Oh, do not play great lord with me! I Chagor, mighty swordsman. When I want, by Erlik I take—"

Conan snapped to his feet and brought his fist up in a whistling arc to Chagor's jaw. The fist connected with a jarring smack, and the Turanian fell backward as if poleaxed. His face expressionless, Conan sat down and took a swallow of wine.

But the Turanian's facilities soon returned to him. He reached out feebly, trying to regain his feet. Conan rose again, turned Chagor over with his boot, and grasped him by the slack of his jacket and trews. Carrying the man to the door, he kicked it open, strode out, and dropped the Turanian into the horse trough. After pulling him out of the water and dipping him back several times, he dropped him in the dirt and reentered the inn.

Scarcely had the door closed when he found himself facing Chagor's three companions, each with scimitar bared. With the quickness of a pouncing panther, Conan swept out his own blade. He was about to launch a headlong attack, knowing that only by tigerish speed could he hope to keep his three adversaries from surrounding him and cutting him down. Then from behind the Turanians, a voice commanded in Hyrkanian:

"Hold! Put up your swords! Back to your table, clods!"

The graybeard with the skullcap had risen to thunder his orders in a voice like the crack of a whip. To Conan's astonishment, the lumbering Turanians obeyed promptly. They backed away, sheathed their sabers, and returned, sullen and grumbling, to their table.

Conan scabbarded his own sword and strode back to his table. There he found that Rudabeh, sitting with her back to the corner, had dozed off and slept through the noisy confrontation.

The harper had disappeared. The young priest who had been in conversation with the Stygian scholar rose, nodded to his acquaintance, and hurried out.

Conan took a draft of wine and looked up to see Parvez standing by his table. The diplomat said: "Good even, Captain Conan! And how are things in Ye-zud?"

Conan growled: "I thank you for stopping the brawl, sir, but I am Nial the blacksmith."

With a chuckle, the Turanian pulled up a vacant stool and sat down. "So that is what you go by here, eh? Very well, you shall be Nial to me. But think not that I do not know you. By the way, what did you with Chagor?"

"I gave him a much-needed bath; you could smell him half a league upwind. Here he comes now."

Chagor had staggered in dripping. He glared about the room; but when Parvez pointed a stern finger, he went meekly back to the table whereat sat the other three.

"At least, I am glad you did him no lasting harm," said Parvez. "They are good enough fellows, but betimes the devil gets into them."

Conan pushed Rudabeh's goblet toward Parvez. "You may as well finish this, since my companion sleeps."

Parvez sniffed and tasted. "Kyrian, eh? You must be in funds."

"What are you doing here?" countered Conan.

"Diplomatic business." Parvez lowered his voice and glanced around. "Perchance we can be of service to each other. I will tell you a thing or two, since I think I can trust you further than most of the wights hereabouts. I have a hold on you, and I know more about you than you suspect; so it behooves us to put some faith in each other. In Aghrapur you had the name of a man of his word, despite your proclivity for violence."

Tensely, Conan growled: "I'll keep your secrets exactly as well as you keep mine."

"We agree, then? What know you of the abduction of Princess Jamilah?"

Conan told Parvez of his encounter with Harpagus in the Marshes of Mehar. Then he repeated what Rudabeh had told him of the veiled woman. The Cimmerian ended by saying: "How did you trace the lady hither?"

"That required no skill. The High Priest of Zath sent a message to His Majesty, stating that Her Royal Highness was safe and well and would be detained until Feridun's plans had attained fruition."

"But what in the nine hells," asked Conan, "does the temple of Zath want with the princess? They already have all the wealth any mortals could desire. Would they force the worship of Zath upon the kingdom of Turan?"

"Nay—at least not for the nonce. I visited the High Priest this day for the answer to that very question. Feridun scornfully rejected any talk of ransom; and in the course of our speech he revealed more by his omissions than by his admissions. When I put his hints and blusters together, I was convinced that he plans to launch some sort of revolution in Zamora, to cast down the sovereign he terms 'corrupt and effete.' Apparently he seized the princess to make certain that King Yildiz shall not intervene to save his brother monarch, as called for by an ancient treaty. He assured me that the lady will be well cared for until his great 'cleansing' is accomplished."

"I had naught to do with that abduction, as some may think," said Conan gruffly. "I do not use women as counters in a game."

Lord Parvez raised quizzical eyebrows. "I myself first thought that you had helped to carry off the lady, because of your simultaneous disappearance; and it was I who sent forth a warrant for your capture. It was fortunate that you made your escape, for now I think you innocent of that offense, although you remain in bad odor in Turan because of Orkhan's slaying."

"I killed in self-defense," growled Conan, "whatever that bitch Narkia has averred."

Parvez shrugged. "That concerns me not, whatever be the truth of it. High Priest Tughril swears to have your heart for the death of his son, but that is his affair, and yours." Parvez rubbed his chin thoughtfully.

"I know about that, too," said Conan, telling of the assassin Varathran's attack on Catigern and the price that had been placed on Conan's head.

"I don't understand," Conan continued, "why this scum should attack the Brythunian instead of me. We look not alike."

"I can imagine it," said Parvez. "Suppose Tughril sends a man to recruit a trusty murderer. In the gutters of Shadizar, his messenger finds Varathran and tells him: 'Go slay Conan the Cimmerian, a great hulking fellow who has fled to Yezud, to seek service in the temple guard.' With no further description to go by, Varathran arrives here and discovers two great, hulking men enmeshed in battle. One is a palpable civilian, whilst the other wears the habiliments of a captain of mercenaries. Naturally, he takes Catigern for his quarry."

"You seem to have followed my every move hither," said Conan uncomfortably.

"Gathering information is my trade, just as fighting is yours. And now, friend—ah—Nial, I have a proposal to make."

"Well?" growled Conan, his blue eyes lighting with interest.

"I want Jamilah, unharmed. You are the one man whom I count upon to get her."

Conan pondered, then said: "How am I supposed to do that? The lady is hidden in that maze of corridors within the temple, just where I know not. Even if I could locate her, how could I smuggle her past the Brythunian guards? There must be at least a score of those fellows on duty there, day and night."

Parvez waved a negligent hand. "In your former and less respectable days — and don't think I know not of them, too — you performed feats of stealth, daring, and cunning no whit the less."

"But even then, I never learned the art of picking locks. My fellow th — my associates said my thick fingers were too clumsy to make it worth their while to teach me. So how could I enter her locked chamber? I am no weakling, but those stout oaken doors are beyond my power to burst by main force. I should need an axe, the sound of whose strokes would bring the guards on the run."

The Turanian smiled. "As to that, I can help you. When I came hither, it was with His Majesty's orders to recover the lady, by personally invading the temple if need be, or face loss of my head on my return. To tip the odds further in my favor, he caused the royal sorcerer to present me with this bauble."

Parvez produced a bejeweled silver arrow, as long as a man's finger. "This," he said, "is the Clavis of Gazrik, one of the magical gimcracks in the royal strongbox. With it you can unlock any door. Having no practical experience at burglary, I dreaded this undertaking; but your appearance simplifies my task."

"How does that thing work?" queried Conan.

"Touch the point of the arrow to the lock and say *kapinin achilir genishi!* and the lock will unlock itself. The Clavis will even make a bolt slide back, if it be not too heavy. I can lend you the object until your mission be accomplished."

"Hm. What shall be my price for this work?"

"Let me think," said the Turanian. "I can pay you fifty pieces of gold from what I have with me. I must needs keep enough to assure my return to Turan with the lady."

"Hah!" ejaculated Conan. "For such a risk? Not so, my lord. It would have to be much, much more."

"I could recommend you to high office and an additional emolument when I got home. I have influence, and I am sure I could at least assure you of a senior captainship."

Conan shook his head. "Had this come ere my unfortunate encounter with Tughril's son . . . But as things stand, Tughril has already set one assassin on my trail, and he is likely to set others. From what I know of his little ways with traps and poisons, in Turan I shouldn't have the chance of a snowball in Kush."

"Well, young man, what *do* you wish that is within my power to grant?"

Conan's eyes blazed bluely across the table. "I'll take your fifty pieces of gold — in advance, mind you — and also that silver arrow, but not as a loan. I'll take it to keep."

Parvez argued briefly against giving up the Clavis of Gazrik; but Conan was firm, and the older man gave in. "It is yours," he said at last. "His Majesty will not be pleased, but gratitude for the return of Jamilah may outweigh his resentment at the loss of the bauble." Parvez handed over the arrow and counted out the gold. "I suspect you have further plans for the use of the device. King Yildiz would pay handsomely for the Eyes of Zath."

He winked at Conan and extended a hand, which the Cimmerian gripped to seal the bargain. With a glance at the still-sleeping Rudabeh, Parvez added: "How will you get your fair companion home? At least, I presume she is fair beneath all those swathings."

Conan reached over and shook the girl. He even slapped her lightly, to no avail. Rudabeh slumbered on.

"I'll carry her," grunted Conan, rising. He gathered the dancing girl in his arms and bade Parvez a curt goodnight. As he passed the table at which sat the four Turanians of Parvez's suite, Chagor spat on the floor and muttered something that sounded like a threat. Ignoring it, Conan strode out into the starlit night.

The cooler air outside failed to revive Rudabeh, who was still dead to the world. So Conan marched up the hillside path to the gate of Yezud with the girl in his arms. He endured in silence the gibes of the Brythunian guards who opened the small door in the gate for him. He was confident that they would not carry tales to the priests, because to do so might spoil their own off-duty amusements.

Conan had meant to lead Rudabeh directly to the back door of the temple. But it occurred to him that, if he delivered her in this unconscious state, he might get her into the gods only knew what kind of trouble. The priests might ask Conan awkward questions, too. After a moment's thought, he carried her through his smithy and into his private abode.

Since the night was moonless, Conan's room was pitch-dark, save for a few dull red coals in the brazier. Feeling his way, he laid Rudabeh on his pallet and loosed her veils. She stirred but did not awaken.

Conan ignited a splinter from the coals in the brazier and lit a candle. When he brought the light closer to Rudabeh, he saw that she was indeed a beautiful girl. As he looked down upon her, his passions rose. The blood pounded in his temples; he set down the candle and began gently to unfasten the girl's garments.

He untied her cloak and spread it out. He unlaced the flimsy jacket and spread it, baring Rudabeh's firm breasts.

The dim-lit room swam to Conan's gaze as he looked upon his prize. His breath quickened. He started to unfasten his own garments when a thought made him pause.

Conan prided himself upon never having forced or deceived a woman. If one wanted to extend her ultimate hospitality to him, he would quickly accept; but he had never coerced a girl or tried to befool her with false promises. To take advantage of Rudabeh's present condition would offend his code almost as gravely as an outright rape.

Still, his passions were strong. For an instant he stood immobile as a statue while the two opposing urges battled within him.

A fleeting vision of his aged mother, back in her Cimmerian village, tipped the balance. Telling himself that there would be other chances openly to solicit Rudabeh's love, he stooped and was just tying up her jacket when she stirred and opened her eyes.

"What do you?" she mumbled.

"Oh," said Conan. "You're alive, thank Mitra. I was going to listen to your heart to see if it still beat."

"I think you had something else in mind," she said as he helped her up. "*Ulp*—I am going to be sick!"

"Not on the floor! Over here!" he pushed her to the washstand and bent her head over the basin.

Half an hour later, just before midnight, Conan delivered Rudabeh, clean and sober, to the back door of the temple, on the north side. "I thank you," she said, "but you should not have been so generous with the wine of Kyros."

"I'll be stingier next time. How can I see you again?"

She sighed. "Ere Feridun became High Priest, you could come to this door and knock four times. Then old Oxyathres would open it, and you could tell him which girl you wished speech with and give him a coin. But Feridun has ended all that. Now you must wait until the priests give me leave to spend an evening at home; and that is something not even the keenest astrologer could predict. We shall have to meet by chance at my mother's house again."

"Would you like another visit to Bartakes's place, when that time comes?"

"Ah, no indeed! I dare not go outside the city wall again; it was godlike luck that the priest Darius failed to mark my presence, and I cannot face such a risk a second time."

She gave him a quick kiss and was gone. Conan walked back to his smithy, scowling and muttering. He wondered: if he had taken advantage of her, would it have left him feeling a bigger fool than he felt now?

chapter viii

The Eight Eyes of Zath

For several days, Conan labored at his craft. He looked forward to seeing Rudabeh again at her mother's home, but the dancing girl failed to appear.

"The way the priests work the poor lass," said Amytis, "a body never knows when she will get home. She is supposed to have four evenings off each month, but it's a lucky month when she gets three."

Once he had caught up with the backlog of work that had piled up in the smithy before his employment, Conan performed his duties in a more leisurely manner. Every day he took an hour or two off to exercise his horse. Once he stopped at Bartakes's Inn to chat with Parvez, who showed increasing impatience.

"I cannot free the woman until I know where she is kept!" expostulated Conan.

"Then you must redouble your efforts to find out," said Parvez. "Rumor tells me that the doom wherewith the High Priest threatens us may be unleashed within a fortnight."

Conan grunted. "Perhaps you are right. I'll do what I can."

The next day, Conan attended another service in the temple of Zath, partly to keep on the good side of the priests and partly to familiarize himself with the layout. He stood through Feridun's harangue predicting the great, purifying revolution. When the dancing girls came on, he stared eagerly to see Rudabeh. At her appearance, he trembled with desire at the sight of her gyrating in nothing but a sparse cobweb of black beads. He tossed a larger coin than before into the acolytes' offering bowl, to give the impression that he was leaning toward the cult of Zath.

He also stared at the great gems that ornamented the statue of the spider-god—eight great opals, each as large as a child's fist; four in a row across the front, one on each side, and two on top. If he could steal them and get away whole, he could go to some far country, buy an estate and a title of nobility, or a high rank in the army, and be secure for life. Not that he would ever cease wandering in search of adventure and danger; but it would be pleasant to know that he had a secure base to return to, where he could rest and enjoy life between bouts of derring-do. He turned over and discarded one plan after another for getting the jewels into his possession.

After the service, he lingered in the vestibule, pretending to get a stone out of his shoe. When the rest of the congregation had streamed out, instead of following them, he entered the corridor leading off from the vestibule to the right as one entered the temple—the side opposite that into which Morcant had led him on his first arrival. He prowled the hallway, glancing keenly to right and left to orient himself and to find clues as to what lay behind the massive oaken doors.

The corridor made a bend, and as Conan came around the corner he found himself facing one of the Brythunian guards. The man stood at the junction of the corridor with another passage, which led off into semidarkness to the right. From his knowledge of the temple's exterior, Conan was sure that this passage occupied the first of the four wings on that side.

The immediate problem was to allay the suspicions of the guard. Casually, Conan said: "Hail, Urien! Have you lost your pay gaming again?"

The guardsman frowned. "I hold my own. But what do you here, Nial? A layman like you should be accompanied by a priest or an acolyte."

"I do but work in the temple's interest . . ." began Conan, but stopped as he saw Urien's eyes look past him. He spun around, to find that Harpagus the Vicar, in black robe and white turban, had come up softly behind him. Conan said:

"It occurred to me, Vicar, that some of the metal furnishings in the temple may need repairs. If I could inspect the place, examining every hinge and fitting, I might save trouble anon."

Harpagus gave a cold little smile. "It is good of you to think of our welfare, Nial. The servants of Zath watch vigilantly for such defects. When they find one, they will inform you in due course. How goes your smithery?"

"Well, I thank you," grumbled Conan. "It keeps me occupied."

"Good! One of your customers complained that your craftsmanship was rough compared with your predecessor's. I explained that you had been soldiering and thus were out of practice. I trust we shall see an improvement."

Conan resisted an impulse to tell the Vicar what the dissatisfied customer could do with the piece Conan had made for him. "I'll do my best, sir. I am now on my way to finish an iron ornament for someone's door."

"One moment, Master Nial. I wish speech with you in my closet; but meanwhile I have a small task to perform. Pray walk with me."

Wondering, Conan followed the priest back to the vestibule and out the front doors of the temple. There Conan found that the worshipers, instead of dispersing to their homes and workshops, were kept on the temple steps by the Brythunian guards, holding pikes parallel to the ground to form a barrier. The reason, Conan saw, was that a flock of sheep was being driven in from the city gate. The animals flowed past the front of the temple and around to the west side, chivvied on their way by two skin-clad shepherds and a dog.

When at last the Brythunians raised their pikes, the Vicar strode around the corner after the sheep, while Conan followed the Vicar. They found the flock huddled near the door at the end of the first wing of the temple they came to on that side. This wing, like its fellow on the opposite side, had a massive door set in its end wall.

The dog raced around the flock, chasing animals back into the mass whenever one started to stray. The shepherds leaned on their crooks and watched. The Vicar pushed through the sheep to the door at the end of the wing. Here he thrust back the massive bolt that secured the door from the outside, unlocked the door with a key, and heaved it open. Stepping back, he waved to indicate that the shepherds should drive their flock in.

With the noisy help of their dog, the shepherds forced the sheep into the opening. When the animals were nearly all inside, the dog behaved strangely, backing away from the opening with its hair bristling and snarling, as if it had encountered a strange and menacing smell. The shepherds drove the remaining beasts into the passage by blows of their crooks.

Harpagus closed the door, locked it, and slammed the big bolt across. He turned, put away his key, and from his robe brought out a small purse, which he handed to the older shepherd. The shepherds bowed, mumbled thanks in their dialect, and walked off with their dog.

"Now, Master Nial," said the Vicar, "we shall repair to my cabinet."

Unable to think of a reason to gainsay the command, Conan followed Harpagus into the chamber where he had received his appointment as blacksmith. Harpagus sat down behind his flat-topped writing table, saying: "Look at me, Nial!"

The priest raised the hand that bore the ring set with the huge gemstone. His piercing eyes caught Conan's and held them as he began to wave the ring-decked fingers back and forth. In a low monotone he intoned:

"You are becoming drowsy—drowsy—drowsy. You are losing your will to think for yourself. You shall tell me, truthfully, all that which I am fain to know. . . ."

The priest's eyes seemed to expand to inhuman size; the room faded away, and Conan stood as in a dense fog, seeing nothing save the priest's huge eyes.

Just in time, Conan recalled the lessons he had received from Kushad, the blind seer of Sultanapur. With a mighty effort, he tore his gaze away and concentrated on his mental picture of the room in which he stood, reciting to himself: "Two threes are six; three threes are nine . . ."

Little by little the fog cleared, and the Vicar's study swam into view. Conan silently faced the Vicar, who said: "Now tell me, Nial, what were you truly doing, loitering in the temple after the service, instead of issuing forth with the others?"

"I had a stone in my shoe, my lord. Then the thought struck me that I could better fulfill my duties as smith to the temple by examining the metalwork in this building for defects."

Harpagus frowned in a puzzled manner and repeated the question, receiving the same reply.

"Are you truly under my influence?" asked the Vicar, "or are you shamming?"

"Ask what you will, sir, and I will answer truly."

"Foolish question," muttered Harpagus. "But let us try another. Tell me of your feelings for and relations with the dancer Rudabeh—everything, even to intimate details."

"Mistress Rudabeh is the daughter of the woman at whose house I take my meals," said Conan. "I once supped with the lass when she visited her home; that is all."

"You have never escorted her out—say, to Bartakes's Inn in Khesron?"

"Nay, sir; she said it were against the temple's rules."

"What did you and she discuss when you met her at her mother's house?"

"We talked of local gossip, and I told of my adventures."

"Have you had carnal knowledge of the wench?"

"Nay, sir; I understand that to be forbidden."

Harpagus sat for a moment, tapping an index finger softly on his desk top. At last he said: "Very well. When I snap my fingers, you shall awaken; but you shall remember none of this discourse. Then you may go."

The priest snapped his fingers. Conan drew a long breath, squared his enormous shoulders, and said: "What did you wish to ask me about, my lord Vicar?"

"Oh, I have forgotten," snapped Harpagus testily. "Go on about your business."

Conan nodded, turned, and started to stride out; but the Vicar called: "Eldoc!"

The Brythunian standing guard before Harpagus's door thrust his head in. "Aye, Vicar?"

"Show Master Nial out. And you, Nial," he added severely, "seem prone to forget that we do not allow laymen to wander the temple unescorted. Do not give me occasion to mention this rule again."

Out in the corridor, Conan wiped his sleeve across his sweat-beaded brow

and ground his teeth in suppressed rage. At least, he hoped that his impersonation of a hypnotic subject had taken in the Vicar.

When Conan reached Amytis's house that day, he again found Rudabeh there
before him. Since the time was close to midsummer and the light lingered late,
they went out after supper into the garden behind the house. Rudabeh said:
"Have a care that you step not on our cabbages!"

When Conan had boasted of his adventures, he asked: "What's this doom
the High Priest is ever threatening to loose?"

"I know not," she replied. "The inner circle keep their secrets."

"It sounds like some plague. I've heard of sorcerous pestilences."

She shrugged. "All will become clear in time, I ween."

"Sorcery ofttimes escapes the sorcerer's control," mused Conan. "We might
well be among the victims."

"You can always flee."

"But what of you?"

She shrugged again. "I must take my chances. Yezud is my home; I am not
a wanderer like you, to whom all places are as one."

"If the plague gets loose in Yezud, you may have no kith or kin left."

"If so," she murmured, "that is my fate."

"Oh, curse your Eastern fatalism! Why not flee with me?"

She gave him a level look. "I wondered how soon you would come to that.
Know, Nial, that I am no man's plaything. When my term ends, I will settle
down with some likely lad, to keep his house and rear his children."

Conan made a wry face. "It sounds as dull as life in my native village. I
could show you some real living."

"Doubtless; but to be the drab of a footloose adventurer is not to my taste."

"How do you know, girl, if you've never tried it?"

"If I found housewifery intolerable, I suppose I could flee with a man like
you. But if I went with you, I could never return to Yezud; the priests would
feed me to Zath."

Conan threw up his hands. "Mitra save me from intelligent women, who
plan their lives like a general setting up a battle! Half the spice of life is not
knowing what the morrow will bring—or even if you will be alive. But still, I
like you better than any other woman I have known, even though you be as
cold as ice to me."

"I like you, too, Nial; but not to the point of folly. Of course if you changed
your ways—if you settled down, as they say—but I must not make rash promises. I pray you to escort me back to the temple."

————

After saying good-night to Rudabeh, Conan returned to his smithy. Finding himself bored and restless, he went down to Khesron, where in the inn he found Parvez studying a map of Zamora. To him Conan said:

"Meseems our enterprise must be done, if done it be, from the outside. The interior is too well guarded." He told of his attempt to prowl the temple corridors and his subsequent interrogation by Harpagus. "For this," he concluded, "I shall need a good length of rope—perhaps forty or fifty cubits. Do you know where I could get one?"

"Not I," said the diplomat; "but our host may. Oh, Bartakes!"

The innkeeper informed them that the nearest rope-walk was in the village of Kharshoi, a couple of leagues down the valley.

"Good," said Conan. "What would be the local price of fifty cubits thereof?" When Bartakes, after a moment of thought, named a sum, Conan held out a hand to Parvez. "Money for the rope, my lord."

"You are a hard man," said the diplomat, fumbling in his wallet. "Now you must excuse me."

With a sour glance, Parvez rose and withdrew. Left alone, Conan glanced around the common room. Captain Catigern came in, and Conan beckoned him. He and Conan ordered wine—the cheap local vintage, for Conan saw no reason to pauperize himself by buying Kyrian when he had no fair companion to savor it with. He and Catigern flipped coins for small sums.

Although Conan drank more wine than usual, Bartakes's liquor seemed to have no effect. After an hour, he and Catigern were almost where they had started, and Conan found himself more bored and restless than ever.

The taverner's daughter wandered over to watch the game. Conan yawned and said: "I've had enough, Captain. Methinks I'll to bed."

"All alone?" said Mandana archly. As Conan looked up, she met his eye and gave a little wriggle.

Conan looked at her without interest. "Smithery is hard work," he grunted. "Hammering out a sword blade is no less laborious than wielding that sword in battle. My trade has sapped my strength."

"Pooh!" retorted Mandana. "It would take more than that to tire a man of your thews! Your head is turned by that dancing girl from the temple. Think not that I did not know her when you brought her hither, for all her mummy wrappings. At least, *I* do not prance indecently around, naked but for a string of beads!"

A choking sound came from across the table, where Catigern was valiantly trying to restrain his mirth. Conan glowered at the captain, then at Bartakes's daughter, growled a curt good-night, and departed.

After Conan sought his pallet late that night, he could not sleep. All he could think of was Rudabeh; her image utterly possessed him. Although he told himself time and again that he should have nothing more to do with her—that she posed a dire threat to the freedom and independence he prized above all—still her face floated before him.

She would, he reflected, ruin him as a fighting man. She would trap him in a sticky web of domesticity, whence he could never honorably escape. Was not the spiderweb the very symbol of Yezud? He would be tied to one place and some dull trade all his life, until he was old and gray, living on soup for want of teeth to chew with. And all this when there were so many places he had not seen, and so many adventures yet untried!

But, though he recoiled with horror from the thought of spending the rest of his life as Yezud's blacksmith, an even stronger urge impelled him—a fiercely burning desire to see Rudabeh again, to gaze on her handsome face, to hear her gentle voice, to admire her proud dancer's carriage, to hold her hand. It was not mere lust, albeit he had a plenty of that.

Nor was his obsession merely a hunger for a woman—any woman. He could have enjoyed a night with the silly wench Mandana any time he chose to pay her father's toll. But he wanted just one woman, no other.

This need, this dependence, was new to Conan's experience, and he did not altogether like it. Time and again he told himself to break out of this invisible web before it was too late. But every time he thought thus, he felt himself weakening, knowing that he could no more brusquely cast Rudabeh aside than he could bring himself to rob an old beggar.

Furthermore, he had agreed with Parvez to rescue Jamilah in return for access to the temple, where he hoped to steal the Eyes of Zath. But, if he took the Eyes, he would have to flee from Yezud as fast as a horse could carry him. If Rudabeh would flee with him—but suppose she refused? Would he give up his quest for the Eyes to settle permanently in Yezud? If he did, would either he or the girl survive Feridun's doom? It would be absurd to undertake the toil and risk of freeing Jamilah and then make no use of the Clavis of Gazrik.

His thoughts whirled round and round, like milk in a butter churn, without coming to a conclusion. At last he gave up trying to sleep and got up.

Some time after midnight, Captain Catigern inspected his Brythunian sentries. As he walked the wall of Yezud, his eye caught a distant movement on the Shadizar road. Then he sighted a man running through Khesron and up the path to the hilltop stronghold. Catigern turned sharply to the lieutenant in command of the watch, saying:

"Who's that? A messenger from the King?"

"Nay," replied the lieutenant. "Unless I mistake me, 'tis none but Nial the blacksmith. He went forth an hour since, saying he needed a good, hard run."

Conan, gasping, waited for the door in the gate valve to open. Then, still panting, he trotted through the gap, flung a surly greeting to the Brythunians, and disappeared.

"I wonder," mused the lieutenant, "has our blacksmith gone mad? Never have I seen a man run so save to escape enemies."

Catigern chuckled. "Aye, he's mad right enough—mad for a wench. Love has made men do stranger things than run a league by the light of the stars!"

chapter  ix

The Powder of Forgetfulness

During his courtship of Rudabeh, if such it could be called, Conan made preparations for sudden flight, despite the fact that he had not yet fully decided to flee. He, long accustomed to making his mind up quickly and following through his decision, right or wrong, found himself vexatiously balanced on a knife-edge of indecision.

Every day he took an hour or so off from his smithery to exercise his horse. He sharpened his sword. He mended and polished his boots, saddlery, and other equipment. He laid in a supply of durable foodstuffs: salted meat, hard biscuits, and a bag of dates brought north by traders from the Zuagir country. He borrowed Parvez's map of Zamora and studied it.

If he fled from Yezud with the Eyes of Zath, which way should he turn? To make his way back to Turan was out of the question so long as Tughril maintained his feud. He did not underestimate the sorcerous powers and lust for revenge of the High Priest of Erlik, whose son he had slain.

West of Yezud, the central ridge of the Karpash Mountains snaked north and south for many leagues. As a born hillman, Conan was sure he could cross the cliff-sided main ridge on foot, but equally sure he would have to abandon any horses he brought. He did not care to flee beyond the mountains only to find himself afoot in a strange land. Besides, if Rudabeh decided to come with him, she also would need a mount.

He could go north to the end of the central ridge and strike west into upper Brythunia. From all he had heard, this was a poor, sparsely-settled land where, though he carried the wealth of ages, there would be nothing to spend it on. In that country he could only buy a farm and settle down to till it. To become a yeoman farmer was the least of Conan's desires; he had seen enough of peasant drudgery in his native Cimmeria.

He could push south, to the other end of the Karpashes, and strike west into Corinthia or south into Khauran. That route would take him through

Shadizar, where a friendly fence would give him a handsome sum for his loot. On the other hand, too many Zamorians, from King Mithridates down, remembering his former depredations in their land, were whetting their knives for a slice of Conan's flesh. Zamora was a poor country to hide in, because Conan's very size, a head taller than most Zamorians, made him all too visible to those who sought him.

A few days after his midnight run, following a three-day absence from his smithy, Conan rode up the valley below Yezud. He was returning from the village of Kharshoi with a coil of rope tied to his saddle.

He jogged peacefully along the narrow, winding route that snaked along the side of the narrow gulch below the wider valley in which Khesron lay. The rocky sides of the valley rose steeply on either hand, carved by erosion into a confused corrugation of pinnacles and detached blocks piled helter-skelter. A fine site for an ambush, he thought, sweeping the tumbled slopes with a wary glance; the stony chaos presented an infinitude of hiding places, while no horse could negotiate such a slope without a broken leg.

Even as this thought crossed his mind, he was jerked to full alertness by a sound that his services in the Turanian army had made all too familiar: the flat snap of a bowstring, followed instantly by the whistling hiss of an arrow in flight.

Instantly, Conan threw himself forward and to the off side of the horse, since the sound came from his left, across the ravine. Holding on with one leg over the saddle and one arm around Ymir's neck, he presented but little target to the unknown archer. As he did so, the arrow sang past the place where his body had been, to shatter against the rocks on his right.

Furiously, Conan whipped back into his saddle and swept out his sword. He turned the horse, glaring at the stony slope as if by the very intensity of his blue-eyed stare he could melt the rocks that concealed his would-be assassin. His excitement communicated itself to Ymir, who danced and snorted. But nothing moved on the rocky incline before him.

He could force the horse down the short slope to the bottom of the valley and across the brook; but then he would have to dismount and climb the facing slope afoot. For a single man to charge uphill on foot, with neither shield nor armor, against a well-placed and competent archer, was equivalent to suicide. His own bow was back in its case in Yezud. For a few heartbeats he swept the rocks with his probing vision, but no sign of his attacker could he see.

At last he turned Ymir's head northward and spurred the animal toward his original destination. If he could not bring his assailant to book, he must quickly get out of range.

Hardly had the horse broken into a canter when the bow twanged again.

Again, Conan ducked; but this had no effect on the arrow, which buried itself with a meaty thump in Ymir's side. The horse gave a great bound and collapsed on the edge of the roadway, rolling off and down the slope.

As his stricken steed fell, Conan flung himself clear. With catlike agility he landed on his feet; but so steep was the slope that he, too, fell and rolled. Halfway down the slope he scrambled to his feet, snatched up the scimitar he had dropped, and covered the rest of the slope in two bounds. At the bottom he jumped across the gurgling run and pounded up the other side, leaping from rock to rock. As rage was replaced by calculation, his ascent became more deliberate, taking cover behind boulders and pinnacles, scanning the slope above him, and then making a quick dash to the shelter of the next prominence.

Soon he had climbed to a level higher than that from which he had started on the other side. He could now look down upon the domes and towers of the craglets that had concealed his assailant. But no sign of his attacker could he discern, even when he had climbed to the top of the valley.

At the top, he reached a small, grassy plateau, which ran horizontally for a bowshot before rising into further slopes and peaks of the rugged Karpash foothills. He walked about the flat, frowning. Presently he sighted something that made his breath quicken: the print of a horse's hoof in a patch of sandy soil. Casting about, he found more hoofprints and a stake driven into the ground. Evidently, someone had recently ridden up to this plateau, bringing the stake with him. At the top he had dismounted, driven the stake into the ground, and tethered his horse while he went about his business—probably trying to put an arrow through Conan. Failing to do so, he had returned to his mount, departing in too much haste to take the stake with him.

Conan cast about, like a hound on the scent, for a clue as to his murderer's direction. But the plateau's surface was either too grassy or too stony to hold the spoor of Conan's unknown foe.

At length Conan gave up and returned down the slope to where, across the little stream, his horse lay dead. He unfastened the saddle and bridle and grimly set out afoot, up the slope to the road and then north toward Yezud, with rope and saddle slung over one shoulder. As he plodded, he wondered how the assassin could have reached the top of the slope without Conan's seeing him, unless magic were involved.

This, Conan suspected, was indeed the explanation. It would not have been magic of the most fell and powerful kind, to strike Conan dead by force of a spell alone; rather it was the magic of a petty illusionist—a spell related to the hypnotic suggestions of the Vicar. For the actual killing, his attacker depended upon material weapons, using unnatural means only to keep himself hidden from Conan's sight.

———

Back in Yezud that evening, Conan's fury at the loss of his horse and his failure to exact payment from his attacker was mitigated by his pleasure in finding Rudabeh at her mother's house.

But Rudabeh did not look happy. "Step out into the garden, Nial," she said tensely. "I have tidings."

"Well?" asked Conan as he followed her into the cabbage patch.

"You know the Vicar, Harpagus? He has learned of our visit to Khesron."

"How so?"

"He called me in and told me that someone—he named no names, but spoke of his informant as 'she'—had carried tales to him."

"By Set!" growled Conan. "I'll wager it was that tavern slut, Mandana."

"Why should she do a thing like that? I have never harmed her."

"I think she's jealous of you, my girl; you know how women are. What does Harpagus intend?"

"He would have me yield to him that which I have denied to you. If I do not, he threatens to denounce me to Lord Feridun."

Conan's voice became the snarl of a hunting leopard. "One more score against the dog! If it wasn't he behind that attempt to murder me on the road today, I'm a Stygian!"

"What's this? Who tried to murder you?"

Briefly, Conan told the tale of his encounter on the road from Kharshoi. Rudabeh exclaimed:

"Oh, how sorry I am for the loss of your horse! But at least you survived, which is more important."

"Never mind that. What will Harpagus do if you resist?"

"It would mean death by the spider-god," said Rudabeh somberly, blanching in the ruddy light of the setting sun. "Or at least a flogging and reduction to the lowest rank in the temple service. As I see it, my choices are these: I can give in to Harpagus and, if it issues badly, end up in Zath's belly anyway. I can defy the Vicar, threatening to tell the High Priest of his lubricity. Or I can go forthwith to Feridun with my tale. But it were my word against the Vicar's, and I am sure his would prevail."

"You haven't mentioned a fourth choice: to run away with me," rumbled Conan.

She shook her head. "We have been all over that. I had almost as lief face Zath as plunge into the life you envision. And you, too, are caught in this cleft stick; for if Feridun thought you had debauched a temple virgin, your fate would be as mine."

"Debauched!" snorted Conan. "A pretty tame sort of debauchery! Your priests, like other rulers, are wont to lay down strict rules for their subjects but themselves to do as they please."

"The rules had fallen into abeyance under Feridun's predecessor, a glutton-

ous voluptuary; but Feridun is a man of such stern morality that the sight of
another enjoying life offends him. But about Harpagus—have you decided
whither your own future lies?"

She meant: Are you ready to become my prudent, unadventurous husband?
Conan clenched his fists and ground his teeth with the passions that were tearing him apart. Then he had a thought that might put off the fatal decision. He
said:

"Do you know of the Powder of Forgetfulness?"

"Nay. What is it?"

"A magical stuff; a witch of my acquaintance gave me some. Throw a pinch
into your enemy's face, she said, and it will make him forget all about you, as
if he had never heard of you. If you will step around to my chamber—" He
checked himself as she began to protest. "Nay, I understand; we cannot be seen
entering my place together. Wait here."

He soon returned with the pouch he had received from Nyssa. Handing it
over, he sighed: "I truly love you, girl; I could show you such loving as these
local clods never dreamed of."

"And what of me when you gallop off to new loves and wilder adventurers;
perchance leaving me with a fatherless child?"

Conan snorted. "You, mistress, should debate with philosophers in the temple courtyards and put them all to shame! I'm no match for you in argument."

"You have a keener mind than you think; you do but lack for schooling."

"I'm schooled in handling swords and bows and horses, not in polite arts
like literature."

"That can be remedied. Darius, the young priest, conducts a school for children, and he could teach you."

Conan growled: "Crom's devils, girl! Are you trying to make me over? I
won't have it!"

When they tired of argument, Conan escorted Rudabeh back to the temple
door. Seeing that the nighted streets were deserted, Conan seized her, crushed
her to him, and covered her with burning kisses. "Come with me!" he murmured in a voice thick with passion.

When he released her, she said gently: "I confess, Nial, that I could learn to
love you—but only if you would, as you say, permit me to 'make you over.'
That would mean giving up your wild ways to settle in Yezud as a proper
householder and husband."

Conan grunted. "I wouldn't even consider such a thing for any other
woman. But for you—I'll think on it."

At his smithy the following morning, Conan gave Lar the day off and began
work on a new project, which he preferred not to have the boy know about.

By afternoon he had a foot-long grapnel ending in three hooks. He was securing the grapnel to his new rope by threading the rope through the eye at the other end of the grapnel and making a splice, when a tense voice called: "Nial!"

A woman stood before the open front of the smithy; Conan recognized Rudabeh despite her heavy veiling. He dropped his work and threw open the door to his private room.

"Step in," he said. "We cannot talk here where everybody can see us. Fear not for your cursed virtue." When both were in the room, he closed the door. "Now what's happened?"

"There is such confusion at the temple that I knew none would miss me."

"Yes, yes; but what's up?"

"Your powder worked—if anything, too well. Harpagus came to my cubicle today, bolted the door, and began his advances by threats and wheedling intermixed. When he laid lustful hands upon me, I raised the pouch and threw the contents in his face."

"A pinch would have sufficed."

The girl shrugged. "Doubtless; but in the excitement I could not measure out the dose with such nicety. He sneezed and coughed and wiped his eyes; and when he had finished he gazed upon me blankly, with no more guile in his face than a babe's! Then he asked me who and where he was. Here's your empty pouch."

"Crom, the powder seems to have blasted his mind for fair! What then?"

"I pushed him out of the room, and he wandered off muttering. I heard that other priests found him thus and took him to the High Priest, who tried by his arcane arts to restore the Vicar's memory. But at last accounts he had not succeeded. I am truly grateful, dear Nial—"

Conan interrupted: "Then there's a favor you can do me in return—oh, not what you're thinking," he added as she shrank away, "although I hope we shall come to that, too. Right now I must know where the Turanian woman is kept captive."

"I must not reveal the temple's secrets—" began Rudabeh.

"Nonsense!" growled Conan. "Haven't you learned that priests are as avid for their own selfish pleasure as other men? The lady is but a pawn in Feridun's play for unlimited power, and I must learn where she abides. Besides, I'm not a stranger; I work for the temple just as you do. Now will you tell me, girl?"

"Well—ah—know you the second story at the north end of the temple?"

"Aye; from a distance I have seen windows high up all the way round the temple."

"The lady is in a chamber on that level, betwixt the northernmost of the west wings and the wing next to it."

"Like this?" Conan squatted on the floor and drew lines in the dust with his finger.

"Exactly! The wall runs from one wing to the other, enclosing a three-sided space below the chamber."

"What's behind that wall? A pleasure garden?"

"Nay; there Feridun keeps his pet Hyrkanian tiger, called Kirmizi. Therefore, when the priests wish to isolate a guest, they house him in that apartment."

Conan grunted. "A tiger, eh? A nice tame kitty?"

"Nay; he's a fierce creature, who can be governed only by the High Priest. Lord Feridun has magical powers over animals. It may be merely a coincidence, but when he and the priest Zariadris were competing for the post of High Priest, and Feridun was elected, Zariadris set out for Shadizar to protest to the King that the election had been fraudulent. He was dragged from his horse by wolves and devoured. Surely you do not plan—"

"Never mind what I plan," grunted Conan. "You'd better start for your mother's house; I'll join you there."

Late that night, the pale face of the full moon gazed down upon Conan of Cimmeria as he cautiously moved around the great wall of the temple. When he came to the section enclosing the area beneath Jamilah's chamber, he uncoiled the rope he carried and tossed the grapnel over the top of the wall. On his second try, the hooks caught.

It was but the work of a moment for the Cimmerian to clamber up the rope and balance himself on the top of the wall. He glanced down into the thoroughfare; but the streets of Yezud were deserted. With no alehouses or other places of public entertainment, most of the citizens retired early. The town watch had already made its nightly sweep of the streets, and had disbanded and gone home, while Catigern's Brythunians on night duty were posted around the city wall or else inside the temple. Yezud had so little crime that no massive precautions against it were deemed necessary.

Conan then studied the triangular area bounded by the wall and the adjacent wings of the temple. Trees and shrubs cast velvety shadows, black pools in the moonlight. Conan's keen vision roved the ground until it lighted upon a bulk lying stretched out beneath a tree.

As if sensing Conan's gaze upon it, the beast heaved itself to its feet and took a step toward the wall, which Conan straddled. From the tiger's throat issued a prolonged grunt—a sound like that of a saw cutting through a log.

An upward glance told Conan that the window of Jamilah's room was thrice man-height above the ground of Kirmizi's enclosure. As the tiger advanced, Conan wrenched his grapnel out of the masonry and leaped to the ground outside the wall. Coiling his rope again, he headed back toward the smithy.

chapter x

The Tiger's Fang

The following noon, Conan strode into Bartakes's Inn. Seated at a small table, Parvez was bent over a board game with Psamitek, the Stygian scholar. Save for two of Parvez's Turanian retainers and a trader from the South, the common room was otherwise deserted. As Conan approached, the diplomat and the scholar looked up.

"Greeting, friend Nial!" said Parvez. "You have been exercising your steed?"

"I would have been; but, two days since, some swine shot the poor beast dead under me. That's not what I came to tell you, though." He looked significantly at Psamitek.

"You must excuse us," said Parvez to the Stygian. "Let Chagor take my side of the game."

Psamitek rose, bowed, murmured an apology, and carried the game board away, holding it carefully level so that the pieces should not slide off. Presently he and Chagor had their heads close together over the board, scowling at the pieces and occasionally making a move.

Conan sat down on the vacant stool and in a low voice said: "I have found out about your captive princess." He told the Turanian of his cursory investigation of the night before.

"A tiger, eh?" mused the Turanian. "To one of your thews, slaying such a beast were not impossible."

"No, thank you!" growled Conan. "I once slew a lion under similar circumstance, in the grounds of a sorcerer who used such cats as watchdogs. But my success was more one of luck than of skill. I came closer to entering the land of the shades at that moment than in any of my brawls and battles."

"What, then, do you propose?" asked Parvez. "To seek the lady's chamber through the interior of the temple?"

"Not with the corridors crawling with guards, as they are day and night.

Have you some magical means to slay this tiger, or at least cast it into a deep slumber?"

"Alas, no! I do not traffic in magic, save for that silver arrow you extorted from me. Now that I think, I do have a means for immobilizing Feridun's striped pet." He fumbled in his scrip and brought out a phial containing a greenish liquid. "An accessory of my trade; three drops of this in a man's drink will waft him to dreamland for hours. But I know not how we shall persuade the tiger to consume the stuff—"

"That's easy," said Conan. "Wait here."

He pushed through the door of the kitchen, where he found Bartakes laboring over provisions for the evening's cookery. When the innkeeper looked up, Conan asked: "Mine host, have you a stout roast of beef, uncooked, that you will sell?"

"What—ah—what in the nine hells do you want with—" began Bartakes, but under Conan's baleful glare he changed his tune. "Well, yes I have. It will cost—"

"The lord Parvez will pay," said Conan, jerking his thumb toward the door to the common room. "Fetch it; he and I are planning a surprise party for a friend."

Bartakes disappeared and shortly returned bearing a platter, on which reposed a haunch of beef large enough to feed a score of warriors. He set it on a vacant table and went out to collect the price from Parvez.

Drawing his scimitar, Conan made a series of cuts into the beef, as deep as the width of his blade. Then he sprinkled the contents of the phial into the cuts. While he was doing this, Bartakes returned.

"What is that?" asked the taverner. "Some kind of seasoning?"

"Aye; a rare condiment from a far land. Now, have you some sacking in which to wrap this thing?"

When the beef had been packaged; Conan returned to the common room with the bundle on his shoulder, pausing at Parvez's table. The diplomat whispered: "When do you plan your attempt?"

"Tonight. We have no time to dawdle; the priests are suspicious of me already. Have you something I can show the lady, to prove I am not merely one more abductor?"

"Take this," said Parvez, pulling off a seal ring and handing it to Conan. "It will identify you."

Conan slipped the ring over his little finger and, carrying the raw beef swathed in sacking over his shoulder, marched out.

The moon, barely past full, thrust its silvern beams through rents in the cloud-crowded sky. It had not yet reached the meridian when Conan, moving quietly down the deserted street, reached the wall that bounded Kirmizi's domain. Halting, he grasped the raw meat with both hands and, whirling it twice about, with a mighty heave sent it soaring across the barrier. It landed inside with a moist thump. Instantly came the grunt of an aroused tiger, and then rending and slobbering sounds told of the beast's enjoyment of the unexpected meal.

Conan squatted in the angle of the wall that furnished the deepest shadow against the light of the fickle moon. With the patience of a hunter in the wild, there he remained, immobile and scarcely breathing, while the moon pursued her cloud-enshrouded path toward the western horizon.

When Conan's ears at last picked up the wheezy sounds of a colossal yawn, he took off his boots and hitched his baldric around so that his sword hung down between his massive shoulders. Pausing no longer, he uncoiled his rope, flung the grapnel over the wall, and swarmed up to the top.

For a moment he could make out nothing in the night-drenched darkness below, for a large, dense cloud had cast the temple and its environs into shadow. When the moon peeped through again, she showed the tiger stretched out peacefully, head on paws and eyes closed. Glancing up at the broken sky, Conan was unpleasantly reminded of the night he had scaled the wall to Nar-kia's apartment. He wondered if there were some omen in this celestial aspect.

At last he whistled softly, then waited. When the beast still did not stir, Conan loosened his grapnel, lowered himself down the inner side of the wall until he hung by his huge hands, then dropped the remaining distance. Kirmizi slumbered on.

Warily, Conan surveyed the occupant of the pen. The tiger lay motionless save for the slow rise and fall of its ribs. While Conan could clearly discern its black stripes, the orange-red of its fur was faded to tarnished silver by the uncertain moonlight.

Beyond the sleeping cat rose the narrow expanse of masonry that separated the inner ends of the two adjacent wings of the temple. An iron gate, set in this wall at ground level, permitted entry and egress for him who tended to the tiger's needs; while, directly above this gate, the window of Jamilah's cham-ber, the shutters of which were open to the warm summer breezes, formed a black rectangular patch in the dimly reflective marble of the temple wall. No lights were to be seen.

A gliding shadow, Conan stole past the sleeping tiger to the apex of the enclosure. Again he uncoiled his rope and, whirling the trefoil grapnel round and round, sent it flying toward the dark aperture above. At the first throw, the grapnel struck the wall with a metallic clank, loud in the stillness, and fell back to earth. A second throw accomplished no more.

As he coiled the rope for another try, Conan cursed himself for not having practiced this maneuver before attempting it in earnest. A third throw sent the grapnel into the window, but the hooks failed to catch when Conan pulled on the free end. His fourth attempt succeeded.

Conan hoisted himself up, hand over hand, while the bulging muscles of his arms writhed like pythons. He clambered over the sill and landed on the uncarpeted floor with a faint slap of bare feet.

The vagrant moon shot a narrow beam of silver slantwise through the window, where it cast an oblong of argent upon the silken hangings of the chamber. The faint illumination outlined a bedstead on which lay a slender form. The night being warm, the sleeper had thrown back the coverlet, disclosing to the Cimmerian's probing gaze the graceful body of a woman, whose dark hair fell loosely across her opalescent shoulders and parted to reveal the pale moons of her splendid breasts.

Conan glided to the bed and whispered: "Lady Jamilah!"

The woman slept on. Conan grasped the curve of her soft shoulder and gently shook her, whereupon Jamilah's eyes slowly opened. Then her eyelids fluttered, and her lips parted with a sharp intake of breath. Conan clapped a broad hand over her mouth to smother her scream; all that emerged was a faint gurgle.

"Hush, lady!" he hissed. "I'm here to rescue you!"

He raised his hand from the pale oval of her face, holding it close enough to clap it down again.

"Who—who are you?" she whispered at last.

"Call me Nial," growled Conan. "King Yildiz's ambassador, Lord Parvez, has sent me to get you out of here. He waits nearby."

"How know I that you speak true?"

Conan pulled off the seal ring and thrust it at her. "He gave me this to show you. It's too dark to see the design on the seal, but you can feel it with your thumb."

She fondled the ring. "How did you enter here?"

"Through the window."

"But the tiger?"

"Kirmizi sleeps with a drug in his belly. Come! You'll have to trust me, unless you'd liefer remain a prisoner here."

Suddenly conscious of her nudity, Jamilah reached for the coverlet. "I cannot rise, with you staring down at me! Turn your back at least."

"Women!" grunted Conan disgustedly. "With our lives hanging on one thread, this is no time for your civilized niceties." But he went to the window and stared out, listening alertly lest Jamilah, moved by doubts about the truth of his tale, attempt to stab him in the back. There he heard nothing but the rustle of rich attire hastily donned. At last Jamilah murmured:

"You may turn, Master Nial. What would you now?"

Conan hauled in his rope; and when it was neatly coiled upon the chamber floor, he tied a loop in the free end and lowered this oval an arm's length down the wall outside.

"Wait," he said. "Have you a proper cloak, besides those frilly garments? If you're seen in the street . . ."

"I understand." She went to a chest and brought out a black velvet cloak with a hood. She handed the bundle to Conan, who tossed it out the window, taking care that it should not strike the sleeping tiger.

"Come here," he said. "Sit on the casement sill, and I'll support you while you place your feet in the loop. Do not look down, but hold my arm while you feel for the rope. There! Now grasp the rope with both hands."

"The rough rope pricks my fingers," complained Jamilah as she lowered herself into position. "And heights do terrify me."

"That cannot be helped, lady. Steady, now; here we go!"

Hand over hand, Conan paid out the rope until the princess reached the ground. Then he examined the hook of the grapnel, which was firmly embedded in the wood of the windowsill. If he lowered himself by the way he had come up, Conan realized that he would be unable to dislodge the rope by jerking it from below, and he needed the rope to get himself and Jamilah over the outer wall of the enclosure.

At last he pulled the entire rope back into the chamber, wrenched the hook out of the sill, and dragged the massive bed across the floor to the window. He passed one end of the rope around the nearest bedpost and hauled briskly until the bight of the rope was at the center of its length.

Dropping the two free ends over the windowsill and firmly gripping the two strands together, he lowered himself over the sill and rappelled down until he hung just above the ground. Then he released the looped end and dropped, as lithely as a pouncing panther, to the ground, and pulled on the grapnel end of the rope until the entire rope tumbled down upon him.

He found a terrified Jamilah pressed back against the wall, gazing wide-eyed at the tiger, whose heavy odor filled his nostrils. Hastily coiling the rope and picking up the woman's cloak, Conan threw a protective arm around the fear-frozen woman and, shadow-silent on the greensward, walked her past the slumbering Kirmizi.

At the outer wall, Conan whirled his grapnel once again and again caught it in the masonry. As he prepared to ascend, a sudden intake of Jamilah's breath warned him of impending danger. Whirling, he saw the tiger rise on unsteady paws and stalk toward him. Evidently the soporific dose had not been adequate, even though he had emptied Parvez's flask into the cloven meat.

Conan swept out his scimitar as the beast, with a rumbling snarl, broke into a lope and, like a coiled spring released, leaped straight at him, its great jaws open and slavering. As the giant cat, fangs bared and talons unsheathed, hurtled toward him, Conan whipped his scimitar up over his head and, with legs braced and both powerful hands gripping the hilt, brought the heavy curved blade whistling down between the glowing emerald eyes. The tiger's body slammed into him and hurled him back against the wall, so that man and tiger fell in a tangled heap at the foot of the enclosure.

As Conan's body disappeared beneath the striped form, Jamilah stifled a little shriek, clapping a jeweled hand over her mouth. "Are you dead, Nial?" she breathed.

"Not quite," grumbled Conan, crawling out from under the limp carcass like an insect emerging from under a stone. Rising, he looked down upon the animal, which lay prone with Conan's scimitar still fixed in its cloven skull. With one bare foot planted on the tiger's head, Conan tugged with all his might to wrench the weapon free.

"Damn!" he muttered. "I swore that never again would I be caught in such a fix; so much for mortal plans. At least this good Kothian steel survived the blow."

"Are you hurt?" inquired Jamilah, her low-pitched voice vibrant with concern.

"I think no bones are broken, albeit I have scratches and bruises aplenty. I feel like a man who has run the gauntlet between lines of foes with clubs."

He wiped his sword on the tiger's fur and sheathed it. Then, climbing the rope to the top of the wall, he sat astride it to haul the princess up and lower her down the other side. At last he released the rope from its attachment in the masonry and dropped down himself. He pulled on his boots, saying:

"Put on the cloak, and pull the hood well down. There will be guards at the city gate, so you'll have to play the part of my sweetheart—one of the village girls from Khesron. Do you understand?"

"I trust, Master Nial," she said, "that you do not plan some improper liberty. After all, I am of royal rank."

"Fear not; but you'll have to forget your royal rank if you want to get away from Yezud!"

"But—"

"But me no buts, lady! Your choice is between staying here and doing what I tell you. Make up your mind."

"Oh, very well," she said. Limping from his bruises, Conan hustled the noblewoman away.

As they passed another of the walls connecting the end of adjacent wings of the temple, Conan suddenly halted, also stopping Jamilah.

"What is it?" she whispered.

"Listen!" He put his ear against the stone, motioning her to silence.

From the enclosure on the other side of this wall came two voices in grave discussion. Conan picked out the deep, bell-like tones of High Priest Feridun; the other voice he could not identify but assumed to be that of a lesser priest. The High Priest said:

". . . fear me the Children will not have reached their full growth for several months."

"But, Holiness!" said the other voice. "We cannot continue to put off the King with bootless threats. He thinks we do but try to frighten him with imaginary bogles."

"But my dear Mirzes, it is not we but he who is bluffing. Well he knows that let his raggle-taggle army but sight one of the Children of Zath, they will dissolve in panic flight. We have the most terrible weapon since the invention of the sword."

"How shall we convince him?"

"Another embassy will soon arrive. If all else fails, I shall take Mithridates's envoy below and show him."

"Suppose he still rejects our just demands?"

"Then we shall set the Great Plan in motion. Even if not fully grown, the Children will perform their duty."

"Zath grant that all work as planned, master," murmured the priest Mirzes.

"Fear not," replied Feridun's tolling voice. "I can govern the Children, as I can beasts of all kinds. As my new Vicar, you must trust me to know best. . . ."

The voices faded away, as if the speakers were withdrawing into the temple. Conan motioned to Jamilah to resume their progress. But the delicate, high-born Turanian woman found it hard to keep up with Conan's lengthy stride, and her thin slippers slipped on the rounded cobblestones.

"Here, let me carry you!" muttered Conan. When she uttered some faint protest, he swept her off her feet and pounded toward the city gate.

Soon afterward, as the moon hung low over the Karpashes, Conan astonished the Brythunians at the front gate by appearing, carrying the cloak-wrapped form of a woman. He set her on her feet but kept one brawny arm around her waist. He whispered in her ear:

"Now play your part, damn it; but don't speak! They'd catch your accent."

"Nial the lady-killer, at it again!" smirked one of the guards.

"Keep it quiet, lads," said Conan. "I'm taking her home; but her people are narrow-minded."

He tightened his grip on Jamilah's waist with a little jerk. She forced a giggle and leaned her head on Conan's shoulder. At a ribald remark from the other guard about what she and Conan had been doing, he felt her stiffen with indignation. But then they were through the small door and moving swiftly down the long incline to the bottom of the crag.

———

A thunderous knocking on the front door of his inn aroused Bartakes. He dragged himself out of bed to shout imprecations down from his bedroom window, adding: "Any fool can see we are closed for the night!"

Conan roared back: "I don't want you; I want Lord Parvez. Rouse him, unless you wish me to tear down your pigsty board by board! Tell him there's a noble traveler here."

Moments later, the yawning Turanian appeared at the door, clutching his flowered night-robe about him.

"Here she is," said Conan's rough voice, "sound but weary."

Parvez dropped to one knee. "My lady Jamilah!" he exclaimed. "Come in at once!" A tear glistened on his cheek in the moonlight, so strong was his emotion. Rising, he said to Conan: "You have done the miraculous, young man. May I have my seal ring back, pray?"

"Oh, I forgot about it," said Conan, slipping off the ring and handing it over.

"And one more thing. Have you seen my servant Chagor?"

"No, I have not. What of him?"

"The fellow has vanished, with his horse. No explanation. Ah, well; I must now bid you a hasty farewell, for it would not do to be here when the priests discover their captive has been enlarged. Bartakes, be so good as to rouse my retainers; we must be on the road ere dawn."

"Permit me to thank you, Master Nial," said Jamilah. "If ever you come to Turan, feel free to ask a boon of me, and if possible I will persuade the King to grant it. Farewell!" She disappeared into the inn.

Back at his quarters, Conan caught a little sleep and was lustily banging away at his anvil next morning when a party of four priests and two Brythunian soldiers appeared before his smithy. A priest in a scarlet turban and a dark-blue robe stepped into the smithy and, raising his voice above the clang of the hammer, said in a sharp, abrupt manner:

"You are Nial the blacksmith, are you not? A lady has been abducted. Hast seen such a person?"

"What sort of lady?" growled Conan, keeping his eyes on his workpiece. After a few more blows he returned it to the furnace and turned to face his questioner.

"Tall, black-haired, and fair to see," said the priest, "albeit past her thirtieth year."

Conan shook his head. "I know naught of such a woman."

"Moreover, Ambassador Parvez and his Turanians hastily departed from Khesron last night. What know you of that?"

"Again, naught. I knew the man; we sometimes drank together of an evening."

"What did you and he talk about?"

"Horses and swords and such things."

"Someone," persisted the priest in a hectoring tone, "slew the High Priest's tiger with a single mighty blow of a sword or axe. Who but you has the thews for such a blow?"

Conan shrugged. "Many Brythunians are large, strong men. To you Zamorians, anyone else looks like a mountain of muscle. As for me, this is the first I have heard of it."

"All barbarians are liars!" sneered the priest. "Fear not, we will get to the bottom of this, and you had better be ready to prove your innocence." He took a step forward and thrust his face close to Conan's.

Conan picked his workpiece out of the furnace with tongs and held the ruddily glowing iron before him. "Be careful around a forge, friend priest. If you get too close, this may set your whiskers afire." When the priest hastily backed away, Conan laid the piece on the anvil and resumed his pounding.

The priest turned and rejoined his group, who marched away. Lar, who had watched the exchange big-eyed, said: "Oh, Master Nial, you all but defied the priests of Zath! They can call upon divine powers to blast you, if you use them with insolence!"

"What's the name of the one who questioned me just now?" growled Conan.

"That is the holy father Mirzes."

"I thought I knew the voice," mused Conan. "He's the new Vicar, I hear. Come on, lad; put some thews into working the bellows! Your fire is barely hot enough to boil water."

chapter xi

The Stench of Carrion

For several days Conan did not see Rudabeh, save when she danced during a service to Zath. He entered the temple early, so as to stand in the front row, whence he had the best view of the spider-idol. Since this was a fair day and sunlight came through the clerestory windows above, Conan could clearly make out the four Eyes across the front of the creature, even at a distance of twenty cubits.

The barbarian's keen vision caught sight of a thin ring around each Eye, lighter in color than the black stone of the statue. This, Conan reasoned, must be a ring of metal or cement let into the stone to hold the gem in place. To remove the Eyes he would have to dislodge these retaining rings, and do so very gently, so as not to crack the jewels. Conan had a good working knowledge of gems from his days as a thief, and he knew the fragility of opals.

Meanwhile his passion for Rudabeh, instead of subsiding, tormented him more and more. When Amytis told him that she expected her daughter home for supper, he impatiently awaited her in the garden, brooding.

On one hand, a fierce desire, like a tornado whirling along its serpentine path of destruction, surged up within him, to give up his rootless, adventurous life, to wed Rudabeh according to the laws of Zamora, and to become, as best he might, a solid citizen who cherished his growing family, joined the municipal watch, worshiped at the temple, and paid his tithes.

Yet, on the other hand, Conan's wild, free, undisciplined spirit recoiled from this tableau as from a venomous serpent. But his other choice was to forget the girl and flee instanter, with the Eyes of Zath if he could obtain them, without them if he could not. If Feridun loosed his promised devastation upon the land, he might have to flee anyway, with or without Rudabeh.

When she appeared, he held out his arms. She shook her head, saying: "Do not torment me, Nial. I do truly love you, but you know under what conditions I would give myself to you."

"But, my girl—" began Conan.

She held up a hand saying: "I have news of moment. You've heard of the disappearance of the princess Jamilah?"

"Aye; some such gossip has smitten my ears."

"The High Priest is furious, as you might expect. Some of the priests suspect you of complicity."

"Who, me?" said Conan with an air of injured innocence. "What have I to do with a Turanian noblewoman?"

"They know you were thick with that diplomat at Bartakes's Inn, who vanished the same night as Jamilah. You would have been seized already, but that Feridun insists he have solid evidence against you ere he acts. I must say the old man tries to live up to his principles.

"Furthermore," continued Rudabeh, "if gossip be true, the High Priest has advanced the date of his revolution. He held Jamilah as a hostage for the good conduct of the King of Turan. Now he must needs move quickly ere the Turanians learn of the princess's escape. So he has warned all the temple folk to hold themselves ready seven days hence. When the alarm gong sounds, we must all go to our quarters and bolt ourselves in."

Conan grunted as he digested this information. He must, he thought, get rid of that telltale coil of rope before some snooping priest stumbled upon it.

Amytis called, and they went in for supper. Afterward, Conan escorted Rudabeh back to the temple and took his way to Khesron. He would have to plan his raid on the temple quickly, and he thought he could map his campaign best sitting alone with a stoup of wine before him.

"Hail, Nial!" At the inn, Catigern's booming voice jogged Conan's elbow. "How about a game?" The Brythunian rattled a pair of dice in his fist.

"I thank you, but not tonight," said Conan. "I need to be alone."

Catigern shrugged and went off to seek other companionship. Conan resumed his broodings. Several jacks of wine later, another voice, with a slight lisp and a guttural accent, invaded his musings. It was Psamitek the Stygian.

"Master Nial," said the slim, swarthy scholar. "Someone wishes to see you beyond the inn."

"Well," growled Conan ungraciously, "tell that someone to come in. He can see me better here in the light."

The scholar smiled a crooked little smile. "It is a lady," he murmured. "It would not be proper for her to enter a vulgar barrelhouse like this."

"Lady?" grunted Conan. "What the devil . . ." He rose, wondering if Jamilah, for some unaccountable reason, had returned to Khesron; but no, that would be insane. He followed Psamitek out.

In the courtyard of Bartakes's Inn, illuminated by the bitumen lamp over the front door and the light of the gibbous moon, stood Rudabeh. Conan gasped as he viewed her; for, instead of the modest street garb she normally wore outside the temple, she was clad in her dancing costume of a few strings of beads and nothing else.

"Conan, darling!" she said in a low, thrilling voice. "You were right and I was wrong. Come, and I will show you that I am as much a woman as you are a man. I know a place where the grass is thick and soft."

She turned and walked deliberately out of the courtyard, while Conan followed like a man in a daze. In the back of his mind, reason tried to warn him that all was not as it seemed; but the warning was swept aside by his rising tide of passion. His blood roared in his ears.

Rudabeh led Conan past a few hovels and out of the village. Her well-rounded form swayed seductively as she walked. Away from the houses of Khesron, the stony ground sloped up, and Conan became impatient to reach the promised meadow.

The ground leveled again, and Rudabeh turned to face Conan. She held out welcoming arms—and in that instant she disappeared. In her place stood Chagor the Turanian, Parvez's vanished retainer, whom Conan had bathed in the horse trough. Chagor held a thick, double-curved Hyrkanian compound bow, with an arrow drawn to the head.

"Ha!" cried the Turanian. "Now you see!" And he released his shaft with the same sharp, flat twang that Conan had heard when he lost his horse. At that range it was impossible to miss.

But as Chagor let fly his shaft, something flew from behind Conan and struck the Turanian with a thump in the chest. As a result, the arrow whistled past Conan's ear.

Before Chagor could whip another shaft from his quiver, Conan swept out his scimitar and charged with the roar of an angry lion. The Turanian dropped his bow and likewise drew, just in time to meet Conan's rush.

Steel clanged and scraped in the moonlight. Behind him, Conan heard sounds of struggle but had no leisure to investigate. The Turanian was a strong swordsman, and Conan found his hands full. Slash backhand—parry—a forehand cut—parry—feint—parry . . . The dancing blades clashed, ground, and twirled to the accompaniment of the stamp of booted feet, heavy breathing, and muttered curses.

The curses were Chagor's, for Conan fought in grim silence. Chagor gasped. "I show you, dog. . . . Your head go to priest of Erlik. . . . Then me rich, you dead. . . ."

Once Chagor was a fraction slow in bringing his blade to a proper parry. Conan's heavier sword sliced into his forearm. Uttering a yell of dismay, Chagor dropped his scimitar. With a catlike leap, Conan sprang forward and, with the power born of frenzy, swung his sword in a wide horizontal arc. The blade sheared through the Turanian's thick neck; his head flew off, to land like a thrown melon in a nearby clump of shrubbery. The body, spouting a fountain of blood, black in the moonlight, tumbled to earth like a felled tree.

At the continuing sounds of struggle behind him, Conan whirled and perceived a tangle of limbs, which resolved itself into Captain Catigern struggling on the ground with Psamitek the Stygian.

Conan seized one of the Stygian's arms with his free hand and twisted. Between him and Catigern, they subdued the scholar, who sat up with his arms gripped behind him and Catigern's dagger pricking his throat.

"How came you to help me so timely?" asked Conan.

"I saw you follow this dog out," explained Catigern, "after you said you wished to be alone; so I became suspicious. I never trusted this Stygian dung; and the next thing I saw was you following Chagor up the hill, bleating endearments, while Psamitek followed you, mumbling some spell. Since this did not sound like you, Nial, I followed Psamitek. When the Turanian drew an arrow on you, I cast a stone to spoil his aim and went for the Stygian. Have a care with this devil; he's stronger than he looks. He bit me."

"All right, Psamitek," said Conan. "Explain this business. There's a small chance that, if we like your explanation, we'll let you live."

"You heard Chagor," said Psamitek. "He overheard Ambassador Parvez address you as 'Conan,' and I knew about Tughril's offer for Conan's head. So we put *our* heads together and arranged that he should desert Parvez's escort, and we should divide the reward betwixt us. Even your limited minds could grasp this simple scheme. . . ."

Psamitek's hypnotic voice so absorbed the attention of Conan and Catigern that they relaxed their grip upon him. Instantly the Stygian, lithe as an eel, squirmed out of their grasp and sprang to his feet. Conan leaped up, swinging his scimitar in a blow that would have cut the slender Stygian in two.

But the blade only swished through empty air. Psamitek had vanished like a blown-out candle flame.

"Come back here!" roared Conan, rushing this way and that with his blade bared and crashing through thorny bushes. The only reply was a peal of cynical, mocking laughter.

"You have your tricks, Conan," said the lisping voice, "but I have mine also, as you shall yet see. Farewell, barbarian lout!"

Conan dashed toward the voice, his sword cleaving the air; but he found nothing. Catigern said: "Save your breath, Nial. The fellow is evidently an expert caster of illusions, and he has made himself invisible. What's this about your being Conan, with a price on your head?"

"You should know better than to ask a fellow mercenary about his past," growled Conan.

"True; forget what I said. We had better drag the Turanian's remains back to the village. The priests will want another report."

"Why not leave him for the hyenas?"

"His ghost would haunt us."

"Oh, very well," said Conan, grasping one ankle of the corpse and dragging it. "You can carry the head, though I'd rather send it as a gift to Tughril. And thanks for saving my life."

As the Festival of All Gods approached, the temple of Zath hummed with activity. Rudabeh's time was taken up with her duties, so Conan had no more personal meetings with her. Bartakes's Inn filled up with the retinues of priestly parties from far parts of Zamora, and latecomers were obliged to rent space in the cramped houses of the villagers or pitch tents in the surrounding fields.

The festival began three days after the slaying of Chagor. Delegations from opulent sanctuaries and lowly shrines of the various Zamorian gods paraded up the broad steps of the temple with pomp and ceremony. Catigern's Brythunians, their polished mail flashing in the sun, stood facing one another in two lines at opposite ends of the temple steps. As each pontiff, in glittering robe and jewel-bedight headdress, marched slowly up the stairs, the soldiers raised their pikes and halberds in salute, then grounded their weapons with a thunderous crash. The priesthoods of the different deities were riven by venomous rivalries, Conan knew, and ceaselessly intrigued to damage one another. But for today each legate beamed upon his fellow clerics and bowed benignly to the assembled priests of Zath.

During the procession of the priests, Conan stood in an inconspicuous corner of the square that fronted on the temple. But after the entrance of the last delegation, when the folk of Yezud and the spellbound pilgrims streamed in to honor the assembled gods of the Zamorian pantheon, Conan mingled with the motley crowd. In the vestibule he thought of slipping away for another attempt to explore the corridors; but this was impossible with a Brythunian firmly planted in front of the entrance to each hallway. So Conan resigned himself to standing through one more endless suite of rituals.

He took a place at the rear of the naos and stood through three hours of ceremony, in which the high priests of the other gods took turns invoking their deities and begging them for favors. Conan ignored their pronouncements but admired the glitter of their bejeweled regalia. If he could only strip a few of these pontiffs of their robes and miters, he thought, the jewels in them would ease his life for years, even though their value would be but a fraction of that of the Eyes of Zath.

Two days later, shafts of rain, hurled from a leaden sky, flogged the worn cobblestones of Yezud as the Festival of All Gods ended. The visiting priests, wrapped in voluminious hooded cloaks against the rain, bid ceremonious farewells to Feridun and his new Vicar on the steps of the temple before turning away to take their places in carriages and horse litters or to mount horses, mules, and camels.

That night, while rain still fell, a giant figure in a dark cloak slipped through the streets of Yezud on noiseless moccasins. At the southernmost wing on the east side of the temple of Zath, Conan fumbled for the silver arrow he had received from Parvez. Touching the lock with the point, he murmured: *"Ka-pinin achilir genishi!"*

A faint, rusty squeal, as if someone within were turning a key in the long-disused lock, made itself heard above the patter of rain. Conan pushed the door, but it failed to open.

Angrily, Conan threw his great weight against the door, striking it with his massive shoulder. Still it did not yield. Then he paused to think.

Perhaps the priests, not trusting in an ordinary lock alone, also warded the door with an inside bolt, like that outside the portal on the other side of the temple, into which the sheep had been driven. Pointing the silver arrow at various heights, Conan repeated *kapinin achilir genishi* several times. At last he was rewarded by the muffled clank of a bolt's being thrown back. At his next push, the door opened.

The hall inside was dark, save for a rectangle of dim light thirty cubits away, where this passage joined the main circumferential corridor. Conan paused to listen; the temple was as silent as a Stygian tomb. The temple people from High Priest to slaves must be sleeping a sleep of exhaustion after the last three days' activities.

Conan stole down the hall, alert for a sign of the Brythunian guards. Cautiously he peeked around corners at the end, but no guards did he see in the main corridor in either direction. As he had hoped, the guards were taking advantage of their employers' fatigue to cluster somewhere, perhaps in the vestibule, for gaming and talk, rather than spend the night in lonely patrolling of the silent hallways.

The corridor into which Conan emerged was lit by a single bitumen lamp in a wall bracket. He turned right and, continuing his strides, walked to a door on the left. If his estimates of distance had been correct, this should be one of the side entrances to the naos.

Again he applied the Clavis of Gazrik to the door and whispered the incantation; again the lock unlocked itself, with no sound except a well-oiled click. When he opened the door, though, he recoiled. Instead of the naos, he found himself surveying a small bedchamber occupied by two narrow bunks, on which lay a pair of acolytes, one snoring. Conan softly closed the door and stole away.

The next door proved to be the one he sought. He slipped into the naos and hurried across the floor of the sanctum, fitfully illuminated by the flickering orange light of the eternal flame. He stopped at the black stone statue of Zath.

Again he was struck by the lifelike aspect of the carving. The work was a perfect replica of a giant arachnid, save that the sculptor, unable to reproduce in stone the hairs along the legs, had indicated them by cross-hatching.

Conan stripped off his cloak and dropped it. Beneath it he wore his blacksmith's apron, with pockets and loops holding the tools of his trade. He pulled out his blacksmith's hammer and, holding his breath for instant flight, gingerly tapped the nearest leg. The sound was reassuringly like that of honest stone; the statue showed no sign of animation.

Conan moved closer to reach the front of the creature's body. The four forward Eyes gleamed in the wavering light of the eternal flame, so that a six-rayed crimson star seemed to dance in the blue-green mistiness of each Eye.

Conan saw that he would need a stronger light than that of the burning bitumen to operate on the Eyes. Reaching under his apron, he brought out a stick of wood, a cubit in length, one end of which was wrapped in an oil-soaked rag. Moving to the luminous bowl that sheltered the eternal fire, he held the unguent-coated cloth on the end of his torch above the lambent flame until the oil caught fire and blazed up.

Conan returned to the statue and wedged his torch into the angle between two of Zath's eight legs, so that it cast a wavering yellow light upon the Eyes on that side. He leaned forward to examine the Eyes, running his fingers over their smooth, spherical surfaces and feeling the retaining rings that held them in place. The Eyes were girasols as large as a small boy's fist. The retaining rings were of lead. This, thought Conan, should make his task easy.

From a pocket of his apron he brought out a handful of drills and stylets. Among these he chose a flat drill with a narrow chisel point. Setting the point into the crack between one of the retaining rings and the surrounding stone, he gave a gentle tap with his hammer, then another. He rejoiced to see that the tool had sunk visibly into the lead; a few more taps and he should be able to pry the ring out.

Sounds from without snatched Conan's attention away from the statue. Voices murmured, feet tramped, doors opened and shut. Amid the sounds, Conan thought he detected the clank of the Brythunians' arms. Now what in the nine hells was arousing the temple at this hour?

Then a key clicked in the side door facing that through which he had come. Before he could retreat, the door swung open.

Snatching his tools away from the statue, Conan whirled, lips drawn back in a voiceless snarl. When he saw Rudabeh in the doorway, he growled: "What are you doing here, girl?"

At that instant the dancer, eyes dilated with apprehension, also spoke: "What do you here, Nial?"

Conan answered with feigned carelessness: "The priests told me to fix a loose fitting on the offering chest."

"At this time of night? Which priest?" The girl's voice was sharp with tension.

Conan shrugged. "I don't remember."

"I do not believe you."

"And why not, pray?" said Conan with an air of offended innocence.

"Because such orders would have come only through me as Mistress of the Properties. You came here to steal. That is sacrilege."

"Now Rudabeh dear, you know what fakers and lechers these priests are—"

"But Zath is still a god, whatever the shortcomings of his—but Nial darling, whatever you came for, you must get you hence at once! The priests from Arenjun have just arrived. They were held up by a storm, which washed out the roads, and so missed the Festival of All Gods. Now Lord Feridun is showing them round the temple; they will soon be here. The new Vicar, Mirzes, sent me hither to see that the reservoir of the eternal flame was full, since we haven't had time to fill it lately."

To confirm her words, the sound of many men moving and talking outside the huge front doors of the naos smote Conan's ears.

"Go quickly!" cried Rudabeh, "or you will be lost!"

"I'm going," growled Conan. Instead of heading for a door, he gathered his tools and torch and ran to the far left corner of the sacred enclosure, where the oil pipe jutted out from the wall. Directly beneath it lay a large trapdoor.

As Conan stooped and shot back the bolt that held down the trapdoor, Rudabeh gave a cry of consternation. "What are you doing?"

"Going below," grunted Conan as he grasped the handle and raised the trapdoor. An overpowering stench of carrion wafted up out of the square black opening.

"Do not go there!" cried Rudabeh in anguished tones, her voice rising with terror. "You know not what you—oh, gods, here come the priests!"

The handles of the great bronze front doors clanked, and the doors themselves began to creak open, as a confabulation of voices reached the chamber from the vestibule. With a rush of feet and a slam of the side door, Rudabeh dashed out of the naos; Conan, glaring about like a hunted animal, bounded down the stair that descended from the temple floor into the reeking darkness below. He dropped the trapdoor into place over his head, leaving himself in darkness save for the flickering orange light of the small torch.

The massive doors groaned open, and the swell of conversation rolled across the marble floor and through the thin planking of the trapdoor. Conan caught the deep, bell-like tones of High Priest Feridun, but he could not distinguish words through the babble. At least the murmur of conversation, bland and unctuous, betrayed no excitement, which it surely would have if any of those entering had caught sight of Rudabeh or himself.

Cautiously, Conan felt his way down the stone stair, peering ahead as far as the torch could throw its feeble beams. He found himself in a spacious passage, higher than his head and wider than his outstretched arms. No sound save the hiss of the flaring torch, so faint as to be barely audible even to his keen ears, dispelled the sepulchral silence. The smell of carrion roweled his nostrils.

As Conan prowled along the rock-hewn floor of the passage, he stumbled over a large object of irregular shape. It proved to be the skull of a bovine—or rather such a skull to which scraps of flesh still adhered. Conan kicked this noisome bit of carrion aside and plodded on, stepping over more fragments of kine—legs, ribs, and other parts. Although no stranger to the stink of corpses and cadavers, the soft squilch of a patch of rotting entrails, on which he stepped, so revolted him that for an instant he almost vomited, and fought down a panicky urge to run screaming.

Coming to a cross tunnel, Conan turned left and walked a few steps along that corridor, which sloped sharply up. He was, he reckoned, still beneath the temple. At the top of the slope, he thought, he would find the door on the west side, through which he had seen the flock of sheep driven.

He went back to the crossing and took the branch that ran straight from the steps down which he had come. This passage, he found, sloped down. Conan continued for some moments, spurning desiccated animal fragments with his moccasins. When the tunnel turned this way and that and sent out branches, so that Conan feared getting lost in the maze, he retraced his steps to the first crossing.

Then he tried the remaining passage, which had been the right-hand branch when he first reached the intersection. The corridor ran straight for a bowshot, then wavered and sent out side passages as the downward-sloping tunnel had done.

Conan began to worry about his torch. It would not last much longer, and to be lost in this catacomb in utter darkness might prove fatal. He had a spare torch thrust through his belt under the apron; but, if he let the first torch die completely before lighting the second from it, he would have the devil's own time igniting the other with flint and steel in darkness. On the other hand, if he lit the second torch sooner than necessary, it, too, would be exhausted that much sooner.

Conan continued warily, thrusting the weak amber glow of the torch into openings in the sides of the tunnel and peering as far as the feeble light allowed his vision to range. He still came upon bones and other fragments of animals. Above the reek of carrion, another smell assailed his keen barbarian nostrils—the scent of a living creature, but one completely alien to him. The odor emanated from no beast or reptile that he knew of; nor yet from any plant or foodstuff with which he was familiar. The odor was unique—acrid but not altogether unpleasant.

As he moved stealthily, straining his eyes and ears, he thought he heard a faint repeated click, such as would be made by a horny object striking against the stone. He could not be sure that he heard aright, realizing that the horror of the tunnel had disoriented his senses and might be leading him to imagine things.

For one wild instant, he wondered whether the statue of Zath in the naos had, in fact, come to life and followed him down into the tunnels. Reason assured him that the onyx spider-god still squatted on its pedestal in the temple. If it had come to life while the High Priest was showing the place to his sacerdotal visitors, Conan would have heard some susurrant echo of the resulting hubbub in the sanctum above.

Still, *something*—and of gigantic dimensions—had devoured the animals whose remains littered the floor of the tunnels. Suddenly Conan, who feared little on the earth that he trod, or in the seas, or in the ambient air above, found himself trembling at the implications of this thought.

He took a few steps down one of the side tunnels, holding high his torch, but saw nothing save some ghostly, whitened bones of a sheep or a goat. He worked his way back to the main corridor and tried another branch, with no happier result; for this branch soon came to a blind end.

He was certain, now, that the clicking sounds were not born of his febrile imagination. The cadenced crepitation seemed to be coming closer, although from which direction he could not tell. With a horror of being cornered at the end of the short branch tunnel, he hastened back to the main corridor.

For an instant Conan stood statuelike, his torch upraised and his head turning from side to side as he strove to locate the source of the sound. It came, he was now convinced, from farther on in this branch of the tunnel, and rapidly waxed in volume.

His skin crawled with nameless terror as the clicks became louder, although he could not perceive their source. Then, just beyond the limit of his torchlight, something moved. As this object approached, Conan saw, reflected in the light of his torch, four spots of brightness in the tunnel at about breast level.

As the unwavering lights grew larger, they seemed to spread out and become four great jewels, such as might decorate the breastplate of an approaching warrior-king. But they were no such ornaments. Behind the four lights loomed an indeterminate bulk. Unable to distinguish details, Conan drew his blacksmith's hammer from its belt loop. Because of the need for silence, he had left his sword back in his quarters.

The lights seemed to halt at the periphery of his torchlight. The clicking stopped, then resumed; the lights drew closer, and behind them Conan caught a nightmarish impression of a vast hairy bulk propelled by many legs.

Conan whirled and ran, the wind of his motion causing his torch to flare up to a bright golden flame. Behind him came the relentless clicking of colossal claws on the stone, closer and ever closer.

Before he realized it, Conan had crossed the main intersection of the tunnels; the one he had first come upon after entering the subterranean system. Too late he decided that his best chance for escape would have been to go back to the trapdoor, burst out, and—if the priests were still in the naos—to confront them openly. The next best alternative would have been to turn to the right and take the downward-sloping tunnel, on the chance that it would issue into the outer world beyond the bounds of wall-girt Yezud.

He started to turn back. But it was too late for that; the four glowing eyes, reflecting the saffron light of the torch, had already reached the main crossing and blocked his way. He was trapped in this branch of the tunnel.

Conan continued his flight up the rising slope. At the top he came to a massive door, which he felt certain was the temple door through which the sheep had been admitted. Shaking with apprehension, he set down his hammer, fumbled for the Clavis of Gazrik, and applied it to the keyhole. When he uttered the spell, he heard the lock clank, and pushed on the knob. But the door would not yield. Then Conan remembered that this door was also closed by a heavy bolt on the outside.

Remembering how he had used the silver arrow on his way into the temple, Conan aimed the arrow to the height where he supposed this bolt to be and repeated: *"Kapinin achilir genishi!"* more loudly. When nothing happened, he shouted the phrase with the full power of his huge lungs.

Instead of the sound of the bolt's motion, the next thing that Conan noticed was that the silver arrow was growing hot in his fingers. When it became too hot to hold, he dropped it. As he did so, it glowed, briefly, dull red; as it struck the floor, it softened and melted into an amorphous puddle, which quickly cooled and solidified. Then Conan remembered Parvez's words, that the Clavis of Gazrik would move a door bolt *if* it were not too heavy. He had evidently overtaxed the powers of the talisman and ruined it. It served him right, he thought, for using magic.

Conan pulled out his hammer and gave the door a furious blow. The portal boomed but remained immobile. Conan could see where he had dented the tough ironwood, without affecting the door's security. With such hard wood, it would take him an hour with hammer and chisel to force his way through the barrier.

He would have struck again, in a frenzy of desperation, but clickings behind him warned him to turn. As he did so, he found that the colossal spider—a living duplicate of the statue in the temple, save that this creature was covered with stiff hairs as long as a man's fingers—was upon him. Reflections of the flame of his torch danced in the four great round eyes across the creature's front.

Below these eyes, a pair of hairy, jointed appendages extended forward like arms. As these organs reached out for Conan, he smote one of them with his hammer, feeling the horny integument yield as it cracked. The spider recoiled a step, folding its injured limb beneath its hairy body.

Then the monster advanced again. It reared up on its six hindmost legs and spread the first pair, together with the uninjured palm, to seize its prey. Conan felt like a fly caught in a web, awaiting its fate.

Below the palps he could see the spider's fangs, a pair of curved, shiny, sharp-pointed organs like the horns of a bull, curving out and then inward, so that the points almost met. They, too, now spread horizontally to pierce Conan's body from opposite sides; green venom dripped from their hollow points. Between and below the fangs, the jointed mouth parts worked hungrily.

For a heartbeat the pair confronted each other, Conan with his hammer raised to deliver one last crushing blow before he died, the spider with its monstrous, hairy appendages spread to grip the man in a last embrace.

From behind Zath, Conan heard Rudabeh's voice, raised in shrill tones of terror: "Nial! Dearest! I have—"

At this anguished cry, the spider backed away from Conan. It turned, so that one of its lateral eyes flashed briefly in the torchlight. Its great sac of an abdomen brushed against the wall of the narrow space, and Zath started toward the voice. Conan heard one frightful shriek; then silence, save for the diminishing click of horny claws on stone. At that instant, Conan's torch went out.

With a yell of fury, Conan started to run after the spider in total darkness, but he missed his direction and crashed into the wall of the tunnel. Getting shakily to his feet, he pulled the second torch from his belt. He cursed like a madman. The rag at the end of the first torch still glowed a dull red, like a lump of lava spat from a volcano.

Conan touched the ends together and blew frantic breaths until the second torch flared up. Dropping the exhausted torch, Conan ran down the ramp in pursuit of Zath.

At the main crossing, he slowed as his torch illumined something sprawled on the floor of the tunnel—something that was not the putrid remains of a cow or a sheep. Dreading what he knew he would find, he approached Rudabeh's body. She looked as if she slept; but when he knelt and pressed an ear to her breast, he could detect no heartbeat.

He leaned his torch against the tunnel wall to free both hands and examined her more closely. She wore the gauzy, fluttery garments that the dancing girls appeared in when they sang in chorus. He ripped away these obscuring filaments and turned over her finely-formed torso. On one shoulder and in the middle of her back he found a pair of puncture wounds, each surrounded by an area of blackened flesh where the injected spider's venom had taken effect.

He called: "Rudabeh! My love! Speak!" He chafed her hands and rhythmically pressed her ribs in hope of starting her breathing. Nothing had any effect.

Hot tears ran down Conan's rugged countenance—the first he had shed in many years. He angrily wiped them away, but still they flowed. Those who knew Conan as a man of iron, hard, merciless, and self-seeking, would have been astonished to see him weeping in that charnel house, heedless of his own safety.

The girl must, he thought, have braved these stinking tunnels, after the priests had gone, to warn him of his peril. To have another lay down life to save his was a unique event in Conan's experience, and the knowledge of her sacrifice filled him with pity, shame, and self-loathing.

Then rage surged like molten iron through his veins, and he picked up his torch and hammer, glaring about. The spider, he thought, must have dropped its burden when the light of Conan's torch alarmed it, and then retreated to that part of the tunnel where he first had met the brute.

With a yell of uncontrolled fury, Conan ran headlong down the tunnel branch where he had first encountered Zath, his torch flaring up with the fetid wind of his motion. He must have run a quarter of a league, shouting: "Zath! Show yourself and fight!" But no sign of the giant arachnid did he see.

Breathing heavily, he gave up the chase. If Zath were in this branch of the tunnel, he would surely have by now overtaken it in its lumbering flight. Perhaps it was hiding in one of the many cross passages and side chambers, but to explore them all would require days.

He retraced his steps until he found himself back at the main crossing. Now cold to the touch, Rudabeh lay where he had left her. He would not abandon her in this stinking hellhole for Zath to consume, because he had a barbarian's superstitious fear of failing to bury the body of one of his kith and kin.

Such a person's ghost, he had learned as a boy, would haunt him in revenge for his neglect. Since he had few friends and no kinsmen in civilized lands, he had not felt compelled to bury any of the many corpses that he had seen in late years. Besides, Rudabeh had been the one human being whom he had truly loved and who had loved him in return since he had left his bleak homeland, and he would not desert her now. He would somehow get her out of the tunnels to some lonely place, where he would dig a grave, with his bare hands if need be, and lay her in it. He would pile rocks on the grave against wolves and hyenas, place a single wildflower atop the stones, and go his way.

He picked up the girl's body, slung it over one massive shoulder, and started back along the tunnel that led to the trapdoor. Surely, he thought, the priests would have retired by this late hour, leaving the naos deserted. At the end of the corridor he set down the cold corpse, climbed the steps, and listened against the underside of the trapdoor.

To his surprise, the sound of voices filtered through to him. He made out the deep tones of the High Priest, the higher ones of Mirzes, and a third voice he did not know. Feridun's leonine roar came through to him:

"Zath curse your eyeballs, Darius! You promised us fair weather for the three days of the festival; instead of which, you allowed our guests to depart in a downpour! Where is the skill at commanding the spirits of the air whereof you have boasted? If you cannot do better than that, we shall have to give the task of weather magic to another."

Darius mumbled something apologetic, but then Mirzes the new Vicar spoke: "I suspect, Holiness, that Darius did it a-purpose, to diminish your repute and thus further his own political designs."

"Naught of the sort!" protested Darius. "I have never . . ." Then all three spoke at once, so that Conan could no longer distinguish words.

Conan thought of bursting into the naos, laying Rudabeh's body on the offering chest, chiseling out the Eyes of Zath, and fleeing. This was obviously impractical while the chamber was occupied. A wild idea crossed his mind, of pushing up the trapdoor and confronting the priests with the body. But Conan had no sword, and the priests had only to shout to bring the Brythunian guards on the run.

He quickly abandoned this suicidal idea. If the priests discovered, as they surely would, that Rudabeh had been in collusion with Conan, they might not bury her properly, either. Nor could he pry out the Eyes with one hand while fighting off Catigern's mercenaries with the other. There was nothing for it but to manage the burial himself and come back later for the jewels, when the naos was vacant.

With a heavy sigh he descended, picked up the body, and set forth. At the main crossing he continued straight on, down the slope of the central passage. Where the tunnel branched, he followed what seemed to be the main corridor.

chapter xii

The Children of Zath

Suddenly, the tunnel opened out into a vast cavern, where stalactites hung from the roof over stalagmites that reared up from the floor to meet them. Directly before Conan, half a dozen stone steps led down to the floor of the cavern, so that he had a clear view across to the farther wall. The feeble light of his torch could not throw its amber beams so far; but in the midst of the distant blackness appeared an opening to the outer world. Through this aperture Conan sighted a patch of night sky, in which a star glimmered. Evidently the rain clouds of the previous day had rolled away.

Within the cave entrance, below the actual aperture, was another patch of dim luminescence. Conan's keen vision identified this as a circular pool of water, reflecting the night sky outside and blocking the entrance to the cave. The strange odor which he had sensed before his encounter with Zath assailed his nostrils with nauseating intensity.

All about the floor of the cave, the flickering orange light showed large, lumpish things scattered here and there among the stalagmites, like giant mushrooms of mottled gray-and-brown coloring. As Conan began to descend the steps, intending to pick his way among these obstacles to the exit, motion caught his eye. When he looked more closely, he saw that one of the supposed fungi was coming to life. It unfolded jointed legs, raised its body from the ground, and turned four gleaming eyes on Conan.

The thing was a duplicate, in miniature, of Zath, although its dimensions were only half those of the original spider god. Still, it was larger than the giant spider that Conan had fought in the Tower of the Elephant years before. One such monster could easily kill Conan, and there must be hundreds in the cavern.

The first spider to awaken started toward Conan, while on all sides other giant spiders were coming to life and rising to their clawed feet. Within a few heartbeats of Conan's first appearance in the cave, the monster arachnids were streaming toward him. The click of their claws on the stone rose to a continuous rattle. Wherever Conan looked, quartets of gleaming eyes caught the light of his torch.

Conan whirled and ran back up the long slope of the tunnel, while his hearing told him that the entire swarm was crowding into the tunnel behind him and racing after him, like a jointed-legged flood. On, on he went. At first, to judge from the diminishing sounds behind him, he gained on his pursuers. But, heavily burdened, he was forced to slow down, while his heart labored and his breath came in gasps. Then the castanet-like sound of hundreds of horny claws on the stone came closer. These, he realized, must be the Children of Zath of whom the High Priest had spoken.

Ever the rough walls of the tunnel fled past. Without the body, Conan was sure he could outrun the spiders; but it inevitably slowed him down. Still, he would not abandon it. He had the feeling of being in a nightmare, where one runs and runs through darkness while an unseen menace comes ever closer behind. He feared that he must have taken a wrong fork and would be lost forever in this maze.

When he was almost in despair, he found himself at the main crossing. He kept straight on and soon reached the stair to the trapdoor.

At the end of the tunnel, Conan climbed the steps and listened. He heard no sound from above—no talking, shuffling, or other indication of human activity. Perhaps the accursed priests had gone to bed at last. In these hours between midnight and morning, all in the temple, save the Brythunian guards on night duty, should be sound asleep. Conan did not know how he could escape unnoticed from the temple with Rudabeh's body; but, with the clatter of claws of the Children of Zath coming closer, he had no time to concoct a clever scheme.

With the fist that held the torch, he pushed against the trapdoor. The square of planking failed to move. With a silent curse, Conan wondered if someone had noticed that the bolt had been shot back and replaced it.

With the crepitation of the Children's claws coming closer, Conan was not about to let a mere bolt stop him now. If a good push would not dislodge it, he could break through the trap with his hammer, although he would have preferred not to do so because of the noise.

He stepped back down to the tunnel floor and set down Rudabeh's body. Then he leaned his torch against the tunnel wall. Again he mounted the steps, put both hands against the underside of the trap, and gave a terrific heave.

The trap rose against resistance, as if someone had placed a heavy weight upon it. Then suddenly the resistance ceased; there was a sharp cry, the thump of a falling body, and the trap flew open.

As Conan leaped out into the gloom, a stream of oil struck him and cascaded over his clothing. By the wavering light of the eternal flame in its bowl, he saw a priest, whom he recognized as Mirzes, the Vicar, sprawled on the floor and beginning to rise. Beside him lay a large pitcher on its side, and a pool of oil spread out from it across the marble.

In a flash, Conan understood. When Rudabeh had disappeared instead of reporting back to the Vicar, Mirzes had doubtless searched for her. Failing to find her, he had undertaken the task of refilling the reservoir himself. He had been standing on the trapdoor and directing the stream of bitumen into his pitcher when Conan's sudden emergence had thrown him off the planking.

Mirzes started to scramble up, crying: "Who—what—Nial! What in the seven hells—" But then his feet slipped on the oily surface, and he fell again.

Conan leaped out on the floor and turned toward Mirzes, but his feet skidded also. He staggered and recovered.

"Help!" croaked Mirzes. "Guards!"

Slipping and scrambling, Conan reached Mirzes just as the priest regained his feet. As Mirzes opened his mouth to cry another alarm, Conan whipped his fist up against the Vicar's chin with a meaty smack, hurling the slight priest back on the mosaic floor unconscious.

Standing over his victim, Conan thought of finishing him off with a skull-cracking blow of his hammer. But with the hammer in his hand, he drew back from his bloodthirsty resolution. To slay a man while that man was asleep or otherwise helpless went against his notions of honor. He thought of cutting Mirzes's turban into lengths to bind and gag the priest.

But it was more urgent to recover his torch and Rudabeh's body and to bolt the trapdoor, before the Children of Zath swarmed up into the naos. Conan started back toward the recess in the wall, aware that the faucet had remained open and that the abundant stream of bitumen continued to pour down into the tunnel. He must quickly turn off the valve; once the flow was stopped and the trap securely bolted, he could turn his attention back to Mirzes.

After that, Conan thought, he would try to pry out the Eyes from the spider idol. To escape from the temple, he would pound on the front door and shout for help. When the Brythunians unlocked and opened the doors, Conan would cry: "Murder! Robbery! Help the Vicar!" When the guards rushed in, he would slip past them and out.

Conan had taken but two steps toward the trapdoor when, with a thunderous belching sound, a mass of flame, and smoke erupted out of the square opening in the floor. The oil had come in contact with Conan's torch in the tunnel. Conan made one desperate effort to reach the faucet, but the flames drove him back with singed hair and eyebrows, frantically beating out a small fire started in his oil-soaked clothing.

Realizing at last that he could do nothing more for Rudabeh's body, he sprang to the statue and began fumbling for tools, to extract at least one Eye before the conflagration drove him forth. Smoke rolled out, thicker and thicker, until it set Conan to coughing and prevented him from even seeing clearly enough to work on the jewels in the statue.

Stubbornly, he continued to try to place a drill in the proper position. He got in one stroke of his hammer and was pleased to see the point of the drill bite into the lead. But the smoke so afflicted him with coughing that he could only clutch at the nearest stone spider-leg, gasping and retching.

Then the light in the naos brightened, and through the billowing smoke Conan saw that a wall hanging was going up in flame. From outside the naos he heard cries of "Fire! Fire!"

The smoke momentarily lifted; and Conan, glancing toward the flaming recess with the trapdoor, saw a sight that wrung a shudder from him. A colossal gray-and-brown spider was hoisting itself out of the trapdoor. Its massive bulk scraped against the sides of the opening as it forced its hairy body through the aperture, like some demon rising from a flaming hell. Zath had escaped its tunnel-prison at last.

Out it came, swiveling about on its jointed legs, and sighted Conan. As the scuttling horror started for its prey, the Cimmerian ran for the front door, putting away his tools as he went. He seized the bronzen door handles and tried to thrust open the doors, but they were still locked. A glance behind showed that the spider was close upon him.

Then a key clicked in the lock and the doors opened. Conan found himself facing the startled countenances of two Brythunians; one of whom held a large key. Others crowded behind the mercenaries. Smoke had already seeped out the cracks around these doors, alerting the people of the temple.

Conan staggered, coughing, out of the naos and into a scene of wild confusion. Priests of Zath, visiting priests from Arenjun, acolytes, dancing girls, mercenaries, and slaves ran in all directions. Priests bawled commands.

Through the smoke loomed Zath in the doorway. At the sight, everyone in the vestibule broke into mad flight for the nearest exit. The small door in the outer valves was jammed with several fugitives trying to get through it at once.

Forcing his way to the door by sheer strength, Conan seized the handles of the main door, wrenched them around, and pushed the groaning valves open. Those clustered against the door boiled out, falling, tripping over one another, and scrambling up to run. Conan glimpsed a pair of acolytes hustling the former Vicar out of the temple, while Harpagus stared about in childlike wonder.

Conan bounded down the front steps two at a time. Halfway down he turned to snatch a look back. Thick smoke poured out of the open portal. Overhead the night was clear and star-dusted, while a half moon stood high in the eastern sky.

In the open front portal stood two figures. One was the giant spider; its long hairs had been mostly singed off, but it seemed otherwise uninjured. The other, almost within arm's length of the monster, was the lean, hawk-nosed figure of High Priest Feridun, in his white robe and black turban. The priest was making passes with his hands and chanting some rigmarole.

With its forelegs raised as if to seize Feridun, Zath paused. The priest continued his incantation, raising his voice to a shout and frantically gesturing, so that his long white beard lashed the smoky night air. The two grotesque figures were silhouetted against the lurid glare of the fire behind them. The spider retreated a step, back toward the naos; then another step. The priest's fabled control over animals could even force this monster to immolate itself in the blaze.

Then Feridun got a lungful of smoke and went into a spell of coughing. Instantly, the spider, no longer constrained by its master's voice, darted forward. Its great jointed limbs enfolded the priest, who screamed once.

A burly figure in mail dashed past Conan up the steps, waving a sword. From the flowing red hair Conan recognized Captain Catigern. Reaching the top, the Brythunian took a cut at the spider's body, opening a gash from which a dark fluid seeped. Zath, who had issued from the portal and now stood on the topmost step, dropped the priest's body and turned upon its new adversary. As it spread its appendages, Catigern backed away, swinging his sword right and left. The spider followed, keeping just beyond reach of the blade.

"Hold on, Catigern!" shouted Conan between coughs. He had sighted, lying on the steps, a halberd belonging to one of the guards on duty at the main entrance. The Brythunian had dropped it when he fled.

Pounding up the steps, Conan snatched up the pole-arm. Coming up on the side of Zath, he swung the halberd high over his head and, with every ounce of power that he possessed, brought it whistling down on the forward segment of the monster.

The axe blade sank deeply into the spider's leathery flesh, and such was the force of the stroke that the shaft broke off midway from butt to head. Ponderously, Zath turned toward Conan. Running in from the other side, Catigern drove his sword in deeply above the base of the second leg and wrenched it out.

Zath began to turn back toward the Brythunian, but it moved more and more slowly. Before it completed its turn, its legs gave way, dropping its body to the marble steps, which became fouled with the dark ichor that dripped from its wounds. Its sprawling legs continued to twitch, but these movements slowly dwindled. Zath was dead.

Catigern seized Conan around the shoulders in a fierce hug. "Thank all the gods you came along! Any time you want a lieutenancy in my company, do but ask."

"I'll think about it," said Conan, coughing.

Another Brythunian approached. "Captain, the priest Dinak wants our help in fighting the fire."

Seeing the spider dead, Yezudites began crowding back into the square before the temple. The citizens boiled out of their houses, some in nightwear and some in hastily donned work garments. The priests dashed about, organizing firefighting. Thick, oily smoke continued to roll out the doors of the temple.

"Bear a hand!" shouted Catigern in Conan's ear, shoving a bucket into his grip. "Get into yonder line!"

Conan had been about to turn away and go to the smithy, collect his gear, and shake the dust of Yezud from his feet. The temple of Zath was an evil fane; even more obnoxious than most Zamorian cults. He cared nothing for its architectural splendor, and if more priests were destroyed in the conflagration, that was all right with him. If he could not bury Rudabeh, to burn the temple for her funeral pyre was the next best thing. With her gone, there was no one in Yezud for whose fate Conan cared.

Well, that was not quite true. Captain Catigern had become a friend, and each had saved the other's life. If the Brythunian were locked in battle with the fire, it behooved Conan to give him a hand.

The sky had begun to pale with the approach of dawn; but then it suddenly clouded over. A small but very black cloud formed over Yezud. A flash of lightning paled the flames licking out around the base of the central dome, and a roll of thunder drowned out the roar of the flames. Down came rain, but such rain as Conan had never seen. It was like standing under a waterfall.

Conan took his place in the bucket line and, with rain running down his face, handed buckets back and forth in a steady rhythm. The buckets were filled at the fountain in the temple square and were passed back to Yezudites around and within the fane.

With a roaring crash, the central dome collapsed and disappeared. A cloud of sparks, smoke, and dust billowed up from the gap; rain poured into it. Little by little, between the firefighters and the rain, the fire was beaten back; it had been confined to the naos.

The Yezudites were still battling the flames, and the sun, though not yet visible, was tinging the scattered dawn clouds crimson when Conan slipped away from the temple. Soon after, somewhat cleaned up and booted, he appeared at the stable with his saddle over one shoulder and a blanket roll over the other. The groom on duty, a stolid youth named Yazdan, looked up as the Cimmerian pushed into the stalls. He asked:

"What would you, Master Nial? I thought you had lost your steed!"

"One of them," grunted Conan, striding down the row of stalls to that housing Egil. "This one's mine, also."

"Ho? What say you?" cried Yazdan. "You must be mad! That unmanageable beast belongs to the temple; Vicar Harpagus brought him back from his travels."

"After he stole him from me!" roared Conan. "Stand aside, boy, if you don't wish to be hurt!"

"I cannot—Zath's curse would—" protested the youth, striving to block Conan's advance with outstretched arms.

"I'm sorry to do this," grated Conan, dropping his burdens. "But you give me no choice."

He picked up Yazdan, who kicked and flailed the air, and slammed the groom against the wall. Yazdan sagged to the floor, half unconscious. Minutes later, Conan led a saddled Egil out of the stable; the horse whinnied and took little dancing steps with the pleasure of being reunited with his old master.

Conan stopped at Bartakes's Inn to buy extra provisions—a loaf, a slab of meat, and a leather bottle of ale—for his journey. He was counting out coins to a yawning Bartakes, whom he had routed out of bed, when a familiar voice said:

"Aha, there you are! I wondered what had become of you." Captain Catigern, still filthy with soot and ash, had his arm in a sling. He continued: "From the blanket roll on your horse, I'd say you were planning to leave us."

"I might," said Conan, "if I had a better prospect elsewhere. What befell your arm?"

"A beam fell on me, and I think the bone is cracked. I'll get a chirurgeon as soon as may be. When I saw the fire was under control, I turned command over to Gwotelin."

"How much of the temple burned?"

"The naos is an indescribable mess; the falling roof timbers smashed that damned spider idol into a hundred pieces. But elsewhere the damage was only slight; most of the building is stone, and the oil stopped flowing out that pipe in the naos. I suppose the pool that feeds it ran dry."

"Will this end the cult of Zath?"

"Mitra, no! They are already talking of rebuilding. I'll wager they'll choose Darius their new High Priest, for that his rain spell saved most of the building. There should be plenty of work for a craftsman like you."

"No doubt, but I have other plans." Conan thought, the Eyes of Zath, if not smashed to fragments by the fall of the dome, would have been baked by the heat to plain white stones of no value. At least, he thought with vindictive relish, if he could not enjoy them, neither could anyone else.

"That is your business," said Catigern. "By the bye, that black stallion looks uncommonly like one of the temple's horses."

"Egil is mine," growled Conan. "Some day I'll tell you how Harpagus stole him from me. If you doubt me, I'll show you how he answers to my voice."

"I am in no condition to gainsay you," said Catigern. "At least, with a new High Priest, let us hope there will be no more giant spiders."

"Whence did Feridun get that one?"

Catigern shrugged, then winced at the sudden pain in his injured arm. "I know not. Perchance it was a leftover from some bygone era; or perchance he grew it by sorcery from an ordinary tarantula."

"What's become of the last two Vicars?"

"Harpagus is still out of his mind, and Mirzes is dead. We found him in the naos, apparently suffocated by smoke."

"Good!" growled Conan.

Catigern looked keenly at the Cimmerian. "That reminds me. One of my men swears he saw you come rushing out of the naos with the spider hot behind you, although no one had seen you go in. Might there be a connection betwixt your unauthorized visit and the death of Mirzes?"

"There might," said Conan. "But there is something else you should know." He described the cavern with the swarming Children of Zath. "The spider must have laid a clutch of eggs after Feridun installed her in the tunnels. If the King didn't give in, Feridun would unleash the horde on Zamora. I think there must be some means of draining that pool, to let the Children escape their cave and scatter over the countryside."

Catigern whistled. "Then the real spider was a female, for all that they call Zath a male god! And these creatures are still there?"

"Unless the river of flaming oil, running down into the cavern, has cooked them. I suppose it did, or they'd have swarmed up out of their burrow as did the big one."

"This I must see," mused the Brythunian. "Can you show me the cave entrance?"

Conan shook his head. "It is somewhere in these hills; but you could search for a month without finding it. You'd better go down through the trapdoor, as I did."

Catigern shuddered. "I must lead my men into that hole with pikes and torches, to make sure all those vermin are dead," he muttered. "Feridun was honest in his way, but the gods preserve me from fanatics!"

"I'm told he controlled beasts of all kinds," said Conan, yawning prodigiously. "If he'd lost his spiders but survived, he might have set wolves or lions or eagles on the Zamorians. Well, I must away."

Catigern accompanied Conan out the door, musing: "There are mysteries here, which the priests will want me to investigate. I shall be glad not to pry into the doings of one who has twice saved my hide, not to mention thwarting the High Priest's mad plan."

Conan wrung the hand of the Catigern's uninjured arm and began to unhitch his horse when he spied the barrel of bitumen, for Bartakes's lamps, standing around the corner of the inn.

Conan left the horse and opened the door. "Mandana!" he called.

"Aye?" The innkeeper's daughter came out of the kitchen, wiping her hands on her apron.

Conan turned to Catigern. "Farewell, friend. I would have a word with the damsel alone."

Catigern grinned wolfishly and entered the tavern. Conan said: "Mandana, will you step out here? I have somewhat to say."

Misinterpreting Conan's grim smile, the girl came forward with alacrity, simpering. "So, have you tired of that skinny temple wench at last?"

"I shall never see her again," said Conan. "Ere he went mad, Harpagus the Vicar told me that you had informed him of Rudabeh's visit to the inn."

"What if I did? She deserved it for violating her temple's rules and coming down here to lure away my patrons. How are we to live, with such unfair competition?"

Conan nodded sagely. "I'll show you something." He stepped to the barrel and threw off the lid. "Now," he said, clutching Mandana about the waist and swinging her off her feet.

"Nial!" she cried. "Not here in the mud! You barbarians are so impetuous! I have a fine bed upstairs—"

"Aye," grunted Conan. With a stride he towered over the barrel. Bending over, with the laughing girl still clutched about the waist, he dipped her flowing black mane into the tarlike fluid.

So speedy and so accurate was his move that Mandana did not suspect his true intention until her scalp was immersed in the black, sticky oil. Then she screamed.

In a single, sweeping motion, Conan raised and set her on her feet. She stood for a moment transfixed, with tar running down her plump, pink cheeks to drip on her bodice. Frantically, she ran her hands through the ropelike strands of hair, stared at the viscous substance that befouled them, and shrieked wordlessly.

"Your just desert for tattling," rumbled Conan. "By the time your shaven skull has grown a new crop, perhaps you'll have learned to mind your own affairs."

Conan unhitched his horse and swung into the saddle. Pursued by screams of "I hate you! I hate you!" he trotted briskly away on the Shadizar road.

Where the narrow valley below Yezud opened out, Conan rode past Kharshoi and into the more spacious lands of central Zamora. The sun being well past its zenith, Conan drew rein on a rise in the road, whence he had a good view of the route by which he had come. Yawning, he pulled a fowl's leg and a biscuit out of his saddle bag and sat cross-legged on the ground, eating, while Egil, reins trailing, cropped the grass behind him. Sleep plucked seductively at Conan's elbow, for he had had none the night before; but he dared not relax until he was farther from Yezud.

Suddenly there came a disturbance in the air before Conan, as if a tiny dust-devil had formed. The dust cleared, and there stood Psamitek the Stygian, holding a small brass tripod with a little smoking brazier at its apex. While Conan gaped with astonishment, the Stygian stooped and set the tripod on the ground. He made passes over it, chanting in some guttural tongue that Conan did not know.

"What the devil?" cried Conan, scrambling to his feet and reaching for his scimitar. "By Crom, this time—"

As he spoke, Psamitek shouted a word. Thereupon the sapphire smoke from the tripod instantly compacted itself into a ropelike column, writhing like a pale-blue, translucent serpent in the still afternoon air.

Another gesture and word from the Stygian, and the blue serpentine of smoke whipped toward Conan like a striking snake. The smoky cord threw coils around Conan's body, like some ghostly python, pinioning his sword arm with his scimitar half drawn. Another coil wrapped itself around Conan's neck and tightened, cutting off the Cimmerian's breath.

Conan struggled until he foamed at the mouth. With his free left hand he clawed at the loop of smoke around his throat, so that his tunic bulged with the desperate bunching of muscles beneath it. To his touch the smoke felt like a cable of some slick, yielding, but animate substance, like a live eel, but dry.

He forced his thumb between the noose and his neck, although he had to gouge his own flesh with his thumbnail. He pulled the loop far enough from his throat to allow a wheezy, strangulated breath, but he might as well have tugged at a steel cable. The loop tightened, and Conan's face purpled. The veins in his temples swelled until they seemed likely to burst.

Psamitek smiled thinly. "I said you should see more of my little tricks. Now I shall at leisure collect your head and the reward therefor. I need not even divide it with that Turanian savage. I shall have the finest occult library in Stygia!"

Conan tried to bite into the noose but could not pull it far enough from his chin to get his teeth into it. He thought of trying to throw his dagger, but one of the loops of smoke had pinioned the weapon against his side. Behind him he heard Egil moving uneasily, watching the drama with anxious incomprehension.

At the spectacle of Conan's violent but unavailing struggles, Psamitek gave a coldly cynical laugh. "This," he purred, "gives me more pleasure than even the gladiatorial games of Argos!"

Before Conan's eyes, the landscape swam and darkened. With a final effort, he pulled the noose far enough from his throat to emit one shout. "Egil!" he croaked. "Kill him!"

With a snort, the well-trained warhorse sprang past Conan and reared up at Psamitek. Conan had a glimpse of the Stygian's sallow countenance, suddenly wide-eyed with alarm at this unexpected intervention. And then one of Egil's hooves descended on Psamitek's shaven head with a crunch of shattered cranium.

Instantly the magical rope faded away, dissolving into wisps of ordinary smoke. Freed, Conan sank down, gasping great lungfuls of air.

When he had recovered, Conan heaved himself erect and tottered over to where Psamitek lay. He went through the Stygian's purse, finding an assortment of coins, some of them gold, and the roll of parchment bearing Tughril's offer for Conan's head. The money Conan transferred to his own purse.

The scroll he stared at, trying to puzzle out its spidery glyphs. It would not do, he thought, to leave such a document adrift in the world. Someone else might get his hands on it and be inspired, like Psamitek, to try to collect the reward.

Conan bent and gently blew upon the tiny, smoldering fire in the brazier; the little tripod still stood upright. When he had coaxed a flame into being, he dipped a corner of the parchment into the blaze and held it there until the writing surface caught fire. He held the sheet, turning it to spread the fire across it. The cryptic writings glowed red for an instant and disappeared. Soon the entire document, save the corner by which Conan held it, was reduced to ash.

Then Conan swung into the saddle and cantered off, leaving the Stygian's body for the hyenas.

Hyborian Names

Acknowledgments

The article "Hyborian Names" is expanded from the following articles by L. Sprague de Camp: "An Exegesis of Howard's Hyborian Tales" in *Amra*, II, 4, 5, and 6, copyright © 1959 by L. Sprague de Camp: "Addenda to the Exegesis" in *Amra*, II, 6, copyright © 1959 by George H. Scithers; "Exegetical Addenda" in *Amra*, II, 9, copyright © 1960 by George H. Scithers; "Addenda to the Exegesis" in *Amra*, II, 40, copyright © 1966 by the Terminus, Owlswick, and Ft. Mudge Electrick Street Railway Gazette; "Superaddendum to the Exegesis" in *Amra*, II, 45, copyright © 1967 by L. Sprague de Camp; "An Exegesis of Howard's Hyborian Tales" in *The Conan Reader* (Baltimore: Mirage Press, 1968), copyright © 1968 by L. Sprague de Camp; and "An Exegesis of Names Discarded by REH" in *Amra*, II, 51, copyright © 1969 by L. Sprague de Camp.

N.B. This article was originally published as part of *Conan the Swordsman*. It has been placed at the end of this omnibus for the sake of clarity and narrative flow.

In choosing names for the people and places in his stories of the Hyborian Age, Robert E. Howard revealed a number of facts about his sources, his reading, and the writers who had influenced him. Concerning these names, H. P. Lovecraft once remarked (in a letter to Donald A. Wollheim about Howard's essay "The Hyborian Age," reprinted in *The Coming of Conan*): "The only flaw in this stuff is R. E. H.'s incurable tendency to devise names too closely resembling actual names of ancient history—names which, for us, have a very different set of associations. In many cases he does this designedly—on the theory that familiar names descend from the fabulous realms he describes—but such a design is invalidated by the fact that we clearly know the etymology of many of the historic terms, hence cannot accept the pedigree he suggests."

Many of the personal names used by Howard in his Conan stories are ordinary Latin personal names (Publius, Constantius, Valeria) or Greek names (Dion, Pelias, Tiberias) or modern Italian versions of these (Publio, Tito, Demetrio). Others are modern Asiatic or Arabic names, sometimes modified (Aram Baksh, Yar Afzal, Jungir Khan, Bhunda Chand, Shah Amurath) while still others are apparently made up (Thak, Thaug, Thog, Yara, Yog, Yogah, Zang, Zogar Sag). In RN occur a number of Aztec or pseudo-Aztec names; in BR, TT, and BB, pseudo-Iroquois names.

Perhaps Lovecraft had especially in mind the Asiatic names that originated in the conquests of Alexander the Great in −IV, or in those of the Muslim Arabs in +VII. It is interesting to note that the three made-up names above, beginning with "Th," are all names of monsters.

Despite Lovecraft's criticism, there was much to be said for Howard's use of real ancient names and names derived from these, because his purely made-up names show a disagreeable sameness (Ka, Kaa-u, Ka-nu, Kaanuub; Thak, Thaug, Thog, etc.). The reason for this is probably a lack of linguistic sophistication on Howard's part. When he graduated from the Kull stories to the Conan stories, he seems to have sworn off made-up names in favor of real names from history and geography, sometimes slightly modified. These borrowed names are usually well-chosen and euphonious. They convey the glamor of antiquity by their near-familiarity without being too difficult for the modern reader, who, having been taught to read by sight-reading methods, is apt to boggle at any name more exotic than "Smith."

Moreover, Lovecraft sometimes borrowed real ancient names (Menes, Kranon, Sarnath) in exactly the manner which he chided Howard for doing.

Howard's geographical names come mainly from the more accessible bodies of myth: Classical (e.g., Stygia), Norse (Asgard), or biblical (Kush); and from the kind of geographical lore to be had from an atlas. Besides the names of obvious derivation, there are many whose origin is more complex, showing wide reading by Howard.

Anybody who made a practice of reading *Adventure Magazine* during the 1920s will recognize, in Howard's Hyborian stories, the influence of the historical adventure stories by Harold Lamb and Talbot Mundy, published in this magazine at this time. Lamb's tales were usually set in an Asiatic locale, dealing with such events as the Crusades, the Mongol and Turkish conquests, and the rise of the Russian state. Howard's stories of Conan and the *kozaki* are closely derived from Lamb's yarns of sixteenth- and seventeenth-century Cossacks.

Mundy's stories were usually laid in modern India, Afghanistan, Tibet, or Egypt. Mundy's picture of these countries is highly romanticized, full of assumptions of ancient sorceries and occult wisdom. Howard's Stygia and Vendhya are essentially Mundy's Egypt and India, respectively, with the names changed. There may also have been some Kipling influence on Howard.

Besides Lamb and Mundy, Howard must have read many other stories in *Adventure*. A search reveals derivations from other leading adventure-story writers of the time, such as Frederick Faust, A. D. Howden Smith, and Sax Rohmer. The stories "Beyond the Black River," "The Treasure of Tranicos," and "Wolves Beyond the Border" are derived from the Indian-fighting novels of Robert W. Chambers, which were often laid in upstate New York in late +XVIII, and possibly also from the novels of J. Fenimore Cooper.

Other fictional influences on Howard were Jack London (whom he much admired), Howard Pyle, and Edgar Rice Burroughs. He also read travel books, such as those of Sir Richard Burton and (possibly) Rosita Forbes. And he read a lot of history. His knowledge of the medieval Muslim world was not negligible, as was shown by the original manuscript of "Hawks over Shem" (entitled, before I rewrote it as a Conan story, "Hawks over Egypt"). This story dealt with the reign and disappearance of the mad eleventh-century Caliph Hakîm.

The fantastic side of Howard's stories seems to have been derived largely from Lovecraft and from Clark Ashton Smith, as is shown by several of How-

ard's names (Crom, Valusia, Commoria, etc.). There is some slight, inconclu-
sive evidence that Howard had read Eddison's *The Worm Ouroboros*: the Iron
Tower of Tarantia and the Iron Tower of King Gorice of Carcë; Eddison's
Gallandus and Howard's Gallanus; and the mention of Hyperboreans by both.
He had also read some of Lord Dunsany's stories.

Here follows a glossary of personal and place names in the fifty Conan stories
professionally published so far. Besides the names devised by Howard for his
original Conan stories, I have also included (a) names adopted by the living
Conan authors for their stories, including stories written in posthumous collaboration with Howard, and (b) names discarded by Howard in the course of
his writing. The living authors have tried to follow the same system in choosing
names that Howard did. Howard often changed the names of places and persons between his first and his final draft; Glenn Lord, working from Howard's
rough drafts, has furnished a list of these discarded names. When an entry is
followed by another name in boldface, in parentheses and preceded by =, the
first name was discarded in favor of the second before the story reached final
form.

As far as possible, supposed derivations are given for all names. Where no
derivation is given, either the source of the name is not known, or it has been
forgotten by the author responsible for it, or it is thought that the name is a
purely made-up one. Stories are referred to by code letters, as shown below.
Stories are listed in the chronological order in which they occur in Conan's life.
The lower-case letters in parentheses following each title refer to authorship,
thus: *c* for Carter, *d* for de Camp, *h* for Howard, and *n* for Nyberg. Here are
the stories:

LD—Legions of the Dead (cd)
TC—The Thing in the Crypt (cd)
TE—The Tower of the Elephant (h)
HD—The Hall of the Dead (dh)
GB—The God in the Bowl (h)
RH—Rogues in the House (h)
HN—The Hand of Nergal (ch)
PP—The People of the Summit (dn)
CS—The City of Skulls (cd)
CM—The Curse of the Monolith (cd)
BG—The Bloodstained God (dh)
FD—The Frost Giant's Daughter (h)
LW—The Lair of the Ice Worm (cd)
QC—Queen of the Black Coast (h)

VW—The Vale of Lost Women (h)
CT—The Castle of Terror (cd)
SD—The Snout in the Dark (cdh)
HS—Hawks Over Shem (dh)
BC—Black Colossus (h)
SI—Shadows in the Dark (cd)
SM—Shadows in the Moonlight (h)
RE—The Road of the Eagles (dh)
WB—A Witch Shall Be Born (h)
BT—Black Tears (cd)
SZ—Shadows in Zamboula (h)
SK—The Star of Khorala (dn)
DI—The Devil in Iron (h)
FK—The Flame Knife (dh)
PC—The People of the Black Circle (h)
SS—The Slithering Shadow (h)
DT—The Drums of Tombalku (dh)
GT—The Gem in the Tower (cd)
PO—The Pool of the Black One (h)
CB—Conan the Buccaneer (cd)
RN—Red Nails (h)
JG—Jewels of Gwahlur (h)
IG—The Ivory Goddess (cd)
BR—Beyond the Black River (h)
MB—Moon of Blood (cd)
TT—The Treasure of Tranicos (ex-The Black Stranger) (dh)
BB—Wolves Beyond the Border (dh)
PS—The Phoenix on the Sword (h)
SC—The Scarlet Citadel (h)
CC—Conan the Conqueror (ex-The Hour of the Dragon) (h)
CA—Conan the Avenger (ex-The Return of Conan) (dn)
WM—The Witch of the Mists (cd)
BS—Black Sphinx of Nebthu (cd)
RZ—Red Moon of Zembabwei (cd)
SH—Shadows in the Skull (cd)
CI—Conan of the Isles (cd)

Dates are indicated thus: Arabic numerals mean years; Roman numerals, centuries; Arabic numerals followed by M, millennia. The signs + and − mean A.D. and B.C. respectively, although + is omitted for years after +1000. Hence −65 means 65 B.C.; +III denotes the third century of the Christian Era; −2M means the second millennium B.C.

Abdashtarth In HS, the high priest of Pteor in Asgalun. A Phoenician name.

Abimael In GT, a Shemitish sailor in the crew of the *Hawk*. A biblical name (Gen. 10:28).

Abombi In SC, a town on the Black Coast sacked by Conan and Bêlit. From Abomey, West Africa.

Acheron In CC, an empire that fell 3,000 years before Conan's time, sometimes called the "northern Stygian kingdom." In Greek mythology, one of the four rivers of Hades; also the name of several rivers in ancient Greece, the largest (modern Gourla) being in Thesprotia.

Adonis In QC, a Shemitish god. In HS, Asgalun has a "Square of Adonis." The Greek name for a Semitic god of vegetation and agriculture, called Adonai ("Lord"), Tammuz, or (in Babylonia) Dumuzi.

Æsir In FD, QC, PS, &c., the blond folk of the northern country of Asgard. In Norse myth, the chief gods (singular, As): Odin, Thor, &c.

Afari In SD, a henchman of the Kushite nobleman Tuthmes. From the Afar, a Hamitic or Erythriotic tribe of Abyssinia (Ethiopia) and Somaliland; their name may be connected with ancient Ophir (q.v.).

Afghuli In PC, CA, one of the people of Afghulistan (q.v.).

Afghulistan In PC, a region of the Himelias. A mixture of Ghulistan (q.v.) and Afghanistan. The Afghuli tribe, of which Conan becomes chief, dwells here.

Ageera In SD, a Kushite witch-smeller.

Agha This title occurs in the names of Agha Shupras (BC) and Jehungir Agha (DI). From *ăgâ*, a Turkish title of respect.

Aghrapur, Agrapur In HN, SZ, DI, &c., the capital of Turan. After Agrâ, India, the site of the Taj Mahal, + the Hindustani *pur*, "town."

Ahriman In CC, BN, RZ, the Heart of Ahriman is a magical jewel. The evil god of Mazdaism or Zoroastrianism (Old Persian, *angra mainyu*, "evil spirit").

Ahrunga (=**Gwarunga**) In the first draft of JG; discarded.

Aja In VW, the chief of the Bakalah. Possibly from Jaja, an enterprising king of the Ibo or Igbo of Nigeria in the 1870s.

Ajaga In SC, a Kushite king. Possibly from the same source as Jaja or Ajonga (q.v.).

Ajonga In CC, a Negro galley slave. Possibly from Wajanga, a place in southern Libya mentioned by Rosita Forbes; or from *ajoga* (or *ajonga*) meaning "wizard" in the speech of the Lango of Uganda.

Ajujo In DT, the god of the black tribesmen of Tombalku. Possibly from "juju," a West African fetish, which comes from the French *joujou*, toy.

Akbatana, Akbitana In BC and JG, a Shemitish city. From Agbatana or Ecbatana, the Greco-Roman names for Hagmatana or Hangmatana (mod. Hamadan), the capital of ancient Media.

Akeb Man In CA, a Turanian officer. A pseudo-Arabic name.

Akhirom In HS, the mad king of Pelishtia. A Phoenician name, Hiram in Hebrew.

Akhlat In BT, a Shemitish town in the Zuagir deserts.

Akif In SZ, CA, a Turanian city. A Turkish proper name; e.g., 'Akif Pasha, a Turkish poet of +XIX.

Akivasha In CC, an evil immortal princess. From the Egyptian name (Ekwesh or Akkaiwasha) for the Achaioi or Achaeans (in archaic Greek, Achaiwoi).

Akkharia, Akkharim In HS, WB, BT, a Shemitish city-state and its people. Possibly from Akkad (Agade) in ancient Iraq.

Akkutho In SC, a former king of Koth. Possibly from the same source as Akkharia (q.v.).

Akrel In PC, an oasis in the desert near Khauran.

Akrim In RE, a river entering the Vilayet Sea from the southeast.

Alafdhal, Yar Afzal Respectively a Turanian guardsman in SZ and a Wazuli chief in PC. From al-Afdal (literally, "the most generous"), an Arabic name.

Alarkar In SK, a count, ancestor to Queen Marala.

Albiona In SK, CC, an Aquilonian countess, formerly Queen Marala of Ophir. From Albion, an old name for Britain, which in turn comes from the Albiones, the name given the Britons by several ancient geographers, such as Pytheas of Massilia (paraphrased by the late-Roman poet Avienus).

Alcemides In WB, TT, a Nemedian philosopher. From various Greek names like Alkides (Herakles), Alkimenes (Bellerophon's brother), Alkman (a poet of −VII), &c.

Alimane In CC, BS, a river between Aquilonia and Zingara, a tributary of the Khorotas. Probably from Allemagne, French for "Germany."

Alkmeenon In JG, IG, a deserted place in Keshan, once the capital of white rulers of the country. From one or more of the Greek names Alkman, Alkmaion, or Alkmenê.

Almuric In SS and CC, a prince of Koth. The name was used in Howard's posthumously published interplanetary novel, *Almuric*, as the name of the distant planet to which the hero is transported.

Altaku In BC, a well in the Oasis of Aphaka. From Altaqu or Eltekeh, a place in ancient Judah, about 12 miles northwest of Jerusalem, where Sennacherib's Assyrians defeated the Egyptians in −700.

Altaro In CC, a Nemedian priest, subordinate to Orastes. Possibly from Altare, Italy.

Alvaro In CI, a Zingaran pirate of the Barachas. A Spanish given name.

Amalric In BC, a Nemedian soldier of fortune; in CC, the Nemedian baron of Tor—perhaps intended as the same man, although the stories do not clearly so state; also, in DT, a young Aquilonian mercenary soldier. An old Germanic name (Gothic *Amalreiks*, French *Amaury*, English *Emery, Emory, Amory*), common in the Middle Ages; e.g., the name of two Christian kings of Jerusalem.

Howard probably took the name from these last, since he wrote a historical novelette, "Gates of Empire" (*Golden Fleece* for Jan. 1939) wherein one of these Kings Amalric of Jerusalem appears.

Amalrus In SK, SC, a noble and later king of Ophir. Probably from Amalric (q.v.).

Amazons In CB and mentioned in "The Hyborian Age," a southern Negro nation ruled by women. In Classical legend, nations of warrior women in Asia Minor and North Africa. The legend may be based upon the Sarmatians, a nomadic Iranic tribe of the Kuban, whose women were required to slay an enemy before they might marry.

Amboola In SD, an officer of the black spearmen of the kingdom of Kush. Probably from *bamboula*, a drum used in West African and Voodoo ceremonies and the dance performed to it. Cf. Bambula.

Amerus (=**Posthumo**) In the first draft of GB, discarded; from the same source as Amalric (q.v.).

Amilio (=**Tiberias**) In first draft of BR, discarded; from the same source as Amilius (q.v.).

Amilius A barony in Aquilonia mentioned in CC. From Æmilia (mod. Emilia), a province in northern Italy, and Æmilius, the corresponding Roman gentile name.

Amir In PC, the Amir Jehun pass is in Ghulistan. Arabic for "commander."

Amra In CC, the name, meaning "lion," by which Conan was known when he sailed with the black corsairs. Howard had used the name before, as Am-ra, a young Atlantean in the Kull story "Exile of Atlantis," and again as the hero of the story "Gods of the North," rewritten from a Conan story, "The Frost Giant's Daughter," but when it was rejected published in a fan magazine with the title and the hero's name changed. Several possible derivations have been suggested. Amra is the name of a small place in Kâthiâvâr, western India. In Arabic, *'umara* or *'amara* means "princes." *Amra* ("strange") is the title of a poem in praise of St. Columba, allegedly by the Irish bard Dallán Forgaill (+VI), although the poem is by some scholars considered a pseudographic work of later date. None of these derivations seems completely satisfactory.

Amric In BN, a Kothian soldier in Conan's guard. From Amalric (q.v.) and Alric, a +VIII king of Kent, England.

Amurath In SM, Shah Amurath is a Turanian noble. A Turkish proper name, also rendered as Murad.

Anakia, Anakim In HS, WB, CA, a Shemitish city-state and its people. A race of tall mountaineers in southern Palestine before its conquest by Joshua, mentioned in Deut. 1:28; 9:2; Josh. 11:21f.

Andarra In SS, a dream place mentioned by a man of Xuthal. From Andorra, a small Pyrenean principality.

Angharzeb In PS, a onetime king of Turan. From Aurangzeb Almagir, a +XVII Mughal emperor of India.

Angkhor In WM, RZ, the capital of Kambuja. From Angkor Wat, the ancient capital of Cambodia.

Anshan In FK, the capital of Iranistan. A city in ancient Elam.

Antar In FK, a Zuagir. From Antara, a legendary Arab hero.

Antillia In CI, an archipelago between the former site of Atlantis and the American coast. The name given a suppositious land in the western Atlantic by pre-Columbian geographers; the name (Italian, Antigla; Portuguese, Antilha; all pronounced the same way) means "counter-island."

Anu In RH, a Hyborian god. The Babylonian sky god.

Aphaka In BC, an oasis in the Shemitish desert. Probably from the Lebanese village known to the Classical Greeks as Aphaka, mod. 'Afqa, near al-Munteira. It was destroyed by a landslide in 1911.

Aphaki In DT, the former ruling caste of Tombalku, of mixed Shemite-Negroid ancestry. Probably from the same source as Aphaka (q.v.).

Aquilonia In TE, QC, RN, &c., the leading Hyborian kingdom, of which Conan eventually becomes king. The name of an ancient city in southern Italy, between modern Venosa and Benevento; ultimately from Latin *aquilo,-onis*, "north wind."

Arallu In FK, a hell referred to by Antar. The Babylonian hell.

Aram In SZ, Aram Baksh is a villainous innkeeper of Zamboula. An Armenian proper name, going back to a king of Urartu in −IX. Also the Hebrew name for Syria, whence "Aramaic."

Aratus In SM, a Brythunian pirate. From the Greek proper name Aratos, borne by a statesman of −III among others.

Arbanus In SC, the general of King Strabonus of Koth. From Artabanus, the Latin form of Artabanush (later Artaban, Artavan), borne by various Persian and Armenian notables including four Parthian kings.

Ardashir In CS, a Turanian officer. An Iranian name, originally Artaxerxes or Artakhshathra. In CA, another Turanian officer.

Arenjun In TC, HD, BG, &c., the "thief-city" of Zamora. From Erzincan, Turkey (the Turks use *c* for the sound of English *j*).

Argos In QC, WB,. PO, &c., a maritime Hyborian nation. A Peloponnesian city in classical Greece, reputedly the oldest city in Greece, at the head of the Gulf of Argolis near modern Nafplion. Howard calls the people of his Argos "Argosseans," whereas the folk of the historical Argos were called "Argives."

Argus In QC, an Argossean ship. From Argos, a Greek name borne by a mythical hundred-eyed giant, Odysseus' dog, and others. Cf. Argos.

Arideus In CC, the squire of Tarascus. Possibly from Philip Arrhidaeus (Arridaios), a half-brother of Alexander the Great.

Ariostro In BN, CI, the young king of Argos, successor to Milo. From Lodovico Ariosto, the Italian poet of +XV and +XVI, author of *Orlando Furioso*.

Arno In MB, an Aquilonian officer. A North European given name; also a river in Italy.

Arpello In SC, an Aquilonian noble. Possibly from Rapallo, Italy, or Apelles, a Greek painter of −IV, or a combination of the two.

Arshak In BG, a Turanian prince; in FK, the successor to Kobad Shah as king of Iranistan. An Iranian name (also Arshaka or Arsaces) borne by the founder of the Parthian dynasty among others.

Artaban In RE, a Turanian general. From the same source as Arbanus. (q.v.).

Artanes In CI, a Zamorian pirate in Conan's crew. A Persian name (later Arten) borne by various Achaemenid and Armenian notables.

Artus In CA, a Vilayet pirate. A form of "Arthur."

Arus In "The Hyborian Age," a Nemedian priest of Mitra, missionary to the Picts. In GB, a Nemedian watchman. In CA, a name taken by Conan on his way to Khanyria. Possibly from Arûs, a medieval sultan of Wadai (q.v.), Africa.

Aryan, Aryas In the prolegomenon to CC (see the introduction to the Ace Books edition of *Conan*), Howard speaks of the Hyborian Age as the time "between the years when the oceans drank Atlantis and the gleaming cities, and the years of the rise of the Sons of Aryas." I do not know whether "Aryas" is an individual or an error for "sons of *the* Aryas." In "The Hyborian Age," Howard speaks of the Aryans as the people of mixed Vanir, Æsir, and Cimmerian descent who conquered lands in Europe and Asia after the Picts and the Hyrkanians had overthrown the Hyborian nations and a convulsion of nature sank much of the Hyborian land beneath the Atlantic Ocean and the North and Mediterranean seas.

The true history of the term "Aryan" is complex. *Ârya* is a Sanskrit word meaning "noble." Between −1500 and −1000, nomadic, cattle-raising barbarians calling themselves Ârya, "noble ones," overran Iran and northern India. About the same time other nomads, speaking similar tongues, conquered most of Europe and parts of the Near East. They ruled the natives, imposed their languages upon them, and finally mixed with them. On linguistic evidence, these nomads probably radiated out originally, perhaps before −2000, from what are now Poland and the Ukraine. They were enabled to conquer their neighbors and their neighbors' neighbors by having been the first people to tame the horse.

In +XIX, scholars discovered the relation of the speech of Iran and northern India on one hand and of Europe on the other, and also came upon this word Ârya. They called this family of languages Indo-European or, sometimes, "Aryan." Since then, "Aryan" has been used in several senses: (a) the Indo-European family of languages; (b) the Indo-Iranian or eastern branch of this family; (c) the original Indo-European-speaking, horse-taming nomads; (d) the descendants of these nomads; or (e), loosely, anybody of the Caucasoid or white race speaking an Indo-European language. Strictly speaking, the term has no racial meaning and is avoided by most scientists because of its equivocality.

In addition, in the late +XIX and early +XX, "Aryan" was used by a number of writers, cultists, demagogues, and politicians (notably Gobineau, Chamberlain, and Hitler) who built up a pseudoscientific cult about the supposedly pure, superior Aryan race. They used the term as a vague equivalent of "Nordic," which describes the tall, blond, long-headed type of the Caucasoid race found most commonly in northern Europe. Actually, there is no reason to think that the original horsemen were Nordics. Since the Alpine type predominates in their land of origin, it is most likely that they were Alpines. And, whatever their racial type, it soon disappeared by intermixture with those whom they conquered.

Although, like other pulp writers of his time, Howard was given to national and racial stereotypes, he was as far as I can tell no crackpot Aryanist. In his introduction to "The Hyborian Age," he was careful to state that the essay was a mere fictional background for his stories and not to be taken as a serious theory of prehistory. And some of the most vigorous peoples in his pseudo-history are racially mixed.

Ascalante In PS, BN, an Aquilonian outlaw, formerly count of Thune; in the Kull story "Exile of Atlantis," a minor character alluded to—an Atlantean once enslaved in Valusia. From Escalante, a town in Spain near Santander. Howard probably took the name from Father Silvestre Vélez de Escalante, a missionary of +XVIII who explored the country that became the southwestern United States and whose name is borne by several places (towns, a river, a mountain range) in Colorado and Utah.

Asgalun, Askalon In QC, HS, JG, the capital of Pelishtia, a Shemitish city-state. From Ascalon or Ashkelon, an ancient city of Palestine.

Asgard In LD, FD, PS, &c., a northern land (cf. Æsir). From ´Asgarə, in Norse mythology the home of the Æsir or principal gods.

Ashkhaurian Dynasty In WB, the ruling family of Khauran (q.v.).

Ashtoreth In QC, a Shemitish deity. (*See* Ishtar.)

Askia In DT, a black wizard, servant of King Sakumbe. From Askia Muhammad or Askia the Great, king of the Songhoi Negroes, who ruled the Songhoi Empire from Timbuktu, 1492–1529.

Asshuri In BC, RE, WB, Shemitish mercenary soldiers. From Asshur, (Assur, Ashur, Aššur), the original name of Assyria, of one of its capital cities, and of its patron gods.

Astreas In WB, a Nemedian philosopher. Possibly from the Greek name Asterios, borne by the mythical Minotaur among others.

Asura In PC, CC, a god of an eastern religion flourishing secretly in Aquilonia. In Indian mythology, a term for a god, spirit, or demon, cognate with the Persian *ahura*.

Atali In FD, the daughter of Ymir. Possibly from Attila the Hun, who appears in the *Völsungá Saga* as Atli.

Atalis In HN, a philosopher of Yaralet in Turan. Probably from the Greek name Attalos or the Hunnish Attila.

Athicus In RH, a prison guard. From Æthicus, a Byzantine geographer.

Atlaia, Atlaians In DT and "The Hyborian Age," a Negro nation far to the south. Possibly from Atlas (cf. Atlantis).

Atlantis An imaginary sunken continent in the Atlantic Ocean, conceived by Plato for his dialogues (*Timaios* and *Kritias* and named for the demigod Atlas; used by Howard (along with many fantasy writers, geographical speculators, and cultists) as part of the background for his King Kull stories and mentioned in TE, PC, the prolegomenon to CC, &c.

Attalus In PS, CC, an Aquilonian barony. From Attalos, a common Macedonian personal name, borne in Roman times by three kings of Pergamon in Asia Minor.

Attelius In BB, a baron of the Westermarck. Possibly from Attila, or Attalus, or both.

Auzakia In CS, one of the seven sacred cities of Meru.

Ayodhya In FK, PC, CA, the capital of Vendhya. From Ayuthya, the former capital of Thailand, and Ayodha, the legendary capital of India in the Golden Age of King Rama.

Aztrias Petanius In GB, a Nemedian noble. "Aztrias" is probably from the same source as Astreas (q.v.); "Petanius" may be from any of several Classical names like Petines and Prytanis.

Azweri In CS, a people of Meru.

Baal In CC, a minion of Xaltotun; (also =Baal-Pteor, discarded). From *ba'al*, Hebrew-Phoenician for "lord." Cf. Bel, Baal-Pteor.

Baal-Pteor In SZ, a Kosalan strangler. From Baal-Peor, a place in Moab (Num. 25). Cf. Pteor. In Howard's preliminary drafts, this character was called Baal or Bel.

Badb In PS, a Cimmerian deity. An Irish goddess, more exactly Badhbh (pronounced BAHV, BAHDHV).

Bajujh In VW, the Negro king of Bakalah. There was a piratical tribe of Borneo, the Bajau, but the derivation is dubious.

Bakalah In VW, a Negro village and tribe of Kush. From a Central African tribe, the Bakalai or Bakalei.

Bakhariot, Bakhauriot In WB, PC, CA, an adjective describing a kind of broad belt. From Bokhara, Turkestan.

Bakhr In BN, a Stygian river, an affluent of the Styx. From the Arabic *bahr*, "river."

Bakra In HN, a Turanian general.

Baksh See Aram. Probably from *bakshi, bakshish*, used in the Near East and India for "giver" and "gratuity" respectively (from the Persian *bakhshi, bakhshish*, or the Arabic *baqshîsh*).

Balardus In BN, the king of Koth, successor to Strabonus. A pseudo-Latin name.

Balash In RK, chief of the Kushafi tribe in the Ilbars Mts. A Persian name (Balas, Valash, Valagash, &c.) of Parthian and Sassanid times.

Balthus In BR, a young Tauranian settler in Conajohara. Possibly from Baltia, a Latin name for Scandinavia (whence the Baltic Sea).

Bamula In VW, CT, a Kushite tribe. Possibly from Bambuba, an existing Negro tribe near Lake Edward; or from Bambara, a tribe on the upper Niger; or from *bamboula*, for which see Amboola.

Baraccus In CA, an exiled Aquilonian nobleman. From Galaccus, in TT.

Baracha In PO, GT, JG, &c., an archipelago in the Western Ocean, used as a pirate base. From Barataria, Louisiana, used as a base by Jean Lafitte, a pirate of the early +XIX.

Bardiya In FK, an official of Kobad Shah's court. An ancient Persian name (Greek, Smerdis).

Barras In SK, a henchman of Count Rigello. A French place name; the Comte de Barras was a French Revolutionary and Napoleonic politician.

Bel In TE, QC, BC, &c., the Shemitish god of thieves. An Assyro-Babylonian word meaning "lord" (cognate with the Hebrew-Phoenician *ba'al*) applied originally to En-lil, an old Babylonian earth god, and later to Marduk, the Babylonian Zeus. A discarded name for Baal-Pteor (q.v.) in the first draft of SZ.

Belesa, Beloso Respectively, the Zingaran heroine of TT and a Zingaran man-at-arms in CC. Origin uncertain; remote possibilities are Belesis, a Babylonian priest of −VII mentioned by Ktesias; a Belesa River in Ethiopia; and Berosos (or Berossus, &c.), a Hellenized Babylonian priest and writer of early −III.

Bêlit In QC, CI, a Shemitish woman pirate. Assyro-Babylonian for "goddess."

Belverus In CC, the capital of Nemedia. Possibly from Belverde, Italy.

Bhalkhana In PC, an adjective describing a breed of horse. Probably from the Balkans or from Balkh, a city in Afghanistan.

Bhambar Pass In PS, a pass in Hyrkania.

Bhunda In PC, Bhunda Chand is king of Vendhva. From various Indian names: Bundelkhand, Bhândârkar, &c.

Bigharma In DT, Howard's manuscript spoke of "the Baghirmi, the Mandingo, and the Bornu" as peoples of the Tombalku Empire. All are modern: the Baghirmi, a Negro tribe near Lake Chad; the Mandingo, a Sudanic people widely spread about West Africa; Bornu, a province of northern Nigeria, once an independent sultanate. I changed the sentence to "the Bigharma, the Mindanga, and the Borni," thinking that the use of so many well-known, modern tribal and geographical names, unmodified, would put too great a strain on the reader's sense of illusion.

Bît-Yakin In JG, a Pelishti wizard. In Assyrian times, the capital of Chaldea (Kaldi) or, sometimes, Chaldea (modern southern Iraq) itself.

Black River In BR, BB, a river on the western Aquilonian frontier. Probably from the Black River in upstate New York, mentioned in the frontier stories of Robert W. Chambers.

Bombaata In HS, a Kushite captain in Asgalun. A pseudo-Bantu name.

Bori In "The Hyborian Age," the deified eponymous ancestor of the Hyboreans or Hybori; from Hyperborea (qq.v.).

Borni In DT, a people of the Tombalku Empire. *See* Bigharma.

Borus In GT, the first mate of Captain Gonzago's *Hawk*. From Boros, an uncommon Greek name.

Bossonian Marches In GB and all the stories from BR to CC, the western frontier province of Aquilonia. Possibly from Bossiney, a former Parliamentary borough in Cornwall, England, which included Tintagel Castle, connected with the Arthurian legends.

Bragi In FD, a chief of the Vanir. The Norse god of poetry.

Bragoras In DT, a former Nemedian king.

Brant In BB, Brant Drago's son is the elected governor of Thandara. "Brant" is probably from Joseph Brant, the English name of Theyendanegea, a Mohawk chief of American Revolutionary times.

Brocas In MB, BB, the baron of Torh, lord of Conawaga. Possibly from the Roman cognomen Brocchus, borne by several relatively obscure Romans of the Senatorial class.

Brythunia In TE, SM, DI, &c., an easterly Hyborian land. From the Welsh Brython, "Briton," derived from the same root as the Latin Brito, Britannia.

Bubastes In BN, the Styx is crossed at the Ford of Bubastes. From Bubastis (ancient Egyptian, Perbaste), a city in ancient Egypt, near modern Zagazig.

Bwatu In CB, a man of Juma's tribe. A pseudo-Bantu name.

Byatis In RZ, a deity of the serpent-men of Valusia. From "serpent-bearded Byatis," an entity in Robert Bloch's Cthulhuvian tales.

Caranthes In GB, a priest of Ibis. *See* Kalanthes.

Castria In RZ, an Aquilonian barony. From various European places named Castra (ancient Roman), Castries (French), and Kastri (Greek).

Catlaxoc In CI, a harlot of Ptahuacan. A pseudo-Mayan name.

Cenwulf In BN, a captain of Bossonian archers. From the Anglo-Saxon names Cenric and Ceolwulf.

Cernunnos In BN, a god invoked by Diviatix. A stag-horned Gaulish god.

Chabela In CB, BN, the daughter of King Ferdrugo of Zingara. The common

Spanish nickname for Isabel. Since Isabel is Spanish for Elizabeth, Chabela is the exact equivalent of Betty.

Chaga In SD, one of the ruling caste of the Kushite capital of Jumballa, of mixed Stygian-Negroid ancestry. From the Chaga or Chagga, an advanced, progressive Negro tribe of Tanzania.

Chakan In BB, one of the race of Pithecanthropoid sub-men dwelling in the Pictish wilderness. Possibly from the same source as Chaga (q.v.) or from Chaka or Tshaka, the Zulu emperor, 1783–1828.

Chand *See* Bhunda. An Indian proper name, also spelled Cand, Chund.

Chelkus In VW, the Ophirean family to which Livia belongs. Possibly from Chelkias, a Judaean mercenary soldier and a favorite of Queen Kleopatra III of Egypt at the end of −II.

Chengir Khan In CA, a Vendhyan nobleman. From Chiang Kaishek (or from Jengis, Genghis, or Chingiz) + Khan (q.v.).

Cherkees In WB, an adjective designating a broad, curved knife. From Cherkess, a name for the Circassians or Adighe of the Caucasus.

Chicmec In RN, a man of Xuchotl. From the Chichimecs, a tribe of Mexican Indians.

Chiron In CC, a minion of Xaltotun. A wise centaur (Cheiron) of Greek myth. Howard may also have been thinking of Charon, in Greek mythology the supernatural boatman who ferried souls across the Styx.

Chunder In PC, Chunder Shan is the governor of Peshkauri. A common Indian proper name, also spelled Chandra or Candra.

Cimmeria, Cimmerians In all the Conan stories, a land and people north of the Hyborian nations, from whom the Gaels or Celts are descended. Historically, the Gimirai or Cimmerians were a nomadic people who invaded Asia Minor in −VII; the modern Armenian language descends from theirs. In Homer, a people (the Kimmerioi) living in a foggy western land. Howard may have had in mind a once proposed but now discredited connection between the Kimmerioi and the Cymry or Welsh.

Codrus In FK, a lieutenant of Conan. From Kodros, a legendary king of Athens.

Colchian Mts. In CA, a range south of the Vilayet Sea. From Colchis, a Caucasian land of Classical times (modern Georgia).

Commoria In TE, a kingdom of Atlantean times. From Commorion, the capital of Hyperborea in Clark Ashton Smith's stories "The Testament of Athammaus," "The Seven Geases," &c.; or from the probable source of these, Comoria or Comorin, the cape at the southern tip of India.

Conajohara In BR, BB, MB, a province on the Aquilonian frontier between the Black and Thunder Rivers. From Canajoharie, a town on the Mohawk River, New York State. Upstate New York also has a Black River, and Howard probably derived both town and river from Robert W. Chambers's stories.

Conan The hero of the Conan stories, a gigantic Cimmerian adventurer. A common Celtic name (e.g., A. Conan Doyle and the Dukes Conan of medieval Brittany), from Conann, a king of the Fomorians (Fomór, pron. "fuh-WORE" or Fomhóraigh) in Irish mythology, in which Conann was killed in battle with the Nemedians (q.v.). Howard also wrote stores of medieval Ireland, unconnected with the Hyborian Age series, with heroes named Conan or Conn (q.v.).

Conawaga In BB, MB, a province of the Westermarck, the borderland between the Pictish Wilderness and Bossonia. From Caughnawaga (or less probably, Conewago), New York.

Conn In the stories from WM to CI, the nickname of Conan's elder son, later King Conan II. A legendary ancient king of Tara, Ireland, claimed as ancestor by various Irish and Scottish dynasties.

Constantius In WB, a Kothic adventurer. The name of three Roman emperors of + IV.

Corinthia In JG, IG, a southeasterly Hyborian nation. From Corinth (Korinthos), a rich city in Classical Greece. Possibly suggested to Howard by the Biblical book of Corinthians.

Couthen In CA, CI, a county of Aquilonia.

Coyoga In BB, a province of the Westermarck, the borderland between Pictland and Bossonia. From Lake Cayuga, New York.

Crassides In CA, captain of the guard at the gate of Khanyria. From Crassus, a common Roman cognomen, + the Greek patronymic suffix-*ides*.

Cratos In CB, a physician of Kordava. From Kratos, a Greek mythological figure.

Crom In all the Conan stories, the chief Cimmerian god and Conan's favorite oath. Usually translated from the Irish as "bent," as in Crom Cruaich, "the bloody bent one," a famous Irish pagan idol. An alternative translation of Crom Cruaich is "lord of the mound."

Ctesphon In TT, PS, the king of Stygia. From Ctesiphon, an ancient ruined city in Iraq, near Baghdad, which flourished in Parthian and Sassanid times.

Cush *See* Kush.

Dagon, Dagonia In DI, Dagonia is an ancient kingdom on the Vilayet Sea, and Dagon, its ruined capital on the isle of Xapur. In JG, Dagon is a god of Zembabwei. Dagon was a fish-god of the Philistines and Phoenicians.

Dagoth In SC, a hill in Koth. Probably from Dagon (q.v.) + Koth (q.v.).

Dagozai In PC, a Himelian or Ghulistani tribe. Probably from Dagon (q.v.) + the Pakhtun (Pashtun, Pathan) tribal ending-*zai* (from *zoe*, "son") as such modern Pakhtun tribes as the Ghilzai and Yusufzai.

Damballah In WM, RZ, another name for Set. The serpent god of Haitian Voodoo, of Dahomean (West African) origin.

Danu In BN, a deity invoked by Diviatix. A Celtic mother goddess, also Dana.

Darfar In SZ, RN, a land of Negro cannibals. Howard derived this name from the region of Darfur in north-central Africa. Darfur is an Arabic name, meaning "abode (*dâr*) of the Fur," the dominant Negroid people of the area. In changing the name to Darfar, Howard unwittingly changed the Arabic meaning to "abode of mice"! The original Darfur is now the westernmost part of the Sudanese Republic.

Dathan In SD, an official of the king of Eruk. A biblical name (Num. 16:1).

Dayuki In RE, a Hyrkanian chief. From Dayaukku or Deioces, a Median ruler of −VIII.

Dekanawatha In BN, RZ, a Pictish chief. From the historical Iroquois leaders Hiawatha and Dekanawida.

Demetrio In GB, a Nemedian magistrate; in CC, an Argossean sea captain. Italian for Demetrios, a common Greek name, from Demeter, goddess of agriculture.

Derketa In RN, a Kushite goddess. From Derketo (q.v.).

Derketo In QC, BC, SS, &c., a Shemitish and Stygian goddess, also worshiped in Zembabwei. A Greek name for the Syrian fertility goddess 'Atar'ata. (Cf. Ishtar.)

Devi In PC, CA, the title of the sister of the king of Vendhya. Hindi for "goddess."

Dexitheus In TT, CI, a priest of Mitra. From Greek names like Dexippos and Dorotheus.

Diana In SD, a Nemedian slave girl in Jumballa. Originally an Italian goddess of light, mountains, and woods, early identified or merged with the Greek Artemis.

Dion In PS, an Aquilonian noble. A common Greek name, borne by, among others, a tyrant of Syracuse in−IV.

Dionus In GB, a Nemedian prefect of police. From Dion (q.v.) and possibly also Dianus, an old spelling of the Roman god Janus.

Dirk In BB, Dirk Strom's son is the commandant of Fort Kwanyara. "Dirk" is the Dutch and Danish form of the old Gothic name Theodoric or Theiudareiks (German Dietrich, English Derek, French Thierry).

Diviatix In BN, RZ, a Ligurean Druid. From the Gaulish chieftains in Caesar's army, Diviciacus and Dumnorix.

Dongola In DT, a Negro tribe mentioned in the synopsis but not in the unfinished rough draft. From a town and province of that name in the Sudan, on the Nile. The people are the Dongolavi.

Drago *See* Brant.

Drujistan In FK, a place in the Ilbars Mountains. Persian for "land of demons."

Duali In CA, a Zuagir tribe. Possibly from Dooala, a place somewhere in Africa.

Edric In MB, an Aquilonian scout. A Saxon king of Kent in +VII.

Egil In LD, an As. A common Nordic name, e.g., of a Swedish king of the legendary Yngling dynasty, before +VI, and of Egil Skallagrimsson, an Icelandic poet of +IX.

Eiglophian Mts. In LW, a range south of Asgard. From Clark Ashton Smith's story, "The Seven Geases."

Emilius In CC, Emilius Scavonus is an Aquilonian noble. From Æmilius, a Roman gentile name (cf. Amilius, Scavonus).

Enaro, Enaros In GB, a Nemedian charioteer; in the King Kull story "By this Axe I Rule!" (later rewritten as PS), Enaros is the commander of the Black Legion. Both probably from Inaros, the Greek name for a Libyan rebel against Persian rule in Egypt, −V, mentioned by Herodotus; the original Egyptian name was probably An-ha-heru-ra-u.

Enosh In BT, the chief of Akhlat. A Biblical name, a variant of Enos (Gen. 5:9).

Epemitreus PS, CI, a long-dead sage. From Epimetheus, in Greek legend Pandora's husband.

Epeus In DT, a former king of Aquilonia. Probably from Epeius or Epeios, in Greek legend the builder of the Trojan horse.

Epona In BN, a deity invoked by Diviatix. The Gaulish goddess of horses.

Erlik In SZ, CA, a Turanian god. The name of a god of the underworld of the Altai Tatars. Howard possibly got his Erlik from Robert W. Chambers's novel *The Slayer of Souls*, which exploits this deity. Howard also brought "priests of Erlik" into a fantasy with a modern setting, "Black Hound of Death" (*Weird Tales*, Nov. 1936).

Erlikites In FK, worshipers of Erlik (q.v.).

Eruk In QC, SD, a Shemitish city-state. From ancient Uruk, Erech, or Orchoê in Babylonia (modern Warka, Iraq).

Escelan In RN, a man of Xuchotl. Probably from the same source as Ascalante (q.v.).

Fabio In GT, an Argossean sailor in the crew of the *Hawk*. An Italian name, from the Roman gentile name Fabius.

Farouz In HS, a name assumed by Mazdak. From the common Persian name Peroch, Peroz, Firuz, &c.

Femesh Valley In CA, site of a battle fought by Conan in Vendhya.

Feng In CM, a duke of Kusan. A common Chinese surname, rhyming with "hung."

Ferdrugo In CS, CB, BN, the king of Zingara. From Federigo, Spanish for Frederick.

Flavius In MB, an Aquilonian officer. A Roman gentile name.

Fronto In SD, an Ophirean thief. A common Roman cognomen.

Frosol In SK, a feudal county in Ophir.

Fulk In WM, an Aquilonian. A name borne by several medieval French notables (French, Foulques).

Galacus In TT, a Kothic pirate. Latin for "Galician."

Galannus *See* Servius. Probably from either the Roman emperor Galienus or Gallandus, a Carcean pirate in E. R. Eddison's *The Worm Ouroboros*.

Galbro In TT, a Zingaran seneschal. Possibly from Gabriello, Italian for "Gabriel."

Gallah In SD, the lower, Negroid caste of Jumballa. From the Galla, an Erythriotic-Negroid people of Abyssinia (Ethiopia) and Kenya.

Galparan, Galporan In CC, a place in western Aquilonia. The former spelling is Howard's; the latter appears only on Kyle's end-paper maps in the Gnome Press editions of the Conan stories.

Galter *See* Jon. An English occupational surname, meaning "clay-digger."

Galzai In PC, CA, a Himelian or Ghulistani tribe. From the Ghilzai, a modern Afghan-Pakhtun tribe.

Gamburu In CB, the capital of the Amazons. From various African place names, e.g., Gambaga (Ghana) and Omaruru (Namibia).

Garma In PS, a road.

Garogh (=**Teyanoga**) In first draft of BB; discarded. Probably from Caroga (also Lake and Creek), Fulton County, New York.

Garus In SK, an adherent of Queen Marala of Ophir.

Gath (=**Aphaka**) In first draft of BC; discarded. A town in western Judea.

Gault In BB, Gault Hagar's son is the narrator. "Gault" is an old English word for stiff clay, also used in the form "Galt" as a surname.

Gazal In DT, a city in the desert of northern Darfar. From the Bahr al-Ghazâl (Arabic for "the gazelle river"), an eastward-flowing river, which joins the White Nile at Lake No.

Gebal *See* Djebal. Possibly either from the Arabic *jabal*, "mountain," or from the town of Gebal (Jebeil or Jubayl), Lebanon—Classical Byblos, Phoenician Gubla.

Gebellez In TT, a Zingaran. The name was Gebbrelo in the original manuscript (probably from the same source as Galbro, q.v.), but I changed it because it was too much like Galbro, another character in the same story.

Ghanara, Ghanata In SZ, CB, CC, adjectives designating a desert south of Stygia and its people. From Ghana, a medieval empire in the western Sudan. The name has been revived for the Dominion of the Commonwealth formerly called the Gold Coast.

Ghandar Chen In CA, a spy of King Yezdigerd of Turan in Tarantia. From the Swedish name Gunder (that of a Swedish world champion runner in the 1940s) + "Chen" from "Shan" or "Shah" (qq.v.).

Gharat In CA, a ruined temple in the Zuagir desert. From "carat," the unit of weight.

Ghaznavi In DI, a Turanian councillor. From Ghaznavid, an adjective designating the dynasty founded by the +XI Afghan conqueror Mahmud of Ghazna, which in turn is the city called Gazaka in ancient times.

Ghemur In CA, a Vendhyan conspirator. From "lemur," a member of the Lemuroidea, a suborder of primitive primates (bush-baby, galago, loris, &c.).

Ghor In PC, a place in Afghulistan. From Ghor or Ghur, a medieval Afghan kingdom. (Ghor is also the name of the Dead Sea Valley in Palestine, but Howard probably got the name from the other source.)

Ghorbal In first draft of CC, the demesne of a Nemedian lord at the execution of Albiona; discarded. Probably from the same sources as Ghor and Khorbul (qq.v.).

Ghori In DI, a fort near Khawarizm. A subprovince of modern Afghanistan. The adjective "Ghorid" designates the medieval dynasties of Ghor (q.v.).

Ghoufags In PS, a Hyrkanian mountain tribe.

Ghulistan In PC, CA, a region of the Himelian Mts. A combination of Arabic *ghûl*, "ghoul," + Persian *istân, estân*, "country"; hence "land of ghouls." (In Persian, Ghulistan would mean "land of roses," but I do not think that is what Howard had in mind.)

Ghurran (=Tauran) In first draft of BR; discarded. Probably from Ghurian, Afghanistan.

Gilzan In DI, a Shemitish torturer. Probably from the same source as Galzai (q.v.).

Gitara In PC, Yasmina's maid. From *gitana*, Spanish for "Gypsy woman." Like "Gypsy," the word is a corruption of that for "Egyptian," although the real Gypsies originally came from India. (Cf. Zingara.)

Gleg In RE, a Zaporoskan robber lord. An old Russian name.

Glyco In MB, an Aquilonian officer. From Glykon, the name of several Greek writers.

Gobir In DT, a Ghanata brigand. The name of a medieval Negro kingdom in the western Sudan.

Godrigo In CB, a Zingaran philosopher. From the Spanish name Rodrigo.

Golamira In PS, CI, a magical mountain.

Gomani In CB, a Kushite slave. A minor +XIX African king and his kingdom, on the border of Tanzania and Mozambique.

Gonzago In GT, captain of the *Hawk*, a Barachan pirate ship. From Gonzaga, an Italian princely family, lords and eventually dukes of Milan, +XIII to +XVIII.

Gonzalvio In CI, Trocero's son. From the Spanish name Gonsalvo, e.g. Gonzalo or Gonsalvo de Córdoba, a Spanish general of +XV.

Goralian Hills In CC, a region in western Aquilonia. Possibly from the Gor-alians or Gorales, mountaineers of southern Poland.

Goram Singh In CI, a Vendhyan pirate in the Barachas. An Indian name; Singh (Hindi for "lion") is regularly used as a surname by adherents of the Sikh religion.

Gorm In FD, an As (see Æsir); in LD, a bard of the Æsir; in BB, Otho Gorm's son is a forest ranger of Schohira (*see* Strom); in "The Hyborian Age," a Pictish chief after Conan's time. The first king of Denmark, in +X.

Gorthangpo In CS, a Meruvian. A pseudo-Tibetan name.

Gorulga In JG, a Keshian priest. Possibly from the Goruol River, a tributary of the Niger.

Gotarza In FK, the captain of Kobad Shah's royal guard. An ancient Persian name (also Gotarzes, Godarz, Guderz, &c.).

Graaskal Mts. In CA, a range on the borders of Hyperborea. Possibly from the Norwegian *gr°a sk°al*, "gray bowl."

Gromel In PS, a Bossonian commanding Conan's Black Legion.

Grondar In FK and the Kull stories, a pre-Catastrophic kingdom, coeval with Valusia.

Guarralid In BN, a Zingaran dukedom. From Spanish place names like Gua-darrema and Valladolid.

Guilaime In WM, CI, an Aquilonian baron. From Guillaume, French for Wil-liam.

Gullah In FK, BR, the Pictish gorilla-god. One of a group of American Ne-groes living along the coast of Georgia and speaking a distinctive Afro-American dialect.

Gunderland, Gundermen In TE, GB, RH, &c., the northernmost province of Aquilonia and its people. Probably from Gunther (Gundicar) or Gunderic, +V kings of the Burgundians.

Gurasha In PC, a valley in Afghulistan.

Gwahlur In JG, IG, the Teeth of Gwahlur are the treasure of Alkmeenon. From Gwalior, India.

Gwarunga In JG, a Keshian priest. Possibly from Garua, West Africa.

Gwawela In BR, a Pictish village. Gwalia is an old name for Wales, and there is a Gwala, Egypt, but such derivations seem unlikely.

Hadrathus In CC, a priest of Asura. Possibly from the Roman name Hadri-anus, an emperor of +II.

Hagar *See* Gault. A Germanic personal name, also Hager.

Hakhamani In FK, an informer for Kobad Shah. The original Persian for Achaemenes, legendary founder of the Achaemenid dynasty.

Hakon In BB, Hakon Strom's son is a commander of rangers in Schohira.

"Hakon" is from the Norse name, Haakon or Hákon; e.g., Hakon the Dane in the *Völsungá Saga*. For "Strom," *see* Dirk, Strom.

Haloga In LD, the stronghold of Queen Vammatar in Hyperborea. From Halogaland, in the *Heimskringla*, a place in Lapland.

Hamar Kur In CA, a Turanian officer. From the Norwegian city Hamar, and "Kur" from Kurdistan.

Han In RZ, a deity of the serpent-men of Valusia.

Hanuman In SZ, FK, a monkey-god of Zamboula. The Indian monkey-god.

Hanumar In GB, a Nemedian city. Probably from Hanuman (q.v.).

Hatupep In CI, a merchant of Ptahuacan. A synthetic Egypto-Mayan name.

Hattusas In FK, a Zamorian serving under Conan. The capital of the Hittite kingdom, near modern Bğazköi (renamed Boğazköi).

Heimdul In FD, a Van or Vanaheimer. From Heimdall, in Norse myth, the guardian of the gates of Valhalla.

Hildico In HN, a Brythunian slave girl in Yaralet. From Hilda or Ildico, the last of the many wives of Attila the Hun.

Himelian Mts. In PC, CA, a range north or north-west of Vendhya. From the Himalayas or Himalayan Mountains.

Hormaz In CS, a Turanian officer. From Hormazd or Ahura Mazda, the good god of the dualistic Zoroastrian universe.

Horsa In FD, an As (*see* Æsir). A half-legendary Saxon chief who, with his brother Hengist or Hengest, led the Saxon invasion of Britain in the middle of +V.

Hotep In HS, a Stygian servant of Zeriti; in CA, a name assumed by Conan in Fort Wakla. An old Egyptian name meaning "contented."

Hsia In CM, a former king of Kusan. A semi-legendary early dynasty of China.

Hyborian, Hyborean, Hybori In RN, BR, TT, &c., the race that overthrew the empire of Acheron and set up in its place the kingdoms of Nemedia, Aquilonia, Brythunia, Argos, and the Border Kingdom. From Hyperborea (q.v.). *See* Bori.

Hyperborea In TE and GB, a northeasterly land, east of Asgard. In Greek legend, a happy land in the Far North; the name means "beyond the North Wind."

Hyrkania, Hyrcania In TE, QC, BC, &c., the land east of the Vilayet Sea. The Turanians, dwelling west of that sea, are also of Hyrkanian origin and are commonly called Hyrkanians. In Classical geography, a region southeast of the Caspian or Hyrcanian Sea corresponding to modern Iranian Mazanderan + Asterabad. The name is Greek for the Old Persian Varkana, one of the Achaemenid satrapies, and survives in the name of the river Gurgan. The original meaning may have been "wolfland." Hyrkania was briefly an independent kingdom in +I. In Iranian legend, Hyrkania was remarkable for its wizards and demons.

Ianthe In SK, KD, the capital of Ophir. In Greek myth, an oceanid or marine nymph.

Ibis In GB, a god. Any of several species of heron-like birds, one of which, *Threskiornis aethiopica*, was held sacred in ancient Egypt.

Ilbars In SM, a Turanian river; in FK, a range of mountains south of the Vilayet Sea. From the Elburz Mountains, Iran.

Ilga In LW, a Virunian girl. A combination of the Norse names Inga and Helga.

Imbalayo In HS, the commander of the Kushite troops in Pelishtia. A pseudo-Zulu name.

Imirus In CA, WM, CI, a barony of Aquilonia.

Irakzai In PC, a Himelian tribe. From the Orakzai, Pakhtum tribe mentioned in Lowell Thomas's *Beyond Khyber Pass*, which Howard read.

Iranistan In BG, RE, PC, &c., an eastern land corresponding to modern Iran. From Iran + the Persian *istân, estân*, "country."

Irem In SM, Shah Amurath's horse. From "ancient Irem, the City of Pillars," mentioned by H. P. Lovecraft in "The Nameless City," and possibly ultimately from Iram, in Arabian legend a deserted city in Yaman. *See* "The City of Many-Columned Iram and Abdullah Son of Abi Kilabah" in Burton's translation of the *Arabian Nights*, v. IV, pp. 113ff.

Ishbak In HS, a name assumed by Conan in Asgalun. A Phoenician name.

Ishtar In QC, BC, SM, &c., a Shemitish goddess also worshiped in the Hyborian nations. The Assyro-Babylonian goddess of love (Hebrew Ashtoreth, Phoenician 'Atar'ata, Syrian Atargatis, Greek Astartê).

Issedon In CS, one of the seven sacred cities of Meru.

Itzra In CI, an Antillian chief. A synthetic Egypto-Mayan name.

Ivanos In SM, RE, a Corinthian pirate. From Ivan, Russian for "John," + the Greek masculine nominative ending-*os*.

Ivga In WB, Valerius' sweetheart. Possibly from Inga, a Norwegian female given name.

Jaga In CM, a head-hunting tribe of the hill region between Kusan and Hyrkania. A Bantu tribe of southern Zaïre.

Jalung Thongpa In CS, the god-king of Meru. A pseudo-Tibetan name.

Jamal In PS, a Turanian soldier. From the Arabic *jamal*, "camel," often used as a personal name.

Jamankh In IG, a hyena-demon. From Jajamankh or Zazamankh, a legendary Egyptian magician.

Jehun *See* Amir. From Shah Jahan or Jehan, a Mughal emperor of +XVII, the builder of the Taj Mahal.

Jehungir, Jungir Jehungir is a Turanian lord in DI, while Jungir Khan is another in SZ. From Jahangir ("world-conqueror"), Shah Jahan's predecessor as Mughal emperor, +XVII.

Jelal In DI, Jelal Khan is a Turanian noble. From the Arabic proper name Jala.

Jerida In CB, a place in Zingara. From the Spanish place names Jérez, Mérida.

Jhebbal *See* Djebal.

Jhelai In PC, a place in Vendhya. From the Jhelam or Jhelum River, a tributary of the Indus.

Jhil A supernatural being mentioned in BR. Possibly from Chil, the kite in Kipling's *Second Jungle Book*; there is also a Jhal, India, and a Hindi word *jhîl*, "swamp."

Jhumda In PC, a river in Vendhya. From the river Jamna, Jumna, or Yamuna in India, and the river Jhelman in Pakistan.

Jihiji In VW, a village in Kush. Possibly from Jijiga, Abyssinia (Ethiopia).

Jhilites In FK, a cult of followers of Jhil (q.v.).

Jillad In BG, a pseudonym of Zyras. This name was used in Howard's original non-Conan story, "The Trail of the Blood-Stained God."

Joka In RH, a servant of Nabonidus. Possibly from the Djukas, tribal Negroes of Surinam, South America, descendants of escaped slaves. (Cf. Ajonga.)

Jon In BB, Jon Galter's son is a dead friend of the narrator. From "John"; *see* Galter.

Jugra In PC, a Wazuli village. A name for the Magyars or Hungarians.

Julio In CB, a Zingaran goldsmith. A Spanish given name, from the Roman gentile name Julius.

Juma In CS, CM, a Kushite serving in the Turanian army; later, in CB, he becomes the chief of a tribe in Kush. A common East African given name.

Jumballa In SD, the capital of Kush. Howard spelled it "Shumballa" (possibly from Shambalai, a hill region in Tanzania) but I changed the name because Carter and I needed the similar name "Shamballa" (q.v.) for CS.

Junia In SK, the wife of Torgrio the thief. From Junius, a common Roman gentile name, e.g., Decimus Junius Brutus Albinus, one of Caesar's assassins.

Kaa-Yazoth In CI, a ruler of the Atlantean Age.

Kalanthes (=**Caranthes**) In GB, discarded. Kalanthes was Howard's original form, but I changed it to Caranthes because I thought it too much like Kallian (q.v.), the name of another character in the same story.

Kallian In GB, Kallian Publico is an art dealer. From the common Greek name Kallias.

Kambuja In WM, a land east of Vendhya. The original name of Cambodia, now Kampuchea.

Kamula In CB, a long-vanished city of Atlantean times.

Kamelia In TE, a kingdom of Atlantean times. Possibly from the camellia, a shrub of the tea family bearing large white flowers. The Knights of the White

Camelia, formed in 1867, was one of a number of white-supremacist secret societies, of which the Ku Klux Klan is the best known, active in the former Confederate states at that time. Possibly also from Camelot, King Arthur's legendary capital.

Karaban In PS, an Aquilonian county. Possibly from Karaman, Turkey.

Kang Hsiu In CA, a Khitan. Common Chinese names.

Kang Lou-Dze In CA, a Khitan girl. Common Chinese names.

Kapeuez In CB, the captain of the Zingaran royal yacht. A pseudo-Spanish name.

Karlus In BB, an Aquilonian ranger at Fort Kwanyara. From the common German name Karl (Latin, Carolus).

Karnath In the first draft of CC, a Stygian city (discarded). Possibly from Lovecraft's Sarnath, in "The Doom That Came to Sarnath." Lovecraft invented the name and was then surprised to learn that it was the name of a real city near Banaras, India.

Kassali In IG, the capital of Punt. From Kassala, a town in the Sudan.

Kchaka In RZ, the ancestors of the dominant tribe of Zembabwei. From Chaga, an East African tribe, or from Chaka, the Zulu emperor, for which *see* Chagan.

Keluka In HS, a Kushite soldier in Asgalun. A pseudo-Swahili name.

Kemosh In CA, a Zuagir god. From Chemosh, a Canaanite god (Num. 21: 29).

Keraspa In BG, a Kezankian chieftain. From Keresaspa, a legendary Persian hero.

Kerim In PC, Kerim Shah is a Turanian spy in Vendhya. From the Arabic *karîm*, "generous," used as a proper name in Muslim countries.

Keshan, Keshia In JG, IG, RZ, a black kingdom and its capital respectively. Probably from Kesh or Kash, an ancient Egyptian name for Nubia, whence Hebrew (and Howard's) Kush.

Kezankian Mts. In BG, a range separating Turan from Zamora. Suggested by the Russian geographical names Kazan and Kazak.

Khafra In HS, a Stygian servant of Zeriti. The Fourth Dynasty king of Egypt who built the Sphinx (Greek, Chephren).

Khahabul (=**Khorbul q.v.**) In first draft of PC, discarded.

Khajar In CB, BN, an oasis in western Stygia, where Thoth-Amon lived. From Kajar or Qajar, an Iranian tribe and a Persian dynasty, 1794–1925.

Khan *See* Chengir, Jehungir, Khosru. A Turko-Tatar word meaning "lord" or "prince."

Khannon In HS, a Pelishti wine-seller. A Phoenician name.

Khanyria In CA, a city in Khoraja. From Khan + Graeco-Roman names like Syria, Illyria, &c.

Kharamun In SZ, a southeastern desert. Possibly from the same source as Karaban (q.v.).

Kharoya In CA, a Zuagir tribe.

Khauran In WB, CA, a small southeastern Hyborian kingdom. Probably from Mt. Hauran, Syria.

Khawarizm, Khawarism In DI, a Turanian city near the southern end of the Sea of Vilayet. From Khwarasm of Chorasmia, a medieval Muslim kingdom in Turkestan; modern Khurasan or Khorassan, Iran. The name comes from the Old Persian Huvarazmish, a satrapy of the Achaemenid Empire. (Cf. Khorusun.)

Khaza In FK, a Stygian. An Egyptian king of the Fourteenth Dynasty, c. −1700.

Khel *See* Khosatral Khel. Probably from *khel*, a Pakhtu word for family or sept; e.g., "Mal Khel Mahsud," a man of the Mal family of the Mahsud tribe.

Khemi In QC, SZ, TT, &c., the main seaport and administrative capital of Stygia. From Kamt, Kam, Chêm, or Chêmia, ancient names for Egypt, probably connected with *qam*, "black," of "Khem," an Egyptian god of fertility.

Khemsa In PC, a wizard serving the Black Circle. From Khamseh, a tribe of Arabian origin in southern Iran.

Kherdpur In CA, a Turanian city. From the Kurds of Kurdistan.

Kheshatta In VW, a city of magicians in Stygia. Probably from Peshitta, the name of an old Syriac version of the Bible.

Khirgulis In CA, a Himelian tribe. From Kirgiz, a Turko-Tatar people, now the republic of Kyrgyzstan, bordering Sinkiang.

Khitai, Khitans In TE, RH, WB, &c., a far-eastern land and its inhabitants. From "Khitan," a medieval Tatar word for China, whence the English word "Cathay."

Khor In first draft of CC, a valley in Aquilonia (discarded). Probably from the same sources as Ghor and Khorbul (q.v.).

Khoraf In CA, a Vilayet port favored by slavers.

Khoraja, Khorala Respectively, a small southern Hyborian city-state in BC and a place in Vendhya, whence came the jewel "Star of Khorala," in SZ, SK. The first syllable is probably from the Arabic *hor*, "lake" or "marsh," which occurs in many place names. Khôr was also an ancient Egyptian name for the Khurri or Hurrians.

Khoraspa (=**Khoraja**, q.v.) In the first draft of BC (discarded).

Khorbul In PC, a city in the Himelias. From *hor* (*see* Khoraja, above) + Kabul, Afghanistan.

Khorosun, Khorusun, Khurusun In DI, PC, CA, a Turanian city. From Khurasan, Iran (cf. Khawarizm).

Khorotas In CC, the Aquilonian river on which Tarantia stands. Probably from *hor* (*see* Khoraja) + Eurotas, the Greek river on which Sparta stands (modern Iri or Evrotos).

Khorshemish In SC, KD, the capital of Koth. From *hor* (*see* Khoraja) + Carchemish, an ancient Syrian city later called Europus.

Khosala *See* Kosala.

Khosatral Khel In DI, a demon who once ruled Dagonia. "Khosatral" is possibly a combination of Khushal Khan, a Pakhtun poet and leader of + XVII, + Chitral, a Pakhtun tribe. (*See also* Khel.)

Khosru In PC, Khosrun Khan is the governor of Secunderam; in CA, a Turanian fisherman. The name of several Iranian kings, also spelled Khusru, Khosrau, or Chosroês.

Khossus A king of Khoraja in BC, SD, and of Koth in SC. From Knossos or Cnossus, the capital of Minoan Crete.

Khotan In BC, Thugra Khotan is the original name of Natohk, the veiled prophet. A river and a town in Sinkiang or Chinese Turkestan. (Cf. Thugra, Natohk.) "Natohk" is an obvious anagram of "Khotan."

Khozgari In PS, a Turanian mountain tribe. Probably from Kashgar, a city in western Sinkiang or Chinese Turkestan.

Khrosha A volcanic region in Koth alluded to in SM, SD, CC. Possibly from Khorshid, Iran, or from Kosha, Nubia. Kosha, like its neighbor Akasha, probably gets its name from Kash, ancient Egyptian for Nubia (cf. Keshan, Kush).

Khumbanigash In WB, the general of Constantius' Shemitish mercenaries. A king of Elam (modern Khuzistan) in −VIII.

Khurakzai In PC, a Himelian tribe. From Khuram, Afghanistan, + -zai (cf. Dagozai, Khurum).

Khurum In PC, a Wazuli village and a legendary Amir. From Khuram, Afghanistan (cf. Khurakzai).

Khurusun *See* Khorusun.

Khushia In RE, the chief wife of King Yildiz.

Khusro In CM, a Turanian soldier. A variant of Khosru (q.v.).

Kidessa In DT, an oasis in the southern deserts, near Tombalku.

Kobad Shah In FK, the king of Iranistan. A Persian name (also Kavata, Qobadh, &c.; Greek, Kobades) borne by various Iranian notables.

Kordava, Kordafan In the original manuscript and outline of SD, Howard mentioned a black country as "Kordafan" and a wizard from there as "a Kordafan." The name comes from Kordofan, a province of the Sudan. To bring the noun and the adjective into proper relationship, I changed the name of the country to "Kordafa."

Kordava In PO, CB, TT, &c., the capital and main seaport of Zingara. From Cordova (Spanish Córdoba), Spain.

Kordofo In DT, Conan's predecessor as general of the cavalry of Tombalku. From the same source as Kordafa (q.v.).

Kormon In BB, Lord Thasperas of Kormon is patron of Schohira. There is a French surname, "Cormon," but any connection is doubtful.

Korunga (=Gwarunga, q.v.) In one non-final draft of JG, discarded. *See* Ahrunga.

Korveka A place mentioned in WB. Cf. Korvela.

Korvela In TT, a bay on the Pictish coast, so named by Zingaran settlers. Possibly a combination of Cordova + *caravela* ("caravel"), Portuguese for a small, lateen-rigged ship.

Korzetta In TT, a county of Zingara. Possibly suggested by Khorbetta (Hurbeit, Bilbeis, ancient Pharbaëthos), Egypt.

Kosala, Khosala An eastern nation alluded to in SZ, PC, RN. From Kosala or Koshala, a kingdom in northern India in the time of the Buddha (−563 to −483).

Kosha *See* Yag-Kosha, Khrosha.

Koth In TE, QC, SM, &c., a southern Hyborian kingdom. Probably from the "Sign of Koth" in H. P. Lovecraft's "The Dream-Quest of Unknown Kadath." There is a town of Koth in Gujarât, India, but the connection is doubtful. Howard used the same name in his interplanetary novel *Almuric*.

Kozak In SM, WB, DI, &c., one of a brotherhood of outlaws in Turan and Hyrkania. Russian for "Cossack," ultimately from the Turkish *quzak*, "adventurer."

Krallides In WB, a Khauranian councilor. Cf. Trallibes.

Kshatriyas In PC, CA, the Vendhyans or their ruling caste. The warrior caste of ancient India.

Kuigars In CS, CM, a nomadic people of Hyrkania. From the Uigurs, a Turkish people of Mongolia and Turkestan.

Kujala In FK, a Yezmite. From Kujula (q.v.).

Kujula In CS, CM, the khan of the Kuigars. A king of the Yüe-Chi, +I.

Kulalo In CB, Juma's capital. From the Kololo, a Tswana people who ruled an empire in Zambia and Rhodesia in the 1830s and 40s.

Kull In TC, CT, SH, and the Kull stories, an Atlantean who becomes king of Valusia.

Kurush Khan In RE, a Hyrkanian chief. Kûrush is the original Persian form of the name of Cyrus the Great (cf. Kyros).

Kusan In CM, SH, a small kingdom in western Khitai. A pseudo-Chinese name.

Kushaf In FK, a region in the Ilbars Mountains.

Kutamun In BC, a Stygian prince. Possibly from Kutama, a medieval Berber tribe of Algeria.

Kuth In SS, a dream place, probably from the same source as Koth (q.v.).

Kuthchemes In BC, FK, a ruined city in the Shemitish desert. Possibly from

the Hindustani *kut*, "fort," +Chemmis (ancient Khemmis, Shmin, Apu, or Pan-
opolis; modern Akhmîm), Egypt.

Kwanyara In BB, a fort on the borders of Schohira. A pseudo-Iroquois name.

Kwarada In BB, the Witch of Skandaga, Valerian's mistress. A pseudo-
Iroquois name.

Kyros A wine-growing region mentioned in HS, CB, CC. The Greek spelling
of Cyrus (Old Persian, Kûrush; cf. Kurush Khan).

Lalibeha In IG, the king of Punt. From Lalibela, a Zangwe king in Abyssinia
(Ethiopia) in +XII.

Laodamas In MB, an Aquilonian officer. The name of several Greek mythological heroes.

Laranga In CC, a Negro galley slave. A pseudo-Bantu name.

Larsha In HD, a ruined city near Shadizar. From Larsa, a city of ancient Babylonia.

Lazbekri In CA, the Mirror of Lazbekri enables Conan and Pelias to spy on
the sorcerer Yah Chieng.

Lemuria In TE, an eastern archipelago of Atlantean times. A hypothetical land
bridge from India to South Africa, invented by scientists in the late +XIX to
explain the distribution of lemurs and the similarity of some geological formations in India and South Africa; later, in Theosophical and other occult
doctrines, a sunken continent in the Indian or the Pacific Ocean, contemporary
with or preceding Atlantis (q.v.). Lemuria as a scientific hypothesis has been
discredited by the advances of +XX geology.

Leng Chi In CA, a Khitan; common Chinese names.

Libnun Hills In HS, a range near Asgalun. From Libnân, Arabic for Lebanon,
the mountain and the republic. In Howard's original non-Conan story, "Hawks
Over Egypt," these hills were the Mokattam (Arabic, Muqattam) Hills near
Cairo.

Ligureans In BB, BN, a race of light-skinned savages dwelling in small clans
in the Pictish Wilderness, culturally similar to the Picts but racially distinct from
them. From the Ligurians, a pre-Roman people of northwestern Italy and
southern France, who mixed with the invading Celts and were conquered by
the Romans.

Lilit In SH, the ruler of Yanyoga. In Semitic mythology, Lilith or Lilitu is a
nocturnal female demon.

Lir In SS, a god by whom Conan swears. The Irish sea god. (Lir is the ge-
netive; the nominative is properly Lér.) The character also appears as the Welsh
god Llyr and as the "King Lear" of Geoffrey of Monmouth (*Historia Regum
Britanniae*, II, 11–14) and Shakespeare.

Lissa In DT, a girl of the desert city of Gazal. From Elissa, the name of the
Tyrian princess (better known by her nickname of "Dido") who is traditionally

believed to have fled from Tyre during a dynastic struggle and founded Carthage, −XIX or −VII. Howard used another name from the same source, Nalissa, in the King Kull story, "Swords of the Purple Kingdom."

Livia In VW, an Ophirean girl of noble family, carried off by Kushites to Bakalah. The feminine form of Livius, a Roman gentile name. Before the Christianization of the Roman Empire, Roman women had no personal names. They were known by the feminine form of their father's gentile (clan) or middle name only; hence, for instance, Gaius Julius Caesar's daughter was automatically called Julia. If a man had more than one daughter, the later ones were given numbers (Secunda, &c.) or diminuitives (Livilla, &c.) to tell them apart.

Lodier In SK, a barony in Ophir.

Lor In CA, a barony of Aquilonia.

Lotus In TE, the powder of the black lotus of Khitai is a deadly poison. In TE, CA, the "fumes" and the pollen of the yellow lotus of Khitai are narcotics. In CC, the smoke of the burning pollen of the black lotus is a powerful drug. In RH, the dust of the gray lotus, which grows beyond Khitai, is a deadly poison. In SC, the juice of the purple lotus of Stygia paralyzes. In SM, the juice of the golden lotus restores sanity. In Homer (*Odyssey*, IX) the fruit of the lotus (probably the jujube, the shrub *Zizyphus* and its relatives) reduces people to a dreamy, lethargic, forgetful state. In modern botany, any of several Old World water lilies of the genera *Nelumbo* and *Nymphaea*.

Louhi In WM, the witch-mistress of Pohiola. The mistress of Pohjola in the *Kalevala*.

Loulan In FK, a region of eastern Hyrkania. A pseudo-Chinese name.

Lubemba. In RZ, the king of Zembabwei who first tamed the wyverns. The country of the Bemba, in modern Zambia.

Lucian In MB, an Aquilonian general. From the Greek Loukianos (Latin, Lucianus), a common name borne by, among others, the Syrio-Greek satirical writer Lucian of Samosata, +II.

Ludovic In BN, the king of Ophir, successor to Amalrus. A common North European name, also Hlodovic, Ludwig, Clovis, Louis, Lodovico, Luigi, Luís, &c.

Luxur In FK, TT, CC, &c., the capital of Stygia. From Luxor, Egypt (from Arabic al-Aqsur of al-Uqsur, "the castles," in ancient times called Wesi, Opet, No-Amun, or Thebes).

Lyco In CA, a Kothian captive in Paikang. From Lykon, a common Classical Greek name.

Macha In PS, a Cimmerian deity. From Emain Macha (pronounced approximately EV-in MAH-khah), Cúchulainn's home in Irish myth.

Mannanan In SS, a god by whom Conan swears. From Manannán (pronounced mah-nah-NYAWN), in Irish mythology a sea god, the son of Lér.

Manara In CA, a county of Aquilonia.

Marala In SK, the queen of King Moranthes II of Ophir; later the Countess Albiona.

Marco In CI, a Barachan pirate in Conan's crew. An Italian given name, from the Latin praenomen Marcus.

Marinus In CA, a hireling of King Yezdigerd in Tarantia. From the Greek Marinos, a common name borne by, among others, a noted +II Tyrian geographer.

Matamba In CB, a Kushite tribe. A pseudo-Bantu name.

Mattenbaal In HS, a priest of Pteor. A Phoenician name.

Maul In TE, HD, the thieves' quarter in a Zamorian city.

Mayapan In CI, the American coast adjacent to Antillia. The Mayas' own name for their country.

Maypur In CA, a Turanian city. Probably from the Mayan Indians.

Mazdak In HS, a Hyrkanian mercenary in the Pelishti army. A Persian name, notably that of the founder of a communistic religion in +V.

Mbega In RZ, SH, one of the twin kings of Zembabwei. A legendary conquering East African chieftain, c. +1700, in the present Tanzania.

Mbonani In CB, a Ghanata slaver. A +XIX East African chieftain.

Mecanta In SK, a county in Ophir.

Mena In GT, a Shemitish conjuror in Captain Gonzago's crew. The more or less legendary founder of the First Dynasty of Egypt, c. −3100.

Menkara In CB, a priest of Set. The name of a Fourth Dynasty king of Egypt, also Menkaura, Menkure, or Mycerinus.

Meru In CS, CM, SH, a tropical valley between the Talakma and Himelian mountain ranges. In Hindu mythology, the mountain on which the gods dwell.

Mesmerism An obsolete name for hypnotism, after its discoverer Franz Anton Mesmer (1733–1815), an Austrian physician; used in this sense by Howard in SZ, PC.

Messantia In PO, CC, CI, the main seaport of Argos. Probably from Messina, Italy.

Metemphoc In CI, the chief of the thieves of Ptahuacan. A synthetic Egypto-Mayan name.

Milo In CS, BM, the king of Argos; in CI, Conan's boatswain. From the Greek Milon, a legendary athlete of Crotona; also a Roman cognomen.

Mindanga In DT, a people of the Tombalku Empire. *See* Bigharma.

Mithridates In CA, a king of Zamora. The Greek version of the Persian Mithradata, borne by various Achaemenid Persian notables and by several kings of Pontus, especially Mithridates VI, the Great, c. −100.

Mitra In GB, RH, QC, &c., a Hyborian god. In Indian mythology, a sun god, cognate with the Persian Mithra or Mithras.

Mkwana In SH, a Zembabwan officer. A pseudo-Bantu name.

Monargo In CI, the count of Couthen. From Monaco.

Moranthes In SD, SK, the king of Ophir and the second of that name, Amalrus' predecessor. Possibly suggested by Orontes, a Persian name (Aurwand, Alwand) borne by a character in Molière's *The Misanthrope*. Also a river in Syria (modern Nahr al-'Asi).

Morrigan In PS, a Cimmerian deity. An Irish goddess, who appears in Arthurian legend in the guise of Morgan le Fay (Malory's English for the French Morgain la fée).

Mulai In CM, a Turanian soldier. A Turkish name.

Munthassem Khan In HN, a Turanian governor.

Muriela In JG, IG, a Corinthian dancing girl. From the feminine proper name Muriel.

Murilo In RH, HN, a noble of a small city-state west of Zamora. Probably from Murillo, a −XVII Spanish painter.

Murzio In RZ, a Zingaran serving with Conan. From the Italian name Muzio, which comes from the Roman gentile names Mucius and Mutius.

Nabonidus In RH, a priest in a small, unnamed city-state west of Zamora. Latin for Nabu-naid, the last Babylonian king.

Nafertari In DI, the mistress of the satrap Jungir Khan. From Nefertari, the name of several Egyptian queens.

Nahor In IG, a Shemitish merchant in Punt. A biblical name (Gen. 11:23).

Namedides *See* Numedides.

Nanaia In FK, a woman of Kobad Shah's harem. From Nana, an ancient oriental name.

Natala In SS, a Brythunian girl. Presumably from the feminine proper name Natalie or Natalia.

Natohk In BC, SD, the name used by Thugra Khotan; "Khotan" (q.v.) backward.

Nebethet In IG, the dominant goddess of Punt. From Nebthet or Nephthys, an Egyptian goddess.

Nebthu In BN, RZ, SH, a ruined city in northern Stygia. From the Egyptian goddess Nebthet or Nephthys.

Nemain In PS, a Cimmerian deity. An Irish goddess, pronounced approximately NEV-in.

Nemedia, Nemedians In TE, GB, QC, &c., a powerful Hyborian kingdom and its people. In Irish mythology, the Nemedians, descendants of the Scythian chief Nemed, were among the first invaders of Ireland. Cf. Conan; also *Lebor Gabála Erenn*, V, 237–56.

Nenaunir In WM, RZ, SH, one of the twin kings of Zembabwei, also priest of Damballah. A Sudanese name.

Nergal In HN, the Hand of Nergal is a powerful talisman. Nergal or Nerigal was the Babylonian war god.

Nestor In HD, a Gunderman officer of Zamorian troops. In Homer's *Iliad*, a wise old king of Pylos with the Achaean host.

N'Gora In QC, a subchief of the black corsairs. A pseudo-Bantu name.

Nezvaya In HN, a river in Turan. Possibly suggested by the Russian rivers Nyeva and Velikaya, or similar names.

Nilas (=Styx) In the first draft of BC, the Nemedian name for the river (discarded); from Nilus, Neilos, or Nile, also mentioned as "Nilus" in "The Hyborian Age."

Nimed In CC, the king of Nemedia (q.v.). From Nemed, in Irish mythology a Scythian chief whose descendants invaded Ireland.

Ninus In HD, the Fountain of Ninus is west of Shadizar; in CB, RZ, a priest of Mitra. In Greek legend (Ninos), the founder of Nineveh.

Niord In FD, an As (*see* Æsir). From Njorth or Njöro, one of the Vanir (q.v.) of Norse mythology.

Nippr In BC, a Shemitish city-state. From Nippur, an ancient Babylonian city.

Njal In LD, a chief or *jarl* of the Æsir, raiding into Hyperborea. From Njal (pronounced NYAHL) Thorgeirsson, hero of one of the most famous Icelandic sagas, *Njals Saga* or *The Saga of Burnt Njal*.

Nordheim In QC, the land of the Æsir and the Vanir. A medieval German place name, meaning "north home."

Nuadens In BN, a god invoked by Diviatix. A Celtic god, also Nuada or Nodens.

Nuadwyddon In BN, a sacred grove of the Ligurean Druids. A pseudo-Welsh name.

Numa In PS, a king of Nemedia. A legendary king of early Rome.

Numalia In GB, a Nemedian city. From Numa (q.v.).

Numedides, Namedides In DT, MB, TT, &c., a king of Aquilonia slain and superseded by Conan. From Numa and Nimed (q.v.) + the Greek gentile suffix-*ides*. Howard used both spellings, but in current editions of the stories the former is used exclusively.

N'Yaga In QC, a black corsair. A pseudo-Bantu name.

Nzinga In CB, RZ, the queen of the Amazons; in RZ, also, her daughter of the same name. A black warrior queen who fought the Portuguese in Angola in +XVII.

Octavia In DJ, a Nemedian girl. The feminine form of the Roman gentile name Octavius (cf. Livia).

Ogaha In BB, a creek between the provinces of Conawaga and Schohira. A pseudo-Iroquois name, probably suggested by upstate New York place names like Oquaga, Otego, &c.

Olgerd In WB, FK, Olgerd Vladislav is a Zaporoskan chief of the Zuagirs. From Olgierd, a grand duke of Lithuania in +XIV (*see* Vladislav).

Olivero In BN, the husband of Princess Chabela. A Spanish name.

Olivia In SM, an Ophirean princess. An Italian and English feminine proper name.

Ollam-Onga In DT, the god of Gazal.

Olmec In RN, a chief of Xuchotl. From the Olmecs or Olmeca, a tribe of Mexican Indians.

Onagrul In CA, a pirate settlement on the eastern shore of the Vilayet Sea. From "onager," the Asiatic wild ass.

Onyaga In BB, the Hawk Clan of the Picts. A pseudo-Iroquois name.

Ophir In TE, QC, SM, &c., a Hyborian kingdom. A goldmining region in the Old Testament, possibly on the shores of the Red or Arabian seas (e.g., western Arabia) or the country of the Afar, in Eritrea on the opposite side of the Red Sea.

Orastes In CC, a former priest of Mitra. From Orestes, in Greek myth the son of Agamemnon; also regent of Italy in +V for his son Romulus Augustulus, the last West Roman Emperor; executed by order of Odovakar in + 476.

Oriskonie In MB, BB, a province of the Westermarck. From Oriskany (now Oriskany Falls), New York, site of a battle in the Revolutionary War.

Orklaga (=Ogaha) In first draft of BB; discarded. A pseudo-Iroquois name.

Ortho A pirate alluded to in RN. Possibly from Otho, a Roman cognomen or family name.

Ostorio In BG, a Nemedian. From Ostorius, a Roman gentile name.

Othbaal An Anaki intriguer. From Ithobaal or Ethbaal, king of Sidon in −IX.

Otho *See* Ortho, Strom.

Paikang In WB, CA, a city in Khitai. From Peiking, China.

Palian Way In GB, a street in Numalia. Probably from the Mappalian Way, a street in Carthage alluded to in Flaubert's *Salammbô*; possibly also from the river Pallia, a tributary of the Tiber.

Pallantides In PS, CC, CA, &c., an Aquilonian general. In Greek mythology, a collective name for the fifty sons of Pallas, uncle of Theseus, who slew all the Pallantides in a struggle for the throne of Athens. Howard may, however, have derived the name from a combination of Palamedes, a Trojan hero, and Pallancia (modern Palencia), Spain.

Pantho In BN, a Zingaran, the duke of Guarralid. From Sancho Panza (Castillian *z* = English *th*).

Pelias In SC, CA, a Kothian wizard. In Greek myth, a king of Iolkos and Jason's wicked uncle.

Pelishtim In WB, CI, JG, a Shemitish nation. Hebrew for the Philistines, whence "Palestine" is also derived. Howard used "Pelishtim" in the singular, whereas the Hebrew singular would be "Pelishti," which form I have substituted where appropriate in the current editions.

Pellia In SC, CC, a principality in Aquilonia. Probably from Pella, the ancient capital of Macedonia.

Peshkauri In PC, a city in northwestern Vendhya. From Peshawar (or Peshâvar), Pakistan.

Petanius *See* Aztreas.

Petreus In RH, a conspirator against Nabonidus. From Petrus, the Latin form of Peter (Greek, Petros).

Picts In TE, GB, BR, &c., the primitive inhabitants of the Pictish Wilderness, along the west coast of the main continent. The primitive pre-Celtic inhabitants of Britain, who were finally absorbed by the invading Scots from Ireland. The affinities of their language are much disputed, some holding them to have spoken a Celtic tongue, some a non-Celtic Indo-European, and some a non-Indo-European one. In the Conan stories, Howard made the Picts a swarthy folk with an Iroquois-like culture; in other stories, he assumed they were dwarfish and Neanderthaloid. From anthropological considerations, it seems most likely that they were physically much the same as the present people of Scotland.

Pohiola In WM, BN, RZ, a sorcerous Hyperborean stronghold. From Pohjola, in the *Kalevala* the "North Country," corresponding to Lapland or a suppositious land even farther north.

Poitain In TT to BN, the southernmost province of Aquilonia, at times independent of that kingdom. From Poitou, a French province on the west coast. Howard spelled the corresponding adjective "Poitanian."

Posthumo In GB, a Numalian policeman. From the Roman cognomen Posthumus, which originally meant "born after his father's death."

Pra-Eun In WM, RZ, a Kambujan wizard. In Cambodian mythology, the king of the angels.

Promero In GB, a Nemedian clerk.

Prospero In PS, CC, CA, &c., a Poitanian supporter of Conan. The magician in Shakespeare's *The Tempest*; ultimately possibly from Prosper Aquitanicus, a Roman theologian of +V.

Ptahuacan In CI, the capital of Antillia. A synthetic Egypto-Mayan name.

Pteion In CA, a demon-haunted Stygian ruined city.

Pteor In JG, the god of the Pelishtim. From Baal-Pteor, for which *see* Baal-Pteor.

Publico *See* Kallian, Publius. From the Roman names Publicius, Publicola.

Publio In CC, an Argossean merchant. Italian for Publius (q.v.).

Publius In TT to CI, the chancellor of Aquilonia under Conan. A Roman praenomen or personal name.

Punt In RN, JG, IG, &c., a Negro kingdom. A place with which the ancient Egyptians traded, probably Somaliland.

Purasati In FK, a Vendhyan girl in Yanaidar. A Hindi feminine name.

Python In FK, CB, CC, the capital of the fallen empire of Acheron. In Greek mythology, a great snake slain by Apollo at Delphi; hence, in modern zoology, a genus of constrictor snakes found in Africa, Asia, and Australia, including the largest existing snakes; also a Greek personal name.

Qirlata In CA, a Zuagir tribe.

Radegund In BN, Conan's elder daughter. From Radegund or Radegunda, daughter of King Berthar of Thuringia in +VI.

Rakhamon In CA, a Stygian sorcerer of former times. From the Egyptian gods Ra and Amon.

Rakhsha In PC, a kind of oriental wizard. From *râkshasa*, a class of demons in Hindu mythology.

Raman In CA, a county in Aquilonia. From the Indian bull Rama in Kipling's *Jungle Books*.

Ramiro In CB, the founder of King Ferdrugo's Zingaran dynasty. A Spanish given name.

Rammon A wizard or priest alluded to in PS. From Rimmon or Ramman, a Semitic storm god.

Rann In LD, Njal's daughter. A Norse sea goddess.

Rhamdan In CA, a port on the Vilayet Sea. From *Ramadân*, the Muslim Lent.

Rhazes In KD, a Kothian astrologer. The Latinized form of the name of ar-Razi, an Arabic physician of +IX.

Rigello In SK, a powerful nobleman, cousin to the king. Suggested by Lake Regillus in Italy, site of a battle in the Second Punic War.

Rima In SK, a slave girl.

Rimush In RZ, SH, a Shemitish astrologer. A king of Assyria, c. −2000.

Rinaldo In PS, SC, a mad Aquilonian poet. An Italian proper name, cognate with Ronald; one of the heroes of Ariosto's *Orlando Furioso*. In his King Kull story, "By This Axe I Rule!", which Howard rewrote as PS, he called the corresponding character "Ridondo."

Rolf In CA, an As at the court of King Yezdigerd. A common Scandinavian name (Old Norse, Hrolf, cognate with English Ralph), e.g., Hrolf Ganger, the Norse conqueror of Normandy.

Roxana In RE, the Zamorian mistress of Prince Teyaspa. The Greek form of the name of several Persian women of Achaemenid times, e.g., one of the wives of Alexander the Great (Old Persian, Rushanek).

Rufia In HS, the mistress of Mazdak. From the Roman cognomens Rufus, Rufinus.

Ruo-Gen In CA, a Khitan kingdom. A pseudo-Chinese name.

Rustum In BG, a Kezankian tribesman. From Rustam, the legendary Iranian hero.

Sabatea A sinister Shemitish city in HS, CC. From the ancient Arabian kingdoms of Sabaea (Sheba) and Nabataea, or the Arabian city of Sabata (modern Sawa), or a combination of these.

Sabina (=**Zenobia**) In first draft of CC, discarded. The feminine form of Sabinus, a Roman cognomen, which comes from Sabini, a people of central Italy who received Roman citizenship in−III.

Sabral In CB, a taverner in Kordava. From the Portuguese surname Cabral.

Sagayetha In MB, a Pictish shaman. A pseudo-Iroquois name.

Sagoyaga In RZ, a chief of the Picts. A pseudo-Iroquois name.

Saidu In DT, a Ghanata brigand. After King Mallam Saidu of Nupe, Nigeria, *reg.* 1926–34.

Sakumbe In DT, one of the joint kings of Tombalku. Possibly from Sakpe, Nigeria.

Salome In WB, the wicked twin sister of Taramis (q.v.). In Matthew 14, the daughter of Herodias.

Samara In PE, a Turanian outpost. From Samarra, a city in Iraq, once briefly the capital of the Caliphate.

Sancha In PO, a Zingaran girl, the daughter of the duke of Kordava. A Spanish and Provençal proper name.

Sareeta (=**Livia**) In first draft of VW; discarded. Possibly from the feminine given name Serena.

Sarpedon (=**Tuscelan**) In first draft of BR; discarded. A Lycian prince in the *Iliad*, slain at Troy by Patroklos.

Sassan In BG, an Iranistani treasure-hunter. Sasan or Sassan was the legendary founder of the Sassanid dynasty (+III to +VII) in Iran.

Satha In SC, a giant snake. From Sathanas, a Greek form of Satan.

Sathus (=**Set**) In first draft of CC; discarded. From the same source as Satha (q.v.).

Scavonus *See* Emilius. Possibly from Savona, Italy, or from such Roman names as Scaevinus, Scaevola.

Schohira In BB, MB, a province of the Westermarck. From Schoharie Creek or County, New York.

Schondara In BB, the principal town of Schohira. Possibly a combination of Sconodoa and Thendara, New York.

Sebro (=**Gebellez**) In first draft of TT; discarded.

Secunderam In PC, CA, a city between Turan and Vendhya, under Turanian rule. From Secunderabad (Sikandarâbâd, "Alexander's place"), India, named for Sikander Lodi of Jaunpur (f. 1500), whose name in turn may come from that of Alexander the Great, + the common *-am* ending found in many southern Indian cities, e.g., Vizagapatam.

Sergius In SM, a Kothic pirate captain. A Roman gentile name.

Servio In CC, a Messantian innkeeper. Italian for Servius (q.v.).

Servius In CC, a Servius Galannus is an Aquilonian noble. A Roman gentile name.

Set In GB, QC, BC, &c., the Stygian serpent-god. In ancient Egypt, the jackal-headed god of war or, later, a god of evil, called Sêth or Typhon by the Greeks.

Shadizar In TC, HD, PO, &c., the capital of Zamora. Possibly from Shanidar, Iraq. Cf. Shalizah.

Shaf Karaz In PS, a chief of the Khozgari tribesmen of Hyrkania.

Shah *See* Amurath, Kerim. Persian for "king."

Shahpur In DI, CA, a Turanian city. The name of several cities in Iran and India, meaning "king's town."

Shalizah In SC, a pass in Ghulistan. Possibly from the Shalamar Gardens, Lahore, India.

Shamar In SC, a southern Aquilonian city. Probably from the Jabal Shammar, a range in Arabia.

Shamballah In CS, SH, the capital of Meru. A Siberian city in Tibetan legend.

Shamla In BC, a pass in Khoraja. From any of various Asian places like Shamil, Iran; Simla, India; or Shamlegh, a village on the Indo-Tibetan border mentioned in Kipling's *Kim*.

Shamu In SC, a plain in Ophir. Probably from Shamo, a Chinese name for the Gobi Desert.

Shan *See* Chunder Shan. Probably a combination of "khan" and "shah" (q.v.), although it is also the Chinese word for "mountain."

Shan-e-Sorkh In BT, the Red Waste in the Zuagir Desert. Modern Farsi (Persian) for "red sand."

Shangara In PS, the abode of the People of the Summit.

Shanya In PS, the daughter of a chief of the Khozgari.

Shapur In CA, a Turanian soldier. A common Persian name (Greek, Sapor) borne by several Sassanid kings.

Shaulun In CA, a village in Khitai near Paikang.

Shem In TE, QC, BC, &c., a land south of the Hyborian nations, divided into city-states and bordering Stygia. In the Bible, Noah's eldest son, the ancestor of the Hebrews, Arabs, and Assyrians; hence the modern "Semite" and "Semitic" (via Greek Sêm), used properly to designate the family of languages spoken by these peoples.

Shevatas In BC, a Zamorian thief. Possibly from Thevatata, a figure in Indian mythology, or Thevatat, a sorcerer-king of Atlantis in Theosophical pseudo-history, which is also derived from Indian myth.

Shirakma In CA, a wine-growing region of Vendhya. A pseudo-Hindi name.

Shirki In CC, a river in western Aquilonia. Possible sources are Sirki, the original Assyrian name for a town at the confluence of the Euphrates and Khabur rivers, later called Phaliga, Circesium, and Buseira or Bessireh; and *shikari*, an Indo-Iranian word for "hunter."

Shondakor In CS, one of the seven sacred cities of Meru. From the title of Leigh Brackett's story "The Last Days of Shandakor," in *Startling Stories* for April 1952.

Shu In CM, SH, the king of Kusan. One of the Three Kingdoms of China in +II.

Shubba In SD, a servant of Tuthmes. Possibly from *jubbah*, the long, loose Arabian gown.

Shu-Chen In CA, a Khitan kingdom.

Shukeli In SC, a eunuch. Possibly from Shukriya, a Sudanese tribe.

Shumir In QC, BC, KD, a Shemitish city-state. From Shumer or Sumer, the land of the Sumerians, the pre-Semitic inhabitants of ancient southern Iraq.

Shupras In BC, the Agha Shupras is a Khorajan councilor. Possibly from Shuqra, Arabia. (Cf. Agha.)

Shushan In BC, a Shemitish river: in DI, a Shemitish city. One of the names of ancient Shusha, Sousa, Shush, or Sus, Iran; the capital of ancient Elam, Elymais, Hûja, Uvja, Goution, or Sousiana (modern Khuzistan).

Sigtona In LW, WM, a stronghold in southwestern Hyperborea. A town of early medieval Sweden.

Sigurd In CB, CI, a Van sailor. From Sigurð or Siegfried, the great North European mythical dragon-slaying hero.

Simura In HS, a city gate of Asgalun. From Simurgh, in Persian myth a gigantic bird, mentioned in the *Shah Nameh* as dwelling on Mt. Qaf.

Siojina-Kisua In CB, the former name for the Nameless Isle. From Swahili *sijina kisiwa*, "no-name island."

Siptah In GT, a Stygian magician, living in a tower on a nameless island. An Egyptian king of the Nineteenth Dynasty, c. −1200.

Skandaga, Scandaga In BB, Kwarada (q.v.) is called the Witch of Skandaga; Howard in "Notes on Various Peoples" describes it (under the alternative spelling) as the largest town of Conawaga. From the Sacandaga River or Vlaie (Swamp), New York.

Skelos In BC, DI, PC, &c., an ancient author of magical books. Probably from "skeleton," which means "dried up" in Greek. The Greek word *skelos* means "leg."

Skuthus In first draft of CC, a necromancer; discarded.

Socandaga (=**Ligurean**) In first draft of BB; discarded. From the same source as Skandaga (q.v.).

Sogdia In RE, a region in Hyrkania. From Sogdiana, the northern-most province of the Achaemenid Empire; later part of the Seleucid and Bactrian Empires, now the Uzbek Socialist Soviet Republic.

Soractus In BR, an Aquilonian woodsman. Probably from Mt. Soracte, Italy.

Sraosha In CB, a deity of the Mitran pantheon. In Zoroastrianism, the personification of the divine word.

Strabo In CI, an Argossean bully. From Strabon (Latin, Strabo), a common Greek name, borne by the noted geographer Strabon of Amasia, −I and +I.

Strabonus In SD, SC, the king of Koth. From the same source as Strabo (q.v.).

Strom, Strombanni In BB, Hakon Strom's son is an Aquilonian ranger, while his brother Dirk Strom's son is commander of Fort Kwanyara. In the original manuscript of TT, Strom was an Argossean pirate captain; but, since all his other Argossean names are Italianate, I changed it to "Strombanni." In BB, Howard had characters named Strom, Storm, and Gorm; believing that this would confuse readers, I changed "Storm" to "Otho." A rare English and Scandinavian surname.

Stygus (=**Styx, q.v.**) In first draft of BC, the Kothian name for the same river; discarded.

Styx, Stygia In TE, OC, WB, &c., respectively a river and a kingdom south of Shem, from whose people the Egyptians are descended. In Greek mythology, the Styx was the largest of the four rivers of Hades. The name was also applied to a real river in Arcadia and means "horror" or "hateful thing." "Stygia" comes from the English adjective "stygian," which in turn comes from the Latin *stygius* (Greek, *stygios*) meaning "Stygian," "infernal," "hellish."

Subas In DT, the original tribe of Sakumbe, on the Black Coast.

Sukhmet In RN, a southern frontier city in Stygia. From Sekhmet (Sekhet or Skhemit), a lion-headed Egyptian goddess.

Sultanapur In DI, CA, a Turanian city. From Sultanpur ("sultan's town"), India.

Sumeru Tso In CS, the inland sea of Meru. From Sumer (cf. Shumir) + Tso, Tibetan for "lake."

Sumuabi In HS, a king of Akkharia. From Sumuabu, founder of the First Dynasty of Babylon, −3M.

Sura In MB, an Aquilonian physician. A common Roman cognomen.

Swamp Snake (=**Zogar Sag**) In first draft of BR; discarded.

Tachic In RN, a man of Xuchotl. Possibly from Tactic, Guatemala.

Talakma Mts. In CS, CA, a range in Hyrkania north of the Himelias, corresponding to the modern Tien Shan. From the Takla Makan, a desert in Sinkiang.

Tamar In SC, in Howard's original manuscript, the capital of Aquilonia, elsewhere called Tarantia (q.v.). Probably from the city of Tamar ("palm tree") mentioned in I Kings 9:18; this in turn is probably an error for Tadmor (Palmyra), Syria. In current editions, I changed this name to Tarantia for consistency.

Tameris (=Bêlit) In first draft of QC; discarded. From the same source as Taramis (q.v.).

Tammuz In HN, the Heart of Tammuz is a powerful amulet. Another name for Adonis (q.v.).

Tananda In SD, the sister of the king of Kush.

Tanasul In CC, WM, a place in western Aquilonia.

Tanzong Tengri In CS, the chief wizard of Meru. A pseudo-Tibetan name.

Taramis In WB, the queen of Khauran. From the Russian feminine name Tamira; or Tamara, a medieval queen of Georgia; ultimately from Tomyris, a Scythian queen in battle with whom Cyrus the Great is said by Herodotus to have been killed.

Tarantia In MB, TT, CC, &c., the capital of Aquilonia. Probably from Taranto (ancient Tarentum, Taras), Italy. (Cf. Tamar.)

Tarascus In CC, CA, the brother of the king of Nemedia. Possibly from Tarascon, France, or from the Tarascan Indians of Mexico.

Tarim In DI, PC, a Turanian divinity. A river in Sinkiang.

Tartur In CA, a Wigur shaman. From Tartar, a medieval European corruption of the Persian Tâtâr, originally meaning a member of one of the tribes of Siberian Mongoloid nomads, of Turkic or Tungusic stock, but later applied to all Central Asian Mongoloid nomadic peoples, who periodically invaded the civilized lands to the east, west, and south.

Tashudang In CS, a Meruvian. A pseudo-Tibetan name.

Tauran In BR, TT, a northwestern province of Aquilonia. Probably from the Taurini, an ancient Ligurian people for whom Turin (Italian Torino, ancient Augusta Taurinorum) is named.

Taurus In TE, a Nemedian thief; in BC, SD, chancellor of Khoraja; in BN, Conan's younger son. Latin for "bull"; the Greek cognate *tauros* was also used as a personal name.

Techotl In RN, a man of Xuchotl. From Techotlala, an Aztec chief of +XIV.

Tecuhltli In RN, one of the feuding clans of Xuchotl. From *tecuhtli*, Aztec (=Nahuatl) for "grandfather" or "councilor."

Terson In SK, a barony in Ophir.

Teyanoga In BB, a Pictish shaman. A pseudo-Iroquois name.

Teyaspa In RE, a Turanian prince. From the Persian name Tiyasp and other names ending in *-asp* or *-aspa*.

Tezcoti In RN, a chamber in Xuchotl. Possibly from Tezcoco or Texcoco, Mexico.

Thabit In CA, a Zuagir. An Arabic name, e.g., of Thâbit, ibn-Qurra, a +IX Arab scientist.

Thak In RN, a man-ape. Possibly from the Hindi *thag*, "thug." Cf. Zembab-wei.

Than In HN, a nobleman of Yaralet.

Thanara In CA, a woman spy for King Yezdigerd. From the Saxon word *thane* or *thegn*, "chief," "nobleman."

Thandara In BB, the southernmost province of the Westermarck. From Then-dara, a place alluded to in Robert W. Chambers's novel *The Little Red Foot*, set in New York State in Revolutionary times; now the name of a town in Her-kimer County, New York, formerly Fulton Chain.

Thasperas In MB, BB, Lord Thasperas of Kormon is the patron of Schohira. Possibly from Tharypas, a king of the Molossians in −V.

Thaug In WB, a toad-demon. Possibly from the same source as Thak (q.v.).

Theggir In PS, a Hyrkanian mountain tribe.

Thenitea In BB, the location of a Schohiran army arrayed against the Nu-medidean forces of Brocas. Probably a coinage from New York State place names like Thendara and Caneadea.

Theringo In SK, a feudal demesne in Ophir.

Thespides. Thespius Respectively in BC, SD, a Khorajan councilor and in CC a renegade Aquilonian count. From Thespis, a Greek poet of −VI.

Thespius (=Thasperas) In first draft of BB; discarded. From the same source as Thespides (q.v.).

Theteles In VW, Livia's brother, slain by the Bakalah. Probably from Classical names like Thestius.

Thog In SS, the demon-god of Xuthal. Also (=Jhebbal Sag) in first draft of BR; discarded. Probably invented, but cf. Thak.

Thogara In CS, one of the seven sacred cities of Meru.

Thorus In BN, a Gunderman serving with Conan's army. From the Norse Thor pór) + a Latin ending.

Thoth-Amon In GB, TT, PS, &c., a Stygian sorcerer-priest. A compound of the Greek names for two Egyptian gods, Thoth (Thout, Tehuti, Dhuti) and Amon (Ammon, Amun). Howard also used Thoth-Amon's copper ring and its attendant baboon-demon in a story with a modern setting, "The Haunter of the Ring" (*Weird Tales*, June 1934).

Thothmekri In CC, a dead priest of Set From Thoth (*see* Thoth-Amon) + Mekri (Mikerê, Merykara), a Tenth Dynasty king of Egypt.

Thrallos In CC, a fountain outside Belverus. Cf. Trallibes.

Throana In CS, one of the seven sacred cities of Meru.

Thror In LD, a subchief of the Æsir. In the Prose Edda, a dwarf; also one of the names of Oðin.

Thugra In BC, Thugra Khotan is an ancient Stygian wizard brought back to life under the name Natohk. Possibly from the Thugra Gorge near Petra, Jordan. (*See* Khotan, Natohk.)

Thule In HN, a northern kingdom of pre-Cataclysmic (Atlantean) times. From Thule or Thoulê, a northern land reported by the −IV Greek explorer Pytheas of Massilia, identified variously with the Orkney and Shetland Islands, the Faeroes, Norway, and Iceland.

Thune In PS, a county of Aquilonia; also part of the name of the wizard in the Kull story, "The Mirrors of Tuzun Thune." Possibly from the same source as Thule (q.v.).

Thuria In "The Hyborian Age" and CI, the main (Eurasian) continent of Atlantean times. In Burroughs' Martian tales, the Martian name of Phobos, the nearer of the two Martian satellites. Also a town, Thouria, in the ancient Peloponnesos, but any connection thereof with Howard or Burroughs is doubtful.

Thutmekri In JG, IG, a Stygian adventurer. From the same sources as Thothmekri (q.v.).

Thutothmes In CC, a Stygian priest. From Thothmes (Thoutmosis, Tehutimesu), the name of several Eighteenth Dynasty kings of Egypt.

Tiberias In BR, an Aquilonian trader; in CC, an Aquilonian noble. An ancient town in Palestine, modern Tabariya.

Tiberio In CC, Publio's secretary. Italian for Tiberius, a Roman praenomen or personal name.

Tibu In DT, a desert tribe of Kush, subject to Tombalku. From the Tibbu or Tibu, a Saharan tribe living around the Tibesti Mountains.

Tilutan In DT, a Ghanata brigand.

Tina In TT, a young Ophirean girl. Diminutive of feminine names like Albertina, Christina, &c.

Tito In QC, an Argossean sea captain. Italian for Titus, a Roman praenomen or personal name.

Tlazitlan In RN, the race that built Xuchotl. Possibly from Tiazatlan, Mexico; or a combination of Tlascala or Tlaxcala, Mexico, and Zatlan, a place in Aztec mythology.

Tolkamec In RN, a wizard of Xuchotl. Possibly a combination of Toltec and Chichimec, two dynasties or dominant tribes from pre-Conquest Mexican history.

Tombalku In DT, a city on the southern edge of the desert south of Stygia. From Timbuktu or Timbouctou, in the République du Soudan, the capital of a succession of Negro empires in medieval times.

Topal In RN, a man of Xuchotl. Possibly from copal, a resinous gum collected from various tropical American trees and used as incense.

Tor In CC, a Nemedian barony. The word means "hill" or "peak" in English.

Toragis In first draft of RN, the place near which Conan's ship was sunk; discarded. Possibly from the same source as Tortage (q.v.).

Torgrio In SK, a thief of Ianthe.

Torh See Brocas. Probably from the same source as Tor (q.v.).

Tortage In PO, a pirate town in the Barachas. From Tortuga (Spanish for "turtle") the name of two Caribbean islands with a piratical history.

Tothmekri In TT, a Stygian prince. From the same sources as Thothmekri (q.v.).

Tothra In SS, a dream place. Possibly a combination of the names of the Egyptian gods Thoth and Ra.

Totrasmek In SZ, a priest of Hanuman.

Tovarro In CB, the brother of King Ferdrugo. From the Spanish surnames Tovar and Navarro.

Trallibes In TT, a place on the coast of the Western Ocean. Possibly from Tralles in Roman Asia Minor.

Tranicos In TT, CI, a pirate admiral. Possibly from the Portuguese name Trancoso.

Trocero In TT to CI, the count of Poitain. Possibly from the Trocadéro Palace, a museum in Paris whose name has been appropriated by many American movie and burlesque theaters.

Tsathoggua In CB, CA, a toad-shaped idol on the Nameless Isle. A god mentioned in Clark Ashton Smith's story "The Ice Demon" (*Weird Tales*, April 1933).

Tsotha-Lanti In SC, a Kothian wizard. Possibly suggested by Thoth + Atlantis.

Tubal In FK, a Shemite serving under Conan. A Biblical name (Gen. 4:22).

Turan In WB, DI, QC, &c., the kingdom set up west of the Vilayet Sea by Hyrkanian invaders. The Old Persian name for Turkestan. In Firdausi's *Shah Nameh*, the main repository of ancient Persian legend, Feridun (Old Persian, Traetaona) divided the world among his three sons, giving Rum (Europe) to Silim, Turan to Tur, and Iran to Irij. Much of the *Shah Nameh* is taken up with the efforts of King Afrasiyab (Frangrasiyan) of Turan to conquer Iran, and his successive defeats by the Persian hero Rustam under various Iranian kings.

Tuscelan In BR, MB, an Aquilonian fort on the Pictish frontier. From ancient Tusculum, Italy.

Tuthamon In FK, CC, a former king of Stygia, the father of Akivasha. From the same sources as Thoth-Amon (q.v.).

Tuthmes In SD, a nobleman of the kingdom of Kush. From the same sources as Thutothmes (q.v.).

Tybor In SC, a river in southeastern Aquilonia. From the Tiber River, Italy.

Upas In TE, PS, a poisonous tree. A Javanese tree, *Antigris toxicaria*, yielding a poisonous sap; formerly reputed to destroy any living thing near it.

Ura In FK, a legendary king of Yanaidar.

Uriaz In HS, a former king of Pelishtia. From the Hebrew name Uriah (Greco-Latin Urias).

Uthghiz In CA, a Turanian admiral. From Utgård or Utgarðar, the land of giants in Norse mythology.

Uttara Kuru In CA, a region east of Vendhya. A legendary land in Hindu mythology.

Valadelad In first draft of RN, a town burned by Conan just before the sinking of his ship by the Zingarans; discarded. From Valladolid, Spain.

Valannus In BR, MB, an Aquilonian officer commanding Fort Tuscelan; in CC, another Aquilonian officer. Probably from the Roman names Valens, Valentius.

Valbroso In CC, a Zingaran robber-count. From Vallombroso ("shady valley"), Italy.

Valenso In TT, a Zingaran count. Probably from Valencia (ancient Valentia), Spain.

Valeria In RN, an Aquilonian woman pirate. The feminine form of Valerius (q.v.). Cf. Livia.

Valerian In BB, a nobleman of Schohira. From Valerianus, a common Roman cognomen, borne by one emperor. It is the adoptive form of the Roman gentile name Valerius, indicating that the bearer has been adopted into the Valerian gens.

Valerio In CB, a Zingaran fencing master. From Valerius (q.v.).

Valerius In WB, a young Khaurani soldier; in CC, an Aquilonian noble. A Roman gentile name.

Valkia In CC, a river and its valley in eastern Aquilonia. Possibly from Valkyrie (Old Norse *valkyrja*), in Norse mythology one of Oðin's maidens. Valka, a god mentioned in the Kull stories, is probably from the same source.

Valusia In TE, CB, RZ, and the Kull stories, a kingdom of Atlantean times. The place name Volusia (possibly connected with the Volusci or Volsci of ancient Italy) occurs in New York State and Florida.

Vammatar In LD, the queen of Haloga. In the *Kalevala*, the daughter of evil.

Vanaheim In FD, TT, PS, &c., a northern land, west of Asgard. In Norse mythology, the home of the Vanir (q.v.).

Vancho In CB, the first officer of Zarono's *Petrel*. From the Spanish name Sancho.

Vanir In FD, QC, TC, &c., the people of Vanaheim (q.v.). In Norse mythology, a class of deities (singular Vanr or Van) originally of fertility and later of weather, agriculture, and commerce.

Varanna(=Velitrium) In first draft of BR; discarded. Probably from the same source as Valannus (q.v.).

Vardan In CA, a Turanian soldier. A common Persian name (Greek Ouardanes, Latin Vardanes), borne by various Parthian and Armenian kings.

Vardanes In BT, a Zamorian adventurer. From the same source as Vardan (q.v.).

Varuna In BN, a god invoked by Conan. The creator-god of ancient Brahmanism.

Vateesa In BC, SD, a Khorajan lady. Probably from Vanessa, a name constructed by Dean Swift from that of his sweetheart Esther Vanhomrigh.

Vathathas In first draft of BC, a legendary king of thieves; discarded. Possibly from the same source as Vathelos (q.v.).

Vathelos, Vezek Respectively the blind author of magical books in BC and a Turanian outpost in WB. Possibly from Vathek, William Beckford's spelling of the name of the Caliph Wathiq (+IX), in Beckford's Gothic novel of that name (1786).

Velitrium In BR, MB, a frontier city on the western borders of Aquilonia. From Velitrae (modern Vellitri), Italy.

Venar (=Venarium, q.v.) In first draft of BR; discarded.

Venarium A frontier fort in Gunderland referred to in BR; probably from Virunum, capital of Roman Noricum, near modern Klagenfurt, Austria.

Vendhya In WB, PC, TT, &c., a land to the far southeast, corresponding to modern India. From the Vindhya Mountains, India. The name means "rent" or "ragged," i.e., having many passes.

Ventrium (=Thenitea) In first draft of BB; discarded. From the same source as Venarium (q.v.).

Verulia A kingdom of Atlantean times, mentioned in "The Hyborian Age." Probably from Verulamium, a Romano-British town, later Verulam; near modern St. Albans.

Veziz Shah In CA, a Turanian city governor. From Vezir, the Arabic ministerial title, and Shah (q.v.).

Vilayet In SM, DI, BR, &c., an inland sea east of Turan, corresponding to the modern Caspian (also in former times called the Hyrcanian Sea and the Sea of Ghel). Turkish for "province."

Vilerus In DT, a former king of Aquilonia. Probably from Valerius (q.v.).

Villagro In CB, the duke of Kordava. A pseudo-Spanish name.

Vinashko In RE, a chief of the Yuetshi. From Kanishka, a Yüe-Chi or Kushana king in India, c. +100.

Virata In FK, a Kosalan magus of Yanaidar. The king of Matsya in the *Mahâbhârata*.

Virunians In LW, a people of Hyperborean descent dwelling in the Border Kingdom. From Virunum (*see* Varanium).

Vladislav *See* Olgerd. A Russian proper name.

Voivode In WB, the title of the mercenary captain Constantius. A title of me-

HYBORIAN NAMES

dieval Slavic generals and governors and of Romanian princes.

Volmana In PS, an Aquilonian noble. Possibly from the Vomano River, Italy.

Wadai In SZ, a Negro country. A part of the Republic of Chad, Africa; formerly, a powerful black kingdom in that area, conquered by the French in 1908–12.

Wakla In CA, a Turanian fort in the Zuagir desert. Originally "Whagra," from the verb "wager."

Wamadzi In CA, a Himelian tribe.

Wazuli In PC, a Himelian tribe. From the Wazirs, a Pakhtun tribe of Pakistan. Burroughs used Waziri as the name of an African tribe.

Westermarck In BB, MB, the borderland between Bossonia and Pictland. From "western" and "mark," an old variant of "march" in the sense of "border."

Wigurs In CA, a tribe of Hyrkanian nomads. From the Uigurs, for which *see* Kuigars.

Wodan In WB, Conan's horse. From the North European creator-god, Oðin, Odin, or Wotan.

Wuhuan In CA, a desert west of Khitai. A pseudo-Chinese name.

Wulfhere In FD, an Æsir chief. An old Saxon name, meaning "wolf army," borne by a pious +VII king of Mercia. Also a character in the stories of Howard's Dark Age hero, Cormac Mac Art.

Xag In first draft of DI, the Yuetshi fisherman; discarded.

Xaltotun In CC, CA, BN, an Acheronian wizard. Probably from Xulun, Mexico.

Xapur In TE, an island in the Sea of Vilayet. Probably from Shahpur (q.v.).

Xatmec In RN, a man of Xuchotl. A pseudo-Aztec name.

Xotalanc In RN, one of the feuding clans of Xuchotl. Probably from Xicalanco, Mexico.

Xotli In CI, the devil-god of Antillia. A pseudo-Aztec name.

Xuthal, Xuthol In SS, a city south of the kingdom of Kush. The former spelling is Howard's; the latter appears only on Kyle's end-paper maps for the Gnome Press editions of the Conan stories.

Yag In TE, SC, a distant planet; also a place (spelled "Yagg") in Howard's novel *Almuric*.

Yagkoolan An expletive in SM, SC. Possibly from Yaxchilan, Guatemala, a city of the so-called Mayan Old Empire on the Usumacinta River.

Yag-Kosha or Yogah In TE, an elephant-headed native of the planet Yag (q.v.). *See* Khrosha.

Yah Chieng In CA, a Khitan magician. A pseudo-Chinese name. From the names of the Chinese leaders Sun Yat-sen and Chiang Kaishek.

Yajur In SZ, FK, a god of Kosala. From Yajur-Veda, a section of the Vedas (Hindu scriptures) dealing with ritual.

Yakov In CI, a Zaporoskan pirate in the Barachas. A Russian name, cognate with "Jacob."

Yama In CS, the Meruvian creator-god. In Hindu myth, the god of the underworld.

Yamad Al-Aphta In CA, a name of Conan among the Zuagirs. From the villain Jamal in the movie *Sinbad the Sailor* (with Douglas Fairbanks, Jr.) and the Arabic definite article *al*, and "Aphta" from "naptha."

Yanaidar In FK, a sinister city in the Ilbars Mts. From Janaidar, a legendary city in Central Asia.

Yanak In CA, a Vilayet pirate. From *Kanaka*, Polynesian for a native man.

Yanyoga In SH, the stronghold of the Valusian serpent-folk south of Kush.

Yar *See* Alafdal. A Pakhtun name.

Yar Allal In CA, a Zuagir.

Yaralet In HN, a city in Turan. Probably from Tokalet, an abandoned Berber city in the western Sahara.

Yasala In RN, a woman of Xuchotl.

Yasmela, Yasmina Respectively the queen regent of Khoraja in BC, KD, and the Devi of Vendhya in PC, CA. From the Arabic *yasmin*, "jasmine," whence the feminine names.

Yasunga In CC, a Negro galley slave; in CI, a black Barachan pirate.

Yateli In DI, a Dagonian girl.

Yelaya In JG, IG, the long-dead princess of Alkmeenon. Possibly from the Spanish surname Zelaya, e.g., José Santos Zelaya, dictator of Nicaragua, 1893–1909.

Yelba River In CA, a stream in southwestern Turan. From the German *gelb*, "yellow."

Yezdigerd In DI, PC, CA, &c., the king of Turan. From Yazdegerd or Yezdijird, the name of three Sassanid kings of Persia, +IV to +VII.

Yezm In FK, the eponym of a cult of assassins in the Ilbars Mts.

Yezud In HD, TC, PC, a city in Zamora where a spider-god is worshiped. Possibly from the Yezidis or "devil-worshipers," a Mazdean sect among the Kurds of Armenia and the Caucasus.

Yig In RZ, a god of the serpent-men of Valusia. From H. P. Lovecraft's story "The Curse of Yig" (with Zealia Bishop).

Yildiz In SM, HN, CM, &c., the king of Turan, the predecessor of Yezdigerd. From *yıldız*, Turkish for "star," used in Turkey as a woman's name (but never as a man's), and also commercially: Yıldız Construction Co. &c. Howard probably got the name from the Yıldız Palace in Istanbul. (The Turkish letter ı stands for a vowel between those of "pit" and "put.")

Yimsha In PC, CA, the mountain stronghold of the Black Circle. Possibly from Yashma, in Azerbaijan.

Yin Allal In CA, a Zuagir chief. A pseudo-Arabic name, suggested by "Allah."

Yizil In PC, a god or demon. Probably from the Turkish *kizil*, "red," which appears in many geographical names.

Ymir In FD, PS, SC, a supernatural giant. In Norse mythology, a primeval giant.

Yo La-Gu In CA, a Khitan soldier. A pseudo-Chinese name.

Yog In DI, a Zamboulan god.

Yogah *See* Yag-Kosha. In Howard's novel *Almuric*, Yogh is the name of a river.

Yota-Pong In JG, a place in Kosala referred to.

Yothga In SC, a magical plant.

Yuetshi In DI, RE, a primitive tribe living around the southern end of the Sea of Vilayet. From the Yüe-Chi or Kushana, a Turko-Tatar people that conquered an Indian empire in +I.

Yukkub In CA, a Turanian city. Possibly from *kub*, Swedish for "cube."

Yun In TE, a Khitan god.

Zabhela A coastal place mentioned in RN. Possibly from the same source as Zargheba (q.v.).

Zahak In FK, a Hyrkanian captain in Yanaidar. A demon in Persian mythology, also Zohak and Dahaka.

Zaheemi In BC, a clan living near the Pass of Shamla.

Zal In BG, a Zamorian. In Persian legend, Rustam's father.

Zamboula In SZ, SK, TT, a city in the southeastern deserts. From Stamboul, a French spelling of Istanbul, the former Constantinople or Byzantium.

Zamora In TE, QC, SM, &c., an ancient kingdom east of the Hyborian lands. A town and a province in Spain, also used as a Spanish surname.

Zang In WB, a priest.

Zapayo Da Kova In DT, the commander of the mercenary force that invades Stygia. "Zapayo" is pseudo-Spanish; "Da Kova" is possibly from Reginald De Koven, an American composer (*Robin Hood*, 1900).

Zaporavo, Zaporoska Respectively a Zingaran pirate captain in PO and a Hyrkanian river in WB, CA. From "Zaporogian," which comes from the Russian *zaporozhets*, "beyond the rapids," used in +XVI and +XVII to designate the Dniepr Cossacks.

Zarallo In RN, the chief of a band of mercenaries in Stygian service. Possibly from the Spanish surname Zorilla.

Zaramba In IG, the chief priest of Punt.

Zargheba, Zarkheba Respectively a Shemitish adventurer in JG, IG, and a southern river in QC. Possibly from Zariba, Arabia.

Zarono In CB, TT, CI, a Zingaran buccaneer captain. A pseudo-Spanish name.

Zebah In CA, a name assumed by the leader of a band of Zuagir raiders. From Sheba or Sabaea in southern Arabia.

Zelata In CC, an Aquilonian wise woman. Possibly from the Spanish surname Zelaya (cf. Yelaya).

Zeltran In CB, the first officer of Conan's *Wastrel*. From the Franco-Spanish surname Beltran.

Zelvar Af In CA, a Himelian hunter. From Halvar, a common Scandinavian name, and Af, a made-up syllable.

Zembabwei, Zimbabwe In JG, WM, RZ, &c., a black kingdom. (The first spelling is used in JG; the second in "The Hyborian Age.") From Zimbabwe, a ruined fortified town in Rhodesia, first built about 1,300 years ago and used in +XVIII and early +XIX as the capital of the Monomotapa Empire. The name was used again by Howard in the form "Zambabwei" in a story, "The Grisly Horror," in *Weird Tales* for Feb. 1935. Although this tale was laid in the United States, it alluded to Zambabwei as a place in Africa where people were sacrificed to a man-eating ape.

Zenobia In CC, WM, BN, &c., a Nemedian girl wedded by Conan. The Greek version of the name of Septimia Bath-Zabbai or Bat-Sabdai, queen of Palmyra in +III.

Zeriti In HS, the witch-mistress of King Akhîrom. A pseudo-Egyptian name.

Zhaibar In PC, CA, a pass northwest of Vendhya into the Himelian Mts. From the Khaibar (Khyber) Pass in Pakistan. Howard's description closely follows Talbot Mundy's account of the Khyber Pass in *King of the Khyber Rifles*.

Zhemri In "The Hyborian Age," HD, a people surviving from Atlantean times to become the Zamorians.

Zhurazi Archipelago In CA, a group of islands in the Vilayet Sea.

Zikamba River In CB, a stream in Kush. A pseudo-Bantu name.

Zillah In BT, the daughter of Enosh of Akhlat. A biblical name (Gen. 4:19).

Zingara In QC, WB, BR, &c., a southwestern maritime kingdom. Italian for "Gypsy." (Cf. Gitara.) The name is probably also connected with Zalgara, a hill region mentioned in the Kull stories.

Zingelito In TT, a Zingaran. A pseudo-Spanish name.

Zingg In "The Hyborian Age," the valley in which the nation of Zingara (q.v.) arose. A remote possibility is a connection with the Zing or Zinj, a Sudanese people mentioned by the medieval Muslim writer Mas'ûdi.

Zlanath In RN, a man of Xuchotl.

Zogar Sag In BR, MB, a Pictish wizard.

Zorathus In CC, a Kothic merchant. Probably from Zaratas, a Greek form of Zoroaster (Old Persian Zarathushtra, modern Zardusht).

Zosara In CS, CM, the daughter of King Yildiz of Turan. The Greek spelling of Zeresh, wife of Haman in the Book of Esther.

Zuagirs In WB, SZ, RN, &c., Shemitish nomads dwelling in the eastern deserts. Probably from the Shagia (Shaigiya, Shaikiyeh), a tribe of Egyptian Arabs, and the Zouia or Zuia, a tribe of Libyan Arabs.

Zuagros In first draft of SZ, Conan's destination at the end of the story; discarded. From the same source as Zuagirs (q.v.) + the Zagros Mts. of western Iran.

Zugites In BC, an ancient and degraded Stygian cult.

Zuru In CB, a Ghanata slaver. A chief of the Ngoni of East Africa in +XIX.

Zurvan In CB, a deity of the Mitran pantheon. From Zarvan or Zarwan, in Zoroastrianism a personification of time.

Zyras In BG, a Corinthian. A pseudo-Greek name.

About the Authors

L. Sprague de Camp was well-known for his fantasies, science popularizations, and historical novels, as well as his work in the science fiction world. His writing appeared in many of the science fiction magazines of the 1930s, including *Astounding* and *The Magazine of Fantasy and Science Fiction*. De Camp also worked on unfinished manuscripts of Robert E. Howard and, with Lin Carter and Björn Nyberg, created new Conan stories. He was the co-author of *Dark Valley Destiny*, the definitive biography of Robert E. Howard. De Camp died in 2000.

Lin Carter was a full-time freelance writer and editor/anthologist of fantasy and science fiction stories. As an editorial consultant, he was the key figure behind the popular Ballantine Adult Fantasy Series of the 1970s. He died in 1988.

Björn Nyberg first began collaborating with de Camp on Conan works in the 1950s. He lives in France.